TESS GERRITSEN

Tess Gerritsen studied medicine at the University of California, and was awarded her MD in 1979. After completing her internship she practised as a doctor in Honolulu, Hawaii. While on maternity leave Gerritsen first started writing and in 1987 her first novel, *Call After Midnight*, was published. However, it was *Harvest*, Gerritsen's first medical thriller, which brought her major commercial success on its publication in 1996. It was a *New York Times* bestseller and was translated into twenty foreign languages. With later successes including *Bloodstream*, *Gravity*, *The Surgeon* and *The Apprentice*, Tess Gerritsen is now recognized as one of the forerunners in the field of gripping medical thrillers.

Tess Gerritsen lives with her family in Maine, where she writes full-time.

D0860643

By the same author

TESS GERRITSEN

Gravity

Bloodstream

HARPER

HarperCollins*Publishers*
77–85 Fulham Palace Road,
London, W6 8JB

The HarperCollins website address is:
www.harpercollins.co.uk

This omnibus edition 2008
Reprinted 2008

Typeset in Meridien by Palimpsest Book Production Limited,
Grangemouth, Stirlingshire

Printed and bound in Great Britain by
Clays Ltd, St Ives plc

Gravity

*To the men and women who
have made spaceflight a reality.*

*Mankind's greatest achievements
are launched on dreams.*

Acknowledgments

I could not have written this book without the generous assistance of people from NASA. My warmest thanks to:

Ed Campion, NASA Public Affairs, for personally guiding me on a fascinating inside tour of Johnson Space Center.

Flight Directors Mark Kirasich (ISS) and Wayne Hale (shuttle) for insights into their demanding roles.

Ned Penley, for explaining the process of payloads selection.

John Hooper, for introducing me to the new Crew Return Vehicle.

Jim Reuter (MSFC), for explaining the space station's environmental and life-support systems.

Flight Surgeons Tom Marshburn, M.D., and Smith Johnston, M.D., for the details of emergency medicine in weightlessness.

Jim Ruhnke, for answering my sometimes bizarre engineering questions.

Ted Sasseen (NASA retired) for sharing memories of his long career as an aerospace engineer.

I'm also grateful for the help of experts from a variety of other fields:

Bob Truax and Bud Meyer, the real-life rocket boys of Truax Engineering, for the inside scoop on reusable launch vehicles.

Steve Waterman, for his knowledge of decompression chambers.

Charles D. Sullivan and Jim Burkhart, for the information on amphibian viruses.

Ross Davis, M.D., for the neurosurgical details.

Bo Barber, my fountain of information about aircraft and runways. (Bo, I'll fly with you anytime!)

Finally, I must once again thank:

Emily Bestler, who let me spread my wings.

Don Cleary and Jane Berkey, of the Jane Rotrosen Agency, for knowing what makes a great story.

Meg Ruley, who makes dreams come true.

and –

My husband, Jacob. Honey, we're in this together.

THE SEA

1

The Galápagos Rift
.30 Degrees South, 90.30 Degrees West

He was gliding on the edge of the abyss.

Below him yawned the watery blackness of a frigid underworld, where the sun had never penetrated, where the only light was the fleeting spark of a bioluminescent creature. Lying prone in the form-fitting body pan of *Deep Flight IV*, his head cradled in the clear acrylic nose cone, Dr Stephen D. Ahearn had the exhilarating sensation of soaring, untethered, through the vastness of space. In the beams of his wing lights he saw the gentle and continuous drizzle of organic debris falling from the light-drenched waters far above. They were the corpses of protozoans, drifting down through thousands of feet of water to their final graveyard on the ocean floor.

Gliding through that soft rain of debris, he guided *Deep Flight* along the underwater canyon's rim, keeping the abyss to his port side, the plateau floor beneath him. Though the sediment was seemingly barren, the evidence of life was everywhere. Etched in the ocean floor were the tracks and plow marks of wandering creatures, now safely concealed in their cloak of sediment. He saw evidence of man as well: a rusted length of chain, sinuously draped around a fallen anchor; a soda pop bottle, half-submerged in ooze. Ghostly remnants from the alien world above.

A startling sight suddenly loomed into view. It was like coming across an underwater grove of charred tree trunks. The objects were blacksmoker chimneys, twenty-foot tubes formed by dissolved minerals swirling out of cracks in the earth's crust. With the joysticks, he maneuvered *Deep Flight* gently starboard, to avoid the chimneys.

'I've reached the hydrothermal vent,' he said. 'Moving at two knots, smoker chimneys to port side.'

'How's she handling?' Helen's voice crackled through his earpiece.

'Beautifully. I want one of these babies for my own.'

She laughed. 'Be prepared to write a very big check, Steve. You spot the nodule field yet? It should be dead ahead.'

Ahearn was silent for a moment as he peered through the watery murk. A moment later he said, 'I see them.'

The manganese nodules looked like lumps of

4

coal scattered across the ocean floor. Strangely, almost bizarrely, smooth, formed by minerals solidifying around stones or grains of sand, they were a highly prized source of titanium and other precious metals. But he ignored the nodules. He was in search of a prize far more valuable.

'I'm heading down into the canyon,' he said.

With the joysticks he steered *Deep Flight* over the plateau's edge. As his velocity increased to two and a half knots, the wings, designed to produce the opposite effect of an airplane wing, dragged the sub downward. He began his descent into the abyss.

'Eleven hundred meters,' he counted off. 'Eleven fifty . . .'

'Watch your clearance. It's a narrow rift. You monitoring water temperature?'

'It's starting to rise. Up to fifty-five degrees now.'

'Still a ways from the vent. You'll be in hot water in another two thousand meters.'

A shadow suddenly swooped right past Ahearn's face. He flinched, inadvertently jerking the joystick, sending the craft rolling to starboard. The hard jolt of the sub against the canyon wall sent a clanging shock wave through the hull.

'Jesus!'

'Status?' said Helen. 'Steve, what's your status?'

He was hyperventilating, his heart slamming in panic against the body pan. *The hull. Have I damaged the hull?* Through the harsh sound of his own breathing, he listened for the groan of steel giving way, for the fatal blast of water. He was thirty-six hundred feet beneath the surface, and over one hundred atmospheres of pressure were squeezing in on all sides like a fist. A breach in the hull, a burst of water, and he would be crushed.

'Steve, talk to me!'

Cold sweat soaked his body. He finally managed to speak. 'I got startled – collided with the canyon wall –'

'Is there any damage?'

He looked out the dome. 'I can't tell. I think I bumped against the cliff with the forward sonar unit.'

'Can you still maneuver?'

He tried the joysticks, nudging the craft to port. 'Yes. Yes.' He released a deep breath. 'I think I'm okay. Something swam right past my dome. Got me rattled.'

'Something?'

'It went by so fast! Just this streak – like a snake whipping by.'

'Did it look like a fish's head on an eel's body?'

'Yes. Yes, that's what I saw.'

'Then it was an eelpout. *Thermarces cerberus*.'

Cerberus, thought Ahearn with a shudder. The three-headed dog guarding the gates of hell.

'It's attracted to the heat and sulfur,' said Helen. 'You'll see more of them as you get closer to the vent.'

If you say so. Ahearn knew next to nothing about marine biology. The creatures now drifting past his acrylic head dome were merely objects of

6

curiosity to him, living signposts pointing the way to his goal. With both hands steady at the controls now, he maneuvered *Deep Flight IV* deeper into the abyss.

Two thousand meters. Three thousand.

What if he had damaged the hull?

Four thousand meters, the crushing pressure of water increasing linearly as he descended. The water was blacker now, colored by plumes of sulfur from the vent below. The wing lights scarcely penetrated that thick mineral suspension. Blinded by the swirls of sediment, he maneuvered out of the sulfur-tinged water, and his visibility improved. He was descending to one side of the hydrothermal vent, out of the plume of magma-heated water, yet the external temperature continued to climb.

One hundred twenty degrees Fahrenheit.

Another streak of movement slashed across his field of vision. This time he managed to maintain his grip on the controls. He saw more eelpouts, like fat snakes hanging head down as though suspended in space. The water spewing from the vent below was rich in heated hydrogen sulfide, a chemical that was toxic and incompatible with life. But even in these black and poisonous waters, life had managed to bloom, in shapes fantastic and beautiful. Attached to the canyon wall were swaying *Riftia* worms, six feet long, topped with feathery scarlet headdresses. He saw clusters of giant clams, white-shelled, with tongues of velvety red peeking out. And he saw crabs, eerily pale and ghostlike as they scuttled among the crevices.

Even with the air-conditioning unit running, he was starting to feel the heat.

Six thousand meters. Water temperature one hundred eighty degrees. In the plume itself, heated by boiling magma, the temperatures would be over five hundred degrees. That life could exist even here, in utter darkness, in these poisonous and superheated waters, seemed miraculous.

'I'm at six thousand sixty,' he said. 'I don't see it.'

In his earphone, Helen's voice was faint and crackling. 'There's a shelf jutting out from the wall. You should see it at around six thousand eighty meters.'

'I'm looking.'

'Slow your descent. It'll come up quickly.'

'Six thousand seventy, still looking. It's like pea soup down here. Maybe I'm at the wrong position.'

'. . . sonar readings . . . collapsing above you!' Her frantic message was lost in static.

'I didn't copy that. Repeat.'

'The canyon wall is giving way! There's debris falling toward you. *Get out of there!*'

The loud *pings* of rocks hitting the hull made him jam the joysticks forward in panic. A massive shadow plummeted down through the murk just ahead and bounced off a canyon shelf, sending a fresh rain of debris into the abyss. The *pings* accelerated. Then there was a deafening clang, and the accompanying jolt was like a fist slamming into him.

His head jerked, his jaw slamming into the body pan. He felt himself tilting sideways, heard the sickening groan of metal as the starboard wing scraped over jutting rocks. The sub kept rolling, sediment swirling past the dome in a disorienting cloud.

He hit the emergency-weight-drop lever and fumbled with the joysticks, directing the sub to ascend. *Deep Flight IV* lurched forward, metal screeching against rock, and came to an unexpected halt. He was frozen in place, the sub tilted starboard. Frantically he worked at the joysticks, thrusters at full ahead.

No response.

He paused, his heart pounding as he struggled to maintain control over his rising panic. Why wasn't he moving? Why was the sub not responding? He forced himself to scan the two digital display units. Battery power intact. AC unit still functioning. Depth gauge reading, six thousand eighty-two meters.

The sediment slowly cleared, and shapes took form in the beam of his port wing light. Peering straight ahead through the dome, he saw an alien landscape of jagged black stones and bloodred *Riftia* worms. He craned his neck sideways to look at his starboard wing. What he saw sent his stomach into a sickening tumble.

The wing was tightly wedged between two rocks. He could not move forward. Nor could he move backward. *I am trapped in a tomb, nineteen thousand feet under the sea.*

'. . . copy? Steve, do you copy?'

He heard his own voice, weak with fear: 'Can't move – starboard wing wedged –'

'. . . port-side wing flaps. A little yaw might wiggle you loose.'

'I've tried it. I've tried everything. I'm not moving.'

There was dead silence over the earphones. Had he lost them? Had he been cut off? He thought of the ship far above, the deck gently rolling on the swells. He thought of sunshine. It had been a beautiful sunny day on the surface, birds gliding overhead. The sea a bottomless blue . . .

Now a man's voice came on. It was that of Palmer Gabriel, the man who had financed the expedition, speaking calmly and in control, as always. 'We're starting rescue procedures, Steve. The other sub is already being lowered. We'll get you up to the surface as soon as we can.' There was a pause, then: 'Can you see anything? What are your surroundings?'

'I – I'm resting on a shelf just above the vent.'

'How much detail can you make out?'

'What?'

'You're at six thousand eighty-two meters. Right at the depth we were interested in. What about that shelf you're on? The rocks?'

I am going to die, and he is asking about the fucking rocks.

'Steve, use the strobe. Tell us what you see.'

He forced his gaze to the instrument panel and flicked the strobe switch.

Bright bursts of light flashed in the murk. He stared at the newly revealed landscape flickering before his retinas. Earlier he had focused on the worms. Now his attention shifted to the immense field of debris scattered across the shelf floor. The rocks were coal black, like magnesium nodules, but these had jagged edges, like congealed shards of glass. Peering to his right, at the freshly fractured rocks trapping his wing, he suddenly realized what he was looking at.

'Helen's right,' he whispered.

'I didn't copy that.'

'She was right! The iridium source – I have it in clear view –'

'You're fading out. Recommend you . . .' Gabriel's voice broke up into static and went dead.

'I did not copy. Repeat, I did not copy!' said Ahearn.

There was no answer.

He heard the pounding of his heart, the roar of his own breathing. *Slow down, slow down. Using up my oxygen too fast . . .*

Beyond the acrylic dome, life drifted past in a delicate dance through poisonous water. As the minutes stretched to hours, he watched the *Riftia* worms sway, scarlet plumes combing for nutrients.

11

He saw an eyeless crab slowly scuttle across the field of stones.

The lights dimmed. The air-conditioning fans abruptly fell silent.

The battery was dying.

He turned off the strobe light. Only the faint beam of the port wing light was shining now. In a few minutes he would begin to feel the heat of that one-hundred-eighty-degree magma-charged water. It would radiate through the hull, would slowly cook him alive in his own sweat. Already he felt a drop trickle from his scalp and slide down his cheek. He kept his gaze focused on that single crab, delicately prancing its way across the stony shelf.

The wing light flickered.

And went out.

THE LAUNCH

2

July 7
Two Years Later

Abort.

Through the thunder of the solid propellant rocket boosters and the teeth-jarring rattle of the orbiter, the command *abort* sprang so clearly into Mission Specialist Emma Watson's mind she might have heard it shouted through her comm unit. None of the crew had, in fact, said the word aloud, but in that instant she knew the choice had to be made, and quickly. She hadn't heard the verdict yet from Commander Bob Kittredge or Pilot Jill Hewitt, seated in the cockpit in front of her. She didn't need to. They had worked so long together as a team they could read each other's minds, and the amber warning lights flashing on the shuttle's flight console clearly dictated their next actions.

Seconds before, *Endeavour* had reached Max Q, the point during launch of greatest aerodynamic

15

stress, when the orbiter, thrusting against the resistance of the atmosphere, begins to shudder violently. Kittredge had briefly throttled back to seventy percent to ease the vibrations. Now the console warning lights told them they'd lost two of their three main engines. Even with one main engine and two solid rocket boosters still firing, they would never make it to orbit.

They had to abort the launch.

'Control, this is *Endeavour*,' said Kittredge, his voice crisp and steady. Not a hint of apprehension. 'Unable to throttle up. Left and center MEs* went out at Max Q. We are stuck in the bucket. Going to RTLS abort.'

'Roger, *Endeavour*. We confirm two MEs out. Proceed to RTLS abort after SRB burnout.'

Emma was already rifling through the stack of checklists, and she retrieved the card for 'Return to Launch Site Abort.' The crew knew every step of the procedure by heart, but in the frantic pace of an emergency abort, some vital action might be forgotten. The checklist was their security blanket.

Her heart racing, Emma scanned the appropriate path of action, clearly marked in blue. A two-engine-down RTLS abort was survivable – but only theoretically. A sequence of near miracles had to happen next. First they had to dump fuel and cut off the last main engine before separating from

* There is a Glossary at the end of this book that contains many of these abbreviations.

the huge external fuel tank. Then Kittredge would pitch the orbiter around to a heads-up attitude, pointing back toward the launch site. He would have one chance, and only one, to guide them to a safe touchdown at Kennedy. A single mistake would send *Endeavour* plunging into the sca.

Their lives were now in the hands of Commander Kittredge.

His voice, in constant communication with Mission Control, still sounded steady, even a little bored, as they approached the two-minute mark. The next crisis point. The CRT display flashed the Pc<50 signal. The solid rocket boosters were burning out, on schedule.

Emma felt it at once, the startling deceleration as the boosters consumed the last of the fuel. Then a brilliant flash of light in the window made her squint as the SRBs exploded away from the tank.

The roar of launch fell ominously silent, the violent shudder calming to a smooth, almost tranquil ride. In the abrupt calm, she was aware of her own pulse accelerating, her heart thudding like a fist against her chest restraint.

'Control, this is *Endeavour*,' said Kittredge, still unnaturally calm. 'We have SRB sep.'

'Roger, we see it.'

'Initiating abort.' Kittredge depressed the Abort push button, the rotary switch already positioned at the RTLS option.

Over her comm unit, Emma heard Jill Hewitt call out, 'Emma, let's hear the checklist!'

17

'I've got it.' Emma began to read aloud, and the sound of her own voice was as startlingly calm as Kittredge's and Hewitt's. Anyone listening to their dialogue would never have guessed they faced catastrophe. They had assumed machine mode, their panic suppressed, every action guided by rote memory and training. Their onboard computers would automatically set their return course. They were continuing downrange, still climbing to four hundred thousand feet as they dissipated fuel.

Now she felt the dizzying spin as the orbiter began its pitch-around maneuver, rolling tail over nose. The horizon, which had been upside down, suddenly righted itself as they turned back toward Kennedy, almost four hundred miles away.

'*Endeavour*, this is Control. Go for main engine cutoff.'

'Roger,' responded Kittredge. 'MECO now.'

On the instrument panel, the three engine-status indicators suddenly flashed red. He had shut off the main engines, and in twenty seconds, the external fuel tank would drop away into the sea.

Altitude dropping fast, thought Emma. *But we're headed for home.*

She gave a start. A warning buzzed, and new panel lights flashed on the console.

'Control, we've lost computer number three!' cried Hewitt. 'We have lost a nav-state vector! Repeat, we've lost a nav-state vector!'

'It could be an inertial-measurement malf,' said

18

Andy Mercer, the other mission specialist seated beside Emma. 'Take it off-line.'

'No! It might be a broken data bus!' cut in Emma. 'I say we engage the backup.'

'Agreed,' snapped Kittredge.

'Going to backup,' said Hewitt. She switched to computer number five.

The vector reappeared. Everyone heaved a sigh of relief.

The burst of explosive charges signaled the separation of the empty fuel tank. They couldn't see it fall away into the sea, but they knew another crisis point had just passed. The orbiter was flying free now, a fat and awkward bird gliding homeward.

Hewitt barked, 'Shit! We've lost an APU!'

Emma's chin jerked up as a new buzzer sounded. An auxiliary power unit was out. Then another alarm screamed, and her gaze flew in panic to the consoles. A multitude of amber warning lights were flashing. On the video screens, all the data had vanished. Instead there were only ominous black and white stripes. *A catastrophic computer failure*. They were flying without navigation data. Without flap control.

'Andy and I are on the APU malf!' yelled Emma.

'Reengage backup!'

Hewitt flicked the switch and cursed. 'I'm getting no joy, guys. Nothing's happening –'

'Do it again!'

'Still not reengaging.'

19

'She's banking!' cried Emma, and felt her stomach lurch sideways.

Kittredge wrestled with the joystick, but they had already rolled too far starboard. The horizon reeled to vertical and flipped upside down. Emma's stomach lurched again as they spun right side up. The next rotation came faster, the horizon twisting in a sickening whirl of sky and sea and sky.

A death spiral.

She heard Hewitt groan, heard Kittredge say, with flat resignation, 'I've lost her.'

Then the fatal spin accelerated, plunging to an abrupt and shocking end.

There was only silence.

An amused voice said over their comm units, 'Sorry, guys. You didn't make it that time.'

Emma yanked off her headset. 'That wasn't fair, Hazel!'

Jill Hewitt chimed in with a protesting, 'Hey, you *meant* to kill us. There was no way to save it.'

Emma was the first crew member to scramble out of the shuttle flight simulator. With the others right behind her, she marched into the windowless control room, where their three instructors sat at the row of consoles.

Team Leader Hazel Barra, wearing a mischievous smile, swiveled around to face Commander Kittredge's irate crew of four. Though Hazel looked like a buxom earth mother with her gloriously frizzy brown hair, she was, in truth, a ruthless

20

gameplayer who ran her flight crews through the most difficult of simulations and seemed to count it as a victory whenever the crew failed to survive. Hazel was well aware of the fact that every launch could end in disaster, and she wanted her astronauts equipped with the skills to survive. Losing one of her teams was a nightmare she hoped never to face.

'That sim really was below the belt, Hazel,' complained Kittredge.

'Hey, you guys keep surviving. We have to knock down your cockiness a notch.'

'Come on,' said Andy. '*Two* engines down on liftoff? A broken data bus? An APU out? And then you throw in a failed number five computer? How many malfs and nits is that? It's not realistic.'

Patrick, one of the other instructors, swiveled around with a grin. 'You guys didn't even notice the other stuff we did.'

'What else was there?'

'I threw in a nit on your oxygen tank sensor. None of you saw the change in the pressure gauge, did you?'

Kittredge gave a laugh. 'When did we have time? We were juggling a dozen other malfunctions.'

Hazel raised a stout arm in a call for a truce. 'Okay, guys. Maybe we did overdo it. Frankly, we were surprised you got as far as you did with the RTLS abort. We wanted to throw in another wrench, to make it more interesting.'

'You threw in the whole damn toolbox,' snorted Hewitt.

'The truth is,' said Patrick, 'you guys are a little cocky.'

'The word is *confident*,' said Emma.

'Which is good,' Hazel admitted. 'It's good to be confident. You showed great teamwork at the integrated sim last week. Even Gordon Obie said he was impressed.'

'The Sphinx said that?' Kittredge's eyebrow lifted in surprise. Gordon Obie was the director of Flight Crew Operations, a man so bafflingly silent and aloof that no one at JSC really knew him. He would sit through entire mission management meetings without uttering a single word, yet no one doubted he was mentally recording every detail. Among the astronauts, Obie was viewed with both awe and more than a little fear. With his power over final flight assignments, he could make or break your career. The fact that he had praised Kittredge's team was good news indeed.

In her next breath, though, Hazel kicked the pedestal out from under them. 'However,' she said, 'Obie is also concerned that you guys are too lighthearted about this. That it's still a game to you.'

'What does Obie expect us to do?' said Hewitt. 'Obsess over the ten thousand ways we could crash and burn?'

'Disaster is not theoretical.'

Hazel's statement, so quietly spoken, made them

22

fall momentarily silent. Since *Challenger*, every member of the astronaut corps was fully aware that it was only a matter of time before there was another major mishap. Human beings sitting atop rockets primed to explode with five million pounds of thrust can't afford to be sanguine about the hazards of their profession. Yet they seldom spoke about dying in space; to talk about it was to admit its possibility, to acknowledge that the next *Challenger* might carry one's name on the crew roster.

Hazel realized she'd thrown a damper on their high spirits. It was not a good way to end a training session, and now she backpedaled on her earlier criticism.

'I'm only saying this because you guys are already so well integrated. I have to work hard to trip you up. You've got three months till launch, and you're already in good shape. But I want you in even *better* shape.'

'In other words, guys,' said Patrick from his console. 'Not so cocky.'

Bob Kittredge dipped his head in mock humility. 'We'll go home now and put on the hair shirts.'

'Overconfidence is dangerous,' said Hazel. She rose from the chair and stood up to face Kittredge. A veteran of three shuttle flights, Kittredge was half a head taller, and he had the confident bearing of a naval pilot, which he had once been. Hazel was not intimidated by Kittredge, or by any of her astronauts. Whether they were rocket scientists

23

or military heroes, they inspired in her the same maternal concern: the wish that they make it back from their missions alive.

She said, 'You're so good at command, Bob, you've lulled your crew into thinking it's easy.'

'No, they make it look easy. Because *they're* good.'

'We'll see. The integrated sim's on for Tuesday, with Hawley and Higuchi aboard. We'll be pulling some new tricks out of the hat.'

Kittredge grinned. 'Okay, try to kill us. But be fair about it.'

'Fate seldom plays fair,' Hazel said solemnly. 'Don't expect me to.'

Emma and Bob Kittredge sat in a booth in the Fly By Night saloon, sipping beers as they dissected the day's simulations. It was a ritual they'd established eleven months ago, early in their team building, when the four of them had first come together as the crew for shuttle flight 162. Every Friday evening, they would meet in the Fly By Night, located just up NASA Road 1 from Johnson Space Center, and review the progress of their training. What they'd done right, what still needed improvement. Kittredge, who'd personally selected each member of his crew, had started the ritual. Though they were already working together more than sixty hours a week, he never seemed eager to go home. Emma had thought it was because the recently divorced Kittredge now lived alone and dreaded returning to his empty house. But as she'd come to know him better, she realized these meetings were simply his way of prolonging the adrenaline high of his job. Kittredge lived to fly. For sheer entertainment he read the painfully dry shuttle manuals. He spent every free moment at the controls of one of NASA's T-38s. It was almost as if he resented the force of gravity binding his feet to the earth.

He couldn't understand why the rest of his crew might want to go home at the end of the day, and tonight he seemed a little melancholy that just the two of them were sitting at their usual table in the Fly By Night. Jill Hewitt was at her nephew's piano recital, and Andy Mercer was home celebrating his tenth wedding anniversary. Only Emma and Kittredge had shown up at the appointed hour, and now that they'd finished hashing over the week's sims, there was a long silence between them. The conversation had run out of shop talk and therefore out of steam.

'I'm taking one of the T-38s up to White Sands tomorrow,' he said. 'You want to join me?'

'Can't. I have an appointment with my lawyer.'

'So you and Jack are forging ahead with it?'

She sighed. 'The momentum's established. Jack has his lawyer, and I have mine. This divorce has turned into a runaway train.'

'It sounds like you're having second thoughts.'

Firmly she set down her beer. 'I don't have any second thoughts.'

'Then why're you still wearing his ring?'

She looked down at the gold wedding band. With sudden ferocity she tried to yank it off, but found it wouldn't budge. After seven years on her finger, the ring seemed to have molded itself to her flesh, refusing to be dislodged. She cursed and gave another tug, this time pulling so hard the ring scraped off skin as it slid over her knuckle. She set the ring down on the table. 'There. A free woman.'

Kittredge laughed. 'You two have been dragging out your divorce longer than I was married. What are you two still haggling over, anyway?'

She sank back in her chair, suddenly weary. 'Everything. I admit it, I haven't been reasonable either. A few weeks ago, we tried to sit down and make a list of all our possessions. What I want, what he wants. We promised ourselves we were going to be civilized about it. Two calm and mature adults. Well, by the time we got halfway down the list, it was out-and-out war. Take no prisoners.' She sighed. In truth, that was the way she and Jack had always been. Equally obstinate, fiercely passionate. Whether in love or at war, the sparks were always flying between them. 'There was only one thing we could both agree on,' she said. 'I get to keep the cat.'

'Lucky you.'

She looked at him. 'Do you ever have any regrets?'

'You mean about my divorce? Never.' Though

his answer was flatly unequivocal, his gaze had dropped, as though he was trying to hide a truth they both knew: he was still mourning the failure of his marriage. Even a man fearless enough to strap himself atop millions of pounds of explosive fuel could suffer from an ordinary case of loneliness.

'This is the problem, you see. I've finally figured it out,' he said. 'Civilians don't understand us because they can't share the dream. The only ones who'll stay married to an astronaut are the saints and the martyrs. Or the ones who just don't give a shit whether we live or die.' He gave a bitter laugh. 'Bonnie, she was no martyr. And she sure as hell didn't understand the dream.'

Emma stared down at her wedding ring, gleaming on the table. 'Jack understands it,' she said softly. 'It was his dream too. That's what ruined it for us, you know. That I'm going up and he can't. That he's the one left behind.'

'Then he needs to grow up and face reality. Not everyone's got the right stuff.'

'You know, I really wish you wouldn't refer to him as some sort of reject.'

'Hey, he's the one who resigned.'

'What else could he do? He knew he wasn't going to get any flight assignments. If they won't let you fly, there's no point being in the corps.'

'They grounded him for his own good.'

'It was medical guesswork. Having one kidney stone doesn't mean you'll get another.'

'Okay, Dr Watson. You're the physician. Tell me this: Would you want Jack on your shuttle crew? Knowing his medical problem?'

She paused. 'Yes. As a physician, yes, I would. Chances are, Jack would do perfectly fine in space. He has so much to offer I can't imagine why they *wouldn't* want him up there. I may be divorcing him, but I do respect him.'

Kittredge laughed and then drained his beer mug. 'You're not exactly objective about this, are you?'

She started to argue the point, then realized she had no defense. Kittredge was right. Where Jack McCallum was concerned, she had never been objective.

Outside, in the humid heat of a Houston summer night, she stopped in the Fly By Night's parking lot and glanced up at the sky. The glare of city lights washed out the stars, but she could still make out comfortingly familiar constellations. Cassiopeia and Andromeda and the Seven Sisters. Every time she looked at them, she remembered what Jack had told her as they'd lain side by side on the grass one summer night, gazing at the stars. The night she had first realized she was in love with him. *The heavens are full of women, Emma. You belong up there too.*

She said, softly, 'So do you, Jack.'

She unlocked her car and slid into the driver's seat. Reaching into her pocket, she fished out the wedding ring. Gazing at it in the gloom of her car, she thought of the seven years of marriage it represented. Almost over now.

She slipped the ring back into her pocket. Her left hand felt naked, exposed. *I'll have to get used to it*, she thought, and started the car.

3

July 10

Dr Jack McCallum heard the scream of the first ambulance siren and said, 'It's show time, folks!' Stepping outside to the ER loading dock, he felt his pulse kick into a tachycardia, felt the jolt of adrenaline priming his nervous system into crackling live wires. He had no idea what was coming to Miles Memorial Hospital, only that there was more than one patient on the way. Over the ER radio they'd been told a fifteen-car pileup on I-45 had left two fatalities at the scene and a score of injured. Although the most critical patients would be taken to Bayshore or Texas Med, all the area's smaller hospitals, including Miles Memorial, were braced for the overflow.

Jack glanced around the ambulance dock to confirm his team was ready. The other ER doctor, Anna Slezak, stood right beside him, looking grimly pugnacious. Their support staff included four nurses, a lab runner, and a scared-looking intern. Only a month out of med school, the intern was the greenest member of the ER team and hopelessly fumble-fingered. *Destined for the field of psychiatry*, thought Jack.

The siren cut off with a *whoop* as the ambulance swung up the ramp and backed up to the dock. Jack yanked open the rear door and got his first glimpse of the patient – a young woman, head and neck immobilized in a cervical collar, her blond hair matted with blood. As they pulled her out of the ambulance and he got a closer look at her face, Jack felt the sudden chill of recognition.

'Debbie,' he said.

She looked up at him, her gaze unfocused, and did not seem to know who he was.

'It's Jack McCallum,' he said.

'Oh. Jack.' She closed her eyes and groaned. 'My head hurts.'

He gave her a comforting pat on the shoulder. 'We'll take good care of you, sweetheart. Don't worry about a thing.'

They wheeled her through the ER doors, toward the trauma room.

'You know her?' Anna asked him.

'Her husband's Bill Haning. The astronaut.'

'You mean one of the guys up on the space station?' Anna laughed. 'Now, *there's* a long distance phone call.'

'It's no problem reaching him, if we have to. JSC can put a call right through.'

'You want me to take this patient?' It was a reasonable question to ask. Doctors usually avoided treating friends and family; you cannot remain objective when the patient in cardiac arrest on the table is someone you know and like. Although he and Debbie had once attended the same social functions, Jack considered her merely an acquaintance, not a friend, and he felt comfortable acting as her physician.

'I'll take her,' he said, and followed the gurney into the trauma room. His mind was already leaping ahead to what needed to be done. Her only visible injury was the scalp laceration, but since she had clearly suffered trauma to her head, he had to rule out fractures of the skull and cervical spine.

As the nurses drew blood for labs and gently pulled off the rest of Debbie's clothing, the ambulance attendant gave Jack a quick history.

'She was about the fifth car in the pileup. Far as we could tell, she got rear-ended, her car spun sideways, and then she got hit again, on the driver's side. Door was caved in.'

'Was she awake when you got to her?'

'She was unconscious for a few minutes. Woke up while we were putting in the IV. We got her spine immobilized right away. BP and heart rhythm have been stable. She's one of the lucky ones.' The attendant shook his head. 'You should've seen the guy behind her.'

Jack moved to the gurney to examine the patient. Both of Debbie's pupils reacted to light, and her extraocular movements were normal. She knew her own name and where she was, but could not recall the date. Oriented only times two, he thought. It was reason enough to admit her, if only for overnight observation.

'Debbie, I'm going to send you for X rays,' he said. 'We need to make sure you haven't fractured anything.' He looked at the nurse. 'Stat CT, skull, and C-spine. And . . .' He paused, listening.

Another ambulance siren was approaching.

'Get those films done,' he ordered, and trotted back outside to the loading dock, where his staff had reassembled.

A second siren, fainter, had joined the first wail. Jack and Anna glanced at each other in alarm. Two ambulances on the way?

'It's going to be one of those days,' he muttered.

'Trauma room cleared out?' asked Anna.

'Patient's on her way to X-ray.' He stepped forward as the first ambulance backed up. The instant it rolled to a stop, he yanked open the door.

It was a man this time, middle-aged and over-weight, his skin pale and clammy. *Going into shock* was Jack's first assessment, but he saw no blood, no signs of injury.

'He was one of the fender benders,' said the EMT as they wheeled the man into the treatment room. 'Got chest pain when we pulled him out of his car. Rhythm's been stable, a little tachycardic, but no PVCs. Systolic's ninety. We gave morphine and nitro at the scene, and oxygen's going at six liters.'

Everyone was right on the ball. While Anna took the history and physical, the nurses hooked up the cardiac leads. An EKG blipped out of the machine. Jack tore off the sheet and immediately focused on the ST elevations in leads V1 and V2.

'Anterior MI,' he said to Anna.

She nodded. 'I figured he was a tPA special.'

A nurse called through the doorway, 'The other ambulance is here!'

Jack and two nurses ran outside.

A young woman was screaming and writhing on the stretcher. Jack took one look at her shortened right leg, the foot rotated almost completely sideways, and knew this patient was going straight to surgery. Jack quickly cut away her clothes, to reveal an impacted hip fracture, her thigh bone rammed into the socket by the force of her knees hitting the car's dashboard. Just looking at her grotesquely deformed leg made him queasy.

'Morphine?' the nurse asked.

He nodded. 'Give her as much as she needs. She's in a world of hurt. Type and cross six units. And get an orthopod in here as soon as –'

'Dr McCallum, stat, X-ray. Dr McCallum, stat, X-ray.'

Jack glanced up in alarm. *Debbie Haning*. He ran out of the room.

He found Debbie lying on the X-ray table, hovered over by the ER nurse and the technician.

'We'd just finished doing the spine and skull films,' said the tech, 'and we couldn't wake her up. She doesn't even respond to pain.'

'How long's she been out?'

'I don't know. She was lying on the table ten, fifteen minutes before we noticed she wasn't talking to us anymore.'

'Did you get the CT scan done?'

'Computer's down. It should be up and running in a few hours.'

Jack flashed a penlight in Debbie's eyes and felt his stomach go into a sickening free fall. Her left pupil was dilated and unreactive.

'Show me the films,' he said.

'C-spine's already up on the light box.'

Jack swiftly moved into the next room and eyed the X rays clipped to the backlit viewing box. He saw no fractures on the neck films; her cervical spine was stable. He yanked down the neck films and replaced them with the skull X rays. At first glance he saw nothing immediately obvious. Then his gaze focused on an almost imperceptible line tracing across the left temporal bone. It was so subtle it looked like a pin scratch on the film. A fracture.

Had the fracture torn the left middle meningeal artery? That would cause bleeding inside her cranium. As the blood accumulated and pressure built up, the brain would be squeezed. It explained the rapid deterioration of her mental status and the blown pupil.

The blood had to be drained at once.

'Get her back to ER!' he said.

Within seconds they had Debbie strapped to the gurney and were wheeling her at a run down the hallway. As they swung her into an empty treatment room, he yelled to the clerk, 'Page neurosurgery *stat!* Tell them we have an epidural bleed, and we're prepping for emergency burr holes.'

He knew what Debbie really needed was the operating room, but her condition was deteriorating so quickly they had no time to wait. The treatment room would have to serve as their OR. They slid her onto the table and attached a tangle of EKG leads to her chest. Her breathing had turned erratic; it was time to intubate.

He had just torn open the package containing the endotracheal tube when a nurse said, 'She's stopped breathing!'

He slipped the laryngoscope into Debbie's throat. Seconds later, the ET tube was in place and oxygen was being bagged into her lungs.

A nurse plugged in the electric shaver. Debbie's blond hair began to fall to the floor in silky clumps, exposing the scalp.

The clerk poked her head in the room. 'Neurosurgeon's stuck in traffic! He can't get here for at least another hour.'

'Then get someone else!'

'They're all at Texas Med! They've got all the head injuries.'

Jesus, we're screwed, thought Jack, looking down

36

at Debbie. Every minute that went by, the pressure inside her skull was building. Brain cells were dying. *If this was my wife, I wouldn't wait. Not another second.*

He swallowed hard. 'Get out the Hudson brace drill. I'll do the burr holes myself.' He saw the nurses' startled looks, and added, with more bravado than he was feeling. 'It's like drilling holes in a wall. I've done it before.'

While the nurses prepped the newly shorn scalp, Jack put on a surgical gown and snapped on gloves. He positioned the sterile drapes and was amazed to find his hands were still steady, even while his heart was racing. It was true he had drilled burr holes before, but only once, and it was years ago, under the supervision of a neurosurgeon.

There's no more time. She's dying. Do it.

He reached for the scalpel and made a linear incision in the scalp, over the left temporal bone. Blood oozed out. He sponged it away and cauterized the bleeders. With a retractor holding back the skin flap, he sliced deeper through the galea and reached the pericranium, which he scraped back, exposing the skull surface.

He picked up the Hudson brace drill. It was a mechanical device, powered by hand and almost antique looking, the sort of tool you might find in your grandfather's woodshop. First he used the perforator, a spade-shaped drill bit that dug just deeply enough into the bone to establish the hole. Then he changed to the rose bit, round-tipped, with multiedged burrs. He took a deep breath, positioned the bit, and began to drill deeper. Toward the brain. The first beads of sweat broke out on his forehead. He was drilling without CT confirmation, acting purely on his clinical judgment. He did not even know if he was tapping the right spot.

A sudden gush of blood spilled out of the hole and splattered the surgical drapes.

A nurse handed him a basin. He withdrew the drill and watched as a steady stream of red drained out of the skull and gathered in a glistening pool in the basin. He'd tapped the right place. With every trickle of blood, the pressure was easing from Debbie Haning's brain.

He released a deep breath, and the tension suddenly eased from his shoulders, leaving his muscles spent and aching.

'Get the bone wax ready,' he said. Then he put down the drill and reached for the suction catheter.

A white mouse hung in midair, as though suspended in a transparent sea. Dr Emma Watson drifted toward it, slender-limbed and graceful as an underwater dancer, the curlicue strands of her dark brown hair splayed out in a ghostly halo. She grasped the mouse and slowly spun around to face the camera. She held up a syringe and needle.

The footage was over two years old, filmed aboard the shuttle *Atlantis* during STS 141, but it remained Gordon Obie's favorite PR film, which is why it was now playing on all the video monitors in NASA's Teague Auditorium. Who wouldn't enjoy watching Emma Watson? She was quick and lithe, and she possessed what one could only call *sparkle*, with the fire of curiosity in her eyes. From the tiny scar over her eyebrow, to the slightly chipped front tooth (a souvenir, he'd heard, of reckless skiing) her face was a record of an exuberant life. But to Gordon, her primary appeal was her intelligence. Her competence. He had been following Emma's NASA career with an interest that had nothing to do with the fact she was an attractive woman.

As director of Flight Crew Operations, Gordon Obie wielded considerable power over crew selection, and he strove to maintain a safe – some would call it heartless – emotional distance from all his astronauts. He had been an astronaut himself, twice a shuttle commander, and even then he'd been known as the Sphinx, an aloof and mysterious man not given to small talk. He was comfortable with his own silence and relative anonymity. Although he was now sitting onstage with an array of NASA officials, most of the people in the audience did not know who Gordon Obie was. He was here merely for set decoration. Just as the footage of Emma Watson was set decoration, an attractive face to hold the audience's interest.

The video suddenly ended, replaced on the

screen with the NASA logo, affectionately known as the meatball, a star-spangled blue circle embellished with an orbital ellipse and a forked slash of red. NASA administrator Leroy Cornell and JSC director Ken Blankenship stepped up to the lectern to field questions. Their mission, quite bluntly, was to beg for money, and they faced a skeptical gathering of congressmen and senators, members of the various subcommittees that determined NASA's budget. For the second straight year, NASA had suffered devastating cutbacks, and lately an air of abject gloom wafted through the halls of Johnson Space Center.

Gazing at the audience of well-dressed men and women, Gordon felt as though he were staring at an alien culture. What was wrong with these politicians? How could they be so shortsighted? It bewildered him that they did not share his most passionate belief: What sets the human race apart from the beasts is man's hunger for knowledge. Every child asks the universal question: *Why?* They are programmed from birth to be curious, to be explorers, to seek scientific truths.

Yet these elected officials had lost the curiosity that makes man unique. They'd come to Houston not to ask *why*, but *why should we?*

It was Cornell's idea to woo them with what he cynically called 'the Tom Hanks tour,' a reference to the movie *Apollo 13*, which still ranked as the best PR NASA had ever known. Cornell had already presented the latest achievements aboard the orbiting International Space Station. He'd let them shake the hands of some real live astronauts. Wasn't that what everyone wanted? To touch a golden boy, a hero? Next there'd be a tour of Johnson Space Center, starting with Building 30 and the Flight Control Room. Never mind the fact that this audience couldn't tell the difference between a flight console and a Nintendo set; all that gleaming technology would surely dazzle them and make them true believers.

But it isn't working, thought Gordon in dismay. *These politicians aren't buying it.*

NASA faced powerful opponents, starting with Senator Phil Parish, sitting in the front row. Seventy-six years old, an uncompromising hawk from South Carolina, Parish's first priority was preserving the defense budget, NASA be damned. Now he hauled his three-hundred-pound frame out of his seat and stood up to address Cornell in a gentleman's drawl.

'Your agency is billions of dollars overbudget on that space station,' he said. 'Now, I don't think the American people expected to sacrifice their defense capabilities just so you can tinker around up there with your nifty lab experiments. This is supposed to be an international effort, isn't it? Well, far as I can see, we-all are picking up most of the tab. How am I supposed to justify this white elephant to the good folks of South Carolina?'

NASA administrator Cornell responded with a

41

camera-ready smile. He was a political animal, the glad-hander whose personal charm and charisma made him a star with the press and in Washington, where he spent most of his time cajoling Congress and the White House for more money, ever more money, to fund the space agency's perennially insufficient budget. His was the public face of NASA, while Ken Blankenship, the man in charge of day-to-day operations at JSC, was the private face known only to agency insiders. They were the yin and yang of NASA leadership, so completely different in temperament it was hard to imagine how they functioned as a team. The inside joke at NASA was that Leroy Cornell was all style and no substance, and Blankenship was all substance and no style.

Cornell smoothly responded to Senator Parish's question. 'You asked why other countries aren't contributing. Senator, the answer is, they already have. This truly is an international space station. Yes, the Russians are badly strapped for cash. Yes, we had to make up the difference. But they're committed to this station. They've got a cosmonaut up there now, and they have every reason to help us keep ISS running. As for *why* we need the station, just look at the research that's being conducted in biology and medicine. Materials science. Geophysics. We'll see the benefits of this research in our own lifetimes.'

Another member of the audience stood, and Gordon felt his blood pressure rise. If there was anyone he despised more than Senator Parish, it was Montana congressman Joe Bellingham, whose Marlboro Man good looks couldn't disguise the fact he was a scientific moron. During his last campaign, he'd demanded that public schools teach Creationism. Throw out the biology books and open the Bible instead. *He probably thinks rockets are powered by angels.*

'What about all that sharing of technology with the Russians and Japanese?' said Bellingham. 'I'm concerned that we're giving away high-tech secrets for free. This international cooperation sounds high-minded and all, but what's to stop them from turning right around and using the knowledge against us? Why should we trust the Russians?'

Fear and paranoia. Ignorance and superstition. There was too much of it in the country, and Gordon grew depressed just listening to Bellingham. He turned away in disgust.

That's when he noticed a somber-faced Hank Millar step into the auditorium. Millar was head of the Astronaut Office. He looked straight at Gordon, who understood at once that a problem was brewing.

Quietly Gordon left the stage, and the two men stepped out into the hallway. 'What's going on?'

'There's been an accident. It's Bill Haning's wife. We hear it doesn't look good.'

'Jesus.'

'Bob Kittredge and Woody Ellis are waiting over in Public Affairs. We all need to talk.'

Gordon nodded. He glanced through the auditorium door at Congressman Bellingham, who was still blathering on about the dangers of sharing technology with the Commies. Grimly he followed Hank out the auditorium exit and across the courtyard, to the next building.

They met in a back office. Kittredge, the shuttle commander for STS 162, was flushed and agitated. Woody Ellis, flight director for the International Space Station, appeared far calmer, but then, Gordon had never seen Ellis look upset, even in the midst of crisis.

'How serious was the accident?' Gordon asked.

'Mrs Haning's car was in a giant pileup on I-45,' said Hank. 'The ambulance brought her over to Miles Memorial. Jack McCallum saw her in the ER.'

Gordon nodded. They all knew Jack well. Although he was no longer in the astronaut corps, Jack was still on NASA's active flight surgeon roster. A year ago, he had pulled back from most of his NASA duties, to work as an ER physician in the private sector.

'Jack's the one who called our office about Debbie,' said Hank.

'Did he say anything about her condition?'

'Severe head injury. She's in ICU, in a coma.'

'Prognosis?'

'He couldn't answer that question.' There was a silence as they all considered what this tragedy meant to NASA. Hank sighed. 'We're going to have to tell Bill. We can't keep this news from him. The problem is . . .' He didn't finish. He didn't need to; they all understood the problem.

Bill Haning was now in orbit aboard ISS, only a month into his scheduled four-month stay. This news would devastate him. Of all the factors that made prolonged habitation in space difficult, it was the emotional toll that NASA worried about most. A depressed astronaut could wreak havoc on a mission. Years before, on *Mir*, a similar situation had occurred when Cosmonaut Volodya Dezhurov was informed of his mother's death. For days, he'd shut himself away in one of *Mir*'s modules and refused to speak to Mission Control Moscow. His grief had disrupted the work of everyone aboard *Mir*.

'They have a very close marriage,' said Hank. 'I can tell you now, Bill's not going to handle this well.'

'You're recommending we replace him?' asked Gordon.

'At the next scheduled shuttle flight. He'll have a tough enough time being stuck up there for the next two weeks. We can't ask him to serve out his full four months.' Hank added quietly, 'They have two young kids, you know.'

'His backup for ISS is Emma Watson,' said Woody Ellis. 'We could send her up on STS 160. With Vance's crew.'

At the mention of Emma's name, Gordon was careful not to reveal any sign of special interest.

45

Any emotion whatsoever. 'What do you think about Watson? Is she ready to go up three months early?'

'She's slated to relieve Bill. She's already up to speed on most of the onboard experiments. So I think that option is viable.'

'Well, I'm not happy about it,' said Bob Kittredge.

Gordon gave a tired sigh and turned to the shuttle commander. 'I didn't think you would be.'

'Watson's an integral part of *my* crew. We've crystallized as a team. I hate to break it up.'

'Your team's three months away from launch. You have time to make adjustments.'

'You're making my job hard.'

'Are you saying you can't get a new team crystallized in that time?'

Kittredge's mouth tightened. 'All I'm saying is, my crew is already a working unit. We're not going to be happy about losing Watson.'

Gordon looked at Hank. 'What about the STS 160 crew? Vance and his team?'

'No problem from their end. Watson would just be another passenger on middeck. They'd deliver her to ISS like any other payload.'

Gordon thought it over. They were still talking about options, not certainties. Perhaps Debbie Haning would wake up fine and Bill could stay on ISS as scheduled. But like everyone else at NASA, Gordon had taught himself to plan for every contingency, to carry in his head a mental flow chart of what actions to follow should a, b, or c occur.

He looked at Woody Ellis for final confirmation. Woody gave a nod.

'Okay,' said Gordon. 'Find me Emma Watson.'

She spotted him at the far end of the hospital hall-way. He was talking to Hank Millar, and though his back was turned to her and he was wearing standard green surgical scrubs, Emma knew it was Jack. Seven years of marriage had left ties of familiarity that went beyond the mere recognition of his face.

This was, in fact, the same view she'd had of Jack McCallum the first time they'd met, when they'd both been ER residents in San Francisco General Hospital. He had been standing at the nurses' station, writing in a chart, his broad shoulders sloping from fatigue, his hair ruffled as though he'd just rolled out of bed. In fact, he had; it was the morning after a hectic night on call, and though he was unshaven and bleary-eyed, when he'd turned and looked at her for the first time, the attraction between them had been instantaneous.

Now Jack was ten years older, his dark hair was threaded with gray, and fatigue was once again weighing down on his shoulders. She had not seen him in three weeks, had spoken to him only briefly on the phone a few days ago, a con-versation that had deteriorated into yet another noisy disagreement. These days they could not seem to be reasonable with each other, could not carry on a civilized conversation, however brief.

So it was with apprehension that she continued down the hall in his direction.

Hank Millar spotted her first, and his face instantly tensed, as though he knew a battle was imminent, and he wanted to get the hell out of there before the shooting started. Jack must have seen the change in Hank's expression as well, because he turned to see what had inspired it.

At his first glimpse of Emma, he seemed to freeze, a spontaneous smile of greeting half-formed on his face. It was almost, but not quite, a look of both surprise and gladness to see her. Then something else took control, and his smile vanished, replaced by a look that was neither friendly nor unfriendly, merely neutral. The face of a stranger, she thought, and that was somehow more painful than if he had greeted her with outright hostility. At least then there would've been *some* emotion left, some remnant, however tattered, of a marriage that had once been happy.

She found herself responding to his flat look with an expression that was every bit as neutral. When she spoke, she addressed both men at the same time, favoring neither.

'Gordon told me about Debbie,' she said. 'How is she doing?'

Hank glanced at Jack, waiting for him to answer first. Finally Hank said, 'She's still unconscious.

We're sort of holding a vigil in the waiting room. If you want to join us.'

'Yes. Of course.' She started toward the visitors' waiting room.

'Emma,' Jack called out. 'Can we talk?'

'I'll see you both later,' said Hank, and he made a hasty retreat down the hall. They waited for him to disappear around the corner, then looked at each other.

'Debbie's not doing well,' said Jack.

'What happened?'

'She had an epidural bleed. Came in conscious and talking. In a matter of minutes, she went straight downhill. I was busy with another patient. I didn't realize it in time. Didn't drill the burr hole until . . .' He paused and looked away. 'She's on a ventilator.'

Emma reached out to touch him, then stopped herself, knowing that he would only shake her off. It had been so long since he'd accepted any words of comfort from her. No matter what she said, how sincerely she meant it, he would regard it as pity. And that he despised.

'It's a hard diagnosis to make, Jack,' was all she could say.

'I should have made it sooner.'

'You said she went downhill fast. Don't second-guess yourself.'

'That doesn't make me feel a hell of a lot better.'

'I'm not trying to make you feel better!' she said in exasperation. 'I'm just pointing out the simple

49

fact that you did make the right diagnosis. And you acted on it. For once, can't you cut yourself some slack?'

'Look, this isn't about me, okay?' he shot back. 'It's about *you*.'

'What do you mean?'

'Debbie won't be leaving the hospital anytime soon. And that means Bill . . .'

'I know. Gordon Obie gave me the heads-up.'

Jack paused. 'It's been decided?'

She nodded. 'Bill's coming home. I'll replace him on the next flight.' Her gaze drifted toward the ICU. 'They have two kids,' she said softly. 'He can't stay up there. Not for another three months.'

'You're not ready. You haven't had time –'

'I'll *be* ready.' She turned.

'Emma.' He reached out to stop her, and the touch of his hand took her by surprise. She looked back at him. At once he released her.

'When are you leaving for Kennedy?' he asked.

'A week. Quarantine.'

He looked stunned. He said nothing, still trying to absorb the news.

'That reminds me,' she said. 'Could you take care of Humphrey while I'm gone?'

'Why not a kennel?'

'It's cruel to keep a cat penned up for three months.'

'Has the little monster been declawed yet?'

'Come on, Jack. He only shreds things when

50

he's feeling ignored. Pay attention to him, and he'll leave your furniture alone.'

Jack glanced up as a page was announced over the address system: 'Dr McCallum to ER. Dr McCallum to ER.'

'I guess you have to go,' she said, already turning away.

'Wait. This is happening so fast. We haven't had time to talk.'

'If it's about the divorce, my lawyer can answer any questions while I'm gone.'

'No.' He startled her with his sharp note of anger. 'No, I *don't* want to talk to your lawyer!'

'Then what do you need to tell me?'

He stared at her for a moment, as though hunting for words. 'It's about this mission,' he finally said. 'It's too rushed. It doesn't feel right to me.'

'What does that mean?'

'You're a last-minute replacement. You're going up with a different crew.'

'Vance runs a tight ship. I'm perfectly comfortable with this launch.'

'What about on the station? This could stretch your stay to six months in orbit.'

'I can deal with it.'

'But it wasn't planned. It's been thrown together at the last minute.'

'What are you saying I should do, Jack? Wimp out?'

'I don't know!' He ran his hand through his hair in frustration. 'I don't know.'

They stood in silence for a moment, neither one of them quite sure what to say, yet neither one ready to end the conversation. *Seven years of marriage*, she thought, *and this is what it's come to. Two people who can't stay together, yet can't walk away from each other. And now there's no time left to work things out between us.*

A new page came over the address system: 'Dr McCallum stat to ER.'

Jack looked at her, his expression torn. 'Emma –'

'Go, Jack,' she urged him. 'They need you.'

He gave a groan of frustration and took off at a run for the ER.

And she turned and walked the other way.

4

July 12
Aboard ISS

From the observation windows of the Node 1 cupola, Dr William Haning could see clouds swirling over the Atlantic Ocean two hundred twenty miles below. He touched the glass, his fingers skimming the barrier that protected him from the vacuum of space. It was one more obstacle that separated him from home. From his wife. He watched the earth turn beneath him, saw the Atlantic Ocean slip away as North Africa and then the Indian Ocean slowly spun by, the darkness of night approaching. Though his body was weightless and floating, the burden of grief seemed to squeeze down on his chest, making it difficult for him to breathe.

At that moment, in a Houston hospital, his wife was fighting for her life, and he could do nothing to help her. For the next two weeks he would be trapped here, able to gaze down at the very city where Debbie might be dying, yet unable to reach her, touch her. The best he could do was close his eyes and try to imagine he was at her side, that their fingers were entwined.

You have to hang on. You have to fight. I'm coming home to you.

'Bill? Are you okay?'

He turned and saw Diana Estes float from the U.S. lab module into the node. He was surprised she was the one inquiring as to his well-being. Even after a month of living together in close quarters, he had not warmed up to the English-woman. She was too cool, too clinical. Despite her icy blond good looks, she was not a woman he'd ever feel attracted to, and she had certainly never favored him with the least hint of interest. But then, her attention was usually focused on Michael Griggs. The fact that Griggs had a wife waiting for him down on earth seemed irrelevant to them both. Up here on ISS, Diana and Griggs were like the two halves of a double star, orbiting each other, linked by some powerful gravitational pull.

This was one of the unfortunate realities of being one of six human beings from four different countries trapped in close quarters. There were always shifting alliances and schisms, a changing sense of *us* versus *them*. The stress of living so long in confinement had affected each of them in different ways. Russian Nicolai Rudenko, who had been living aboard ISS the longest, had lately turned sullen and irritable. Kenichi Hirai, from Japan's NASDA, was so frustrated by his poor command of English, he often lapsed into uneasy silence. Only Luther Ames had remained everyone's friend. When Houston broke the bad news about Debbie, Luther was the one who had known instinctively what to say to Bill, the one who had spoken from his heart, from the human part of him. Luther was the Alabama-born son of a well-loved black minister, and he had inherited his father's gift for bestowing comfort.

'There's no question about it, Bill,' Luther had said. 'You gotta go home to your wife. You tell Houston they'd better send the limo to get you, or they'll have to deal with me.'

How different from the way Diana had reacted. Ever logical, she had calmly pointed out that there was nothing Bill could do to speed his wife's recovery. Debbie was comatose; she wouldn't even know he was there. *As cold and brittle as the crystals she grows in her lab*, was what Bill thought of Diana.

That's why he was puzzled that she was now asking about him. She hung back in the node, as remote as always. Her long blond hair waved about her face like drifting sea grass.

He turned to look out the window again. 'I'm waiting for Houston to come into view,' he said.

'You've got a new batch of E-mail from Payloads.'

He said nothing. He just stared down at the twinkling lights of Tokyo, now poised at the knife edge of dawn.

'Bill, there are items that require your attention. If you don't feel up to it, we'll have to split up your duties among the rest of us.'

Duties. So that's what she had come to discuss. Not the pain he was feeling, but whether she could count on him to perform his assigned tasks in the lab. Every day aboard ISS was tightly scheduled, with little time to spare for reflection or grief. If one crew member was incapacitated, the others had to pick up the slack, or experiments went untended.

'Sometimes,' said Diana with crisp logic, 'work is the best thing to keep grief at bay.'

He touched his finger to the blur of light that was Tokyo. 'Don't pretend to have a heart, Diana. It doesn't fool anyone.'

For a moment she said nothing. He heard only the continuous background hum of the space station, a sound he'd grown so accustomed to he was scarcely aware of it now.

She said, unruffled, 'I do understand you're having a hard time. I know it's not easy to be trapped up here, with no way to get home. But there's nothing you can do about it. You just have to wait for the shuttle.'

He gave a bitter laugh. 'Why wait? When I could be home in four hours.'

'Come on, Bill. Get serious.'

'I am serious. I should just get in the CRV and *go*.'

'Leaving us with no lifeboat? You're not thinking straight.' She paused. 'You know, you might feel better with some medication. Just to help you get through this period.'

He turned to face her, all his pain, all his grief, giving way to rage. 'Take a pill and cure everything, is that it?'

'It could help. Bill, I just need to know you won't do something irrational.'

'Fuck you, Diana.' He pushed off from the cupola and floated past her, toward the lab hatchway.

'Bill!'

'As you so kindly pointed out, I've got work to do.'

'I told you, we can divide up your duties. If you're not feeling up to it –'

'I'll do my own goddamn work!'

He drifted into the U.S. lab. He was relieved she didn't follow him. Glancing back, he saw her float toward the habitation module, no doubt to check the status of the Crew Return Vehicle. Capable of evacuating all six astronauts, the CRV was their only lifeboat home should a catastrophe befall the station. He had spooked her with his mutterings about hijacking the CRV, and he regretted it. Now she'd be watching him for signs of emotional meltdown.

It was painful enough to be trapped in this glorified sardine can two hundred twenty miles above earth. To also be watched with suspicion made the ordeal worse. He might be desperate to go home, but he was not unstable. All those years of training, the psychological screening tests, had confirmed the fact Bill Haning was a professional – certainly not a man who'd ever endanger his colleagues.

Propelling himself with a practiced push-off from one wall, he floated across the lab module to his workstation. There he checked the latest batch of E-mail. Diana was right about one thing: Work would distract him from thoughts of Debbie.

Most of the E-mail had come from NASA's Ames Biological Research Center in California, and the messages were routine requests for data confirmation. Many of the experiments were monitored from the ground, and scientists sometimes questioned the data they received. He scrolled down the messages, grimacing at yet another request for astronaut urine and feces samples. He kept scrolling, and paused at a new message.

This one was different. It did not come from Ames, but from a private-sector payload operations center. Private industry paid for a number of experiments aboard the station, and he often received E-mail from scientists outside NASA.

This message was from SeaScience in La Jolla, California.

To: Dr William Haning, ISS Bioscience
Sender: Helen Koenig, Principal Investigator

Re: Experiment CCU#23 (Archaeon Cell Culture)

Message: Our most recent downlinked data indicates rapid and unexpected increase in cell culture mass. Please confirm with your onboard micro mass measurement device.

Another jiggle-the-handle request, he thought wearily. Many of the orbital experiments were controlled by commands from scientists on the ground. Data was recorded within the various lab racks, using video or automatic sampling devices, and the results downlinked directly to researchers on earth. With all the sophisticated equipment aboard ISS, there were bound to be occasional glitches. That's the real reason humans were needed up here – to troubleshoot the temperamental electronics.

He called up the file for CCU#23 on the payloads computer and reviewed the protocol. The cells in the culture were *Archaeons*, bacterialike marine organisms collected from deep-sea thermal vents. They were harmless to humans.

He floated across the lab to the cell culture unit and slipped his stockinged feet into the holding stirrups to maintain his position. The unit was a box-shaped device with its own fluid-handling and delivery system to continuously perfuse two dozen cell cultures and tissue specimens. Most of the experiments were completely self-contained and without need of human intervention. In his four weeks aboard ISS, Bill had only once laid eyes on the tube #23.

He pulled open the cell specimen chamber tray. Inside were twenty-four culture tubes arrayed around the periphery of the unit. He identified #23 and removed it from the tray.

At once he was alarmed. The cap appeared to be bulging out, as though under pressure. Instead of a slightly turbid liquid, which was what he'd expected to see, the contents was a vivid blue-green. He tipped the tube upside down, and the culture did not shift. It was no longer liquid, but thickly viscous.

He calibrated the micro mass measurement device and slipped the tube into the specimen slot. A moment later, the data appeared on the screen.

Something is very wrong, he thought. *There has been some sort of contamination. Either the original sample of cells was not pure, or another organism has found its way into the tube and has destroyed the primary culture.*

He typed out his response to Dr Koenig:

. . . Your downlinked data confirmed. Culture appears drastically altered. It is no longer liquid, but seems to be a gelatinous mass, bright, almost neon blue-green. Must consider the possibility of contamination . . .

He paused. There was another possibility: the effect of microgravity. On earth, tissue cultures tended to grow in flat sheets, expanding in only two dimensions across the surface of their containers. In the weightlessness of space, freed from the effects of gravity, those same cultures behaved differently. They grew in three dimensions, taking on shapes they never could on earth.

What if #23 was not contaminated? What if this was simply how Archaeons behaved without gravity to keep them in check?

Almost immediately he discarded that notion. These changes were too drastic. Weightlessness alone could not have turned a single-celled organism into this startling green mass.

He typed:

... Will return a sample of culture #23 to you on next shuttle flight. Please advise if you have further instructions –

The sudden clang of a drawer startled him. He turned and saw Kenichi Hirai working at his own research rack. How long had he been there? The man had drifted so quietly into the lab Bill had not even known he'd entered. In a world where there is no up or down, where the sound of footsteps is never heard, a verbal greeting is sometimes the only way to alert others to your presence.

Noticing Bill's glance, Kenichi merely nodded in greeting and continued with his work. The man's silence irritated Bill. Kenichi was like the station's resident ghost, creeping around without a

61

word, startling everyone. Bill knew it was because Kenichi was insecure about his English and, to avoid humiliation, chose to converse little if at all. Still, the man could at least call out a 'hello' when he entered a module to avoid rattling the nerves of his five colleagues.

Bill turned his attention back to tube #23. What would this gelatinous mass look like under the microscope?

He slid tube #23 into the Plexiglas glove box, closed the hatch, and inserted his hands in the attached gloves. If there was any spillage, it would be confined to the box. Loose fluids floating around in microgravity could wreak havoc on the station's electrical wiring. Gently he loosened the tube seal. He knew the contents were under pressure; he could see the cap was bulging. Even so, he was shocked when the top suddenly exploded off like a champagne cork.

He jerked back as a blue-green glob splatted against the inside of the glove box. It clung there for a moment, quivering as though alive. It *was* alive; a mass of microorganisms, joined in a gelatinous matrix.

'Bill, we need to talk.'

The voice startled him. Quickly he recapped the culture tube and turned to face Michael Griggs, who had just entered the module. Floating right behind Griggs was Diana. *The beautiful people*, Bill thought. Both of them looked sleek and athletic in their navy blue NASA shirts and cobalt shorts.

'Diana tells me you're having problems,' said Griggs. 'We just spoke to Houston, and they think it might help if you considered some medication. Just to get you through the next few days.'

'You've got Houston worried now, have you?'

'They're concerned about you. We all are.'

'Look, my crack about the CRV was purely sarcastic.'

'But it makes us all nervous.'

'I don't need any Valium. Just leave me alone.' He removed the tube from the glove box and returned it to its slot in the cell culture unit. He was too angry to work on it now.

'We have to be able to trust you, Bill. We have to depend on each other up here.'

In fury, Bill turned to face him. 'Do you see a raving lunatic in front of you? Is that it?'

'Your wife is on your mind now. I understand that. And —'

'You wouldn't understand. I doubt you give *your* wife much thought these days.' He shot a knowing glance at Diana, then launched himself down the length of the module and into the connecting node. He started to enter the hab module, but stopped when he saw Luther was there, setting up the midday meal.

There's nowhere to hide. Nowhere to be alone.

Suddenly in tears, he backed out of the hatchway and retreated into the cupola.

Turning his back to the others, he stared through the windows at the earth. Already, the Pacific coast was rotating into view. Another sunrise, another sunset.

Another eternity of waiting.

Kenichi watched Griggs and Diana float out of the lab module, each propelled by a well-gauged push-off. They moved with such grace, like fair-haired gods. He often studied them when they weren't watching; in particular, he enjoyed looking at Diana Estes, a woman so blond and pale she seemed translucent.

Their departure left him alone in the lab, and he was able to relax. So much conflict on this station. It unsettled his nerves and affected his concentration. He was tranquil by nature, a man content to work in solitude. Though he could understand English well enough, it was an effort for him to speak it, and he found conversation exhausting. He was far more comfortable working alone, and in silence, with only the lab animals as company.

He peered through the viewing window at the mice in the animal habitat, and he smiled. On one side of the screened divider were twelve males; on the other were twelve females. As a boy growing up in Japan, he had raised rabbits and had enjoyed cuddling them in his lap. These mice, however, were not pets, and they were isolated from human contact, their air filtered and conditioned before being allowed to mix with the space station's environment. Any handling of the animals was done in the adjoining glove box, where all biological specimens, from bacteria to lab rats, could be manipulated without fear of contaminating the station's air.

Today was blood-sampling day. Not a task he enjoyed, because it involved pricking the skin of the mice with a needle. He murmured an apology in Japanese as he inserted his hands in the gloves and transferred the first mouse into the sealed work area. It struggled to escape his grasp. He released it, allowing it to float free as he prepared the needle. It was a pitiful sight to watch, the mouse frantically thrashing its limbs, attempting to propel itself forward. With nothing to push off against, it drifted helplessly in midair.

The needle now ready, he reached up with his gloved hand to recapture the mouse. Only then did he notice the blue-green globule floating beside the mouse. So close to it, in fact, that with one dart of a pink tongue, the mouse gave it an experimental lick. Kenichi laughed out loud. Drinking floating globules was something the astronauts did for fun, and that's what the mouse appeared to be doing now, playing with its newfound toy.

Then the thought occurred to him: Where had the blue-green substance come from? Bill had been using the glove box. Was whatever he'd spilled toxic?

Kenichi floated to the computer workstation and looked at the experimental protocol Bill had last called up. It was CCU#23, a cell culture.

The protocol reassured him that the globule contained nothing dangerous. *Archaeons* were harmless single-celled marine organisms, without infectious properties.

Satisfied, he returned to the glove box and inserted his hands. He reached for the needle.

5

July 16

We have no downlink.

Jack stared up at the plume of exhaust streaking into the azure sky, and terror knifed deep into his soul. The sun was beating down on his face, but his sweat had chilled to ice. He scanned the heavens. Where was the shuttle? Only seconds before, he had watched it arc into a cloudless sky, had felt the ground shake from the thunder of liftoff. As it had climbed, he'd felt his heart soar with it, borne aloft by the roar of rockets, and had followed its path heavenward until it was just a glinting pinprick of reflected sunlight.

He could not see it. What had been a straight white plume was now a jagged trail of black smoke.

Frantically he searched the sky and caught a dizzying whirl of images. Fire in the heavens. A devil's fork of smoke. Shattered fragments tumbling toward the sea.

We have no downlink.

He woke up, gasping, his body steeped in sweat. It was daylight, and the sun shone, piercingly hot, through his bedroom window.

With a groan he sat up on the side of the bed and dropped his head in his hands. He had left the air conditioner off last night, and now the room felt like an oven. He stumbled across his bedroom to flip the switch, then sank down on the bed again and breathed a sigh of relief as chill air began to spill from the vent.

The old nightmare.

He rubbed his face, trying to banish the images, but they were too deeply engraved in his memory. He had been a college freshman when *Challenger* exploded, had been walking through the dorm lounge when the first film footage of the disaster had aired on the television. That day, and in the days that followed, he'd watched the horrifying footage again and again, had incorporated it so deeply into his subconscious that it had become as real to him as if he himself had been standing in the bleachers at Cape Canaveral that morning.

And now the memory had resurfaced in his nightmares.

It's because of Emma's launch.

In the shower he stood with head bowed under a pounding stream of cool water, waiting for the last traces of his dream to wash away. He had three weeks of vacation starting next week, but he was a long way from being in a holiday mood. He had not taken out the sailboat in months. Maybe a few weeks out on the water, away from the glare of city lights, would be the best therapy. Just him, and the sea, and the stars.

It had been so long since he'd really looked at the stars. Lately it seemed he had avoided even glancing at them. As a boy, his gaze had always been drawn heavenward. His mother once told him that, as a toddler, he had stood on the lawn one night and reached up with both hands, trying to touch the moon. When he could not reach it, he had howled in frustration.

The moon, the stars, the blackness of space – it was beyond his reach now, and he often felt like that little boy he once was, howling in frustration, his feet trapped on earth, his hands still reaching for the sky.

He shut off the shower and stood leaning with both hands pressed against the tiles, head bent, hair dripping. *Today is July sixteenth*, he thought. *Eight days till Emma's launch*. He felt the water chill on his skin.

In ten minutes he was dressed and in the car.

It was a Tuesday. Emma and her new flight team would be wrapping up their three-day integrated simulation, and she'd be tired and in no mood to see him. But tomorrow she'd be on her way to Cape Canaveral. Tomorrow she'd be out of reach.

At Johnson Space Center, he parked in the

Building 30 lot, flashed his NASA badge at Security, and trotted upstairs to the shuttle Flight Control Room. Inside, he found everyone hushed and tense. The three-day integrated simulation was like the final exam for both the astronauts and the ground control crew, a crisis-packed run-through of the mission from launch to touchdown, with assorted malfunctions thrown in to keep everyone on their toes. Three shifts of controllers had rotated through this room several times in the last three days, and the two dozen men and women now sitting at the consoles looked haggard. The rubbish can was overflowing with coffee cups and diet Pepsi cans. Though a few of the controllers saw Jack and nodded hello, there was no time for a real greeting; they had a major crisis on their hands, and everyone's attention was focused on the problem. It was the first time in months Jack had visited the FCR, and once again he felt the old excitement, the electricity, that seemed to crackle in this room whenever a mission was underway.

He moved to the third row of consoles, to stand beside Flight Director Randy Carpenter, who was too busy at the moment to talk to him. Carpenter was the shuttle program's high priest of flight directors. At two hundred eighty pounds, he was an imposing presence in the FCR, his stomach bulging over his belt, his feet planted apart like a ship's captain steadying himself on a heaving bridge. In this room, Carpenter was in command. 'I'm a prime example,' he liked to say, 'of just how far a fat boy with glasses can get in life.' Unlike the legendary flight director Gene Kranz, whose quote 'Failure is not an option' made him a media hero, Carpenter was well known only within NASA. His lack of photogenic qualities made him an unlikely movie hero, in any event.

Listening in on the loop chatter, Jack quickly pieced together the nature of the crisis Carpenter was now dealing with. Jack had faced just such a problem in his own integrated sim two years ago, when he was still in the astronaut corps, preparing for STS 145. The shuttle crew had reported a precipitous drop in cabin pressure, indicating a rapid air leak. There was no time to track down the source; they had to go to emergency deorbit.

The flight dynamics officer, sitting at the front row of consoles known as the Trench, was rapidly plotting out the flight trajectories to determine the best landing site. No one considered this a game; they were too aware that if this crisis were real, the lives of seven people would be in jeopardy.

'Cabin pressure down to thirteen point nine psi,' reported Environmental Control.

'Edwards Air Force Base,' announced Flight Dynamics. 'Touchdown at approximately thirteen hundred.'

'Cabin pressure will be down to seven psi at this rate,' said Environmental. 'Recommend they don helmets now. Before initiating reentry sequence.'

Capcom relayed the advice to *Atlantis*.

'Roger that,' responded Commander Vance. 'Helmets are on. We are initiating deorbit burn.'

Against his will, Jack was caught up in the urgency of the game. As the moments ticked by, he kept his gaze fixed on the central screen at the front of the room, where the orbiter's path was plotted on a global map. Even though he knew that every crisis was artificially introduced by a mischievous sim team, the grim seriousness of this exercise had rubbed off on him. He was scarcely aware that his muscles had tensed as he focused on the changing data flickering on the screen.

The cabin pressure dropped to seven psi.

Atlantis hit the upper atmosphere. They were in radio blackout, twelve long minutes of silence when the friction of reentry ionizes the air around the orbiter, cutting off all communications.

'*Atlantis*, do you copy?' said Capcom.

Suddenly Commander Vance's voice broke through: 'We hear you loud and clear, Houston.'

Touchdown, moments later, was perfect. Game over.

Applause broke out in the FCR.

'Okay, folks! Good job,' said Flight Director Carpenter. 'Debriefing at fifteen hundred. Let's all take a break for lunch.' Grinning, he pulled off his headset and for the first time looked at Jack. 'Hey, haven't seen you around here in ages.'

'Been playing doctor with civilians.'

'Going for the big bucks, huh?'

Jack laughed. 'Yeah, tell me what to do with

all my money.' He glanced around at the flight controllers, now relaxing at their consoles with sodas and bag lunches. 'Did the sim go okay?'

'I'm happy. We made it through every glitch.'

'And the shuttle crew?'

'They're ready.' Carpenter gave him a knowing look. 'Including Emma. She's in her element, Jack, so don't rattle her. Right now she needs to focus.' This was more than just friendly advice. It was a warning: *Keep your personal issues to yourself. Don't screw around with my flight crew's morale.*

Jack was subdued, even a little contrite, as he waited outside in the sweltering heat for Emma to emerge from Building 5, where the flight simulators were housed. She walked out with the rest of her crew. Obviously they had just shared a joke, because they were all laughing. Then she saw Jack, and her smile faded.

'I didn't know you were coming,' she said.

He shrugged and said sheepishly, 'Neither did I.'

'Debriefing's in ten minutes,' said Vance.

'I'll be there,' she said. 'You all go on ahead.' She waited for her team to walk away; then she turned to face Jack again. 'I've really got to join them. Look, I know this launch complicates everything. If you're here about the divorce papers, I promise I'll sign them as soon as I get back.'

'I didn't come about that.'

'Is there something else, then?'

He paused. 'Yeah. Humphrey. What's the name

of his vet? In case he swallows a hair ball or something.'

She fixed him with a perplexed look. 'The same vet he's always had. Dr Goldsmith.'

'Oh. Yeah.'

They stood in silence for a moment, the sun beating on their heads. Sweat trickled down his back. She suddenly seemed so small to him and insubstantial. Yet this was a woman who'd jumped out of an airplane. She could outrace him on horseback, spin circles around him on the dance floor. His beautiful, fearless wife.

She turned to look at Building 30, where her team was waiting for her. 'I have to go, Jack.'

'What time are you leaving for the Cape?'

'Six in the morning.'

'All your cousins flying out for the launch?'

'Of course.' She paused. 'You won't be there. Will you?'

The *Challenger* nightmare was still fresh in his mind, the angry trails of smoke etching across a blue sky. *I can't be there to watch it*, he thought. *I can't deal with the possibilities*. He shook his head.

She accepted his answer with a chilly nod and a look that said: *I can be every bit as detached as you are*. Already she was withdrawing from him, turning to leave.

'Emma.' He reached for her arm and gently tugged her around to face him. 'I'll miss you.'

She sighed. 'Sure, Jack.'

'I really will.'

'Weeks go by without a single call from you. And now you say you're going to miss me.' She laughed.

He was stung by the bitterness in her voice. And by the truth of her words. For the past few months he *had* avoided her. It had been painful to be anywhere near her because her success only magnified his own sense of failure.

There was no hope of reconciliation; he could see that now, in the coolness of her gaze. Nothing left to do but be civilized about it.

He glanced away, suddenly unable to look at her. 'I just came by to wish you a safe trip. And a great ride. Give me a wave every so often, when you pass over Houston. I'll watch for you.' A moving star was what ISS would look like, brighter than Venus, hurtling through the sky.

'You wave too, okay?'

They both managed a smile. So it would be a civilized parting after all. He held open his arms, and she leaned toward him for a hug. It was a brief and awkward one, as though they were strangers coming together for the first time. He felt her body, so warm and alive, press against him. Then she pulled away and started toward the Mission Control building.

She paused only once, to wave good-bye. The sunlight was sharp in his eyes, and squinting against its brightness, he saw her only as a dark silhouette, her hair flying in the hot wind. And he knew that he had never loved her as much as he did at that very moment, watching her walk away.

July 19
Cape Canaveral

Even from a distance, the sight took Emma's breath away. Poised on launchpad 39B, awash in brilliant floodlights, the shuttle *Atlantis*, mated to its giant orange fuel tank and the paired solid rocket boosters, was a towering beacon in the blackness of night. No matter how many times she experienced it, that first glimpse of a shuttle lit up on the pad never failed to awe her.

The rest of the crew, standing beside her on the blacktop, were equally silent. To shift their sleep cycle, they'd awakened at two that morning and had emerged from their quarters on the third floor of the Operations and Checkout building to catch a nighttime glimpse of the behemoth that would carry them into space. Emma heard the cry of a night bird and felt a cool wind blow in from the Gulf, freshening the air, sweeping away the stagnant scent of the wetlands surrounding them.

'Kind of makes you feel humble, doesn't it?' said Commander Vance in his soft Texas drawl.

The others murmured in agreement.

'Small as an ant,' said Chenoweth, the lone rookie on the crew. This would be his first trip aboard the shuttle, and he was so excited he seemed to generate his own field of electricity.

76

'I always forget how big she is, and then I take another look at her and I think, Jesus, all that power. And I'm the lucky son of a bitch who gets to ride her.'

They all laughed, but it was the hushed, uneasy laughter of parishioners in a church.

'I never thought a week could go by so slowly,' said Chenoweth.

'This man's tired of being a virgin,' said Vance.

'Damn right I am. I want *up* there.' Chenoweth's gaze lifted hungrily to the sky. To the stars. 'You guys all know the secret, and I can't wait to share it.'

The secret. It belonged only to the privileged few who had made the ascent. It wasn't a secret that could be imparted to another; you yourself had to live it, to see, with your own eyes, the blackness of space and the blue of earth far below. To be pressed backward into your seat by the thrust of the rockets. Astronauts returning from space often wear a knowing smile, a look that says, *I am privy to something that few human beings will ever know.*

Emma had worn such a smile when she'd emerged from *Atlantis*'s hatch over two years ago. On weak legs she had walked into the sunshine, had stared up at a sky that was startlingly blue. In the span of eight days aboard the orbiter, she had lived through one hundred thirty sunrises, had seen forest fires burning in Brazil and the eye of a hurricane whirling over Samoa, had viewed an earth that seemed heartbreakingly fragile. She had returned forever changed.

In five days, barring a catastrophe, Chenoweth would share the secret.

'Time to shine some light on these retinas,' said Chenoweth. 'My brain still thinks it's the middle of the night.'

'It *is* the middle of the night,' said Emma.

'For us it's the crack of dawn, folks,' Vance said. Of all of them, he had been the quickest to readjust his circadian rhythm to the new sleep-wake schedule. Now he strode back into the O and C building to begin a full day's work at three in the morning.

The others followed him. Only Emma lingered outside for a moment, gazing at the shuttle. The day before, they had driven over to the launchpad for a last review of crew escape procedures. Viewed up close, in the sunlight, the shuttle had seemed glaringly bright and too massive to fully comprehend. One could focus on only a single part of her at a time. The nose. The wings. The black tiles, like reptilian scales on the belly. In the light of day, the shuttle had been real and solid. Now she seemed unearthly, lit up against the black sky.

With all the frantic preparation, Emma had not allowed herself to feel any apprehension, had firmly banished all misgivings. She was ready to go up. She wanted to go up. But now she felt a sliver of fear.

She looked up at the sky, saw the stars disappear

behind an advancing veil of clouds. The weather was about to change. Shivering, she turned and went into the building. Into the light.

July 23
Houston

Half a dozen tubes snaked into Debbie Haning's body. In her throat was a tracheotomy tube, through which oxygen was forced into her lungs. A nasogastric tube had been threaded up her left nostril and down her esophagus into the stomach. A catheter drained urine, and two intravenous catheters fed fluids into her veins. In her wrist was an arterial line, and a continuous blood pressure tracing danced across the oscilloscope. Jack glanced at the IV bags hanging over the bed and saw they contained powerful antibiotics. A bad sign; it meant she'd acquired an infection – not unusual when a patient has spent two weeks in a coma. Every breach in the skin, every plastic tube, is a portal for bacteria, and in Debbie's bloodstream, a battle was now being waged.

With one glance, Jack understood all of this, but he said nothing to Debbie's mother, who sat beside the bed, clasping her daughter's hand. Debbie's face was flaccid, the jaw limp, the eyelids only partially closed. She remained deeply comatose, unaware of anything, even pain.

Margaret looked up as Jack came into the cubicle, and gave a nod of greeting. 'She had a bad night,'

79

said Margaret. 'A fever. They don't know where it's coming from.'

'The antibiotics will help.'

'And then what? We treat the infection, but what happens next?' Margaret took a deep breath. 'She wouldn't want it this way. All these tubes. All these needles. She'd want us to let her go.'

'This isn't the time to give up. Her EEG is still active. She's not brain dead.'

'Then why doesn't she wake up?'

'She's young. She has everything to live for.'

'This isn't *living*.' Margaret stared down at her daughter's hand. It was bruised and puffy from IVs and needle sticks. 'When her father was dying, Debbie told me she never wanted to end up like that. Tied down and force-fed. I keep thinking about that. About what she said . . .' Margaret looked up again. 'What would you do? If this was your wife?'

'I wouldn't think about giving up.'

'Even if she'd told you she didn't want to end up this way?'

He thought about it for a moment. Then said with conviction, 'It would be *my* decision, in the end. No matter what she or anyone else told me. I wouldn't give up on someone I loved. Ever. Not if there was the smallest chance I could save her.'

His words offered no comfort to Margaret. He didn't have the right to question her beliefs, her instincts, but she had asked his opinion, and his answer had come from his heart, not his head.

80

Feeling guilty now, he gave Margaret one last pat on the shoulder and left the cubicle. Nature would most likely take the decision out of their hands. A comatose patient with a systemic infection is already on death's threshold.

He left the ICU and glumly stepped into the elevator. This was a depressing way to kick off his vacation. First stop, he decided as he stepped off on the lobby level, would be the corner grocery store for a six-pack. An ice-cold beer and an afternoon loading up the sailboat was what he needed right now. It would get his mind off Debbie Haning.

'Code Blue, SICU. Code Blue, SICU.'

His head snapped up at the announcement over the hospital address system. *Debbie*, he thought, and dashed for the stairwell.

Her SICU cubicle was already crowded with personnel. He pushed his way in and shot a glance at the monitor. *Ventricular fibrillation!* Her heart was a quivering bundle of muscles, unable to pump, unable to keep her brain alive.

'One amp epinephrine going in now!' one of the nurses called out.

'Everyone stand back!' a doctor ordered, placing the defibrillator paddles on the chest.

Jack saw the body give a jolt as the paddles discharged, and saw the line shoot up on the monitor, then sink back to baseline. Still in V fib.

A nurse was performing CPR, her short blond hair flipping up with each pump on the chest.

Debbie's neurologist, Dr Salomon, glanced up as Jack joined him at the bedside.

'Is the amiodarone in?' asked Jack.

'Going in now, but it's not working.'

Jack glanced at the tracing again. The V fib had gone from coarse to fine. Deteriorating toward a flat line.

'We've shocked her four times,' said Salomon. 'Can't get a rhythm.'

'Intracardiac epi?'

'We're down to Hail Marys. Go ahead!'

The code nurse prepared the syringe of epinephrine and attached a long cardiac needle. Even as Jack took it, he knew that the battle was already over. This procedure would change nothing. But he thought about Bill Haning, waiting to come home to his wife. And he thought about what he had said to Margaret only moments ago.

I wouldn't give up on someone I loved. Ever. Not if there was the smallest chance I could save her.

He looked down at Debbie, and for one disconcerting moment the image of Emma's face flashed through his mind. He swallowed hard and said, 'Hold compressions.'

The nurse lifted her hands from the sternum.

Jack gave the skin a quick swab of Betadine and positioned the tip of the needle beneath the xiphoid process. His own pulse was bounding as he pierced the skin. He advanced the needle into the chest, exerting gentle negative pressure.

A flash of blood told him he was in the heart.

With one squeeze of the plunger, he injected the entire dose of epinephrine and pulled out the needle. 'Resume compressions,' he said, and looked up at the monitor. *Come on, Debbie. Fight, damn it. Don't give up on us. Don't give up on Bill.*

The room was silent, everyone's gaze fixed on the monitor. The tracing flattened, the myocardium dying, cell by cell. No one needed to say a word; the look of defeat was on their faces.

She is so young, thought Jack. Thirty-six years old.

The same age as Emma.

It was Dr Salomon who made the decision. 'Let's end it,' he said quietly. 'Time of death is eleven-fifteen.'

The nurse administering compressions solemnly stepped away from the body. Under the bright cubicle lights, Debbie's torso looked like pale plastic. A mannequin. Not the bright and lively woman Jack had met five years ago at a NASA party held under the stars.

Margaret stepped into the cubicle. For a moment she stood in silence, as though not recognizing her own daughter. Dr Salomon placed his hand on her shoulder and said gently, 'It happened so quickly. There was nothing we could do.'

'He should have been here,' said Margaret, her voice breaking.

'We tried to keep her alive,' said Dr Salomon. 'I'm sorry.'

'It's Bill I feel sorry for,' said Margaret, and she

took her daughter's hand and kissed it. 'He wanted to be here. And now he'll never forgive himself.'

Jack walked out of the cubicle and sank into a chair in the nurses' station. Margaret's words were still ringing in his head. *He should have been here. He'll never forgive himself.*

He looked at the phone. *And what am I still doing here?* he wondered.

He took the Yellow Pages from the ward clerk's desk, picked up the phone, and dialed.

'Lone Star Travel,' a woman answered.

'I need to get to Cape Canaveral.'

6

Cape Canaveral

Through the open window of his rental car, Jack inhaled the humid air of Merritt Island and smelled the jungle odors of damp soil and vegetation. The gateway to Kennedy Space Center was a surprisingly rural road slashing through orange groves, past ramshackle doughnut stands and weed-filled junkyards littered with discarded missile parts. Daylight was fading, and up ahead he saw the taillights of hundreds of cars, slowed to a crawl. Traffic was backing up, and soon his car would be trapped in the conga line of tourists searching for parking spots from which to view the morning launch.

There was no point trying to work his way through this mess. Nor did he see the point of trying to make it through the Port Canaveral gate. At this hour, the astronauts were asleep, anyway. He had arrived too late to say good-bye.

He pulled out of traffic, turned the car around, and headed back to Highway AIA. The road to Cocoa Beach.

Since the era of Alan Shepard and the original Mercury seven, Cocoa Beach had been party central for the astronauts, a slightly seedy strip of hotels and bars and T-shirt shops stretching along a spit of land trapped between the Banana River to the west and the Atlantic Ocean to the east. Jack knew the strip well, from the Tokyo Steak House to the Moon Shot Bar. Once he had jogged the same beach where John Glenn used to run. Only two years ago, he had stood on Jetty Park and gazed across the Banana River at launchpad 39A. At *his* shuttle, the bird that was supposed to take him into space. The memories were still clouded by pain. He remembered a long run on a sweltering afternoon. The sudden, excruciating stab in his flank, an agony so terrible he was brought to his knees. And then, through a haze of narcotics, the somber face of his flight surgeon gazing down at him in the ER, telling him the bad news. A kidney stone.

He'd been scrubbed from the mission.

Even worse, his future in spaceflight was in doubt. A history of kidney stones was one of the few conditions that could permanently ground an astronaut. Microgravity caused physiologic shifts in body fluids, resulting in dehydration. It also caused bones to leach out calcium. Together, these factors raised the risk of new kidney stones while in space – a risk NASA did not want to take. Though still in the astronaut corps, Jack had effectively been grounded. He had hung on for another year, hoping for a new flight assignment, but his name never again came up. He'd been reduced to an astronaut ghost, condemned to wander the halls of JSC forever in search of a mission.

Fast-forward to the present. Here he was, back in Canaveral, no longer an astronaut but just another tourist cruising down A1A, hungry and grumpy, with nowhere to go. Every hotel within forty miles was booked solid, and he was tired of driving.

He turned into the parking lot of the Hilton Hotel and headed for the bar.

The place had been spiffed up considerably since the last time he had been here. New carpet, new barstools, ferns hanging from the ceiling. It used to be a slightly shabby hangout, a tired old Hilton on a tired old tourist strip. There were no four-star hotels on Cocoa Beach. This was as close as you came to luxury digs.

He ordered a scotch and water and focused on the TV above the bar. It was tuned to the official NASA channel, and the shuttle *Atlantis* was on the screen, aglow with floodlights, ghostly vapor rising around it. Emma's ride into space. He stared at the image, thinking of the miles of wiring inside that hull, the countless switches and data buses, the screws and joints and O-rings. Millions of things that could go wrong. It was a wonder that so little *did* go wrong, that men, imperfect as they were, could design and build a craft of such reliability that seven people are willing to strap themselves inside. *Please let this launch be one of the perfect ones*, he thought. *A launch where everyone has done their job right, and not a screw is loose. It has to be perfect because my Emma will be aboard.*

A woman sat down on the barstool beside him and said, 'I wonder what they're thinking now.'

He turned to look at her, his interest momentarily captured by a glimpse of thigh. She was a sleek and sunny blonde, with one of those blandly perfect faces whose features one forgets within an hour of parting. 'What who's thinking?' he asked.

'The astronauts. I wonder if they're thinking, "Oh, shit, what'd I get myself into?"'

He shrugged and took a sip of scotch. 'They're not thinking anything right now. They're all asleep.'

'I wouldn't be able to sleep.'

'Their circadian rhythm's completely readjusted. They probably went to bed two hours ago.'

'No, I mean, I wouldn't be able to sleep at *all*. I'd be lying awake thinking up ways to get out of it.'

He laughed. 'I guarantee you, if they're awake, it's because they can't wait to climb on board that baby and blast off.'

She looked at him curiously. 'You're with the program, aren't you?'

'Was. Astronaut corps.'

'Not now?'

He lifted the drink to his lips, felt the ice cubes clink sharply against his teeth. 'I retired.' Setting down his empty glass, he rose to his feet and saw disappointment flash in the woman's eyes. He allowed himself a moment's consideration of how the rest of the evening *could* go were he to stay and continue the conversation. Pleasant company. The promise of more to follow.

Instead he paid his bar tab and walked out of the Hilton.

At midnight, standing on the beach at Jetty Park, he gazed across the water toward pad 39B. *I'm here*, he thought. *Even if you don't know it, I'm with you.*

He sat down on the sand and waited for dawn.

July 24

Houston

'There's a high-pressure system over the Gulf, which is expected to keep skies clear over Cape Canaveral, so RTLS landing is a go. Edwards Air Force Base is seeing intermittent clouds, but that's expected to clear by launch. TAL site in Zaragoza, Spain, is still current and forecast go. TAL site in Morón, Spain, is also current and go. Ben Guerir, Morocco, is experiencing high winds and sandstorms, and at this time is not a viable TAL site.'

The first weather briefing of the day, broadcast simultaneously to Cape Canaveral, brought satisfactory news, and Flight Director Carpenter was happy. The launch was still a go. The poor landing conditions at Ben Guerir airport was only a minor concern, since the two alternate transatlantic-abort landing sites in Spain were clear. It was all backups within backups, anyway; the sites would be needed only in case of a major malfunction.

He glanced around at the rest of the ascent team to see if there were any new concerns. The nervous tension in the Flight Control Room was palpable and mounting, as it always was prior to a launch, and that was good. The day they *weren't* tense was the day they made mistakes. Carpenter wanted his people on edge, with all synapses snapping – a level of alertness that, at midnight, required an extra dose of adrenaline.

Carpenter's nerves were as taut as everyone else's, despite the fact that the countdown was right on schedule. The inspection team at Kennedy had finished their checks. The flight dynamics team had reconfirmed the launch time to the second. In the meantime, a far-flung cast of thousands was watching the same countdown clock.

At Cape Canaveral, where the shuttle was poised for launch, the same tension would be building in the firing room of the Launch Control Center, where a parallel team sat at their consoles, preparing for liftoff. As soon as the solid rocket boosters ignited, Houston's Mission Control would take over. Though thousands of miles apart, the two control rooms in Houston and Canaveral were so closely interconnected by communications they might as well have been located in the same building.

In Huntsville, Alabama, at Marshall Space Flight

Center, research teams were waiting for their experiments to be launched.

One hundred sixty miles north-northeast of Cape Canaveral, Navy ships waited at sea to recover the solid rocket boosters, which would separate from the shuttle after burnout.

At contingency landing sites and tracking stations around the world, from NORAD in Colorado to the international airfield at Banjul, Gambia, men and women watched the clock.

And at this moment, seven people are preparing to place their lives in our hands.

Carpenter could see the astronauts now on closed-circuit TV as they were helped into their orange launch-and-entry suits. The images were live from Florida, but without audio. Carpenter found himself pausing for a moment to study their faces. Though none of them revealed a trace of fear, he knew it had to be there, beneath their beaming expressions. The racing pulse, the zing of nervousness. They knew the risks, and they had to be scared. Seeing them on the screen was a sobering reminder to ground personnel that seven human beings were counting on them to do their jobs right.

Carpenter tore his gaze from the video monitor and focused his attention back on his team of flight controllers, seated at the sixteen consoles. Though he knew each member of the team by name, he addressed them by their mission-command positions, their titles reduced to the shorthand call signs that was NASA-speak. The guidance officer was nicknamed GDO. The spacecraft communicator was Capcom. The propulsion systems engineer was Prop. The trajectory officer was Traj. Flight surgeon was shortened to Surgeon. And Carpenter went by the call sign of Flight.

The countdown came out of the scheduled T-minus-three-hours hold. The mission was still a go.

Carpenter stuck his hand in his pocket and gave his shamrock key ring a jingle. It was his private good-luck ritual. Even engineers have their superstitions.

Let nothing go wrong, he thought. *Not on my watch.*

Cape Canaveral

The Astrovan ride from the O and C building to launchpad 39B took fifteen minutes. It was a strangely silent ride, none of the crew saying much. Just a half hour before, while suiting up, they had been joking and laughing in that sharp and electric tone that comes when one's nerves are raw with excitement. The tension had been building since the moment they had been awakened at two-thirty for the traditional steak and eggs breakfast. Through the weather briefing, the suiting up, the prelaunch ritual of dealing out playing cards for the best poker hand, they had all been a little too noisy and cheerful, all engines roaring with confidence.

Now they'd fallen silent.

The van came to a stop. Chenoweth, the rookie, seated beside Emma, muttered, 'I never thought diaper rash would be one of the job hazards.'

She had to laugh. They were all wearing Depend adult diapers under their bulky flight suits; it would be a long three hours until liftoff.

With help from the launchpad technicians, Emma stepped out of the van. For a moment she paused on the pad, gazing up in wonder at the thirty-story shuttle, ablaze with spotlights. The last time she'd visited the pad, five days ago, the only sounds she'd heard were the sea wind and the birds. Now the spacecraft itself had come to life, rumbling and smoking like a waking dragon, as volatile propellants boiled inside the fuel tank.

They rode the elevator up to Level 195 and stepped onto the grated catwalk. It was still night, but the sky was washed out by the pad lights, and she could barely get a glimpse of the stars overhead. The blackness of space was waiting.

In the sterile white room, technicians in lint-free 'bunny' suits helped the crew, one by one, through the hatch and into the orbiter. The commander and pilot were seated first. Emma, assigned to mid-deck, was the last to be assisted. She settled back into her padded seat, buckles secured, helmet in place, and gave a thumbs-up.

The hatch swung shut, closing the crew off from the outside.

Emma could hear her own heartbeat. Even

through the air-to-ground voice checks chattering over her comm unit, through the gurgles and groans of the awakening shuttle, the thud of her own heart came through in a steady drumbeat. As a middeck passenger, she had little to do in the next two hours but sit and think; the preflight checks would be conducted by the flight-deck crew. She had no view of the outside, nothing to stare at except the stowage area and food pantry.

Outside, dawn would soon light the sky, and pelicans would skim the surf at Playalinda Beach.

She took a deep breath and settled back to wait.

Jack sat on the beach and watched the sun come up.

He was not alone in Jetty Park. The sightseers had been gathering since before midnight, the arriving cars forming an endless line of headlights creeping along the Bee Line Expressway, some peeling north toward Merritt Island Wildlife Refuge, the others continuing across the Banana River to the city of Cape Canaveral. The viewing would be good from either location. The crowd around him was in a holiday mood, with beach towels and picnic baskets. He heard laughter and loud radios and the bawling of sleepy children. Surrounded by that swirl of celebrants, he was a silent presence, a man alone with his thoughts and fears.

As the sun cleared the horizon, he stared north,

toward the launchpad. She would be aboard *Atlantis* now, strapped in and waiting. Excited and happy and a little afraid.

He heard a child say, 'That's a bad man, Mommy,' and he turned to look at the girl. They gazed at each other for a moment, a tiny blond princess locking eyes with an unshaven and very disheveled man. The mother snatched the girl into her arms and quickly moved to a safer spot on the beach.

Jack gave a wry shake of his head and once again turned his gaze northward. Toward Emma.

Houston

The Flight Control Room had turned deceptively quiet. It was twenty minutes till launch – time to confirm it was still a go. All the back-room controllers had completed their systems checks, and now the front room was ready to be polled.

In a calm voice, Carpenter went down the list, requesting verbal confirmation from each front-room controller.

'Fido?' asked Carpenter.

'Fido is go,' said the flight dynamics officer.

'Guido?'

'Guidance is go.'

'Surgeon?'

'Surgeon is go.'

'DPS?'

'Data Processing is go.'

When Carpenter had polled them all and received

affirmatives from all, he gave a brisk nod to the room.

'Houston, are you go?' asked the launch director in Cape Canaveral.

'Mission Control is go,' affirmed Carpenter.

The launch director's traditional message to the shuttle crew was heard by everyone at Houston's Mission Control.

'*Atlantis*, you are a go. From all of us at the Cape, good luck and Godspeed.'

'Launch Control, this is *Atlantis*,' they heard Commander Vance respond. 'Thanks for gettin' this bird ready to fly.'

Cape Canaveral

Emma closed and locked her visor and turned on her oxygen supply. Two minutes till liftoff. Cocooned and isolated in her suit, she had nothing to do but count the seconds. She felt the shudder of the main engines gimballing into launch position.

T minus thirty seconds. The electrical link to ground control was now severed, and the onboard computers took control.

Her heart accelerated, the adrenaline roaring through her veins. As she listened to the countdown, she knew, second by second, what to expect, could see in her mind's eye the sequence of events that were now playing out.

At T minus eight seconds, thousands of gallons

of water were dumped beneath the launchpad to suppress the roar of the engines.

At T minus five, the onboard computers opened the valves to allow liquid oxygen and hydrogen to travel into the main engines.

She felt the shuttle jerk sideways as the three main engines ignited, the spacecraft straining against the bolts that still harnessed it to the launchpad.

Four. Three. Two . . . The point of no return.

She held her breath, hands gripped tight, as the solid rocket boosters ignited. The turbulence was bone-shaking, the roar so painfully loud she could not hear communications through her headset. She had to clamp her jaw shut to stop her teeth from slamming together. Now she felt the shuttle roll into its planned arc over the Atlantic, and her body was shoved back against the seat by the acceleration to three g's. Her limbs were so heavy she could barely move them, the vibrations so violent it seemed the orbiter would surely fly apart into pieces. They were at Max Q, the peak of turbulence, and Commander Vance announced he was throttling back the main engines. In less than a minute, he would throttle up again to full thrust.

As the seconds ticked by, as the helmet rattled around her head, and the force of liftoff pressed like an unyielding hand against her chest, she felt a fresh lick of apprehension. This was the point during launch when *Challenger* had exploded.

Emma closed her eyes and remembered the simulation with Hazel two weeks ago. They were now approaching the point where everything in the sim had started to go wrong, where they'd been forced into an RTLS abort, and then Kittredge had lost control of the orbiter. This was a critical moment in the launch, and there was nothing she could do but lie back and hope that real life was more forgiving than a simulation.

Over the headset she heard Vance say, 'Control, this is *Atlantis*. Throttling up.'

'Roger, *Atlantis*. Throttle up.'

Jack stood with his gaze cast skyward, his heart in his throat, as the shuttle lifted into the sky. He heard the crackling of the solid rocket boosters as they spewed out twin fountains of fire. The trail of exhaust climbed higher, sketched by the glinting pinpoint of the shuttle. All around him, the crowd burst out in applause. A perfect launch, they all thought. But Jack knew there were too many things that could still go wrong.

Suddenly he was frantic that he'd lost track of the seconds. How much time had elapsed? Had they passed through Max Q? He shielded his eyes against the morning sunlight, straining to see *Atlantis*, but able to make out only the plume of exhaust.

Already the crowd had started to drift back to their cars.

He remained frozen, waiting in dread. He saw no terrible explosion. No black smoke. No nightmare.

Atlantis had safely escaped the earth and was now hurtling through space.

He felt tears trickle down his cheeks, but he didn't bother to wipe them away. He let them fall as he continued to gaze at the sky, at the dissipating trail of smoke that marked his wife's ascent into the heavens.

THE STATION

7

July 25
Beatty, Nevada

Sullivan Obie awakened with a groan to the sound of the ringing telephone. His head felt as if cymbals were banging on it, and his mouth tasted like an old ashtray. He reached for the phone and accidentally knocked it off the cradle. The loud thud made him wince with pain. *Aw, forget it*, he thought, and turned away, burrowing his face into a nest of tangled hair.

A woman?

Squinting against the morning light, he confirmed that there was indeed a woman lying in bed with him. A blonde. Snoring. He closed his eyes, hoping that if he just went back to sleep, she would be gone when he woke up again.

But he could not sleep now. Not with the voice yelling from the fallen receiver.

He fished around at the side of the bed and found the phone. 'What, Bridget?' he said. 'What?'

'Why aren't you here?' Bridget demanded.

''Cause I'm in bed.'

'It's ten-thirty! Hel-*lo*? Meeting with the new investors? I might as well warn you, Casper is wavering between crucifixion and strangulation.'

The investors. Shit.

Sullivan sat up and clutched his head, waiting for the dizziness to pass.

'Look, just leave the bimbo and get over here,' said Bridget. 'Casper's already walking them over to the hangar.'

'Ten minutes,' he said. He hung up and stumbled to his feet. The bimbo didn't stir. He had no idea who she was, but he left her asleep in his bed, figuring he had nothing worth stealing, anyway.

There was no time to shower or shave. He tossed back three aspirins, chased them with a cup of nuked coffee, and roared off on his Harley.

Bridget was waiting for him outside the hangar. She *looked* like a Bridget, sturdy and redheaded, with a bad temper to match. Sometimes, unfortunately, stereotypes do ring true.

'They're about to leave,' she hissed. 'Get your butt in there.'

'Who are these guys again?'

'A Mr Lucas and a Mr Rashad. They represent a consortium of twelve investors. You blow this, Sully, and we're toast.' She paused, eyeing him in disgust. 'Ah, hell, we're already toast. Look at you. Couldn't you at least have shaved?'

'You want me to go back home? I can rent a tuxedo on the way.'

'Forget it.' She thrust a folded newspaper into his hand.

'What's this?'

'Casper wants it. Give it to him. Now get in there and convince 'em to write us a check. A big check.'

Sighing, he stepped into the hangar. After the harsh desert glare, the relative darkness was a comfort to his eyes. It took him a moment to spot the three men, standing by the black thermal barrier tiles of the orbiter *Apogee II*. The two visitors, both in business suits, looked out of place among all the aircraft tools and equipment.

'Good morning, gentlemen!' he called. 'Sorry I'm late, but I got hung up on a conference call. You know how things can drag on . . .' He glimpsed Casper Mulholland's warning look of *Don't push it, asshole* and swallowed hard. 'I'm Sullivan Obie,' he said. 'Mr Mulholland's partner.'

'Mr Obie knows every nut and bolt of this RLV,' said Casper. 'He used to work with the old master himself, Bob Truax out in California. In fact, he can explain the system better than I can. Around here, we call him our Obie-Wan.'

The two visitors merely blinked. It was not a good sign when the universal language of *Star Wars* failed to elicit a smile.

105

Sullivan shook hands, first with Lucas, then with Rashad, grinning broadly even as his hopes sank. Even as he felt a surge of resentment toward these two well-dressed gentlemen whose money he and Casper so desperately needed. Apogee Engineering, their baby, the dream they had nurtured for the past thirteen years, was about to go under, and only a fresh infusion of cash, from a new set of investors, could save it. He and Casper had to make the sales pitch of their lives. If it didn't work, they might as well pack up their tools and sell off the orbiter as a carnival ride.

With a flourish, Sullivan waved his arm at *Apogee II*, which looked less like a rocket plane and more like a fat fireplug with windows.

'I know she may not look like much,' he said, 'but what we've built here is the most cost-effective and practical reusable launch vehicle now in existence. She uses an assisted SSTO launch system. After vertical takeoff, upon climbing to twelve kilometers, pressure-fed rockets accelerate the vehicle to a Mach four staging point at low-dynamic pressures. This orbiter is fully reusable, and weighs only eight and a half tons. It fulfills the principles we believe are the future of commercial space travel. Smaller. Faster. Cheaper.'

'What sort of lift engine do you use?' asked Rashad.

'Rybinsk RD-38 air-breathing engines imported from Russia.'

'Why Russian?'

'Because, Mr Rashad – between you, me, and the wall – the Russians know more about rocketry than anyone else on earth. They've developed dozens of liquid-fueled rocket motors, using advanced materials which can operate at higher pressures. Our country, I'm sorry to say, has developed only one new liquid-fueled rocket motor since Apollo. This is now an international industry. We believe in choosing the best components for our product – wherever those components may come from.'

'And how does this . . . *thing* land?' asked Mr Lucas, looking dubiously at the fireplug orbiter.

'Well, that's the beauty of *Apogee II*. As you'll notice, she has no wings. She doesn't need a runway. Instead she drops straight down, using parachutes to slow her descent and air bags to cushion touchdown. She can land anywhere, even in the ocean. Again, we have to tip our hats to the Russians, because we've borrowed features from their old *Soyuz* capsule. It was their reliable workhorse for decades.'

'You like that old Russki technology, huh?' said Lucas.

Sullivan stiffened. 'I like technology that works. Say what you want about the Russians, they knew what they were doing.'

'So what you have here,' said Lucas, 'is something of a hybrid. *Soyuz* mixed in with space shuttle.'

'A very *small* space shuttle. We've spent thirteen

years in development and only sixty-five million dollars to get this far – that's amazingly inexpensive when you compare it to what the shuttle cost. With multiple spacecraft, we believe you'll get an annual return on investment of thirty percent, if we launch twelve hundred times a year. Cost per flight would be eighty thousand dollars; the price per kilogram would be dirt cheap at two hundred seventy. Smaller, faster, cheaper. That's our mantra.'

'How small are we talking about, Mr Obie? What's your payload capacity?'

Sullivan hesitated. This was the point where they might lose them. 'We can launch a payload of three hundred kilograms, plus a pilot, to low earth orbit.'

There was a long silence.

Mr Rashad said, 'That's all?'

'That's almost seven hundred pounds. You can fit a lot of research experiments in –'

'I know how much three hundred kilos is. It's not much.'

'So we make up for it by more frequent launches. You can almost think of it as an airplane to space.'

'In fact – in fact, we've already got NASA's interest!' Casper interjected with a note of desperation. 'This is just the kind of system they might purchase for quick hops to the space station.'

Lucas's eyebrow shot up. 'NASA is interested?'

'Well, we have something of an inside track.'

Aw, shit, Casper, thought Sullivan. *Don't go there.*

'Show them the newspaper, Sully.'

'What?'

'*Los Angeles Times*. Second page.'

Sullivan looked down at the L.A. *Times* that Bridget had thrust in his hand. He turned to the second page and saw the article: 'NASA Launches Astronaut Replacement.' Next to it was a photograph of JSC high-muck-a-mucks at a press conference. He recognized the homely guy with the big ears and the bad haircut. It was Gordon Obie.

Casper snatched the paper and showed it to their visitors. 'See this man here, standing next to Leroy Cornell? That's the director of Flight Crew Operations. Mr Obie's brother.'

The two visitors, obviously impressed, turned and looked at Sullivan.

'Well?' said Casper. 'Would you gentlemen care to talk business?'

'We might as well tell you this up front,' said Lucas. 'Mr Rashad and I have already taken a look at what other aerospace companies have in development. We've looked over the Kelly Astroliner, the Roton, the Kistler K-1. We were impressed by all of them, especially the K-1. But we figured we should give your little company a chance to make a pitch as well.'

Your little company.

Fuck this, thought Sullivan. He hated begging for money, hated getting down on his knees before stuffed shirts. This was a hopeless campaign. His head ached, his stomach was growling, and these two-suits had wasted his time.

'Tell us why we should bet on your horse,' said Lucas. 'What makes Apogee our best choice?'

'Frankly, gentlemen, I don't think we are your best choice,' Sullivan answered bluntly. And he turned and walked away.

'Uh – excuse me,' said Casper, and he went chasing after his partner. 'Sully!' he whispered. 'What the hell are you doing?'

'These guys aren't interested in us. You heard them. They love the K-1. They want *big* rockets. To match their dicks.'

'Don't screw this up! Go back and talk to them.'

'Why? They're not writing us any checks.'

'We lose them, we lose everything.'

'We've already lost.'

'No. No, you can *sell* this to them. All you have to do is tell the truth. Tell them what we really believe. Because you know and I know we've got the best.'

Sullivan rubbed his eyes. The aspirin was wearing off, and his head pounded. He was sick of begging. He was an engineer and a pilot, and he'd happily spend the rest of his life with his hands blackened by engine grease. But it would not happen, not without new investors. Not without new cash.

He turned and walked back to the visitors. To his surprise, both men seemed to regard him with wary respect. Perhaps because he had told the truth.

'Okay,' said Sullivan, emboldened by the fact he had nothing to lose. He might as well go down like a man. 'Here's the deal. We can back up everything we've said with one simple demonstration. Are the other companies ready to launch at the drop of a hat? No, they are not. They need *preparation* time,' he sneered. 'Months and months of it. But we can launch anytime. All we need to do is load this baby onto its booster and we can shoot her up to low earth orbit. Hell, we can send her up to hotdog the space station. So give us a date. Tell us when you want liftoff, and we'll do it.'

Casper turned as white as a – well, a ghost. And not a friendly one. Sullivan had just taken them so far out on a limb they were clawing at thin air. *Apogee II* hadn't been tested yet. She had been sitting in this hangar for over fourteen months, gathering dust while they scrounged for money. On this, her maiden voyage, Sully wanted to launch her all the way to orbit?

'In fact, I'm so confident she'll pass muster,' said Sullivan, raising the stakes even higher, 'I'll ride in the pilot's seat myself.'

Casper clutched his stomach. 'Uh . . . that's just a figure of speech, gentlemen. She can be flown perfectly well unmanned –'

'But there's no real drama in that,' said Sullivan. 'Let me take her up. It'll make it more interesting for everyone. What do you say?'

I say you're outta your fucking mind, Casper's eyes told him.

The two businessmen exchanged looks, a few whispered words. Then Lucas said, 'We'd be very interested in a demonstration. It will take us time to round up all our partners. Coordinate travel schedules. So let's say ... a month. Can you do it?'

They were calling his bluff. Sullivan merely laughed. 'A month? No problem.' He looked at Casper, who now had his eyes closed as though in pain.

'We'll be in touch,' said Lucas, and turned toward the door.

'One last question, if I may,' said Mr Rashad. He pointed to the orbiter. 'I notice the name on your prototype is *Apogee II*. Is there an *Apogee I?*'

Casper and Sullivan looked at each other.

'Uh, yes,' said Casper. 'There was ...'

'And what happened to her?'

Casper went mute.

What the hell, thought Sullivan. Telling the truth seemed to work with these guys; he might as well do it again.

'She crashed and burned,' he said. And walked out of the hangar.

Crashed and burned. That was the only way to describe what had happened on that cold, clear morning a year and a half ago. The morning his dreams had crashed and burned as well. Sitting at

112

his battered desk in the company office, nursing his hangover with a cup of coffee, he couldn't help replaying every painful detail of that day. The busload of NASA officials pulling up at the launch site. His brother, Gordie, grinning with pride. The air of celebration among the dozen Apogee employees and the score of investors who had assembled under the tent for prelaunch coffee and doughnuts.

The countdown. The liftoff. Everyone squinting up at the sky as *Apogee I* streaked toward the heavens and receded to a glinting pinpoint.

Then the flash of light, and it was all over.

Afterward, his brother had not said very much, barely a few words of condolence. But that's how it was with Gordon. All their lives, whenever Sullivan screwed up – and it seemed to happen all too often – Gordon would just give that sad and disappointed shake of the head. Gordon was the older brother, the sober and reliable son who had distinguished himself as a shuttle commander.

Sullivan had never even made it into the astronaut corps. Though he, too, was a pilot and an aerospace engineer, things never seemed to go Sullivan's way. If he climbed into the cockpit, that was precisely the moment a wire would short out or a line would rupture. He often thought the words *Not My Fault* should be tattooed on his forehead, because more often than not, it *wasn't* his fault when things went wrong. But Gordon didn't see it that way. Things never went wrong for *him*. Gordon thought the concept of bad luck was an excuse to cover up incompetence.

'Why don't you call him?' said Bridget.

He looked up. She was standing by his desk, her arms crossed like a disapproving schoolteacher's. 'Call who?' he asked.

'Your brother, who else? Tell him we're launching the second prototype. Invite him to watch. Maybe he'll bring the rest of NASA.'

'I don't want anyone from NASA.'

'Sully, if we impress them, we'll turn this company around.'

'Like the last time, huh?'

'A fluke. We've fixed the problem.'

'So maybe there'll be another fluke.'

'You're gonna jinx us, you know that?' She shoved the phone in front of him. 'Call Gordon. If we're gonna roll the dice, we might as well bet the whole house.'

He eyed the phone, thinking about *Apogee I*. About how a lifetime of dreams can be vaporized in an instant.

'Sully?'

'Forget it,' he said. 'My brother's got better things to do than hang out with losers.' And he tossed the newspaper into the rubbish can.

July 26
Aboard *Atlantis*

'Hey, Watson,' Commander Vance called down to the middeck. 'Come up and take a look at your new home.'

Emma floated up the access ladder and emerged on the flight deck, right behind Vance's seat. At her first glimpse through the windows, she inhaled a sharp breath of wonder. This was the closest she had ever come to the station. During her first mission, two and a half years ago, they had not docked with ISS, but had observed it only from a distance.

'Gorgeous, isn't she?' said Vance.

'She's the most beautiful thing I've ever seen,' Emma said softly.

And she was. With her vast solar arrays fanning out from the massive main truss, ISS looked like a majestic sailing ship soaring through the heavens. Built by sixteen different countries, the components had been delivered into space on forty-five separate launches. It had taken five years to assemble her, piece by piece, in orbit. Far more than merely a marvel of engineering, she was a symbol of what man can achieve when he lays down his weapons and turns his gaze skyward.

'Now, that's a nice piece of real estate,' said Vance. 'I'd call that a view apartment.'

'We're right on the R-bar,' said shuttle pilot DeWitt. 'Nice flying.'

Vance left the command seat and stationed himself at the flight deck's overhead window for visual approach as they neared the ISS docking module. This was the most delicate phase in the complicated process of rendezvous. *Atlantis* had been launched into a lower orbit than ISS, and for the last two days she had been playing a game of catch-up with the hurtling space station. They would approach her from below, using their RCS jets to fine-tune their position for docking. Emma could hear the whomp of the thrusters' firing now and felt the orbiter shudder.

'Look,' said DeWitt. 'There's that solar array that got dinged last month.' He pointed to one of the solar panels, scarred by a gaping hole. One of the inescapable perils of space is the constant rain of meteorites and manmade debris. Even a tiny fragment can be a devastating missile when it's hurtling at thousands of miles per hour.

As they drew closer and the station filled the window, Emma felt such overwhelming awe and pride that tears suddenly flashed in her eyes. *Home*, she thought. *I'm coming home*.

The air-lock hatch swung open, and a wide brown face grinned at them from the other end of the vestibule connecting *Atlantis* with ISS. 'They brought oranges!' Luther Ames called out to his station mates. 'I can smell 'em!'

'NASA home delivery service,' deadpanned Commander Vance. 'Your groceries have arrived.' Bearing a nylon sack of fresh fruit, Vance floated through *Atlantis*'s air lock into the space station.

It had been a perfect docking. With both spacecrafts traveling at a speed of 17,500 miles per hour above the earth, Vance had approached ISS at the delicate rate of two inches per second, lining up *Atlantis*'s docking module to the ISS port for a good, tight lock.

Now the hatches were open and *Atlantis*'s crew floated one by one into the space station to be greeted with handshakes and hugs, and the welcoming smiles of people who have not seen new faces in over a month. The node was too small to hold thirteen people, and the crews quickly spilled into the adjoining modules.

Emma was the fifth to cross into the station. She popped out of the vestibule and inhaled a mélange of scents, the slightly sour and meaty odors of humans confined too long in a closed space. Luther Ames, an old friend from astronaut training, was the first to greet her.

'Dr Watson, I presume!' he boomed out, pulling her into a hug. 'Welcome aboard. The more ladies, the merrier.'

'Hey, you know I'm no lady.'

He winked. 'We'll keep that between us.' Luther had always been larger than life, a man whose good cheer could fill a room. Everyone liked Luther because Luther liked everyone. Emma was glad to have him aboard.

Especially when she turned to look at her other station mates. She shook hands first with Michael Griggs, the ISS commander, and found his greeting polite but almost military. Diana Estes, the Englishwoman sent up by the European Space Agency, was not much warmer. She smiled, but her eyes were a strange glacial blue. Cool and distant.

Emma turned next to the Russian, Nicolai Rudenko, who had been aboard ISS the longest – almost five months. The module lights seemed to wash all the color from his face, turning it as drab as the gray-flecked stubble of his beard. As they shook hands, his gaze barely met hers. *This man*, she thought, *needs to go home. He is depressed. Exhausted.*

Kenichi Hirai, the astronaut from NASDA, floated forward to greet her next. He, at least, had a smile on his face and a firm handshake. He stammered a greeting and quickly retreated.

By now the module had emptied out, the rest of the group dispersing to other parts of the station. She found herself alone with Bill Haning.

Debbie Haning had died three days ago. *Atlantis* would be bringing Bill home, not to his wife's bedside, but to her funeral. Emma floated across to him. 'I'm sorry,' she said softly. 'I'm so sorry.'

He merely nodded and looked away. 'It's strange,'

he said. 'We always thought – if something ever happened – it would happen to me. Because I'm the big hero in the family. The one who takes all the risks. It never occurred to us that she would be the one . . .' He took a deep breath. She saw that he was fighting to maintain his composure, and she knew this was not the time for words of sympathy. Even a gentle touch might destroy his fragile control over his emotions.

'Well, Watson,' he finally said. 'I guess I should be the one to show you the ropes. Since you'll be taking on my load.'

She nodded. 'Whenever you're ready, Bill.'

'Let's do it now. There's a lot to tell you. And not much time for the changeover.'

Though Emma was familiar with the layout of the station, her first interior glimpse of the actual structure was a dizzying experience. The weightlessness of orbit meant there was no up or down, no floor or ceiling. Every surface was functional workspace, and if she turned too quickly in midair, she instantly lost all sense of direction. That, and the twinges of nausea, made her move slowly, focusing her eyes on one spot as she turned.

She knew that the core of ISS had as much inhabitable airspace as two Boeing 747s, but it was distributed among a dozen bus-sized modules, plugged together like Tinkertoys into connecting points called nodes. The shuttle had docked on Node 2. Attached to that same node were the European Space Agency lab, the Japanese lab, and the U.S. lab, which served as the gateway into the rest of the station.

Bill led her out of the U.S. lab into the next connecting point, Node 1. Here they paused for a moment to look out the observation cupola. The earth slowly spun beneath them, milky clouds swirling over seas.

'This is where I spend every spare moment,' said Bill. 'Just looking out these windows. It feels almost sacred to me. I call this the Church of Mother Earth.' He tore his gaze away from the view and turned to point out the other node hatchways. 'Directly opposite is the EVA air lock,' he said. 'And the hatchway below us leads into the hab module. Your sleep station's in there. The CRV is docked at the other end of the hab, for quick evac access.'

'Three crew members sleep in this hab?'

He nodded. 'The other three sleep in the Russian service module. It's through this hatchway here. Let's head there now.'

They left Node 1, and like fish swimming through a maze of tunnels, they floated into the Russian half of the station.

This was the oldest part of ISS, the section that had been in orbit longest, and its age showed. As they passed through Zarya – the power and propulsion plant – she saw smudges on the walls, the occasional scratch and dent. What had been only a set of blueprints in her head now took on texture and sensory detail. The station was more than just a maze of gleaming labs; it was also a home for human beings, and the wear and tear of constant occupancy was evident.

They floated into the Russian service module, and Emma confronted a disorienting view of Griggs and Vance, both of them upside down. *Or am I the one who's upside down?* thought Emma, amused by this topsy-turvy world of weightlessness. Like the U.S. hab, the RSM contained a galley, toilet, and sleep stations for three crew members. At the far end, she spotted another hatchway.

'Does that go to the old *Soyuz?*' she asked.

Bill nodded. 'We use it for storing junk now. That's about all we can do with it.' The *Soyuz* capsule, which had once served as an emergency lifeboat, was now obsolete, and its batteries had long since drained.

Luther Ames popped his head into the RSM. 'Hey, everyone, it's show time! Group hug in the media conferencing center. NASA wants the taxpayers to see our international love fest up here.'

Bill gave a weary sigh. 'We're like animals in a zoo. Every day it's *smile* for the damn cameras.'

Emma was the last to join the exodus to the hab module. By the time she reached it, a dozen people were already crowded inside. It looked like a tangle of arms and legs in there, everyone bobbing, trying not to collide with each other.

While Griggs struggled to get things organized,

Emma hung back in Node 1. Drifting in mid-air, she found herself slowly turning toward the cupola. The view beyond those windows took her breath away.

The earth stretched below in all its magnificence, a rim of stars crowning the gentle curve of the horizon. They were passing into night now, and below, she saw familiar landmarks slipping into darkness. Houston. It was their first passover of the night.

She leaned close to the window, pressing her hand to the glass. *Oh, Jack*, she thought. *I wish you were here. I wish you could see this.*

Then she waved. And she knew, without the slightest doubt, that somewhere in the darkness below, Jack was waving back.

8

July 28

Personal E-mail to: Dr Emma Watson (ISS)
From: Jack McCallum

Like a diamond in the sky. That's what you look like from down here. Last night I stayed up to watch you pass over. Gave you a big wave.

This morning on CNN, you were being touted as Ms Right Stuff. 'Girl astronaut blasts off, doesn't chip a nail,' or something equally hokey. They interviewed Woody Ellis and Leroy Cornell, and both of them were beaming like proud daddies. Congratulations. You're America's sweetheart.

Vance and crew made a picture-perfect landing. Bloodsucking reporters were all over poor Bill when he arrived in Houston. I caught a glimpse of him on TV – he looks like he's aged twenty years. Services for Debbie are this afternoon. I'll be there.

Tomorrow, I'll be sailing on the Gulf.

Em, I got the divorce papers today, and I'll be honest with you. It doesn't feel good. But then, I guess it's not supposed to, is it?

Anyway, they're ready for us to sign. Maybe now that it's finally over, we can get back to being friends again. The way we used to be.

Jack

P.S.: Humphrey's a little shit. You owe me a new couch.

Personal E-mail to: Jack McCallum
From: Emma Watson

America's sweetheart? Puh-leeze. This has turned into a high-wire act, with everyone on earth watching and waiting for me to screw up. And when I do, I'll be the shoulda-sent-a-man Exhibit #1. I hate that.

On the other hand, I do love it up here. How I wish you could see this view! When I look down at the earth and see how incredibly beautiful she is, I want to shake some sense into everyone living down there. If only they could see how small and fragile and very alone the earth is, surrounded by all this cold black space. They'd take much better care of her.

(Uh, oh, here she goes again, getting teary-eyed about the home planet. Shoulda sent a man.)

I'm happy to report the nausea's gone. I can

zip around from mod to mod with scarcely a twinge. I still get a little woozy when I catch an unexpected glimpse of earth through a window. It screws up my sense of up and down, and it takes me a few seconds to reorient. I'm trying to keep up the exercise, but two hours every day is a big chunk of time, especially when I've got so much to do. Dozens of experiments to monitor, a zillion E-mails from Payload Operations, every scientist demanding top priority for their pet projects. Eventually, I'll get up to speed. But this morning I was so tired, I slept right through Houston's wakeup music. (And Luther says they blasted us with Wagner's Valkyrie!)

As for the divorce being final, it doesn't feel good for me, either. But, Jack, at least we had seven good years. That's more than a lot of couples can say. I know you must be anxious to finish this business. I promise I'll sign the papers as soon as I get home.

Don't stop waving.

Em

P.S.: Humphrey never attacked my furniture. What did you do to upset him?

Emma turned off her laptop computer and folded it shut. Answering personal E-mail was the last task of the day. She had looked forward to hearing from home, but Jack's mention of the divorce had stung her. *So he's ready to move on*, she thought. *He's ready to 'be friends' again.*

As she zipped herself into her sleep restraint bag, she was angry at him, at how easily he'd accepted the end of their marriage. Early in their divorce, when their arguments were still raging, she'd felt strangely reassured by every noisy disagreement. But now the conflicts had ended, and Jack had reached the stage of calm acceptance. No pain, no regrets.

And here I am, still missing you. And I hate myself for it.

Kenichi hesitated to wake her. He lingered outside her sleep station privacy curtain, wondering if he should call out again. It was such a small matter, and he hated to disturb her. She had looked so tired at supper, had actually dozed off still clutching her fork. Without the constant pull of gravity, the body does not crumple when you fall unconscious, and there is no warning jerk of the head to startle you awake. Tired astronauts had been known to fall asleep in the midst of repairs, while still holding a tool in their hand.

He decided not to wake her and returned, alone, to the U.S. lab.

Kenichi had never needed more than five hours of rest a night, and while the others slept, he would often wander the labyrinth of the space station, checking on his various experiments. Inspecting, exploring. It seemed that only when the human crew slept did the station assert its own gleaming personality. It became an autonomous being that hummed and clicked, its computers directing a thousand different functions, electronic commands zinging through its nervous system of wires and circuits. As Kenichi drifted through the maze of tunnels, he thought of all the human hands that had worked to fashion just a single square inch of this structure. The electronics and metal workers, the molders of plastic. The glassmakers. Because of their labor, a farmer's son who had grown up in a mountain village of Japan now floated two hundred twenty miles above the earth.

Kenichi had been aboard the station for a month, and the wonder of it all had not left him.

He knew his stay here was limited. He knew the toll now being exacted on his body: the steady seepage of calcium from his bones, the wasting of his muscles, the declining vigor of arteries and heart, now freed from the challenge of pumping against gravity. Every moment aboard ISS was precious, and he did not want to waste a minute of it. So, during the hours scheduled for sleep, he roamed the station, lingering at windows, visited the animals in the lab.

That was how he had discovered the dead mouse.

It had been floating with legs frozen and extended, pink mouth gaping open. Another one of the males. It was the fourth mouse to die in sixteen days.

He confirmed that the habitat was functioning properly, that the temperature set points had not been violated and the airflow rate was maintained at the standard twelve changes per hour. Why were they dying? Could it be contamination of the water or food? Several months ago, the station had lost a dozen rats when toxic chemicals had seeped into the animal habitat's water supply.

The mouse floated in a corner of the enclosure. The other males were bunched at the far end, as though repulsed by the corpse of their cage mate. They seemed frantic to get away from it, paws clinging to the cage screen. On the other side of the wire divider, the females, too, were bunched together. All except one. She was twitching, spiraling slowly in midair, her claws thrashing in seizure-like movements.

Another one is sick.

Even as he watched, the female gave what looked like a last tortured gasp and suddenly went limp.

The other females bunched even tighter, a panicked mass of writhing white fur. He had to remove the corpses, before the contagion – if it was a contagion – spread to the other mice.

He interfaced the habitat to the life-sciences glove box, snapped on latex gloves, and inserted his hands through the rubber dams. Reaching first into the male side of the enclosure, he removed the corpse and bagged it in plastic. Then he opened the females' enclosure and reached in for the second

128

dead mouse. As he removed it, a flash of white fur shot out past his hand.

One of the mice had escaped into the glove box.

He snatched her in midair. And almost immediately released her when he felt the sharp nip of pain. She had bitten right through the glove.

At once he pulled his hands out of the box, quickly peeled off the gloves, and stared at his finger. A drop of blood welled up, the sight of it so unexpected, he felt nauseated. He closed his eyes, berating himself. This was nothing – barely a prick. The mouse's rightful vengeance for all those needles he had stuck in them. He opened his eyes again, but the nausea was still there.

I need to rest, he thought.

He recaptured the struggling mouse and thrust it into the cage. Then he removed the two bagged corpses and placed them in the refrigerator. Tomorrow, he'd deal with the problem. Tomorrow, when he felt better.

July 30

'I found this one dead today,' said Kenichi. 'It is number six.'

Emma frowned at the mice in the animal habitat. They were housed in a divided cage, the males separated from the females only by a wire barrier. They shared the same air, the same food and water supply. On the male side, a dead mouse floated motionless, limbs extended and rigid. The other males were clustered at the opposite end of the enclosure, scrabbling at the screen as though frantic to escape.

'You've lost six mice in seventeen days?' said Emma.

'Five males. One female.'

Emma studied the remaining live animals for signs of illness. They all appeared alert, their eyes bright, with no mucus discharge from their nostrils.

'First, let's get this dead one out,' she said. 'Then we'll take a close look at the others.'

Using the glove box, she reached into the cage and removed the corpse. It was already in rigor mortis, the legs stiff, the spine inflexible. The mouth was partly open, and the tip of the tongue protruded in a soft flap of pink. It was not unusual for lab animals to die in space. On one shuttle flight in 1998, there had been almost a hundred percent mortality among newborn rats. Microgravity was an alien environment, and not all species adapted well.

Prior to launch, these mice would have been screened for a number of bacteria, fungi, and viruses. If this was an infection, then they had picked it up while aboard ISS.

She put the dead mouse in a plastic pouch, changed gloves, and reached into the enclosure for one of the live mice. It squirmed with great vigor, showing no signs of illness. The only unusual feature was a tattered ear that had been chewed by its cage mates. She flipped it over to look at its belly and gave an exclamation of surprise.

'This is a female,' she said.

'What?'

'You had a female in the male enclosure.'

Kenichi leaned close to peer through the glove box window at the mouse's genitals. The evidence was plain to see. His face flushed deep red with embarrassment.

'Last night,' he explained. 'She bit me. I put her back in a hurry.'

Emma gave him a sympathetic smile. 'Well, the worst that can happen is an unexpected baby boom.'

Kenichi slipped on gloves and inserted his hands in the second pair of glove box armholes. 'I make the mistake,' he said. 'I fix it.'

Together they examined the rest of the mice in the enclosure, but found no other misplaced specimens. All appeared healthy.

'This is very strange,' said Emma. 'If we're dealing with a contagious disease, there ought to be some evidence of infection . . .'

'Watson?' a voice called over the module intercom.

'In the lab, Griggs,' she answered.

'You've got priority E-mail from Payloads.'

'I'll get it now.' She sealed off the animal enclosure and said to Kenichi, 'Let me check my message. Why don't you take out the dead mice you put in cold storage. We'll look at them.'

He nodded and floated across to the refrigerator.

At the workstation computer, she called up her priority E-mail.

To: Dr Emma Watson
From: Helen Koenig, Principal Investigator
   Re: Experiment CCU#23 (Archaeon Cell Culture)
   Message: Immediately abort this experiment. Latest specimens returned by Atlantis show fungal contamination. All Archaeon cultures, along with the containers holding them, should be incinerated in onboard crucible and the ashes jettisoned.

Emma read and reread the message on the screen. Never before had she received such a strange request. Fungal contamination was not dangerous. To incinerate the cultures seemed a drastic overreaction. She was so preoccupied by this puzzling request she paid no attention to Kenichi, who was taking the dead mice out of the refrigerator. Only when she heard him gasp did she turn to look at him.

At first all she saw was his shocked face, splattered with a foul slurry of entrails. Then she looked at the plastic bag that had just burst open. In his horror, he had released it, and it floated free, hanging in the air between them.

'What is *that*?' she said.

He said, in disbelief, 'The mouse.'

But it was not a dead mouse she saw in the bag. It was a mass of disintegrated tissue, a putrefied gumbo of flesh and fur that even now was leaking out foul-smelling globules.

Biohazard!

She shot the length of the module to the caution-and-warning panel and hit the button to shut off airflow between modules. Kenichi had already opened the emergency rack and pulled out two filter masks. He tossed one to her, and she clapped it over her nose and mouth. They didn't need to exchange a word; they both knew what had to be done.

Quickly they closed the hatches on either end of the module, effectively isolating the lab from the rest of the station. Then Emma took out a biocontainment bag and carefully moved toward the drifting bag of liquefied flesh. Surface tension had bound the liquids together in one globule; if she was careful not to stir the air, she could trap it in the bag, without scattering droplets. Gently she lowered the containment bag over the free-floating specimen and quickly sealed it off. She heard Kenichi give a sigh of relief. Hazard contained.

'Did it leak into the refrigerator?' she asked.

'No. Only when I took it out.' He wiped his face with an alcohol swab and sealed the swab for safe disposal. 'The bag, it was . . . you know, blown up big. Like a balloon.'

The contents had been under pressure, the process of decomposition releasing gases. Through the plastic containment bag, she could see the date of death on the label. *This is impossible*, she thought. In just five days, the corpse had deteriorated to a black puree of rotted flesh. The bag was cold to the touch, so the refrigerator was functioning. Despite cold storage, something had accelerated the body's decomposition. Flesh-eating *streptococcus?* she wondered. Or another bacteria, equally destructive?

She looked at Kenichi and thought, *It splashed him in the eye*.

'We need to talk to your principal investigator,' she said. 'The one who sent up these mice.'

It was only five A.M., Pacific Daylight Time, but the voice of Dr Michael Loomis, principal investigator for the experiment 'Conception and gestation in mice during spaceflight,' was fully alert and obviously concerned. He was speaking to Emma from Ames Research Center in California. Though she couldn't see him, she could picture the man who belonged to this reedy voice: tall, energetic. A man for whom five in the morning is a normal part of the workday.

'We've been monitoring these animals for over a month,' said Loomis. 'It's a relatively low-stress experiment for the animals. We'd planned to mingle the males and females next week, in hopes they'd successfully mate and conceive. This research has important applications for long-term space-flight. Planetary colonization. As you can imagine, these deaths are pretty upsetting.'

'We've already got cultures incubating,' said Emma. 'All the dead mice appear to be decomposing more quickly than they should. Based on the condition of the corpses, I'm concerned about *clostridia* or *streptococcus* infections.'

'Dangerous bugs like that on the station? That would be a serious problem.'

'Exactly. Especially in a closed environment like ours. We'd all be vulnerable.'

'What about autopsying the dead mice?'

Emma hesitated. 'We're only set up to deal with Level Two contamination up here. Nothing more dangerous. If this is a serious pathogen, I can't afford to risk infecting other animals. Or people.'

There was a silence. Then Loomis said, 'I understand. And I guess I have to agree with you. So you'll be safely disposing of all the corpses?'

'Immediately,' said Emma.

July 31

For the first time since he'd arrived on ISS, Kenichi could not sleep. He had zipped himself into his restraint bag hours ago, yet he was still awake, still mulling over the puzzle of the dead mice. Though no one had uttered a word of reproach, somehow he felt responsible for the failed experiment. He tried to think of what he might have done wrong. Had he used a contaminated needle, perhaps, when he'd sampled their blood, or a bad setting in the animal rack's environmental controls? Thoughts of all the possible mistakes he might have made kept sleep at bay.

Also, his head was throbbing.

He had first noticed the discomfort this morning, when it had started as a vague tingling around his eye. As the day wore on, the tingling had become an ache, and now the left half of his head hurt. Not an excruciating pain, just a nagging annoyance.

He unzipped his bag. He was getting no rest in any event; he might as well check on the mice again.

He floated past Nicolai's curtained sleep station and headed through the series of connecting modules that led to the U.S. half of the station. Only when he'd entered the lab did he realize someone else was awake.

Voices murmured in the adjoining NASDA lab. Silently he floated into Node 2 and peered through the open hatch. He saw Diana Estes and Michael Griggs, limbs tangled together, mouths locked in hungry exploration. At once he backed out unnoticed, his face burning with embarrassment at what he'd just witnessed.

Now what? Should he grant them their privacy and return to his sleep station? *This is not right*, he thought with sudden resentment. *I am here to work, to fulfill my duties.*

He floated to the animal habitat. Deliberately

136

he made a great deal of noise as he opened and closed the rack drawers. A moment later, as he'd expected, Diana and Griggs suddenly appeared, both of them looking flushed. *And well they should be*, he thought, *considering what they've been up to*.

'We had a problem with the centrifuge,' lied Diana. 'I think it's fixed now.'

Kenichi merely nodded, betraying no sign that he knew the truth. Diana was cool as ice about it, and that both appalled and angered him. Griggs, at least, had the decency to look a little guilty.

Kenichi watched as they floated out of the lab and disappeared through the hatch. Then he turned his attention back to the animal habitat. He peered into the cage.

Another mouse was dead. A female.

August 1

Diana Estes calmly held out her arm for the tourniquet and squeezed her hand open and shut several times to plump up her antecubital vein. She did not flinch or look away as the needle pierced her skin; indeed, Diana was so detached, she might have been watching someone else's blood being drawn. Every astronaut was poked and prodded many times during the course of his or her career. At selection screening, they endured multiple blood draws and physical exams and the most probing of questions. Their serum chemistries and EKGs and cell counts were on permanent record, to be pored over by aerospace physiologists. They panted and sweated on treadmills with electrodes attached to their chests; their body fluids were cultured, their bowels probed; every inch of skin was examined. Astronauts were not just highly trained personnel; they were also experimental subjects. They were the equivalent of lab rats, and while in orbit, they resigned themselves to a sometimes painful battery of tests.

Today was specimen collection day. As the physician on board, Emma was the one wielding the needles and syringes. No wonder most of her crewmates groaned when they saw her coming.

Diana, though, had simply held out her arm and submitted to the needle. As Emma waited for the syringe to fill with blood, she sensed the other woman's gaze appraising her skill and technique. If Princess Diana had been England's rose, went the joke at JSC, then Diana Estes was England's ice cube, an astronaut whose poise never cracked, even in the heat of real calamity.

Four years ago, Diana had been aboard *Atlantis* when a main engine failed. On tapes of the crew transmissions, the voices of the shuttle commander and pilot had risen in alarm as they scrambled to guide the shuttle in a transatlantic abort. But not Diana's voice. She could be heard coolly reading the checklist as *Atlantis* hurtled to an uncertain landing in North Africa. What had sealed her icy reputation were the biotelemetry readings. On that particular launch, the entire crew had been

138

wired to record their blood pressure and pulse. While the heart rates of everyone else had sky-rocketed, Diana's had barely accelerated to a leisurely ninety-six beats per minute. 'That's because she's not human,' Jack had joked. 'She's really an android. The first in NASA's newest line of astronauts.'

Emma had to admit there was something not quite human about the woman.

Diana glanced at the puncture site on her arm, saw that the bleeding had stopped, and matter-of-factly turned back to her protein crystal growth experiments. She was indeed almost android perfect, long-limbed and slender, her flawless skin paled to milky white from a month in space. All that plus a genius IQ, according to Jack, who had trained with Diana for the shuttle mission he had never completed.

Diana had a doctorate in materials science and had published over a dozen research papers on zeolites – crystalline materials used in petroleum refinement – prior to being accepted into the astronaut program. Now she was the scientist in charge of both organic and inorganic crystals research. On earth, crystal formation was distorted by gravity. In space, crystals grew larger and more elaborate, allowing thorough analysis of their structure. Hundreds of human proteins, from angiotensin to chorionic gonadotropin, were being grown as crystals aboard ISS – vital pharmaceutical research that could lead to the development of new drugs.

Finished with Diana, Emma left the ESA lab and floated into the hab, to find Mike Griggs. 'You're next,' she said.

He groaned and reluctantly held out his arm. 'All in the name of science.'

'It's just one tube this time,' said Emma, tying on the tourniquet.

'We've gotten so many needle sticks we look like junkies.'

She gave his skin a few gentle slaps to bring out the antecubital vein. It plumped up, blue and cordlike on his muscular arm. Griggs had been compulsive about staying in condition – not a simple thing while in orbit. Life in space took its toll on the human body. Astronauts' faces were bloated, swollen by shifts in fluids. Their thigh and calf muscles shrank until they had 'chicken legs,' poking out pale and scrawny from their bloomerlike shorts. Duties were exhausting, the irritations too numerous to count. And then there was the emotional toll of being confined for months with crewmates who were under stress, scarcely bathed, and wearing dirty clothes.

Emma swabbed the skin with alcohol and pierced the vein. Blood shot back into the syringe. She glanced at him and saw his gaze was averted. 'Okay?'

'Yeah. I do appreciate a skillful vampire.'

She released the tourniquet and heard his sigh of relief when she withdrew the needle. 'You can eat breakfast now. I've drawn everyone's blood but

140

Kenichi's.' She glanced around the hab. 'Where is he?'

'I haven't seen him this morning.'

'I hope he hasn't eaten. That'll screw up his glucose level.'

Nicolai, who'd been floating off in a corner, quietly finishing his breakfast, said, 'He is still asleep.'

'Strange,' said Griggs. 'He's always up before everyone else.'

'His sleep is not so good,' said Nicolai. 'Last night, I hear him vomit. I ask if he needs help, and he tells me no.'

'I'll check on him,' said Emma.

She left the hab and headed up the long tunnel to the RSM, where Kenichi's sleep station was. She found his privacy curtain was closed.

'Kenichi?' she called out. There was no response. 'Kenichi?' She hesitated a moment, then opened the curtain and saw his face.

His eyes were a brilliant bloodred.

'Oh, my God,' she said.

THE SICKNESS

9

The flight surgeon manning the console for ISS Mission Control was Dr Todd Cutler, a physician who was so fresh-faced and youthful the astronauts had dubbed him 'Doogie Howser' after the TV show about a teenage doctor. Cutler was, in reality, a ripe old thirty-two and known for his cool competence. He acted as Emma's personal physician while she was in orbit, and once a week, during their private medical conference, she spoke to him on a closed communications loop, reporting the most intimate details about her health. She trusted Todd's medical skills and was relieved that he was the surgeon on duty at that hour in the ISS control room at Johnson.

'He's got scleral hemorrhages in both eyes,' she said. 'It scared the hell out of me when I first saw it. I think he got them from vomiting so hard last night – the sudden changes in pressure popped a few vessels in his eyes.'

'That's a relatively minor concern right now. The

hemorrhages will clear up,' said Todd. 'What about the rest of the exam?'

'He's got a fever of thirty-eight point six. Pulse one twenty, blood pressure one hundred over sixty. The heart and lungs sound fine. He does complain of a headache, but I can't find any neurologic changes. What really worries me is the fact he has no bowel sounds, and his abdomen is diffusely tender. He's vomited several times in just the last hour – so far, it's negative for blood.' She paused. 'Todd, he looks *sick*. And here's the bad news. I just ran his amylase level. It's six hundred.'

'Oh, shit. You think he's got pancreatitis?'

'With a rising amylase, it's certainly possible.' Amylase was an enzyme produced by the pancreas, and its levels usually skyrocketed when the organ became inflamed. But a high amylase level could also indicate other acute abdominal processes. A bowel perforation or a duodenal ulcer.

'His white blood cell count is also high,' said Emma. 'I've drawn blood cultures, just in case.'

'What's the history? Anything worth noting?'

'Two things. First, he's been under some emotional stress. One of his experiments is crashing on him, and he feels responsible.'

'And the second thing?'

'He was splashed in the eye two days ago, with body fluids from a dead lab mouse.'

'Tell me more.' Todd's voice had gone very quiet.

'The mice in his experiment have been dying, for reasons unknown. The corpses have decomposed at an amazing rate. I was concerned about pathogenic bacteria, so I took samples of the body fluids for culture. Unfortunately, all those cultures are ruined.'

'How?'

'I think it's fungal contamination. The plates have all turned green. No known pathogens can be identified. I had to discard the plates. The same thing happened to another experiment, a cell culture of marine organisms. We had to abort that project because fungi got into the culture tube.'

Fungal overgrowth, unfortunately, was not an uncommon problem in closed environments like ISS, despite the continually recirculating air. Aboard the old *Mir* station, the windows were sometimes coated with a fuzzy layer of fungi. Once the air of a spacecraft has been contaminated by these organisms, it is next to impossible to eliminate them. Luckily, they were by and large harmless to people and lab animals.

'So we don't know if he's been exposed to any pathogens,' said Todd.

'No. Right now, it looks more like a case of pancreatitis, not a bacterial infection. I've got an IV started, and I think it's time for a nasogastric tube.' She paused, then added reluctantly, 'We need to think about emergency evacuation.'

There was a long silence. This was the scenario everyone dreaded, the decision no one wanted to make. The Crew Return Vehicle, which remained docked to ISS whenever personnel were aboard, was large enough to evacuate all six astronauts. Since the *Soyuz* capsules were no longer functioning, the CRV was the only escape vehicle on the station. If it left, they would all have to be aboard it. For the sake of one sick crew member, they would be forced to abandon ISS, ending hundreds of in-flight experiments. It would be a crippling setback to the station.

But there was an alternative. They could wait for the next shuttle flight to evacuate Kenichi. Now it came down to a medical decision. *Could* he wait? Emma knew NASA was relying on her clinical judgment, and the responsibility weighed heavily on her shoulders.

'What about a shuttle evac?' she asked.

Todd Cutler understood the dilemma. 'We have *Discovery* on the pad for STS 161, launch minus fifteen days. But her mission is classified military. Satellite retrieval and repair. One sixty-one's crew hasn't been prepping for ISS docking and rendezvous.'

'What about replacing them with Kittredge's team? My old crew from 162? They're scheduled to dock here in seven weeks. They're fully prepared.'

Emma glanced at Mike Griggs, who was hovering nearby, listening to the conversation. As ISS commander, his primary goal was to keep the station up and running, and he was firmly opposed to abandoning her. He joined the conversation.

'Cutler, this is Griggs. If my crew evacuates, we lose experiments. That's months of work down the drain. A shuttle rescue makes the most sense. If Kenichi needs to get home, then you folks come pick him up. Let the rest of us stay here and do our jobs.'

'Can a rescue wait that long?' asked Todd.

'How soon can you get that bird up here?' said Griggs.

'We have to talk logistics. Launch windows –'

'Just tell us how long.'

Cutler paused. 'Flight Director Ellis is standing by. Go ahead, Flight.'

What had started as a closed and confidential loop between two physicians was now open to the flight director. They heard Woody Ellis say, 'Thirty-six hours. That's the earliest possible launch.'

A lot could change in thirty-six hours, Emma thought. An ulcer could perforate or hemorrhage. Pancreatitis could lead to shock and circulatory collapse.

Or Kenichi could recover completely, the victim of nothing worse than a severe intestinal infection.

'Dr Watson's the one examining the patient,' Ellis said. 'We're relying on her judgment here. What's the clinical call?'

Emma thought about it. 'He doesn't have an acute surgical abdomen – not at the moment. But things could go bad fast.'

'So you're not sure.'

'No, I'm not.'

'The instant you give us the word, we'll still need twenty-four hours for fueling.'

A whole day's lag between a call for rescue, and the actual launch, plus additional time for rendez-vous. If Kenichi suddenly took a turn for the worse, could she keep him alive that long? The situation had turned nerve-racking. She was a physician, not a fortune-teller. She had no X rays at her disposal, no operating room. The physical exam and blood tests were abnormal but non-specific. If she chose to delay rescue, Kenichi might die. If she called for help too soon, millions of dollars would be wasted on an unnecessary launch.

A wrong decision either way would end her career with NASA.

This was the tightrope Jack had warned her about. *I screw up, and the whole world knows. They're waiting to see if I've got the right stuff.*

She looked down at the printout of Kenichi's blood tests. Nothing she saw there justified hitting the panic button. Not yet.

She said, 'Flight, I'm going to keep him on IVs and start NG suction. Right now his vital signs are looking stable. I just wish I knew what was going on in his belly.'

'So in your opinion, emergency shuttle launch is not yet indicated?'

She released a deep breath. 'No. Not yet.'

'We will nevertheless be poised and ready to light *Discovery*'s candle, should it be necessary.'

'I appreciate that. I'll get back to you later with a medical update.' She signed off and looked at Griggs. 'I hope I'm making the right call.'

'Just cure him, okay?'

She went to check on Kenichi. Because he would need attention throughout the night, she'd moved him out of the hab module and into the U.S. lab, so the rest of the crew would not have their sleep disturbed. He was zipped into a restraint bag. An infusion pump fed a steady flow of saline solution into his intravenous line. He was awake and obviously in discomfort.

Luther and Diana, who'd been watching the patient, both looked relieved to see Emma. 'He vomited again,' said Diana.

Emma anchored her feet to hold her position and slipped the stethoscope on her ears. Gently she placed the diaphragm on Kenichi's abdomen. Still no bowel sounds. His digestive tract had shut down, and fluid would begin to accumulate in his stomach. That fluid needed to be drained.

'Kenichi,' she said, 'I'm going to insert a tube into your stomach. It will help the pain, and maybe stop the vomiting.'

'What – what tube?'

'A nasogastric tube.' She opened the ALSP medical kit. Inside was a broad array of supplies and drugs, a collection as complete as a modern ambulance's. In the drawer marked 'Airway' were various tubes, suction devices, collection bags; and a laryngoscope. She tore open the packet containing the long nasogastric tube. It was thin and coiled, made of flexible plastic, with a perforated tip.

Kenichi's bloodred eyes widened.

'I'll be as gentle as I can,' she said. 'You can help it go faster by taking a sip of water when I ask you to. I'm going to insert this end into your nostril. The tube will go down the back of your throat, and when you swallow the water, the tube will pass into your stomach. The only uncomfortable part will be right at the beginning, when I first slip it in. After it's in place, it should hardly bother you at all.'

'How long does it stay inside?'

'A day, at least. Until your intestines start working again.' She added, gently, 'It really is necessary, Kenichi.'

He sighed and nodded.

Emma glanced at Luther, who was looking more and more horrified by the idea of this tube. 'He'll need water to sip. Could you get some?' Then she looked at Diana, who was floating nearby. As usual, Diana looked unperturbed, coolly detached from the crisis. 'I need NG suction set up.'

Diana automatically reached into the ALSP kit for the suction device and collection bag.

Emma uncoiled the NG tube. First she dipped the tip in lubricant gel, to ease its passage through the nasopharynx. Then she handed Kenichi the pouch of water, which Luther had filled.

She gave Kenichi's arm a reassuring squeeze. Though dread was plain to see in his eyes, he returned a nod of consent.

The perforated end of the tube glistened with lubricant. She inserted the tip into his right nostril and gently advanced it deeper, into his nasopharynx. He gagged, eyes watering, and began to cough in protest as the tube slid down the back of his throat. She threaded it deeper. He was twitching now, fighting the overwhelming instinct to thrust her away, to yank the tube out of his nose.

'Swallow some water,' she urged.

He wheezed and with a trembling hand brought the straw to his lips.

'Swallow, Kenichi,' she said.

When a bolus of water is passed from the throat into the esophagus, the epiglottis reflexively closes over the opening to the trachea, preventing any leakage into the lungs. It would also direct an NG tube down the correct passageway. The instant she saw him begin to swallow, she swiftly advanced the tube, threading it past the throat and down the esophagus, until it slid in far enough for the tip to be in the stomach.

'All done,' she said, taping the tube to his nose. 'You did fine.'

'Suction's ready,' said Diana.

Emma connected the NG tube to the suction device. They heard a few gurgles, then fluid suddenly appeared in the tube, flowing out of Kenichi's stomach, into the drainage bag. It was a bilious green; no blood, Emma noted with relief. Perhaps this was all the treatment he needed – bowel rest, NG suction, and intravenous fluids. If he did indeed have pancreatitis, this therapy alone would carry him through the next few days, until the shuttle arrived.

'My head – it hurts,' said Kenichi, closing his eyes.

'I'll give you something for the pain,' said Emma.

'So what do you think? Crisis averted?' It was Griggs speaking. He had watched the procedure from the hatchway, and even though the tube was now inserted, Griggs hung back, as though repulsed by the mere sight of illness. He did not even look at the patient, but kept his gaze focused on Emma.

'We'll have to see,' she said.

'What do I tell Houston?'

'I just got the tube in. It's too early.'

'They need to know soon.'

'Well, I *don't* know!' she snapped. Then, swallowing her temper, she said more calmly, 'Can we discuss this in the hab?' She left Luther to stay with the patient and headed through the hatchway.

In the hab module, she and Griggs were joined by Nicolai. They gathered around the galley table as though sharing a meal. What they were sharing, instead, were their frustrations over an uncertain situation.

'You're the M.D.,' said Griggs. 'Can't you make a decision?'

'I'm still trying to stabilize him,' said Emma. 'Right now I don't know what I'm dealing with.

It could resolve in another day or two. Or it could suddenly get worse.'

'And you can't tell us which is going to happen.'

'Without an X ray, without an OR, I can't see what's going on inside him. I can't predict what his condition will be tomorrow.'

'Great.'

'I do think he should go home. I'd like the launch moved up as soon as possible.'

'What about a CRV evac?' asked Nicolai.

'A controlled shuttle ride is always better for transporting a sick patient,' said Emma. A CRV return was a rough ride, and depending on weather conditions on earth, they might not be able to touch down in the best possible location for medical transport.

'Forget CRV evac,' said Griggs flatly. 'We're not abandoning this station.'

Nicolai said, 'If he becomes critical –'

'Emma will just have to keep him alive long enough for *Discovery* to get here. Hell, this station's like an orbiting ambulance! She *should* be able to keep him stable.'

'What if she cannot?' pressed Nicolai. 'A man's life is worth more than these experiments.'

'It's the option of last resort,' said Griggs. 'We all jump on the CRV, we're abandoning months of work.'

'Look, Griggs,' said Emma. 'I don't want to leave the station any more than you do. I fought like hell to make it up here, and I'm not about to cut my

155

stay short. But if my patient needs instant evac, then it's *my* call.'

'Excuse me, Emma,' said Diana, floating in the hatchway. 'I just finished running Kenichi's last blood tests. I think you should see this.' She handed Emma a computer printout.

Emma stared at the results: *Creatine kinase: 20.6 (normal 0–3.08).*

This illness was more than pancreatitis, more than just a gastrointestinal disturbance. A high CK meant there had been damage to either his muscles or his heart.

Vomiting is sometimes a symptom of a heart attack.

She looked at Griggs. 'I've just made the decision,' she said. 'Tell Houston to fire up the shuttle. Kenichi has to get home.'

August 2

Jack tightened the jib sheet, his sunburned arms gleaming with sweat as he strained against the crank. With a satisfying *whomp* the sail went taut, and *Sanneke* heeled leeward, her bow suddenly slicing faster through the muddy waters of Galveston Bay. He had left the Gulf of Mexico behind him, had sailed around Point Bolivar earlier that afternoon, dodging the ferry from Galveston Island, and was now tacking past the string of refineries on the shores of Texas City as he sailed north toward Clear Lake. Toward home.

Four days at sea on the Gulf had turned him

brown and shaggy. He had informed no one of his plans, had simply stocked up on food and set sail toward open water, beyond sight of land, into nights so black his eyes had been dazzled by the stars. Lying on his back on deck, the Gulf waters gently rocking the hull beneath him, he'd gazed for hours at the night sky. With that field of stars stretching in every direction, as far as he could see, he could almost imagine he was hurtling through space, that each rise of the swells was thrusting him deeper into the coil of another galaxy. He had emptied his mind of everything but the stars and the sea. Then a meteor had streaked by in a brilliant slash of light, and suddenly he'd thought of Emma. He could not put up barricades high enough to keep her out. She was always there, hovering at the edges, waiting to slip into his thoughts when he least expected it. Least wanted it. He had gone rigid, his eyes fixed on that dying streak of the meteor's trail, and even though nothing else had changed, not the direction of the wind nor the rise and fall of the swells, he had felt suddenly, deeply, alone.

It was still dark when he'd raised the sails and turned back for home.

Now, as he motored up the channel into Clear Lake, past rooflines silhouetted against the glare of sunset, he regretted his decision to return home so soon. On the Gulf there had been a constant breeze, but here, the heat hung unstirred and the humidity was stifling.

He tied up at his slip and stepped onto the dock, his legs unsteady from days at sea. First order of business, he thought, was a cold shower. He'd save the boat cleanup for tonight, when it was cooler. And as for Humphrey, well – another day in the kennel wouldn't hurt the little hair ball. Lugging his duffel bag, he headed up the dock and was walking past the marina's small grocery store when his gaze fell on the newsstand. His duffel bag slipped from his grasp and hit the ground. He stared at the banner headline across that morning's *Houston Chronicle:*

'Emergency Shuttle Countdown Begins – Liftoff Tomorrow.'

What has happened? he thought. *What has gone wrong?*

With shaking hands he pulled quarters from his pockets, fed the coins into the slot, and grabbed a copy from the stand. Two photos accompanied the news article. One was of Kenichi Hirai, the NASDA astronaut from Japan. The other was of Emma.

He snatched up the duffel bag and ran for a phone.

There were three flight surgeons at the meeting – an indication to Jack that the crisis they faced was medical. As he walked into the room, heads turned in surprise. He read the unspoken question in space station flight director Woody Ellis's eyes: *What's Jack McCallum doing back in the fold?*

Dr Todd Cutler gave the answer. 'Jack helped

158

develop our emergency medical procedures protocol for the station's first crew. I thought he should join us.'

Ellis said, uneasily, 'The personal angle makes this complicated.' *Emma* was what he meant.

'Every member of that crew is like family to us,' said Todd. 'So in a way, it's *all* personal.'

Jack took a seat beside Todd. Sitting at the table were the NSTS deputy director, the ISS mission operations director, flight surgeons, and several program managers. Also present was NASA's public affairs officer, Gretchen Liu. With the exception of launch days, the news media largely ignored NASA operations. Today, though, journalists from every news agency were crammed into the tiny pressroom in NASA's Public Information building, awaiting Gretchen's appearance. What a difference a day made, thought Jack. Public attention was fickle. It demanded explosions, tragedy. Crisis. The miracle of a flawless operation drew no one's attention.

Todd passed a sheaf of papers to him, with a note scrawled on top: '*Hirai's labs and clinical findings last 24 hours. Welcome back.*'

Jack flipped through the medical reports while he listened to the meeting. He had a day's worth of developments to catch up on, and it took him a while to absorb the essentials. Astronaut Kenichi Hirai was seriously ill, his lab findings puzzling to everyone. The shuttle *Discovery* was poised for a six A.M. EDT launch manned by Kittredge's crew, along with an astronaut-physician. Countdown was on schedule.

'Any change in your recommendations?' the NSTS deputy director asked the flight surgeons. 'Do you still think Hirai can wait for a shuttle evac?'

Todd Cutler answered. 'We still believe a shuttle evac is the safest option. We aren't changing our recommendations in that regard. ISS is a fairly well-equipped medical facility, with all the drugs and equipment needed for cardiopulmonary resuscitation.'

'So you still believe he's had a heart attack?'

Todd looked at his fellow flight surgeons. 'Frankly,' he admitted, 'we're not entirely certain. There are things that do point to a myocardial infarction – a heart attack, in layman's terms. Mainly, the rising levels of cardiac enzymes in his blood.'

'Then why are you still unsure?'

'The EKG shows only nonspecific changes – a few T wave inversions. It's not a classic pattern for an MI. Also, Hirai was thoroughly screened for cardiovascular disease prior to his acceptance in the program. He had no risk factors. Frankly, we're not sure what's going on. But we do have to assume he has had a heart attack. Which makes a shuttle evac the best option. It's a gentler reentry and a controlled landing. Far less stress on the patient than coming home in the CRV. In the meantime, ISS can deal with any arrhythmias he may have.'

Jack looked up from the lab reports he'd been scanning. 'Without the necessary lab equipment, the station can't fractionate these CK levels. So how can we be sure this enzyme is really from the heart?'

Everyone's attention turned to him.

'What do you mean by "fractionate"?' asked Woody Ellis.

'Creatine kinase is an enzyme that helps muscle cells utilize stored energy. It's found in both striated and cardiac muscle. When there's damage to heart cells, say, in a heart attack, the CK levels rise in the blood. That's why we're assuming he had a heart attack. But what if it's not the heart?'

'What else could it be?'

'Some other type of muscle damage. Trauma, for instance, or convulsions. Inflammation. In fact, just a simple intramuscular injection can cause the CK to rise. You need to fractionate the CK in order to tell if it's from heart muscle. The station can't do that test.'

'So he may not have had a heart attack at all.'

'Correct. And here's another puzzling detail. After acute muscle damage, his CK levels should drop back to normal. But look at the pattern.' Jack flipped through the lab sheets and read off the numbers. 'In the last twenty-four hours, his levels have been steadily *rising*. Which indicates continued damage.'

'It's just part of the bigger puzzle,' said Todd.

'We've got abnormal results all over the board, without any recognizable pattern. Liver enzymes, renal abnormalities, sedimentation rate, white blood cell counts. Some labs go up while others are dropping. It's as though different organ systems are taking turns being attacked.'

Jack looked at him. 'Attacked?'

'Just a figure of speech, Jack. I don't know *what* process we're dealing with. I know it's not lab error. We've run controls on the other crew members, and they're perfectly normal.'

'But is he sick enough to warrant *any* evac?' The question was asked by the mission operations director for the shuttle. He was not happy about any of this. *Discovery*'s original mission was to retrieve and repair the classified *Capricorn* satellite. Now her mission had been usurped by this crisis. 'Washington is not happy about postponing the satellite repair. You've commandeered their flight so *Discovery* can play flying ambulance. Is it really necessary? Can't Hirai recover on the station?'

'We can't predict it. We don't know what's wrong with him,' said Todd.

'You have a physician up there, for God's sake. Can't *she* figure it out?'

Jack tensed. This was an attack on Emma. 'She doesn't have X-ray vision,' he said.

'She's got just about everything else at her disposal. What'd you call the station, Dr Cutler? "A well-equipped medical facility"?'

'Astronaut Hirai needs to get home, as expeditiously as possible,' said Todd. 'That remains our position. If you want to second-guess your flight surgeons, that's your choice. All I can say is, I'd never presume to second-guess an engineer on propulsion systems.'

That effectively ended the argument.

The NSTS deputy director said, 'Are there any other concerns?'

'Weather,' said the NASA forecaster. 'I just thought I'd mention there's a storm system developing west of Guadeloupe and moving very slowly westward. It won't affect the launch. But depending on its path, it could be a problem for Kennedy in the next week or so.'

'Thanks for the heads up.' The deputy director glanced around the room and saw no further questions. 'Then launch is still a go for five A.M. CDT. See you all there.'

10

Punta Arena, Mexico

The Sea of Cortez shimmered like beaten silver in the fading light. From her table on the outdoor deck of the Las Tres Virgenes café, Helen Koenig could see fishing boats heading back to Punta Colorado. This was the time of day she loved best, the evening breeze cool against her sun-flushed skin, her muscles pleasantly weary from an afternoon's swim. A waiter brought the margarita she'd ordered and set the drink before her.

'*Gracias, señor*,' she murmured.

For an instant he met her gaze. She saw a quiet and dignified man with tired eyes and silver-streaked hair, and she felt a prick of discomfort. Yankee guilt, she thought as she watched him walk back to the bar. A feeling she experienced every time she drove down to Baja. She sipped her drink and gazed at the sea, listening to the whining trumpets of a mariachi band playing somewhere up the beach.

It had been a good day, and she'd spent almost all of it in the sea. A two-tank dive in the morning followed by a shallower dive in the afternoon. And then, just before dinner, a swim in the sunset-gilded waters. The sea was her comfort, her sanctuary. It had always been so. Unlike the love of a man, the sea was constant and it never disappointed her. It was always ready to embrace her, soothe her, and in moments of crisis she found herself fleeing into its waiting arms.

This was why she had come to Baja. To swim in warm waters and to be alone, where no one could reach her. Not even Palmer Gabriel.

Her lips puckered from the tang of the margarita. She drank it down and ordered a second. Already the alcohol made her feel as if she were floating. No matter; she was now a free woman. The project was finished, aborted. The cultures destroyed. Even though Palmer was furious with her, she knew she had done the right thing. The safe thing. Tomorrow she would sleep in, order hot chocolate and huevos rancheros for breakfast. Then she'd slip beneath the waters for another dive, another return to her sea-green lover.

A woman's laughter drew her attention. Helen looked at the bar, where a couple was flirting, the woman slim and tanned, the man with muscles like steel cord. A vacation fling in the making. They would probably have dinner together, walk along the beach, hold hands. Then there would be a kiss, an embrace, all the hormone-charged rituals of mating. Helen watched them with both a scientist's interest and a woman's envy. She knew such rituals did not apply to her. She was forty-nine years old and she looked it. Her waist was thick, her hair more than half gray, and her face was unremarkable save for the intelligence of her eyes. She was not the sort of woman who attracted looks from sun-bronzed Adonises.

She finished the second margarita. By now the floating sensation had spread to her whole body, and she knew it was time to get some food in her stomach. She opened the menu. '*Restaurante de Las Tres Virgenes*' it said at the top. The Three Virgins. An appropriate place for her to eat. She might as well be a virgin.

The waiter came to take her order. She looked up at him and had just requested the grilled dorado when her eyes focused on the TV over the bar, on the image of the space shuttle poised on the launchpad.

'What's happening?' she said, pointing to the TV.

The waiter shrugged.

'Turn up the sound,' she called out to the bar-tender. 'Please, I need to hear it!'

He reached for the volume knob, and the broadcast spilled out in English. An American channel. Helen crossed to the bar counter and stared at the television.

'. . . medical evacuation of astronaut Kenichi Hirai. NASA has not released any further information, but reports indicate their flight surgeons remain baffled by his illness. Based on today's blood tests, they felt it was prudent to launch a shuttle rescue. *Discovery* is expected to lift off tomorrow at six A.M. Eastern Daylight Time.'

'*Señora?*' said the waiter.

Helen turned and saw he was still holding his order pad. 'Do you wish another drink?'

'No. No, I have to leave.'

'But your food –'

'Cancel my order. Please.' She opened her purse, handed him fifteen dollars, and hurried out of the restaurant.

Back in her hotel room she tried to call Palmer Gabriel in San Diego. It took half a dozen tries to connect with the international operator, and when the call finally went through, she got only Palmer's voice mail.

'They have a sick astronaut on ISS,' she said. 'Palmer, this is what I was afraid of. What I warned all of you about. If it's confirmed, we have to move fast. Before . . .' She paused, glancing at the clock. *To hell with this*, she thought, and hung up. *I have to get home to San Diego. I'm the only one who knows how to deal with this. They'll need me.*

She threw her clothes into the suitcase, checked out of the hotel, and climbed into a taxi for the fifteen-mile ride to the tiny airstrip in Buena Vista. A small plane would be waiting for her there to fly her to La Paz, where she could catch a commercial flight to San Diego.

It was a rough taxi ride, the road bumpy and winding, the dust flying in the open windows. But the part of the trip she truly dreaded was the flight coming up. Small planes terrified her. If not for her rush to get home, she would have made the long drive up the Baja Peninsula in her own car, which was now safely parked at the resort. She clung to the armrest with sweaty palms, imagining what sort of aviation disaster awaited her.

Then she glimpsed the night sky, clear and velvety black, and she thought of the people aboard the space station. Thought of the risks other, braver human beings took. It was all a matter of perspective. A ride in a small plane is nothing compared to the dangers an astronaut faces.

This was not the time to be a coward. Lives might hang in the balance. And she was the only one who knew what to do about it.

The spine-rattling ride suddenly smoothed out. They were now on a paved road, thank God, and Buena Vista was just a few miles away.

Sensing the urgency of this journey, her driver accelerated, and the wind whipped through the open windows, stinging her face with dust. She reached down to crank up the glass. Suddenly she felt the taxi swerve left to pass a slow-moving car. She glanced up and saw to her horror they were on a curve.

'*Señor! Más despacio!*' she said. *Slow down*.

They were neck and neck with the other car now, the taxi just pulling ahead, the driver unwilling to surrender his gain. The road ahead wound to the left, dipping out of sight.

'Don't pass!' she said. 'Please, don't—' Her gaze shot forward and froze on the blinding lights of another car.

She raised her arms to cover her face, blotting out the brilliance of those lights. But she could not shut out the scream of the tires or the shriek of her own voice as the headlights leaped toward them.

August 3

From his seat behind the glass partition of the crowded visitors' gallery, Jack had a clear view down into the Flight Control Room, where every console was manned, every controller neatly attired for the TV cameras. Though the men and women working below might be intently focused on their duties, they never entirely forgot they were being observed, that the public eye was trained on them, and every gesture, every nervous shake of the head, could be seen through the wall of glass behind them. Only a year ago, Jack had manned the flight surgeon's console during a shuttle launch, and he had felt the gaze of strangers, like a vague but uncomfortable heat trained on the back of his neck. He knew the people below were feeling it now.

The atmosphere in the FCR appeared icy calm,

as were the voices on the comm loop. It was the image NASA strove to maintain, of professionals doing their job and doing it well. What the public seldom saw were the crises in the back controller rooms, the near-disasters, the Chinese fire drills when things went wrong and confusion reigned.

Not today, he thought. *Carpenter's at the helm. Things will go right.*

Flight Director Randy Carpenter was leading the ascent team. He was old enough and experienced enough to have witnessed a multitude of crises during his career. It was his belief that space-flight tragedies were not usually the result of one major malfunction, but rather a series of small problems that piled up until they resulted in disaster. He was therefore a stickler for details, a man for whom every problem was a potential crisis. His team looked up to him – quite literally, because Carpenter was a giant of a man, six foot four and nearly three hundred pounds.

Gretchen Liu, the public affairs officer, was sitting at the far left, last-row console. Jack saw her turn and give the viewing gallery an A-OK smile. She was dressed in her TV best today, a navy blue suit and gray silk scarf. This mission had caught the world's attention, and although most of the press was gathered at the launch site in Cape Canaveral, there were enough reporters here in JSC's Mission Control to pack the observation gallery.

The ten-minute countdown hold ended. On

audio, they heard final weather clearance, and then the countdown proceeded. Jack leaned forward, his muscles tensing as events cascaded toward liftoff. That old launch fever was back. A year ago, when he'd walked away from the space program, he thought he'd left all this behind. But here he was, caught up once again in the excitement. The dream. He imagined the crew strapped into their seats, the vehicle trembling beneath them as the chambers of liquid oxygen and hydrogen built up pressure. He thought of their claustrophobia as they closed their visors. The hiss of oxygen. The quickening of their pulses.

'We have SRB ignition,' said the public affairs officer in KSC's Launch Control. 'And liftoff! We have liftoff! Control has now shifted to Houston's JSC . . .'

Tracing across the central screen, the shuttle's course arced eastward along its planned flight path. Jack was still tense, his heart racing. On the TV screens mounted above the gallery, images of the shuttle were being transmitted from Kennedy. Communications between Capcom and shuttle commander Kittredge played on the speakers. *Discovery* had gone into its roll and was climbing into the upper reaches of the atmosphere, where blue sky would soon darken to the blackness of space.

'We're looking good,' said Gretchen over the media loop. In her voice they heard the triumph of a perfect launch. And so far it *was* perfect. Right through Max Q, through SRB sep, through main engine cutoff.

In the FCR, Flight Director Carpenter stood immobile, his gaze fixed on the front screen.

'*Discovery*, you are go for ET sep,' said Capcom.

'Roger, Houston,' said Kittredge. 'We have ET sep.'

It was the sudden jerking up of Carpenter's massive head that told Jack something had just changed. In the FCR, a flutter of activity seemed to animate all the flight controllers at once. Several of them glanced sideways at Carpenter, whose normally slouching shoulders had snapped up to attention. Gretchen had her hand pressed to her earpiece as she listened intently to the loop.

Something has gone wrong, thought Jack.

The air-to-ground loop continued to play on the gallery audio.

'*Discovery*,' said Capcom, 'MMACS reports umbilical doors have failed to close. Please confirm.'

'Roger that, and we confirm. The doors are not closing.'

'Suggest you go to manual command.'

There was an ominous silence. Then they heard Kittredge say, 'Houston, we're A-OK now. The doors have just closed.'

Only then, when Jack released a sharp breath, did he realize he'd been holding it. So far this was the only glitch. Everything else, he thought, is perfect. Yet the effects of that sudden surge of adrenaline still lingered, and his hands were sweating. They'd just been reminded of how many things can go wrong, and he could not shake off this new sense of uneasiness.

He stared down at the FCR and wondered if Randy Carpenter, the best of the best, felt the same sense of foreboding.

August 4

It was as though the clock in his brain had automatically reset itself, shifting his sleep and wake cycles so that his mind snapped to alertness at one A.M. Jack lay in bed, eyes wide open, the luminous glow of his nightstand clock staring back at him. Like the shuttle *Discovery*, he thought, I am racing to catch up with ISS. With Emma. Already his body was synchronizing itself to hers. In an hour, she would be waking up, and her workday would begin. And here was Jack, awake already, their rhythms in near parallel.

He did not try to go back to sleep, but rose and got dressed.

At one-thirty A.M., Mission Control was quietly humming with activity. He glanced first in the FCR, where the shuttle controllers sat. So far, no crises had occurred aboard *Discovery*.

He went down the hall to Special Vehicle Operations, the separate control room for ISS. It was much smaller than the shuttle's FCR, with its own array of consoles and personnel. Jack headed straight to the flight surgeon's console and sank into the chair next to Roy Bloomfeld, the physician on duty. Bloomfeld glanced at him with surprise.

'Hey, Jack. I guess you're really back in the program.'

'Couldn't stay away.'

'Well, it can't be the money. So it must be the thrill of the job.' He leaned back, yawning. 'Not many thrills tonight.'

'Patient's stable?'

'Has been for the last twelve hours.' Bloomfeld nodded to the biotelemetry readings on his console. Kenichi Hirai's EKG and blood pressure readings blipped across the screen. 'Rhythm's steady as a rock.'

'No new developments?'

'Last status report was four hours ago. His headache's worse, and he still has that fever. Antibiotics don't seem to be doing much of anything. We're all scratching our heads over this one.'

'Does Emma have any ideas?'

'At this point, she's probably too exhausted to think. I told her to get some sleep, since we're watching the monitor anyway. So far, it's been pretty boring.' Bloomfeld yawned again. 'Listen, I gotta take a leak. Can you watch the console for a few minutes?'

'No problem.'

Bloomfeld left the room, and Jack slipped on the headset. It felt familiar and good to be sitting in front of a console again. To hear the muted conversation from the other controllers, to watch the front screen, where the station's orbital path traced a sine wave across the map. This might not be a seat on the shuttle, but it was as close as he could get to one. *I won't ever touch the stars, but I can be here to see that others do.* It was a startling revelation to him, that he had accepted that bitter twist in his life. That he could stand on the periphery of his old dream and still admire the view from afar.

His gaze suddenly focused on Kenichi Hirai's EKG, and he leaned forward. The heart tracing had shuddered up and down in a few rapid oscillations. Now it sketched a completely straight line across the top of the screen.

Jack relaxed. This was nothing to worry about; he recognized it as an electrical anomaly – probably a loose EKG lead. The blood pressure tracing continued across the screen, unchanged. Perhaps the patient had moved, accidentally pulling off a lead. Or Emma had disconnected the monitor, to allow him to use the toilet in private. Now the blood pressure tracing abruptly cut off – another indication that Kenichi was off the monitors. He watched the screen for a moment longer, expecting the readings to reappear.

When they did not, he got on the loop.

'Capcom, this is Surgeon. I'm seeing a loose lead pattern on the patient's EKG.'

'Loose lead?'

'Looks like he's been disconnected from his monitor. There's no heart tracing coming across. Could you check with Emma to confirm?'

'Roger, Surgeon. I'll give her a jingle.'

A soft whine pulled Emma from a dreamless sleep, and she awakened to the cold kiss of moisture on her face. She had not intended to doze. Though Mission Control was continually monitoring Kenichi's EKG on biotelemetry and would alert her to any changes in his status, she had planned to stay awake throughout the crew's designated sleep period. But in the last two days, she had caught only brief snatches of rest, and those were often interrupted by her crewmates, waking her with questions about her patient's status. Exhaustion, and the utter relaxation of weightlessness, had finally caught up with her. Her last waking memory was of watching Kenichi's heart rhythm blip across the screen in a hypnotic squiggle, the line fading to a blur of green. To black.

Aware of the cold splash of water clinging to her cheek, she opened her eyes and saw a globule float toward her, twirling with a rainbow of reflections. It took her a few dazed seconds to understand what she was looking at, another few seconds to register the dozens of other globules dancing like silvery Christmas ornaments all around her.

Static, then a voice, crackled over her comm unit. 'Uh, Watson, this is Capcom. We hate to wake you, but we need to confirm status of the patient's EKG leads.'

Hoarse with exhaustion, Emma replied, 'I'm awake, Capcom. I think.'

'Biotelemetry shows an anomaly on your patient's EKG. Surgeon thinks you've got a loose lead up there.'

She had been drifting, turning in midair while asleep, and now she reoriented herself in the module and turned to where her patient should be.

His sleep restraint bag was empty. The disconnected IV tube floated free, the catheter end releasing drops of glistening saline into the air. Loose electrode wires drifted in a tangle.

At once she shut off the infusion pump and quickly glanced around. 'Capcom, he's not here. He's left the module! Stand by.' She pushed off the wall, shot into Node 2, leading to the NASDA and ESA labs. A glance through the hatchways told her he was not there.

'Have you located him?' Capcom asked.

'Negative. I'm still looking.'

Had he become disoriented, wandered away in confusion? Backtracking through the U.S. lab, she shot through the node hatchway. A droplet splattered her face. She swiped at the pinpoint of moisture and was startled to see her finger was smeared with blood.

'Capcom, he's passed through Node One. Bleeding from his IV puncture site.'

'Recommend you shut off airflow between modules.'

'Roger that.' She glided through the hatchway of the hab module. The lights had been dimmed, and in the gloom, she saw Griggs and Luther, both sound asleep and zipped into their restraint bags. No Kenichi.

Don't panic, she thought as she shut off the intermodule airflow. *Think. Where would he go?*

Back to his own sleep station, at the Russian end of ISS.

Without waking Griggs or Luther, she left the hab and moved quickly into the tunnel of connecting nodes and modules, her gaze darting left and right in search of her fugitive patient. 'Capcom, I still haven't located him. I'm through Zarya and heading for the RSM.'

She slipped into the Russian service module, where Kenichi normally slept. In the gloom she saw Diana and Nicolai both asleep, floating as though drowned, their arms drifting free of their restraint bags. Kenichi's station was empty.

Her anxiety turned to real fear.

She gave Nicolai a shake. He was slow to awaken, and even after he opened his eyes, it took him a moment to understand what she was telling him.

'I can't find Kenichi,' she repeated. 'We need to search every module.'

'Watson,' said Capcom over her headset. 'Engineering reports intermittent anomaly in Node One air lock. Please check status.'

'What anomaly?'

'Off and on readings indicate the hatch between the equipment and crew locks may not be fully secure.'

Kenichi. He's in the air lock.

With Nicolai right behind her, she shot like a flying bird through the station and dove into Node 1. At her first frantic glance through the open hatch, into the equipment lock, Emma caught a startling glimpse of what looked like three bodies. Two were only the pair of EVA suits, the hard-shelled torsos mounted on the air lock walls for easy donning.

Hanging in midair, his body arched backward in a convulsive spasm, was Kenichi.

'Help me get him out of here!' said Emma. She maneuvered behind him and, bracing her feet against the outer hatch, shoved him toward Nicolai, who pulled him out of the air lock. Together, they propelled him toward the lab module, where the medical equipment had been set up.

'Capcom, we've located the patient,' said Emma. 'He appears to be seizing – grand mal. I need Surgeon on the loop!'

'Stand by, Watson. Go ahead, Surgeon.'

Emma heard a startlingly familiar voice over her headset. 'Hey, Em. Hear you've got yourself a problem up there.'

'*Jack?* What are you doing –'

'How's your patient?'

Still in a state of shock, she focused her attention on Kenichi. Even as she restarted the IV, attached EKG wires, she was wondering what Jack was doing in Mission Control. He had not sat at a flight surgeon's console in a year; now here he was on the comm loop, his voice calm, even casual, as he asked about Kenichi's status.

'Is he still seizing?'

'No. No, he's making purposeful movements now – fighting us –'

'Vital signs?'

'Pulse is rapid – one twenty, one thirty. He's moving air.'

'Good. So he's breathing.'

'We're just getting the EKG hooked up now.' She glanced at the monitor, at the cardiac rhythm racing across the screen. 'Sinus tach, rate of one twenty-four. Occasional PVCs.'

'I see it on biotelemetry.'

'Taking BP now . . .' She whiffed up the cuff, listened to the brachial pulse as the pressure was slowly released. 'Ninety-five over sixty. Not significantly –'

The blow caught her by surprise. She gave a sharp cry of pain as Kenichi's hand flailed out, striking her across the mouth. The impact spun her away, and she flew across the module, colliding with the opposite wall.

'Emma?' said Jack. '*Emma?*'

Dazed, she reached up to touch her throbbing lip.

'You're bleeding!' said Nicolai.

Over her headset, Jack's frantic voice demanded, 'What the hell is going on up there?'

'I'm okay,' she murmured. And repeated, irritably, 'I'm okay, Jack. Don't have a cow.'

But her head was still buzzing from the blow. As Nicolai strapped Kenichi to the patient restraint board, she hung back, waiting for her dizziness to pass. At first she did not register what Nicolai was saying.

Then she saw the look of disbelief in his eyes. 'Look at his stomach,' Nicolai whispered. '*Look!*'

Emma moved closer. 'What the hell is that?' she whispered.

'Talk to me, Emma,' said Jack. 'Tell me what's going on.'

She stared at Kenichi's abdomen, where the skin seemed to ripple and boil. 'There's something moving – under his skin –'

'What do you mean, moving?'

'It looks like muscle fasciculations. But it's migrating across the belly . . .'

'Not peristalsis?'

'No. No, it's moving *upwards*. It's not following the intestinal tract.' She paused. The squirming had suddenly stopped, and she was staring at the smooth, unworried surface of Kenichi's abdomen.

Fasciculations, she thought. The uncoordinated twitching of muscle fibers. It was the most likely explanation, except for one detail: Fasciculations do not migrate in waves.

Suddenly Kenichi's eyes shot open, and he stared at Emma.

The cardiac alarm squealed. Emma turned to see the EKG whipsawing up and down on the screen.

'V tach!' said Jack.

'I see it, I see it!' She flipped on the defibrillator charge button, then felt for a carotid pulse.

There it was. Faint, barely palpable.

His eyes had rolled up, and only the bloodred sclerae were visible. He was still breathing.

She slapped on defibrillator pads, positioned the paddles on the chest, and pressed the discharge buttons. An electric charge of one hundred joules shot through Kenichi's body.

His muscles contracted in a violent and simultaneous spasm. His legs thrashed against the board. Only the restraints kept him from flying across the module.

'Still in V tach!' said Emma.

Diana came flying into the module. 'What can I do?' she asked.

'Get the lidocaine ready!' snapped Emma. 'CDK drawer, right side!'

'Found it.'

'He's not breathing!' said Nicolai.

Emma grabbed the ambu-bag and said, 'Nicolai, brace me!'

He maneuvered into position, planting his feet on the opposite wall, his back pressed against Emma's to hold her in place as she applied the oxygen mask. On earth, performing cardiopulmonary resuscitation is demanding enough; in microgravity, it is a nightmare of complex acrobatics, with drifting equipment, tubes twisting and tangling in midair, syringes filled with precious drugs floating away. The simple act of pressing your hands against a patient's chest can send you tumbling across the room. Although the crew had practiced this scenario, no rehearsal could reproduce the genuine chaos of bodies frantically maneuvering in a closed space, racing against the clock of a dying heart.

With the mask over Kenichi's mouth and nose, she squeezed the ambu-bag, forcing oxygen into his lungs. The EKG line continued to thrash across the screen.

'One amp lidocaine IV push now,' said Diana.

'Nicolai, shock him again!' said Emma.

After the briefest hesitation, he reached for the paddles, placed them on the chest, and pressed the discharge buttons. This time two hundred joules arced through Kenichi's heart.

Emma glanced at the monitor. 'He's gone into V fib! Nicolai, start cardiac compressions. I'm going to intubate!'

Nicolai released the defib paddles, and they floated off, dangling at the ends of the wires. Bracing his feet against the opposite wall of the module, he was about to place his palms on Kenichi's sternum when he suddenly jerked his hands away.

Emma looked at him. 'What is it?'

'His chest. Look at his chest!'

They stared.

The skin on Kenichi's chest was boiling, squirming. At the contact points where the defib paddles had delivered their electric jolts, two raised circles had formed and were now spreading, like ripples cast by a stone in water.

'Asystole!' came Jack's voice over her headset.

Nicolai was still frozen, staring at Kenichi's chest.

It was Emma who swung into position, bracing her back against Nicolai's.

Asystole. The heart has stopped. He will die without cardiac compressions.

She felt nothing moving, nothing unusual. Just skin stretched over the bony landmarks of his breastbone. *Muscle fasciculations*, she thought. *It had to be. There's no other explanation.* With her body braced in position, she began chest compressions, her hands performing the work for Kenichi's heart, pumping blood to his vital organs.

'Diana, one amp IV epinephrine!' she ordered.

Diana injected the drug into the IV line.

They all looked at the monitor, hoping for, praying for, a blip on the screen.

11

'There has to be an autopsy,' said Todd Cutler.

Gordon Obie, director of Flight Crew Operations, flashed him an irritated look. Some of the others in the conference room gave Cutler dismissive nods as well, because he had merely stated the obvious. Of course there would be an autopsy.

Over a dozen people had gathered together for this crisis meeting. An autopsy was the least of their concerns. Right now, Obie was dealing with more urgent issues. Normally a man of few words, he'd suddenly found himself in the uncomfortable position of having reporters' microphones thrust at his face whenever he appeared in public. The excruciating process of assigning blame had begun.

Obie had to accept a portion of responsibility for this tragedy, because he had approved the choice of every member of the flight crew. If the crew screwed up, in essence, *he* had screwed up. And his choice of Emma Watson was starting to look like a major error.

That, at least, was the message he was hearing in this room. As the only physician aboard ISS Emma Watson should have realized Hirai was dying. An immediate CRV evac might have saved him. Now a shuttle had been launched, and a multimillion-dollar rescue mission had turned into nothing more than a morgue run. Washington was hungry for scapegoats, and the foreign press was asking a politically incendiary question: Would an *American* astronaut have been allowed to die?

The PR fallout was, in fact, this meeting's major topic of discussion.

Gretchen Liu said, 'Senator Parish has gone on the record with a statement.'

JSC director Ken Blankenship groaned. 'I'm afraid to ask.'

'CNN-Atlanta faxed it over. And I quote: "Millions of tax dollars went into the development of the emergency Crew Return Vehicle. Yet NASA chose not to use it. They had a critically ill man up there whose life might have been saved. Now that courageous astronaut is dead, and it's apparent to everyone that a terrible mistake was made. One death in space is one death too many. A congressional inquiry is in order."' Gretchen looked up with a grim expression. 'Our favorite senator speaks.'

'I wonder how many people remember that he tried to kill our Crew Return Vehicle program?' said Blankenship. 'I'd love to rub that in his face right now.'

'You can't,' said Leroy Cornell. As NASA administrator, it was second nature for Cornell to weigh all the political ramifications. He was their link to Congress and the White House, and he never lost sight of how things would play out in Washington. 'You launch a direct attack on the senator, and things will really hit the fan.'

'He's attacking *us*.'

'That's nothing new, and everyone knows it.'

'The public doesn't,' said Gretchen. 'He's making headlines with these attacks.'

'That's the whole point – the senator wants headlines,' said Cornell. 'We fire back, it'll feed the media beast. Look, Parish has never been our friend. He's fought every budget increase we've ever asked for. He wants to buy gunships, not spaceships, and we'll never change his mind.' Cornell took a deep breath and looked around the room. 'So we might as well take a good hard look at his criticism. And ask ourselves if it isn't justified.'

The room went momentarily silent.

'Obviously, mistakes were made,' said Blankenship. 'Errors in medical judgment. Why didn't we know how sick the man was?'

Obie saw an uneasy glance fly between the two flight surgeons. Everyone was now focused on the performance of the medical team. And on Emma Watson.

She wasn't here to defend herself; Obie would have to speak up for her.

Todd Cutler beat him to it. 'Watson's at a disadvantage up there. Any doctor would be,' he said. 'No X ray, no OR. The truth is, none of us know why Hirai died. That's why we need the autopsy. We have to know what went wrong. And whether microgravity was a contributing factor.'

'There's no question about an autopsy,' said Blankenship. 'Everyone's agreed on that point.'

'No, the reason I mention it is because of the . . .' Cutler dropped his voice, 'preservation problem.'

There was a pause. Obie saw gazes drop in uneasy contemplation of what that meant.

'The lack of refrigeration on the station is what he's talking about,' said Obie. 'Not for something as large as a human body. Not in a pressurized environment.'

ISS flight director Woody Ellis said, 'Shuttle rendezvous is in seventeen hours. How badly can the body deteriorate in that time?'

'There's no refrigeration aboard the shuttle either,' pointed out Cutler. 'Death occurred seven hours ago. Add to that the time for rendezvous, the transfer of the corpse, as well as other cargo, and the undocking. We're talking at least three days with the body at room temperature. And that's if everything goes like clockwork. Which, as we all know, is not a given.'

Three days. Obie thought of what could happen to a dead body in two days. Of how badly raw chicken parts stank if he left them in his garbage can for just one night . . .

'You're saying *Discovery* can't delay her return home, even for an extra day?' said Ellis. 'We were hoping there'd be time for other tasks. There are numerous experiments on ISS ready to come home. Scientists on the ground are waiting for them.'

'An autopsy won't be of much help if the body's deteriorated,' said Cutler.

'Isn't there some way to preserve it? Embalm it?'

'Not without affecting its chemistry. We need an unembalmed body. And we need it home soon.'

Ellis sighed. 'There has to be a compromise. A way to get *something* else accomplished while they're docked.'

Gretchen said, 'From a PR point of view, it looks bad, going about your usual business while a corpse is stored in the middeck. Besides, isn't there some, well, health hazard? And then there's . . . the odor.'

'The body is sealed in a plastic shroud,' said Cutler. 'They can curtain it off out of view in a sleep station.'

The subject had turned so grim that most faces in the room were looking pale. They could talk about the political fallout and the media crisis. They could talk about hostile senators and mechanical anomalies. But dead bodies and bad smells and deteriorating flesh were not things they wanted to concentrate on.

Leroy Cornell finally broke the silence. 'I understand your sense of urgency about getting the body

189

back for autopsy, Dr Cutler. And I understand the PR angle as well. The seeming . . . lack of sensitivity if we go about our business. But there *are* things we have to do, even in light of our losses.' He looked around the table. 'That is our prime objective, isn't it? One of our strengths as an organization? No matter what goes wrong, no matter what we suffer, we always strive to get the job done?'

That's the moment Obie sensed the sudden shift of mood in the room. Up till then, they had been laboring under the pall of tragedy, the pressure of media attention. He had seen gloom and defeat in these faces, and defensiveness. Now the pall was lifting. He met Cornell's gaze and felt some of his old disdain toward the man fall away. Obie had never trusted smooth talkers like Cornell. He thought of NASA administrators as a necessary evil and tolerated them only as long as they kept their noses out of operational decisions.

At times, Cornell had strayed over that line. Today, though, he had done them a service by making them step back and view the big picture. Everyone had come to this meeting with his or her private concerns. Cutler wanted a fresh corpse to autopsy. Gretchen Liu wanted the right media spin. The shuttle management team wanted *Discovery*'s mission expanded.

Cornell had just reminded them that they had to look beyond this death, beyond their individual concerns, and focus on what was best for the space program.

Obie gave a small nod of agreement, which was noted by others at the table. The Sphinx had finally made his opinion known.

'Every successful launch is a gift from heaven,' he said. 'Let's not waste this one.'

August 5

Dead.

Emma's running shoes pounded rhythmically on the TVIS treadmill, and every slap of her soles against the moving belt, every impact jolting her bones and joints and muscles, was another self-administered blow of punishment.

Dead.

I lost him. I fucked up and I lost him.

I should have realized how sick he was. I should have pushed for a CRV evac. But I delayed, because I thought I could handle it. I thought I could keep him alive.

Muscles aching, sweat beading on her forehead, she continued to punish herself, enraged by her own failure. She had not used the TVIS in three days because she'd been too busy tending to Kenichi. Now she was making up for it, had snapped on the side restraints, turned the treadmill to active mode, and started her run.

On earth she enjoyed running. She was not particularly fast, but she'd developed endurance and had learned to slip into that hypnotic trance that comes to long-distance runners as the miles melt

191

away beneath their feet, as the burn of working muscles gives way to euphoria. Day after day she had worked to build up that endurance, had forced herself, through sheer stubbornness, to go longer, farther, always in competition with her last run, never cutting herself a break. It was the way she'd been since she was a girl, smaller than the others, but fiercer. All her life she had been fierce, but never more so than with herself.

I made mistakes. And now my patient's dead.

Sweat soaked through her shirt, a big wet blotch spreading between her breasts. Her calves and thighs were beyond the burn stage. The muscles were twitching, on the verge of collapse from the constant tension of the restraints.

A hand reached over and flicked off the TVIS power switch. The running belt abruptly shuddered to a halt. She glanced up and met Luther's gaze.

'I think that's more than enough, Watson,' he said quietly.

'Not yet.'

'You've been at it for more than three hours.'

'I'm just getting started,' she muttered grimly. She switched on the power, and once again her shoes pounded on the moving belt.

Luther watched her for a moment, his body floating at her eye level, his gaze unavoidable. She hated being studied, even hated *him* at that instant, because she thought he could see right through to her pain, her self-disgust.

'Wouldn't it be quicker just to smash your head against a wall?' he said.

'Quicker. But not painful enough.'

'I get it. To be punishment, it's gotta hurt, huh?'

'Right.'

'Would it make a difference if I told you this is bullshit? Because it is. It's a waste of energy. Kenichi died because he was sick.'

'That's where I'm supposed to come in.'

'And you couldn't save him. So now you're the corps fuckup, huh?'

'That's right.'

'Well, you're wrong. Because *I* claimed that title before you.'

'Is this some sort of contest?'

Again, he shut off the TVIS power. Again the treadmill belt ground to a halt. He was staring her right in the eye, his gaze angry. As fierce as hers.

'Remember *my* fuckup? On *Columbia?*'

She said nothing; she didn't have to. Everyone at NASA remembered it. It had happened four years ago, during a mission to repair an orbiting comm satellite. Luther had been the mission specialist responsible for redeploying the satellite after repairs were completed. The crew had ejected it from its cradle in the payload bay and watched it drift away. The rockets had ignited right on schedule, sending the satellite into its correct altitude.

Where it failed to respond to any commands. It was dead in orbit, a multimillion-dollar piece of junk uselessly circling the earth. Who was responsible for this calamity?

Almost immediately, the blame fell on the shoulders of Luther Ames. In his haste to deploy, he had forgotten to key in vital software codes – or so the private contractor claimed. Luther insisted he *had* keyed in the codes, that he was the scapegoat for mistakes made by the satellite's manufacturer. Though the public heard very little about the controversy, within NASA, the story was known by all. Luther's flight assignments dried up. He was condemned to the status of astronaut ghost, still in the corps, but invisible to those who chose shuttle crews.

Complicating the mess was the fact Luther was black.

For three years, he suffered in obscurity, his resentment mounting. Only the support of close friends among the other astronauts – Emma most of all – had kept him in the corps. He knew he'd made no mistakes, but few at NASA believed him. He knew people talked behind his back. Luther was the man the bigots pointed to as evidence minorities didn't have the 'right stuff.' He'd struggled to maintain his dignity, even as he'd felt despair closing in.

Then the truth came out. The satellite had been flawed. Luther Ames was officially absolved of blame. Within a week, Gordon Obie offered him a flight assignment: a four-month mission aboard ISS.

But even now, Luther felt the lingering stain on his reputation. He knew, only too painfully, what Emma was now going through.

He stuck his face right in front of hers, forcing her to look at him. 'You're not perfect, okay? We're all human.' He paused, and added dryly, 'With the possible exception of Diana Estes.'

Against her will, she laughed.

'Punishment over. Time to move on, Watson.'

Her respirations had returned to normal, even though her heart continued pounding, because she was still angry at herself. But Luther was right; she had to move on. It was time to deal with the aftermath of her mistakes. A final report still needed to be transmitted to Houston. Medical summary, clinical course. Diagnosis. Cause of death.

Doctor fuckup.

'*Discovery* docks in two hours,' said Luther. 'You've got work to do.'

After a moment, she nodded and unclipped the TVIS restraints. Time to get on with the job; the hearse was on its way.

August 7

The tethered corpse, sealed in its shroud, slowly spun in the gloom. Surrounded by the clutter of excess equipment and spare lithium canisters, Kenichi's body was like one more unneeded station part stowed away in the old *Soyuz* capsule. *Soyuz* had not been operational in over a year, and the station crew used its service compartment as excess storage space. It seemed a terrible indignity to keep Kenichi in here, but the crew had been shaken badly by his death. To be confronted repeatedly with his corpse, floating in one of the modules where they worked or slept, would have been too upsetting.

Emma turned to Commander Kittredge and Medical Officer O'Leary of the shuttle *Discovery*. 'I sealed the remains immediately after death,' she said. 'It hasn't been touched since.' She paused, her gaze returning to the corpse. The shroud was black, and small pouches of plastic billowed out, obscuring the human form within.

'The tubes are still in?' asked O'Leary.

'Yes. Two IVs, the endotracheal, and the NG.' She had disturbed nothing; she knew the pathologists performing the autopsy would want everything left in place. 'You have all the blood cultures, all the specimens we collected from him. Everything.'

Kittredge gave a grim nod of the head. 'Let's do it.'

Emma unhooked the tether and reached for the corpse. It felt stiff, bloated, as though its tissues were already undergoing anaerobic decomposition. She refused to think about what Kenichi must look like beneath the layer of dark plastic.

It was a silent procession, as grim as a funeral cortege, the mourners floating like wraiths as they escorted the corpse through the long tunnel of modules. Kittredge and O'Leary led the way, gently guiding the body through hatchways. They were followed by Jill Hewitt and Andy Mercer, no one saying a word. When the orbiter had docked a day and a half ago, Kittredge and his crew had brought smiles and hugs, fresh apples and lemons, and a long-awaited copy of the Sunday *New York Times*. This was Emma's old team, the people she had trained with for a year, and seeing them again had been like having a bittersweet family reunion. Now the reunion was over, and the last item to be moved aboard *Discovery* was making its ghostly passage toward the docking module.

Kittredge and O'Leary floated the corpse through the hatchway and into *Discovery*'s middeck. Here, where the shuttle crew slept and ate, was where the body would be stowed until landing. O'Leary maneuvered it into one of the horizontal sleep pallets. Prior to launch, the pallet had been reconfigured to serve as a medical station for the ailing patient. Now it would be used as a temporary coffin for the returning corpse.

'It's not going in,' said O'Leary. 'I think the body's too distended. Was it exposed to heat?' He looked at Emma.

'No. *Soyuz* temperature was maintained.'

'Here's your problem,' said Jill. 'The shroud's snagged on the vent.' She reached in and freed the plastic. 'Try it now.'

This time the corpse fit. O'Leary slid the panel

197

shut so no one would have to look at the pallet's occupant.

There followed a solemn ceremony of farewell between the two crews. Kittredge pulled Emma into a hug and whispered, 'Next mission, Watson, you're my first choice.' When they separated, she was crying.

It ended with the traditional handshake between the two commanders, Kittredge and Griggs. Emma caught one last glimpse of the orbiter crew – *her* crew – waving good-bye, and then the hatches swung shut. Though *Discovery* would remain attached to ISS for another twenty-four hours while its crew rested and prepared for the undocking, the closing of those airtight hatches effectively ended all human contact between them. They were once again separate vehicles, temporarily attached, like two dragonflies hurtling together in a mating dance through space.

Pilot Jill Hewitt was having trouble getting to sleep.

Insomnia was new to her. Even on the night before a launch, she could manage to drop off cleanly into a deep sleep, trusting in a lifetime of good luck to carry her through the next day. It was a point of pride for her that she'd never needed a sleeping pill. Pills were for nervous Nellies who fretted about a thousand awful possibilities. For the neurotics and obsessives. As a naval pilot, Jill had known more than her share of mortal danger. She'd flown missions over Iraq, had landed a crippled jet on a heaving carrier, had ejected into a stormy sea. She figured she'd cheated Death so many times that surely he'd given up on her and gone home in defeat. And so she usually slept just fine at night.

But tonight, sleep was not coming. It was because of the corpse.

No one wanted to be near it. Though the privacy panel was shut, concealing the body, they all felt its presence. Death shared their living space, cast its shadow over their evening meal, stifled their usual jokes. It was the unwanted fifth member of their crew.

As though to escape it, Kittredge, O'Leary, and Mercer had abandoned their usual sleep stations and had moved up to the flight deck. Only Jill remained on the middeck, as though to prove to the men that she was less squeamish than they were, that she, a woman, wasn't bothered by a corpse.

But now, with the cabin lights dimmed, she found that sleep was eluding her. She kept thinking about what lay beyond that closed-off panel. About Kenichi Hirai, when he was alive.

She remembered him quite vividly as pale and soft-spoken, with black hair stiff as wire. Once, in weightlessness training, she had brushed against his hair and had been surprised by its boarlike bristliness. She wondered what he looked like now. She felt a sudden, sickening curiosity about what had become of his face, what changes Death had wrought. It was the same curiosity that used to compel her, as a child, to poke twigs into the corpses of the dead animals she sometimes encountered in the woods.

She decided to move further away from the body.

She brought her sleep restraint bag to the port side and anchored it behind the flight-deck access ladder. It was as far away as she could get, yet still be on the same deck. Once again she zipped herself into the bag. Tomorrow she would need every reflex, every brain cell, to be operating at peak performance for reentry and landing. Through sheer strength of will, she forced herself into a deepening trance.

She was asleep when the swirl of iridescent liquid began to seep through Kenichi Hirai's shroud.

It had begun with a few glistening droplets oozing through a tiny rent in the plastic, torn open when the shroud had snagged. For hours the pressure had been building, the plastic slowly inflating as the contents swelled. Now the breach widened, and a shimmering ribbon streamed out. Escaping through the pallet ventilation holes, the ribbon broke apart into blue-green droplets that briefly danced in weightless abandon before recongealing into large globules that undulated in the dimly lit cabin. The opalescent fluid continued to spill forth. The globules spread, riding the gentle currents of circulating air. Drifting across the cabin, they found their way to the limp form of Jill Hewitt, who slept unaware of the shimmering cloud enveloping her, unaware of the mist she inhaled with every soft breath or of the droplets that settled like condensation on her face. Only briefly did she stir, to brush the tickle on her cheek as the opalescent drops slid toward her eye.

Rising with the air currents, the dancing droplets passed through the opening of the interdeck access and began to spread through the gloom of the flight deck, where three men drifted in the utter relaxation of weightless sleep.

12

The ominous swirl had begun to take shape over the eastern Caribbean days before. It had started as a short wave trough aloft, a gentle undulation of clouds formed from the evaporated waters of the sun-baked equatorial sea. Butting up against a bank of cooler air from the north, the clouds had begun to rotate, spinning around a calm eye of dry air. Now it was a definite spiral that seemed to grow with every new image transmitted by the geostationary GOES weather satellite. The NOAA National Weather Service had been tracking it since its birth, had watched as it meandered, directionless, off the eastern end of Cuba. Now the newest buoy data was coming in, with measurements of temperature, wind speed and direction. This data reinforced what the meteorologists were now seeing on their computer screens.

It was a tropical storm. And it was moving northwest, toward the tip of Florida.

This was the sort of news shuttle flight director Randy Carpenter dreaded. They could tinker with engineering problems. They could troubleshoot multiple systems failures. But against the forces of Mother Nature, they were helpless. The primary concern of this morning's mission management team meeting was a go-no-go decision on deorbit, and they had planned for shuttle undocking and deorbit burn in six hours' time. The weather briefing changed everything.

'NOAA Spaceflight Meteorology Group reports the tropical storm is moving north-northwest, bearing toward the Florida Keys,' said the forecaster. 'Radar from Patrick Air Force Base and NexRad Doppler from the National Weather Service in Melbourne show radial wind velocities of up to sixty-five knots, with intensifying rain. Rawinsonde balloon and Jimsphere balloon both confirm. Also, both the Field Mill network around Canaveral as well as LDAR show increasing lightning activity. These conditions will probably continue for the next forty-eight hours. Possibly longer.'

'In other words,' said Carpenter, 'we're not landing at Kennedy.'

'Kennedy is definitely out. At least for the next three to four days.'

Carpenter sighed. 'Okay, we sorta guessed that was coming. Let's hear about Edwards.'

Edwards Air Force Base, tucked into a valley east of the Sierra Nevada in California, was not their first choice. A landing at Edwards delayed shuttle processing and turnaround for the next mission because the shuttle would have to be transported back to Kennedy, piggybacked to a 747.

'Unfortunately,' said the forecaster, 'there's a problem with Edwards as well.'

A knot had formed in Carpenter's stomach. A premonition that this was the beginning of a bad chain of events. As lead shuttle flight director, he had made it his personal mission to review every mishap on record and analyze what had gone wrong. With the advantage of hindsight, he could usually trace the problem backward, through a succession of bad but seemingly innocuous decisions. Sometimes it started back at the factory with a distracted technician, a miswired panel. Hell, even something as big and expensive as the Hubble Telescope lens had started off screwed up from the very beginning.

Now he could not shake off the feeling that he would later think back to this very meeting and ask himself, *What should I have done differently? What could I have done to prevent a catastrophe?*

He asked, 'What are the conditions at Edwards?'

'Currently they're looking at a cloud ceiling at seven thousand feet.'

'That's an automatic no-go.'

'Right. So much for sunny California. But there's the possibility of partial clearing within the next

204

twenty-four to thirty-six hours. We might have reasonable landing conditions if we just wait it out. Otherwise, it's off to New Mexico we go. I just checked the MIDDS, and White Sands looks good. Clear skies, head winds at five to ten knots. No adverse weather forecast.'

'So it's down to a choice,' said Carpenter. 'Wait till Edwards clears up. Or go for White Sands.' He looked around the room at the rest of the team, seeking opinions.

One of the program managers said, 'They're fine up there right now. We could leave them docked to ISS as long as we need to, until the weather cooperates. I don't see the necessity of rushing them home to a less than optimal site.'

Less than optimal was an understatement. White Sands was little more than an isolated landing strip equipped with heading alignment cylinders.

'There's the matter of getting the corpse back as soon as possible,' said Todd Cutler. 'While an autopsy's still useful.'

'We're all aware of that,' said the program manager. 'But weigh it against the negatives. White Sands is limited. Civilian medical backup just isn't there, if we have any problems on landing. In fact, all things considered, I'd suggest we wait it out even longer, till Kennedy's clear. Logistically, it's the best thing for the program. Quicker orbiter turnaround, get her right back on the pad for the next mission. In the meantime, the flight crew can use ISS as a hotel for the next few days.'

Several other program managers nodded. They were all taking the most conservative approach. The crew was safe where they were; the urgency of bringing home Hirai's corpse paled in light of all the problems of a White Sands landing. Carpenter thought of all the ways he could be second-guessed should there, God forbid, be a catastrophic landing at White Sands. He thought of the questions *he* would ask, were he reviewing the decisions of another flight director. *Why didn't you wait out the weather? Why did you hurry them home?*

The right decision was the one that minimized risk, yet met mission goals.

He decided to choose the middle ground.

'Three days is stretching it out too long,' he said. 'So Kennedy's out. Let's go for Edwards. Maybe we'll get clear skies tomorrow.' He looked at the forecaster. 'Make those clouds go away.'

'Sure. I'll just do a reverse rain dance.'

Carpenter glanced at the wall clock. 'Okay, crew's wake-up call is in four hours. We'll give 'em the news then. They can't come home quite yet.'

August 9

Jill Hewitt woke up gasping. Her first conscious thought was that she was drowning, that with every breath, she was inhaling water.

She opened her eyes, and with her first panicked

206

glance saw what looked like a swarm of jellyfish drifting around her. She coughed, at last managed to draw in a deep breath, and coughed again. The sharply expelled air sent all the jellyfish tumbling away.

She scrambled out of her restraint bag and turned up the cabin lights. In amazement she stared at the shimmering air.

'Bob!' she yelled. 'We've got a spill!'

She heard O'Leary say, up on flight deck, 'Jesus, what the hell is *this*?'

'Get out the masks!' ordered Kittredge. 'Until we know this isn't toxic.'

Jill opened the emergency locker, pulled out the contaminant-protection kit, and tossed masks and goggles to Kittredge, O'Leary, and Mercer as they came diving down the access opening into middeck. There'd been no time to get dressed; everyone was still in their underwear, still shaking off sleep.

Now, with their masks on, they stared at the blue-green globules drifting around them.

Mercer reached out and captured one in his hand. 'Weird,' he said, rubbing it between his fingers. 'It feels thick. Slimy. Like some sort of mucus.'

Now O'Leary, the medical officer, caught one and held it up to his goggles for a closer look. 'It's not even liquid.'

'Looks to me like a liquid,' said Jill. 'It behaves like one.'

'But it's more gelatinous. Almost like –'

They all gave a start as loud music abruptly blared out. It was Elvis Presley's velvet voice singing 'Blue Suede Shoes.' Their morning wake-up call from Mission Control.

'And a good mornin' to you, *Discovery*,' came Capcom's cheery voice. 'Time to rise and shine, folks!'

Kittredge responded, 'Capcom, we're already awake. We've, uh, got ourselves a strange situation up here.'

'Situation?'

'We have some sort of spill in the cabin. We're trying to identify it. It's a viscous substance. Sort of a milky blue-green. Almost looks like little opals floating around. It's already spread to both decks.'

'You guys wearing your masks?'

'Affirmative.'

'You know where it's coming from?'

'Not a clue.'

'Okay, we're consulting ECLSS right now. They may have an idea what it is.'

'Whatever it is, it doesn't seem to be toxic. We've all been asleep with this stuff hanging in the air. None of us seems to be sick.' Kittredge glanced around at his masked crew, and they all shook their heads.

'Is there any odor to the spill?' asked Capcom. 'ECLSS wants to know if it could be from the waste collection system.'

Suddenly Jill felt queasy. Was this stuff they'd been breathing in, swimming in, leaked toilet waste?

'Uh – I guess one of us has to take a sniff,' said Kittredge. He looked around at his crew, who merely stared back. 'Gee, guys, don't all volunteer at once,' he muttered, and finally lifted his mask. He smeared a globule between his fingers and took a whiff. 'I don't think this is sewage. It doesn't smell chemical, either. At least, not petroleum-based.'

'What does it smell like?' asked Capcom.

'Sort of . . . fishy. Like the slime off a trout. Something from the galley, maybe?'

'Or it could be leakage from one of the life-science payloads. You're carrying a few experiments back from ISS. Aren't there aquarium enclosures onboard?'

'This stuff does sort of remind me of frog eggs. We'll inspect the enclosures,' said Kittredge. He looked around the cabin, at the glistening clumps adhering to the walls. 'It's landing on everything now. We're gonna be cleaning up the splatters for a while. It'll set back our reentry.'

'Uh, *Discovery*, I hate to break the news,' said Capcom. 'But reentry's going to be delayed in any event. You'll have to sit tight.'

'What's the problem?'

'We've got some weather down here. Kennedy's looking at crosswinds of up to forty knots, with thunderstorm anvils in the vicinity. Tropical storm's moving in from the southeast. She's already made a mess of the Dominican Republic, and she's headed for the Keys.'

'What about Edwards?'

'They're currently reporting a seven-thousand-foot cloud ceiling. It should clear up in the next two days. So unless you guys are anxious to land at White Sands, we're looking at a delay of at least thirty-six hours. We may have you reopen the hatches and join the crew on ISS again.'

Kittredge eyed the globules drifting by. 'Negative on that, Capcom. We'd contaminate the station with this spill. We've gotta get things cleaned up.'

'Roger that. Surgeon is standing by here, wants to confirm that your crew is experiencing no adverse effects. Is that correct?'

'The spill appears harmless. No one's showing any signs of illness.' He batted away a clump of globules, and they went spinning off like scattered pearls. 'They're really kind of pretty. But I hate to think of them gunking up our electronics, so we'd better get cracking on cleanup detail.'

'We'll update you on the weather as it changes, *Discovery*. Now get out those mops and buckets.'

'Yeah,' laughed Kittredge. 'Just call us the sky-high cleaning service. We even do windows.' He pulled off his mask. 'I guess it's safe to take 'em off.'

Jill took off her mask and goggles and glided across to the emergency locker. She had just stowed the equipment when she found Mercer staring at her.

'What?' she said.

'Your eye – what happened to it?'

'What's wrong with my eye?'

'You'd better take a look.'

She floated across to the hygiene station. Her first glimpse in the mirror was shocking. The sclera of one of her eyes was blood red. Not merely streaked, but a solid crimson.

'Jesus,' she murmured, horrified by her own reflection. *I'm a pilot. I need my eyes. And one of them looks like a bag of blood.*

O'Leary turned her around by the shoulders and examined her eye. 'It's nothing to worry about, okay?' he said. 'It's just a scleral hemorrhage.'

'*Just?*'

'A small bleed into the white of your eye. It looks more serious than it is. It'll clear up without any effect on your vision.'

'How did I get it?'

'Sudden changes in intracranial pressure can do it. Sometimes a violent cough or heavy vomiting is all it takes to pop a tiny vessel.'

She gave a relieved sigh. 'That must be it. I woke up coughing on one of those floating goombahs.'

'See? Nothing to worry about.' He gave her a pat. 'That'll be fifty bucks. Next patient!'

Reassured, Jill turned back to the mirror. *It's merely a small bleed*, she thought. *Nothing to worry about*. But the image staring back horrified her. One normal eye, one eye an evil and brilliant red. Something alien. Satanic.

August 10

'They're the houseguests from hell,' said Luther. 'We shut the door on 'em and they still refuse to leave.'

Everyone in the galley laughed, even Emma. In the last few days there had not been much in the way of humor aboard ISS, and it was a relief to hear people joking again. Since they'd transferred Kenichi's corpse to *Discovery*, everyone's mood seemed brighter. His shrouded body had been a grim and constant reminder of death, and Emma was relieved she no longer had to confront the evidence of her own failure. She could focus, once again, on her work.

She could even laugh at Luther's crack, although the subject of his humor – the orbiter's failure to depart – was not, in fact, very funny. It complicated their day. They had expected *Discovery* to undock early yesterday morning. Now it was a day later, and she was still mated and could not leave for at least the next twelve hours. Her uncertain departure time threw the station's work schedule into uncertainty as well. Undocking was more than just a simple matter of the orbiter detaching itself and flying away. It was a delicate dance between two massive objects hurtling at 17,500 miles per hour, and it required the cooperation of both the orbiter and ISS crews. During undocking, the space station's control software had to be temporarily reconfigured for proximity operations, and its crew suspended many of its research activities. Everyone had to be focused on the orbiter's departure.

On avoiding calamity.

Now a cloudy day over an air force base in California had delayed everything, wreaking havoc on the space station's work schedule. But this was the nature of spaceflight; the only thing predictable about it was the unpredictable.

An alarming blob of grape juice came floating by Emma's head. And here was more unpredictability, she thought, laughing, as a sheepish Luther went chasing after it with a straw. You let your attention wander for just an instant, and there goes a vital tool or a sip's worth of juice drifting away. Without gravity, an unrestrained object could end up anywhere.

This was something the crew of *Discovery* was now confronting. 'We had glops of this stuff land all over our aft DAP controls,' she heard Kittredge say over the radio. *Discovery*'s commander was conversing with Griggs on the space-to-space subsystem. 'We're still trying to clean off the toggle switches, but it's like thick mucus when it dries. I just hope it hasn't plugged up any data ports.'

'You find out where it's coming from?' asked Griggs.

213

'We found a small crack in the toadfish enclosure. But it doesn't look like much leaked out – not enough to account for what's flying around the cabin.'

'Where else could it be coming from?'

'We're checking the galley and commode now. We've been so busy cleaning up, we haven't had a chance to identify the source. I just can't figure out what this stuff is. It sort of reminds me of frog eggs. Round clumps, in this sticky green mass. You should see my crew – it's like they've been slimed on *Ghostbusters*. And then Hewitt's got this evil red eye. Man, we're scary looking.'

Evil red eye? Emma turned to Griggs. 'What's wrong with Hewitt's eye?' she said. 'I didn't hear about it.'

Griggs relayed the question to *Discovery*.

'It's just a scleral bleed,' answered Kittredge. 'Nothing serious, according to O'Leary.'

'Let me talk to Kittredge,' said Emma.

'Go ahead.'

'Bob, this is Emma,' she said. 'How did Jill get that scleral bleed?'

'She woke up coughing yesterday. We think that's what did it.'

'Is she having any abdominal pains? Headaches?'

'She did complain of a headache a little while ago. And we've all got muscle aches. But we've been working like dogs here.'

'Nausea? Vomiting?'

'Mercer's got an upset stomach. Why?'

'Kenichi had a scleral bleed too.'

'But that's not a serious condition,' said Kittredge. 'That's what O'Leary says.'

'No, it's the *cluster* of symptoms that concerns me,' said Emma. 'Kenichi's illness started with vomiting and a scleral hemorrhage. Abdominal pains. A headache.'

'Are you saying this is some sort of contagion? Then why aren't *you* sick? You took care of him.'

A good question. She couldn't answer that.

'What disease are we talking about?' asked Kittredge.

'I don't know. I do know Kenichi was incapacitated within a day of his first symptoms. You guys need to undock and go home now. Before anyone on *Discovery* gets sick.'

'No can do. Edwards is still under clouds.'

'Then White Sands.'

'Not a good option right now. They've got a problem with one of their TACANs. Hey, we're doing fine. We'll just wait out the weather. It shouldn't be more than another twenty-four hours.'

Emma looked at Griggs. 'I want to talk to Houston.'

'They're not going to head for White Sands just because Hewitt's got a red eye.'

'It could be more than just a scleral hemorrhage.'

'How would they catch Kenichi's illness? They weren't exposed to him.'

The corpse, she thought. *His corpse is on the orbiter.*

'Bob,' she said. 'This is Emma again. I want you to check the shroud.'

'What?'

'Check Kenichi's shroud for a breach.'

'You saw for yourself it's sealed tight.'

'Are you sure it still is?'

'Okay,' he sighed. 'I have to admit, we haven't checked the body since it came aboard. I guess we were all a little creeped-out about it. We've kept the pallet panel closed so we wouldn't have to look at him.'

'How does the shroud look?'

'I'm trying to get the panel open now. It seems to be sticking a little, but . . .' There was a silence. Then a murmured 'Jesus.'

'Bob?'

'The spill's coming from the shroud!'

'What is it? Blood, serum?'

'There's a tear in the plastic. I can see it leaking out!'

What was leaking out?

She heard other voices in the background. Loud groans of disgust, and the sound of someone retching.

'Seal it off. *Seal it off!*' said Emma. But they didn't answer.

Jill Hewitt said, 'His body feels like mush. As if he's . . . *dissolving*. We should find out what's happening to it.'

'*No!*' cried Emma. '*Discovery*, do *not* open the shroud!'

To her relief, Kittredge finally responded, 'Roger that, Watson. O'Leary, seal it up. We're not going to let any more of . . . that stuff . . . leak out.'

'Maybe we should jettison the body,' said Jill.

'No,' Kittredge answered. 'They want it for autopsy.'

'What sort of fluid is it?' asked Emma. 'Bob, answer me!'

There was a silence. Then he said, 'I don't know. But whatever it is, I hope it's not infectious. Because we've all been exposed.'

Twenty-eight pounds of flab and fur. That was Humphrey, sprawled like a fat pasha on Jack's chest. *This cat is trying to murder me*, thought Jack, staring up into Humphrey's malevolent green eyes. He'd fallen asleep on the couch, and the next thing he knew, a ton of kitty lard was crushing his ribs, squeezing the air out of his lungs.

Purring, Humphrey sank a claw into Jack's chest.

With a yelp, Jack shoved him away, and Humphrey landed on all fours with a ponderous thump.

'Go catch a mouse,' Jack muttered, and turned on his side to resume his nap, but it was hopeless. Humphrey was yowling to be fed. Again. Yawning, Jack dragged himself off the couch and stumbled into the kitchen. As soon as he opened the cupboard where the cat food was stored, Humphrey began to yowl louder. Jack filled the cat bowl with Little Friskies and stood watching in disgust as his nemesis chowed down. It was only three in the afternoon, and Jack had not yet caught up on his sleep. He'd been awake all night, manning the surgeon's console in the space station control room, and then had come home and settled on the couch to review the ECLSS subsystems for the space station. He was back in the game, and it felt good. It even felt good to wade through a bone-dry MOD training manual. But fatigue had finally caught up with him, and he'd dropped off to sleep around noon, surrounded by stacks of flight manuals.

Humphrey's bowl was already half empty. Unbelievable.

As Jack turned to leave the kitchen, the phone rang.

It was Todd Cutler. 'We're rounding up medical personnel to meet *Discovery* at White Sands,' he said. 'The plane's leaving Ellington in thirty minutes.'

'Why White Sands? I thought *Discovery* was going to wait for Edwards to clear up.'

'We've got a medical situation on board, and we can't wait for the weather to clear. They're going to deorbit in an hour. Plan on infectious precautions.'

'What's the infection?'

'Not yet identified. We're just playing it safe. Are you with us?'

'Yeah, I'm with you,' said Jack, without an instant's hesitation.

'Then you'd better get moving or you'll miss the plane.'

'Wait. Who's the patient? Which one's sick?'

'They all are,' said Cutler. 'The entire crew.'

13

Infectious precautions. Emergency deorbit. What are we dealing with?

The wind was blowing, kicking up dust as Jack trotted across the tarmac toward the waiting jet. Squinting against flying grit, he climbed the steps and ducked into the aircraft. It was a Gulfstream IV seating fifteen passengers, one of a fleet of sturdy and reliable workhorses that NASA used to shuttle personnel between its many far-flung centers of operation. There were already a dozen people aboard, including a number of nurses and doctors from the Flight Medicine Clinic. Several of them gave Jack waves of greeting.

'We've got to get going, sir,' said the copilot. 'So if you could buckle right in.'

Jack took a window seat near the front of the plane.

Roy Bloomfeld was the last to step aboard, his bright red hair stiff from the wind. As soon as Bloomfeld took his seat, the copilot closed the hatch.

'Todd isn't coming?' asked Jack.

'He's manning the console for landing. Looks like we're gonna be the shock troops.'

The plane began to taxi out onto the runway. They could waste no time; it was an hour-and-a-half flight to White Sands.

'You know what's going on?' Jack asked. 'Cause I'm in the dark.'

'I got a brief rundown. You know that spill they had on *Discovery* yesterday? The one they've been trying to identify? Turns out it was fluids leaking from Kenichi Hirai's body bag.'

'That bag was sealed tight. How did it leak?'

'Tear in the plastic. The crew says the contents seem to be under pressure. Some sort of advanced decomposition going on.'

'Kittredge described the fluid as green and only mildly fishy smelling. That hardly sounds like fluid from a decomposing corpse.'

'We're all puzzled. The bag's been resealed. We'll have to wait till they land to find out what's going on inside. It's the first time we've dealt with human remains in microgravity. Maybe there's something different about the process of decomposition. Maybe the anaerobic bacteria die off, and that's why it's not giving off foul odors.'

'How sick is the crew?'

'Both Hewitt and Kittredge are complaining of severe headaches. Mercer's throwing up like a dog now, and O'Leary's got abdominal pain. We're not sure how much of it is psychological. There's

221

gotta be an emotional reaction when you've been gulping in a decomposing colleague.'

Psychological factors certainly complicated the picture. Whenever there is an outbreak of food poisoning, a significant percentage of victims are, in fact, uninfected. The power of suggestion is so strong it can produce vomiting as severe as any real illness.

'They had to put off the undocking. White Sands has been having problems too – one of their TACANs was transmitting erroneous signals. They needed a few hours to get it up and functioning again.'

The TACAN, or tactical air navigation locating system, was a series of ground transmitters that provided the orbiter with updates on its navigation-state vector. A bad TACAN signal could cause the shuttle to miss the runway entirely.

'Now they've decided they can't wait,' said Bloomfeld. 'In just the last hour, the crew's gotten sicker. Kittredge and Hewitt *both* have scleral hemorrhages. That's how it started with Hirai.'

Their plane began its takeoff roll. The roar of the engines filled their ears, and the ground dropped away.

Jack yelled over the noise, 'What about ISS? Is anyone sick on the station?'

'No. They kept the hatches closed between vehicles to contain the spill.'

'So it's confined to *Discovery?*'

'So far as we know.'

Then Emma's okay, he thought, releasing a deep breath. *Emma's safe.* But if a contagion had been brought aboard *Discovery* inside Hirai's corpse, why wasn't the space station crew infected as well?

'What's the shuttle's ETA?' he asked.

'They're undocking now. Burn target's in forty-five minutes, and touchdown should be around seventeen hundred.'

Which didn't give the ground crew much time to prepare. He stared out the window as they broke through the clouds into a golden bath of sunlight. *Everything is working against us*, he thought. *An emergency landing. A broken TACAN shack. A sick crew.*

And it will all come together on a runway in the middle of nowhere.

Jill Hewitt's head hurt, and her eyeballs were aching so badly she could barely focus on the undocking checklist. In just the last hour pain had crept into every muscle of her body, and now it felt as if jagged bolts were ripping through her back, her thighs. Both her sclerae had turned red; so had Kittredge's. His eyeballs looked like twin bags of blood. Glowing. Red. He was in pain too; she could see it in the way he moved, the slow and guarded turning of his head. They were both in agony, yet neither of them dared accept an injection of narcotics. Undocking and landing required peak alertness, and they could not risk losing even the slightest edge of performance.

Get us home. Get us home. That was the mantra that kept running through Jill's head as she struggled to stay on task, as sweat drenched her shirt and the pain ate into her concentration.

They were racing through the departure checklist. She had plugged the IBM ThinkPad's computer cable into the aft console data port, booted up, and opened the Rendezvous and Proximity Operations program.

'There's no data flow,' she said.

'What?'

'The port must be gunked up by the spill. I'll try the middeck PCMMU.' She unplugged the cable. Every bone in her face screamed with pain as she made her way through the interdeck access, carrying the ThinkPad. Her eyes were throbbing so badly they felt as if they were about to pop out of their sockets. Down on middeck, she saw Mercer was already dressed in his launch-and-entry suit and strapped in for reentry. He was unconscious – probably from the dose of narcotics. O'Leary, also strapped in, was still awake but looking dazed. Jill floated across to the middeck data port and plugged in the ThinkPad.

Still no data stream.

'Shit. *Shit.*'

Now struggling to focus, she made her way back to the flight deck.

'No luck?' said Kittredge.

'I'll change out the source cable and try this port again.' Her head was pounding so badly now it brought tears to her eyes. Teeth gritted, she pulled out the cable, replaced it with a new one. Rebooted. From Windows, she opened RPOP.

The *Rendezvous and Proximity Operations* logo appeared on the screen.

Sweat broke out on her upper lip as she began to type in the mission elapsed time. Days, hours, minutes, seconds. Her fingers weren't obeying as they should. They were sluggish, clumsy. She had to back up to correct the numbers. At last she selected 'Prox Ops' and clicked on 'OK.'

'RPOP initialized,' she said with relief. 'Ready to process data.'

Kittredge said, 'Capcom, are we go for sep?'

'Stand by, *Discovery*.'

The wait was excruciating. Jill looked down at her hand and saw that her fingers had started to twitch, that the muscles of her forearm were contracting like a dozen writhing worms beneath the skin. As if something alive were tunneling through her flesh. She fought to keep her hand steady, but her fingers kept twitching in electric spasms. *Get us home now. While we can still fly this bird.*

'*Discovery*,' said Capcom. 'You are a go for undocking.'

'Roger that. Digital autopilot on low Z. Go for undocking.' Kittredge shot Jill a look of profound relief. 'Now let's get the hell home,' he muttered, and grasped the hand controls.

* * *

Flight Director Randy Carpenter stood like the statue of Colossus, his gaze fixed on the front screen, his engineer's brain coolly monitoring simultaneous streams of visual data and loop conversations. As always, Carpenter was thinking several steps ahead. The docking base was now depressurized. The latches connecting the orbiter to ISS would unhook, and preloaded springs in the docking system would gently push the two vehicles apart, causing them to free drift away from each other. Only when they were two feet apart would *Discovery*'s RCS jets be turned on to steer the orbiter away. At any point in this delicate sequence of events, things could go wrong, but for every possible failure, Carpenter had a contingency plan. If the docking latches failed to unhook, they'd fire pyrotechnic charges and shear off the latch retention bolts. If that failed, two crew members from ISS could perform an EVA and manually remove the bolts. They had backup plans for backup plans, a contingency for every failure.

At least, every failure they could predict. What Carpenter dreaded was the glitch that no one had thought about. And now he asked himself the same question he always did at the beginning of a new mission phase: *What have we failed to anticipate?*

'ODS has successfully disengaged,' he heard Kittredge announce. 'Latches have released. We're now in free drift.'

The flight controller beside Carpenter gave a little punch of triumph in the air.

226

Carpenter thought ahead, to the landing. The weather at White Sands was holding steady, head winds at fifteen knots. The TACAN would be up and operational in time for the shuttle's arrival. Ground crews were at this moment converging on the runway. There were no new glitches in sight, yet he knew one had to be waiting just around the corner.

All this was going through his mind, but not a flicker of expression crossed his face. Not a hint to any of the flight controllers in the room that he was feeling dread, as sour as bile, in his throat.

Aboard ISS, Emma and her crewmates also watched and waited. All research activities were at a temporary standstill. They had gathered at the Node 1 cupola to look at the massive shuttle as it undocked. Griggs was also monitoring the operation on an IBM ThinkPad, which showed the same RPOP wireframe display that Houston's Mission Control was now looking at.

Through the cupola windows, Emma saw *Discovery* begin to inch away, and she gave a sigh of relief. The orbiter was now in free drift, and on its way home.

Medical Officer O'Leary floated in a narcotic daze. He'd injected fifty milligrams of Demerol into his own arm, just enough to take the edge off his pain, to allow him to strap in Mercer, to prepare the cabin for reentry. Even that small dose of narcotic was clouding his mental processes.

He sat strapped in his middeck seat, ready for deorbit. The cabin seemed to drift in and out of focus, as though he were seeing it underwater. The light hurt his eyes, and he closed them. Moments ago, he thought he'd seen Jill Hewitt float past with the ThinkPad; now she was gone, but he could hear her strained voice over his headset, along with Kittredge's and Capcom's. They had undocked.

Even in his mental fog, he felt a sense of impotence, of shame, that he was strapped into his seat like an invalid while his crewmates up on flight deck were laboring to get them home. Pride made him fight his way back from the comfortable oblivion of sleep, and he surfaced into the hard glare of the middeck lights. He felt for his harness release, and as the straps came free, he floated out of his seat. The middeck began to shift around him, and he had to close his eyes to stem the sudden tide of nausea. *Fight it*, he thought. *Mind over matter. I'm the one who always had the iron stomach.* But he could not bring himself to open his eyes, to confront that disorienting drift of the room.

Until he heard the sound. It was a creaking, so close by that he thought it must be Mercer, stirring in his sleep. O'Leary turned toward the sound – and found that he was not facing Mercer. He was staring at Kenichi Hirai's body bag.

It was bulging. Expanding.

My eyes, he thought. *They're playing tricks on me.*

He blinked and refocused. The shroud was still swollen, the plastic ballooning out over the corpse's abdomen. Hours ago, they had patched the leak; now the pressure inside must be building up again.

Moving through a dreamlike haze, he floated across to the sleeping pallet. He placed his hand on the bulging body bag.

And jerked away in horror. For in that brief moment of contact, he had felt it swell, retract, and swell again.

The corpse was pulsating.

Sweat beading her upper lip, Jill Hewitt watched through the overhead window as *Discovery* unlatched from ISS. Slowly the gap widened between them, and she glanced at the data streaming across her computer screen. One foot separation. Two feet. *Going home.* Pain suddenly arced through her head, its stab so unbearable she felt herself beginning to black out. She fought back, holding on to consciousness with the stubbornness of a bulldog.

'ODS is clear,' she said through clenched teeth.

Kittredge responded with, 'Switching to RCS OP, low Z.'

Using the reaction-control-system thrusters, Kittredge would now gently steer away from ISS, moving to a point three thousand feet below the station, where their differing orbits would automatically begin to pull them farther apart.

Jill heard the *whomp* of the thrusters firing and felt the orbiter shudder as Kittredge, at the aft controls, slowly backed them down the R-bar. His hand shook, and his face went tight with the effort to retain control of his grip. He, not the computer, was flying the orbiter, and a wayward jerk of the control stick could send them careening off course.

Five feet apart. Ten. They were past the crucial separation phase now, moving further and further away from the station.

Jill began to relax.

And then she heard the shriek on middeck. A cry of horror and disbelief. *O'Leary.*

She turned, just as a gruesome fountain of human debris burst onto the flight deck and exploded toward her.

Kittredge, nearest the interdeck access, caught the brunt of the force and went flying against the rotational hand controller. Jill tumbled backward, her headset flying off, her body pummelled by foul-smelling fragments of intestine and skin and clumps of black hair, still attached to scalp. *Kenichi's hair.* She heard the *whomps* of firing thrusters, and the orbiter seemed to lurch around her. The cloud of disintegrated human parts had spread throughout the flight deck, and a nightmarish galaxy swirled, floating bits of plastic shroud and shattered organs and those strange greenish clumps. A grapelike mass of them floated by and splattered against a nearby wall.

When droplets collide with, and adhere to, flat surfaces in microgravity, they tremble briefly from the impact, then fall still. This splatter had not stopped moving.

In disbelief, she watched as the quivering intensified, as a ripple disturbed the surface. Only then did she see, embedded deep within the gelatinous mass, a core of something black, something moving. It writhed like the larva of a mosquito.

Suddenly a new image caught her eye, even more startling. She stared up through the window above the flight deck and saw the space station rapidly zooming toward them, so close now she could almost make out the rivets on the solar array truss.

In a burst of panic, she shoved against the wall and dove through that gruesome cloud of exploded flesh, her arms outstretched in desperation toward the orbiter control stick.

'Collision course!' yelled Griggs over space-to-space radio. '*Discovery*, you are on a collision course!'

There was no response.

'*Discovery! Reverse course!*'

Emma watched in horror as disaster hurtled toward them. Through the space station's cupola window, she saw the orbiter simultaneously pitch up and roll to starboard. She saw *Discovery*'s delta wing slicing toward them with enough momentum to ram it through the station's aluminum hull. She saw, in the imminent collision, the approach of her own death.

The plumes of firing rockets suddenly spewed out from the forward RCS thruster in the orbiter's nose. *Discovery* began to pitch downward, reversing momentum. Simultaneously the starboard delta wing rolled upward, but not quickly enough to clear the space station's main solar truss. She felt her heartbeat freeze.

Heard Luther whisper, 'Lord Jesus.'

'CRV!' Griggs shouted in panic. 'Everyone to the evac vehicle!'

Arms and legs churned in midair, feet flying in every direction as the crew scrambled to evacuate the node. Nicolai and Luther were first through the hatch, into the hab. Emma had just grabbed the hatch handhold when her ears filled with the squeal of rending metal, the groan of aluminum being twisted and deformed by the collision of two massive objects.

The space station shuddered, and in the ensuing quake, she caught a disorienting glimpse of the node walls tilting away, of Griggs's ThinkPad spinning in midair and Diana's terrified face, slick with sweat.

The lights flickered and went out. In the darkness, a red warning light flashed on and off, on and off.

A siren shrieked.

14

Shuttle flight director Randy Carpenter was watching death on the front screen.

At the instant of the orbiter's impact, he felt the blow as surely as if a fist had been rammed into his own sternum, and he actually lifted his hand and pressed it to his chest.

For a few seconds, the Flight Control Room went absolutely silent. Stunned faces stared at the front wall. On the center screen was the world map with the shuttle trajectory trace. To the right was the frozen RPOP display, *Discovery* and ISS represented by wireframe diagrams. The orbiter was now melded like a crumpled toy to the silhouette of ISS. Carpenter felt his lungs suddenly expand, realized that, in his horror, he had forgotten to breathe.

The FCR erupted in chaos.

'Flight, we have no voice downlink,' he heard Capcom say. '*Discovery* is not responding.'

'Flight, we're still getting data stream from TCS –'

'Flight, no drop in orbiter cabin pressure. No indication of oxygen leak –'

'What about ISS?' Carpenter snapped. 'Do we have downlink from them?'

'SVO's trying to hail them. The station pressure is dropping –'

'How low?'

'It's down to seven hundred ten . . . six hundred ninety. Shit, they're decompressing fast!'

Breach in the station's hull! thought Carpenter. But that wasn't his problem to fix; it belonged to Special Vehicle Operations, down the hall.

The propulsion systems engineer suddenly broke into the comm loop. 'Flight, I'm reading RCS ignition, F2U, F3U, and F1U. *Someone's* working the orbiter controls.'

Carpenter's head snapped to attention. The RPOP display was still locked and frozen, with no new images appearing. But Propulsion's report told him that *Discovery's* steering rockets had just fired. It had to be more than just a random discharge; the crew was trying to move the orbiter away from ISS. But until they had radio downlink, they could not confirm the orbiter crew's status. They could not confirm they were alive.

It was the most terrible scenario of all, the one he feared most. A dead crew on an orbiting shuttle. Though Houston could control most of the orbiter's maneuvers by ground command, they could not bring it home without crew help. A functioning human being was necessary to flip the arming switches for the OMS deorbit burn. It took a human hand to deploy the air-data probes and to lower the landing gear for touchdown. Without someone at the controls to perform these functions, *Discovery* would remain in orbit, a ghost ship circling silently around the earth until its orbit decayed months from now, and it fell to earth in a streak of fire. It was this nightmare that passed through Carpenter's head as the seconds ticked by, as panic slowly gathered force around him in the FCR. He could not afford to think about the space station, whose crew even now might be in the agonal throes of a decompressive death. His focus had to remain on *Discovery*. On *his* crew, whose survival seemed less and less likely with every second of silence that passed.

Then, suddenly, they heard the voice. Faint, halting.

'Control, this is *Discovery*. Houston. Houston . . .'

'It's Hewitt!' said Capcom. 'Go ahead, *Discovery*!'

'. . . major anomaly . . . could not avoid collision. Structural damage to orbiter appears minimal . . .'

'*Discovery*, we need visual on ISS.'

'Can't deploy Ku antenna – closed circuit gone –'

'Do you know the extent of their damage?'

'Impact tore off their solar truss. I think we punched a hole in their hull . . .'

Carpenter felt sick. They still had heard no word from the ISS crew. No confirmation they had survived.

'What is your crew's status?' asked Capcom.

'Kittredge is barely responding. Hit his head on the aft control panel. And the crew on middeck – I don't know about them –'

'What's your status, Hewitt?'

'Trying to . . . oh, God, my head . . .' There was a soft sob. Then she said, 'It's alive.'

'Did not copy.'

'The stuff floating around – the spill from the body bag. It's moving all around me. It's *inside* me. I can see it moving under my skin, and it's *alive*.'

A chill crawled all the way up Carpenter's spine. Hallucinations. A head injury. They were losing her, losing their only chance of getting the orbiter down intact.

'Flight, we're approaching burn target,' warned FDO. 'We can't afford to miss it.'

'Tell her to go for deorbit,' Carpenter ordered.

'*Discovery*,' said Capcom. 'Go to APU prestart.'

There was no response.

'*Discovery?*' repeated Capcom. 'You're going to miss your burn target!'

As the seconds stretched to minutes, Carpenter's muscles tensed, and his nerves felt like live wires. He gave a sigh of relief when Hewitt finally responded.

'Middeck crew's in landing position. They're both unconscious. I've strapped them in. But I can't get Kittredge into his LES –'

'Screw his reentry suit!' said Carpenter. 'Let's not miss that target. Just get the bird down!'

'*Discovery*, we advise you proceed directly to APU

prestart. Just strap him into the starboard seat, and you get on with deorbit.'

They heard a ragged sigh of pain. Then Hewitt said, 'My head – having trouble focusing . . .'

'We roger that, Hewitt.' Capcom's voice became gentler. Almost soothing. 'Look, Jill. We know you're the one in the commander's seat now. We know you're hurting. But we can guide you in on autoland, all the way to wheel stop. If you just *stay with us*.'

She let out a tortured sob. 'APU prestart complete,' she whispered. 'Loading OPS 3-0-2. Tell me when, Houston.'

'Go for deorbit burn,' said Carpenter.

Capcom relayed the decision. 'Go for deorbit burn, *Discovery*.' And he added softly, 'Now, let's get you home.'

In the hellish darkness, Emma braced herself for the shock of decompression. She knew exactly what to expect. How she would die. There would be the roar of air rushing out of the hull. The sudden popping of her eardrums. The rapid crescendo of pain as her lungs expanded and her alveoli exploded. As the air pressure drops toward vacuum, the boiling temperature of liquid also drops, until it becomes the same as the freezing temperature. One instant, the blood is boiling. In the next, it freezes solid in the veins.

The red warning lights, the siren, confirmed her worst fears. It was a Class 1 emergency. They had a breached hull, and their air was leaking into space.

She felt her ears pop. *Evacuate now!*

She and Diana dove into the hab, flying through gloom lit only by the bright red flashes of the warning panels. The siren was so loud everyone had to yell to hear each other. In her panic, Emma bounced into Luther, who grabbed her before she could ricochet off in a new direction.

'Nicolai's already in the CRV. You and Diana next!' he shouted.

'Wait. Where's Griggs?' said Diana.

'Just *get in!*'

Emma turned. In the psychedelic flash of red warning lights, she saw no one else in the hab. Griggs had not followed them. A strange, fine mist seemed to hang in the gloom, but there was no hurricane whoosh of air sucking them toward the breach.

And no pain, she suddenly realized. She'd felt her ears pop, but there was no chest pain, no symptoms of explosive decompression.

We can save this station. We have time to isolate the leak.

She did a quick swimmer's turn, kicked off the wall, and went flying back toward the node.

'Hey! What the fuck, Watson?' yelled Luther.

'Don't give up the ship!'

She was moving so fast she slammed against the edge of the hatchway, bashing her elbow. *Here* was the pain now, not from decompression but from her own stupid clumsiness. Her arm was throbbing as she kicked off again, into the node.

Griggs wasn't there, but she saw his ThinkPad, drifting at the end of its data cord. The screen flashed a bright red 'Decompression' warning. The air pressure was down to six hundred fifty and dropping. They had only minutes to work, minutes before their brains would not function.

He must have gone in search of the leak, she thought. *He's going to close off the damaged module.*

She dove into the U.S. lab, through that thickening white mist. *Was* it mist or was it her vision fogging over from hypoxia? A warning that unconsciousness was closing in? She shot through the darkness and felt disoriented by the warning lights continuing to flash like a strobe. She banged into the far hatchway. Her coordination was off, and her clumsiness getting worse. She slipped through the hatch opening, into Node 2.

Griggs was there. He was struggling to disconnect a tangle of cables strung between the NASDA and European modules.

'The leak's in NASDA!' he yelled over the screaming sirens. 'If we can clear the cables from this hatchway and close it off, we can isolate the module.'

She dove forward to help him yank the cables apart. Then she found one that could not be disconnected. 'What the hell's this?' she said. All cables leading through hatchways were supposed to be easy to pull apart in case of an emergency.

This one was continuous – a violation of safety rules. 'It doesn't have a quick release!' she yelled.

'Get me a knife and I'll cut it!'

She spun around, dove back into the U.S. lab. *A knife. Where the hell is a knife?* Through the red flashes of light, she saw the medical locker. *A scalpel.* She yanked open the drawer, reached into the instrument tray, and went flying back into Node 2.

Griggs took the scalpel and began to sever the cable.

'What can we do to help?' came Luther's shout.

Emma turned and saw him, along with Nicolai and Diana, hovering anxiously in the hatchway.

'The breach is in NASDA!' she said. 'We're gonna close off the module!'

Sparks suddenly shot out like fireworks. Griggs yelped and jerked away from the cable. 'Shit! It's a live wire!'

'We've got to cut it!' said Emma.

'And get fried to a crisp? I don't think so.'

'Then how do we seal the hatch?'

Luther said, 'Pull back! Pull back into the lab! We'll close off the whole node. Isolate this end of the station.'

Griggs looked at the sparking wire. He didn't want to close off Node 2, because it meant sacrificing both the NASDA and European modules, which would be completely depressurized and unreachable. And it meant sacrificing the shuttle docking port, which also led off Node 2.

'Pressure's dropping, folks!' called Diana, reading a handheld pressure gauge. 'We're down to six hundred twenty-five millimeters! Just pull the fuck back, and let's close off the node!'

Emma could already feel herself breathing faster, trying to catch her breath. Hypoxia. They were all going to black out if they didn't do something soon.

She tugged Griggs's arm. 'Pull back! It's the only way to save the station!'

He gave a stunned nod and retreated with Emma into the U.S. lab.

Luther tried to tug the hatch shut, but he couldn't get it to budge. Now that they were outside Node 2, they had to pull, not push the hatch shut. And they were working against the rush of escaping air, in a rapidly depressurizing atmosphere.

'We'll have to abandon this module too!' yelled Luther. 'Retreat to Node 1 and close off the next hatch!'

'Hell no!' Griggs said. 'I'm not giving up this module as well!'

'Griggs, we've got no choice. I can't pull this hatch shut!'

'Then let me do it!' Griggs grabbed the handle and strained to pull it shut, but the hatch moved only a few inches before he had to let go in exhaustion.

'You're gonna kill us all just to save this fucking module!' shouted Luther.

It was Nicolai who suddenly yelled out the solution. '*Mir!* Feed the leak! Feed the leak!' He shot out of the lab, headed toward the Russian end of the station.

Mir. Everyone immediately knew what he was talking about. 1997. The *Progress* collision with *Mir*'s Spektr module. There had been a breach in the hull, and *Mir* had begun to leak its precious air into space. The Russians, with years more experience in manned space stations, were ready with their emergency response: feeding the leak. Pour extra oxygen into the module to raise the pressure. Not only would it buy them time to work, it might narrow the pressure gradient enough so they could pull the hatch shut.

Nicolai came flying back into the lab with two oxygen tanks. Frantically he opened the valves all the way. Even over the screaming sirens, they could hear the screech of air escaping from the tanks. Nicolai tossed both tanks into Node 2. *Feeding the leak.* They were building air pressure on the other side of the hatch.

They were also pouring oxygen into a module with a live wire, thought Emma, remembering the sparks. It could trigger an explosion.

'Now!' Nicolai shouted. 'Try to close the hatch!'

Luther and Griggs both grabbed the handle and pulled. They would never know if it was due to their combined desperation or if the oxygen tanks had succeeded in dropping the pressure gradient across that hatchway, but the hatch slowly began to swing shut.

Griggs locked it in place.

For a moment he and Luther simply hung limp in midair, both of them too exhausted to say a word. Then Griggs turned, his face bright with sweat in the flashing lights.

'Now let's shut off that fucking racket,' he said.

The ThinkPad was still floating where he'd left it in Node 1. Peering at the glowing screen, he rapidly tapped in a series of commands. To everyone's relief, the sirens stopped screaming. The flashing red lights also stopped, leaving only a constant yellow glow on the caution-and-warning panels. At last they could communicate without shouting.

'Air pressure is back up to six hundred ninety and rising,' he said, and gave a laugh of relief. 'Looks like we're home free.'

'Why are we still at Class 3 caution?' asked Emma, pointing to the yellow light on the screen. A Class 3 caution meant one of three possibilities: Their backup guidance computer was down, one of their control motion gyros was inoperative, or they'd lost their S-band radio link to Mission Control.

Griggs tapped a few more keys. 'It's the S-band. We've lost it. *Discovery* must have hit our P-1 truss and taken out the radio. Looks like they also hit our port solar arrays. We've lost a photovoltaic module. That's why we're still in power down.'

'Houston must be going bonkers, wondering

what's happening,' said Emma. 'And now they can't reach us. What about *Discovery?* What's happened to them?'

Diana, already working the space-to-space radio, said, '*Discovery* isn't responding. They may be out of UHF range.'

Or they were all dead and couldn't respond.

'Can we get these lights back?' said Luther. 'Cross-strap primary power?'

Griggs began to tap on the keyboard again. Part of the beauty of ISS's design lay in its redundancy. Each of its power channels were configured to supply electricity for specific loads, but those channels could be rerouted – 'cross-strapped' – as needed. Though they'd lost one photovoltaic module, they had three others to tap into.

Griggs said, 'I know this is a cliché, but "let there be light."' He hit a computer key, and the module lights barely brightened. But it was enough to navigate through hatchways. 'I've rerouted power. Nonessential payload functions are now off the grid.' He released a deep breath and looked at Nicolai. 'We need to contact Houston. It's your show, Nicolai.'

The Russian understood at once what he had to do. Moscow's Mission Control maintained its own separate communications link with the station. The collision should not have affected the Russian end of ISS.

Nicolai gave a terse nod. 'Let us hope Moscow has paid its electric bill.'

*   *   *

ITEM 3–7-EXEC
ITEM 3–8-EXEC
OPS 3–0–4 PRO

Jill Hewitt was gasping in pain, short little whimpers that punctuated every push of a new button on the control panel. Her head felt like a melon ripe to explode. Her field of vision had contracted so that it seemed as if she were peering down a long black tunnel and the controls had receded almost beyond her reach. It took every ounce of concentration for her to focus on each switch she had to flip, on each button wavering beyond her finger. Now she struggled to make out the attitude-direction indicator, her vision blurring as the eight-ball display seemed to spin wildly in its casing. *I can't see it. I can't read pitch or yaw* . . .

'*Discovery*, you are at entry interface,' said Capcom. 'Body flap on auto.'

Jill squinted at the panel and reached for the switch, but it seemed so far away . . .

'*Discovery?*'

Her trembling finger made contact. She switched to 'auto.' 'Confirm,' she whispered, and let her shoulders go slack. The computers were now in control, flying the ship. She did not trust herself on the stick. She did not even know how long she could stay conscious. Already the black tunnels were closing over her vision, swallowing the light. For the first time she could hear the sound of rushing air across the hull, could feel her body being shoved back against her seat.

Capcom had gone silent. She was in communications blackout, the spacecraft hurtling against the atmosphere with such force it stripped the electrons from air molecules. That electromagnetic storm interrupted all radio waves, cut off all communication. For the next twelve minutes it was only her, and the ship, and the roaring air.

She had never felt so alone.

She felt the autopilot begin to steer into the first high bank, rolling the spacecraft on its side, slowing it down. She imagined the glow of heat on the cockpit windows, could feel its warmth, like the sun radiating on her face.

She opened her eyes. And saw only darkness.

Where are the lights? she thought. *Where is the glow on the window?*

She blinked, again and again. Rubbed her eyes, as though to force them to see, to force her retinas to draw in light. She reached out toward the control panel. Unless she flipped the right switches, unless she deployed the air-data probes and lowered the landing gear, Houston could not land the ship. They could not get her home alive. Her fingers brushed against a mind-numbing array of dials and buttons, and she gave a howl of despair.

She was blind.

15

At 4,093 feet above sea level, the air at White
Sands Missile Proving Grounds was dry and thin.
The landing strip traced across an ancient dried-out
seabed located in a desert valley formed between
the Sacramento and Guadalupe mountain ranges
to the east, and the San Andres Mountains to
the west. The closest town was Alamogordo, New
Mexico. The terrain was stark and arid, and only
the hardiest of desert vegetation could survive.

The area had long served as a training base for
fighter pilots. It had also seen other uses through
the decades. During World War II, it was the site
of a German prisoner of war camp. It was also
the location of the Trinity site, where the U.S.
exploded its first atomic bomb, assembled not far
away in Los Alamos, New Mexico. Barbed wire and
unmarked government buildings had sprouted up
in this desert valley, their functions a mystery even
to the residents of nearby Alamogordo.

Through binoculars, Jack could see the landing

strip shimmering with heat in the distance. Runway 16/34 was oriented just slightly off due north-south. It was fifteen thousand feet long and three hundred feet wide – large enough to accept the heaviest of jets, even in that rarefied air, which forces long landing and takeoff rolls.

Just west of the touchdown point, Jack and the medical team waited, along with a small convoy of NASA and United Space Alliance vehicles, for *Discovery*'s arrival. They had stretchers, oxygen, defibrillators, and ACLS kits – everything one could find in a modern ambulance, and more. For landings at Kennedy, there would be over one hundred fifty ground team members prepared to meet the orbiter. Here, on this desert strip, they had barely three dozen, and eight of them were medical personnel. Some of the ground crew were wearing self-contained atmospheric protective suits, to insulate them from any propellant leaks. They would be the first to meet the orbiter and, with atmospheric sensors, would quickly assess the potential for explosions before allowing doctors and nurses to approach.

A distant rumble made Jack lower his binoculars and glance due east. Choppers were approaching, so many of them they looked like an ominous swarm of black wasps.

'What's this?' said Bloomfeld, also noticing the choppers. Now the rest of the ground crew was staring at the sky, many of them murmuring in bewilderment.

'Could be backup,' said Jack.

The convoy leader, listening on his comm unit, shook his head. 'Mission Control says they're not ours.'

'This airspace should be clear,' said Bloomfeld.

'We're trying to hail the choppers, but they're not responding.'

The rumble had crescendoed, and Jack could feel it in his bones now, a deep and constant thrum in his sternum. They were going to invade the orbiter's airspace. In fifteen minutes, *Discovery* would drop out of the sky and find those choppers in her flight path. He could hear the convoy leader talking urgently into his headset, could feel panic begin to ripple through the ground crew.

'They're holding position,' said Bloomfeld.

Jack raised his binoculars. He counted almost a dozen choppers. They had indeed halted their approach and were now landing like a flock of vultures, due east of the orbiter's touchdown point.

'What do you suppose that's all about?' said Bloomfeld.

Two minutes left of communications blackout. Fifteen minutes till touchdown.

Randy Carpenter was feeling the first flush of optimism. He knew they could bring *Discovery* down safely. Barring a catastrophic computer failure, they could fly that bird from the ground. The key was Hewitt. She had to stay conscious, had to be able to flip two switches at the right times. Minimal tasks, but crucial. At their last radio contact, ten minutes before, Hewitt had sounded alert, but in pain. She was a good pilot, a woman with a steel backbone tempered by the refiner's fire of the U.S. Navy. All she had to do was stay conscious.

'Flight, we have good news from NASCOM,' said Ground Control. 'Mission Control Moscow has made radio contact with ISS on Regul S-Band.'

Regul was the Russian S-band radio system aboard ISS. It was completely separate and independent of the U.S. system, and it operated via Russian ground stations and their LUCH satellite.

'Contact was brief. They were on the tail end of LUCH satellite comm pass,' said Ground Control. 'But the crew is all alive and well.'

Carpenter's optimism flared even brighter, and he tightened his plump fingers in a triumphant fist. 'Damage report?'

'They had a breach of the NASDA module and had to close off Node Two and everything forward of that. They've also lost at least two solar arrays and several truss segments. But no one's hurt.'

'Flight, we should be coming out of comm blackout,' said Capcom.

At once Carpenter's attention snapped back to *Discovery*. He was happy about the news from ISS, but his first responsibility was to the shuttle.

'*Discovery*, do you copy?' said Capcom. '*Discovery?*'

The minutes went by. Too many. Suddenly Carpenter was back dancing on the brink of panic.

Guidance said, 'Second S-turn completed. All systems look good.'

Then why wasn't Hewitt responding?

'*Discovery*,' repeated Capcom, his voice now urgent. 'Do you copy?'

'Going into third S-turn,' said Guidance.

We've lost her, thought Carpenter.

Then they heard her voice. Soft and unsteady. 'This is *Discovery*.'

Capcom's sigh of relief huffed loudly over the loop. '*Discovery*, welcome back! It's good to hear your voice! Now you need to deploy your air-data probes.'

'I – I'm trying to find the switches.'

'Your air-data probes,' Capcom repeated.

'I know, I know! *I can't see the panel!*'

Carpenter felt as if his blood had just frozen in his veins. *Dear God, she's blind. And she's seated in the commander's seat. Not in her own.*

'*Discovery*, you need to deploy now!' said Capcom. 'Panel C-three –'

'I *know* which panel!' she cried. There was silence. Then the sound of her breath rushing out in a whoosh of pain.

'Probes have been deployed,' said MMACS. 'She did it. She found the switch!'

Carpenter allowed himself to breathe again. To hope again.

'Fourth S-turn,' said Guidance. 'Now at TAEM interface.'

'*Discovery*, how ya doing?' said Capcom.

One minute, thirty seconds to touchdown. *Discovery* was now traveling at six hundred miles per hour, at an altitude of eight thousand feet and dropping rapidly. The pilots called it the 'flying brick' – heavy, with no engines, gliding in on delta-wing slivers. There'd be no second chances, no abort and fly around for another try. It was going to land, one way or the other.

'*Discovery?*' said Capcom.

Jack could see it glinting in the sky, puffs of smoke trailing from its yaw jets. It looked like a bright chip of silver as it swept around on its final turn to line up with the runway.

'Come on, baby. You're lookin' good!' whooped Bloomfeld.

His enthusiasm was shared by all three dozen members of the ground crew. Every shuttle landing is a celebratory event, a victory so moving it brings tears to the eyes of those who watch from the ground. Every eye was now turned to the sky, every heart pounding as they watched that chip of silver, *their* baby, gliding toward the runway.

'Gorgeous. God, she's beautiful!'

'Yee-haw!'

'Linin' up just fine! Yes *sir!*'

The convoy leader, listening on his earpiece to Houston, suddenly snapped straight, his spine rigid in alarm. 'Oh, shit,' he said. 'Landing gear isn't down!'

Jack turned to him. '*What?*'

'Crew hasn't deployed the landing gear!'

Jack's head whipped around to stare at the approaching shuttle. It was barely one hundred feet above the ground, moving at over three hundred miles an hour. He could not see the wheels.

The crowd suddenly went dead silent. Their celebration had just turned into disbelief. Horror.

Get them down. Get those wheels down! Jack wanted to scream.

The shuttle was seventy-five feet above the runway, lined up perfectly. Ten seconds till touchdown.

Only the flight crew could lower the landing gear. No computer could flip the switch, could perform the task meant for a human hand. No computer could save them.

Fifty feet and still traveling over two hundred miles an hour.

Jack did not want to see the final event, but he could not help himself. He could not turn away. He saw *Discovery*'s tail slam down first, spewing up a shower of sparks and shattered heat tiles. He heard the screams and sobs of the crowd as *Discovery*'s nose slammed down next. The shuttle began to slide sideways, trailing a maelstrom of debris. A delta wing broke off, went flying like a black scythe through the air. The shuttle kept scraping sideways in a deafening screech.

The other wing broke off, tumbling, shattering.

Discovery slid off the tarmac, onto the desert sand. A tornado of dust flew up, obscuring Jack's view of the final seconds. His ears rang with the crowd's screams, but he could not utter a sound. Nor could he move; shock had numbed him so profoundly he felt as if he had left his own body and were hovering, ghostlike, in some nightmare dimension.

Then the cloud of dust began to clear, and he saw the shuttle, lying like a broken bird, in a terrible landscape of scattered debris.

Suddenly the ground convoy was moving. As engines roared to life, Jack and Bloomfeld jumped in back of the medical vehicle and began the bouncing ride across the desert floor to the crash site. Even over the roar of the convoy engines, Jack heard another sound, throbbing and ominous.

The choppers were moving in too.

Their vehicle suddenly braked to a halt. Jack and Bloomfeld, both clutching emergency medical kits, jumped to the ground in a cloud of dust. *Discovery* was still a hundred yards ahead. The choppers had already landed, forming a ring around the shuttle. Barring the convoy.

Jack began to run toward *Discovery*, ready to duck his head beneath the whirring rotor blades. He was stopped before he reached the ring of choppers.

'What the hell is going on?' yelled Bloomfeld as uniformed soldiers suddenly poured out of the choppers and formed an armed wall against the NASA ground crew.

'Back off! Back off!' one of the soldiers yelled.

The convoy leader pushed to the front. 'My crew needs to get to the orbiter!'

'You people will stay back!'

'You have no authority here! This is a NASA operation!'

'Everyone get the fuck back *now!*'

Rifles suddenly came up, barrels pointed at the unarmed ground crew. NASA personnel began to back away, all eyes focused on the guns, on the implied threat of mass slaughter.

Looking past the soldiers, Jack saw that a white plastic tent was rapidly being erected over *Discovery*'s hatch, closing it off from the outside air. A dozen hooded figures, completely clad in bright orange suits, emerged from two of the choppers and approached the orbiter.

'Those are Racal biological space suits,' said Bloomfeld.

The orbiter hatch was now completely hidden by the plastic tent. They could not see the hatch being opened. They could not see those space-suited men enter the middeck.

That's our *flight crew in there, thought Jack. Our people who might be dying in that orbiter. And we can't reach them. We've got doctors and nurses standing here, with a truck full of medical equipment, and they won't let us do our jobs.*

He pushed toward the line of soldiers, stepping

directly in front of the Army officer who appeared to be in charge. 'My medical crew is coming in,' he said.

The officer gave a smirk. 'I don't think so, sir.'

'We're employees of NASA. We're doctors, charged with the health and well-being of that flight crew. You can shoot us if you'd like. But then you'd have to kill everyone else here too, because they'd be witnesses. And I don't think you're going to do that.'

The rifle came up, the barrel pointed directly at Jack's chest. His throat was dry, and his heart was slamming against his ribs, but he stepped around the soldier, ducked under the chopper blades, and kept walking. He didn't even glance back as the soldier ordered,

'Halt, or I'll shoot!'

He walked on, his gaze fixed on the billowing tent ahead of him. He saw the men in their Racal space suits turn and stare at him in surprise. He saw the wind kick up a puff of dust and send it swirling across his path. He was almost at the tent when he heard Bloomfeld yell.

'Jack, look out!'

The blow caught him right at the base of the skull. He went down on his knees, pain exploding in bright bursts in his head. Another blow slammed into his flank, and he sprawled forward, tasting sand, hot as ash in his face. He rolled over, onto his back, and saw the soldier looming over him, rifle butt raised to deliver yet another blow.

'That's enough,' said an oddly muffled voice. 'Leave him alone.'

The soldier backed away. Now another face loomed into view, staring down at Jack through a clear Racal hood.

'Who are you?' the man said.

'Dr Jack McCallum.' The words came out in barely a whisper. He sat up, and his vision suddenly blurred, danced on the edge of darkness. He clutched his head, willing himself to stay conscious, fighting the blackness threatening to drag him down. 'Those are *my* patients in that orbiter,' Jack said. 'I demand to see them.'

'That's not possible.'

'They need medical attention –'

'They're dead, Dr McCallum. All of them.'

Jack froze. Slowly he raised his head and met the man's gaze through the clear face shield. He could read no expression there, could see nothing that reflected the tragedy of four lost lives.

'I'm sorry about your astronauts,' the man said, and turned to walk away.

Jack struggled to stand up. Though swaying and dizzy, he managed to stay on his feet. 'And who the fuck are *you?*' he demanded.

The man paused and turned back. 'I'm Dr Isaac Roman, USAMRIID,' he said. 'That orbiter is now a hot zone. The Army is assuming control.'

USAMRIID. Dr Roman had pronounced it as one word, but Jack knew what the letters stood for. The

U.S. Army Medical Research Institute of Infectious Diseases. Why was the Army here? Since when had this turned into a military operation?

Jack squinted in the flying dust, his skull still ringing from the blow, and struggled to absorb this bewildering information. An eternity seemed to pass, a surreal progression of images in slow motion. Men in Racal suits striding toward the orbiter. The soldier staring at him with expressionless eyes. The isolation tent billowing in the wind like a living, breathing organism. He looked at the ring of soldiers, still holding the ground crew at bay. He looked at the orbiter and saw the men in space suits carry the first stretcher out of the tent. The body was sealed in a bag. The plastic had been stamped repeatedly with the bright red biohazard symbol, like blossoms strewn across a corpse.

The sight of that stretcher made Jack's mind snap back into focus. He said, 'Where are you taking the bodies?'

Dr Roman did not even turn to look at him, but directed the stretcher to a waiting chopper. Jack started to walk toward the orbiter, and once again found a soldier standing in front of him, rifle butt raised to deliver another blow.

'Hey!' came a shout from the ground crew. 'You dare to hit him again and we've got thirty witnesses!'

The soldier turned and stared at the angry NASA and United Space Alliance employees, who were now surging forward, voices raised in outrage.

'You think this is Nazi Germany?'

'— think you can beat up civilians now?'

'Who the hell *are* you guys?'

The nervous soldiers tightened ranks as the ground crew continued to push forward, shouting, feet churning up dust.

A rifle shot exploded into the air. The crowd went dead still.

There is something terribly wrong here, thought Jack. *Something we don't understand*. These soldiers were fully prepared to shoot. To kill.

The convoy leader understood this as well, because he blurted out in panic, 'I'm in comm link with Houston! At this moment, a hundred men and women in Mission Control are listening!'

Slowly the soldiers lowered their rifles and glanced toward their officer. A long silence passed, broken only by the wind and the scatter shot of sand pinging the choppers.

Dr Roman appeared at Jack's side. 'You people don't understand the situation,' he said.

'Explain it to us.'

'We are dealing with a serious biohazard. The White House Security Council has activated the Army's Biological Rapid Response Team — a team created by an act of Congress, Dr McCallum. We're here on orders from the White House.'

'What biohazard?'

Roman hesitated. He glanced toward the NASA ground crew, who stood in a tense huddle beyond the line of soldiers.

'What is the organism?' Jack said.

At last Roman met his gaze through the plastic face shield. 'That information is classified.'

'We're the medical team, charged with the health of that flight crew. Why weren't we told about this?'

'NASA doesn't realize what it's dealing with.'

'And how is it that you do?' The question, heavy with significance, went unanswered.

Another stretcher emerged from the tent. And whose body was that? Jack wondered. The faces of the four crew members flashed through his mind. All dead now. He could not grasp that fact. He could not imagine those vibrant, healthy people reduced to shattered bones and ruptured organs.

'Where are you taking the bodies?' he asked.

'A Level Four facility for autopsy.'

'Who's doing the autopsy?'

'I am.'

'As the crew's flight surgeon, I should be present.'

'Why? Are you a pathologist?'

'No.'

'Then I don't see how you could contribute anything useful.'

'How many dead pilots have you examined?' Jack shot back. 'How many aircraft accidents have you investigated? Aerospace trauma is *my* training. My field of expertise. You might need me.'

'I don't think so,' said Roman. And he walked away.

Stiff with rage, Jack crossed back to the NASA ground crew and said to Bloomfeld. 'The Army's in control of this site. They're taking the bodies.'

'By what authority?'

'He says it comes straight from the White House. They've activated something called a Biological Rapid Response Team.'

'That's an antiterrorist team,' said Bloomfeld. 'I've heard about them. They were created to deal with bioterrorism.'

They watched a chopper lift off, carrying two of the bodies. *What the hell is really going on?* Jack wondered. *What are they hiding from us?*

He turned to the convoy leader. 'Can you patch me through to JSC?'

'Anyone in particular?'

Jack thought of whom he could trust, and who was high enough in the NASA bureaucracy to carry the battle to the very top.

'Get me Gordon Obie,' he said. 'Flight Crew Operations.'

THE AUTOPSY

16

Gordon Obie walked into the video conference room prepared for bloody battle, but none of the officials sitting around the table suspected the depth of his rage. And no wonder; Obie was wearing his usual poker face, and he didn't say a word as he took his place at the table, next to a tearful and puffy-eyed Public Affairs Officer Gretchen Liu. Everyone looked shell-shocked. They didn't even notice Gordon's entrance.

Also at the table was NASA administrator Leroy Cornell, JSC director Ken Blankenship, and a half dozen senior NASA officials, all of them grimly staring at the two video display screens. On the first screen was a Colonel Lawrence Harrison from USAMRIID, speaking from the Army base in Fort Detrick, Maryland. On the second monitor was a solemn, dark-haired man in civilian clothes, identified as 'Jared Profitt, White House Security Council.' He did not look like a bureaucrat. With his mournful eyes and his gaunt, almost ascetic features, he looked like a medieval monk, unwillingly transported into a modern age of suits and ties.

Blankenship was talking, his comments directed at Colonel Harrison. 'Not only did your soldiers prevent my people from doing their jobs, they threatened them at gunpoint. One of our flight surgeons was assaulted – knocked to the ground with a rifle butt. We have three dozen witnesses –'

'Dr McCallum broke through our security cordon. He refused to halt as ordered,' Colonel Harrison responded. 'We had a hot zone to protect.'

'So now the U.S. Army is prepared to attack, even shoot, civilians?'

'Ken, let's try to look at it from USAMRIID's point of view,' said Cornell, placing a calming hand on Blankenship's arm. The diplomat's touch, thought Gordon with distaste. Cornell might be NASA's spokesman at the White House and their best asset when it came to cajoling Congress for money, but many at NASA had never really trusted him. They could never trust any man who thought more like a politician than an engineer. 'Protecting a hot zone is a valid reason to apply force,' said Cornell. 'Dr McCallum did breach the security line.'

'And the results could have been disastrous,' said Harrison over the audio feed. 'Our intelligence reports that Marburg virus may have been purposefully introduced to the space station. Marburg is a cousin of Ebola virus.'

'How would it get aboard?' said Blankenship. 'Every experimental protocol is reviewed for safety. Every lab animal is certified healthy. We don't send up biohazards.'

'That's your agency line, of course. But you receive your experimental payloads from scientists all around the country. You may screen their protocols, but you can't examine every bacteria or tissue culture as it arrives for launch. To keep biological materials alive, the payloads are loaded right onto the shuttle. What if one of those experiments was contaminated? Consider how easy it is to replace a harmless culture with a dangerous organism like Marburg.'

'Are you saying this was a deliberate sabotage attempt on the station?' said Blankenship. 'An act of bioterrorism?'

'That's precisely what I'm saying. Let me describe what happens to you if you are infected with this particular virus. First your muscles begin to ache and you have a fever. The ache is so severe, so agonizing, you can scarcely bear to be touched. An intramuscular injection makes you shriek in pain. Then your eyes turn red. Your belly begins to hurt, and you vomit, again and again. You begin to throw up blood. It comes up black at first, because of digestive processes. Then it comes faster and turns bright red, as rapid as a gushing pump. Your liver swells, cracks. Your kidneys fail. Your internal organs are being destroyed, turning to foul, black mush. And suddenly, disastrously,

your blood pressure crashes. And you're dead.'
Harrison paused. 'That's what we may be dealing
with, gentlemen.'

'This is *bullshit!*' blurted Gordon Obie.

Everyone at the table stared at him in astonishment. The Sphinx had spoken. On the rare
occasions Obie did say anything at a meeting, it
was usually in a monotone, his words used to
convey data and information, not emotion. This
outburst had shocked them all.

'May I ask who just spoke?' asked Colonel
Harrison.

'I'm Gordon Obie, director of Flight Crew Operations.'

'Oh. The astronauts' top dog.'

'You could call me that.'

'And why is this bullshit?'

'I don't believe this is Marburg virus. I don't
know what it is, but I do know you're not telling
us the truth.'

Colonel Harrison's face froze into a rigid mask.
He said nothing.

It was Jared Profitt who spoke. His voice sounded
exactly as Gordon had expected, thin and reedy.
He was not a bully like Harrison, but a man who
preferred to appeal to one's intellect and reason.
'I understand your frustration, Mr Obie,' Profitt
said. 'There's so much we're unable to tell you
because of security concerns. But Marburg is not
something we can be careless about.'

'If you already know it's Marburg, then why

are you excluding our flight surgeons from the autopsy? Are you afraid we'll learn the truth?'

'Gordon,' Cornell said quietly, 'why don't we discuss this in private?'

Gordon ignored him and said to the screen, 'What disease are we really talking about? An infection? A toxin? Something loaded on board the shuttle in a military payload, perhaps?'

There was a silence. Then Harrison blustered, 'There's that NASA paranoia! Your agency likes to blame the military for everything that goes wrong.'

'Why do you refuse to allow my flight surgeon into the autopsy?'

'Are we speaking of Dr McCallum?' asked Profitt.

'Yes. McCallum has training in aviation trauma and pathology. He is a flight surgeon as well as a former member of the astronaut corps. The fact you refuse to let him or *any* of our doctors view the autopsies makes me wonder what you don't want NASA to see.'

Colonel Harrison glanced sideways, as though to look at someone else in the room. When he gazed back at the camera, his face was flushed and angry. 'This is absurd. You people just crashed the shuttle! You screw up the landing, kill your own crew, and then you point an accusing finger at the U.S. *Army?*'

'The entire astronaut corps is up in arms about this,' said Gordon. 'We want to know what really happened to our colleagues. We insist you allow one of *our* doctors to view the bodies.'

Leroy Cornell again tried to intercede. 'Gordon, you can't make unreasonable demands like this,' he said quietly. 'They know what they're doing.'

'So do I.'

'I'm going to ask you to back down *now*.'

Gordon looked Cornell in the eye. Cornell was NASA's representative to the White House, NASA's voice in Congress. Opposing him was career suicide.

He did it anyway. 'I speak for the astronauts,' he said. '*My* people.' He turned to the video screen, his gaze fixed on the stony face of Colonel Harrison. 'And we're not above taking our concerns to the press. We don't consider this move lightly – exposing confidential NASA matters. The astronaut corps has always been discreet. But if we're forced to, we will demand a public inquiry.'

Gretchen Liu's jaw dropped. 'Gordon,' she whispered, 'what the hell are you doing?'

'What I have to do.'

The silence at the table stretched to a full minute.

Then, to everyone's astonishment, Ken Blankenship said, 'I side with our astronauts.'

'So do I,' said another voice.

'Me too –'

'–and me.'

Gordon looked around the table at his colleagues. Most of these people were engineers and operational managers whose names seldom turned up in the press. More often than not, they were in conflict with the astronauts, whom they considered flyboys with big egos. The astronauts got all the glory, but these men and women, who performed the unseen and unglamorous jobs that made spaceflight a reality, were the heart and soul of NASA. And they were now united behind Gordon.

Leroy Cornell looked stricken, the leader abandoned by his own troops. He was a proud man, and this was a humiliatingly public blow. He cleared his throat and slowly squared his shoulders. Then he faced the video image of Colonel Harrison. 'I have no choice but to support my astronauts as well,' he said. 'I insist that one of our flight surgeons be allowed to view the autopsies.'

Colonel Harrison said nothing. It was Jared Profitt who made the final decision – Jared Profitt who was obviously the real man in charge. He turned to confer with someone standing offscreen. Then he looked at the camera and nodded.

Both screens went blank. The video conference had ended.

'Well, you certainly thumbed your nose at the U.S. Army,' said Gretchen. 'Did you see how pissed-off Harrison looked?'

No, thought Gordon, remembering Colonel Harrison's expression just before the image went blank. *That wasn't anger I saw on his face. It was fear.*

The bodies had not been taken to USAMRIID

headquarters in Fort Detrick, Maryland, as Jack had expected. They'd been transported barely sixty miles away from the White Sands landing strip to a windowless concrete-block building, much like the dozens of other anonymous government buildings that had sprung up in that dry desert valley. But this one had a distinguishing feature: a series of ventilation pipes jutting up from the roofline. Barbed wire bristled atop the perimeter fence. As they drove through the military checkpoint, Jack heard the hum of high-voltage wires.

Flanked by his armed escort, Jack approached the front entrance – the only entrance, he realized. On the door was a chillingly familiar symbol: the bright red biohazard blossom. *What is this facility doing in the middle of nowhere?* he wondered. Then he scanned the featureless horizon, and his question was answered. The building was here precisely because it *was* in the middle of nowhere.

He was escorted through the door and into a series of stark corridors heading deeper into the heart of the building. He saw men and women in Army uniforms, others in lab coats. All lighting was artificial, and the faces appeared bluish and sickly.

The guards stopped outside a door labeled 'Men's Lockers.'

'Go in,' he was told. 'Follow the written instructions to the letter. Then go through the next door. They're waiting for you.'

Jack entered the room. Inside were lockers, a laundry cart containing various sizes of green surgical scrub suits, a shelf with paper caps, a sink, and a mirror. A list of instructions was posted on the wall, starting with *'Remove ALL street clothes, including underwear.'*

He took off his clothes, left them in an unsecured locker, and dressed in a scrub suit. Then he pushed through the next door, again labeled with the universal biohazard symbol, into an ultraviolet-lit room. There he paused, wondering what to do next.

A voice over the intercom said, 'There's a shelf of socks beside you. Put on a pair and walk through the door.'

He did.

A woman in a scrub suit was waiting for him in the next room. She was brusque, unsmiling, as she told him to don sterile gloves. Then she angrily ripped off strips of tape and sealed his sleeves and pant cuffs. The Army may have resigned themselves to Jack's visit, but they weren't going to make it a friendly one. She slipped an audio headset over his head, then gave him a 'Snoopy' hat, like a swimming cap, to hold the equipment in place.

'Now suit up,' she barked.

Time for the space suit. This one was blue, with the gloves already attached. As his hostile assistant lowered the hood over his head, Jack felt a dart of anxiety about the woman. In her anger, she could sabotage the process, see to it that he wasn't completely sealed off from contamination.

She closed the seal on his chest, hooked him up to a wall hose, and he felt the whoosh of air blow into his suit. It was too late now to worry about what could go wrong. He was ready to cross into the hot area.

The woman unplugged his hose and pointed to the next door.

He stepped through, into the air lock. The door slammed shut behind him. A man in a space suit was waiting for him. He did not speak, but gestured to Jack to follow him through the far door.

They stepped through and walked down a hallway to the autopsy room.

Inside was a stainless steel table with a body on it, still sealed in its bag. Two men in space suits were already standing on either side of the body. One of the men was Dr Roman. He turned and saw Jack.

'Don't touch anything. Don't interfere. You're only here to observe, Dr McCallum, so stay the hell out of our way.'

Nice welcome.

The space-suited escort plugged a wall hose into Jack's suit, and once again air hissed into his helmet. If not for the audio headset, he'd be unable to hear anything the other three men said.

Dr Roman and his two associates opened the body bag.

Jack felt his breath catch, his throat constrict.

The corpse was Jill Hewitt's. Her helmet had been removed, but she was still wearing the orange launch-and-entry suit, embroidered with her name. Even without that identification, he would have known it was Jill, because of her hair. It was a silky chestnut, cut in a bob and streaked with the first hints of gray. Her face was strangely intact. Her eyes were half open. Both sclerae were a bright and shocking red.

Roman and his colleagues unzipped the LES and stripped the corpse. The fabric was fire-retardant, too tough to cut through. They had to peel it off. They worked efficiently, their comments matter-of-fact and without even a hint of emotion. When they had removed her clothing, she looked like a broken doll. Both her hands were deformed by fractures, reduced to masses of crushed bone. Her legs, too, were broken and akilter, the shins bent at impossible angles. The tips of two broken ribs penetrated her chest wall, and black bruises marked the strap lines of her seat restraint.

Jack felt his breaths coming too fast, and he had to quell his rising horror. He had witnessed many autopsies, on bodies in much worse shape. He had seen aviators burned into little more than charred twigs, skulls exploded from the pressure of cooking brains. He had seen a corpse whose face had been sliced off from walking into a chopper's tail rotor. He had seen a Navy pilot's spine broken in half and folded backward from ejecting through a closed canopy.

This was far, far worse because he knew the deceased. He remembered her as a living, breathing woman. His horror was mingled with rage, because these three men viewed Jill's exposed body with such cold dispassion. She was a slab of meat on the table, nothing more. They ignored her injuries, her grotesquely fractured limbs. The cause of death was only of secondary concern to them. They were more interested in the microbiological hitchhiker harbored within her corpse.

Roman began his Y incision. In one hand he gripped a scalpel; the other hand was safely encased in a steel-mesh glove. One slash ran from the right shoulder, diagonally through the breast, to the xiphoid process. Another diagonal slash ran from the left shoulder and met the first slash at the xiphoid. The incision continued straight down the abdomen, with a small jag around the umbilicus, ending near the pubic bone. He cut through the ribs, freeing the sternum. The bony shield was lifted to reveal the chest cavity.

The cause of death was immediately apparent.

When a plane crashes, or an automobile slams into a wall, or a despondent lover makes a suicide leap from a ten-story building, the same forces of deceleration apply. A human body traveling at great speed is abruptly brought to a halt. The impact itself can shatter ribs and send missiles of bone shards into vital organs. It can fracture vertebrae, rupture spinal cords, crush skulls against dashboards or instrument panels. But even when pilots are fully strapped in and helmeted, even when no part of their body makes contact with the aircraft, the force of deceleration alone can be fatal, because although the torso may be restrained, the internal organs are not. The heart and lungs and great vessels are suspended inside the chest by only tissue attachments. When the torso comes to an abrupt halt, the heart continues to swing forward like a pendulum, moving with such force it shears tissues and rips open the aorta. Blood explodes into the mediastinum and pleural cavity.

Jill Hewitt's chest was a lake of blood.

Roman suctioned it out, then frowned at the heart and lungs. 'I can't see where she bled out,' he said.

'Why don't we remove the entire block?' said his assistant. 'We'd have better visibility.'

'The tear is most likely in the ascending aorta,' said Jack. 'Sixty-five percent of the time, it's located just above the aortic valve.'

Roman glanced at him in annoyance. Up till then, he'd managed to ignore Jack; now he resented this intrusive comment. Without a word, he positioned his scalpel to sever the great vessels.

'I advise examining the heart in situ first,' said Jack. 'Before you cut.'

'How and where she bled out is not my primary concern,' Roman retorted.

They don't really care what killed her, thought

Jack. *All they want to know is what organism might be growing, multiplying, inside her.*

Roman sliced through the trachea, esophagus, and great vessels, then removed the heart and lungs in one block. The lungs were covered with hemorrhages. Traumatic or infectious? Jack didn't know. Next Roman examined the abdominal organs. The small bowel, like the lungs, was splotchy with mucosal hemorrhages. He removed it and set the glistening coils of intestines in a bowl. He resected the stomach, pancreas, and liver. All would be sectioned and examined microscopically. All tissue would be cultured for bacteria and viruses.

The body was now missing almost all its internal organs. Jill Hewitt, Navy pilot, triathlete, lover of J&B scotch and high-stakes poker and Jim Carrey movies, was now nothing but a hollow shell.

Roman straightened, looking vaguely relieved. So far, the autopsy had revealed nothing unexpected. If there was gross evidence of Marburg virus, Jack did not see it.

Roman circled behind the corpse, to the head.

This was the part Jack dreaded. He had to force himself to watch as Roman sliced the scalp, his incision running across the top of the crown, from ear to ear. He peeled the scalp forward and folded the flap over the face, a fringe of chestnut hair flopping down over her chin. With a rongeur, they cracked the skull. No saws, no flying bone dust, could be allowed in a Level 4 autopsy. They pried off the cap of bone.

A fist-sized mass of clotted blood plopped out, splattering the stainless steel table.

'Big subdural hematoma,' said one of Roman's associates. 'From the trauma?'

'I don't think so,' said Roman. 'You saw the aorta – death would have been nearly instantaneous on impact. I'm not sure her heart was pumping long enough to produce this much intracranial bleeding.' Gently he slid his gloved fingers into the cranial cavity, probing the surface of gray matter.

A gelatinous mass slithered out and splashed onto the table.

Roman jerked back, startled.

'What the hell is *that?*' his assistant said.

Roman didn't answer. He just stared at the clump of tissue. It was covered with a blue-green membrane. Through the glistening veil, the mass appeared irregular, a knot of formless flesh. He was about to slit the membrane open, then he stopped himself and shot a glance toward Jack. 'It's a tumor of some kind,' he said. 'Or a cyst. That would explain the headache she reported.'

'No it wouldn't,' Jack spoke up. 'Her headache came on suddenly – within hours. A tumor takes months to grow.'

'How do you know she hasn't been hiding her symptoms these past months?' countered Roman. 'Keeping it a secret so she wouldn't get scrubbed from the launch?'

Jack had to concede that was a possibility.

Astronauts were so eager for flight assignments they might well conceal any symptoms that would pull them from a mission.

Roman looked at his associate standing across the table from him. The other man nodded, slid the mass into a specimen container, and carried it out of the room.

'Aren't you going to section it?' said Jack.

'It needs to be fixed and stained first. If I start slicing now, I could deform the cellular architecture.'

'You don't know if it *is* a tumor.'

'What else would it be?'

Jack had no answer. He had never seen anything like it.

Roman continued his examination of Jill Hewitt's cranial cavity. Clearly the mass, whatever it was, had increased pressure on her brain, deforming its structures. How long had it been there? Months, years? How was it possible that Jill had been able to function normally, much less pilot a complicated vehicle like the shuttle? All this raced through Jack's head as he watched Roman remove the brain and slide it into a steel basin.

'She was close to herniating through the tentorium,' said Roman.

No wonder Jill had gone blind. No wonder she hadn't lowered the landing gear. She had already been unconscious, her brain about to be squeezed like toothpaste out the base of her skull.

Jill's corpse – what remained of it – was sealed into a new body bag and wheeled out of the room, along with the biohazard containers holding her organs.

A second body was brought in. It was Andy Mercer.

With fresh gloves pulled over his space suit gloves, and a clean scalpel, Roman set to work on the Y incision. He was moving more quickly, as though Jill had just been the warm-up and he was only now hitting his stride.

Mercer had complained of abdominal pain and vomiting, Jack remembered as he watched Roman's scalpel slice through skin and subcutaneous fat. Mercer hadn't complained of a headache, as Jill had, but he'd had a fever and had coughed up a little blood. Would his lungs show the effects of Marburg virus?

Again, Roman's diagonal cuts met below the xiphoid, and he sliced a shallow line down the abdomen to the pubis. Again he cut through the ribs, freeing up the triangular shield that covered the heart. He lifted the sternum.

Gasping, he stumbled backward, dropping his scalpel. It clanged onto the table. His assistants stood frozen in disbelief.

In Mercer's chest cavity was a cluster of blue-green cysts, identical to the cyst in Jill Hewitt's brain. They were massed around his heart, like tiny translucent eggs.

Roman stood paralyzed, his gaze fixed on the

gaping torso. Then his gaze shifted to the glistening peritoneal membrane. It was distended, full of blood and bulging out through the abdominal incision.

Roman stepped toward the body, staring at the outpouching of peritoneal membrane. When he'd made his incision through the abdominal wall, his scalpel had nicked the surface of that membrane. A trickle of blood-tinged fluid leaked out. At first it was barely a few drops. Then, even as they watched, the trickle turned into a stream. The slit suddenly burst open into a gaping rent as blood gushed out, carrying with it a slippery flood of blue-green cysts.

Roman gave a cry of horror as the cysts plopped onto the floor in splatters of blood and mucus.

One of them skittered across the concrete and bumped against Jack's rubber boot. He bent down, to touch it with his gloved hand. Abruptly he was yanked backward as Roman's associates pulled him away from the table.

'Get him out of here!' Roman ordered. 'Get him out of the room!'

The two men pushed Jack toward the door. He resisted, shoving away the gloved hand now grasping his shoulder. The man stumbled backward, tipped over a tray of surgical instruments, and sprawled to the floor, slippery with cysts and blood.

The second man wrenched Jack's air hose from its connection and held up the kinked end. 'I advise you to walk out with us, Dr McCallum,' he said. 'While you've still got breathable air.'

'My suit! Jesus, I've got a breach!' It was the man who'd stumbled into the instrument tray. He was now staring in horror at a two-inch-long tear in his space suit sleeve – a sleeve that was coated with Mercer's body fluids.

'It's wet. I can feel it. My inner sleeve is wet –'

'*Go!*' barked Roman. 'Decon *now!*'

The man unplugged his suit and went running in panic out of the room. Jack followed him to the air lock door, and they both stepped through, into the decon shower. Water shot out of the overhead jets, pounding down like hard rain on their shoulders. Then the shower of disinfectant began, a torrent of green liquid that splattered noisily against their plastic helmets.

When it finally stopped, they stepped through the next door and pulled off their suits. The man immediately peeled off his already-wet scrub suit and thrust his arm under a faucet of running water, to rinse away any body fluids that had leaked through the sleeve.

'You have any breaks in your skin?' asked Jack. 'Cuts, hangnails?'

'My daughter's cat scratched me last night.'

Jack looked down at the man's arm and saw the claw marks, three scabbed lines raking up the inner arm. The same arm as the torn space suit. He looked at the man's eyes and saw fear.

'What happens now?' said Jack.

'Quarantine. I go to lockup. Shit . . .'

'I already know it's not Marburg,' said Jack.

The man released a deep breath. 'No. It's not.'

'Then what is it? Tell me what we're dealing with,' said Jack.

The man clutched the sink with both hands and stared down at the water gurgling into the drain. He said softly, 'We don't know.'

17

Sullivan Obie was riding his Harley on Mars.

At midnight, with the full moon shining down and the pock-marked desert stretched out before him, he could imagine it was the Martian wind whipping his hair and red Martian dust churning beneath his tires. This was an old fantasy from boyhood, from the days when those precocious Obie brothers shot off homemade rockets and built cardboard moon landers and donned space suits of crinkled foil. The days when he and Gordie knew, just knew, that their futures lay in the heavens.

And this is where those big dreams end up, he thought. *Drunk on tequila, popping wheelies in the desert*. No way was he ever getting to Mars, or to the moon either. Chances were he wouldn't even get off the goddamn launchpad, but would be instantly atomized. A quick, spectacular death. What the hell; it beat dying at seventy-five with cancer.

He skidded to a stop, his bike spitting up dirt,

and stared across the moonlit ripples of sand at *Apogee II*, gleaming like a streak of silver, her nose cone pointed at the stars. They had moved her to the launchpad yesterday. It was a slow and celebratory procession, the dozen Apogee employees honking horns and beating on their car roofs as they followed the flatbed truck across the desert. When she had finally been hoisted into position and everyone squinted up against the blazing sun to look at her, they had suddenly fallen silent. They all knew this was the last roll of the dice. In three weeks, when *Apogee II* lifted off, she would be carrying all their hopes and dreams.

And my sorry carcass as well, thought Sullivan.

A chill shot through him as he realized he might be staring at his own coffin.

He goosed the Harley and roared back toward the road, bouncing across dunes, leaping over dips. He rode with abandon, his recklessness fueled by tequila and by the sudden and unshakable certainty that he was already a dead man. That in three weeks he would be riding that rocket to oblivion. Until then, nothing could touch him, nothing could hurt him.

The promise of death had made him invincible.

He accelerated, flying across the bleak moonscape of his boyhood fantasies. *And here I am in the lunar rover, speeding across the Sea of Tranquility. Roaring up a lunar hill. Launching off to a soft landing . . .*

He felt the ground drop away. Felt himself

soaring through the night, the Harley growling between his knees, the moon shining in his eyes. Still soaring. How far? How high?

The ground hit with such force he lost control and tumbled sideways, the Harley falling on top of him. For a moment he lay stunned, pinned between his bike and a flat rock. *Well, this is one fucking stupid position to be in*, he thought.

Then the pain hit him. Deep and grinding, as though his hips were crushed to splinters.

He gave a cry and fell back, his face turned to the sky. The moon shone down, mocking him.

'His pelvis is fractured in three places,' said Bridget. 'The doctors pinned it last night. They tell me he's gonna be confined to bed for at least six weeks.'

Casper Mulholland could almost hear the sound of his dreams popping, like the loud burst of a balloon. 'Six . . . *weeks?*'

'And then he'll be in rehab for another three or four months.'

'Four *months?*'

'For God's sake, Casper. Say something original.'

'We're screwed.' He slapped his palm against his forehead, as though to punish himself for daring to dream they could ever succeed. It was that old Apogee curse again, cutting them off at the ankles just as they reached the finish line. Blowing up their rockets. Burning down their first office. And now, taking their only pilot out of commission.

He paced the waiting room, thinking, *Nothing has ever gone right for us*. They'd invested all their combined savings, their reputations, and the last thirteen years of their lives. This was God's way of telling them to give up. To cut their losses before something *really* bad happened.

'He was drunk,' said Bridget.

Casper halted and turned to look at her. She stood with her arms grimly crossed, her red hair like the flaming halo of an avenging angel.

'The doctors told me,' she said. 'Blood alcohol level of point one nine. As pickled as a herring. This isn't just our usual bad luck. This is our own dear Sully fucking up again. My only consolation is that for the next six weeks, he's gonna have a big tube stuck up his dick.'

Without a word, Casper walked out of the visitors' waiting room, headed up the hall, and pushed into Sullivan's hospital room. 'You moron,' he said.

Sully looked up at him with morphine-glazed eyes. 'Thanks for the sympathy.'

'You don't deserve any. Three weeks before launch and you pull some goddamn Chuck Yeager stunt in the desert? Why didn't you just finish the job? Splatter your brains while you were at it? Hell, we wouldn't have known the difference!'

Sully closed his eyes. 'I'm sorry.'

'You always are.'

'I screwed up. I know . . .'

'You promised them a manned flight. It wasn't

my idea, it was *yours*. Now they're expecting it. They're excited about it. When was the last time any investor was excited about us? This could have made the difference. If you'd just kept the bottle corked –'

'I was scared.'

Sully had spoken so softly Casper wasn't sure he'd heard him right. 'What?' he said.

'About the launch. Had a . . . bad feeling.'

A bad feeling. Slowly Casper sank into the bed-side chair, all his anger instantly dissolving. Fear is not something a man readily admits to. The fact that Sully, who regularly courted destruction, would confess to being afraid left Casper feeling shaken.

And, at last, sympathetic.

'You don't need me for the launch,' said Sully.

'They expect to see a pilot climb into that cock-pit.'

'You could put a goddamn monkey in my seat and they'd never know the difference. She doesn't need a pilot, Cap. You can uplink all the commands from the ground.'

Casper sighed. They had no choice now; it would have to be an unmanned flight. Clearly they had a valid excuse not to launch Sully, but would the investors accept it? Or would they believe, instead, that Apogee had lost its nerve? That it lacked the confidence to risk a human life?

'I guess I just lost my nerve,' said Sully softly. 'Got to drinking last night. Couldn't stop . . .'

Casper understood his partner's fear – the way he understood how one defeat can lead inexorably to another and then another until the only certainty in a man's life is failure. No wonder Sully was scared; he had lost faith in their dream. In Apogee.

Maybe they all had.

Casper said, 'We can still make this launch work. Even without a monkey in the cockpit.'

'Yeah. You could send up Bridget instead.'

'Then who'd answer the phones?'

'The monkey.'

Both men laughed. They were like two old soldiers, mustering up a shred of cheer on the eve of certain defeat.

'So we're gonna do it?' said Sully. 'We're gonna launch?'

'That was the whole idea of building a rocket.'

'Well, then.' Sully took a deep breath, and a ghost of the old bravado returned to his face. 'Let's do it right. Press release to all the wire services. One mother of a tent party with champagne. Hell, invite my sainted brother and his NASA pals. If she blows up on the pad, at least we'll go outta business in style.'

'Yeah. We always had an excess of style.'

They grinned.

Casper rose to leave. 'Get better, Sully,' he said. 'We'll need you for *Apogee III*.'

He found Bridget still sitting in the visitors' waiting room. 'So what happens now?' she said.

'We launch on schedule.'

'Unmanned?'

He nodded. 'We fly her from the control room.'

To his surprise, she huffed out a sigh of relief. 'Hallelujah!'

'What're you so happy about? Our man's laid up in a hospital bed.'

'Exactly.' She slung her purse over her shoulder and turned to leave. 'It means he won't be up there to fuck things up.'

August 11

Nicolai Rudenko floated in the air lock, watching as Luther wriggled his hips into the lower torso assembly of the EVA suit. To the diminutive Nicolai, Luther was an exotic giant, with those broad shoulders and legs like pistons. And his skin! While Nicolai had turned pasty during his months aboard ISS, Luther was still a deep and polished brown, a startling contrast to the pale faces that inhabited their otherwise colorless world. Nicolai had already suited up, and now he hovered beside Luther, ready to assist his partner into the EVA suit's upper torso assembly. They said little to each other; neither man was in the mood for idle chatter.

The two of them had spent a mostly conversationless night sleeping in the air lock, allowing their bodies to adjust to a lower atmospheric pressure of 10.2 pounds per square inch – two thirds that of the space station. The pressure in their suits would be even less, at 4.3. The suits could not be inflated any higher, or the limbs would be too stiff and bulky, the joints impossible to flex. Moving directly from a fully pressurized spacecraft into the lower air pressure of an EVA suit was like surfacing too fast from the depths of the ocean. An astronaut could suffer the bends. Nitrogen bubbles formed in the blood, clogging capillaries, cutting off precious oxygen to the brain and spinal cord. The consequences could be devastating: paralysis and stroke. Like deep-sea divers, astronauts had to give their bodies time to adjust to the changing pressures. The night before a space walk, the EVA crew washed out their lungs with a hundred percent oxygen and shut themselves into the air lock for 'the camp-out.' For hours they were trapped together in a small chamber already crammed full of equipment. It was not a place for claustrophobics.

With his arms extended over his head, Luther squirmed into the suit's hard-shelled upper torso, which was mounted on the air lock wall. It was an exhausting dance, like wriggling into an impossibly small tunnel. At last his head popped out through the neck hole, and Nicolai helped him close the waist ring, sealing the two halves of the suit.

They put on their helmets. As Nicolai looked down to fit his helmet to the torso assembly, he noticed something glistening on the rim of the suit's neck ring. Just spittle, he thought, and locked on the helmet. They donned their gloves. Sealed into their suits, they opened the equipment lock hatch, floated into the adjoining crew lock, and shut the hatch behind them. They were now in an even smaller compartment, barely large enough to contain both the men and their bulky life-support backpacks.

Thirty minutes of 'prebreathe' came next. While they inhaled pure oxygen, purging their blood of any last nitrogen, Nicolai floated with his eyes closed, mentally preparing for the space walk ahead. If they could not get the beta gimbal assembly to unlock, if they could not reorient the solar panels toward the sun, they would be starved for power. Crippled. What Nicolai and Luther accomplished in the next six hours could well determine the fate of the space station.

Though this responsibility weighed heavily on his tired shoulders, Nicolai was anxious to open the hatch and float out of the air lock. To go EVA was like being reborn, the fetus emerging from that small, tight opening, the umbilical restraint dangling as one swims out into the vastness of space. Were the situation not so grave, he would be looking forward to it, would be giddily anticipating the freedom of floating in a universe without walls, the dazzling blue earth spinning beneath him.

But the images that came to mind, as he waited with his eyes closed for the thirty minutes to pass, were not of spacewalking. What he saw instead were the faces of the dead. He imagined

Discovery as she plunged from the sky. He saw the crew, strapped into their seats, bodies shaken like dolls, spines snapping, hearts exploding. Though Mission Control had not told them the details of the catastrophe, the nightmarish visions filled his head, made his heart pound, his mouth turn dry.

'Your thirty minutes are up, guys,' came Emma's voice over the intercom. 'Time for depress.'

Hands clammy with sweat, Nicolai opened his eyes and saw Luther start the depressurization pump. The air was being sucked out, the pressure in the crew lock slowly dropping. If there was a leak in their suits, they would now detect it.

'A-OK?' asked Luther, checking the latches on their umbilical tethers.

'I am ready.'

Luther vented the crew lock atmosphere to space. Then he released the handle and pulled open the hatch.

The last air hissed out.

They paused for a moment, clutching the side of the hatch, staring out in awe. Then Nicolai swam out, into the blackness of space.

'They're coming out now,' said Emma, watching on closed-circuit TV as the two men emerged from the crew lock, umbilical tethers trailing after them. They removed tools from the storage box outside the airlock. Then, pulling themselves from hand-hold to handhold, they made their way toward the main truss. As they passed by the camera mounted just under the truss, Luther gave a wave.

'You watching the show?' came his voice over the UHF audio system.

'We see you fine on external camera,' said Griggs. 'But your EMU cameras aren't feeding in.'

'Nicolai's too?'

'Neither one. We'll try to track down the problem.'

'Okay, well, we're heading up onto the truss to check out the damage.'

The two men moved out of the first camera's range. For a moment they disappeared from view. Then Griggs said, 'There they are,' and pointed to a new screen, where the space-suited men were moving toward the second camera, propelling themselves hand over hand along the top of the truss. Again they passed out of range. They were now in the blind zone of the damaged camera and could no longer be seen.

'Getting close, guys?' asked Emma.

'Almost – almost there,' said Luther, sounding short of breath. *Slow down*, she thought. *Pace yourselves*.

For what seemed like an endless wait, there was only silence from the EVA crew. Emma felt her pulse quicken, her anxiety rising. The station was already crippled and starved for power. Nothing must go wrong with these repairs. *If only Jack was here*, she thought. Jack was a talented tinkerer who could rebuild any boat engine or cobble together a shortwave radio from junkyard scraps. In orbit, the most valuable tools are a clever pair of hands.

'Luther?' said Griggs.

There was no answer.

'Nicolai? Luther? Please respond.'

'Shit,' said Luther's voice.

'What is it? What do you see?' said Griggs.

'I'm looking at the problem right now, and man, it's a mess. The whole P-6 end of the main truss is twisted around. *Discovery* must've clipped the 2-B array and bent that end right up. Then she swung over and snapped off the S-band antennas.'

'What do you think? Can you fix anything?'

'The S-band's no problem. We got an ORU for the antennas, and we'll just replace 'em. But the port-side solar arrays – forget it. We need a whole new truss on that end.'

'Okay.' Wearily Griggs rubbed his face. 'Okay, so we're definitely down one PVM. I guess we can deal with that. But we need the P-4 arrays reoriented, or we're screwed.'

There was a pause as Luther and Nicolai headed back along the main truss. Suddenly they were in camera range; Emma saw them moving slowly past in their bulky suits and enormous backpacks, like deep-sea divers moving through water. They stopped at the P-4 arrays. One of the men floated down the side of the truss and peered at the mechanism joining the enormous solar wings to the truss backbone.

'The gimbal assembly is bent,' said Nicolai. 'It cannot turn.'

'Can you free it up?' asked Griggs.

They heard a rapid exchange of dialogue between Luther and Nicolai. Then Luther said, 'How elegant do you want this repair to be?'

'Whatever it takes. We need the juice soon, or we're in trouble, guys.'

'I guess we can try the body shop approach.'

Emma looked at Griggs. 'Does that mean what I think it means?'

It was Luther who answered the question. 'We're gonna get out a hammer and bang this sucker back into shape.'

He was still alive.

Dr Isaac Roman gazed through the viewing window at his unfortunate colleague, who was sitting in a hospital bed watching TV. Cartoons, believe it or not. The Nickelodeon channel, which the patient stared at with almost desperate concentration. He didn't even glance at the space-suited nurse who'd come into the room to remove the untouched lunch tray.

Roman pressed the intercom button. 'How are you feeling today, Nathan?'

Dr Nathan Helsinger turned his startled gaze to the viewing window, and for the first time noticed that Roman was standing on the other side of the glass. 'I'm fine. I'm perfectly healthy.'

'You have no symptoms whatsoever?'

'I told you, I'm *fine*.'

Roman studied him for a moment. The man looked healthy enough, but his face was pale and tense. Scared.

'When can I come out of isolation?' said Helsinger.

'It's been scarcely thirty hours.'

'The astronauts had symptoms by eighteen hours.'

'That was in microgravity. We don't know what to expect here, and we can't take chances. You know that.'

Abruptly Helsinger turned to stare at the TV again, but not before Roman saw the flash of tears in his eyes. 'It's my daughter's birthday today.'

'We sent a gift in your name. Your wife was informed you couldn't make it. That you're on a plane to Kenya.'

Helsinger gave a bitter laugh. 'You do tie up those loose ends well, don't you? And what if I die? What will you tell her?'

'That it happened in Kenya.'

'As good a place as any, I suppose.' He sighed. 'So what did you get her?'

'Your daughter? I believe it was a Dr Barbie.'

'That's exactly what she wanted. How did you know?'

Roman's cell phone rang. 'I'll check back on you later,' he said, then turned from the window to answer the phone.

'Dr Roman, this is Carlos. We've got some of the DNA results. You'd better come up and see this.'

'I'm on my way.'

He found Dr Carlos Mixtal sitting in front of the lab computer. Data was scrolling down the monitor in a continuous stream:

```
GTGATTAAAGTGGTTAAAGTTGCTCATGTTC
AATTATGCAGTTGTTGCGGTTGCTTAGTGT
CTTTAGCAGACACATATGAAAAGCTTTTAG
ATGTTTTGAATTCAATTGAGTTGGTTTATTG
TCAAACTTTAGCAGATGCAAGAGAAATT
CCTGAATGCGATATTGCTTTAGTTGAAGG
CTCTGT . . .
```

The data was made up of only four letters, *G*, *T*, *A*, and *C*. It was a nucleotide sequence, and each of the letters represented the building blocks that make up DNA, the genetic blueprint for all living organisms.

Carlos turned at the sound of Roman's footsteps, and the expression on his face was unmistakable. Carlos looked scared. *Just like Helsinger*, Roman thought. *Everyone is scared*.

Roman sat down beside him. 'Is that it?' he asked, pointing to the screen.

'This is from the organism infecting Kenichi Hirai. We took it from the remains that we were able to . . . scrape from the walls of *Discovery*.'

Remains was the appropriate word for what was left of Hirai's body. Ragged clumps of tissue, splattered throughout the walls of the orbiter. 'Most of the DNA remains unidentifiable. We have no idea what it codes for. But this particular sequence, here on the screen, we can identify. It's the gene for coenzyme F420.'

'Which is?'

'An enzyme specific to the Archaeon domain.'

Roman sat back, feeling faintly nauseated. 'So it's confirmed,' he murmured.

'Yes. The organism definitely has Archaeon DNA.' Carlos paused. 'I'm afraid there's bad news.'

'What do you mean, "bad news"? Isn't this bad enough?'

Carlos tapped on the keyboard and the nucleotide sequence scrolled to a different segment. 'This is another gene cluster we found. I thought at first it had to be a mistake, but I've since confirmed it. It's a match with *Rana pipiens*. The northern leopard frog.'

'What?'

'That's right. Lord knows how it picked up frog genes. Now here's where it gets really scary.' Carlos scrolled to yet another segment of the genome. 'Another identifiable cluster,' he said.

Roman felt a chill creeping up his spine. 'And what are these genes?'

'This DNA is specific to *Mus musculis*. The common mouse.'

Roman stared at him. 'That's impossible.'

'I've confirmed it. This life-form has somehow incorporated mammalian DNA into its genome. It's added new enzymatic capabilities. It's changing. Evolving.'

Into what? Roman wondered.

'There's more.' Again Carlos tapped on the keyboard, and a new sequence of nucleotide bases scrolled onto the monitor. 'This cluster is not of Archaeon origin, either.'

'What is this? More mouse DNA?'

'No. This part is human.'

The chill shot all the way up Roman's spine. The hairs on the back of his neck were bristling. Numbly he reached for the telephone.

'Connect me to the White House,' he said. 'I need to speak to Jared Profitt.'

His call was answered on the second ring. 'This is Profitt.'

'We've analyzed the DNA,' said Roman.

'And?'

'The situation is worse than we thought.'

18

Nicolai paused to rest, his arms trembling from fatigue. After months of living in space, his body had grown weak and unaccustomed to physical labor. In microgravity there is no heavy lifting and little need to exert one's muscles. In the last five hours, he and Luther had worked nonstop, had repaired the S-band antennas, had dismantled and reassembled the gimbal. Now he was exhausted. Just the extra effort of bending his arms in the turgid EVA suit made simple tasks difficult.

Working in the suit was an ordeal in itself. To insulate the human body from extreme temperatures ranging from -250 to 250 degrees Fahrenheit and to maintain pressure against the vacuum of space, the suit was constructed of multiple layers of aluminized Mylar insulation, nylon ripstop, an Ortho-fabric cover, and a pressure-garment bladder. Beneath the suit, an astronaut wore an undergarment laced with water-cooling tubes. He also had to wear a life-support backpack containing water, oxygen, self-rescue jet pack, and radio equipment. In essence, the EVA suit was a personal spacecraft, bulky and difficult to maneuver in, and just the act of tightening a screw required strength and concentration.

The work had exhausted Nicolai. His hands were cramping in the clumsy space suit gloves, and he was sweating.

He was also hungry.

He took a sip of water from the mouthpiece mounted inside his suit and released a heavy sigh. Though the water tasted strange, almost fishy, he thought nothing of it. Everything tasted strange in microgravity. He took another sip and felt wetness splash onto his jaw. He could not reach into his helmet to brush it away, so he ignored it and gazed down at the earth. That sudden glimpse of it, spread out in breathtaking glory beneath him, made him feel a little dizzy, a little nauseated. He closed his eyes, waiting for the feeling to pass. It was motion sickness, nothing more; it often happened when you unexpectedly caught sight of earth. As his stomach settled, he became aware of a new sensation: The spilled water was now trickling up his cheek. He twitched his face, trying to shake off the droplet, but it continued to slide across his skin.

But I am in microgravity, where there is no up or down. Water should not be trickling at all.

He began to shake his head, tapped his gloved hand on his helmet.

Still he felt the droplet moving up his face, tracing a wet line up his jaw. Toward his ear. It had reached the edge of his comm-assembly cap now. Surely the fabric would soak up the moisture, would prevent it from trickling further . . .

All at once his body went rigid. The wetness had slid beneath the edge of the cap. It was now squirming toward his ear. Not a droplet of water, not a stray trickle, but something that moved with purpose. *Something alive.*

He thrashed left, then right, trying to dislodge it. He banged hard on his helmet. And still he felt it moving, sliding under his comm assembly.

He caught dizzying glimpses of earth, then black space, then earth again, as he flailed and twisted around in a frantic dance.

The wetness slithered into his ear.

'Nicolai? Nicolai, please respond!' said Emma, watching him on the TV monitor. He was turning around and around, gloved hands battering frantically at his helmet. 'Luther, he looks like he's having a seizure!'

Luther appeared on camera, moving quickly to assist his EVA partner. Nicolai kept thrashing, shaking his head back and forth. Emma could hear them on UHF, Luther asking frantically, 'What is it, what is it?'

'My ear – It is in my ear –'

'Pain? Does your ear hurt? *Look* at me!'

Nicolai slapped his helmet again. 'It's going *deeper!*' he screamed. 'Get it out! Get it out!'

'What's wrong with him?' cried Emma.

'I don't know! Jesus, he's panicking –'

'He's getting too close to the tool stanchion. Get him away before he damages his suit!'

On the TV monitor, Luther grabbed his partner by the arm. 'Come on, Nicolai! We're going back in the air lock.'

Suddenly Nicolai clutched at his helmet, as though to rip it off.

'No! *Don't!*' screamed Luther, clutching at both of his partner's arms in a desperate attempt to restrain him. The men thrashed together, umbilical tethers winding, tangling around them.

Griggs and Diana had joined Emma at the TV monitor, and the three of them watched in horror as the drama unfolded outside the station.

'Luther, the tool stanchion!' said Griggs. 'Watch your suits!'

Even as he said it, Nicolai suddenly and violently twisted in Luther's grasp. His helmet slammed into the tool stanchion. A fine stream of what looked like white mist suddenly spurted out of his faceplate.

'Luther!' cried Emma. 'Check his helmet! Check his helmet!'

Luther stared at Nicolai's faceplate. 'Shit, he's got a crack!' he yelled. 'I can see air leaking out! He's decompressing!'

'Tap his emergency O_2 and get him in *now!*'

Luther reached over and flipped the emergency oxygen supply switch on Nicolai's suit. The extra

305

airflow might keep the suit inflated long enough for Nicolai to make it back alive. Still struggling to keep his partner under control, Luther began to haul him toward the air lock.

'Hurry,' murmured Griggs. 'Jesus, *hurry.*'

It took precious minutes for Luther to drag his partner into the crew lock, for the hatch to be closed and the atmosphere repressurized. They didn't wait for the usual air-lock integrity check, but pumped the pressure straight up to one atmosphere.

The hatch swung open, and Emma dove through into the equipment lock.

Luther had already removed Nicolai's helmet and was frantically trying to pull him out of the upper torso shell. Working together, they wriggled a struggling Nicolai out of the rest of his EVA suit. Emma and Griggs dragged him through the station and into the RSM, where there was full power and light. He was screaming all the way, clawing at the left side of his comm-assembly cap. Both eyes were swollen shut, the lids ballooned out. She touched his cheeks and felt crepitus – air trapped in the subcutaneous tissues from the decompression. A line of spittle glistened on his jaw.

'Nicolai, calm down!' said Emma. 'You're all right, do you hear me? You'll be all right!'

He shrieked and yanked off the comm cap. It went flying away.

'Help me get him onto the board!' said Emma.

It took all hands to set up the medical restraint board, strip off Nicolai's ventilation long johns, and strap him down. They had him fully restrained now. Even as Emma checked his heart and lungs and examined his abdomen, he continued to whimper and rock his head from side to side.

'It's his ear,' said Luther. He had shed his bulky EVA suit and was staring wide-eyed at the tormented Nicolai. 'He said there was something in his ear.'

Emma looked closer at Nicolai's face. At the line of spittle that traced from his chin, up the curve of his left jaw. To his ear. A drop of moisture was smeared on the pinna.

She turned on the battery-powered otoscope and inserted the earpiece into Nicolai's canal.

The first thing she saw was blood. A bright drop of it, glistening in the otoscope's light. Then she focused on the eardrum.

It was perforated. Instead of the gleam of the tympanic membrane, she saw a black and gaping hole. *Barotrauma* was her first thought. Had the sudden decompression blown out his eardrum? She checked the other eardrum, but it was intact.

Puzzled, she turned off the otoscope and looked at Luther. 'What happened out there?'

'I don't know. We were both taking a breather. Resting up before we brought the tools back in. One minute he's fine, the next minute he's panicking.'

'I need to look at his helmet.'

She left the RSM and headed back to the equipment lock. She swung open the hatch and gazed in, at the two EVA suits, which Luther had remounted on the wall.

'What are you doing, Watson?' said Griggs, who'd followed her.

'I want to see how big the crack was. How fast he was decompressing.'

She went to the smaller EVA suit, labeled 'Rudenko,' and removed the helmet. Peering inside, she saw a dab of moisture adhering to the cracked faceplate. She took out a cotton swab from one of her patch pockets and touched the tip to the fluid. It was thick and gelatinous. Blue-green.

A chill slithered up her spine.

Kenichi was in here, she suddenly remembered. *The night he died, we found him in this air lock. He has somehow contaminated it.*

At once she was backing out in panic, colliding with Griggs in the hatchway. 'Out!' she cried. 'Get out now!'

'What is it?'

'I think we've got a biohazard! Close the hatch! Close it!'

They both scrambled out of the air lock, into the node. Together they slammed the hatch shut and sealed it tight. They exchanged tense glances.

'You think anything leaked out?' Griggs said.

Emma scanned the node, searching for any droplets spinning through the air. At first glance she saw nothing. Then a flash of movement, a telltale sparkle, seemed to dance at the furthest periphery of her vision.

She turned to stare at it. And it was gone.

Jack sat at the surgeon's console in Special Vehicle Operations, his tension growing with every passing minute as he watched the clock on the front screen. The voices coming over his headset were speaking with new urgency, the chatter fast and staccato, as status reports flew back and forth between the controllers and ISS flight director Woody Ellis. Similar in layout to the shuttle Flight Control Room and housed in the same building, the SVO room was a smaller, more specialized version, manned by a team dedicated only to space station operations. Over the last thirty-six hours, ever since *Discovery* had collided with ISS, this room had been the scene of relentlessly mounting anxiety, laced with intermittent panic. With so many people in the room, so many hours of unrelieved stress, the air itself smelled of crisis, the mingled odors of sweat and stale coffee.

Nicolai Rudenko was suffering from decompression injuries and clearly needed to be evacuated. Because there was only one lifeboat – the Crew Return Vehicle – the entire crew was coming home. This would be a controlled evacuation. No shortcuts, no mistakes. No panic. NASA had run through this simulation many times before, but a CRV evac had never actually been done, not with five living, breathing human beings aboard.

Not with someone I love aboard.

Jack was sweating, almost sick with dread.

He kept glancing at the clock, cross-checking it with his watch. They had waited for ISS's orbital path to reach the right position before vehicle separation could proceed. The goal was to bring the CRV down in the most direct approach possible to a landing site immediately accessible to medical personnel. The entire crew would need assistance. After weeks of living in space, they would be weak as kittens, their muscles unable to support them.

The time for separation was approaching. It would take them twenty-five minutes to coast away from ISS and acquire GPS guidance, fifteen minutes for the deorbit burn setup. An hour to land.

In less than two hours, Emma would be back on earth. *One way or another.* The thought came before he could suppress it. Before he could stop himself from remembering the terrible sight of Jill Hewitt's flayed body on the autopsy table.

He clenched his hands into fists, forcing himself to concentrate on Nicolai Rudenko's biotelemetry readings. The heart rate was fast but regular; blood pressure holding steady. *Come on, come on. Let's bring them home now.*

He heard Griggs, on board ISS, report, 'Capcom, my crew is all aboard the CRV and the hatch is closed. It's a little cozy in here, but we're ready when you are.'

'Stand by to power up,' said Capcom.

'Standing by.'

'How is the patient doing?'

Jack's heart gave a leap as he heard Emma's voice join the loop. 'His vitals remain stable, but he's disoriented times three. The crepitus has migrated to his neck and upper torso, and it's causing him some discomfort. I've given him another dose of morphine.'

The sudden decompression had caused air bubbles to form in his soft tissues. The condition was harmless, but painful. What Jack worried about were air bubbles in the nervous system. Could that be the reason Nicolai was confused?

Woody Ellis said, 'Go for power up. Remove ECCLES seals.'

'ISS,' said Capcom, 'you are now go for –'

'Belay that!' a voice cut in.

Jack looked at Flight Director Ellis in confusion. Ellis looked just as confused. He turned to face JSC director Ken Blankenship, who'd just walked into the room, accompanied by a dark-haired man in a suit and a half dozen Air Force officers.

'I'm sorry, Woody,' said Blankenship. 'Believe me, this is not my decision.'

'What decision?' said Ellis.

'The evacuation is off.'

'We have a sick man up there! The CRV's ready to go –'

'He can't come home.'

'Whose decision is that?'

The dark-haired man stepped forward. He said, with what was almost a quiet note of apology, 'The decision is mine. I'm Jared Profitt, White House Security Council. Please tell your crew to reopen the hatches and exit the CRV.'

'My crew is in trouble,' said Ellis. 'I'm bringing them home.'

Trajectory cut in, 'Flight, we have to go to sep now if we want them landing on target.'

Ellis nodded to Capcom. 'Proceed to CRV power up. Let's go to sep.'

Before Capcom could utter another word, his headset was yanked off and he was hauled from his chair and pushed aside. An Air Force officer took Capcom's place at the console.

'Hey!' yelled Ellis. '*Hey!*'

All the flight controllers froze as the other Air Force officers immediately fanned out across the room. Not a weapon was drawn, but the threat was apparent.

'ISS, do not power up,' said the new Capcom. 'The evacuation has been canceled. Reopen the hatches and exit the CRV.'

A baffled Griggs responded, 'I don't think I copied that, Houston.'

'The evacuation is off. Exit the CRV. We are experiencing difficulties with both TOPO and GNC computers. Flight has decided it's best to hold off the evac.'

'How long?'

'Indefinitely.'

Jack shot to his feet, ready to wrestle away Capcom's headset.

Jared Profitt suddenly stepped in front of him, barring his way. 'You don't understand the situation, sir.'

'My wife is on that station. We're bringing her home.'

'They can't come home. They may all be infected.'

'With what?'

Profitt didn't answer.

In fury, Jack lunged toward him, but was hauled back by two Air Force officers.

'Infected with *what?*' Jack yelled.

'A new organism,' said Profitt. 'A chimera.'

Jack looked at Blankenship's stricken face. He looked at the Air Force officers who now stood poised to assume control of the consoles. Then he noticed another familiar face: that of Leroy Cornell, who'd just come into the room. Cornell looked pale and shaken. That's when Jack understood that this decision had been made at the very top. That nothing he, or Blankenship, or Woody Ellis said would make a difference.

NASA was no longer in control.

THE CHIMERA

19

They gathered at Jack's house, where all the shades were drawn. They didn't dare meet at JSC, where they would most certainly be noticed. They were all so stunned by the sudden takeover of NASA operations they had no idea how to proceed. This was one crisis for which they had no operations manual, no contingency plans. Jack had invited only a handful of people, all of them from inside NASA operations: Todd Cutler, Gordon Obie, Flight Directors Woody Ellis and Randy Carpenter, and Liz Gianni from the Payload Directorate.

The doorbell rang, and everyone tensed.

'He's here,' said Jack, and he opened the door.

Dr Eli Petrovitch from NASA's Life Sciences Directorate stepped in, clutching a laptop carrying case. He was a thin and fragile man who, for the past two years, had been battling lymphoma. Clearly he was losing the war. Most of his hair had fallen out, and only a few brittle white strands remained. His skin looked like yellowed parchment, stretched over the jutting bones of his face. But there was the glow of excitement in his eyes, lit by a scientist's unflagging curiosity.

'Did we get it?' asked Jack.

Petrovitch nodded and patted his briefcase. On that skeletal face, his smile looked ghoulish. 'USAMRIID has agreed to share some of its data.'

'Some?'

'Not all. Much of the genome remains classified. We were given only parts of the sequence, with large gaps. They're showing us just enough to prove that the situation is grave.' He carried the laptop to the dining room table and flipped it open. As everyone crowded around to watch, Petrovitch booted up the computer, then slipped in a floppy disk.

Data began to scroll down, line after line of seemingly random letters marching at a dizzying pace down the screen. It was not text; these letters did not spell out words at all, but a code. The same four letters reappeared again and again, in a changing sequence: *A*, *T*, *G*, and *C*. They represented the nucleotides adenine, thymine, guanine, and cytosine. The building blocks that made up DNA. This string of letters was a genome, the chemical blueprint for a living organism.

'This,' said Petrovitch, 'is their chimera. The organism that killed Kenichi Hirai.'

'What *is* this "*ky-mir-ra*" thing I keep hearing

about?' asked Randy Carpenter. 'For the sake of us ignorant engineers, maybe you could explain it?'

'Certainly,' said Petrovitch. 'And there's no reason to feel ignorant. It's not a term used much outside of molecular biology. The word comes from the ancient Greeks. Chimera was a mythological beast, said to be unconquerable. A fire-breathing creature with a lion's head, a goat's body, and a serpent's tail. She was eventually slain by a hero named Bellerophon. It wasn't exactly a fair fight, because he cheated. He hitched a ride on Pegasus, the winged horse, and shot arrows down at Chimera from above.'

'This mythology is interesting,' cut in Carpenter impatiently, 'but what's the relevance?'

'The Greek Chimera was a bizarre creature made up of three different animals. Lion, goat, and serpent, all combined into one. And that's exactly what we're seeing here, in this chromosome. A creature as bizarre as the beast killed by Bellerophon. This is a *biological* chimera whose DNA comes from at least three unrelated species.'

'Can you identify those species?' asked Carpenter.

Petrovitch nodded. 'Over the years, scientists around the world have amassed a library of gene sequences from a variety of species, from viruses to elephants. But collecting this data is slow and tedious. It's taken decades just to analyze the human genome. So as you can imagine, there are a number of species that haven't been sequenced. Large areas of this chimera's genome can't be identified; they're nowhere in the library. But here's what we have been able to identify so far.' He clicked on the icon for 'species matches.'

On the screen appeared:

Mus musculis (common mouse)
Rana pipiens (northern leopard frog)
Homo sapiens

'This organism is part mouse, part amphibian. And part human.' He paused. 'In a sense,' he said, 'the enemy is *us*.'

The room fell silent.

'Which of our genes is on that chromosome?' Jack asked softly. 'What part of Chimera is human?'

'An interesting question,' said Petrovitch, nodding in approval. 'It deserves an interesting answer. You and Dr Cutler will appreciate the significance of this list.' He typed on the keyboard.

On the screen appeared:

Amylase
Lipase
Phospholipase A
Trypsin
Chymotrypsin
Elastase
Enterokinase

'My God,' murmured Todd Cutler. 'These are all digestive enzymes.'

The organism is primed to devour its host, thought Jack. *It uses these enzymes to digest us from the inside, reducing our muscles and organs and connective tissue to little more than a foul soup.*

'Jill Hewitt – she told us Hirai's body had disintegrated,' said Randy Carpenter. 'I thought she was hallucinating.'

Jack said suddenly, 'This has got to be a bioengineered organism! Someone cooked this thing up in a lab. Took a bacteria or virus and grafted on genes from other species, to make it a more effective killing machine.'

'But *which* bacteria? *Which* virus?' said Petrovitch. 'That's the mystery here. Without more of the genome to examine, we can't identify which species they started off with. USAMRIID refuses to show us the most important part of this organism's chromosome. The part that identifies this killer.' He looked at Jack. 'You're the only one here who's actually seen the pathology at autopsy.'

'It was only a glimpse. They pushed me out of the room so fast I barely got a look. What I saw appeared to be some sort of cysts. The size of pearls, embedded in a blue-green matrix. They were in Mercer's thorax and abdomen. In Hewitt's cranium. I've never seen anything like it before.'

'Could they have been hydatid cysts?' asked Petrovitch.

'What's that?' asked Woody.

'It's an infection by the larval stage of a parasitic tapeworm called *echinococcus*. It causes cysts in the liver and lungs. For that matter, in any organ.'

'You think this could be a parasite?'

Jack shook his head. 'Hydatid cysts take a long time to grow. Years, not days. I don't think this was a parasite.'

'Maybe they weren't cysts at all,' said Todd. 'Maybe they were spores. Fungus balls. *Aspergillus* or *cryptococcus*.'

Liz Gianni from Payloads cut in, 'The crew reported a problem with fungal contamination. One of the experiments had to be destroyed because of overgrowth.'

'Which experiment?' asked Todd.

'I'd have to look it up. I remember it was one of the cell cultures.'

'But simple fungal contamination wouldn't account for these deaths,' said Petrovitch. 'Remember, there were fungi floating around *Mir* all the time, and no one died of it.' He looked at the computer screen. 'This genome tells us we're dealing with an entirely new life-form. I agree with Jack. It must have been engineered.'

'So it's bioterrorism,' said Woody Ellis. 'Someone's sabotaged our station. They must have sent it up in one of the payloads.'

Liz Gianni vigorously shook her head. Aggressive and intense, she was a forceful presence at any meeting, and she spoke up now with absolute assurance. 'Every payload goes through safety review. There are hazard reports, three-phase analyses of all containment devices. Believe me, we would have nixed anything this dangerous.'

'Assuming you knew it was dangerous,' said Ellis.

'Of course we'd know!'

'What if there was a breach in security?' said Jack. 'Many of the experimental payloads arrive directly from the principal investigators – the scientists themselves. We don't know what *their* security is like. We don't know if they have a terrorist working in their lab. If they switched a bacterial culture at the last minute, would we necessarily know?'

For the first time Liz looked uncertain. 'It . . . it's unlikely.'

'But it could happen.'

Though she wouldn't admit the possibility, dismay registered in her eyes. 'We'll grill every principal investigator,' she said. 'Every scientist who sent up an experiment. If they had a lapse in security, I'm fucking well gonna find out about it.'

She probably will, thought Jack. Like the other men in the room, he was a little afraid of Liz Gianni.

'There's one question we haven't asked yet,' said Gordon Obie, speaking up for the first time. As always, he'd been the Sphinx, listening without comment, silently processing information. 'The question is *Why?* Why would anyone sabotage

323

the station? Is this someone with a grudge against us? A fanatic opposed to technology?'

'The biological equivalent of the Unabomber,' said Todd Cutler.

'Then why not just release the organism at JSC and kill off our infrastructure? That would be easier, and far more logical.'

'You can't apply logic to a fanatic,' Cutler pointed out.

'You can apply logic to everyone, including fanatics,' Gordon responded. 'As long as you know the framework in which they operate. And that's why this bothers me. That's why I wonder if we're really dealing with sabotage.'

'What else would it be,' said Jack, 'if *not* sabotage?'

'There is another possibility. It could be something just as frightening,' said Gordon, his troubled gaze lifting to Jack's. 'A mistake.'

Dr Isaac Roman ran down the hall, his pager alarm squealing on his belt, dreading what he was about to face. He silenced the pager and opened the door leading into the Level 4 isolation suite. He did not enter the patient's room, but stood safely outside and stared at the horror unfolding beyond the observation window.

There was blood splattered on the walls and pooling on the floor where Dr Nathan Helsinger lay seizing. Two nurses and a physician in space suits were trying to stop him from injuring himself, but his spasms were so violent and so powerful they could not restrain him. His leg shot out and a nurse went sprawling, sliding across the blood-slicked concrete floor.

Roman hit the intercom button. 'Your suit! Is there a breach?'

As she slowly rose to her feet, he could see her expression of terror. She looked down at her gloves, her sleeves, then at the juncture where the hose fed air into her suit. 'No,' she said, and it was almost a sob of relief. 'No breach.'

Blood splattered the window. Roman jerked back as bright droplets trickled down the glass. Helsinger was banging his head against the floor now, his spine relaxing, then hyperextending. Opisthotonos. Roman had seen this bizarre posture only once before, in a victim of strychnine poisoning, the body curved backward like a bow strung under tension. Helsinger spasmed again, and his skull slammed backward against the concrete. Blood sprayed the faceplates of the two nurses.

'Back off!' Roman commanded through the intercom.

'He's hurting himself!' said the physician.

'I don't want anyone else exposed.'

'If we could get these seizures under control –'

'There's nothing you can do to save him. I want you all to move away *now*. Before you get hurt.'

Reluctantly the two nurses backed away. After a pause, so did the physician. They stood in silent tableau as the scene of horror played out at their feet.

New convulsions sent Helsinger's head whipping backward. The scalp split open, like cloth ripping along a seam. The pool of blood widened into a lake.

'Oh, God, look at his eyes!' one of the nurses cried.

The eyes were popping out, like two giant marbles straining to burst out of the sockets. *Traumatic proptosis*, thought Roman. The eyeballs thrust forward by catastrophic intracranial pressure, the lids shoved apart, wide and staring.

The seizures continued, unrelenting, the head battering the floor. Splinters of bone flew up and ticked against the window. It was as though he were trying to crack open his own skull, to release whatever was trapped inside.

Another crack. Another spattering of blood and bone.

He should have been dead. Why was he still seizing?

But even decapitated chickens continue to twitch and thrash, and Helsinger's death throes were not yet over. His head lifted off the floor, his spine curling forward like a spring winding up to unbearable tension just before it snaps. His neck lashed backward. There was a *crack*, and the skull split open like an egg. Shards of bone flew. A lump of gray matter splashed the window.

Roman gasped and stumbled backward, nausea

rising in his throat. He dropped his head, fighting to stay in control. Fighting the darkness that threatened to envelop his vision.

Sweating, shaking, he managed to lift his head. To look, once again, through the window.

Nathan Helsinger at last lay still. What was left of his head rested in a lake of blood. There was so much blood that for a moment Roman could not focus on anything else but that spreading pool of scarlet. Then his gaze settled on the dead man's face. On the blue-green mass that clung, quivering, to his forehead. Cysts.

Chimera.

August 14

'Nicolai? Nicolai, please respond!'

'My ear – It is in my ear –'

'Pain? Does your ear hurt? Look *at me!'*

'It's going deeper! Get it out! Get it . . .'

White House Security Council science adviser Jared Profitt pressed the OFF button on the cassette recorder and looked at the men and women seated around the table. All of them wore expressions of horror. 'What happened to Nicolai Rudenko was more than just a decompressive accident,' he said. 'That's why we took the action we did. That's why I urge you all to stay the course. There's too much at stake. Until we learn more about this organism – how it reproduces, how it infects – we can't let those astronauts come home.'

The response was stunned silence. Even NASA administrator Leroy Cornell, who had led off the meeting with an outraged protest about the takeover of his agency, sat utterly speechless.

It was the president who asked the first question. 'What *do* we know about this organism?'

'Dr Isaac Roman from USAMRIID can answer that better than I can,' said Profitt, and he nodded to Roman, who was not seated at the table, but on the periphery, where he'd been largely unnoticed by everyone in the room. Now he stood so that he could be seen, a tall and graying man with the look of exhaustion in his eyes.

'I'm afraid the news is not good,' he said. 'We've injected Chimera into a number of different mammalian species including dogs and spider monkeys. Within ninety-six hours, all were dead. A mortality rate of one hundred percent.'

'And there's no treatment? Nothing has worked?' asked the secretary of defense.

'Nothing. Which is frightening enough. But there's worse news.'

The room went very still as fear rippled across faces. How could this get any worse?

'We have repeated the DNA analysis of the most recent generation of eggs, collected from the dead monkeys. Chimera has acquired yet a new cluster of genes, specific to *Ateles geoffroyi*. The spider monkey.'

The president blanched. He looked at Profitt. 'Does this mean what I think it means?'

'It's devastating,' said Profitt. 'Every time this life-form cycles through a new host, every time it produces a new generation, it seems to acquire new DNA. It has the ability to stay several steps ahead of us by picking up new genes, new capabilities it's never had before.'

'How the hell can it do this?' asked General Moray of the Joint Chiefs of Staff. 'An organism that picks up new genes? That keeps remaking itself? It sounds impossible.'

Roman said, 'It's not impossible, sir. In fact, a similar process occurs in nature. Bacteria often share genes with each other, trading them back and forth by using viruses as couriers. That's how they develop antibiotic resistance so quickly. They spread around the genes for resistance, adding new DNA to their chromosomes. Like everything else in nature, they'll use every weapon they have to survive. To perpetuate their species. That's what this organism is doing.' He moved to the head of the table, where a blowup of an electron micrograph was displayed. 'You can see here, in this photograph of the cell, what looks like tiny granules. They're clumps of helper virus. Couriers that travel into the host cell, raid its DNA, and bring back bits and pieces of genetic material to Chimera. Adding new genes, new weapons to its arsenal.' Roman looked at the president. 'This organism came equipped to survive any environmental conditions. All it needs to do is raid the local fauna's DNA.'

The president looked ill. 'So it's still changing. Still evolving.'

There were murmurs of dismay around the table. Frightened glances, creaking chairs.

'What about that doctor who got infected?' asked a woman from the Pentagon. 'The one USAMRIID had in Level Four isolation? Is he still alive?'

Roman paused, a look of pain in his eyes. 'Dr Helsinger died late last night. I witnessed the terminal event and it was . . . a horrible death. He began to convulse so violently we didn't dare control him for fear someone's space suit would be torn and someone else exposed. These were seizures unlike any I've ever seen. It was as though every single neuron in his brain fired at once in a massive electrical storm. He broke the bed rail. Snapped it cleanly off the frame. Rolled off the mattress and began to – to batter his head on the floor. So hard, we could . . .' He swallowed. 'We could hear the skull crack. By then there was blood flying everywhere. He kept smashing his head against the floor, almost as if he was trying to break it open. To release the pressure building up inside. The trauma only made it worse, because he began to bleed into his brain. At the end, the intracranial pressure was so great, it bulged his eyes out of their sockets. Like a cartoon character. Like an animal you see squashed on the road.' He took a deep breath. 'That,' he said quietly, 'was the terminal event.'

'Now you understand the possible epidemic we

330

face,' said Profitt. 'This is why we can't afford to be weak or careless. Or sentimental.'

There was another long silence. Everyone looked at the president. They were all waiting for – hoping for – an unequivocal decision.

Instead, he swiveled his chair toward the window and stared outside. 'I wanted to be an astronaut, once,' he said sadly.

Didn't we all? thought Profitt. *Which child in this country has not dreamed of riding a rocket into space?*

'I was there when they launched John Glenn on the shuttle,' the president said. 'And I cried. Just like everyone else. Goddamn it, but I cried like a baby. Because I was proud of him. And proud of this country. And proud of just being part of the human race . . .' He paused. Took a deep breath and wiped his hand across his eyes. 'How the hell do I condemn those people to death?'

Profitt and Roman exchanged unhappy glances.

'We have no choice, sir,' said Profitt. 'It's five lives versus the lives of God knows how many people here on earth.'

'They're *heroes*. Honest-to-God heroes. And we're going to leave them up there to die.'

'The chances are, Mr President, we wouldn't be able to save them anyway,' said Roman. 'All of them are probably infected. Or they soon will be.'

'Then some of them may *not* be infected?'

'We don't know. We do know Rudenko definitely is. We believe he was exposed while in his EVA suit. If you'll recall, Astronaut Hirai was

331

found seizing in the EVA equipment lock ten days ago. That would explain how the suit got contaminated.'

'Why aren't the others sick yet? Why only Rudenko?'

'Our studies indicate this organism needs incubation time before it reaches the infectious stage. We think it's most contagious around the time the host dies, or afterwards, when it's released from the corpse. But we're not certain. We can't afford to be wrong. We have to assume they're all carriers.'

'Then keep them in Level Four isolation until you know. But at least get them *home*.'

'Sir, that's where the risk comes in,' said Profitt. 'In just bringing them home. The CRV's not like the shuttle, which you actually guide down to a specific landing strip. They'd be coming home in a far less controllable vehicle – essentially a pod with parachutes. What if something goes wrong? What if the CRV breaks up in the atmosphere, or crashes on landing? This organism would be released into the air. The wind could carry it anywhere! By then, it will have so much human DNA in its genome, we won't be able to fight it. It will be too much like *us*. Any drug we use against it would kill humans as well.' Profitt paused, letting the impact of his words sink in. 'We can't let emotions affect our decision. Not with so much at stake.'

'Mr President,' cut in Leroy Cornell, 'with all due respect, may I point out that this would be a politically disastrous move. The public will not allow five heroes to die in space.'

'Politics should be our last concern right now!' said Profitt. 'Our first priority is public health!'

'Then why the secrecy? Why have you cut NASA out of the loop? You've shown us only parts of the organism's genome. Our life-sciences people are ready and willing to contribute their expertise. We want to find a cure every bit as much as – even more than – you do. If USAMRIID would just share all its data with us, we could work together.'

'Our concern is security,' said General Moray. 'A hostile country could turn this into a devastating bioweapon. Giving out Chimera's genetic code is like handing out a blueprint for that weapon.'

'Meaning you don't trust NASA with that information?'

General Moray met Cornell's gaze head-on. 'I'm afraid NASA's new philosophy of sharing technology with every two-bit country under the sun does not make your agency a good security risk.'

Cornell flushed with anger but said nothing.

Profitt looked at the president. 'Sir, it *is* a tragedy that five astronauts must be left up there to die. But we have to look beyond that, to the possibility of a far greater tragedy. A worldwide epidemic, caused by an organism we're just beginning to understand. USAMRIID is working around the clock to learn what makes it tick. Until then, I urge you to stay the course. NASA is not equipped to deal with a biological disaster. They have one planetary-protection officer. *One*. The Army's Biological Rapid Response Team is prepared for just this sort of crisis. As for NASA operations, leave that under the control of U.S. Space Command, backed up by the Fourteenth Air Force. NASA has too many personal and emotional ties to the astronauts. We need a firm grip on the helm. We need absolute discipline.' Profitt slowly looked around at the men and women seated at the long table. Only a few of these people did he truly respect. Some were interested only in prestige and power. Others had earned a seat here because of political connections. Still others were easily swayed by public sentiment. Few had motives as uncomplicated as his.

Few had suffered his nightmares, had awakened soaked with sweat in the darkness, shaken by the terrible vision of what they might face.

'Then you're saying the astronauts can never come home,' said Cornell.

Profitt looked at the NASA administrator's ashen face and felt genuine sympathy. 'When we find a way to cure it, when we know we can kill this organism, then we can talk about bringing your people home.'

'If they're still alive,' murmured the president.

Profitt and Roman glanced at each other, but neither responded. They already understood the obvious. They would not find a cure in time. The astronauts would not be coming home alive.

*   *   *

Jared Profitt wore his jacket and tie as he walked through that sweltering day, but he scarcely noticed the heat. Others might complain of the miseries of a D.C. summer. He did not mind the soaring temperatures. It was winter he dreaded, because he was so sensitive to cold, and on frosty days his lips would turn blue and he'd shiver under layers of scarves and sweaters. Even in summer he kept a sweater in his office to combat the effects of the air conditioner. Today the temperature was in the nineties, and perspiration gleamed on all the faces he passed on the street, but he did not remove his jacket or loosen his tie.

The meeting had left him deeply chilled, both in body and soul.

He was carrying his lunch in a brown paper bag, the identical lunch he packed every morning before he left for work. The route he walked was the one he always took, west toward the Potomac, the Reflecting Pool on his left. He took comfort in the routine, the familiar. There were so few things in his life that offered much reassurance these days, and as he grew older, he found himself adhering to certain rituals, much as a monk in a religious order adheres to the daily rhythm of work and prayer and meditation. In many ways, he was like those ancient ascetics, a man who ate only to fuel his body and dressed in suits only because it was required of him. A man for whom wealth meant nothing.

The name *Profitt* could not be further from the reality of the man.

He slowed his pace as he walked along the grassy slope past the Vietnam War Memorial, and gazed down at the solemn line of visitors shuffling past the wall etched with names of the dead. He knew what they were all thinking as they confronted those panels of black granite, as they considered the horrors of war: *So many names. So many dead.*

And he thought, *You have no idea.*

He found an empty bench in the shade and sat down to eat. From his brown bag he removed an apple, a wedge of cheddar, and a bottle of water. Not Evian or Perrier, but straight from the tap. He ate slowly, watching the tourists as they made the circuit from memorial to memorial. *And so we honor our war heroes*, he thought. Society erected statues, engraved marble plaques, raised flags. It shuddered at the number of lives lost on both sides in the slaughterhouse of war. Two million soldiers and civilians dead in Vietnam. Fifty million dead in World War II. Twenty-one million dead in World War I. The numbers were appalling. People might ask: Could man have a more lethal enemy than himself?

The answer was yes.

Though humans could not see it, the enemy was all around them. Inside them. In the air they breathed, the food they drank. Throughout the history of mankind, it has been their nemesis, and it would survive them long after they have vanished from the face of the earth. The enemy was the microbial world, and over the centuries, it has killed more people than all of man's wars combined.

From A.D. 542 to 767, forty million dead of the plague in the Justinian pandemic.

In the 1300s, twenty-five million dead when the Black Death returned.

In 1918 and 1919, thirty million dead of influenza.

And in 1997, Amy Sorensen Profitt, age forty-three, dead of pneumococcal pneumonia.

He finished his apple, placed the core in the brown bag, and carefully rolled his rubbish into a tight bundle. Though the lunch had been meager, he felt satisfied, and he remained on the bench for a while, sipping the last of the water.

A tourist walked by, a woman with light brown hair. When she turned just so and the light slanted across her face, she looked like Amy. She felt him staring, and she glanced his way. They regarded each other for a moment, she with wariness, he with silent apology. Then she walked away, and he decided she did not look like his dead wife after all. No one did. No one could.

He rose to his feet, discarded his trash in a receptacle, and began to walk back the way he'd come. Past the wall. Past the uniformed veterans, gray and shaggy now, keeping vigil. Honoring the memory of the dead.

But even the memories fade, he thought. The image

of her smile across the kitchen table, the echo of her laughter – all those were receding as time went by. Only the painful memories hung on. A San Francisco hotel room. A late-night phone call. Frantic images of airports and taxis and phone booths as he raced across the country to reach Bethesda Hospital in time.

But necrotizing streptococcus has its own agenda, its own timetable for killing. *Just like Chimera*.

He drew in a breath of air and wondered how many viruses, how many bacteria, how many fungi, had just swirled into his lungs. And which of those might kill him.

20

'I say fuck'em,' said Luther. The air-to-ground comm was off, their conversation unmonitored by Mission Control. 'Let's get back on the CRV, flip the switches, and *go*. They can't make us turn around and come back.'

Once they left the station, they *couldn't* turn around. The CRV was essentially a glider with drag chutes. After separation from ISS, it could travel a maximum of four revolutions around the earth before it was forced to deorbit and land.

'We've been advised to sit tight,' said Griggs. 'That's exactly what we're going to do.'

'Follow stupid shit orders? Nicolai's going to *die* on us if we don't get him home!'

Griggs looked at Emma. 'Opinion, Watson?'

For the last twenty-four hours, Emma had been hovering by her patient, monitoring Nicolai's condition. They could all see for themselves that he

339

was in critical condition. Tied down to the medical restraint board, he twitched and trembled, his limbs sometimes flailing out with such violence Emma was afraid he'd snap his bones. He looked like a boxer who had been pummeled mercilessly in the ring. Subcutaneous emphysema had bloated the soft tissues of his face, swelling his eyelids shut. Through the narrow slits, his sclerae were a brilliant, demonic red.

She didn't know how much Nicolai could hear and understand, so she didn't dare say aloud what she was thinking. She motioned her crewmates out of the Russian service module.

They met in the hab, where Nicolai could not hear them, and where they could safely remove their goggles and masks.

'Houston needs to clear our evac now,' she said, 'or we're going to lose him.'

'They're aware of the situation,' said Griggs. 'They can't authorize an evac until the White House clears it.'

'So we're just gonna hang around up here and watch each other get sick?' said Luther. 'What if we just got in the CRV and left? What're they gonna do, shoot us down?'

Diana said quietly, 'They could.'

The truth of what she'd just said made them all fall silent. Every astronaut who had ever climbed aboard the shuttle and sweated through a countdown knew that sitting in a bunker at KSC was a team of Air Force officers whose only job was to blow up the shuttle, incinerating the crew. Should the steering system go awry during launch, should the shuttle veer disastrously toward a populated area, it was the duty of these range-safety officers to press the destruct buttons. They had met every member of the shuttle's flight crew. They had probably seen photographs of the astronauts' families. They knew exactly who they would be killing. It was a terrible responsibility, yet no one doubted those Air Force officers would carry it out.

Just as they would almost certainly destroy the CRV if so ordered. When faced with the specter of a new and lethal epidemic, the lives of five astronauts would seem trivial.

Luther said, 'I'm willing to bet they'll let us land safely. Why wouldn't they? Four of us are still healthy. *We* haven't caught anything.'

'But we've already been exposed,' said Diana. 'We've breathed the same air, shared the same quarters. Luther, you and Nicolai slept together in that air lock.'

'I feel perfectly fine.'

'So do I. So do Griggs and Watson. But if this is an infection, we may already be in the incubation stages.'

'That's why we have to follow orders,' said Griggs. 'We stay right where we are.'

Luther turned to Emma. 'Do you go along with this martyr shit?'

'No,' she said. 'I don't.'

Griggs looked at her in surprise. 'Watson?'

'I'm not thinking about myself,' said Emma. 'I'm thinking about my patient. Nicolai can't talk, so I have to do it for him. I want him in a hospital, Griggs.'

'You heard what Houston said.'

'What I heard was a lot of confusion. Evac Orders being given, then belayed. First they tell us it's Marburg virus. Then they say it's not a virus at all, but some new organism cooked up by bioterrorists. I don't know what the hell's going on down there. All I know is, my patient is . . .' She abruptly lowered her voice. 'He's dying,' she said softly. 'My primary responsibility is to keep him alive.'

'And my responsibility is to act as commander of this station,' said Griggs. 'I have to believe that Houston is calling the shots the best they can. They wouldn't put us in this danger unless the situation was truly grave.'

Emma could not disagree. Mission Control was manned by people she knew, people she trusted. *And Jack is there*, she thought. There was no human being she trusted more than him.

'Looks like we have data being uplinked,' said Diana, glancing at the computer. 'It's for Watson.'

Emma glided across the module to read the message glowing on the screen. It was from NASA Life Sciences.

Dr Watson,
    We think you should know exactly what you're dealing with – what we're all dealing

with. This is the DNA analysis of the organism infecting Kenichi Hirai.

Emma called up the attached file.

It took her a moment to mentally process the nucleotide sequence that flowed across the screen. A few minutes more to actually *believe* the conclusions.

Genes from three *different* species were on one chromosome. Leopard frog. Mouse. And human.

'What is this organism?' asked Diana.

Emma said softly, 'A new life-form.'

It was a Frankenstein's monster. An abomination of nature. She suddenly focused on the word 'mouse,' and she thought, *The mice. They were the first to get sick*. Over the past week and a half they had continued to die. The last time she had checked the cage, only one mouse, a female, was still alive.

She left the hab and headed deeper into the powered-down half of the station.

The U.S. lab was deep in gloom. She floated across the semi-darkness to the animal holding rack. Had the mice been the original carriers for this organism, the vessels in which the chimera had been brought aboard ISS? Or were they just the accidental victims, infected through exposure to something else aboard the station?

And was the last mouse alive?

She opened the rack drawer and peered into the cage at the lone resident.

343

Her heart sank. The mouse was dead.

She had come to think of this female with the chewed-up ear as a fighter, the scrappy survivor who, through sheer orneriness, had outlasted its cage mates. Now Emma felt an unexpected pang of grief as she gazed at the lifeless body floating at the far end of the cage. Its abdomen already looked bloated. The corpse would have to be removed immediately and discarded with the contaminated trash.

She interfaced the cage to the glove box, inserted her hands into the gloves, and reached in to grab the mouse. The instant her fingers closed over it, the corpse suddenly scrabbled to life. Emma gave a scream of surprise and released it.

The mouse flipped over and glared at her, whiskers twitching in irritation.

Emma gave a startled laugh. 'So you're not dead after all,' she murmured.

'Watson!'

She turned toward the intercom, which had just spat out her name. 'I'm in the lab.'

'Get in here! The RSM. Nicolai's seizing!'

She flew out of the lab, caroming off walls in the gloom as she shot toward the Russian end. The first thing she saw as she popped into the RSM were the faces of her crewmates, their horror evident even through their goggles. Then they moved aside and she saw Nicolai.

His left arm was jerking spasmodically and with such power the whole restraint board shuddered.

The seizures marched down the left side of his body, and his leg began to thrash as well. Now his hips were lurching, thrusting off the board as the seizures continued their inexorable march across his body. The jerking intensified, the wrist restraints scraping his skin bloody. Emma heard a sickening *crack* as the bones of his left forearm snapped. The right wrist restraint flew apart, and his arm thrashed unchecked, the back of his hand pummeling the edge of the table, smashing bones and flesh.

'Hold him still! I'm going to pump him full of Valium!' yelled Emma, frantically rummaging inside the medical kit.

Griggs and Luther each grabbed an arm, but even Luther was not powerful enough to control the unrestrained limb. Nicolai's right arm flew up like a whip, flinging Luther aside. Luther went tumbling, and his foot clipped Diana on the cheek, knocking her goggles askew.

Nicolai's head suddenly slammed backward against the table. He gasped in a gurgling breath, and his chest bloated up with air. A cough exploded from his throat.

Phlegm sprayed out, catching Diana in the face. She gave a yelp of disgust and released her grip, drifting backward as she wiped her exposed eye.

A globule of blue-green mucus floated past Emma. Encased in that gelatinous mass was a pearllike kernel. Only as it drifted past the luminaire assembly of the lighting system did Emma realize what she was looking at. When a hen's egg is held in front of a candle flame, the contents can be seen through the shell. Now the luminaire assembly was acting as the candle, its glow penetrating the kernel's opaque membrane.

Inside, something was moving. Something was alive.

The cardiac monitor squealed. Emma spun around to look at Nicolai, and she saw that he had stopped breathing. A flat line traced across the monitor.

August 16

Jack slipped the comm unit on his head. He was alone in a back room of Mission Control, and this conversation was supposed to be confidential, but he knew that what he and Emma said today would not, in fact, be private. He suspected that all communications with ISS were now being monitored by the Air Force and U.S. Space Command.

He said, 'Capcom, this is Surgeon. I'm ready for private family conference.'

'Roger, Surgeon,' said Capcom. 'Ground Control, secure air to ground loop.' There was a pause, then: 'Surgeon, proceed to PFC.'

Jack's heart was pounding. He took a deep breath and said, 'Emma, it's me.'

'He might have lived if we'd gotten him home,' she said. 'He might have had a chance.'

'We weren't the ones who stopped the evac! Again and again, NASA's been overruled. We're

346

fighting to get you home, as soon as possible. If you'll just hang in –'

'It won't be soon enough, Jack.' She said it quietly. Matter-of-factly. Her words chilled him to the marrow. 'Diana is infected,' she said.

'Are you sure?'

'I just ran her amylase level. It's rising. We're watching her now. Waiting for the first symptoms. The stuff flew all over the module. We've cleaned it up, but we're not sure who else was exposed.' She paused, and he heard her take a shaky breath. 'You know those things you saw inside Andy and Jill? The things you thought were cysts? I sectioned one under the microscope. I've just downlinked the images to Life Sciences. They're not cysts, Jack. And they're not spores.'

'What are they?'

'They're eggs. Something is inside them. Something is growing.'

'Growing? Are you saying they're multicellular?'

'Yes. That's exactly what I'm saying.'

He was stunned. He had assumed they were dealing with a microbe, nothing larger than a single-celled bacteria. Mankind's deadliest enemies have always been microbial – bacteria and viruses and protozoa, too small to be seen by the human eye. If Chimera was multicellular, then it was far more advanced than a simple bacteria.

'The one I saw was still unformed,' she said. 'It was more like a – a *cluster* of cells than anything else. But with vascular channels. And contractile movements. As though the whole thing was pulsating, like a culture of myocardial cells.'

'Maybe it *was* a culture. A group of single cells clumped together.'

'No. No, I think it was all one organism. And it was still young, still developing.'

'Into what?'

'USAMRIID knows,' she said. 'These things were growing inside Kenichi Hirai's corpse. Digesting his organs. When his body disintegrated, they must have been splashed all over that orbiter.'

Which the military immediately placed under quarantine, thought Jack, remembering the choppers. The space-suited men.

'They're growing in Nicolai's corpse as well.'

He said, 'Jettison his body, Emma! Don't waste any time.'

'We're doing it now. Luther's preparing to release the body from the air lock. We have to hope the vacuum of space will kill this thing. It's a historic event, Jack. The first human burial in space.' She gave a strange laugh, but it quickly choked off into silence.

'Listen to me,' he said. 'I'm going to bring you home. If I have to ride a goddamn rocket myself and come pick you up.'

'They won't let us come home. I know that now.'

He had never heard such defeat in her voice, and it made him angry. Desperate. 'Don't wimp out on me, Emma!'

'I'm only being realistic. I've seen the enemy, Jack. Chimera is a complex multicellular life-form. It moves. It reproduces. It uses *our* DNA, *our* genes, against us. If this is a bioengineered organism, some terrorist has just created the perfect weapon.'

'Then he must have designed a defense as well. No one unleashes a new weapon without knowing how to protect himself against it.'

'A fanatic might. A terrorist whose only interest is in killing people – lots of people. And this thing could do that. Not only does it kill, it reproduces. It *spreads*.' She paused. And the sound of exhaustion seeped into her voice. 'Given those facts, it's clear we won't be coming home.'

Jack pulled off the comm unit and dropped his head in his hands. For a long time he sat alone in the room, the sound of Emma's voice still vivid in his mind. *I don't know how to save you*, he thought. *I don't even know where to begin*.

He did not hear the door open. Only when Liz Gianni from Payload Operations said his name did he finally look up.

'We have a name,' she said.

He shook his head in bewilderment. 'What?'

'I told you, I was going to look up which experiment had to be destroyed because of fungal over-growth. It turns out it was a cell culture. The principal investigator is a Dr Helen Koenig, a marine biologist out in California.'

'What about her?'

'She's disappeared. She resigned two weeks ago from the lab at SeaScience where she works. Hasn't been heard from since. And Jack, here's the kicker. I just spoke to someone at SeaScience. She told me that federal investigators raided Koenig's lab on August ninth. They removed all her files.'

Jack sat up straight. 'What was Koenig's experiment? What kind of cell culture did she send up?'

'A single-celled marine organism. They're called Archaeons.'

21

'It was supposed to be a three-month protocol,' said Liz. 'A study of how Archaeons multiply in microgravity. The culture began to show some bizarre results. Rapid growth, clump formation. It was multiplying at amazing rates.'

They were walking along one of the pathways that wound through the JSC campus, past a pond where a fountain sprayed water into the listless air. The day was uncomfortably hot and muggy, but they felt safer talking outside; here, at least, they could speak in private.

'Cells behave differently in space,' said Jack. That, in fact, was the reason cultures were grown in orbit. On earth, tissue grows flat like a sheet, covering the surface of the culture plate. In space, the absence of gravity allows tissues to grow in three dimensions, assuming shapes it can never achieve on earth.

'Considering how exciting these developments were,' said Liz, 'it's surprising the experiment was abruptly terminated at six and a half weeks.'

'Who terminated the experiment?' asked Jack.

'The order came directly from Helen Koenig. Apparently, she analyzed the Archaeon samples which had been returned to earth aboard *Atlantis* and found them contaminated by fungi. She ordered the culture on ISS destroyed.'

'And was it?'

'Yes. But the weird part was *how* it was destroyed. The crew wasn't allowed to just bag and dispose of it in the contaminated wet trash, which is what they'd normally do with a nonhazardous organism. No, Koenig told them to put the cultures in the crucible and *incinerate* them. And then to jettison the ash.'

Jack stopped on the path and stared at her. 'If Dr Koenig is a bioterrorist, why would she destroy her own weapon?'

'Your guess is as good as mine.'

He thought about it for a moment, trying to make sense of it, but not coming up with an answer.

'Tell me more about her experiment,' he said. 'What, exactly, *is* an Archaeon?'

'Petrovitch and I reviewed the scientific literature. *Archaeons* are a bizarre domain of single-celled organisms called *extremophiles* – "lovers of extreme conditions." They were discovered only twenty years ago, living – and thriving – near boiling volcanic vents on the sea floor. They've also been found buried in polar ice caps and in rocks deep in the earth's crust. Places we thought life couldn't exist.'

'So they're sort of like hardy bacteria?'

'No, they're a completely separate branch of life. Literally, their name means "the ancient ones." They're so ancient, their origins date back to the universal ancestor of *all* life. A time before even bacteria existed. Archaeons were some of the first inhabitants of our planet, and they'll probably be the last to survive. No matter what happens – nuclear war, asteroid impact – they'll be here, long after we're extinct.' She paused. 'In a sense, they're earth's ultimate conquerors.'

'Are they infectious?'

'No. They're harmless to humans.'

'Then this isn't our killer organism.'

'But what if something *else* was in that culture instead? What if she slipped in a different organism just before she shipped us the payload? I find it interesting that Helen Koenig vanished just as this crisis was heating up.'

Jack said nothing for a moment, his thoughts focused on why Helen Koenig would abruptly order her own experiment incinerated. He remembered what Gordon Obie had said at their meeting. Perhaps this was not an act of sabotage at all, but something just as frightening. A mistake.

'There's more,' said Liz. 'Something else about this experiment that raises the red flag for me.'

'What?'

'How it got funded. Experiments that come from

outside NASA have to compete for room aboard the station. The scientist fills out the OLMSA application, explaining the possible commercial uses for the experiment. It gets reviewed by us and goes through various committees before we prioritize which ones get launched. The process takes a long time – at least a year or more.'

'How long did the Archaeon application take?'

'Six months.'

He frowned. 'It was rushed through that quickly?'

Liz nodded. 'Fast track. It didn't have to compete for NASA funding, like most experiments do. It was a commercial reimbursable. Someone *paid* to send up that experiment.'

That was, in fact, one of the ways NASA kept ISS financially viable – by selling payload space aboard the station to commercial users.

'So why would a company spend big bucks – and I do mean big bucks – to grow a test tube of essentially worthless organisms? Scientific curiosity?' She gave a skeptical snort. 'I don't *think* so.'

'Which company paid for it?'

'The firm Dr Koenig worked for. SeaScience in La Jolla, California. They develop commercial products from the sea.'

The despair Jack had felt earlier was finally lifting. Now he had information to work with. A plan of action. At last he could *do* something.

He said, 'I need the address and phone number

of SeaScience. And the name of that employee you spoke to.'

Liz gave a brisk nod. 'You got it, Jack.'

August 17

Diana awakened from a restless sleep, her head aching, the dreams still clouding her mind. Dreams of England, of her childhood home in Cornwall. Of the neat brick pathway leading to the front door, overhung by climbing roses. In her dream, she had pushed open the little gate and heard it squeal as it always did, the hinges in need of oil. She had started up the walkway to the stone cottage. Only half a dozen paces and she would be on the front stoop, opening the door. Calling out that she was home, at last home. She wanted her mother's hugs, her mother's forgiveness. But the half dozen paces became a dozen. Two dozen. And still the cottage was out of reach, the pathway stretching longer and longer until the house had receded to the size of a doll's.

Diana awakened with both arms reaching out, a cry of despair bursting from her throat.

She opened her eyes and saw Michael Griggs staring at her. Though his face was partly obscured by a protective filter mask and goggles, she could see his expression of horror.

She unzipped her sleep restraint and floated across the Russian service module. Even before she looked in the mirror at her own reflection, she knew what she would see.

A flame of brilliant red was splashed across the white of her left eye.

Emma and Luther spoke in hushed voices as they floated together in the dimly lit hab. Most of the station was still in power down; only the Russian segment, which had its own self-contained electrical supply, was operating at full power. The U.S. end of the station was reduced to an eerie maze of shadowy tunnels, and in the gloom of the hab, the brightest source of light was the computer screen, on which the Environmental Control and Life Support System diagrams were currently displayed. Emma and Luther were already familiar with the ECLS system, had memorized its components and subsystems during their training on earth. Now they had an urgent reason to review the system. They had a contagion on board, and they could not be certain if the entire station was contaminated. When Nicolai had coughed, spraying eggs throughout the Russian service module, the hatch had been open. Within seconds, the station's circulation system, designed to keep pockets of dead air from building up, had swirled the airborne droplets into other parts of the station. Had the environmental-control system filtered out and trapped the airborne particles, as it was designed to do? Or was the contagion everywhere now, in every module?

On the computer screen were diagrams of air-flow into and out of the station's atmosphere. Oxygen was supplied by several independent sources. The primary source was the Russian Elektron generator, which electrolyzed water into hydrogen and oxygen. A solid-fuel generator using chemical cartridges was one of the backup sources, as were the oxygen storage tanks, which were recharged by the shuttle. A plumbed system distributed the oxygen, mixed with nitrogen, throughout the station, and fans kept the air circulating between modules. Fans also drew in air through various scrubbers and filters, removing carbon dioxide, water, and airborne particles.

'These HEPA filters should've trapped every egg or larva within fifteen minutes,' said Luther, pointing to the high-efficiency particulate air filters in the diagram. 'The system's ninety-nine point nine percent efficient. Everything bigger than a third of a micron should've been filtered out.'

'Assuming the eggs stayed airborne,' said Emma. 'The problem is, they adhere to surfaces. And I've seen them move. They could crawl into crevices, hide behind panels where we can't see them.'

'It'd take months for us to rip out every panel and look for them. Even then, we'd probably miss a few.'

'Forget ripping out the panels. That's hopeless. I'll change out the rest of the HEPA filters. Recheck the microbial air samplers tomorrow. We have to assume that'll do it. But if those larvae have crawled into the electrical conduits, we'll never find them.' She sighed, her fatigue so heavy she had to struggle to think. 'Whatever we do, it may not make a difference. It may be too late.'

'It's definitely too late for Diana,' Luther said softly.

Today, the scleral hemorrhages had appeared in Diana's eyes. She was now confined to the Russian service module. A plastic sheet had been draped over the hatchway, and no one was allowed in without a respiratory mask and goggles. *A useless exercise*, thought Emma. They had all breathed the same air; they had all touched Nicolai. Perhaps they were all infected.

'We have to assume the Russian service module is now hopelessly contaminated,' said Emma.

'That's the only livable module with full power. We can't close it off entirely.'

'Then I guess you know what we have to do.'

Luther gave a weary sigh. 'Another EVA.'

'We need to restore full power to this end,' she said. 'You've got to finish those repairs on the beta gimbal assembly, or we'll be on the edge of catastrophe. If anything else goes wrong with our remaining power supply, we could lose Environmental Control next. Or the Guidance and Nav computers.' It was what the Russians used to call *the coffin scenario*. Without the power to orient itself, the station would begin to spin out of control.

'Even if we do restore power,' said Luther, 'it doesn't address our real problem. The biocontamination.'

'If we can contain it to the Russian end –'

'But she's incubating larvae right now! She's like a bomb, waiting to go off.'

'We jettison her body as soon as she dies,' said Emma. 'Before she sheds any eggs or larvae.'

'That may not be soon enough. Nicolai coughed up those eggs when he was still alive. If we wait till Diana dies . . .'

'What are you suggesting, Luther?' Griggs's voice startled them both, and they turned to look at him. He was staring at them from the hatchway, his face gleaming in the shadows. 'Are you saying we shove her out while she's still alive?'

Luther drifted deeper into the gloom, as though retreating from attack. 'Jesus, that's not what I was saying.'

'Then what *were* you saying?'

'Just that the larvae – we know they're inside her. We know it's a matter of time.'

'Maybe they're inside all of us. Maybe they're inside *you*. Growing, developing right now. Should we jettison your body?'

'If that's what it takes to stop it from spreading. Look, we all know she's going to die. There's nothing we can do about it. We've got to think ahead –'

'Shut up!' Griggs shot across the hab and grabbed Luther by his shirt. Both men slammed into the far wall and bounced off again. They twisted around and around in midair, Luther trying to pry off Griggs's hands, Griggs refusing to release him.

'Stop it!' yelled Emma. 'Griggs, let him *go!*'

Griggs released his hold. The two men drifted apart, still breathing hard. Emma positioned herself like a referee between them.

'Luther's right,' she said to Griggs. 'We have to think ahead. We may not want to do it, but we have no choice.'

'And if it was you, Watson?' Griggs shot back. 'How would you like us discussing what to do with your body? How quickly we can bag you up, dispose of you?'

'I'd *expect* you to be making those plans! There are three other lives at stake, and Diana knows it. I'm trying my best to keep her alive, but right now, I don't have a clue what will work. All I can do is pump her full of antibiotics and wait for Houston to give us some answers. As far as I'm concerned, we're on our own up here. We have to plan for the worst!'

Griggs shook his head. His eyes were red-rimmed, his face haggard with grief. He said softly, 'How can it get any worse?'

She didn't answer. She looked at Luther and read her own thoughts in his eyes. *The worst is yet to come.*

'ISS, we have Surgeon standing by,' said Capcom. 'Go ahead, ISS.'

'Jack?' said Emma.

She was disappointed to hear Todd Cutler's voice instead. 'It's me, Emma. I'm afraid Jack's left JSC for the day. He and Gordon took off for California.'

Damn you, Jack, she thought. *I need you.*

'We're all in agreement down here about the EVA,' said Todd. 'It needs to be done, and soon. My first question to you is, how is Luther Ames? Both physically and mentally? Is he up to it?'

'He's tired. We're all tired. We've hardly slept in the last twenty-four hours. The cleanup is keeping us busy.'

'If we give him a day to rest, could he manage the EVA?'

'Right now, a day of rest seems like an impossible dream.'

'But would it be enough time?'

She considered it for a moment. 'I think so. He just needs to catch up on his sleep.'

'Okay. Then here's my second question. Are *you* up to an EVA?'

Emma paused in surprise. 'You want *me* to be his partner?'

'We don't think Griggs is up to it. He's withdrawn from all communication with the ground. Our psychologist feels he's too unstable at this point.'

'He's grieving, Todd. And very bitter that you won't let us come home. You may not be aware of this, but he and Diana are . . .' She paused.

'We know. And these emotions seriously undercut

361

his effectiveness. It makes an EVA dangerous. That's why you need to be Luther's partner.'

'What about a suit? The other EMU is too big for me.'

'There's an Orlan-M suit stored in the old *Soyuz*. It was tailored for Elena Savitskaya and was left on board several missions ago. Elena was about your height and weight. It should fit.'

'It's my first EVA.'

'You've gone through WET-F training. You can handle it. Luther just needs you out there to assist.'

'What about my patient? If I'm outside doing the EVA, who's going to attend to her?'

'Griggs can change her IVs, see to her needs.'

'And if there's a medical crisis? What if she starts to convulse?'

Todd said quietly, 'She's dying, Emma. We don't think there's anything you can do to change that fact.'

'That's because you haven't given me any useful information to work with! You're more interested in keeping this station alive! It seems you care more about the goddamn solar arrays than the crew. We need a cure, Todd, or we're all going to die up here.'

'We don't have a cure. Not yet –'

'Then get us the fuck home!'

'You think we *want* to leave you stranded up there? You think we have a choice? It's like the Nazi high command down here! They've got Air

362

Force assholes posted all over Mission Control, and –'

There was sudden silence.

'Surgeon?' said Emma. 'Todd?'

Still no answer.

'Capcom, I've lost Surgeon,' she said. 'I need comm link restored.'

A pause. Then, 'Stand by, ISS.'

She waited for what seemed like an eternity. When Todd's voice finally came back on, it was subdued. *Cowed*, thought Emma.

'They're listening, aren't they?' she said.

'That's affirmative.'

'This is supposed to be a PMC! A private loop!'

'Nothing's private anymore. Remember that.'

She swallowed hard, suppressing her anger. 'Okay. Okay, I'll dispense with the ranting. Just tell me what you've got on this organism. Tell me what I can use against it.'

'I'm afraid there's not much to tell you. I just spoke to USAMRIID. To a Dr Isaac Roman, who's in charge of the Chimera project. His news isn't good. All their antibiotic and antihelminth trials have failed. He says Chimera has so much foreign DNA it's now closer to a mammalian genome than anything else. Which means any drug we use against it kills *our* tissues as well.'

'Have they tried cancer drugs? This thing multiplies so fast, it's behaving like a tumor. Could we attack it that way?'

'USAMRIID tried antimitotics, hoping they could

kill it during the cell-division phase. Unfortunately, the doses they needed were so high they ended up killing the hosts as well. The entire gastrointestinal mucosa sloughed off. The host animals bled out.'

The worst death imaginable, thought Emma. Massive hemorrhage into the bowels and stomach. Blood pouring from both mouth and rectum. She had witnessed such a death on earth. In space, it would be even more horrifying, giant globules of blood filling the cabin like bright red balloons, splashing onto every surface, every crew member.

'Then nothing has worked,' she said.

Todd said nothing.

'Isn't there something? Some cure that won't kill the host?'

'There was only one thing they mentioned. But Roman believes it's only a temporary effect. Not a cure.'

'What's the treatment?'

'A hyperbaric chamber. It requires a minimum of ten atmospheres of pressure. The equivalent of diving to a depth of over three hundred feet. Infected animals kept at those high pressures are still alive, six days after exposure.'

'It has to be a *minimum* of ten atmospheres?'

'Anything less, and the infection runs its course. The host dies.'

She let out a cry of frustration. 'Even if we *could* pump our air pressure that high, ten atmospheres is more than this station can tolerate.'

'Even two would stress the hull,' said Todd.

'Plus, you'd need a heli-ox atmosphere. You can't reproduce that on the station. That's why I didn't want to mention it. In your situation, it's useless information. We've already looked into the possibility of flying a hyperbaric chamber up to ISS, but equipment that bulky – something capable of producing pressures that high – needs to go into *Endeavour*'s cargo bay. The problem is, she's already out of horizontal processing. It would take a minimum of two weeks to get a chamber loaded up and launched. And it means docking the orbiter to ISS. Exposing *Endeavour* and its crew to your contamination.' He paused. 'USAMRIID says that's not an option.'

She was silent, her frustration boiling into rage. Their only hope, a hyperbaric chamber, required their return to earth. That was not an option either.

'There has to be something we can do with this information,' she said. 'Explain to me. Why would hyperbaric therapy work? Why did USAMRIID even think of testing it?'

'I asked Dr Roman that same question.'

'What did he say?'

'That this was a new and bizarre organism. That it requires us to consider unconventional therapy.'

'He didn't answer your question.'

'It's all he would tell me.'

Ten atmospheres of pressure was near the upper limit of human tolerance. Emma was an avid scuba diver, but she had never dared go deeper than a hundred twenty feet. A depth of three hundred feet was only for the foolhardy. Why had USAMRIID tested such extreme pressures?

They must have had a reason, she thought. *Something they know about this organism made them think it would work.*

Something they're not telling us.

22

The reason why Gordon Obie was known as the Sphinx had never been more apparent than on their flight to San Diego. They had signed out one of the T-38 jets from Ellington Field, with Obie at the controls and Jack squeezed into the single passenger seat. That they hardly said a word to each other while in the air was not surprising. A T-38 is not conducive to conversation, since passenger and pilot sit one behind the other like two peas crammed in a pod. But even during the refueling stop in El Paso, when they had both climbed out to stretch their legs after an hour and a half in cramped quarters, Obie could not be drawn into conversation. Only once, as they stood on the edge of the tarmac drinking Dr Peppers from the hangar vending machine, did he offer a spontaneous comment. He squinted up at the sun, already past its noon height, and said, 'If she was my wife, I'd be scared shitless too.'

Then he tossed his empty soda can into the trash bin and walked back to the jet.

After landing at Lindbergh Field, Jack took the wheel of their rental car, and they headed north on Interstate 5 to La Jolla. Gordon said almost nothing, but simply stared out the window. Jack had always thought Gordon was more machine than man, and he imagined that computerlike brain registering the passing scenery like bits of data: HILL. OVER-PASS. HOUSING DEVELOPMENT. Though Gordon had once been an astronaut, no one in the corps really knew him. He would dutifully show up at all their social events, but would stand off by himself, a quiet and solitary figure sipping nothing stronger than his favorite Dr Pepper. He seemed perfectly at ease with his own silence, accepted it as part of his personality, just as he'd accepted his comically protruding ears and his bad haircuts. If no one really knew Gordon Obie, it was because he saw no reason to reveal himself.

That was why his comment in El Paso had surprised Jack. *If she was my wife, I'd be scared shitless too.*

Jack could not imagine the Sphinx ever being scared, nor could he imagine him being married. As far as he knew, Gordon had always been a bachelor.

Afternoon fog was already rolling in from the sea by the time they wound their way up the La Jolla coastline. They almost missed the entrance to

SeaScience; the turnoff was marked by one small sign, and the road beyond it seemed to lead into a grove of eucalyptus trees. Only when they'd driven a half mile down the turnoff did they spot the building, a surreal, almost fortresslike complex of white concrete overlooking the sea.

A woman in a white lab coat met them at the security desk. 'Rebecca Gould,' she said, shaking their hands. 'I work down the hall from Helen. I spoke to you this morning.' With her shorn hair and stout build, Rebecca might have passed for either sex. Even her deep voice was ambiguous.

They took the elevator down to the basement level. 'I don't really know why you insisted on coming out here,' said Rebecca. 'As I told you on the phone, USAMRIID's already picked Helen's lab clean.' She pointed to a doorway. 'You can see for yourself how little they left behind.'

Jack and Gordon stepped into the lab and looked around in dismay. Empty filing cabinet drawers hung open. Shelves and countertops had been swept clean of all equipment, and not even a test tube rack was in sight. Only the wall decorations had been left behind, mostly framed travel posters, seductive photographs of tropical beaches and palm trees and brown women glistening in the sun.

'I was in my lab down the hall the day they showed up. Heard a lot of upset voices and breaking glass. I looked out my door and saw men

369

carting out files and computers. They took everything. The incubators with her cultures. Racks of seawater samples. Even the frogs she kept in that terrarium over there. My assistants tried to stop the raid, and they got hauled out for questioning. Naturally, I called upstairs to Dr Gabriel's office.'

'Gabriel?'

'Palmer Gabriel. Our company president. He came down himself, along with a SeaScience attorney. They couldn't stop the raid, either. The Army just came in with their carton boxes and hauled everything away. They even took the employees' lunches!' She opened the refrigerator and pointed to the empty shelves. 'I don't know what the hell they thought they'd find.' She turned to face them. 'I don't know why you're here, either.'

'I think we're all looking for Helen Koenig.'

'I told you. She resigned.'

'Do you know why?'

Rebecca shrugged. 'That's what USAMRIID kept asking. Whether she was angry at SeaScience. Whether she was mentally unstable. I certainly didn't see that. I think she was just tired. Burned out from working here seven days a week, for God knows how long.'

'And now no one can find her.'

Rebecca's chin jutted up in anger. 'It's not a crime to leave town. It doesn't mean she's a bioterrorist. But USAMRIID treated this lab like a crime scene. As if she was growing Ebola virus or something. Helen was studying Archaeons. Harmless sea microbes.'

'Are you certain that was the only project going on in this lab?'

'Are you asking whether I kept tabs on Helen? Of course not. I'm too busy doing my own work. But what else would Helen be doing? She's devoted years to Archaeon research. That particular strain she sent up to ISS was her discovery. She considered it her personal triumph.'

'Is there a commercial application for Archaeons?' Rebecca hesitated. 'Not that I'm aware of.'

'Then why study them in space?'

'Haven't you heard of pure science, Dr McCallum? Knowledge for its own sake? These are weird, fascinating creatures. Helen found her species in the Galápagos Rift, near a volcanic vent, at a depth of nineteen thousand feet. Six hundred atmospheres of pressure, at boiling temperatures, this organism was *thriving*. It shows us how adaptable life can be. It's only natural to wonder what would happen if you took that life-form out of its extreme conditions and brought it up to a friendlier environment. Without thousands of pounds of pressure crushing it. Without even gravity to distort its growth.'

'Excuse me,' interrupted Gordon, and they both turned to look at him. He had been wandering around the lab, poking in empty drawers and looking into trash cans. Now he was standing beside one of the travel posters hanging on the wall. He pointed to a snapshot that had been taped to a corner of the picture frame. It showed a large aircraft parked on a tarmac. Posed under the wing were the two pilots. 'Where did this photo come from?'

Rebecca shrugged. 'How would I know? This is Helen's lab.'

'It's a KC-135,' said Gordon.

Now Jack understood why Gordon had focused on the photo. The KC-135 was the same aircraft NASA used to introduce astronauts to microgravity. When flown in giant parabolic curves, it was like an airborne roller coaster, producing up to thirty seconds of weightlessness per dive.

'Did Dr Koenig use a KC-135 in any of her research?' asked Jack.

'I know she spent four weeks out at some airfield in New Mexico. I have no idea what kind of plane they were using.'

Jack and Gordon exchanged thoughtful looks. Four weeks of KC-135 research would cost a fortune.

'Who would authorize an expense like that?' asked Jack.

'It would have to be approved by Dr Gabriel himself.'

'Could we speak to him?'

Rebecca shook her head. 'You don't just drop in on Palmer Gabriel. Even the scientists who work here hardly ever see him. He has research facilities all over the country, so he may not even be in town right now.'

'Another question,' Gordon interrupted. He had wandered over to the empty terrarium and was peering down at the moss and pebbles lining the bottom. 'What's this enclosure for?'

'The frogs. I told you about them, remember? They were Helen's pets. USAMRIID carted them off along with everything else.'

Gordon suddenly straightened and looked at her. 'What kind of frogs?'

She gave a startled laugh. 'Do you NASA guys always ask such weird questions?'

'I'm just curious what variety one would keep as a pet.'

'I think they were some sort of leopard frog. Me, I'd recommend a poodle instead. They're a lot less slimy.' She glanced at her watch. 'So, gentlemen. Any other questions?'

'I think I'm through here, thank you,' said Gordon. And without another word he walked out of the lab.

They sat in the rental car, the sea mist now swirling past their windows, moisture filming the glass. *Rana pipiens*, thought Jack. The northern leopard frog. One of the three species on Chimera's genome.

'This is where it came from,' he said. 'This lab.'

Gordon nodded.

'USAMRIID knew about this place a week ago,'

said Jack. 'How did they find out? How did they know Chimera came from SeaScience? There has to be some way to force them to share their information with us.'

'Not if it's a matter of national security.'

'NASA is *not* the enemy.'

'Maybe they think we are. Maybe they believe the threat comes from *inside* NASA,' said Gordon.

Jack looked at him. 'One of ours?'

'It's one of two reasons why Defense would keep us out of the loop.'

'And the other reason?'

'Because they're assholes.'

Jack gave a laugh and slumped back against his seat. Neither one of them spoke for a moment. The day had already wearied them both, and they still had the flight back to Houston.

'I feel like I'm punching at thin air,' said Jack, pressing his hand to his eyes. 'I don't know who or what I'm fighting. But I can't afford to *stop* fighting.'

'She's not a woman I'd give up on, either,' said Gordon.

Neither one of them had said her name, but they both knew they were talking about Emma.

'I remember her first day at Johnson,' said Gordon. In the dim light of the misted windows, Gordon's homely face was sketched in shades of gray on gray. He sat very still, his gaze focused straight ahead, a somber and colorless man. 'I addressed her incoming astronaut class. I looked around the room at all those new faces. And there she was, front and center. Not afraid to be picked on. Not afraid of humiliation. Not afraid of anything.' He paused and gave a small shake of his head. 'I didn't like sending her up. Every time she was chosen for a crew assignment, I wanted to scratch her name off the list. Not because she wasn't good. Hell, no. I just didn't like watching her ride off to that launchpad, knowing what I know about everything that can go wrong.' He suddenly stopped talking. It was more than Jack had ever heard him say in one stretch, more than Gordon had ever revealed of his feelings. Yet none of what he'd said came as a surprise to Jack. He thought of the countless ways he loved Emma. *And what man would not love her?* he wondered. *Even Gordon Obie is not immune.*

He started the car, and the windshield cleared as the wipers scraped away the veil of mist. It was already five o'clock; they would be flying back to Houston in darkness. He pulled out of the parking space and drove toward the exit.

Halfway across the lot, Gordon said, 'What the hell is this?'

Jack slammed on the brakes as a black sedan barreled toward them through the mist. Now a second car screeched into the parking lot and skidded to a stop, its front bumper just kissing theirs. Four men emerged.

Jack froze as his door was yanked open and a

voice commanded, 'Gentlemen, please step out of the car. Both of you.'

'Why?'

'You will step out of the car *now*.'

Gordon said softly, 'I get the feeling this is not negotiable.'

Reluctantly they both climbed out and were swiftly patted down and relieved of their wallets.

'He wants to talk to you two. Get in the backseat.' The man pointed to one of the black cars.

Jack glanced around at the four men watching them. *Resistance is futile* just about summed up their situation. He and Gordon walked to the black car and slid into the rear seat.

There was a man sitting in front. All they saw was the back of his head and shoulders. He had thick silvery hair, swept back, and wore a gray suit. His window whisked down, and the two confiscated wallets were handed to him. He slid the window shut again, a darkly tinted barrier against prying eyes. For a few minutes he studied the contents of the wallets. Then he turned to face his backseat visitors. He had dark, almost obsidian eyes, and they seemed strangely devoid of reflected images. Two black holes trapping light. He tossed the wallets into Jack's lap.

'You're a long way from Houston, gentlemen.'

'Must have been that wrong turn in El Paso,' said Jack.

'What does NASA want here?'

'We want to know what was really in that cell culture you sent up.'

'USAMRIID's already been here. They swept the place clean. They have everything. Dr Koenig's research files, her computers. If you have any questions, I suggest you ask *them*.'

'USAMRIID'S not talking to us.'

'That's your problem, not mine.'

'Helen Koenig was working for *you*, Dr Gabriel. Don't you know what goes on in your own labs?'

Jack saw, by the man's expression, that he had guessed correctly. This was the founder of SeaScience. *Palmer Gabriel.* An angelic last name for a man whose eyes gave off no light.

'I have hundreds of scientists working for me,' said Gabriel. 'I have facilities in Massachusetts and Florida. I can't possibly know everything that goes on in those labs. Nor can I be held responsible for any crimes my employees commit.'

'This is not just any crime. This is a bioengineered chimera – an organism that's killed an entire shuttle crew. And it came from your lab.'

'My researchers direct their own projects. I don't interfere. I'm a scientist myself, Dr McCallum, and I know that scientists work best when allowed complete independence. The freedom to indulge their curiosity. Whatever Helen did was her business.'

'Why study Archaeons? What was she hoping to find?'

He turned to face forward, and they saw only

the back of his head, with its silvery sweep of hair. 'Knowledge is always useful. At first we may not recognize its value. For instance, what possible benefit is there to knowing the reproductive habits of the sea slug? Then we learn about all the valuable hormones we can extract from that lowly sea slug. And suddenly, its reproduction is of utmost importance.'

'And what's the importance of Archaeons?'

'That's the question, isn't it? That's what we do here. Study an organism until we learn its usefulness.' He pointed toward his research facility, now shrouded in mist. 'You'll notice it's by the sea. All my buildings are by the sea. It's my oil field. That's where I look for the next new cancer drug, the next miracle cure. It makes perfect sense to look there, because that's where *we* come from. Our birthplace. All life comes from the sea.'

'You haven't answered my question. Is there a commercial value for *Archaeons?*'

'That remains to be seen.'

'And why send them into space? Was there something she discovered on those KC-135 flights? Something to do with weightlessness?'

Gabriel rolled down his window and signaled to the men. The back doors swung open. 'Please step out now.'

'Wait,' said Jack. 'Where is Helen Koenig?'

'I haven't heard from her since she resigned.'

'Why did she order her own cell cultures incinerated?'

Jack and Gordon were hauled out of the backseat and shoved toward their rental car.

'What was she afraid of?' Jack yelled.

Gabriel did not answer. His car window rolled shut, and his face disappeared behind the shield of tinted glass.

23

Luther vented the last air in the crew lock to space and opened the EVA hatch. 'I'll go first,' he said. 'You take it slow. It's always scary the first time out.'

That first glimpse of the emptiness beyond made Emma grasp the edge of the hatchway in panic. She knew the sensation was common, and that it would pass. That brief paralysis of fear gripped almost everyone on their first spacewalk. The mind had trouble accepting the vastness of space, the absence of up or down. Millions of years of evolution had imprinted in the human brain the terror of falling, and this was what Emma now struggled to overcome. Every instinct told her that if she released her grip, if she ventured out the hatchway, she would plummet, shrieking, in an endless fall. On a rational level, she knew this would not happen. She was connected to the crew lock by her tether. If that tether broke, she could use her SAFER jet pack to propel herself back to the station. It would take an unlikely series of independent mishaps to cause a catastrophe.

Yet that is exactly what has happened to this station, she thought. Mishap after mishap. Their own *Titanic* in space. She could not shake the premonition of yet another disaster.

Already they had been forced to violate protocol. Instead of the usual overnight camp-out at reduced air pressures, they had spent only four hours in the air lock. Theoretically, it should be long enough to prevent the bends, but any change in normal procedures added an element of risk.

She took a few deep breaths and felt the paralysis begin to melt away.

'How ya doing?' she heard Luther ask over her comm unit.

'I'm just . . . taking a minute to enjoy the view,' she said.

'No problems?'

'No. I'm A-OK.' She released her grip and floated out of the hatch.

Diana is dying.

Griggs stared with mounting bitterness at the closed-circuit TV monitors showing Luther and Emma at work outside the station. Drones, he thought. Obedient robots, leaping at Houston's command. For so many years, he, too, had been a drone. Only now did he understand his position

381

in the greater scheme of things. He, and everyone else, were disposable. On-orbit replacement units whose real function was to maintain NASA's glorious hardware. *We may all be dying up here, but yes, sir, we'll keep the place in fucking shipshape order.*

They could count him out. NASA had betrayed him, had betrayed all of them. Let Watson and Ames play the good little soldiers; he would have no more of it.

Diana was all he cared about.

He left the hab and headed toward the Russian end of the station. Slipping under the plastic sheeting draped over the hatchway, he entered the RSM. He didn't bother to put on his mask or goggles; what difference did it make? They were all going to die.

Diana was strapped to the treatment board. Her eyes were swollen, the lids puffy. Her abdomen, once so flat and firm, was now bloated. *Filled with eggs*, he thought. He pictured them growing inside her, expanding beneath that pale tent of skin.

Gently he touched her cheek. She opened her blood-streaked eyes and struggled to focus on his face.

'It's me,' he whispered. He saw that she was trying to free her hand from the wrist restraint. He clasped her hand in his. 'You need to keep your arm still, Diana. For the IV.'

'I can't see you.' She gave a sob. 'I can't see anything.'

'I'm here. I'm right with you.'

'I don't want to die this way.'

He blinked away tears and started to say something, false reassurance that she would not die, that he would not let her. But the words wouldn't come. They had always been truthful with each other; he would not lie to her now. So he said nothing.

She said, 'I never thought . . .'

'What?' he prompted gently.

'That this is . . . how it would happen. No chance to play the hero. Just sick and useless.' She gave a laugh, then grimaced in pain. 'Not my idea of going out . . . in a blaze of glory.'

A blaze of glory. That was how every astronaut imagined it would be to die in space. A brief moment of terror, and then the quick demise. Sudden decompression or fire. Never had they imagined a death like this, a slow and painful ebbing away as one's body is consumed and digested by another life-form. Abandoned by the ground. Quietly sacrificed to the greater good of mankind.

Expendable. He could accept it for himself, but he could not accept Diana's expendability. He could not accept the fact he was about to lose her.

It was hard to believe that on the first day they'd met, during training at JSC, he had thought her cold and forbidding, an icy blonde with too much confidence. Her British accent had put him off as well, because it made her sound so superior. It was crisp and cultured compared to his Texas drawl. By

383

the first week, they disliked each other so much they were scarcely speaking to each other.

By the third week, at Gordon Obie's insistence, they'd reluctantly declared a truce.

By the eighth week, Griggs was showing up at her house. Just for a drink at first, two professionals reviewing their upcoming mission. Then the mission talk had given way to conversations of a more personal nature. Griggs's unhappy marriage. The thousand and one interests he and Diana had in common. It all led, of course, to the inevitable.

They had concealed the affair from everyone at JSC. Only here, on the station, had their relationship become apparent to their colleagues. Had there been even a whiff of suspicion before this, Blankenship would have scrubbed them from the mission. Even in this modern day and age, an astronaut's divorce was a black mark against him. And if that divorce had resulted from a liaison with another member of the corps – well, so much for any future flight assignments. Griggs would have been reduced to an invisible member of the corps, neither seen nor heard.

For the last two years he had loved her. For two years, whenever he had lain beside his sleeping wife, he had yearned for Diana and plotted out the ways they might be together. Someday, they *would* be together, even if they had to resign from NASA. That was the dream that had sustained him through all those unhappy nights. Even after these two months with her in close quarters, even after their occasional flares of temper, he had not stopped loving her. He had not surrendered the dream. Until now.

'What day is this?' she murmured.

'It's Friday.' He began to stroke her hair again. 'In Houston, it's five-thirty in the afternoon. Happy hour.'

She smiled. 'TGIF.'

'They're sitting at the bar now. Chips and margaritas. God, I could do with a stiff drink. A nice sunset. You and me, on the lake . . .'

The tears glistening on her lashes almost broke his heart. He no longer gave a damn about biocontamination, about the dangers of infecting himself. With his bare hand he wiped away the tears.

'Are you in pain?' he said. 'Do you need more morphine?'

'No. Save it.' *Someone else will need it soon*, was what she didn't say.

'Tell me what you want. What I can do for you.'

'Thirsty,' she said. 'All that talk of margaritas.'

He gave a laugh. 'I'll mix one up for you. The nonalcoholic version.'

'Please.'

He floated across to the galley and opened the food locker. It was stocked with Russian supplies, not the same items as in the U.S. hab. He saw vacuum-packed pickled fish. Sausages. An array of unappetizing Russian staples. And vodka – a small bottle of it, sent by the Russians, ostensibly for medicinal purposes.

This may be the last drink we'll ever have together.

He shook some vodka into two drink bags and restowed the bottle. Then he added water to the bags, diluting hers so that it was barely alcoholic. Just a taste, he thought, to bring back happy memories. To remind her of the evenings they had spent together, watching sunsets from her patio. He gave the bags a few good shakes to mix the water and vodka. Then he turned to look at her.

A bright red balloon of blood was oozing from her mouth.

She was convulsing. Her eyes were rolled back, her teeth clamped down on her tongue. One raw and ragged slice of it was still hanging on by a thread of tissue.

'Diana!' he screamed.

The balloon of blood broke off and the satiny globule drifted away. At once another began to form, fed by the blood pouring out of the torn flesh.

He grabbed a plastic bite block, already taped to the restraint board, and tried to force it between her teeth, to protect her soft tissues from any more trauma. He could not pry the teeth apart. The human jaw has one of the strongest muscles in the body, and hers was clamped tight. He grabbed the syringe of Valium, premeasured and ready to inject, and shoved the tip into the IV stopcock. Even as he pressed the plunger, her seizure was starting to fade. He gave her the whole dose.

Her face relaxed. Her jaw fell limp.

'Diana?' he said. She didn't respond.

The new bubble of blood was growing, spilling from her mouth. He had to apply pressure, to stop it.

He opened the medical kit, found the sterile gauze, and ripped open the package, sending a few squares flying away. He positioned himself behind her head and gently opened her mouth to expose the torn tongue.

She coughed and tried to turn her face away. She was choking on her own blood. Aspirating it into her lungs.

'Don't move, Diana.' With his right wrist pressing down on her lower teeth, to keep her jaw open, he wadded up a bundle of gauze in his left hand and began to dab away the blood. Her neck suddenly jerked taut in a new convulsion, and her jaw snapped shut.

He screamed, the meaty part of his hand caught between her teeth, the pain at once so terrible his vision began to blacken. He felt warm blood splash against his face, saw a bright globule fountaining up. His blood, mingled with hers. He tried to pull free, but her teeth had sunk in too deeply. The blood was pouring out, the globule inflating to the size of a basketball. *Severed artery!* He could not pry her jaw open; the seizure had caused her muscle to contract with superhuman strength.

Blackness was closing in on his vision.

In desperation, he rammed his free fist against her teeth. The jaw did not relax.

He hit her again. The basketball of blood flew apart in a dozen smaller globules, splashing his face, his eyes. Still he could not open her jaw. There was so much blood now it was as though he were swimming in a lake of it, unable to draw in a breath of clean air.

Blindly he swung his fist against her face and felt bones crack, yet he could not pull free. The pain was crushing, unbearable. Panic seized him, blinding him to anything but making the agony stop. He was scarcely aware of what he was doing as he hit her again. And again.

With a scream he finally yanked his hand free and went flying backward, clutching his wrist, releasing swirls of blood in bright ribbons all around him. It took him a moment to stop caroming off walls, to shake his vision clear. He focused on Diana's broken face, on the bloodied stumps of her teeth. The damage done by his own fist.

His howl of despair echoed off the walls, filling his ears with the sound of his own anguish. *What have I done? What have I done?*

He floated to her side, held her shattered face in his hands. He no longer felt the pain of his own wound; it receded to nothing, overshadowed by the greater horror of his own actions.

He gave another howl, this time of rage. He battered his fist against the module wall. Ripped the plastic sheeting that covered the hatchway. *We're all dying anyway!* Then he focused on the medical kit.

He reached in and grabbed a scalpel.

Flight Surgeon Todd Cutler stared at his console and felt a stab of panic. On his screen were the biotelemetry readings for Diana Estes. Her EKG tracing had just burst into a sawtooth pattern of rapid spikes. To his relief, it was not sustained. Just as abruptly, the tracing reverted back to a rapid sinus rhythm.

'Flight,' he said, 'I'm seeing a problem with my patient's heart rhythm. Her EKG just showed a five-second run of ventricular tachycardia.'

'Significance?' Woody Ellis responded briskly.

'It's a potentially fatal rhythm if it's prolonged. Right now she's back in sinus, around one thirty. That's faster than she's been running. Not danger-ous, but it worries me.'

'Your advice, Surgeon?'

'I'd give her antiarrhythmics. She needs IV lido-caine or amiodarone. They've got both drugs in their ALS pack.'

'Ames and Watson are still out on EVA. Griggs'll have to give it.'

'I'll talk him through it.'

'Okay. Capcom, let's get Griggs on comm.'

As they waited for Griggs to respond, Todd kept a close eye on the monitor. What he saw worried him. Diana's pulse rate was increasing: 135, 140.

Now a brief burst of 160, the spikes almost lost in a flutter of patient movement or electrical interference. What was happening up there?

Capcom said, 'Commander Griggs is not responding.'

'She needs that lidocaine,' said Todd.

'We can't get him on comm.'

Either he can't hear us or he's refusing to answer, thought Todd. They'd been worried about Griggs's emotional health. Had he withdrawn so completely he'd ignore an urgent communication?

Todd's gaze suddenly froze on his console screen. Diana Estes was going in and out of V tach. Her ventricles were contracting so rapidly, they could not pump with any efficiency. They could not maintain her blood pressure.

'She needs that drug *now!*' he snapped.

'Griggs is not responding,' said Capcom.

'Then get the EVA crew inside!'

'*No,*' Flight cut in. 'They're at a delicate point in repairs. We can't interrupt them.'

'She's turning critical.'

'We pull in the EVA crew, that ends all repairs for the next twenty-four hours.' The crew could not pop inside and go right back out again. They needed time to recover, additional time to repeat the decompression cycle. Though Woody Ellis didn't say it aloud, he was probably thinking the same thing as everyone else in the room: Even if they did call the crew inside to assist, it would make little difference to Diana Estes. Her death was inevitable.

To Todd's horror, the EKG tracing was now in sustained V tach. It was not recovering.

'She's going downhill!' he said. 'Get *one* of them inside now! Bring in Watson!'

There was a second's hesitation.

Then Flight said, 'Do it.'

Why isn't Griggs responding?

Frantically Emma pulled herself from handhold to handhold, moving as fast as she could along the main truss. She felt slow and clumsy in the Orlan-M suit, and her hands ached from the effort of flexing against the resistance of bulky gloves. She was already weary from the repair work, and now fresh sweat was soaking into her suit lining, and her muscles quivered from fatigue.

'Griggs, respond. Goddamnit, respond!' she snapped into her comm link.

ISS remained silent.

'What's Diana's status?' she demanded between panted breaths.

Todd's voice came on. 'Still in V tach.'

'Shit.'

'Don't rush, Watson. Don't get careless!'

'She's not going to last. Where the fuck is Griggs?'

She was breathing so hard now she could barely keep up the conversation. She forced herself to concentrate on grabbing the next hand rung, on keeping her tether untangled. Clambering off the truss, she made a lunge for the ladder, but was suddenly snapped to a halt. Her sleeve had caught on a corner of the work platform.

Slow down. You're going to get yourself killed.

Gingerly she unsnagged her sleeve and saw there was no puncture. Heart still hammering, she continued down the ladder and pulled herself into the air lock. Quickly she swung the hatch shut and opened the pressure equalization valve.

'Talk to me, Todd,' she snapped as the air lock began to repressurize. 'What's the rhythm?'

'She's now in coarse V fib. We still can't get Griggs on comm.'

'We're losing her.'

'I know, I know!'

'Okay, I'm up to five psi –'

'Air-lock integrity check. Don't skip it.'

'I don't have time.'

'Watson, *no fucking shortcuts.*'

She paused and took a deep breath. Todd was right. In the hostile environment of space, one must never take shortcuts. She completed the air-lock integrity check, finished repressurization, and opened the next hatch, leading into the equipment lock. There she swiftly removed her gloves. The Russian Orlan-M suit was easier to doff than the American EMU, but it still took time to swing open the rear life-support system and wriggle out. *I'll never make it in time*, she thought as she furiously kicked her feet free from the lower torso.

'Status, Surgeon!' she barked into her comm assembly.

'She's now in fine fib.'

A terminal rhythm, thought Emma. This was their last chance to save Diana.

Now clad only in her water-cooling garment, she opened the hatch leading into the station. Frantic to reach her patient, she pushed off the wall and dove headfirst through the hatch opening.

Wetness splashed her face, blurring her vision. She missed the handhold and collided with the far wall. For a few seconds she drifted in confusion, blinking away the sting. *What did I get in my eyes?* she thought. *Not eggs. Please, not eggs . . .* Slowly her vision cleared, but even then, she could not comprehend what she was seeing.

Floating all around her in the shadowy node were giant globules. She felt more wetness brush her hand, and she looked down at the blackish stain soaking into her sleeve, at the dark splotches blooming here and there on her water-cooling garment. She held her sleeve up to one of the node lights.

The stain was blood.

In horror she gazed at the giant globules hanging in the shadows. So much of it . . .

Quickly she closed the hatch to prevent the contamination from spreading into the air lock. It was too late to protect the rest of the station; the globules had spread everywhere. She dove into the hab, opened the CCPK, and donned protective mask and goggles. Maybe the blood was not infectious. Maybe she could still protect herself.

'Watson?' said Cutler.

'Blood . . . there's blood everywhere!'

'Diana's rhythm is agonal – there's not much left to jump-start!'

'I'm on my way!' She pushed out of the node and entered the tunnellike Zarya. The Russian module seemed blindingly bright after the barely lit U.S. end, the globules of blood like gaily colored balloons floating in the air. Some had collided with the walls, splattering Zarya a brilliant red. Popping out the far end of the module, she could not avoid one giant bubble floating directly in her path. Reflexively she closed her eyes as it splattered her goggles, obscuring her view. Drifting blindly, she wiped her sleeve across the goggles to clear away the blood.

And found herself staring straight at Michael Griggs's chalk-white face.

She screamed. In horror she thrashed uselessly at empty air, going nowhere.

'Watson?'

She stared at the large bubble of blood still clinging to the gaping wound on his neck. This was the source of all the blood – a slashed carotid artery. She forced herself to touch the intact side of his neck, to search for a pulse. She could not feel one.

'Diana's EKG is flat line!' said Todd.

Emma's stunned gaze shifted to the hatch leading to the RSM, where Diana was supposed to be isolated. The plastic sheeting was gone; the module was open to the rest of the station.

In dread, she entered the RSM.

Diana was still strapped to the patient restraint board. Her face had been battered beyond recognition, her teeth smashed to splinters. A balloon of blood was oozing from her mouth.

The squeal of the cardiac monitor at last drew Emma's attention. A flat line traced across the screen. She reached over to turn off the alarm, and her hand froze in midair. Glistening on the power switch was a blue-green gelatinous clump.

Eggs. Diana has already shed eggs. She has already released Chimera into the air.

The monitor alarm seemed to build to an unbearable shriek, yet Emma remained motionless, staring at that cluster of eggs. They seemed to shimmer and recede out of focus. She blinked, and as her vision cleared again, she remembered the moisture hitting her face, stinging her eyes as she had dived through the air-lock hatch. She had not been wearing goggles then. She could still feel the wetness on her cheek, cool and clinging.

She reached up to touch her face, and stared at the eggs, like quivering pearls, on her fingertips.

The squeal of the cardiac alarm had become unbearable. She flipped off the monitor, and the squeal ceased. The silence that followed was just as alarming. She could not hear the hiss of the vent fans. They should be drawing in air, pulling it through the HEPA filters for cleansing. *There's too much blood in the air. It has blocked all the filters.* The rise in the pressure gradient across those filters had tripped the sensors, automatically shutting off the overheated fans.

'Watson, please respond!' said Todd.

'They're dead.' Her voice broke into a sob. 'They're both dead!'

Now Luther's voice broke into the loop. 'I'm coming in.'

'No,' she said. 'No –'

'Just hang on, Emma. I'll be right there.'

'Luther, you can't come in! There's blood and eggs everywhere. This station is no longer habitable. You have to stay in the air lock.'

'That's not a long-term solution.'

'There *is* no fucking long-term solution!'

'Look, I'm in the crew lock now. I'm closing the outer hatch. Starting repress –'

'The vent fans have all shut off. There's no way to clean this air.'

'I'm up to five psi. Pausing for integrity check.'

'If you come in, you'll be exposing yourself!'

'Going to full repress.'

'Luther, I've already been exposed! I got splashed in the eyes.' She took a deep breath. It came out in a sob. 'You're the only one left. The only one with any chance of surviving.'

There was a long silence. 'Jesus, Emma,' he murmured.

'Okay. Okay, listen to me.' She paused to calm herself. To think logically. 'Luther, I want you to move into the equipment lock. It should still be relatively clean in there, and you can take off your helmet. Then turn off your personal comm assembly.'

'What?'

'*Do it.* I'm heading for Node One. I'll be right on the other side of the hatch, talking to you.'

Now Todd broke in: 'Emma? Emma, do *not* break off air-to-ground loop –'

'Sorry, Surgeon,' she murmured, and turned off her comm assembly.

A moment later, she heard Luther say, over the station's hardline intercom system, 'I'm in the equipment lock.'

They were talking in private now, their conversation no longer monitored by Mission Control.

'There's one option left for you,' said Emma. 'The one you've been pushing for all along. I can't take it, but you can. You're still clean. You won't bring the disease home.'

'We already agreed on this. No one stays behind.'

'You've got three hours left of uncontaminated air in your EMU. If you keep your helmet on in the CRV and go straight to deorbit, you could make it down in time.'

'You'll be stranded.'

'I'm stranded here anyway!' She took another deep breath, and spoke more calmly. 'Look, we both know this goes against orders. It could be a very bad idea. How they'll respond is anyone's guess – that's the gamble. But, Luther, it's your choice to make.'

'There'll be no way for you to evac.'

'Take me out of the equation. Don't even think of me.' She added, softly, 'I'm already dead.'

'Emma, no –'

'What do *you* want to do? Answer that. Think only about *yourself*.'

She heard him take a deep breath. 'I want to go home.'

So do I, she thought, blinking away tears. *Oh, God, so do I.*

'Put on your helmet,' she said. 'I'll open the hatch.'

24

Jack ran up the stairs to Building 30, flashed his badge at Security, and headed straight to Special Vehicle Operations.

Gordon Obie intercepted him just outside the control room. 'Jack, wait. You go in there and raise hell, they'll toss you right out. Take a minute to cool down, or you won't be any help to her.'

'I want my wife home *now*.'

'Everyone wants them home! We're trying the best we can, but the situation has changed. The whole station is now contaminated. The filter system's off. The EVA crew never had a chance to complete the gimbal repairs, so they remain in power down. And now they're not talking to us.'

'What?'

'Emma and Luther have cut off communications. We don't know what's going on up there. That's why they rushed you back – to help us get through to them.'

Jack stared through the open doorway, into the Special Vehicle Operations Room. He saw men and women at their consoles, performing their duties as always. It suddenly enraged him that those flight controllers could remain so calm and efficient. That the deaths of two more astronauts did not seem to alter their cold professionalism. The cool demeanor of everyone in the room only magnified his own grief, his own terror.

He walked into the control room. Two uniformed Air Force officers stood beside Flight Director Woody Ellis, monitoring the comm loops. They were a disturbing reminder that the room was not under NASA's control. As Jack moved along the back row, toward the surgeon's console, several controllers shot him sympathetic looks. He said nothing, but sank into the chair next to Todd Cutler. He was acutely aware that just behind him, in the viewing gallery, other Air Force officers from U.S. Space Command were watching the room.

'You've heard the latest?' said Todd softly.

Jack nodded. There was no longer any EKG tracing on the monitor; Diana was dead. So was Griggs.

'Half the station's still in power down. And now they've got eggs floating in the air.'

And blood as well. Jack could picture what it must be like aboard the station. The lights dimmed. The stench of death. Blood splattering the walls, clogging the HEPA filters. An orbiting house of horrors.

'We need you to talk to her, Jack. Get her to tell us what's happening up there.'

'Why aren't they talking?'

'We don't know. Maybe they're pissed at us. They have a right to be. Maybe they're too traumatized.'

'No, they must have a reason.' Jack looked at the front screcn, showing the station's orbital path above the earth. *What are you thinking, Emma?* He slipped on the headset and said, 'Capcom, this is Jack McCallum. I'm ready.'

'Roger, Surgeon. Stand by, and we'll try them again.'

They waited. ISS did not respond.

At the third row of consoles, two of the controllers suddenly glanced back over their shoulders, at Flight Director Ellis. Jack heard nothing over the comm loop, but he saw the Odin controller, the controller in charge of onboard data networks, rise from his chair and lean forward to whisper across his console to the second-row controllers.

Now the OPS controller, in the third row, took off his headset, stood up, and stretched. He started up the side aisle, walking casually, as though headed for a bathroom break. As he passed by the surgeon's console, he dropped a piece of paper in Todd Cutler's lap and continued out of the room.

Todd unfolded the note and shot Jack a stunned look. 'The station's reconfigured their computers to ASCR mode,' he whispered. 'The crew's already started CRV sep sequence.'

Jack stared back in disbelief. ASCR, or assured safe crew return, was the computer config meant to support crew evacuation. He glanced quickly around the room. None of the controllers was saying a word about this over the loop. All Jack saw were rows of squared shoulders, everyone's gaze focused tightly on their consoles. He glanced sideways at Woody Ellis. Ellis stood absolutely motionless. The body language said it all. *He knows what's going on. And he's not saying a thing, either.*

Jack broke out in a sweat. This was why the crew wasn't talking. They had made their own decision, and they were forging ahead with it. The Air Force would not be in the dark for long. Through their Space Surveillance Network of radar and optical sensors, they could monitor objects as small as a baseball in low earth orbit. As soon as the CRV separated, as soon as it became an independent orbital object, it would come to the attention of Space Command's control center in Cheyenne Mountain Air Station. The million-dollar question was: How would they respond?

I hope to God you know what you're doing, Emma.

After CRV sep, it would take twenty-five minutes for the evac vehicle to bring up guidance and landing targets, another fifteen minutes to set up the deorbit burn. Another hour to land. U.S. Space Command would have them identified and tracked long before the CRV could touch down.

In the second row, the OSO flight controller raised his hand in a casual thumbs-up. With that gesture, he'd silently announced the news: The CRV had separated. For better or worse, the crew was on its way home.

Now the game begins.

The tension in the room coiled tighter. Jack hazarded a glance at the two Air Force officers, but the men seemed oblivious to the situation; one of them kept looking at the clock, as though anxious to be elsewhere.

The minutes ticked past, the room strangely quiet. Jack leaned forward, his heart hammering, sweat soaking his shirt. By now the CRV would be drifting outside the station's envelope. Their landing target would be identified, their guidance system locked onto GPS satellites.

Come on, come on, thought Jack. *Go to deorbit now!*

The sound of a ringing telephone cut the silence. Jack glanced sideways and saw one of the Air Force monitors answer it. Suddenly he went rigid and turned to Woody Ellis.

'What the hell is going on here?'

Ellis said nothing.

The officer quickly typed on Ellis's console keyboard and stared at the screen in disbelief. He grabbed the phone. 'Yes, sir. I'm afraid that's a confirmation. The CRV has separated. No, sir, I don't know how it – Yes, sir, we have been monitoring the loop, but—' The officer was red-faced and sweating as he listened to the tirade spewing from the receiver. When he hung up, he was shaking with rage.

'Turn it around!' he ordered.

Woody Ellis answered with barely disguised contempt. 'It isn't a *Soyuz* capsule. You can't command it to drive around like a goddamn automobile.'

'Then stop it from landing!'

'We can't. It's a one-way trip home.'

Three more Air Force officers walked swiftly into the room. Jack recognized General Gregorian of U.S. Space Command – the man now in authority over NASA operations.

'What's the status?' Gregorian snapped.

'The CRV is undocked but still in orbit,' the red-faced officer replied.

'How soon before they reach atmosphere?'

'Uh – I don't have that information, sir.'

Gregorian turned to the flight director. 'How soon, Mr Ellis?'

'It depends. There are a number of options.'

'Don't give me a fucking engineering lecture. I want an answer. I want a number.'

'Okay.' Ellis straightened and looked him hard in the eye. 'Anywhere from one to eight hours. It's up to them. They can stay in orbit for four revolutions max. Or they can deorbit now and be on the ground in an hour.'

Gregorian picked up the phone. 'Mr President, I'm afraid there's not much time to decide. They could deorbit any minute now. Yes, sir, I know it's a hard choice. But my recommendation remains the same as Mr Profitt's.'

What recommendation? thought Jack with a surge of panic.

An Air Force officer called out from one of the flight consoles, 'They've started their deorbit burn!'

'We're running out of time, sir,' said Gregorian. 'We need your answer now.' There was a long pause. Then he nodded, with relief. 'You've made the right decision. Thank you.' He hung up and turned to the Air Force officers. 'It's a go.'

'What's a go?' said Ellis. 'What are you people planning to do?'

His questions were ignored. The Air Force officer picked up the phone and calmly issued the order: 'Stand by for EKV launch.'

What the hell is an EKV? thought Jack. He looked at Todd and saw by his blank expression that he didn't know what was being launched, either.

It was Topo, the trajectory controller, who walked over to their console and quietly answered the question. 'Exoatmospheric kill vehicle,' he whispered. 'They're going to intercept.'

'Target must be neutralized before it descends to atmosphere,' said Gregorian.

Jack shot to his feet in panic. *'No!'*

Almost simultaneously, other controllers rose from their chairs in protest. Their shouts almost drowned out Capcom, who had to yell at the top of his voice to be heard.

'I have ISS on comm! ISS is on comm!'

ISS? Then someone is still aboard the station. Someone has been left behind.

Jack cupped his hand over his earpiece and listened to the downlinked voice.

It was Emma. 'Houston, this is Watson on ISS. Mission Specialist Ames is *not* infected. I repeat, he is *not* infected. He is the only crew member returning aboard CRV. I urgently request you allow the vehicle's safe landing.'

'Roger that, ISS,' said Capcom.

'You see? There's no reason to shoot it down,' Ellis said to Gregorian. 'Stop your EKV launch!'

'How do we know Watson's telling the truth?' countered Gregorian.

'She must be telling the truth. Why else would she stay behind? She's just stranded herself up there. The CRV was the only lifeboat she had!'

The impact of those words made Jack go numb. The heated conversation between Ellis and Gregorian suddenly seemed to fade out. Jack was no longer focusing on the fate of the CRV. He could think only of Emma, alone now, and trapped on the station, with no way to evacuate. *She knows she is infected. She has stayed behind to die.*

'CRV has completed deorbit burn. It's descending. Trajectory is on the front screen.'

Tracing across the world map at the front of the room was a small blip representing the CRV and its lone human passenger. They heard him now, on comm.

'This is Mission Specialist Luther Ames. I am approaching entry altitude, all systems nominal.'

The Air Force officer looked at Gregorian. 'We're still standing by for EKV launch.'

'You don't have to do this,' said Woody Ellis. 'He's not sick. We can bring him home!'

'The craft itself is probably contaminated,' said Gregorian.

'You don't know that!'

'I can't take that chance. I can't risk the lives of people on earth.'

'Godddamnit, this is *murder*.'

'He disobeyed orders. He knew what our response would be.' Gregorian nodded to the Air Force officer.

'EKVs have been launched, sir.'

Instantly the room hushed. Woody Ellis, pale and shaken, stared at the front screen, at the multiple trajectory tracings, hurtling toward an intersecting point.

The minutes went by in dead silence. At the front of the room, one of the women controllers began to cry softly.

'Houston, I'm approaching entry interface.' It was a shock to hear Luther's cheery voice suddenly crackle on the comm. 'I'd greatly 'preciate it if you'd have someone meet me on the ground, 'cause I'm gonna need help getting out of this EMU.'

No one responded. No one had the heart to.

'Houston?' said Luther, after a moment of silence. 'Hey, you guys still there?'

At last Capcom managed to reply, in an uneven voice, 'Uh, roger, CRV. We'll have the beer keg waiting for you, Luther ol' buddy. Dancing girls. The whole works . . .'

'Geez, you guys have loosened up since we last spoke. Okay, looks like I'm 'bout ready for LOS. You keep that beer cold, and I –'

There was a loud burst of static. Then the transmission went dead.

The blip on the front screen exploded into a shocking sunburst of fragments, scattering into delicate pixels of dust.

Woody Ellis crumpled into his chair and dropped his head in his hands.

August 19

'Securing air-to-ground loop,' said Capcom. 'Stand by, ISS.'

Talk to me, Jack. Please talk to me, Emma pleaded silently as she floated in the hab's semidarkness. With the circulation fans shut down, the module was so quiet she could hear the whoosh of her own pulse, the movement of air rushing in and out of her lungs.

She was startled when Capcom's voice suddenly said, 'Air-to-ground secure. You may proceed to PFC.'

'Jack?' she said.

'I'm here. I'm right here, sweetheart.'

'He was clean! I told them he was clean –'

'We tried to stop it! The order came straight from the White House. They didn't want to take any chances.'

'It's my fault.' Her exhaustion suddenly gave way to tears. She was alone and scared. And haunted by her catastrophically wrong decision. 'I thought they'd let him come back. I thought it was his best chance of staying alive.'

'Why did you stay behind, Emma?'

'I had to.' She took a deep breath and said, 'I'm infected.'

'You were *exposed*. That doesn't mean you're infected.'

'I just ran my own blood tests, Jack. My amylase level is rising.'

He said nothing.

'I'm now eight hours postexposure. I should have another twenty-four to forty-eight hours before I . . . can no longer function.' Her voice had steadied. She sounded strangely calm now, as though she were talking about a patient's impending death. Not her own. 'That's enough time to get a few things in order. Jettison the bodies. Change out some of the filters, and get the fans working again. It should make cleanup easier for the next crew. If there is a next crew . . .'

Jack still hadn't spoken.

'As for my own remains . . .' Her voice had

steadied to numb dispassion, all emotions suppressed. 'When the time comes, I think the best
thing I can do, for the good of the station, is to go
EVA. Where I can't contaminate anything after I
die. After my body . . .' She paused. 'The Orlan
is easy enough to get into without assistance. I
have Valium and narcotics on hand. Enough to
put me under. So I'll be asleep when my air runs
out. You know, Jack, it's not such a bad way to
go, when you think about it. Floating outside.
Looking at the earth, the stars. And just drifting
off to sleep . . .'

She heard him then. He was crying.

'Jack,' she said softly. 'I love you. I don't know
why things fell apart between us. I know some of
it had to be my fault.'

He drew in a shuddering breath. 'Emma, *don't*.'

'It's so stupid that I waited this long to tell you.
You probably think I'm only saying it now because
I'm going to die. But, Jack, the honest-to-God
truth is –'

'You're not going to die.' He said it again, with
anger. 'You are not going to die.'

'You've heard Dr Roman's results. Nothing has
worked.'

'The hyperbaric chamber has.'

'They can't get a chamber up here in time. And
without a lifeboat, I can't get home. Even if they'd
let me return.'

'There's got to be a way. Something you can do
to reproduce the chamber's effect. It's working

on infected mice. It's keeping them alive, so it's doing *something*. They're the only ones who've survived.'

No, she suddenly realized. *Not the only ones*.

Slowly, she turned and stared at the hatchway leading into Node 1.

The mouse, she thought. *Is the mouse still alive?*

'Emma?'

'Stand by. I'm going to check something in the lab.'

She swam through Node 1, into the U.S. lab. The stench of dried blood was just as strong in here, and even in the gloom, she could see the dark splatters on the walls. She floated across to the animal habitat, pulled out the mouse enclosure, and shone a flashlight inside.

The beam captured a pitiful sight. The bloated mouse was in its agonal throes, limbs thrashing out, mouth open, drawing in gulps of air.

You can't be dying, she thought. *You're the survivor, the exception to the rule. The proof that there's still hope for me.*

The mouse twisted, body corkscrewing in agony. A thread of blood curled out from between the hind legs, broke off into swirling droplets. Emma knew what would come next: the final flurry of seizures as the brain dissolved into a soup of digested proteins. She saw a fresh pulse of blood stain the white fur of the hindquarters. And then she saw something else, something pink, protruding between the legs.

It was moving.

The mouse thrashed again.

The pink thing slid all the way out, writhing and hairless. Tethered to its abdomen was a single glistening strand. An umbilical cord.

'Jack,' she whispered. *'Jack!'*

'I'm here.'

'The mouse – the female –'

'What about it?'

'These last three weeks, she's been exposed again and again to Chimera, and she hasn't gotten sick. She's the only one who's survived.'

'She's still alive?'

'Yes. And I think I know why. She was pregnant.'

The mouse began to writhe again. Another pup slid out in a glistening veil of blood and mucus.

'It must have happened that night when Kenichi put her with the males,' she said. 'I haven't been handling her. I never realized . . .'

'Why would pregnancy make a difference? Why should it be protective?'

Emma floated in the gloom, struggling to come up with an answer. The recent EVA and the shock of Luther's death had left her physically drained. She knew that Jack was just as exhausted. Two tired brains, working against the ticking time bomb of her infection.

'Okay. Okay, let's think about pregnancy,' she said. 'It's a complex physiological condition. It's more than just the gestation of a fetus. It's an altered metabolic state.'

'Hormones. Pregnant animals are chemically high on hormones. If we can mimic that state, maybe we can reproduce what's happened in that mouse.'

Hormone therapy. She thought of all the different chemicals circulating in a pregnant woman's body. Estrogen. Progesterone. Prolactin. Human chorionic gonadotropin.

'Birth control pills,' said Jack. 'You could mimic pregnancy with contraceptive hormones.'

'We have nothing like that on board. It's not part of the medical kit.'

'Have you checked Diana's personal locker?'

'She wouldn't take contraceptives without my knowledge. I'm the medical officer. I'd know about it.'

'Check it anyway. Do it, Emma.'

She shot out of the lab. In the Russian service module, she quickly pulled open the drawers in Diana's locker. It felt wrong, to be pawing through another woman's private possessions. Even a dead woman's. Among the neatly folded clothes she uncovered a private stash of candy. She hadn't known that Diana loved sweets; there was so much about Diana she would never know. In another drawer she found shampoo and toothpaste and tampons. No birth control pills.

She slammed the drawer shut. 'There's nothing on this station I can use!'

413

'If we launched the shuttle tomorrow – if we got the hormones up to you –'

'They won't launch! And even if you could send up a whole damn pharmacy, it'd still take three days to get to me!'

In three days, she would most likely be dead.

She clung to the blood-splattered locker, her breaths coming hard and fast, every muscle taut with frustration. With despair.

'Then we have to approach this from another angle,' said Jack. 'Emma, stay with me on this! I need you to help me think.'

She released a sharp breath. 'I'm not going anywhere.'

'*Why* would hormones work? What's the mechanism? We know they're chemical signals – an internal communication system at the cellular level. They work by activating or repressing gene expression. By changing the cell's programming . . .' He was rambling now, letting his stream of consciousness lead him toward a solution. 'In order for a hormone to work, it has to bind to a specific receptor on the target cell. It's like a key, in search of the right lock in which to fit. Maybe if we studied the data from Sea Science – if we could find out what other DNA Dr Koenig grafted onto this organism's genome – we might know how to shut off Chimera's reproduction.'

'What do you know about Dr Koenig? What other research has she worked on? That might be a clue.'

'We have her curriculum vitae. We've seen her published papers on Archaeons. Other than that, she's something of a mystery to us. So is SeaScience. We're still trying to dig up more information.'

That will take precious time, she thought. *I don't have much of it left.*

Her hands ached from gripping Diana's locker. She relaxed her hold and drifted away, as though swept along on a tide of despair. Loose items from Diana's locker floated around her in the air, evidence of Diana's sweet tooth. Chocolate bars. M&M's. A cellophane package of crystallized ginger candy. It was that last item that Emma suddenly focused on. Crystallized ginger.

Crystals.

'Jack,' she said. 'I have an idea.'

Her heart was racing as she swam out of the Russian service module and headed back into the U.S. lab. There she turned on the payload computer. The monitor glowed an eerie amber in the darkened module. She called up the operations data files and clicked on 'ESA.' European Space Agency. Here were all the procedures and reference materials required to operate the ESA payload experiments.

'What are you thinking, Emma?' came Jack's voice over her comm unit.

'Diana was working on protein crystal growth, remember? Pharmaceutical research.'

'Which proteins?' he shot back, and she knew he understood exactly what she was thinking.

'I'm scrolling down the list now. There are dozens . . .'

The protein names raced up the screen in a blur. The cursor halted on the entry she'd been searching for: '*Human chorionic gonadotropin.*'

'Jack,' she said softly. 'I think I've just bought myself some time.'

'What've you got?'

'HCG. Diana was growing the crystals. I'd have to do an IVA to get to it. They're in the ESA module, and that's at vacuum. But if I start depress now, I could get to those crystals in four or five hours.'

'How much HCG is on board?'

'I'm checking.' She opened the experiment file and quickly scanned the mass measurement data.

'Emma?'

'Hold on, hold on! I've got the most recent mass here. I'm looking up normal HCG levels in pregnancy.'

'I can get those for you.'

'No, I've found it. Okay. Okay, if I dilute this crystal mass in normal saline . . . plug in my body weight as forty-five kilograms . . .' She typed in the numbers. She was making wild assumptions here. She didn't know how quickly HCG was metabolized, or what its half-life would be. The answer at last appeared onscreen.

'How many doses?' said Jack.

She closed her eyes. *It's not going to last long enough. It's not going to save me.*

'Emma?'

She released a deep breath. It came out as a sob. 'Three days.'

THE ORIGIN

25

It was 1:45 A.M., and Jack's vision was blurred from fatigue, the words on the computer screen fading in and out of focus. 'There must be more,' he said. 'Keep searching.'

Gretchen Liu, seated at the keyboard, glanced up at Jack and Gordon in frustration. She had been sound asleep when they called her to come in, and she'd arrived without her usual camera-ready makeup and contact lenses. They had never seen their normally elegant public affairs officer looking so unglamorous. Or wearing glasses, for that matter – thick horn-rim glasses that magnified her pinched eyes. 'I'm telling you guys, this is all I can find on Lexis-Nexis search. Almost nothing on Helen Koenig. On SeaScience, there's only the usual corporate news releases. And as for the name *Palmer Gabriel*, well, you can see for yourself he doesn't court publicity. In the last five years, the only place his name turns up in the media is on the financial pages of *The Wall*

Street Journal. Business articles about SeaScience and its products. There's no biographical data. There's not even a photo of the man.'

Jack slumped back in his chair and rubbed his eyes. The three of them had spent the last two hours in the Public Affairs Office, combing every article about Helen Koenig and SeaScience they could find on Lexis-Nexis. They had turned up numerous hits for SeaScience, dozens of articles in which its products had been mentioned, from shampoos to pharmaceuticals to fertilizers. But almost nothing had turned up on Koenig or Gabriel.

'Try the name *Koenig* again,' said Jack.

'We've done every possible spelling variation on her name,' said Gretchen. 'There's nothing.'

'Then type in the word *Archaeons*.'

Sighing, Gretchen typed in *Archaeons* and clicked on 'Search.'

A numbingly long string of article citations filled the screen.

'Alien Earth Creatures. Scientists Hail Discovery of New Branch of Life.' *(Washington Post)*

'Archaeons to Be Subject of International Conference.' *(Miami Herald)*

'Deep Sea Organisms Offer Clues to Life's Origins.' *(Philadelphia Inquirer)*

'Guys, this is hopeless,' said Gretchen. 'It'll take

us all night to read every article on this list. Why don't we just call it a night and get some sleep?'

'Wait!' Gordon said. 'Scroll down to this one.' He pointed to a citation at the bottom of the screen: ' "Scientist Dies in Galápagos Diving Accident" *(New York Times)*.'

'The Galápagos,' said Jack. 'That's where Dr Koenig discovered the Archaeon strain. In the Galápagos Rift.'

Gretchen clicked on the article and the text appeared. The story was two years old.

COPYRIGHT: *The New York Times.*
SECTION: International News.
HEADLINE: 'Scientist Dies in Deep Sea Diving Accident.'
BYLINE: Julio Perez, NYT Correspondent.
BODY: An American scientist studying Archaeon marine organisms was killed yesterday when his one-man submersible became wedged in an undersea canyon of the Galápagos Rift. The body of Dr Stephen D. Ahearn was not recovered until this morning, when cables from the research vessel *Gabriella* were able to haul the minisub to the surface.

'We knew he was still alive down there, but there was nothing we could do,' said a fellow scientist aboard *Gabriella*. 'He was trapped at nineteen thousand feet. It took us hours to free his submersible and haul it back to the surface.'

Dr Ahearn was a professor of geology at the University of California, San Diego. He resided in La Jolla, California.

Jack said, 'The ship's name was *Gabriella*.'

He and Gordon looked at each other, both of them struck by the same startling thought: *Gabriella. Palmer Gabriel.*

'I'll bet you this was a SeaScience vessel,' said Jack, 'and Helen Koenig was aboard.'

Gordon's gaze shifted back to the screen. 'Now this is interesting. What do you make of the fact Ahearn was a geologist?'

'So what?' said Gretchen, yawning.

'What was a geologist doing aboard a marine research vessel?'

'Checking out the rocks on the sea floor?'

'Let's do a search on his name.'

Gretchen sighed. 'You guys owe me a night's worth of beauty sleep.' She typed in the name *Stephen D. Ahearn* and clicked on 'Search.'

A list appeared, seven articles in all. Six of them were about his undersea death in the Galápagos.

One article was from the year prior to his death:

'UCSD Professor to Present Latest Findings on Tektite Research. Will Be Keynote Speaker at International Geological Conference in Madrid.' (*San Diego Union*)

Both men stared at the screen, too stunned for a moment to utter a word.

Then Gordon said softly, 'This is it, Jack. This is what they've been trying to hide from us.'

Jack's hands had gone numb, his throat dry. He focused on a single word, the word that told them everything.

Tektite.

JSC director Ken Blankenship's house was one of the anonymous tract homes in the suburb of Clear Lake, where so many JSC officials lived. It was a large house for a bachelor, and in the glare of the security lights, Jack saw that the front yard was immaculately groomed, every hedge clipped into submission. That yard, so well lit at three A.M., was exactly what one would expect of Blankenship, who was notorious for his perfectionism as well as his almost paranoid obsession with security. *There's probably a surveillance camera trained on us right this moment*, thought Jack as he and Obie waited for Blankenship to answer the front door. It took several rings of the doorbell before they saw lights come on inside. Then Blankenship appeared, a squat little Napoleon dressed in a bathrobe.

'It's three in the morning,' said Blankenship. 'What are you guys doing here?'

'We need to talk,' said Gordon.

'Is there something wrong with my phone? You couldn't have called first?'

'We can't use the phone. Not about this.'

They all stepped into the house. Only after the front door swung shut did Jack say, 'We know what the White House is trying to hide. We know where Chimera comes from.'

Blankenship stared at him, his irritation over a disturbed night's sleep instantly forgotten. Then he looked at Gordon, seeking confirmation of Jack's statement.

'It explains everything,' said Gordon. 'USAMRIID's secrecy. The White House's paranoia. And the fact that this organism behaves unlike anything our doctors have ever encountered.'

'What did you find out?'

Jack answered the question. 'We know Chimera has human, mouse, and amphibian DNA. But USAMRIID won't tell us what other DNA is on the genome. They won't tell us what Chimera really is, or where it comes from.'

'You told me last night the bug was sent up in a SeaScience payload. A culture of Archaeons.'

'That's what we thought. But Archaeons are not dangerous organisms. They're incapable of causing disease in humans – that's why the experiment was accepted by NASA. Something about this particular Archaeon is different. Something SeaScience didn't tell us.'

'What do you mean, different?'

'Where it came from. The Galápagos Rift.'

Blankenship shook his head. 'I don't see the significance.'

'This culture was discovered by scientists aboard

the vessel *Gabriella*, a ship belonging to SeaScience. One of those researchers was a Dr Stephen Ahearn, who was flown out to *Gabriella*, apparently as a last-minute consultant. Within a week, he was dead. His minisub became trapped at the bottom of the rift, and he suffocated.'

Blankenship said nothing, but his gaze remained focused on Jack's.

'Dr Ahearn was known for his research on tektites,' said Jack. 'Those are glassy fragments produced whenever a meteor collides with the earth. That was Dr Ahearn's field of expertise. The geology of meteors and asteroids.'

Still Blankenship said nothing. *Why isn't he reacting?* Jack wondered. *Doesn't he understand what this means?*

'SeaScience flew Ahearn to the Galápagos because they needed a geologist's opinion,' said Jack. 'They needed confirmation of what they'd found on the sea floor. An asteroid.'

Blankenship's face had gone rigid. He turned and walked toward the kitchen.

Jack and Gordon followed him. 'That's why the White House is so scared of Chimera!' said Jack. 'They know where it comes from. They know what it is.'

Blankenship picked up the telephone and dialed. A moment later, he said, 'This is JSC director Kenneth Blankenship. I need to speak to Jared Profitt. Yes, I know what time it is. This is an emergency, so if you could connect me to his home . . .' There was a moment's silence. Then he said into the phone, 'They know. No, I did not tell them. They found out on their own.' A pause. 'Jack McCallum and Gordon Obie. Yes, sir, they're standing right here in my kitchen.' He handed the receiver to Jack. 'He wants to speak to you.'

Jack took the phone. 'This is McCallum.'

'How many people know?' was the first thing Jared Profitt asked him.

That question instantly told Jack how sensitive this information was. He said, 'Our medical people know. And a few people in Life Sciences.' That was all he'd say; he knew better than to name names.

'Can you all keep it quiet?' asked Profitt.

'That depends.'

'On what?'

'On whether your people cooperate with us. Share information with us.'

'What do you want, Dr McCallum?'

'Full disclosure. Everything you've learned about Chimera. The autopsy results. The data from your clinical trials.'

'And if we don't share? What happens?'

'My colleagues at NASA start faxing every news agency in the country.'

'Telling them what, exactly?'

'The truth. That this organism is not terrestrial.'

There was a long silence. Jack could hear his own heartbeat thudding in the receiver. *Have we guessed right? Have we really uncovered the truth?*

Profitt said, 'I'll authorize Dr Roman to tell you everything. He'll be expecting you at White Sands.' The phone went dead.

Jack hung up and looked at Blankenship. 'How long have you known?'

Blankenship's silence only fueled Jack's anger. He took a threatening step forward, and Blankenship backed up against the kitchen wall. '*How long have you known?*'

'Only – only a few days. I was sworn to secrecy!'

'Those were *our* people dying up there!'

'I had no choice! This has got everyone terrified! The White House. Defense.' Blankenship took a deep breath and looked Jack straight in the eye. 'You'll understand what I'm talking about. When you get to White Sands.'

August 20

With one end gripped in her teeth, Emma yanked the tourniquet tight, and the veins of her left arm plumped up like blue worms beneath the pale skin. She gave her antecubital vein a quick swipe of alcohol and winced at the prick of the needle. Like a junkie desperate for a fix, she injected the entire contents of the syringe, loosening the tourniquet halfway through. When she was finished, she closed her eyes and allowed herself to drift as she imagined the HCG molecules, like tiny stars of hope, coursing up her veins, swirling into her heart and lungs. Streaming out into arteries and capillaries. She imagined she could already feel its effect, the headache melting away, the hot flames of her fever smothered to a dying glow. *Three doses left*, she thought. *Three more days*.

She imagined herself drifting out of her own body, and she saw herself, as though from a distance, curled up like a mottled fetus in a coffin. A bubble of mucus spilling out of her mouth, breaking into bright squirming threads like maggots.

Abruptly she opened her eyes and realized that she had been sleeping. Dreaming. Her shirt was saturated with sweat. It was a good sign. It meant that her fever had eased off.

She massaged her temples, trying to force out the images from her dream, but she could not; reality and nightmares had merged into one.

She stripped off the sweat-soaked shirt and put on a clean one from Diana's locker. Despite the bad dreams, that brief nap had refreshed her, and she was alert again, ready to search for new solutions. She floated into the U.S. lab and pulled up all the Chimera files on the computer. It was an extraterrestrial organism, Todd Cutler had informed her, and everything NASA now knew about the life-form had been transmitted to her onboard computers. She reviewed the files, hoping to find some new inspiration, some fresh approach that no one else had thought of. Everything she read was dismally familiar.

She opened the genome file. A nucleotide

sequence spilled across the monitor in an unending stream of *A*s, *C*s, *T*s, and *G*s. Here was Chimera's genetic code – parts of it, anyway. The parts USAMRIID had chosen to share with NASA. She stared, hypnotized, as the lines of code marched down the screen. This was the essence of the alien life-form now growing inside her. It was the key to the enemy. If only she knew how to use it.

The key.

She suddenly thought of what Jack had said earlier, about hormones. *In order for a hormone to work, it has to bind to a specific receptor on the target cell. It's like a key in search of just the right lock in which to fit.*

Why would a mammalian hormone like HCG suppress the reproduction of an alien life-form? she wondered. Why would an extraterrestrial organism, so foreign to anything on earth, possess properly fitting locks to *our* keys?

On the computer, the nucleotide sequence had finished scrolling to the end. She stared at the blinking cursor and thought of the earth-born species whose DNA had been raided by Chimera. By acquiring those new genes, this alien life-form had become part human. Part mouse. Part amphibian.

She got on the comm with Houston. 'I need to speak to somebody in Life Sciences,' she said.

'Anyone in particular?' asked Capcom.

'An amphibian expert.'

'Stand by, Watson.'

Ten minutes later, a Dr Wang from NASA Life Sciences came on the loop. 'You had a question about amphibians?' he asked.

'Yes, about *Rana pipiens*, the northern leopard frog.'

'What can I tell you about it?'

'What happens if you expose the leopard frog to human hormones?'

'Any hormone in particular?'

'Estrogen, for instance. Or HCG.'

Dr Wang answered without hesitation. 'Amphibians in general are adversely affected by environmental estrogens. It's been studied quite a bit, actually. A number of experts think the worldwide decline in frog populations is due to estrogenlike substances polluting streams and ponds.'

'What estrogenlike substances?'

'Certain pesticides, for instance, can mimic estrogens. They disrupt the frogs' endocrine systems, making it impossible for them to reproduce or thrive.'

'So it doesn't actually kill them.'

'No, it just disrupts reproduction.'

'Are frogs in particular sensitive to this?'

'Oh, yes. Far more than mammals. Plus, frogs have permeable skin, so they're susceptible to toxins in general. That's sort of their, well, Achilles' heel.'

Achilles' heel. She fell silent for a moment, thinking about that.

'Dr Watson?' said Wang. 'You have any other questions?'

'Yes. Is there any disease or toxin that would kill a frog, but not harm a mammal?'

'That's an interesting question. When it comes to toxins, it would depend on the dose. You give a little arsenic to a frog, you'd kill it. But arsenic would kill a man as well, if he's given a larger dose. Then again, there are microbial diseases, certain bacteria and viruses, that only kill frogs. I'm not a physician, so I'm not absolutely certain they're harmless to humans, but –'

'Viruses?' she cut in. 'Which ones?'

'Well, Ranaviruses, for instance.'

'I've never heard of those.'

'Only amphibian experts are familiar with them. They're DNA viruses. Part of the Iridovirus family. We think they're the cause of tadpole edema syndrome. The tadpoles swell up and hemorrhage.'

'And that's fatal to them?'

'Very much so.'

'Does this virus kill people as well?'

'I don't know. I don't think anyone does. I do know Ranaviruses have killed off whole populations of frogs around the world.'

The Achilles' heel, she thought. *I've found it.*

By adding the leopard frog's DNA to its own genome, Chimera had become part amphibian. It had also acquired an amphibian's vulnerabilities.

She said, 'Is there any way to obtain live

samples of one of these Ranaviruses? To test against Chimera?'

There was a long silence. 'I get it,' said Dr Wang. 'No one's tried that yet. No one's even considered –'

'Can you get the virus?' she cut in.

'Yes. I know two amphibian research labs in California who are working with live Ranaviruses.'

'Then do it. And get hold of Jack McCallum. He needs to know about this.'

'He and Gordon Obie just left for White Sands. I'll reach them there.'

Tumbleweeds skittered across the road, swept along in a stinging cloud of sand. The men drove past the guardhouse, past the electrified fence, and into the barren Army compound. Jack and Gordon stepped out of the vehicle and squinted up at the sky. The sun was a dusky orange, obscured by windblown dust. The color of sunset, not high noon. They had managed to catch only a few hours of sleep before they'd taken off from Ellington, and it hurt Jack's eyes just to see the light of day.

'This way, gentlemen,' the driver said.

They followed the soldier into the building.

It was a different reception from the last time Jack had visited. This time the Army escort was polite and respectful. This time Dr Isaac Roman was waiting at the front desk, although he did not look particularly happy about their arrival.

'Only you are allowed to come with me, Dr

McCallum,' he said. 'Mr Obie will have to wait here. That was the agreement.'

'I made no such agreement,' said Jack.

'Mr Profitt did, on your behalf. He's the only reason you're being allowed in this building. I haven't a great deal of time, so let's get this over with.' He turned and walked to the elevators.

'Now, there's your standard Army-issue asshole,' said Gordon. 'Go on. I'll wait here.'

Jack followed Roman into the elevator.

'First stop is subbasement level two,' said Roman, 'where we house our animal trials.' The elevator door opened, and they confronted a wall of glass. It was a viewing window.

Jack approached the window and stared at the laboratory beyond. Inside were a dozen workers wearing biocontamination suits. Cages held spider monkeys and dogs. Right beside the window were glass-enclosed rat cages. Roman pointed to the rats. 'You'll notice each cage is labeled with the date and time they were infected. I can think of no better way to illustrate Chimera's lethal nature.'

In the Day 1 cage, the six rats appeared healthy, vigorously spinning their exercise wheels.

In the cage labeled 'Day 2,' the first signs of illness appeared. Two of the six rats were shivering, their eyes a bright bloodred. The other four were huddled in a lethargic heap.

'The first two days,' said Dr Roman, 'is Chimera's reproductive phase. You understand, this is completely opposite to what we see on earth. Usually a life-form must reach maturity before it begins to repro-duce. Chimera reproduces *first*, and then begins to mature. It divides at a rapid rate, producing up to a hundred copies of itself by forty-eight hours. They start out microscopic in size – not visible to the naked eye. Small enough so that you could breathe them in, or absorb them through your mucous membranes, and not even know you've been exposed.'

'So they're infectious at this early stage in their life cycle?'

'They're infectious at *any* stage of their life cycle. They only have to be released into the air. Usually it happens around the time of the victim's death, or when the corpse bursts open several days post mortem. Once Chimera's infected you, once it's multiplied inside your body, each individual copy begins to grow. Begins to develop into . . .' He paused. 'We don't really know what to call them. Egg sacs, I suppose. Because they contain a larval life-form inside them.'

Jack's gaze moved on to the Day 3 enclosure. All the mice were twitching, limbs thrashing as though repeatedly jolted by electric shocks.

'By the third day,' said Roman, 'the larvae are growing rapidly. Displacing the victim's brain matter by sheer mass effect. Wreaking havoc with the host's neurologic functions. And by day four . . .'

They looked at the fourth enclosure. All but one

were dead. The corpses had not been removed; they lay stiff-legged, mouths gaping open. There were still three cages to go; the process of decomposition had been allowed to continue.

By day five, the corpses were beginning to bloat.

On day six, the bellies had grown even larger, the skin stretched drum-taut. Viscous fluid seeped from the open eyes and glistened on the nostrils.

And on day seven . . .

Jack halted beside the window, staring into the seventh enclosure. Ruptured corpses littered the bottom like deflated balloons, the skin torn open to reveal a black stew of dissolved organs. And adhering to one rat's face was a gelatinous mass of opaque globes. They were quivering.

'The egg sacs,' said Roman. 'By this stage, the corpse's body cavities are packed with them. They grow at an astonishing rate, feeding on host tissues. Digesting muscles and organs.' He looked at Jack. 'Are you familiar with the life cycle of parasitic wasps?'

Jack shook his head.

'The adult wasp injects its eggs into a living caterpillar. The larvae grow, ingesting their host's hemolymph fluid. All this time, the caterpillar is *alive*. Incubating a foreign life-form that's eating it from the inside, until the larvae finally burst out of their dying host.' Roman looked at the dead rats. 'These larvae, too, multiply and develop inside a living victim. And that's what finally kills the host.

All those larvae, packing into the cranium. Nibbling away at the surface of the gray matter. Damaging capillaries, causing intracranial bleeding. The pressure builds. Vessels in the eyes engorge, burst. The host experiences blinding headaches, confusion. He stumbles around as though drunk. In three or four days, he is dead. And still the life-form continues to feed on the corpse. Raiding its DNA. Using that DNA to speed its own evolution.'

'Into what?'

Roman looked at Jack. 'We don't know the end point. With every generation, Chimera acquires DNA from its host. The Chimera we're working with now is not the same one we started out with. The genome has become more complex. The life-form more advanced.'

More and more human, thought Jack.

'This is the reason for absolute secrecy,' said Roman. 'Any terrorist, any hostile country, could mine the Galápagos Rift for more of these things. This organism, in the wrong hands . . .' His voice trailed off.

'So nothing about this thing is manmade.'

Roman shook his head. 'It was found by chance in the rift. Brought up to the surface by *Gabriella*. At first Dr Koenig thought she'd discovered a new species of Archaeons. Instead, what she found was this.' He looked at the wriggling mass of eggs. 'A thousand years, they've been trapped in the remains of that asteroid. At a depth of nineteen thousand feet. That's what has kept it in check

438

all this time. The fact it came to rest in the deep sea, and not on land.'

'Now I understand why you tested the hyperbaric chamber.'

'All this time Chimera has existed benignly in the rift. We thought, if we reproduced those pressures, we could make it benign again.'

'And can you?'

Roman shook his head. 'Only temporarily. This life-form has been permanently altered by exposure to microgravity. Somehow, when it was brought to ISS, its reproductive switch was turned on. It's as if it was preprogrammed to be lethal. But it needed the *absence* of gravity to start that program running again.'

'How temporary is hyperbaric treatment?'

'Infected mice stay healthy as long as they're in the chamber. We've kept them alive ten days now. But as soon as we take any of them out, the disease continues its progression.'

'What about Ranavirus?' Only an hour ago, Dr Wang from NASA Life Sciences had briefed Jack by phone. At that very moment, a supply of the amphibian virus was winging its way by Air Force jet to Dr Roman's lab. 'Our scientists believe it could work.'

'Theoretically. But it's too early to launch a rescue shuttle. First we have to *prove* Ranavirus works, or you'd risk the lives of another shuttle crew. We need time to test the virus. Several weeks, at least.'

Emma doesn't have weeks, thought Jack. *She has only three days' worth of HCG*. In silence he gazed down at the cage of rat corpses. At the eggs, glistening in their nest of slime. *If only I could buy more time*.

Time. A thought suddenly occurred to him. The memory of something Roman had just said.

'You said the hyperbaric chamber has kept mice alive for ten days so far.'

'That's correct.'

'But it was only ten days ago that *Discovery* crashed.'

Roman avoided his gaze.

'You planned the chamber tests right from the start. Which means you already knew what you were dealing with. Even before you performed the autopsies.'

Roman turned and started to walk back to the elevator. He gave a gasp of surprise when Jack caught him by the collar and spun him around.

'That wasn't a commercial payload,' said Jack. *'Was it?'*

Roman pushed away and stumbled backward, against the wall.

'Defense used SeaScience as a cover,' said Jack. 'You paid them to send up the experiment for you. To hide the fact that this life-form is of military interest.'

Roman sidled toward the elevator. Toward escape.

Jack grabbed the man's lab coat and tightened

his grip on the collar. 'This wasn't bioterrorism. This was your own fucking *mistake!*'

Roman's face had turned purple. 'I can't – can't breathe!'

Jack released him, and Roman slid down the wall, his legs collapsing beneath him. For a moment he didn't speak, but sat slumped on the floor, struggling to catch his breath. When at last he did talk, all he could manage was a whisper.

'We had no way of knowing what it would do. How it would change without gravity . . .'

'But you knew it was alien.'

'Yes.'

'And you knew it was a chimera. That it already had amphibian DNA.'

'No. No, we didn't know that.'

'Don't bullshit me.'

'We don't know how the frog DNA got onto the genome! It must have happened in Dr Koenig's lab. A mistake of some kind. She was the one who found the organism in the rift, the one who finally realized what it was. SeaScience knew we'd be interested. An extraterrestrial organism – of course we were! Defense paid for their KC-135 experiments. We funded the payload space on ISS. It couldn't go up as a military payload. There'd be too many questions asked, too many review committees. NASA would wonder why the Army cared about harmless sea microbes. But no one questions the private sector. So it went up as a commercial payload, with Sea-Science as sponsor. And Dr Koenig as principal investigator.'

'Where is Dr Koenig?'

Slowly Roman rose to his feet. 'She's dead.'

That information took Jack by surprise. 'How?' he asked softly.

'It was an accident.'

'You think I believe that?'

'It's the truth.'

Jack studied the man for a moment and decided Roman was not lying.

'It happened over two weeks ago in Mexico,' said Roman. 'Just after she resigned from SeaScience. The taxi she was riding in was completely destroyed.'

'And USAMRIID's raid on her lab? You weren't there to investigate, were you? You were there to see that all her files were destroyed.'

'We are talking about an alien life-form. An organism more dangerous than we realized. Yes, the experiment was a mistake. A catastrophe. Just imagine what could happen if this information leaked out to the world's terrorists?'

This was why NASA had been kept in the dark. Why the truth could never be revealed.

'And you haven't seen the worst of it yet, Dr McCallum,' said Roman.

'What do you mean?'

'There's one more thing I want to show you.'

They rode the elevator down to the next level, to subbasement three. Deeper into Hades, thought

442

Jack. Once again they stepped out to face a wall of glass, and beyond it, another lab with more space-suited workers.

Roman pressed the intercom button and said, 'Could you bring out the specimen?'

One of the lab workers nodded. She crossed to a walk-in steel vault, spun the massive combination lock, and disappeared inside. When she emerged again, she was wheeling a cart with a steel container on a tray. She rolled it to the viewing window.

Roman nodded.

She unlatched the steel container, lifted out a Plexiglas cylinder, and set it on the tray. The contents bobbed gently in a clear bath of formalin.

'We found this burrowed inside the spinal column of Kenichi Hirai,' said Roman. 'His spine protected it from the force of impact when *Discovery* crashed. When we removed it, it was still alive – but only barely.'

Jack tried to speak, but could not produce a single word. He heard only the hiss of the ventilation fans and the roar of his own pulse as he stared in horror at the contents of the cylinder.

'This is what the larvae grow into,' said Roman. 'This is the next stage.'

He understood, now. The reason for secrecy. What he had seen preserved in formalin, coiled up in that Plexiglas cylinder, had explained everything. Though it had been mangled during extraction, its essential features had been apparent. The glossy amphibian skin. The larval tail. And the fetal curl of the spine – not amphibian, but something far more horrifying, because its genetic origin was recognizable. *Mammalian*, he thought. Maybe even human. It was already beginning to look like its host.

Allowed to infect a different species, it would change its appearance yet again. It could raid the DNA of any organism on earth, assume any shape. Eventually it could evolve to the point where it needed no host at all in which to grow and reproduce. It would be independent and self-sufficient. Perhaps even intelligent.

And Emma was now a living nursery for these things, her body a nourishing cocoon in which they were growing.

Jack shivered as he stood on the tarmac and stared across the barren airstrip. The Army jeep that had brought him and Gordon back to White Sands Air Force Base had receded to barely a glint now, trailing a fantail of dust into the horizon. The sun's white-hot brilliance brought tears to his eyes, and for a moment, the desert shimmered out of focus, as though underwater.

He turned to look at Gordon. 'There's no other way. We have to do it.'

'There are a thousand things that can go wrong.'

'There always are. That's true for every launch,

every mission. Why should this one be any different?'

'There'll be no contingencies. No safety backups. I know what we're dealing with, and it's a cowboy operation.'

'Which makes it possible. What's their motto? *Smaller, faster, cheaper.*'

'Okay,' said Gordon, 'let's say you *don't* blow up on the launchpad. Say the Air Force *doesn't* blast you out of the sky. Once you get up there, you're still faced with the biggest gamble of all: whether the Ranavirus will work.'

'From the very beginning, Gordon, there was one thing I couldn't figure out: Why was amphibian DNA on that genome? How did Chimera get frog genes? Roman thinks it was an accident. A mistake that happened in Koenig's lab.' Jack shook his head. 'I don't think it was an accident at all. I think Koenig *put* those genes there. As a fail-safe.'

'I don't understand.'

'Maybe she was thinking ahead, to the possible dangers. To what could happen if this new life-form changed while in microgravity. If Chimera ever got out of control, she wanted a way to kill it. A back door through its defenses. And this is it.'

'A frog virus.'

'It will work, Gordon. It has to work. I'll bet my life on it.'

A whorl of dust spun between them, kicking

up sand and stray scraps of paper. Gordon turned and gazed across the tarmac at the T-38 they had flown from Houston. And he sighed. 'I was afraid you'd say that.'

26

August 22

Casper Mulholland was gobbling down his third package of Tums, and his stomach still felt like a bubbling cauldron of acid. In the distance, *Apogee II* glinted like a bullet casing planted point up in the desert sand. She was not a particularly impressive sight, especially to this audience. Most of them had heard the earth-shaking roar of a NASA launch, had been awed by the majesty of the shuttle's giant columns of fire streaking into the sky. *Apogee II* looked nothing like the shuttle. She was more like a child's toy rocket, and Casper could see disappointment in the eyes of the dozen or so visitors as they climbed the newly erected viewing stand and gazed across the bleak desert terrain, toward the launchpad. Everyone wanted *big*. Everyone was in love with size and power. The small, the elegantly simple, did not interest them.

Another van pulled up at the site, and a fresh

group of visitors began piling out, hands lifting at once to shield their eyes from the morning sun. He recognized Mark Lucas and Hashemi Rashad, the two businessmen who had visited Apogee over three weeks ago. He saw the same disappointment play across their faces as they squinted toward the launchpad.

'This is as close to the pad as we can get?' said Lucas.

'I'm afraid so,' said Casper. 'It's for your own safety. We're dealing with explosive propellants out there.'

'But I thought we were going to get an in-depth look at your launch operations.'

'You'll have full access to our ground-control facility – our equivalent of Houston's Mission Control. As soon as she's off the pad, we'll drive over to the building and show you how we guide her into low earth orbit. That's the real test of our system, Mr Lucas. Any engineering grad can launch a rocket. But getting one safely into orbit, and then guiding her to a flyby of the station, is a far more complicated matter. That's why we moved up this demonstration four days – to hit just the right launch window for ISS. To show you our system is already rendezvous-capable. *Apogee II* is just the kind of bird NASA's looking to buy.'

'You're not actually going to dock, are you?' said Rashad. 'I heard the station is in quarantine.'

'No, we're not going to dock. *Apogee II*'s just a prototype. She can't physically hook up with ISS because she doesn't have an orbital docking system. But we'll fly her close enough to the station to demonstrate we can do it. You know, just the fact we're able to change our launch schedule on short notice is a selling point. When it comes to spaceflight, flexibility is key. Unexpected things always pop up. My partner's recent accident, for example. Even though Mr Obie's laid up in bed with a broken pelvis, you'll notice we didn't cancel the launch. We'll control the entire mission from the ground. Gentlemen, *that's* flexibility.'

'I can understand why you might delay a launch,' said Lucas. 'Say, for bad weather. By why did you have to move it *up* four days? Some of our partners weren't able to make it here in time.'

Casper could feel the last Tums tablet bubble away in a fresh spurt of stomach acid. 'It's simple, really.' He paused to take out a handkerchief and wipe the sweat from his forehead. 'It has to do with that launch window I mentioned. The space station's orbit is at an inclination of fifty-one point six degrees. If you look at a tracing of its orbital path on a map, it makes a sine wave varying between fifty-one point six degrees north and fifty-one point six degrees south. Since the earth rotates, the station passes over a different place on the map with each orbit. Also, the earth isn't entirely spherical, which adds another complication. When that orbital trace passes over your launch site, that's the most efficient time to lift off. Adding up all those factors, we came up with various launch options. Then there's the question of daytime versus nighttime launches. Allowable launch angles. The most current weather forecasts . . .'

Their eyes had begun to glaze over. He'd already lost them.

'Anyway,' Casper finished with a profound sense of relief, 'today at seven-ten A.M. turns out to be the best choice. That all makes perfect sense to you, right?'

Lucas seemed to give himself a shake, like a startled dog coming out of a nap. 'Yes. Of course.'

'I'd still like to get closer,' said Mr Rashad on a wistful note. He gazed at the rocket, a snub-nosed blip on the horizon. 'From this far away, she's not much to look at, is she? So small.'

Casper smiled, even as he felt his own stomach digest itself in nervous acid. 'Well, you know what they say, Mr Rashad. It's not the size that matters. It's what you do with it.'

This is the last option, thought Jack as a bead of perspiration slid down his temple and soaked into the lining of his flight helmet. He tried to calm his racing pulse, but his heart was like a frantic animal trying to batter its way out of his chest. For so many years, this was the moment he had dreamed of: strapped into the flight seat, helmet closed, oxygen flowing. The countdown ticking toward zero. In those dreams, fear had not been part of the equation, only excitement. Anticipation. He had not expected to be terrified.

'You are at T minus five minutes. The time to back out is now.' It was Gordon Obie's voice over the hardline comm. At every step of the way, Gordon had offered Jack chances to change his mind. During the flight from White Sands to Nevada. In the early morning hours, as Jack suited up in the Apogee Engineering hangar. And finally, on the drive across the pitch-black desert to the launchpad. This was Jack's last opportunity.

'We can stop the countdown now,' said Gordon. 'Nix the whole mission.'

'I'm still a go.'

'Then this will be our last voice contact. There can't be any communication from you. No downlink to the ground, no contact with ISS, or everything's blown. The instant we hear your voice, we'll abort the whole mission and bring you back.' *If we still can*, was what he didn't add.

'I roger that.'

There was a silence. 'You don't have to do this. No one expects you to.'

'Let's get on with it. Just light the damn candle, okay?'

Gordon's answering sigh came through loud and clear. 'Okay. You're a go. We're at T minus three minutes and counting.'

'Thank you, Gordie. For everything.'

'Good luck and Godspeed, Jack McCallum.'

The hard link was severed.

And that may be the last voice I'll ever hear, thought Jack. From this point on, the only uplink from

Apogee ground control would be command data streaming into the onboard guidance and nav computers. The vehicle was flying itself; Jack was nothing more than the dumb monkey in the pilot's seat.

He closed his eyes and focused on the beating of his own heart. It had slowed. He now felt strangely calm and prepared for the inevitable, whatever that might be. He heard the whirs and clicks of the onboard systems preparing for the leap. He imagined the cloudless sky, its atmosphere dense as water, like a sea of air through which he must surface to reach the cold, clear vacuum of space.

Where Emma was dying.

The crowd in the viewing stand had fallen ominously silent. The countdown clock, displayed on the closed-circuit video feed, slid past the T minus sixty seconds mark and kept ticking. *They're going for the launch window*, thought Casper, and the fresh sweat of panic bloomed on his forehead. In his heart, he had never really believed it would come to this moment. He had expected delays, aborts, even a cancellation. He had lived through so many disappointments, so much bad luck with this damn bird, that dread rose like bile in his throat. He glanced at the faces in the stands and saw that many of them were mouthing the seconds as they ticked by. It started as a whisper, a rhythmic disturbance in the air.

'Twenty-nine. Twenty-eight. Twenty-seven . . .'

The whispers became a chorus of murmurs, growing louder with each passing second.

'Twelve. Eleven. Ten . . .'

Casper's hands were shaking so hard he had to clutch the railing. His pulse throbbed in his fingertips.

'Seven. Six. Five . . .'

He closed his eyes. Oh, God, what had they done?

'Three. Two. One . . .'

The crowd sucked in a simultaneous gasp of wonder. Then the roar of the boosters spilled over him, and his eyes flew open. He stared at the sky, at the streak of fire lifting toward the heavens. Any second now it would happen. First the blinding flash, then, lagging behind at the speed of sound, the pulse of the explosion battering their eardrums. That's how it had happened with *Apogee I*.

But the fiery streak kept on rising until it was only a pale dot punched in the deep blue sky.

A hand clapped his back, hard. He gave a start and turned to see Mark Lucas beaming at him.

'Way to go, Mulholland! What a gorgeous launch!'

Casper ventured another terrified glance at the sky. Still no explosion.

'But I guess you never had any doubts, did you?' said Lucas.

Casper swallowed. 'None at all.'

The last dose.

Emma squeezed the plunger, slowly emptying

453

the contents of the syringe into her vein. She removed the needle, pressed gauze to the puncture site, and folded her arm to hold it in place while she disposed of the needle. It felt like a sacred ceremony, every action performed with reverence, with the solemn knowledge that this was the last time she would experience each sensation, from the prick of the needle, to the hard lump of gauze pressing into the flesh at the crook of her arm. And how long would this final dose of HCG keep her alive?

She turned and looked at the mouse cage, which she had moved into the Russian service module, where there was more light. The lone female was now curled in a shivering ball, dying. The hormone's effect was not permanent. The babies had died that morning. *By tomorrow*, thought Emma, *I will be the only one alive aboard this station.*

No, not the only one. There would be the life-form inside her. The scores of larvae that would soon awaken from dormancy and begin to feed and grow.

She pressed her hand to her abdomen, like a pregnant woman sensing the fetus inside her. And like a real fetus, the life-form she now harbored would carry bits and pieces of her DNA. In that way, it was her biological offspring, and it possessed the genetic memory of every host it had ever known. Kenichi Hirai. Nicolai Rudenko. Diana Estes. And now, Emma.

She would be the last. There would be no new

hosts, no new victims, because there would be no rescuers. The station was now a sepulchre of contagion, as forbidden and untouchable as a leper colony had been to the ancients.

She floated out of the RSM and swam toward the powered-down section of the station. There was barely enough light to guide her through the darkened node. Except for the rhythmic sigh of her own breathing, all was silent on this end. She moved through the same molecules of air that had once swirled in the lungs of people now dead. Even now, she sensed the presence of the five who had passed on, could imagine the echoes of their voices, the last faint pulses of sound fracturing at last into silence. This was the very air through which they had moved, and it was still haunted by their passing.

And soon, she thought, *it will be haunted by mine*.

August 24

Jared Profitt was awakened just after midnight. It took only two rings of the phone to propel him from deep sleep to a state of complete alertness. He reached for the receiver.

The voice on the other end was brusque. 'This is General Gregorian. I've just spoken to our control center in Cheyenne Mountain. That so-called demo launch from Nevada continues to be on a rendezvous path with ISS.'

'Which launch?'

'Apogee Engineering.'

Profitt frowned, trying to remember the name. Every week there were numerous launches from sites around the world. A score of commercial aerospace firms were always testing booster systems or sending satellites into orbit or even blasting off cremated human remains. Space Command was already tracking nine thousand manmade objects in orbit. 'Refresh my memory about this Nevada launch,' he asked.

'Apogee is testing a new reusable launch vehicle. They sent it up at oh-seven-ten yesterday morning. They informed the FAA as required, but didn't let us know until after the fact. This flight is billed as an orbital trial of their new RLV. A launch into low earth orbit, a flyby past ISS, and then reentry. We've been tracking it for a day and a half now, and based on its most recent on-orbit burns, it seems possible they'll approach the station closer than they told us.'

'How close will they get?'

'It depends on their next burn maneuvers.'

'Close enough for an actual rendezvous? A docking?'

'That's not possible with this particular vehicle. We have all the specs on their orbiter. It's just a prototype, with no orbital docking system. The best it can do is a flyby and a wave.'

'A wave?' Profitt suddenly sat up in bed. 'Are you telling me this RLV is manned?'

'No, sir. That was just a figure of speech. Apogee

says the vehicle is unmanned. There are animals aboard, including a spider monkey, but no pilot. And we've picked up no voice communication between ground and vehicle.'

A spider monkey, thought Profitt. Its presence aboard the spacecraft meant they could not rule out the possibility of a human pilot. The craft's environmental monitors, the carbon dioxide levels, would not distinguish between animal or human life. He was uneasy about the lack of information. He was even more uneasy about the timing of the launch.

'I'm not certain there's any cause for alarm,' said Gregorian. 'But you did ask to be notified of any orbital approaches.'

'Tell me more about Apogee,' Profitt cut in.

Gregorian gave a dismissive snort. 'A minor player. Twelve-man engineering firm out in Nevada. They haven't had a lot of luck. A year and a half ago, they blew up their first prototype twenty seconds into launch, and all their early investors vanished. I'm sort of surprised they're still hanging in there. Their booster's based on Russian technology. The orbiter's a simple, bare-bones system with a parachute reentry. Payload capacity's only three hundred kilos, plus a pilot.'

'I'll fly out to Nevada at once. We need to get a better handle on this.'

'Sir, we can monitor every move this vehicle makes. Right now, we have no reason to take action. They're just a small firm, trying to impress some new investors. If the orbiter presents any real concern, we can have our ground-based interceptors standing by to bring that bird down.'

General Gregorian was probably right. The fact that some hotshot ground jockeys decided to launch a monkey into space did not constitute a national emergency. He had to move very carefully on this. The death of Luther Ames had unleashed a national uproar of protest. This was not the time to shoot down another spacecraft – one built by a private American firm, no less.

But so much about this Apogee launch disturbed him. The timing. The rendezvous maneuvers. The fact they could neither confirm nor rule out a human presence.

What else could it be but a rescue mission?

He said, 'I'm leaving for Nevada.'

Forty-five minutes later, Profitt was in his car and pulling out of the driveway. The night was clear, the stars like bright pinpricks in blue velvet. There were perhaps one hundred billion galaxies in the universe, and each galaxy contained a hundred billion stars. How many of those stars had planets, and how many planets had life? *Panspermia*, the theory that life exists and is distributed throughout the universe, was no longer merely speculation. The belief that there was life only on this pale blue dot, in this insignificant solar system, now seemed as absurd as the ancients' naive belief that the sun and the stars revolved around the earth. The only strict requirements for life were the presence of carbon-based compounds plus some form of water. Both were in abundance throughout the universe. Which meant that life, however primitive, could be abundant as well, and that interstellar dust might be seeded with bacteria or spores. From such primitive creatures did all other life spring.

And what happened if such life-forms, arriving as bits of cosmic dust, seeded a planet where life already existed?

This was Jared Profitt's nightmare.

Once, he had thought the stars beautiful. Once he had viewed the universe with awe and wonder. Now, when he looked at the night sky, he saw infinite menace. He saw biological Armageddon.

Their conqueror, descending from the heavens.

It was time to die.

Emma's hands were shaking, and the pounding in her head was so severe she had to grit her teeth just to keep herself from crying out. The last morphine shot had barely taken the edge off the pain, and she was so dazed by the narcotic she could barely focus on the computer screen. On the keyboard beneath her fingers. She paused to still the trembling of her hands. Then she began to type.

Personal E-mail to: Jack McCallum

If I could have one wish, it would be to hear your voice again. I don't know where you are, or why I can't speak to you. I only know that this thing inside me is about to claim victory. Even as I write this, I can feel it gaining ground. I can feel my strength retreating. I have fought it as long as I can. But I'm tired now. I'm ready to sleep.

While I can type these words, this is what I most want to say. I love you. I have never stopped loving you. They say that no one who stands poised at the doorway to eternity steps through it with a lie on his lips. They say that deathbed confessions are always to be believed. And this is mine.

Her hands were shaking so badly she could not type any more. She signed off and pressed 'send.'

In the medical kit, she found the supply of Valium. There were two tablets left. She swallowed them both with a gulp of water. The edges of her vision were starting to black out. Her legs felt numb, as though they were not part of her body at all, but the limbs of a stranger.

There was not much time left.

She did not have the strength to don an EVA suit. And what did it matter now where she died? The station was already diseased. Her corpse would be just one more item to clean up.

She made her last passage into the dark side of the station.

The cupola was where she wanted to spend her final waking moments. Floating in darkness, gazing down at the beauty of the earth. From the windows, she could see the blue-gray arc of the Caspian Sea. Clouds swirling over Kazakhstan and snow in the Himalayas. *Down there are billions of people going about their lives*, she thought. *And here am I, a dying speck in the heavens.*

'Emma?' It was Todd Cutler, speaking gently over her comm unit. 'How are you doing?'

'Not . . . feeling so good,' she murmured. 'Pain. Vision's starting to fade. I took the last Valium.'

'You have to hang in there, Emma. Listen to me. Don't give up. Not yet.'

'I've already lost the battle, Todd.'

'No, you haven't! You have to have faith –'

'In miracles?' She gave a soft laugh. 'The real miracle is that I am up here at all. That I'm seeing the earth from a place so few people have ever been . . .' She touched the window of the cupola and felt the warmth of the sun through the glass. 'I only wish I could speak to Jack.'

'We're trying to make that happen.'

'Where is he? Why can't you reach him?'

'He's working like crazy to get you home. You have to believe that.'

She blinked away tears. *I do.*

'Is there anything we can do for you?' said Todd. 'Anyone else you want to speak to?'

'No.' She sighed. 'Only Jack.'

There was a silence.

'I think – I think what I want most now –'

'Yes?' said Todd.

'I'd like to go to sleep. That's all. Just go to sleep.'

He cleared his throat. 'Of course. You get some rest. I'll be right here if you need me.' He closed with a soft, 'Good night, ISS.'

Good night, Houston, she thought. And she took off her headset and let it float away into the gloom.

27

The convoy of black sedans braked to a stop in front of Apogee Engineering, tires churning up a massive cloud of dust. Jared Profitt stepped out of the lead car and gazed up at the building. It looked like an airplane hangar, windowless and bleakly industrial, its rooftop studded with satellite equipment.

He nodded to General Gregorian. 'Secure the building.'

Barely a minute later, Gregorian's men gave the all-secure signal, and Profitt stepped into the building.

Inside, he found a ragtag group of men and women herded into a tense and angry circle. He immediately recognized two of the faces: Director of Flight Crew Operations Gordon Obie and shuttle Flight Director Randy Carpenter. So NASA was here, as he'd suspected, and this featureless building in the middle of the Nevada desert had been turned into a rebel Mission Control.

Unlike the Flight Control Room at NASA, this was clearly a shoestring operation. The floor was bare concrete. Spaghetti tangles of wires and cables were strung everywhere. A grotesquely overweight cat picked its way among a pile of discarded electronic equipment.

Profitt walked over to the flight consoles and saw the data streaming in. 'What's the orbiter's status?' he asked.

One of Gregorian's men, a flight controller from U.S. Space Command, said, 'It's already completed its Ti-burn, sir, and it's now moving up the R-bar. It could rendezvous with ISS within forty-five minutes.'

'Halt the approach.'

'No!' said Gordon Obie. He broke away from the group and stepped forward. 'Don't do this. You don't understand –'

'There can be no evacuation of station crew,' said Profitt.

'It's *not* an evacuation!'

'Then what's it doing up there? It's clearly about to rendezvous with ISS.'

'No, it's not. It *can't*. It has no docking system, no way of connecting with the station. There's no chance of cross-contamination.'

'You haven't answered my question, Mr Obie. What is *Apogee II* doing up there?'

Gordon hesitated. 'It's going through a near-approach sequence, that's all. It's a test of *Apogee*'s rendezvous capabilities.'

'Sir,' said the flight controller from Space Command. 'I'm seeing a major anomaly here.'

Profitt's gaze shot back to the console. 'What anomaly?'

'The cabin atmospheric pressure. It's down to eight psi. It should be at fourteen point seven. Either the orbiter has a serious air leak, or they've purposely allowed it to depressurize.'

'How long has it been that low?'

Quickly the flight controller typed on the keyboard, and a graph appeared, a plot of the cabin pressure over time. 'According to their computers, the cabin was maintained at fourteen point seven for the first twelve hours after launch. Then around thirty-six hours ago, it was depressurized to ten point two, where it held steady until an hour ago.' Suddenly his chin jerked up. 'Sir, I know what they're doing! This appears to be a prebreathe protocol.'

'Protocol for what?'

'An EVA. A spacewalk.' He looked at Profitt. 'I think someone's aboard that orbiter.'

Profitt turned to face Gordon Obie. 'Who's aboard? Who did you send up?'

Gordon could see there was no longer any point in holding back the truth. He said, in quiet defeat, 'It's Jack McCallum.'

Emma Watson's husband.

'So it's a rescue mission,' said Profitt. 'How was it supposed to work? He goes EVA, and then what?'

'The SAFER jet pack. The Orlan-M suit he's wearing is equipped with one. He uses it to propel himself from *Apogee II* to the station. Enters via the ISS airlock.'

'And he retrieves his wife and brings her home.'

'No. That wasn't the plan. Look, he understands – we *all* understand – why she can't come home. The reason Jack went up was to deliver the Ranavirus.'

'And if the virus doesn't work?'

'That's the gamble.'

'He's exposing himself to ISS. We'd never let him come home.'

'He wasn't planning to come home! The orbiter was going to return without him.' Gordon paused, his gaze fixed on Profitt's. 'It's a one-way trip, and Jack knows it. He accepted the conditions. It's his wife dying up there! He won't – he can't – let her die alone.'

Stunned, Profitt fell silent. He looked at the flight console, the monitors streaming with data. As the seconds ticked by, he thought of his own wife, Amy, dying in Bethesda Hospital. Remembered his frantic sprint through the Denver airport to catch the next flight home to her, and remembered his despair as he'd arrived breathless at the gate to see the plane pulling away. He thought of the desperation that must be driving McCallum, the anguish of being so heartbreakingly close to his goal, only to see it drift inexorably out of reach. And he thought, *This will bring no harm to anyone here on earth. To anyone but McCallum. He has made his choice, with full knowledge of the consequences. What right do I have to stop him?*

He said, to the Space Command flight controller, 'Return control of the console to Apogee. Let them resume their mission.'

'Sir?'

'I said, let the orbiter continue its approach.'

There was a moment of stunned silence. Then the Apogee controllers scrambled back into their seats.

'Mr Obie,' said Profitt, turning to look at Gordon. 'You do understand that we'll be monitoring every move McCallum makes. I am not your enemy. But I'm charged with protecting the greater good, and I'll do what's necessary. If I see any indication you plan to bring either of those people home, I will order *Apogee II* destroyed.'

Gordon Obie nodded. 'It's what I'd expect you to do.'

'Then we both know where we stand.' Profitt took a deep breath and turned to face the row of consoles. 'Now. Go ahead and get that man to his wife.'

Jack hung poised at the edge of eternity.

No amount of EVA training in the WET-F pool could have prepared him for this visceral punch of fear, for the paralysis that now seized him as he stared into the emptiness of space. He had swung open the hatch leading into the open payload bay, and his first view, through the bay's gaping clam-shell doors, was of the earth, a dizzying drop below. He could not see ISS; she was floating above him, out of view. To reach her, he would have to swim down past those payload doors and circle around to the opposite side of *Apogee II*. But first, he had to force himself to ignore every instinct that was now screaming at him to retreat back into the air lock.

'Emma,' he said, and the sound of her name was like a murmured prayer. He took a breath and prepared to release his grip on the hatchway, to surrender himself to the heavens.

'*Apogee II*, this is Capcom Houston. *Apogee* – Jack – please respond.'

The transmission over his comm unit caught Jack by surprise. He had not expected any contact from the ground. The fact Houston was openly hailing him by name meant all secrecy had been shattered.

'*Apogee*, we urgently request you respond.'

He remained silent, uncertain if he should con-firm his presence in orbit.

'Jack, we have been advised that the White House will not interfere with your mission. Pro-vided you understand one essential fact: This is a one-way trip.' Capcom paused and then said quietly, 'If you board ISS, you can't leave it again. You can't come home.'

'This is *Apogee II*,' Jack finally answered. 'Mes-sage received and understood.'

'And you still plan to proceed? Think about it.'

'What the hell do you think I came up here for? The fucking view?'

'Uh, we roger that. But before you proceed, you should be aware of this. We lost contact with ISS about six hours ago.'

'What do you mean, "lost contact"?'

'Emma is no longer responding.'

Six hours, he thought. *What has happened in the last six hours?* The launch had been two days ago. It had taken that long for *Apogee II* to catch up with ISS and complete the rendezvous maneuvers. In all that time, he'd been cut off from all communication, from any knowledge of what was happening aboard the station.

'You may already be too late. You might want to reconsider –'

'What does biotelemetry show?' he cut in. 'What's her rhythm?'

'She's not hooked up. She chose to disconnect her leads.'

'Then you don't know. You can't tell me what's going on.'

'Just before she went silent, she sent you a final E-mail.' Capcom added gently, 'Jack, she was saying good-bye.'

No. At once he released his grip on the hatchway and pushed out of the air lock, diving headfirst into the open payload bay. *No.* He grabbed a handhold and scrambled up over the clamshell door, to the other side of *Apogee II*. Suddenly the space station was *right there*, looming above him, so

469

big and sprawling he was momentarily stunned by the wonder of it. Then, in panic, he thought, *Where is the air lock? I don't see the air lock!* There were so many modules, so many solar arrays, fanned out across an area as large as two football fields. He could not orient himself. He was lost, overwhelmed by the dizzying spread.

Then he spotted the dark-green *Soyuz* capsule jutting out. He was underneath the Russian end of the station. Instantly everything snapped into place. His gaze shot to the American end, and he identified the US hab. At the upper end of the hab was Node 1, which led to the air lock.

He knew where he was going.

Here came the leap of faith. With only his SAFER jet pack to propel him, he would be crossing empty space without tethers, without anything to anchor him. He activated the jet pack, pushed off from *Apogee*, and launched himself toward ISS.

It was his first EVA, and he was clumsy and inexperienced, unable to judge how quickly he was closing in on his goal. He slammed into the hab hull with such force he almost caromed off, and barely managed to grab onto a handhold.

Hurry. She is dying.

Sick with dread, he clambered up the length of the hab, his breaths coming hard and fast.

'Houston,' he panted. 'I need Surgeon – have him standing by –'

'Roger that.'

'Almost – I'm almost to Node One –'

'Jack, this is Surgeon.' It was Todd Cutler's voice, speaking with quiet urgency. 'You've been out of the loop for two days. You need to know a few things. Emma's last dose of HCG was fifty-five hours ago. Since then, her labs have deteriorated. Amylase and CPK sky-high. Last transmission, she was complaining of headaches and visual loss. That was six hours ago. We don't know her current condition.'

'I'm at the air-lock hatch!'

'Station control software has been switched to EVA mode. You're a go for repress.'

Jack swung open the hatch and pulled himself into the crew lock. As he twisted around to close the external hatch, he caught a glimpse of *Apogee II*. She was already moving away. His only lifeboat was going home without him. He'd passed the point of no return.

He closed and sealed the hatch. 'Pressure-equalization valve open,' he said. 'Beginning repress.'

'I'm trying to prepare you for the worst,' said Todd. 'In case she –'

'Tell me something useful!'

'Okay. Okay, here's the latest from USAMRIID. The Ranavirus does seem to work on their lab animals. But it's only been effective in early cases. If it's given during the first thirty-six hours after infection.'

'What if it's given after that?'

Cutler didn't respond. His silence confirmed the worst.

471

The crew lock pressure was up to fourteen psi. Jack opened the middle hatch and dove into the equipment lock. Frantically he detached his gloves, then doffed his Orlan-M suit and wriggled out of the cooling garment. From the Orlan's zippered pockets he pulled out various packets containing emergency medications and prefilled syringes of Ranavirus. By now he was shaking with fear, terrified of what he would find inside the station. He swung open the inner hatch.

And confronted his worst nightmare.

She was floating in the gloom of Node 1, like a swimmer adrift in a dark sea. Only this swimmer was drowning. Her limbs jerked in rhythmic spasms. Convulsions wracked her spine, and her head snapped forward and back, her hair lashing like a whip. Death throes.

No, he thought. *I won't let you die. Goddamnit, Emma, you are not going to leave me.*

He grasped her around the waist and began to pull her toward the Russian end of the station. Toward the modules that still had power and light. Her body twitched like a live wire jolted by electric shocks, thrashing in his arms. She was so small, so fragile, yet the strength now coursing through her dying body threatened to overpower his grip on her. Weightlessness was new to him, and he bounced drunkenly off walls and hatchways as he struggled to maneuver them both into the Russian service module.

'Jack, talk to me,' said Todd. 'What's going on?'

'I've moved her into the RSM – getting her onto the restraint board –'

'Have you given the virus?'

'Tying her down first. She's seizing –' He fastened the Velcro straps over her chest and hips, anchoring her torso to the medical restraint board. Her head slammed backward, her eyes rolling up into the orbits. The sclerae were a brilliant and horrifying red. *Give her the virus. Do it now.*

A tourniquet was looped around the restraint-board frame. He whipped it free and tied it around her thrashing arm. It took all his strength to forcibly extend her elbow, to expose the antecubital vein. With his teeth he uncapped the syringe of Ranavirus. Stabbing the needle into her arm, he squeezed the plunger.

'It's in!' he said. 'The whole syringe!'

'What's she doing?'

'She's still seizing!'

'There's IV Dilantin in the med kit.'

'I see it. I'm starting an IV!' The tourniquet floated by, a startling reminder that in weightlessness, what was not tied down would quickly drift out of reach. He snatched it from midair and reached, once again, for Emma's arm.

A moment later he reported, 'Dilantin's going in! IV's running wide open.'

'Any change?'

Jack stared at his wife, silently demanding, *Come on, Emma. Don't die on me.*

Slowly her spine relaxed. Her neck went limp

473

and her head stopped battering the board. Her eyes rolled forward, and he could see her irises now, two dark pools ringed by bloodred sclerae. At his first glimpse of her pupils, a moan rose in his throat.

Her left pupil was fully dilated. Black and lifeless.

He was too late. She was dying.

He cupped her face in his hands, as though by sheer will he could force her to live. But even as he pleaded with her not to leave him, he knew that she would not be saved by mere touch or prayer. Death was an organic process. Biochemical functions, the movement of ions across cell membranes, slowly ceased. The brain waves flattened. The rhythmic contractions of myocardial cells faded to a quiver. Just wishing it so would not make her live.

But she was not dead. Not yet.

'Todd,' he said.

'I'm here.'

'What is the terminal event? What happens to the lab animals?'

'I don't follow –'

'You said Ranavirus works, if given early enough in the infection. Which means it must be killing Chimera. So why doesn't it work when given later?'

'Too much tissue damage has occurred. There's internal bleeding –'

'Bleeding where? What do the autopsies show?'

'Seventy-five percent of the time, in dogs, the fatal hemorrhage is intracranial. Chimera's enzymes damage blood vessels on the surface of the cerebral cortex. The vessels rupture, and the bleeding causes a catastrophic rise in intracranial pressure. It's like a massive head injury, Jack. The brain herniates.'

'What if you stop the bleeding, stop the brain damage? If you get the victims past the acute stage, they might live long enough for Ranavirus to work.'

'Possibly.'

Jack stared down at Emma's dilated left pupil. A terrible memory flashed into his head: Debbie Haning, unconscious on a hospital gurney. He had failed Debbie. He had waited too long to take action, and because of his indecision, he had lost her.

I will not lose you.

He said, 'Todd, she's blown her left pupil. She needs burr holes.'

'What? You're working blind. Without X-ray –'

'It's the only chance she has! I need a drill. Tell me where the work tools are kept!'

'Stand by.' Seconds later, Todd came back on comm. 'We're not sure where the Russians stow their kit. But NASA's are in Node One, in the storage rack. Check the labels on the Nomex bags. The contents are specified.'

Jack shot out of the service module, once again colliding with walls and hatchways as he clumsily barreled his way into Node 1. His hands were shaking as he opened the storage rack. He pulled out three Nomex bags before he found the one labeled 'Power drill/bits/adapters.' He grabbed a second bag containing screwdrivers and a hammer, and shot back out of the node. He'd been away from her for only a moment, yet the fear that he would return to find her dead sent him flying through Zarya and back into the service module.

She was still breathing. Still alive.

He anchored the Nomex bags to the table and removed the power tool. It was meant for space station repair and construction, not neurosurgery. Now that he actually held the drill in his hand and considered what he was about to do, panic seized him. He was operating in unsterile conditions, with a tool meant for steel bolts, not flesh and bone. He looked at Emma, lying flaccid on the table, and thought of what lay beneath that cranial vault, thought of her gray matter, where a lifetime of memories and dreams and emotions were stored. Everything that made her uniquely Emma. All of it dying now.

He reached into the medical kit and took scissors and a shaving razor. Grasping a handful of her hair, he began to snip it away, then shaved the stubble, clearing an incision site over her left temporal bone. *Your beautiful hair. I have always loved your hair. I have always loved you.*

The rest of her hair he bound up and tucked

476

out of the way, so it would not contaminate the site. With a strip of adhesive tape, he restrained her head to the board. Moving more quickly now, he prepared his tools. The suction catheter. The scalpel. The gauze. He swished the drill bits in disinfectant, then wiped them off with alcohol.

He pulled on sterile gloves and picked up the scalpel.

His skin was clammy inside the latex gloves as he made his incision. Blood oozed from the scalp, welling into a gently expanding globule. He dabbed it with gauze and sliced deeper, until his blade scraped bone.

To breach the skull is to expose the brain to a hostile universe of microbial invaders. Yet the human body is resilient; it can survive the most brutal of insults. He kept reminding himself of this as he tapped a nick into the temporal bone, as he positioned the tip of the drill bit. The ancient Egyptians and the Incas had successfully performed skull trephinations, opening holes in the cranium with only the crudest of tools and no thought of sterile technique. It could be done.

His hands were steady, his concentration fierce as he drilled into the bone. A few millimeters too deep, and he could hit brain matter. A thousand precious memories would be destroyed in a second. Or a nick of the middle meningeal artery, and he could unleash an unstoppable fountain of blood. He kept pausing to take a breath, to probe the depth of the hole. *Go slow. Go slow.*

Suddenly he felt the last filigree of bone give way, and the drill broke through. Heart slamming in his throat, he gently withdrew the bit.

A bubble of blood immediately began to form, slowly ballooning out from the breach. It was dark red – venous. He gave a sigh of relief. Not arterial. Even now the pressure on Emma's brain was slowly easing, the intracranial bleed escaping through this new opening. He suctioned the bubble, then used gauze to absorb the continuing ooze as he drilled the next hole, and the next, punching a one-inch-diameter ring of perforations in the skull. By the time the last hole was drilled, and the circle was complete, his hands were cramping, his face beaded with sweat. He could not pause to rest; every second counted.

He reached for a screwdriver and ball peen hammer.

Let this work. Let this save her.

Using the screwdriver as a chisel, he gently dug the tip into the skull. Then, teeth gritted, he pried off the circular cap of bone.

Blood billowed out. The larger opening at last allowed it to escape, and it gradually spilled out of the cranium.

So did something else. *Eggs.* A clump of them gushed out and floated, quivering, into the air. He caught them with the suction catheter, trapping them in the vacuum jar. Throughout history, mankind's most dangerous enemies have been the smallest life-forms. Viruses. Bacteria. Parasites.

And now you, thought Jack, staring into the jar. *But we can defeat you.*

The blood was barely oozing out the cranial hole. With that initial gush, the pressure on her brain had been relieved.

He looked at Emma's left eye. The pupil was still dilated. But when he shone a light into it, he thought – or was he imagining it? – that the edges quivered just the slightest bit, like black water rippling toward the center.

You will *live*, he thought.

He dressed the wound with gauze and started a new IV infusion containing steroids and pheno-barbital to temporarily deepen her coma and protect her brain from further damage. He attached EKG leads to her chest. Only after all these tasks had been done did he finally tie a tourniquet around his own arm and inject himself with a dose of Ranavirus. It would either kill them both or save them both. He would know soon enough.

On the EKG monitor, Emma's heart traced a steady sinus rhythm. He took her hand in his, and waited for a sign.

August 27

Gordon Obie walked into Special Vehicle Oper-ations and gazed around the room at the men and women working at their consoles. On the front screen, the space station traced its sinuous path across the global map. At this moment, in the

479

deserts of Algeria, villagers who chanced to glance up at the night sky would marvel at the strange star, brilliant as Venus, soaring across the heavens. A star unique in all the firmament because it was created not by an all-powerful god, nor by any force of nature, but by the fragile hand of man.

And in this room, halfway around the world from that Algerian desert, were the guardians of that star.

Flight Director Woody Ellis turned and greeted Gordon with a sad nod. 'No word. It's been silent up there.'

'How long since the last transmission?'

'Jack signed off five hours ago to get some sleep. It's been almost three days since he got much rest. We're trying not to disturb him.'

Three days, and still no change in Emma's status. Gordon sighed and headed along the back row to the flight surgeon's console. Todd Cutler, unshaven and haggard, was watching Emma's biotelemetry readings on his monitor. And when had Todd last slept? Gordon wondered. Everyone looked exhausted, but no one was ready to admit defeat.

'She's still hanging in there,' Todd said softly. 'We've withdrawn the phenobarb.'

'But she hasn't come out of the coma?'

'No.' Sighing, Todd slumped back and pinched the bridge of his nose. 'I don't know what else to do. I've never dealt with this before. Neurosurgery in space.'

It was a phrase many of them had uttered over the last few weeks. *I've never dealt with this before. This is new. This is something we've never seen.* Yet wasn't that the essence of exploration? That no crisis could be predicted, that every new problem required its own solution. That every triumph was built on sacrifice.

And there *had* been triumphs, even in the midst of all this tragedy. *Apogee II* had landed safely in the Arizona desert, and Casper Mulholland was now negotiating his company's first contract with the Air Force. Jack was still healthy, even three days after being aboard ISS – an indication that Ranavirus was both a cure and a preventive against Chimera. And the very fact that Emma was alive counted as a triumph as well.

Though perhaps only a temporary one.

Gordon felt a profound sense of sadness as he watched her EKG blip across the screen. *How long can the heart go on beating when the brain is gone?* he wondered. *How long can a body survive a coma?* To watch this slow fading away of a once-vibrant woman was more painful than to witness her sudden and catastrophic death.

Suddenly he sat up straight, his gaze frozen on the monitor. 'Todd,' he said. 'What's happening to her?'

'What?'

'There's something wrong with her heart.'

Todd raised his head and stared at the tracing shuddering across the monitor. 'No,' he said, and reached for the comm switch. 'That's not her heart.'

The high whine of the monitor alarm sliced through Jack's twilight sleep, and he awakened with a start. Years of medical training, of countless nights spent in on-call rooms, had taught him to surface fully alert from the deepest sleep, and the instant he opened his eyes he knew where he was. He knew something was wrong.

He turned toward the sound of the alarm and was briefly disoriented by his upside-down view. Emma appeared to be suspended facedown from the ceiling. One of her three EKG leads floated loose, like a strand of sea grass drifting underwater. He turned a hundred eighty degrees, and everything righted itself.

He reattached her EKG lead. His own heart was racing as he watched the monitor, afraid of what he would see. To his relief, a normal rhythm blipped across the screen.

And then – something else. A shuddering of the line. *Movement.*

He looked down at Emma. And saw that her eyes were open.

'ISS is not responding,' said Capcom.

'Keep trying. We need him on comm now!' snapped Todd.

Gordon stared at the biotelemetry readings, not understanding any of it, and fearing the worst. The

EKG skittered up and down, then suddenly went flat. *No*, he thought. *We've lost her!*

'It's just a disconnect,' said Todd. 'The lead's fallen off. She may be seizing.'

'Still no response from ISS,' said Capcom.

'What the hell is going on up there?'

'Look!' said Gordon.

Both men froze as a blip appeared on the screen. It was followed by another and another.

'Surgeon, I have ISS,' Capcom announced. 'Requesting immediate consultation.'

Todd shot forward in his chair. 'Ground Control, close the loop. Go ahead, Jack.'

It was a private conversation; no one but Todd could hear what Jack was saying. In the sudden hush, everyone in the room turned to look at the surgeon's console. Even Gordon, seated right beside him, could not read Todd's expression. Todd was hunched forward, both hands cupping his headset, as though to shut out any distractions.

Then he said, 'Hold on, Jack. There are a lot of folks down here waiting to hear this. Let's tell them the news.' Todd turned to Flight Director Ellis and gave him a triumphant thumbs-up. 'Watson's awake! She's talking!'

What happened next would remain forever etched in Gordon Obie's memory. He heard voices swell, cresting into noisy cheers. He felt Todd slap him on the back, hard. Liz Gianni gave a rebel whoop. And Woody Ellis fell into his chair with a look of disbelief and joy.

But what Gordon would remember most of all was his own reaction. He looked around the room and suddenly found his throat was aching and his eyes were blurred. In all his years at NASA, no one had ever seen Gordon Obie cry. They were damn well not going to see it now.

They were still cheering as he rose from his chair and walked, unnoticed, out of the room.

Five Months Later
Panama City, Florida

The squeal of hinges and the clank of metal echoed in the vast Navy hangar as the door to the hyperbaric chamber at last swung open. Jared Profitt watched as the two Navy physicians stepped out first, both of them taking in deep breaths as they emerged. They had spent over a month confined to that claustrophobic space, and they seemed a little dazed by their sudden transition into freedom. They turned to assist the last two occupants out of the chamber.

Emma Watson and Jack McCallum stepped out. They both focused on Jared Profitt, crossing toward them.

'Welcome back to the world, Dr Watson,' he said, and held out his hand in greeting.

She hesitated, then shook it. She looked far thinner than her photographs. More fragile. Four months quarantined in space, followed by five weeks in the hyperbaric chamber, had taken its toll. She had lost muscle mass, and her eyes seemed huge and darkly luminous in that pale face. The hair growing back on her shaved scalp was silver, a startling contrast against the rest of her brown mane.

Profitt looked at the two Navy doctors. 'Could you leave us alone, please?' He waited until their footsteps faded away.

Then he asked Emma, 'Are you feeling well?'

'Well enough,' she said. 'They tell me I'm free of disease.'

'None that can be detected,' he corrected her. This was an important distinction. Though they had demonstrated that Ranavirus did indeed eradicate Chimera in lab animals, they could not be certain of Emma's long-term prognosis. The best they could say was that there was no evidence of Chimera in her body. From the moment she'd landed aboard *Endeavour*, she'd been subjected to repeated blood tests, X rays, and biopsies. Though all were negative, USAMRIID had insisted she remain in the hyperbaric chamber while the tests continued. Two weeks ago, the chamber pressure had been dropped to a normal one atmosphere. She had remained healthy.

Even now, she was not entirely free. For the rest of her life she would be a subject of study.

He looked at Jack and saw hostility in the man's eyes. Jack had said nothing, but his arm circled Emma's waist in a protective gesture that said clearly, *You are not taking her from me.*

'Dr McCallum, I hope you understand that every decision I made was for a good reason.'

'I understand your reasons. It doesn't mean I agree with your decisions.'

'Then at least we share that much – an understanding.' He did not offer his hand; he sensed that McCallum would refuse to shake it. So he said simply, 'There are a number of people waiting outside to see you. I won't keep you from your friends any longer.' He turned to leave.

'Wait,' said Jack. 'What happens now?'

'You're free to leave. As long as you both return for periodic testing.'

'No, I mean what happens to the people responsible? The ones who sent up Chimera?'

'They are no longer making decisions.'

'And that's it?' Jack's voice rose in anger. 'No punishment, no consequences?'

'It will be handled in the usual manner. The way it's done at any government agency, including NASA. A discreet shuffle to the sidelines. And then a quiet retirement. There can't be any investigation, any disclosure whatsoever. Chimera is too dangerous to reveal to the rest of the world.'

'But people have died.'

'Marburg virus will be blamed. Accidentally introduced to ISS by an infected monkey. Luther Ames' death will be attributed to a mechanical malfunction of the CRV.'

'*Someone* should be held accountable.'

'For what, a bad decision?' Profitt shook his

head. He turned and looked at the closed hangar door, where a slit of sunlight shone through. 'There's no crime to punish here. These are people who simply made mistakes. People who didn't understand the nature of what they were dealing with. I know it's frustrating for you. I understand your need to blame someone. But there are no real villains in this piece, Dr McCallum. There are only . . . heroes.' He turned and looked directly at Jack.

The two men regarded each other for a moment. Profitt saw no warmth, no trust in Jack's gaze. But he did see respect.

'Your friends are waiting for you,' said Profitt.

Jack nodded. He and Emma crossed to the hangar door. As they stepped out, a burst of sunlight shone in, and Jared Profitt, squinting against the brightness, saw Jack and Emma only in silhouette, his arm around her shoulder, her profile turned to his. To the sound of cheering voices, they walked out and vanished into the blinding light of midday.

THE SEA

28

A shooting star arced across the heavens and shattered into bright bits of glitter. Emma took in a sharp breath in awe, inhaling the smell of the wind over Galveston Bay. Everything about being home again seemed new and strange to her. This unbroken panorama of sky. The rocking of the sailboat's deck beneath her back. The sound of water slapping *Sanneke*'s hull. She had been so long deprived of simple, earthbound experiences that just the sensation of the breeze on her face was something to be treasured. During the last months of quarantine on the station, she had stared down at the earth, homesick for the smell of grass, the taste of salt air, the warmth of the soil under her bare feet. She had thought, *When I am home again, if I am ever home again, I will never leave it.*

Now here she was, savoring the sights and smells of earth. Yet she could not help turning her wistful gaze toward the stars.

'Do you ever wish you could go back?' Jack

asked the question so softly his words were almost lost in the wind. He lay beside her on *Sanneke*'s deck, his hand clasping hers, his gaze also fixed on the night sky. 'Do you ever think, "If they gave me one more chance to go up there, I'd take it"?'

'Every day,' she murmured. 'Isn't it strange? When we were up there, all we talked about was coming home. And now we're home, and we can't stop thinking about going back up.' She brushed her fingers across her scalp, where the shorter hair was growing back as a startling streak of silver. She could still feel the knotty ridge of scar tissue where Jack's scalpel had cut through skin and galea. It was a permanent reminder of what she had survived on the station. An enduring record of horror, carved in her flesh. Yet, when she looked at the sky, she felt the old yearning for the heavens.

'I think I'll always be hoping for another chance,' she said. 'The way sailors always want to go back to sea. No matter how terrible their last voyage. Or how fervently they kiss the ground when they reach land. In time, they miss the sea, and they always want to return.'

But she would never return to space. She was like a sailor trapped on land, with the sea all around her, tantalizing yet forbidden. It was forever out of her reach because of Chimera.

Although the doctors at JSC and USAMRIID could no longer detect any evidence of infection in her body, they could not be certain Chimera had been eradicated. It could be merely dormant, a benign tenant of her body. No one at NASA dared predict what would happen should she return to space.

So she would never return. She was an astronaut ghost now, still a member of the corps, but without hope of any flight assignment. It was up to others to pursue the dream. Already, a new team was aboard the station, completing the repairs and biological cleanup that she and Jack had begun. Next month, the last replacement parts for the damaged main truss and solar arrays would be launched aboard *Columbia*. ISS would not die. Too many lives had been lost to make an orbiting station a reality; to abandon it now would be to render that sacrifice meaningless.

Another shooting star streaked overhead, tumbled like a dying cinder, and winked out. They both waited, hoping, for another. Other people who saw falling stars might think them omens, or angels winging from heaven, or consider them occasions to make a wish. Emma saw them for what they were: bits of cosmic debris, wayward travelers from the cold, dark reaches of space. That they were nothing more than rocks and ice did not make them any less wondrous.

As she tilted her head back and scanned the heavens, *Sanneke* rose upon a swell, and she had the disorienting impression that the stars were rushing toward her, that she was hurtling through space and time. She closed her eyes. And without warning, her heart began to pound with inexplicable dread. She felt the icy kiss of sweat on her face.

Jack touched her trembling hand. 'What's wrong? Are you cold?'

'No. No, not cold . . .' She swallowed hard. 'I suddenly thought of something terrible.'

'What?'

'If USAMRIID's right – if Chimera came to earth on an asteroid – then that's proof other life is out there.'

'Yes. It would prove it.'

'What if it's intelligent life?'

'Chimera's too small, too primitive. It's not intelligent.'

'But whoever sent it here may be,' she whispered.

Jack went very still beside her. 'A colonizer,' he said softly.

'Like seeds cast on the wind. Wherever Chimera landed, on any planet, in any solar system, it would infect the native species. Incorporate their DNA into its own genome. It wouldn't need millions of years of evolution to adapt to its new home. It could acquire all the genetic tools for survival from the species already living there.'

And once established, once it became the dominant species on its new planet, what then? What was its next step? She didn't know. The answer, she thought, must lie in the parts of Chimera's genome they could not yet identify. The sequences of DNA whose function remained a mystery.

A fresh meteor streaked the sky, a reminder that the heavens are ever-changing and turbulent. That the earth is only one lonely traveler through the vastness of space.

'We'll have to be ready,' she said. 'Before the next Chimera arrives.'

Jack sat up and looked at his watch. 'It's getting cold,' he said. 'Let's go home. Gordon will go ballistic if we miss that press conference tomorrow.'

'I've never seen him lose his temper.'

'You don't know him the way I do.' Jack began to haul on the halyard, and the main sail rose, flapping in the wind. 'He's halfway in love with you, you know.'

'Gordie?' She laughed. 'I can't imagine.'

'And you know what I can't imagine?' he said softly, pulling her close beside him in the cockpit. 'That any man wouldn't be.'

The wind suddenly gusted, filling the sail, and *Sanneke* surged ahead, slicing through the waters of Galveston Bay.

'Ready about,' said Jack. And he steered them through the wind, turning the bow west. Guided not by the stars, but by the lights of shore.

The lights of home.

GLOSSARY

NASA has been dubbed the 'National Acronym-Slinging Agency' and with good reason. Conversations between NASA employees are often so peppered with acronyms the uninitiated may believe they are hearing a foreign language. Here are definitions for some of the acronyms and abbreviations used in *Gravity*:

AFB: Air Force Base.

ALSP: Advanced Life Support Pack; the onboard medical kit that provides advanced cardiac life support.

APU: Auxiliary Power Unit.

ASCR: Assured Safe Crew Return; a space-station-control software mode that supports emergency separation and departure of evacuation vehicles.

ATO: Abort to Orbit; an abort mode that allows the vehicle to achieve a temporary orbit prior to returning to earth.

Capcom: Capsule Communicator.

CCPK: Crew Contaminant Protection Kit.

CCTV: Closed-Circuit Television.

CRT: Cathode-Ray Tube.

CRV: Crew Return Vehicle; the space station's lifeboat.

C/W: Caution and Warning.

DAP: Digital Autopilot.

ECLSS: Environmental Control and Life Support System.

ECS: Environmental Control System.

EKG: Electrocardiogram.

EKV: Exoatmospheric Kill Vehicle; missile designed to destroy objects before they enter earth's atmosphere.

EMU: Extravehicular Mobility Unit; a spacewalking suit (American); see also Orlan-M.

EPS: Electrical Power System.

ESA: European Space Agency.

EVA: Extravehicular Activity; a spacewalk.

FAA: Federal Aviation Agency.

Falcon: Flight controller in charge of monitoring ISS power systems and solar arrays.

FCR: Flight Control Room.

FDO: Flight Dynamics Officer.

FGB: (Russian initials) Functional Cargo Block; one of the space station modules; also called *Zarya*.

Flight: Flight Director.

GC: Ground Control.

GDO: Guidance Officer.

GNC: Guidance, Navigation, and Control.

GOES: Geostationary Operational Environmental Satellite; a weather satellite.

GPC: General Purpose Computer.

Hab: (American) Habitation Module.

HCG: Human Chorionic Gonadotropin; a hormone of pregnancy.

HEPA filter: High-Efficiency Particulate Air filter.

ISS: International Space Station.

IVA: Intravehicular Activity; a spacewalk inside a decompressed vehicle or module.

JPL: Jet Propulsion Laboratory.

JSC: Johnson Space Center (Houston).

KSC: Kennedy Space Center (Cape Canaveral, Florida).

Ku-band: Ku-band communication subsystem.

LCC: Launch Control Center.

LEO: Low Earth Orbit; orbit within a few hundred miles of earth.

LES: Launch and Entry Suit; the bright orange suit astronauts wear during liftoff and for return to earth. It is a one-piece partial pressure suit which provides a thermal barrier as well as anti-g protection.

LOS: Loss of Signal.

MCC: Mission Control Center.

ME: Main Engines.

MECO: Main Engine Cutoff.

MMACS: Maintenance, Mechanical Arm, and Crew Systems engineer.

MMT: Mission Management Team.

MMU: Mass Memory Unit.

MOD: Mission Operations Director.

MSFC: Marshall Space Flight Center.

NASA: National Aeronautics and Space Administration.

NASDA: The Japanese space agency.

NOAA: National Oceanic and Atmospheric Administration.

NORAD: North American Air Defense Command.

NSTS: National Space Transportation System.

Odin: Flight controller for ISS onboard data networks and computers.

ODS: Orbital Docking System.

OMS: Orbital Maneuvering System.

Orlan-M: A spacewalking suit (Russian).

ORU: Orbital Replacement Unit.

Oso: Flight controller for ISS Mechanical/Maintenance/Latches.

PAO: Public Affairs Officer.

PFC: Private Family Conference.

PI: Principal Investigator; the earth-based scientist in charge of an on-orbit experiment.

PMC: Private Medical Conference.

POCC: Payload Operations Control Center.

Psi: Pounds per square inch.

PVM: Photovoltaic Module.

RCS: Reaction Control System; one of the shuttle engine systems used on orbit to maneuver the spacecraft.

RLV: Reusable Launch Vehicle.

RPOP: Rendezvous and Proximity Operations Program (software).

RSM: Russian Service Module.

RTLS: Return to Launch Site; a launch-abort mode that requires the shuttle to fly downrange to dissipate fuel, then turn around for a landing at or near the launch site.

SAFER: Simplified Aid for EVA Rescue; a jet pack that allows a spacewalking astronaut to pilot himself to safety in the event he becomes untethered.

Sim: Short for *flight simulation*.

SRB: Solid Rocket Boosters.

STS: Shuttle Transportation System.

Surgeon: The call sign for the mission flight surgeon.

SVOR: Special Vehicle Operations Room; the flight control room for the International Space Station.

TACAN: Tactical Air Navigation.

TAEM: Terminal Area Energy Management.

TAL: Transatlantic Landing; an abort mode in which the shuttle lands on the other side of the Atlantic Ocean.

TDRS: Tracking and Data Relay Satellite.

Topo: Flight controller for ISS trajectory control.

TVIS: Treadmill with Vibration Isolation System.

UHF: Ultrahigh Frequency.

United Space Alliance (USA): A private contractor chartered to maintain and conduct certain aspects of NASA's operations.

USAMRIID: United States Army Medical Research Institute of Infectious Diseases.

U.S. Space Command: Part of the Unified Command of the Department of Defense, USSPACECOM monitors manmade objects orbiting earth and supports military as well as civilian operations involving space.

WET-F: Weightless Environment Training Facility.

Bloodstream

To Tim and Elyse

Acknowledgments

I owe many thanks to:

My husband Jacob, still my best friend after all these years.

Meg Ruley, my guardian angel and miracle worker. You walk on water.

Jane Berkey and Don Cleary for their guiding voices.

My superb editor, Emily Bestler.

The ladies of the breakfast club for delivering my weekly dose of sanity.

The memory of Rockport Police Chief Perley Sprague. Your kindness was an inspiration.

And finally, to the town of Camden, Maine, the best place on earth a writer could call home. Please rest assured this book is not about you.

Prologue

Tranquility, Maine, 1946

If she was still enough, quiet enough, he would not find her. He might think he knew all her hiding places, but he had never discovered her secret niche, this small hollow in the cellar wall, concealed by the shelves of her mother's canning jars. As a young child she had easily slipped into this space, and every game of hide and seek had found her curled up in her lair, giggling at his frustration as he thumped from room to room, searching for her. Sometimes the game would go on so long she'd fall asleep, and would awaken hours later to the sound of her mother's voice worriedly calling her name.

Now here she was again, in her cellar hiding place, but she was no longer a child. She was fourteen and barely able to squeeze into the niche. And this was no lighthearted game of hide and seek.

She could hear him upstairs, roaming the house,

searching for her. He rampaged from room to room, cursing, slamming furniture to the floor.

Please, please, please. Someone help us. Someone make him go away.

She heard him roar out her name: 'IRIS!' His footsteps creaked into the kitchen. Approached the cellar door. Her hands balled into tight fists, and her heart was a banging drum.

I am not here. I am far away, escaping, soaring into the night sky . . .

The cellar door flew open, slamming into the wall. Golden light shone down, framing him in the open doorway at the top of the stairs.

He reached up to pull on the light chain and the bare bulb came on, dimly illuminating the cavernous cellar. Cowering behind the jars of home-canned tomatoes and cucumbers, Iris heard him descend the steep stairs, each creak bringing him toward her. She pressed deeper into the hollow, flattening herself against the crumbling stone and mortar, and closed her eyes, willing herself to be invisible. Through the slamming of her own heartbeat she heard him reach the bottom of the steps.

Don't see me. Don't see me.

The footsteps moved right past the canning shelves and headed toward the far end of the cellar. She heard him kick over a box. Empty jars shattered on the stone floor. Now he was circling back, and she could hear his harsh breathing, punctuated by animal grunts. Her own breaths were coming short and fast, her hands clenched so tightly she thought her bones would shatter. The footsteps moved to the canning shelves and stopped.

Her eyes shot open, and through a chink between two jars she saw him standing right in front of her. She had slid down until her gaze was level with his belt. She cringed even lower, dropping as far below his line of sight as she could. He took a jar off the shelf and smashed it to the ground. The smell of pickles, sharp and vinegary, rose up from the stone floor. He reached for a second jar, then suddenly put it back, as though a better thought had occurred to him. He turned and walked up the cellar steps, yanking the light chain as he exited.

Once again she was in darkness.

She realized she had been crying. Her face was wet, sweat mingling with tears, but she didn't dare release even a whimper.

Upstairs the footsteps creaked toward the front of the house and then there was silence.

Had he left? Had he finally gone away?

She remained frozen, not daring to move. The minutes went by. She counted them off slowly in her head. Ten. Twenty. Her muscles were cramping, the spasms so painful she had to bite her lip to keep from crying out.

An hour.

Two hours.

Still no sound from above.

Slowly she emerged from the hiding place. She

stood in the darkness, waiting for the blood to recirculate in her muscles, for the feeling to come back in her legs. Listening, the whole time listening.

She heard nothing.

The cellar had no window, and she didn't know if it was still dark outside. She stepped through the broken glass on the floor and crossed to the stairs. She climbed them one at a time, pausing after each step to listen some more. When at last she reached the top, her palms were so slick she had to wipe them off on her blouse before she could open the cellar door.

The lights were on in the kitchen, and everything looked startlingly normal. She could almost believe the horror of last night was simply a bad dream. A clock ticked loudly on the wall. It was five A.M., still dark outside.

She tiptoed to the kitchen doorway and peered into the hall. One glimpse at the splintered furniture, the splashes of blood on the wallpaper, told her she had not been dreaming. Her palms were wet again.

The hallway was deserted, and the front door hung open.

She had to get out of the house. Run to the neighbors, run to the police.

She started up the hall, each step bringing her closer to escape. Terror had primed her five senses to such acuity that she registered every fragment of splintered wood on the floral carpet, every tick

4

of the clock in the kitchen behind her. She was almost at the front door.

Then she cleared the banister and came within view of the stairs, where her mother had toppled, head down. She couldn't stop herself from staring at the body. At her mother's long hair draping the steps, like black water rippling downhill.

Nausea surging up her throat, she lurched toward the front door.

He was standing there. In his hand was an ax.

With a sob she spun around and darted up the stairs, almost slipping on her mother's blood. She heard him pounding up the steps after her. She had always been faster than he, and terror made her fly up the stairs like a panicked cat.

On the second floor landing she caught a glimpse of her father's body, lying halfway out of his bedroom doorway. There was no time to think about it, no time to absorb the horror; she was already dashing up the next flight of stairs and into the turret room.

She slammed the door and latched it just in time.

He gave a roar of rage and began pounding on the closed door.

She scurried over to the window and forced it open. Staring down at the ground far below, she knew she could not survive a fall. But there was no other way out of the room.

She yanked on a curtain, pulling it off the rod. *A rope. Have to make a rope!* She tied one end to a radiator pipe, wrenched a second curtain down, and tied the two lengths of fabric together.

A loud thud sent a splinter of wood flying at her. She glanced back and to her horror saw the tip of the ax poking through the door. Saw it pried loose again for the next swing.

He was breaking through!

She yanked down a third curtain, and with shaking hands, knotted it to the first two.

The ax came down again. The wood splintered wider, more chunks flying.

She yanked down a fourth curtain, but even as she frantically tied the last knot, she knew the rope was not long enough. She knew it was too late.

She spun around to face the door just as the ax broke through.

1

The Present

'Someone's going to get hurt out there,' said Dr Claire Elliot, looking out her kitchen window. Morning mist, thick as smoke, hung over the lake, and the trees beyond her window drifted in and out of focus. Another gunshot rang out, closer this time. Since first light, she'd heard the gunfire, and would probably hear it all day until dusk, because it was the first day of November. The start of hunting season. Somewhere in those woods, a man with a rifle was tramping around half-blind through the mist as imagined shadows of white-tailed deer danced around him.

'I don't think you should wait outside for the bus,' said Claire. 'I'll drive you to school.'

Noah, hunched at the breakfast table, said nothing. He scooped up another spoonful of Cheerios and slurped it down. Fourteen years old, and her son still ate like a two-year-old, milk splashing on the

7

table, crumbs of toast littering the floor around his chair. He ate without looking at her, as though to meet her gaze was to come face to face with Medusa. And what difference would it make if he did look at me, she thought wryly. My darling son has already turned to stone.

She said again, 'I'll drive you to school, Noah.'

'That's okay. I'm taking the bus.' He stood up and grabbed his backpack and skateboard.

'Those hunters out there can't possibly see what they're shooting at. At least wear the orange hat. So they won't think you're a deer.'

'But it looks so dorky.'

'You can take it off on the bus. Just put it on now.' She took the knit cap from the mitten shelf and held it out to him.

He looked at it, then finally, at her. He had sprouted up several inches in just one year, and they were now the same height, their gazes meeting straight on, neither one able to claim the advantage. She wondered if Noah was as acutely aware of their new physical equality as she was. Once she could hug him and a child would hug back. Now the child was gone, his softness resculpted into muscle, his face narrowed to a sharp new angularity.

'Please,' she said, still holding out the cap.

At last he sighed and jammed the cap over his dark hair. She had to suppress a smile; he did look dorky.

He had already started down the hallway when she called out: 'Good-bye kiss?'

With a look of exasperation, he turned to give her the barest peck on the cheek, and then he was out of the door.

No hugs anymore, she thought ruefully as she stood at the window and watched him trudge toward the road. It's all grunts and shrugs and awkward silences.

He stopped beneath the maple tree at the end of the driveway, pulled off the cap, and stood with his hands in his pockets, shoulders hunched against the cold. No jacket, just a thin gray sweatshirt against a thirty-seven-degree morning. It was cool to be cold. She had to resist the urge to run outside and bundle him into a coat.

Claire waited until the school bus appeared. She watched her son climb aboard without a backward glance, saw his silhouette move down the aisle and take a seat beside another student – a girl. Who is that girl? she wondered. I don't know the names of my son's friends anymore. I've shrunk to just a small corner of his universe. She knew this was supposed to happen, the pulling away, the child's struggle for independence, but she was not prepared for it. The transformation had occurred suddenly, as though a sweet boy had walked out of the house one day, and a stranger had walked back in. *You're all I have left of Peter. I'm not ready to lose you as well.*

The bus rumbled away.

Claire returned to the kitchen and sat down to her cup of lukewarm coffee. The house felt hollow and silent, a home still in mourning. She sighed and unrolled the weekly *Tranquility Gazette*. HEALTHY DEER HERD PROMISES BOUNTIFUL HARVEST, announced the front page. The hunt was on. Thirty days to bag your deer.

Outside, another gunshot echoed in the woods.

She turned the page to the police blotter. There was no mention yet of last night's Halloween disturbance, or of the seven rowdy teenagers who'd been arrested for taking their annual trick-or-treating too far. But there, buried among the reports of lost dogs and stolen firewood, was her name, under VIOLATIONS: 'Claire Elliot, age forty, operating vehicle with expired safety sticker.' She still hadn't brought the Subaru in for its safety inspection; today she'd have to drive the truck instead, just to avoid getting another citation. Irritably she flipped to the next page and was scanning the day's weather forecast – cold and windy, high in the thirties, low in the twenties – when the telephone rang.

She rose to answer it. 'Hello?'

'Dr Elliot? This is Rachel Sorkin out on Toddy Point Road. I've got something of an emergency out here. Elwyn just shot himself.'

'What?'

'You know, that idiot Elwyn Clyde. He came trespassing on my property, chasing after some poor deer. Killed it too – a beautiful doe, right in my front yard. These stupid men and their stupid guns.'

10

'What about Elwyn?'

'Oh, he tripped and shot his own foot. Serves him right.'

'He should go straight to the hospital.'

'Well you see, that's the problem. He doesn't want to go to the hospital, and he won't let me call an ambulance. He wants me to drive him and the deer home. Well, I'm not going to. So what should I do with him?'

'How badly is he bleeding?'

She heard Rachel call out: 'Hey, Elwyn? *Elwyn!* Are you bleeding?' Then Rachel came back on the line. 'He says he's fine. He just wants a ride home. But I'm not taking him, and I'm certainly not taking the deer.'

Claire sighed. 'I guess I can drive over and take a look. You're on Toddy Point Road?'

'About a mile past the Boulders. My name's on the mail box.'

The mist was starting to lift as Claire turned her pickup truck onto Toddy Point Road. Through stands of white pine, she caught glimpses of Locust Lake, the fog rising like steam. Already beams of sunlight were breaking through, splashing gold onto the rippling water. Across the lake, just visible through fingers of mist, was the north shore with its summer cottages, most of them boarded up for the season, their wealthy owners gone home to Boston or New York. On the south shore, where Claire now drove, were the more modest homes, some of them little more than two-room shacks tucked in among the trees.

She drove past the Boulders, an outcropping of granite stones where the local teenagers gathered to swim in the summertime, and spotted the mailbox with the name *Sorkin*.

A bumpy dirt road brought her to the house. It was a strange and whimsical structure, rooms added haphazardly, corners jutting out in unexpected places. Rising above it all, like the tip of a crystal breaking through the roof, was a glassed-in belfry. An eccentric woman would have an eccentric house, and Rachel Sorkin was one of Tranquility's odd birds, a striking, black-haired woman who strode once a week into town, swathed in a purple hooded cape. This looked like a house in which a caped woman might reside.

By the front steps, next to a neatly tended herb garden, lay the dead deer.

Claire climbed out of her truck. At once two dogs bounded out of the woods and barred her way, barking and growling. Guarding the kill, she realized.

Rachel came out of the house and yelled at the dogs: 'Get out of here, you bloody animals! Go home!' She grabbed a broom from the porch and came tearing down the steps, long black hair flying, the broom thrust forward like a lance.

The dogs backed away.

'Ha! Cowards,' said Rachel, lunging at them with the broom. They retreated toward the woods.

'Hey, you leave my dogs alone!' shouted Elwyn Clyde, who had limped out onto the porch. Elwyn was a prime example of an evolutionary dead end: a fifty-year-old lump bundled in flannel, and doomed to eternal bachelorhood. 'They're not hurtin' nothin'. They're just watchin' after my deer.'

'Elwyn, I got news for you. You killed this poor creature on my property. So she's mine.'

'What you gonna do with a deer? Blasted vegetarian!'

Claire cut in: 'How's the foot, Elwyn?'

He looked at Claire and blinked, as though surprised to see her. 'I tripped,' he said. 'No big deal.'

'A bullet wound is always a big deal. May I take a look at it?'

'Can't pay you . . .' He paused, one scraggly eyebrow lifting as a sly thought occurred. ''Less you want some venison.'

'I just want to make sure you're not bleeding to death. We can settle up some other time. Can I look at your foot?'

'If you really want to,' he said, and limped back into the house.

'This should be a treat,' said Rachel.

It was warm inside the kitchen. Rachel threw a birch log into the wood stove, and sweet smoke puffed out as she dropped the cast iron lid back in place.

'Let's see the foot,' said Claire.

Elwyn hobbled over to a chair, leaving smears of blood on the floor. He had his sock on, and there was a jagged hole at the top, near the big toe, as though a rat had chewed through the wool. 'Hardly bothering me,' he said. 'Not worth all this fuss, if you ask me.'

Claire knelt down and peeled off the sock. It came away slowly, the wool matted to his foot not by blood but by sweat and dead skin.

'Oh God,' said Rachel, cupping her hand over her nose. 'Don't you ever change your socks, Elwyn?'

The bullet had passed through the fleshy web between the first and second toe. Claire found the exit wound underneath the foot. There was only a little blood oozing out now. Trying not to gag on the smell, she tested movement of all the toes, and determined that no nerves had been damaged.

'You'll have to clean it and change the bandages every day,' she said. 'And you need a tetanus shot, Elwyn.'

'Oh, I got one of them already.'

'When?'

'Last year, from ol' Doc Pomeroy. After I shot myself.'

'Is this an annual event?'

'That one went through my other foot. 'Tweren't a big deal.'

Dr Pomeroy had died back in January, and Claire had acquired all his old medical records when she'd bought the practice from his estate eight months

14

ago. She could check Elwyn's file and confirm the date of his last tetanus shot.

'I guess it's up to me to clean that foot,' said Rachel.

Claire took out a small bottle of Betadine from her medical bag and handed it to her. 'Add that to a warm bucket of water. Let him soak in it for a while.'

'Oh, I can do that myself,' said Elwyn, and got up.

'Then we might as well just amputate right now!' snapped Rachel. 'Sit *down*, Elwyn.'

'Gee,' he said, and sat down.

Claire left a few packets of bandages and gauze wrappings on the table. 'Elwyn, you come into my office next week, so I can check the wound.'

'But I got too much to do –'

'If you don't come in, I'll have to hunt you down like a dog.'

He blinked at her in surprise. 'Yes, ma'am,' he said meekly.

Suppressing a smile, Claire picked up her medical bag and walked out of the house.

The two dogs were in the front yard again, fighting over a filthy bone. As Claire came down the steps, they both spun around to stare at her.

The black one trotted forward and growled.

'Shoo,' Claire said, but the dog refused to back down. It took another few steps forward, teeth bared.

The tan dog, spotting opportunity, snatched the

bone in its teeth and began dragging away the prize. It got halfway across the yard before the black dog suddenly noticed the thief and streaked back into the fight. Yelping and growling, they thrashed around the yard in a tangle of black and tan. The bone lay, forgotten, beside Claire's pickup truck.

She opened the door and was just sliding in behind the steering wheel when the image registered in her brain. She looked down at the ground, at the bone.

It was less than a foot long, and stained a rusty brown with dirt. One end had broken off, leaving jagged splinters. The other end was intact, the bony landmarks recognizable.

It was a femur. And it was human.

Ten miles out of town, Tranquility Police Chief Lincoln Kelly finally caught up with his wife.

She was doing about fifty in a stolen Chevy, weaving left and right, the loose tailpipe kicking up sparks every time she hit a dip in the road.

'Man oh man,' said Floyd Spear, sitting beside Lincoln in the cruiser. 'Doreen got her snookerful today.'

'I've been on the road all morning,' said Lincoln. 'Didn't get a chance to check up on her.' He turned on the siren, hoping that would induce Doreen to slow down. She sped up.

'Now what?' asked Floyd. 'Want me to call for backup?'

16

Backup meant Hank Dorr, the only other officer on patrol duty that morning.

'No,' said Lincoln. 'Let's see if we can't talk her into pulling over.'

'At sixty miles an hour?'

'Get on the bullhorn.'

Floyd picked up the mike and his voice boomed out over the speaker: 'Hey, Doreen, pull over! C'mon, Sweetheart, you're gonna hurt someone!'

The Chevy just kept dipping and weaving.

'We could wait till she runs out of gas,' Floyd suggested.

'Keep talking to her.'

Floyd tried the mike again. 'Doreen, Lincoln's here! C'mon, Sweetheart, pull over! He wants ta 'pologize!'

'I want to *what*?'

'Pull over, Doreen, and he'll tell you himself!'

'What in hell are you talking about?' said Lincoln.

'Women always expect a man to apologize.'

'But I didn't do anything!'

Up ahead, the Chevy's brake lights suddenly lit up.

'See?' said Floyd as the Chevy rolled to a stop at the side of the road.

Lincoln pulled up behind it and climbed out of the cruiser.

Doreen sat hunched behind the steering wheel, her red hair wild and tangled, her hands shaking. Lincoln opened the door, reached over his

17

wife's lap, and removed the car keys. 'Doreen,' he said wearily, 'you gotta come back to the station.'

'When are you coming home, Lincoln?' she asked.

'We'll talk about that later. Come on, Honey, let's get in the cruiser.' He reached for her elbow but she shook him off and slapped his hand for good measure.

'I just want to know when you're coming home,' she said.

'We've talked about this and talked about this.'

'You're still married to me. You're still my husband.'

'And there's just no point in talking about it any more.' Again he took her elbow. He already had her out of the Chevy when she hauled off and slugged him in the jaw. He staggered back a few steps, his whole head ringing.

'Hey!' said Floyd, grabbing Doreen's arms. 'Hey now, you don't wanna go doing that!'

'Lemme go!' screeched Doreen. She broke out of Floyd's grasp and took another swing at her husband.

This time Lincoln ducked, which only made his wife madder. She got in one more swing before Lincoln and Floyd managed to get her arms secured.

'I hate to do this,' said Lincoln. 'But you're just not being reasonable today.' He snapped the handcuffs on her wrists. She spat at him. He wiped his sleeve across his face, then patiently guided his wife into the backseat of the cruiser.

'Oh man,' said Floyd. 'You know we're gonna have to book her.'

'I know.' Lincoln sighed and slid in behind the wheel.

'You can't divorce me, Lincoln Kelly!' said Doreen. 'You promised to love and cherish!'

'I didn't know about the bottle,' said Lincoln, and he turned the car around.

They drove at a leisurely speed toward town, Doreen cussing a purple streak the whole time. It was the drinking that did it; it seemed to pop the cork off her bottle of demons.

Two years ago, Lincoln had moved out of their house. He figured he'd given the marriage his best effort and ten years of his life. He wasn't by nature a quitter, but the despair had finally gotten to him. That and the sense that, at forty-five, his life was racing by, joyless and unfruitful. He wished he could do right by Doreen, wished that he could recapture some of that old affection he'd felt for her early on in their marriage, when she'd been bright and sober, not bubbling over with anger as she was now. Sometimes he'd search his own heart for whatever trace of love might still linger, some small spark among the ashes, but there was nothing left. The ashes were cold. And he was tired.

He had tried to stand by her, but Doreen couldn't even see clear to help herself. Every few months, when her rage boiled up, she'd spend the day

19

drinking. Then she'd 'borrow' someone's car and go for one of her famous high-speed drives. People in town knew to stay off the roads when Doreen Kelly got behind the wheel.

Back at the Tranquility police station, Lincoln let Floyd do the booking and locking up. Through the two closed doors leading to the cell, he could hear Doreen yelling for a lawyer. He supposed he should call one for her, though no one in Tranquility wanted to take her on. Even down south as far as Bangor, she'd worn out her welcomes. He sat at his desk, flipping through the Rolodex, trolling for a lawyer's name. Someone he hadn't called in a while. Someone who didn't mind being cussed out by a client.

It was all too much, too early in the morning. He shoved away the Rolodex and ran his hand through his hair. Doreen was still yelling in the back room. This would all be reported in that nosy *Gazette*, and then the Bangor and Portland papers would pick it up because the whole damn state of Maine thought it was funny and so very quaint. *Tranquility police chief arrests own wife. Again.*

He reached for the telephone and was dialing the number for Tom Wiley, attorney at law, when he heard a knock at his door. Glancing up, he saw Claire Elliot walk into his office, and he hung up.

'Hey, Claire,' he said. 'Got your safety sticker yet?'

'I'm still working on it. But I'm not here about

my car. I want to show you something.' She set a dirty bone down on his desk.

'What's this?'

'It's a femur, Lincoln.'

'What?'

'A thigh bone. I think it's human.'

He stared at the dirt-encrusted bone. One end was splintered off, and the shaft showed the gnawings of animal teeth. 'Where did you find this?'

'Rachel Sorkin's place.'

'How did Rachel get it?'

'Elwyn Clyde's dogs dragged it into her yard. She doesn't know where it came from. I was over there this morning, after Elwyn shot himself in the foot.'

'Again?' He rolled his eyes and they both laughed. If every village had an idiot, then Tranquility's would be Elwyn.

'He's okay,' she said. 'But I guess a gunshot wound should be reported.'

'Consider it done. I already have a folder for Elwyn and his gunshot wounds.' He gestured to a chair. 'Now tell me about this bone. Are you sure it's human?'

She sat down. Though they were looking directly at each other, he felt a barrier of reserve between them that was almost physical. He had sensed it the first time they'd met, soon after she'd moved to town, when she had attended to a prisoner suffering from abdominal pain in Tranquility's three-cell jail. Lincoln had been curious about her from the start. Where was her husband? Why was she alone raising her son? But he had not felt comfortable asking her personal questions, and she did not seem to invite such intrusion. Pleasant but intensely private, she seemed reluctant to let anyone get too close to her, which was a shame. She was a pretty woman, short but sturdy, with luminous dark eyes and a mass of curly brown hair just starting to show the first strands of silver.

She leaned forward, her hands resting on his desk. 'I'm not an expert or anything,' she said, 'but I don't know what other animal this bone could come from. Judging by the size, it looks like a child's.'

'Did you see any other bones around?'

'Rachel and I searched the yard, but we didn't find any. The dogs could've picked this up anywhere in the woods. You'll have to search the whole area.'

'Could be from an old Indian burial.'

'Possibly. But doesn't it still have to go to the medical examiner?' Suddenly she turned, her head cocked. 'What's all that commotion?'

Lincoln flushed. Doreen was shouting in her cell again, letting fly a fresh torrent of abuse. 'Damn you, Lincoln! You jerk! You liar! Damn you to hell!'

'It sounds like somebody doesn't like you very much,' said Claire.

He sighed and pressed his hand to his forehead. 'My wife.'

Claire's gaze softened to a look of sympathy. It was apparent she knew about his problems. Everyone in town did.

'I'm sorry,' she said.

'Hey, loser!' Doreen yelled. 'You got no right to treat me like this!'

With deliberate effort, he redirected his attention to the thigh bone. 'How old was the victim, do you think?'

She picked up the femur and turned it over in her hands. For a moment she held it with quiet reverence, fully aware that this broken length of bone had once supported a laughing, running child. 'Young,' she murmured. 'I would guess under ten years old.' She lay it on the desk and stared down in silence.

'We haven't had any missing children reported recently,' he said. 'The area's been settled for hundreds of years, and old bones are always turning up. A century ago, it wasn't all that unusual to die young.'

She was frowning. 'I don't think this child died from natural causes,' she said softly.

'Why do you say that?'

She reached over to turn on his desk lamp, and held the bone close to the light. 'There,' she said. 'It's so crusted over, you can barely see it through the dirt.'

He reached in his pocket for his glasses – another reminder of the years' passage, of his youth slipping away. Bending closer, he tried to see what she was pointing at. Only when she'd scraped away a clot of dirt with her fingernail did he see the wedge-shaped gash.

It was the mark of a hatchet.

2

When Warren Emerson finally regained consciousness, he found he was lying next to the woodpile and the sun was shining in his eyes. His last memory was of shade, of silvery frost on the grass and bulging pockets of soil, heaved up from the cold. He'd been splitting firewood, swinging the ax and enjoying the sharp ring it made in the crisp air. The sun had not yet cleared the pine tree in his front yard.

Now it was well above the tree, which meant he had been lying here for some time, perhaps an hour, judging by its position in the sky.

Slowly Warren sat up, his head aching as it always did afterwards. His hands and face were numb from the cold; both of his gloves had fallen off. He saw the ax lying beside him, its blade buried deep in one end of a maple log. A day's worth of firewood, already split, lay scattered around him. It took him a painfully long time to register these observations, and to consider the significance of each in turn. The thoughts came to him with effort, as though dragged from a great distance, arriving tattered and in disarray. He was patient with himself; eventually it would all make sense.

He had come out soon after sunrise to split his wood for the day. The result of his labor now lay all around him. He had almost completed the morning chore, had just swung his ax into that last log, when the darkness came over him. He had fallen onto the woodpile; that would explain why some of the logs had rolled off the top. His underwear was soaked; he must have wet himself, as he often did during a fit. Looking down at his clothes, he saw that his jeans were saturated.

There was blood on his shirt.

He staggered to his feet and walked slowly back into the old farmhouse.

The kitchen was hot and stuffy from the wood-stove; it made him feel a little dizzy, and his vision had started to fade around the edges by the time he reached the bathroom. He sat down on the chipped toilet lid, clutching his head, waiting for the clouds to lift from his brain. The cat came in and rubbed against his calf, meowing for attention. He reached down to her and drew comfort from the softness of her fur.

His face was no longer numb from the cold, and he was now aware of pain throbbing insistently in his temple. Clutching the sink for support, he rose to his feet and looked in the mirror. Just over his left ear, the gray hair was stiff and matted with blood. A streak of it had dried across his cheek, like war paint. He stared at his own reflection, at a face deeply etched by sixty-six years of hard winters and honest work and loneliness. His only companion was the cat, now meowing at his feet, not from affection but hunger. He loved the cat, and someday he would mourn her passing with tears and a solemn burial and nights of longing for the sound of her purring, but he was under no illusion that she loved him.

He removed his clothes, the frayed and blood-stained shirt, the urine-soaked jeans. He undressed with the same care he devoted to every other task in his life, leaving his clothes in a tidy heap on the toilet lid. He turned on the shower and stepped in without waiting for the water to warm up; the discomfort was only momentary, scarcely worth a shiver in the context of his cold and uncomfortable life. He washed the blood out of his hair, the laceration stinging from the soap. He must have sliced his scalp open when he fell on the woodpile. It would heal, as all his other cuts had. Warren Emerson was a walking testament to the durability of scar tissue.

The cat renewed her meowing as soon as he stepped out of the shower. It was a pitiful sound, despairing, and he could not listen to it without feeling guilty. Still naked, he walked to the kitchen, opened a can of Little Friskies chicken bits, and spooned it into Mona's cat bowl.

She gave a soft growl of pleasure and began to

eat, no longer caring whether he came or went. Except for his skill with a can opener, he was extraneous to her existence.

He went to the bedroom to dress.

Once it had been his parents' room, and it still contained all their possessions. The spindle bed, the bureau with the brass knobs, the photographs hanging up in their tin picture frames. As he buttoned his shirt, his gaze lingered on one photo in particular, of a dark-haired girl with smiling eyes. What was Iris doing at this moment? he wondered, as he did every day of his life. Did she ever think of him? His gaze moved on to another photo. It was the last one taken of his family, his mother plump and smiling, his father ill at ease in a suit and tie. And wedged between them, with his hair slicked to one side, was little Warren.

He reached out, fingers touching the photo of his own twelve-year-old face. He could not remember that boy. Up in the attic were the toy trains and the adventure books and the brittle crayons that once belonged to the child in that photo, but that was a different Warren who'd played in this house, who had stood smiling between his parents for a Sunday photograph. Not the Warren he saw when he looked in the mirror.

Suddenly he felt a terrible longing to touch that child's toys again.

He climbed the steps to the attic and dragged the old blanket chest under the light. With the bare bulb swinging overhead, he lifted the chest lid.

28

Inside were treasures. He took them out one by one and set them on the dusty floor. The cookie tin with all the Matchbox cars. The Lincoln Logs. The leather pouch of marbles. At last he found what he'd been looking for: the set of checkers.

He lay out the board and set up the checkers, red on his side, black on the opposite.

Mona came padding up to the attic and sat beside him, her breath smelling of chicken. For a moment she regarded the board with feline disdain. Then she tiptoed over to it and sniffed at one of the black pieces.

'Is that your first move then?' said Warren. It was not a very smart move, but then, what did one expect from a cat? He moved the black piece for her, and she seemed satisfied.

Outside the wind blew, rattling loose shutters. He could hear the branches of the lilac tree scratch against the clapboards.

Warren advanced a red checker and he smiled at his companion. 'Your move, Mona.'

At six-thirty, as she did every weekday morning, five-year-old Isabel Morrison crept into her older sister's bedroom and climbed under the covers with Mary Rose. There she wriggled like a happy worm in the warm sheets and hummed to herself as she waited for Mary Rose to wake up. There would always be a great deal of sighing and moaning, and Mary Rose would turn from one side to another, her long brown hair tickling

Isabel's face. Isabel thought Mary Rose was the most beautiful girl on earth. She looked like the sleeping Princess Aurora, waiting for her prince to kiss her. Sometimes Isabel would pretend *she* was Prince Charming, and even though she knew girls weren't supposed to kiss each other, she would plant her lips on her sister's mouth and announce: 'Now you have to wake up!'

One time, Mary Rose had been awake all along, and had sprung up like a giggling monster and tickled Isabel so mercilessly that both girls had fallen off the bed in a duet of happy squeals.

If only Mary Rose would tickle her now. If only Mary Rose would be her normal self.

Isabel leaned close to her sister's ear and whispered, 'Aren't you going to wake up?'

Mary Rose pulled the covers over her head. 'Go away, pest.'

'Mommy says it's time for school. You have to wake up.'

'Get out of my room!'

'But it's time for –'

Mary Rose gave a growl and lashed out with an angry kick.

Isabel slithered to the far side of the bed, where she lay in troubled silence, rubbing her sore shin and trying to understand what had just happened. Mary Rose had never kicked her before. Mary Rose always woke up with a smile and called her Dizzy Izzy and braided her hair before school.

She decided to try again. She crawled on hands

and knees to her sister's pillow, peeled back the sheets, and whispered into Mary Rose's ear: 'I know what Mommy and Daddy are getting you for Christmas. You wanna hear?'

Mary Rose's eyes shot open. She turned to look at Isabel.

With a whimper of fear, Isabel scrambled off the bed and stared at a face she scarcely recognized. A face that frightened her. 'Mary Rose?' she whispered.

Then she ran out of the room.

Her mother was downstairs in the kitchen, stirring a pot of oatmeal and trying to hear the radio over the screeches of their parakeet, Rocky. As Isabel came tearing into the kitchen, her mother turned and said, 'It's seven o'clock. Isn't your sister getting up?'

'Mommy,' Isabel wailed in despair. 'That's not Mary Rose!'

Noah Elliot did a 360 kick-flip, popping the skateboard off the curb, into the air, and landing it neatly on the blacktop. *All right! Nailed it!* Baggy clothes flapping in the wind, he rode the board all the way down to the teachers' parking lot, ollied the curb, and came around again, a sweet ride all the way.

It was the only time he felt in control of his life, when he was riding his board, when for once, he determined his own fate, his own course. These days it seemed too many things were decided by other people, that he was being dragged, kicking and screaming, into a future he'd never asked for. But when he was riding his board, with the wind in his face and the pavement streaking by, he owned the moment. He could forget he was trapped in this nowhere town. He could even forget, for one brief and exhilarating ride, that his dad was dead and that nothing could ever be right again.

He felt the freshmen girls watching him. They were standing in a tight group behind the trailer classrooms, glossy heads bent close together as they made giggly girl sounds. All their faces moved in unison as their eyes tracked Noah on his board. He rarely talked to them, and they rarely talked to him, but every lunch period, there they'd be, watching him as he worked through his repertoire.

Noah wasn't the only skateboarder at Knox High School, but he was definitely the best, and the girls kept their focus on him, ignoring the other boys whizzing around on the blacktop. Those boys were just posers anyway, dudes pretending to be skaters, all dressed up in gear straight out of the CCS catalogue. They had the uniform down right – Birdhouse shirts and Kevlar shoes and pants so big the cuffs dragged on the ground – but they were still posers in a hick town. They hadn't skated with the big boys in Baltimore.

As Noah circled around to make his return run, he noticed the gleam of blond hair at the edge of the track field. Amelia Reid was watching him.

She stood off by herself, cradling a book as usual. Amelia was one of those girls who seemed dipped in honey, she was so perfect, so golden. Nothing at all like her two jerky brothers, who were always hassling him in the cafeteria. Noah had never noticed her watching him before, and the realization that her attention was at this very moment focused on *him* made his knees go a little wobbly.

He ollied the board and almost lost it on the landing. *Focus, dude! Don't bite it.* He zipped down to the faculty parking lot, spun around, and came rumbling up the concrete ramp. There was a handrail on one side, slanted downward. He spun around, and popped up onto the railing. It would've been a sweet slide all the way down.

Except for the fact Taylor Darnell chose just that moment to walk in front of him.

Noah yelled, 'Outta the way!' but Taylor didn't react in time.

At the last possible instant, Noah rolled off his board and tumbled to the pavement. The skateboard, its momentum established, slid all the way down the rail and smacked into Taylor's back.

Taylor whirled, yelling: 'What the hell, man? Who threw that?'

'Didn't throw it, dude,' said Noah, picking himself up from the ground. His palms were both scraped, and his knee was throbbing. 'It was an accident. You just got in the way.' Noah bent down to pick up the skateboard, which had landed wheels up. Taylor was an okay kid, one of the first who'd come up to say hello when Noah first arrived in town eight months ago. Sometimes, they even hung out together in the afternoons, showing each other new skateboard tricks. So Noah was shocked when Taylor suddenly shoved him, hard.

'Hey! Hey, what's your problem?' said Noah.

'You threw it at me!'

'No I didn't.'

'Everyone saw it!' Taylor looked around at the bystanders. 'Didn't you see it?'

No one said anything.

'I told you, it was an accident,' said Noah. 'I'm really sorry, man.'

There was laughter over by the trailer classrooms. Taylor glanced at the girls and realized they were watching the exchange, and his face turned a furious red. 'Shut up!' he yelled at them. 'Idiot girls!'

'Geez, Taylor,' said Noah. 'What's your problem?'

The other skaters had popped up their boards and were now standing around, watching. One of them joked,

'Hey, why did Taylor cross the road?'

'Why?'

'Cause he got his dick stuck in the chicken!'

All the skaters laughed, including Noah. He couldn't help it.

He was unprepared for the blow. It seemed to come out of nowhere, a sucker punch to the jaw. His head snapped up and he stumbled backwards

34

and fell, his butt hitting the blacktop. There he sat for a moment, ears roaring and vision blurred as his shock gave way to hurt rage. *He was my friend, and he hit me!*

Noah staggered back to his feet and lunged at Taylor, tackling him head on. They both sprawled to the ground, Noah on top. They rolled over and over, both boys flailing, neither one able to get in a decisive blow. Noah finally pinned him, but it was like holding down a spitting cat.

'Noah Elliot!'

He froze, his hands still trapping Taylor's wrists. Slowly he turned his head and saw the principal, Miss Cornwallis, standing over them. The other kids had all backed away and were watching from a safe distance.

'Get up!' said Miss Cornwallis. 'Both of you!'

At once Noah released Taylor and rose to his feet. Taylor, his face by now almost purple with rage, screamed: 'He shoved me! He shoved me and I tried to defend myself!'

'That's not true! He hit me first!'

'He threw his skateboard!'

'I didn't throw anything. It was an accident!'

'Accident? You liar!'

'Both of you, be quiet!' yelled Miss Cornwallis.

There was shocked silence in the schoolyard as everyone stared at the principal. They'd never heard her yell before. She was a prim but handsome woman who wore suits and low heels to school and kept her blond hair neatly tucked into a

French twist. To see her shouting was a revelation to them all.

Miss C. took a deep breath, swiftly recovering her dignity. 'Give me the skateboard, Noah.'

'It was an accident. I didn't hit him.'

'You were pinning him on the ground. I saw it.'

'But I didn't hit him!'

She held out her hand. 'Give it to me.'

'But –'

'Now.'

Noah walked over to his board, lying a few feet away. It was well-worn, one chipped edge crisscrossed with electrician's tape. The board had been a birthday gift when he turned thirteen. He'd added the decals underneath it – a green dragon with red fire shooting out of its mouth – and had broken in the wheels riding the streets of Baltimore where he used to live. He loved this board, because it reminded him of everything he'd left behind. Everything he still missed. He held it for a moment, then, wordlessly, handed it to Miss C.

She took it with a look of distaste. Turning to address the other students she said, 'There'll be no more skating on school grounds. I want all the skateboards brought home today. And if I see any boards tomorrow, I'll confiscate them. Is that clear?'

There was a silent nodding of heads.

Miss C. turned to Noah. 'You're in detention until three-thirty this afternoon.'

'But I didn't do anything!'

'You come to my office now. You're going to sit and think about what you did do.'

Noah started to argue, then swallowed his words. Everyone was looking at him. He glimpsed Amelia Reid standing by the track field, and his face flushed with humiliation. In silence, head down, he followed Miss C. toward the building.

The other skaters sullenly parted to let them through. Only as Noah was walking away from them did he hear one of the boys mutter:

'Thanks, Elliot. You screwed it up for the rest of us.'

If one wished to take the pulse of the town of Tranquility, the place to go was Monaghan's Diner. This was where the Dinosaur Club met every day at noon. It was not really a club, but a coffee klatch, six or seven retirees who, for want of a job to go to, hung around Nadine's counter, admiring the pies under the plastic bells. Claire had no idea how the club got its name. Her guess was that one of the men's wives, in a fit of pique over her husband's daily absence, one day blurted out something like: 'Oh, you and that bunch of old dinosaurs!' And the name stuck, as good names do. They were all men, all well past sixty. Nadine was only in her fifties, but she was an unofficial Dinosaur because she worked behind the counter and had the good humor to tolerate their bad jokes and cigarette smoke.

Four hours after the thigh bone was found,

Claire stopped in at Monaghan's for lunch. The Dinosaurs, seven of them today, all wearing blaze orange over flannel shirts, sat in their usual place, the far left barstools near the milkshake machine.

Ned Tibbetts turned and nodded as Claire came in the door. Not a warm greeting, but gruffly respectful. 'Mornin', Doc.'

'Morning, Mr Tibbetts.'

'Gonna be a mean wind blowing in today.'

'It's already freezing outside.'

'Coming out of the northwest. Could have snow tonight.'

'Cup of coffee, Doc?' asked Nadine.

'Thank you.'

Ned turned back to the other Dinosaurs, who'd variously acknowledged her entrance, and were now back in conversation. She knew only two of them by name; the others were merely familiar faces. Claire sat alone at her end of the counter, as befitted her outsider status. Oh, people were cordial enough to her. They smiled, they were polite. But to these natives, her eight months in Tranquility was but a temporary sojourn, a city girl's fling with the simple life. Winter, they all seemed to agree, would be the test. Four months of snowstorms and black ice would drive her back to the city, as it had driven off the last two doctors from away.

Nadine slid a steaming cup of coffee in front of Claire. 'Guess you know all about it, don't you?' she said.

38

'All about what?'

'That bone.' Nadine stood watching her, patiently waiting for her contribution to the community pool of knowledge. Like most Maine women, Nadine did a lot of listening. It was the men who seemed to do all the talking. Claire heard them when she walked through the local hardware store or the five-and-dime or the post office. They stood around and gabbed while their wives waited, silent and watchful.

'I hear it's a kid's bone,' said Joe Bartlett, swiveling on the stool to look at Claire. 'A thigh bone.'

'That right, Doc?' another one asked.

The other Dinosaurs turned and looked at Claire.

She said, with a smile, 'You already seem to know everything about it.'

'Heard it was whacked up good. Maybe a knife. Maybe an ax. Then the animals got at it.'

'You boys sure are cheerful today,' snorted Nadine.

'Three days in those woods, raccoons and coyotes clean your bones straight off. Then Elwyn's dogs come along. Hardly ever feeds 'em, y'know. Bone like that's a tasty snack. Maybe his dogs've been chewing on it for weeks. Elwyn, he wouldn't think to give it a second look.'

Joe laughed. 'That Elwyn, he just plain doesn't think.'

'Maybe he shot the kid himself. Mistook it for a deer.'

Claire said, 'It looked like a very old bone.'

Joe Bartlett waved at Nadine. 'I made up my mind. I'll have the Monte Cristo sandwich.'

'Whooee! Joe's goin' fancy on us today!' said Ned Tibbetts.

'What about you, Doc?' asked Nadine.

'A tuna sandwich and a bowl of mushroom soup, please.'

As Claire ate her lunch, she listened to the men talk about whom the bone might belong to. It was impossible not to listen in; three of them wore hearing aids. Most of them could remember as far back as sixty years ago, and they batted the possibilities around like a birdie in play. Maybe it was that young girl who'd fallen off Bald Rock Cliff. No, they'd found her body, remember? Maybe it was the Jewett girl – hadn't she run off when she was sixteen? Ned said no, he'd heard from his mother that she was living in Hartford; the girl'd have to be in her sixties now, probably a grandmother. Fred Moody said his wife Florida said the dead girl had to be from away – one of the summer people. Tranquility kept track of its own, and wouldn't someone remember if a local kid had vanished?

Nadine refilled Claire's cup of coffee. 'Don't they just go on and on?' she said. 'You'd think they was planning world peace.'

'How do they know so much about it, any-way?'

'Joe's second cousin to Floyd Spear, over at the police department.' Nadine began to wipe down

40

the counter, long, brisk strokes that left behind a faintly chlorinated smell. 'They say some bone expert's driving up from Bangor today. Way I figure, it's gotta be one of those summer people.'

That, of course, was the obvious answer – one of the summer people. Whether it was an unsolved crime or an unidentified body, the all-purpose answer served. Every June, Tranquility's population quadrupled when wealthy families from Boston and New York began arriving for their lakeside vacations. Here, in this peaceful summertime colony, they would linger on the porches of their shorefront cottages while their children splashed in the water. In the shops of Tranquility, cash registers would ring merrily as the summer folk pumped dollars into the local economy. Someone had to clean their cottages, repair their fancy cars, bag their groceries. The business from those few short months was enough to keep the local population fed through the winter.

It was the money that made the visitors tolerable. That and the fact that every September, with the falling of the leaves, they would once again vanish, leaving the town to the people who belonged here.

Claire finished her lunch and walked back to her office.

Tranquility's main street followed the curve of the lake. At the top of Elm Street was Joe Bartlett's gas and garage, which he'd run for forty-two years until he retired; now his daughter's two girls pumped gas and changed oil. A sign above the garage proudly proclaimed: Owned and Operated by Joe Bartlett and Granddaughters. Claire had always liked that sign; she thought it said a lot for Joe Bartlett.

At the post office, Elm Street curved north. Already that northwest wind was starting to blow in across the lake. It blasted through the narrow alleys between buildings, and walking along the sidewalk was like passing through a series of icy wind tunnels. In the window above the five-and-dime, a black cat gazed down at her, as though pondering the stupidity of creatures out in such weather.

Next to the five-and-dime was the yellow Victorian where Claire had her medical practice.

The building had once served as Dr Pomeroy's business and residence. The door still had the old frosted glass with the lettering: MEDICAL OFFICE. Although the name *James Pomeroy, M.D.*, had been replaced by *Claire Elliot, M.D., Family Practice*, she sometimes imagined she could see the shadow of the old name lingering like a ghost in the pebbled glass, refusing to yield to the new occupant.

Inside, her receptionist, Vera, was yakking on the phone, her bracelets clattering as she flipped through the appointment book. Vera's hairstyle was like her personality: wild and woolly and a little frazzled. She cupped her hand over the receiver and said to Claire, 'Mairead Temple's in the exam room. Sore throat.'

'How's the rest of the afternoon look?'

'Two more coming in, and that's it.'

Which added up to only six patients all day, worried Claire. Since the summer tourists departed, Claire's practice had contracted. She was the only doctor with an office right in Tranquility, yet most of the locals drove the twenty miles to Two Hills for medical care. She knew why; not many in town believed she'd last through one hard winter, and they saw no point getting attached to a doctor who'd be gone by the following autumn.

Mairead Temple was one of the few patients Claire had managed to attract, but it was only because Mairead owned no car. She'd walked a mile into town, and now she sat on the exam table, still wheezing slightly from the cold weather. Mairead was eighty-one and she had no teeth or tonsils. Nor did she have much deference for authority.

Examining Mairead's throat, Claire said, 'It does look pretty red.'

'I coulda told you that myself,' Mairead answered.

'But you don't have a fever. And your lymph nodes aren't swollen.'

'Hurts wicked bad. Can't hardly swallow.'

'I'll take a throat culture. By tomorrow we'll know if it's strep. But I think it's just a virus.'

Mairead, her eyes small and suspicious, watched Claire peel open a throat swab. 'Dr Pomeroy always gave me penicillin.'

'Antibiotics don't work on a virus, Mrs Temple.'

'Always made me feel better, that penicillin.'

'Say "ah."'

Mairead gagged as Claire swabbed her throat. She looked like a tortoise, leathery neck extended, toothless mouth snapping at the air. Eyes watering, she said: 'Pomeroy was in practice a long time. Always knew what he was doing. All you young doctors, you coulda learned a thing or two from him.'

Claire sighed. Would she always be compared to Dr Pomeroy? His gravestone sat in a place of honor in the Mountain Street Cemetery. Claire saw his cryptic notes in the old medical charts, and sometimes she sensed his ghost dogging her on her rounds. Certainly it was Pomeroy's ghost that now came between her and Mairead. Dead though he was, he would always be remembered as the town doctor.

'Let's listen to your lungs,' said Claire.

Mairead grunted and tugged at her clothes. It was cold outside, and she had dressed for it. A sweater, a cotton shirt, thermal underwear, and a bra all had to be pulled free before Claire could set her stethoscope on her chest.

Through the thump-thump of Mairead's heart, Claire heard a distant tapping and she looked up.

Vera stuck her head in the room. 'Call on line two.'

'Can you take a message?'

'It's your son. He won't talk to me.'

'Excuse me, Mrs Temple,' Claire said, and went into her office to take the call. 'Noah?'

'You have to pick me up. I'm gonna miss the bus.'

'But it's only two-fifteen. The bus hasn't left yet.'

'I'm in detention. I can't leave until three-thirty.'

'Why? What happened?'

'I don't wanna talk about it now.'

'I'm going to find out anyway, honey.'

'Not *now*, Mom.' She heard him sniffle, heard the tears break through his voice. 'Please. Please, can you just come and get me?'

The phone went dead. Haunted by the image of her son, crying and in trouble, Claire quickly dialed the school back. But by the time she reached the secretary, Noah had already left the office, and Miss Cornwallis was not available to speak to her.

Claire had an hour to finish with Mairead Temple, see two new patients, and drive to the school.

Feeling pressured now, and distracted by Noah's crisis, she stepped back into the exam room and was dismayed to see that Mairead already had put her clothes back on.

'I'm not quite finished examining you,' said Claire.

'Yeah, y'are,' grunted Mairead.

'But Mrs Temple –'

'Came for penicillin. Didn't come to get no Q-Tip shoved down my throat.'

'Please, won't you just sit down? I know I do

45

things a little differently from Dr Pomeroy, but there's a reason for it. Antibiotics don't stop a virus, and they can cause side effects.'

'Never caused me no side effects.'

'It only takes a day to get back the culture results. If it's strep, I'll give you the medicine then.'

'Gotta walk all the way into town. Takes up half my day.'

Suddenly Claire understood what the real issue was. Every lab test, every new prescription, meant a mile-long walk into town for Mairead, and then another mile walk home.

With a sigh, she pulled out a prescription pad. And for the first time that visit, she saw Mairead's smile. Satisfied. Triumphant.

Isabel sat quietly on the couch, afraid to move, afraid to say a word.

Mary Rose was very, very mad. Their mother was not home yet, so Isabel was all alone with her sister. She had never seen Mary Rose behave this way, pacing back and forth like a tiger in the zoo, screaming at her. At her, Isabel! Mary Rose was so angry, it turned her face wrinkled and ugly, not like Princess Aurora anymore, but more like an evil queen. This was not her sister. This was a bad person inside her sister's body.

Isabel huddled deeper into the cushions, watching furtively as the bad person in Mary Rose's body stalked through the living room, muttering. *Never get to go anywhere or do anything because of you! Stuck at home all the time. A baby-sitter slave! I wish you were dead. I wish you were dead.*

But I'm your sister! Isabel wanted to wail, though she didn't dare make a peep. She began to cry, silent tears plopping onto the cushions, making big wet stains. Oh no. Mary Rose would be mad about that, too.

Isabel waited until her sister's back was turned, then she quietly slipped off the couch and darted into the kitchen. She would hide in here, out of Mary Rose's way, until their mother came home. She ducked around the corner of a kitchen cabinet and sat down on the cold tiles, hugging her knees to her chest. If she just stayed quiet, Mary Rose wouldn't find her. She could see the clock on the wall, and she knew that when the little hand was on the five, their mother would come home. She needed to pee, now, but she would just have to wait because she was safe here.

Then Rocky the parakeet began to screech. His cage was a few feet away, by the window. She looked up at him, silently imploring him to be quiet, but Rocky was not very smart and he kept screeching at her. Their mother had said it many times: 'Rocky is just a birdbrain,' and he was proving it now by all the noise he made.

Be quiet! Oh please be quiet or she'll find me!

Too late. Footsteps creaked into the kitchen. A drawer was yanked open and silverware clanged to the floor. Mary Rose was flinging around forks and spoons. Isabel wrapped herself into a ball and squeezed more tightly against the cabinet.

Rocky the traitor stared at her as he squawked, as though to shout out: 'There she is! There she is!'

Now Mary Rose paced into view, but she wasn't looking at Isabel. She was staring at Rocky. She went to the cage and stood looking at the parakeet, who continued to screech. She opened the door and thrust in her hand. Rocky's wings flapped in panicked whooshes of flying feathers and birdseed. She captured the struggling bird, a squirming puff of powder blue, and took him out of the cage. With one quick twist, she snapped the bird's neck.

Rocky went limp.

She flung the body against the wall. It plopped to the floor in a sad little heap of feathers.

A silent scream boiled up in Isabel's throat. She choked it back and buried her face against her knees, waiting in terror for her sister to break her neck as well.

But Mary Rose walked right out of the kitchen. Right out of the house.

3

Noah was sitting on the front steps of the high school when Claire arrived at four o'clock. She had rushed through her last two appointments, and had driven straight to the school five miles away, but she was a half hour late, and she could see he was angry about it. He didn't say a word, just climbed into the truck, and slammed the door shut.

'Seat belt, honey,' she said.

He yanked on the shoulder strap and rammed the buckle in. They drove for a moment in silence.

'I've been sitting around forever. What took you so long?' he said.

'I had patients to see, Noah. Why were you in detention?'

'It wasn't my fault.'

'Whose fault was it, then?'

'Taylor. He's turning into such a jerk. I don't know what's wrong with him.' Sighing, he slumped into his seat. 'And I used to think we were friends. Now it's like he hates me.'

49

She glanced at him. 'Is this Taylor Darnell you're talking about?'

'Yeah.'

'What happened?'

'It was an accident. My skateboard ran into him. Next thing I know, he's shoving me around. So I shoved him back, and he fell.'

'Why didn't you call a teacher?'

'There weren't any around. Then Miss Cornwallis comes out and suddenly Taylor starts yelling that it's *my* fault.' He turned away from her, but not before she'd glimpsed the embarrassed swipe of his hand across his eyes. He tries so hard to be grown up, she thought with a twinge of pity, but he's really still a child.

'She took my skateboard, Mom,' he said softly. 'Can you get it back for me?'

'I'll call Miss Cornwallis tomorrow. But I want you to call Taylor and apologize.'

'He turned on me! He's the one who should apologize!'

'Taylor's not having an easy time of it, Noah. His parents just got divorced.'

He looked at her. 'How do you know? Is he your patient?'

'Yes.'

'What did you see him for?'

'You know I can't talk about that.'

'Like you ever talk to me about anything,' he muttered, and turned once again to stare out the window.

She knew better than to rise to the bait, so she said nothing, preferring silence to the argument that would surely erupt between them if she allowed him to provoke her.

When he spoke again, it was so quietly she almost didn't hear him. 'I want to go home, Mom.'

'That's where I'm taking you.'

'No, I mean *home*. To Baltimore. I don't want to stay here anymore. There's nothing here but trees and a bunch of old guys driving around in their pickup trucks. We don't belong here.'

'This is our home now.'

'Not mine.'

'You haven't tried very hard to like it here.'

'Like I had a choice? Like you asked *me* if we should move?'

'We'll both learn to like it. I'm still adjusting, too.'

'So why did we have to move?'

Gripping the steering wheel, she stared straight ahead. 'You know why.' They both knew what she was talking about. They'd left Baltimore because of *him*, because she'd taken a hard look at her son's future and was frightened by what she saw. An enlarging circle of troubled friends. Repeated calls from the police. More courtrooms and lawyers and therapists. She had seen their future in Baltimore, and she'd grabbed her son and run like hell.

'I'm not going to turn into some perfect preppie just because you drag me up to the woods,' he said.

'I can mess things up just as good right here. So we might as well go back.'

She pulled into their driveway and turned to face him. 'Messing up is not going to get you back to Baltimore. Either you get your life together or you don't. It's your choice.'

'When is anything my choice?'

'You have lots of choices. And from now on, I want you to make the right ones.'

'You mean the ones *you* want.' He jumped out of the truck.

'Noah. Noah!'

'Just leave me *alone!*' he yelled. He slammed the door shut and stalked off to the house.

She didn't follow him. She just sat clutching the steering wheel, too tired and upset at that moment to deal with him. Abruptly she shifted into reverse and backed out of the driveway. They both needed time to cool down, to get their emotions under control. She turned onto Toddy Point Road and headed along the shore of Locust Lake. Driving as therapy.

How easy it had all seemed when Peter was alive, when one of his cross-eyed looks was all that was needed to make their son laugh. The days when they were still happy, still whole.

We haven't been happy since you died, Peter. I miss you. I miss you every day, every hour. Every minute of my life.

The lights from lakeside cottages shimmered through her tears as she drove. She rounded the curve, drove past the Boulders, and suddenly the lights were no longer white but blue, and they seemed to be dancing among the trees.

It was a police cruiser, and it was parked on Rachel Sorkin's property.

She pulled to a stop in the driveway. Three vehicles were in the front yard, two police cruisers and a white van. A Maine state trooper was talking to Rachel on the porch. Beneath the trees, flashlight beams zigzagged across the ground.

Claire spotted Lincoln Kelly emerging from the woods. It was his silhouette she recognized as he passed before one of the searchlights. Though not a tall man, Lincoln was straight and solid and he moved with a quiet assuredness that made him seem larger than he was. He stopped to speak to the state trooper, then he noticed Claire and crossed the yard to her truck.

She rolled down the window. 'Have you found any more bones?' she asked.

He leaned in, bringing with him the scent of the forest. Pine trees and earth and wood smoke. 'Yep. The dogs led us over to the streambed,' he said. 'That bank eroded pretty badly this spring, after all those floods. That's what uncovered the bones. But I'm afraid wild animals have already scattered most of them in the woods.'

'Does the ME think it's a homicide?'

'It's no longer an ME's case. The bones are too old. There's a forensic anthropologist in charge now, if you'd like to talk to her. Name's Dr Overlock.'

He opened the truck door and Claire climbed out. Together they walked into the gloom of the woods. Dusk had rapidly thickened to night. The ground was uneven, layered with dead leaves, and she found herself stumbling in the underbrush. Lincoln reached out to steady her. He seemed to have no trouble navigating in the darkness, his heavy boots connecting solidly with the ground.

Lights were shining among the trees, and Claire heard voices and the sound of trickling water. She and Lincoln emerged from the woods, onto the stream bank. A section of the eroded bank had been cordoned off by police tape strung between stakes, and on a tarp lay the mud-encrusted bones that had already been unearthed. Claire recognized a tibia and what looked like fragments of a pelvis. Two men wearing waders and headlamps stood knee-deep in the stream, gingerly excavating the side of the bank.

Lucy Overlock was standing among the trees talking on a cell phone. She was like a tree herself, tall and strapping, dressed in a woodsman's wardrobe of jeans and work boots. Her hair, almost entirely gray, was tied back in a tight, no-nonsense ponytail. She saw Lincoln, gave a harassed wave, and continued with her phone conversation.

'. . . no artifacts yet, just the skeletal remains. But I assure you, this burial doesn't fall under NAGPRA. The skull looks Caucasoid to me, not Indian. What do you mean, how can I tell? It's obvious! The brain-case is too narrow, and the facial breadth just isn't wide enough. No, of course it's not absolute. But the site is on Locust Lake, and there's never been a Penobscot settlement here. The tribe wouldn't even fish in this lake, it's such a taboo place.' She looked up at the sky and shook her head. 'Certainly, you can examine the bones for yourself. But we have to excavate this site now, before the animals do any more damage, or we'll lose the whole thing.' She hung up and looked at Lincoln in frustration. 'Custody battle.'

'Over bones?'

'It's that NAGPRA law. Indian graves protection. Every time we find remains, the tribes demand one hundred percent confirmation it's not one of theirs. Ninety-five percent isn't good enough for them.' Her gaze turned to Claire, who'd stepped forward to introduce herself.

'Lucy Overlock,' said Lincoln. 'And this is Claire Elliot. The doctor who found the thigh bone.'

The two women shook hands, the no-nonsense greeting of two medical professionals meeting over a grim business.

'We're lucky you're the one who spotted the bone,' said Lucy. 'Anyone else might not have realized it was human.'

'To be honest, I wasn't entirely sure,' said Claire. 'I'm glad I didn't drag everyone out here for a cow bone.'

'It's definitely not a cow.'

One of the diggers called out from the streambed: 'We found something else.'

Lucy dropped knee-deep into the stream and aimed a flashlight at the exposed bank.

'There,' said the digger, gently prodding the soil with a trowel. 'Looks like it might be another skull.'

Lucy snapped on gloves. 'Okay, let's ease it out.'

He slid the tip of his trowel deeper into the bank and gingerly pried away caked mud. The object dropped into Lucy's gloved hands. She scrambled out of the water and up onto the bank. Kneeling down, she surveyed her treasure over the tarp.

It was indeed a second skull. Under the floodlight, Lucy carefully turned it over and examined the teeth.

'Another juvenile. No wisdom teeth,' Lucy noted. 'I see decayed molars here and here, but no fillings.'

'Meaning no dental work,' said Claire.

'Yes, these are old bones. A good thing for you, Lincoln. Otherwise, this would be an active homicide case.'

'Why do you say that?'

She rotated the skull, and the light fell on the crown, where fracture lines radiated out from a central depression, the way a soft-boiled egg cracks when it is struck with the back of a spoon.

'I don't think there's any doubt,' she said. 'This child died a violent death.'

The chirp of a beeper cut through the silence,

startling them all. In the stillness of those woods, that electronic sound was strangely foreign. Disconcerting. Both Claire and Lincoln automatically reached for their respective pagers.

'It's mine,' said Lincoln, glancing at his readout. Without another word, he took off through the woods toward his cruiser. Seconds later, Claire saw the dome light flashing through the trees as his vehicle streaked away.

'Must be an emergency,' said Lucy.

Officer Pete Sparks was already at the scene, trying to talk old Vern Fuller into putting down his shotgun. Night had fallen, and Lincoln's first glimpse of the situation was of two wildly gesturing silhouettes intermittently backlit by the flashing dome light of Pete's cruiser. Lincoln pulled to a stop in Vern's driveway and cautiously stepped out of his vehicle. He heard bleating sheep, the restless clucking of chickens. The sounds of a working farm.

'You don't need the gun,' Pete was saying. 'Just go back in the house, Vern, and we'll look into this.'

'Like you looked into it the last time?'

'I didn't find anything the last time.'

'That's because you take so damn long gettin' here!'

'What's the problem?' said Lincoln.

Vern turned to him. 'That you, Chief Kelly? Then you tell this – this boy here that I'm not about to hand over my only protection.'

'I'm not asking you to hand it over,' said a weary-sounding Pete. 'I just want you to stop waving it around. Go inside and put the gun away, so nobody gets hurt.'

'I think that's a good idea,' said Lincoln. 'We don't know what we're dealing with, so you go in and lock the door, Vern. Stay close to the phone, just in case we need you to call for backup.'

'Backup?' Vern gave a grunt. 'Yeah. Okay, I'll do that.'

The two cops waited for the old man to stomp into the house and shut the door.

Then Pete said, 'He's blind as a bat. Wish we could get that shotgun away from him. Every time I come out here, I half expect to get my head blown off.'

'What's the problem, anyway?'

'Aw, it's the third time he's called nine-one-one. I'm so busy runnin' my tail off with all these other calls, it takes me a while to get here. He always has the same complaint about some wild animal stalking his sheep. Probably just seeing his own shadow, that's what.'

'Why does he call us?'

''Cause Fish and Game takes even longer to respond. I been here twice this week, didn't find anything. Not even a coyote print. Today's the first time I seen Vern this riled up. Thought I'd better get you out, just in case he decided to shoot *me* 'stead of some wild animal.'

Lincoln glanced at the house, and saw the old

man's face silhouetted in the window. 'He's watching. Might as well check the property, just to keep him happy.'

'Says he saw the animal over by the barn.'

Pete turned on his flashlight, and they started across the yard, toward the sound of bleating sheep. Lincoln felt the old man's gaze every step of the way. Let's just humor him, he thought. Even if it is a waste of our time.

He was startled when Pete suddenly halted, his flashlight beam trained on the barn door.

It hung open.

Something wasn't right. It was after dark, and the door should have been latched to protect the animals.

He turned on his flashlight as well. They approached more slowly now, their jerky beams guiding the way. At the entrance to the barn they paused. Even through the earthy melange of farmyard odors, they could smell it: the scent of blood.

They stepped into the barn. At once the bleating intensified, the sound as disturbing as the cries of panicked children. Pete swung his flashlight in a wide arc, and they caught glimpses of pitchforks and fluttering chickens and sheep fearfully bunched together in a pen.

Lying on the sawdust floor was the source of that foul odor.

Pete stumbled out of the building first, and retched into the weeds, one hand propped up against the barn wall. 'Jesus. Jesus.'

'It's just a dead sheep,' said Lincoln.

'I never seen a coyote do that. Lay out the offal . . .'

Lincoln aimed his beam at the ground, quickly scanning the area around the barn door. All he saw was a jumble of boot prints, his and Pete's and Vern Fuller's. No tracks. How could an animal leave no tracks?

A twig snapped behind him, and he whirled around to see Vern, still clutching the shotgun.

'It's a bear,' said the old man. 'That's what I seen, a bear.'

'A bear wouldn't do this.'

'I know what I saw. Whyn't you believe me?'

Because everyone knows you're half blind.

'It went that way, into the woods,' said Vern, pointing to the forested edge of his property. 'I followed it over there, just before dark. Then I lost it.'

Lincoln saw that the boot tracks did indeed head toward the forest, but Vern had retraced his steps several times, obscuring any animal footprints.

He followed the trail over to the woods. There he stood for a moment, peering into the blackness. The trees were so thick they seemed to form an impenetrable wall that even his flashlight beam could not pierce.

By now Pete had recovered, and was standing by his side. 'We should wait till daylight,' Pete whispered. 'Don't know what we're dealing with.'

'I know it's not a bear.'

'Yeah, well, I'm not scared of bears. But if it's something else . . .' Pete drew his weapon. 'Rumor has it a cougar was spotted up at Jordan Falls last week.'

Now Lincoln drew his weapon as well as he moved slowly into the woods. He took half a dozen steps, the crack of breaking twigs under his boot as loud as gunfire. All at once he froze, staring at that wall of trees. The forest seemed to close in. The hairs on the back of his neck were standing up.

There's something out there. It's watching us.

Every instinct screamed at him to retreat. He backed away, his heart racing, his boots setting off explosions of noise. Only when he and Pete had emerged completely from the woods did that feeling of imminent danger fade away.

They stood once again in front of Vern Fuller's barn, and the sheep were still bleating. He looked down at the boot prints. Suddenly his head came up.

'What lies beyond those woods?' he asked.

'Goes back a ways,' said Vern. 'Other side's Barnstown Road. Bunch of houses.'

Houses, thought Lincoln.

Families.

Noah was watching TV when Claire got home. As she hung up her coat in the hallway, she recognized the theme music from *The Simpsons* cartoon playing in the other room, and she heard Homer Simpson's loud burp and Lisa Simpson's mutter of disgust. Then she heard her son laugh, and she thought: *I'm so glad my son still laughs at cartoons*.

She went into the front parlor and saw Noah flopped back against the couch cushions, his face briefly lit up with laughter. He looked at her, but didn't say anything.

She sat down beside him and propped her feet up on the coffee table, next to his. Big feet, little feet, she thought with quiet amusement. Noah's feet had grown so huge, they almost looked like a clown's beside hers.

On the TV, an enormously fat Homer was bouncing around in a flowery muumuu, and shoveling food into his mouth.

Noah laughed again, and so did Claire. This was exactly the way she wanted to spend the rest of the evening. They would watch TV together, and eat popcorn for dinner. She leaned toward him, and they affectionately bumped heads together.

'I'm sorry, Mom,' he said.

'It's okay, Honey. I'm sorry I was late picking you up.'

'Grandma Elliot called. A little while ago.'

'Oh? Does she want me to call her back?'

'I guess.' He watched the TV for a while, his silence stretching through the string of commercials. Then he said, 'Grandma wanted to make sure we were okay tonight.'

Claire gave him a puzzled look. 'Why?'

'It's Dad's birthday.'

On the TV, Homer Simpson in his flowered

muumuu had hijacked an ice cream truck and was driving it at breakneck speed, gobbling ice cream the whole way. Claire watched in stunned silence. *Today was your birthday*, she thought. *You've been dead only two years, and already we're losing bits and pieces of your memory.*

'Oh god, Noah,' she whispered. 'I can't believe it. I completely forgot.'

She felt his head droop heavily against her shoulder. And he said, with quiet shame, 'So did I.'

Sitting in her bedroom, Claire returned Margaret Elliot's call. Claire had always liked her mother-in-law, and through the years, their affection had grown to the point that she felt far closer to Margaret than she ever had to her own coldly aloof parents. Sometimes it seemed to Claire that everything she knew about love, about passion, had been taught to her by the Elliot family.

'Hi, Mom. It's me,' said Claire.

'Sixty-two degrees and sunny in Baltimore today,' Margaret replied, and Claire had to laugh. Ever since she'd moved to Tranquility, this had been the running joke between them, their comparison of weather reports. Margaret had not wanted her to leave Baltimore. 'You have no idea what real cold is,' she'd told Claire, 'and I'm going to keep reminding you of what you've left behind.'

'Thirty-five degrees here,' Claire dutifully reported. She looked out her window. 'It's getting colder. Darker.'

'Did Noah tell you I called earlier?'

'Yes. And we're doing fine. We really are.'

'Are you?'

Claire said nothing. Margaret had the uncanny talent for reading emotions from just the simple inflection of one's voice, and already she had sensed something amiss.

'Noah told me he wants to come back here,' said Margaret.

'We just moved.'

'You can always change your mind.'

'Not now. I've made too many commitments here. To this new practice, the house.'

'Those are commitments to *things*, Claire.'

'No, they're really commitments to Noah. I need to stay here, for him.' She paused, suddenly aware that, as much as she loved Margaret, she was feeling a little irritated. She was also weary of the gentle but repeated hints that she should return to Baltimore. 'It's always hard for a kid to make a fresh start, but he'll adjust. He's too young to know what he wants.'

'That's true, I suppose. What about you? Do you still want to be there?'

'Why are you asking, Mom?'

'Because I know it would be hard for me, moving to a new place. Leaving behind my friends.'

Claire stared at the dresser mirror, at her own tired face. At the reflection of her bedroom, which still had few pictures on the wall. It was merely a collection of furniture, a place to sleep, not yet part of a real home.

'A widow needs her friends, Claire,' said Margaret.

'Maybe that was one of the reasons I had to leave.'

'What do you mean?'

'That's what I was to everyone – the widow. I'd walk into my clinic, and people would give me those sad and sympathetic looks. They were all afraid to laugh or tell jokes when I was around. And no one, no one ever dared to talk about Peter. It's as if they thought I'd break down in sobs if they just mentioned his name.'

There was silence on the line, and Claire suddenly regretted having spoken so frankly.

'It doesn't mean I ever stop missing him, Mom,' she said softly. 'I see him every time I look at Noah's face. The resemblance is so amazing. It's like watching Peter grow up.'

'In more ways than one,' Margaret said, and Claire was relieved to hear the warmth had not left her mother-in-law's voice. 'Peter wasn't the easiest child to raise. I don't think I ever told you about all the trouble he got into when he was Noah's age. That's where Noah gets his streak of mischief, you know. From Peter.'

Claire had to laugh. *He certainly didn't get it from me, his boringly scrupulous mother, whose most serious crime was neglecting to get that safety sticker.*

'Noah's got a good heart, but he's still only fourteen,' said Margaret with a friendly note of warning. 'Don't be too terribly shocked if there's more mischief on the way.'

Later, as Claire headed back downstairs, she smelled the odor of burning matches, and she thought: Well, here it comes, then. More mischief. He's sneaking another cigarette. She followed the scent to the kitchen and came to a halt in the doorway.

Noah was holding a lit match. He glanced at her, and quickly shook it out. 'It's all the candles I could find,' he said.

In silence she approached the kitchen table. Her vision suddenly blurred with tears as she gazed at the Sara Lee layer cake he had taken out of the freezer. Flames danced atop eleven candles.

Noah struck another match and lit the twelfth flame on the cake. 'Happy birthday, Dad,' he said softly.

Happy birthday, Peter, she thought, and blinked away her tears.

And she and her son blew out the candles.

4

Mrs Horatio was going to pith a frog.

'It doesn't hurt them a bit, once you've penetrated their brain stem,' she explained. 'The needle goes in at the base of the skull, and you wiggle it around a little to destroy all the sensory tracts running up to the brain. This paralyzes them, stops any conscious movement, but it keeps their spinal reflexes intact for study.' She reached into the jar and picked up a squirming frog in one hand. With her other hand, she reached for the pithing needle. It was humongous.

Though a ripple of nausea stirred in his stomach, Noah sat perfectly still at his desk in the third row. He was careful to keep his legs casually thrown out in front of him, his expression bored.

He could hear the other students squirm in their chairs, the girls mostly. To his right, a horrified Amelia Reid covered her mouth with her hand.

He let his gaze slide around the room and he silently pronounced judgment as he looked at each student in turn. *Nerd. Jock. Kiss-ass preppie.* Except for Amelia Reid, none of them were kids he cared to hang out with. None of them were interested in hanging out with *him*, either, but that was okay. His mom might like it in this town, but he didn't plan on staying forever.

Graduate, and then I'm outta here, outta here, outta here.

'Taylor, stop fidgeting and pay attention,' said Mrs Horatio.

Noah glanced sideways, and saw that Taylor Darnell was gripping his desk with both hands and staring at the exam paper he'd just gotten back that morning. Mrs Horatio had scrawled a giant D plus in red marker. The test paper was covered with Taylor's angry slashes in black ink. Next to the humiliating grade, he'd written: 'Die, Mrs Whoratio.'

'Noah, are you paying attention?'

Noah flushed and turned his gaze back to the front of the class. Mrs Horatio was holding up the frog for all to see. She actually looked like she was enjoying herself as she placed the tip of the pithing needle against the back of the frog's head. Her eyes were bright, her mouth puckered and eager as she jammed the needle into the brainstem. The frog's hind legs thrashed, its webbed feet slapping in pain.

Amelia gave a whimper and dropped her head down, her blond hair cascading over the desk. Chairs were squeaking all over the room now.

Someone called out with a note of desperation: 'Mrs Horatio, can I be excused?'

'. . . have to move the needle back and forth with a certain amount of force. Don't worry about the feet flapping around like this. It's purely reflex action. Just the spine shooting off impulses.'

'Mrs Horatio, I *have* to use the bathroom . . .'

'In a minute. First, you have to see how I do this.' She twisted the needle and there was a soft *crack*.

Noah thought he was going to puke. Struggling to maintain that look of utterly cool nonchalance, he turned away, his hands clenched under his desk. *Don't puke, don't puke, don't puke.* He focused on Amelia's blond hair, which he'd often admired. Rapunzel hair. He stared at it, thinking how much he'd like to stroke it. He'd never even dared talk to Amelia. She was like a girl in a golden bubble, beyond the reach of any mere mortal.

'There now,' said Mrs Horatio. 'That's all there is to it. You see, class? Total paralysis.'

Noah forced his gaze back to the frog. It lay on the teacher's desk, a limp, flappy carcass. Still alive, if you believed old Horatio, but showing no signs of it. He felt a sudden and overwhelming pity for that frog, imagined himself sprawled across that desk, eyes open and aware, body unresponsive. Darts of panic going nowhere, just exploding like firecrackers in your brain. He himself felt paralyzed and numb.

'Now each of you pair up with a lab partner,' said Mrs Horatio. 'And scoot your desks together.'

69

Noah swallowed and looked sideways at Amelia. She gave a helpless nod.

He moved his desk next to hers. They didn't speak to each other; it was a partnership based purely on proximity, but hey, whatever it took to get up close. Amelia's lips were trembling. He wanted very much to comfort her, but he didn't know how to, so he just sat there, his face assuming, by default, its usual bored expression. *Say something nice to her, moron. Something to impress her. You may never get another chance!*

'Frog sure looks dead,' he said.

She shuddered.

Mrs Horatio came walking down the aisle carrying the jar of frogs. She stopped beside Noah and Amelia.

'Take one. Each team works on a frog.'

The blood drained from Amelia's face. It was up to Noah.

He shoved his hand in the jar and grabbed a wriggling frog. Mrs Horatio slapped a pithing needle down on his desk. 'Get started, you two,' she said, and moved on to the next team.

Noah looked down at the frog he was holding. It stared back at him, bug-eyed. He picked up the pithing needle, then he looked at the frog again. Those eyes were begging him, *Let me live, let me live!* He put down the needle, his nausea back full force, and looked hopefully at Amelia. 'You wanna do the honors?'

'I can't,' she whispered. 'Don't make me, *please*.'

One of the girls screamed. Noah glanced sideways and saw Lydia Lipman leap out of her chair and scramble away from her lab partner, Taylor Darnell. There was a wooden *thud, thud, thud,* as Taylor stabbed his pithing needle into the frog. Blood spattered on his desk.

'Taylor! Taylor, stop it!' said Mrs Horatio.

He kept stabbing. *Thud, thud.* The frog looked like green hamburger. 'D plus,' he muttered. 'I studied all week for that test. You can't give me a D plus!'

'Taylor, go to the principal's office.'

He stabbed the frog harder. 'You can't give me a lousy D plus!'

She grabbed his wrist and tried to take the needle away from him. 'Go see Miss Cornwallis *now*!'

Taylor yanked away, knocking the dead frog off his desk. It tumbled into Amelia's lap. With a shriek, she jumped to her feet and the small corpse splatted to the floor.

'Taylor!' Mrs Horatio yelled. Again she grabbed his wrist, this time forcing him to drop the pithing needle. 'Leave this room immediately!'

'Fuck you!'

'What did you say?'

He stood up and shoved his chair to the floor. 'Fuck you!'

'You are suspended as of right now! You've been sullen and disrespectful all week. This is it, buddy. You're out of here!'

He kicked the chair. It bounced up the aisle and

crashed into a desk. Grabbing his shirt, she tried to march him toward the door, but he twisted free and shoved her backwards. She fell against a desk, toppling the jar. It shattered, and frogs leaped free, scattering away in a writhing carpet of green.

Slowly Mrs Horatio rose to her feet, fury blazing in her eyes. 'I'm going to have you expelled!'

Taylor reached into his backpack.

Mrs Horatio's gaze froze on the gun in his hand. 'Put it down,' she said. 'Taylor, put it down!'

The explosion seemed to punch her in the abdomen. She staggered backwards, clutching her belly, and dropped to the floor with a look of disbelief. Time seemed to halt, frozen for one interminable moment as Noah stared down in horror at the bright river of blood streaming toward his sneakers. Then a girl's terrified shriek pierced the silence. In the next instant, chaos exploded all around him. He heard chairs slam to the floor, saw a fleeing girl stumble and fall to her knees in the broken glass. The air itself seemed misted with blood and panic.

Another gunshot exploded.

Noah's gaze swept around in a slow-motion pan of fleeing bodies, and he saw Vernon Hobbs tumble forward and crash into a desk. The room was a blur of flying hair and churning legs. But Noah himself could not seem to move. His feet were mired in a waking nightmare, his body refusing to obey his brain's commands of *Run! Run!*

His gaze panned back across the chaos to Taylor

Darnell, and to his horror he saw that the gun was now pointed at Amelia's head.

No, he thought. *No!*

Taylor fired.

A streak of blood magically appeared on Amelia's temple and the rivulet slowly dripped down her cheek, yet she remained standing, her eyes wide and focused like a condemned animal's on the gun barrel. 'Please, Taylor,' she whispered. 'Please, don't . . .'

Taylor raised the gun again.

All at once, Noah's legs broke free of their nightmare paralysis, his body moving of its own accord. His brain registered a multitude of details at once. He saw Taylor's head come up, face rotating toward Noah. He saw the gun slowly sweep around in an arc. He saw the look of surprise in Taylor's eyes as Noah came flying at him.

Another bullet exploded out of the barrel.

'I've just noticed my patient was admitted. Why didn't anyone call me?'

The ward clerk looked up from her desk and seemed to shrink when she saw it was Claire asking the question. 'Uh . . . which patient, Dr Elliot?'

'Katie Youmans. I saw her name posted on one of the doors, but she's not in the room. I can't find her chart in the rack.'

'She was admitted just a few hours ago, through the ER. She's in X-ray right now.'

'No one notified me.'

The clerk's gaze dropped like a stone to her desk. 'Dr DelRay's taken over as attending physician.'

Claire absorbed this dismaying news in silence. It was not uncommon for patients to switch physicians, sometimes for the most trivial of reasons. Two of Adam DelRay's patients had transferred to Claire's practice as well. But she was surprised that this particular patient would choose to leave her care.

Sixteen years old, and mildly retarded, Katie Youmans had been living with her father when she was brought in to see Claire for a bladder infection. Claire had noticed at once the circumferential bruises on the girl's wrists. Forty-five minutes of gentle questioning and a pelvic examination had confirmed Claire's suspicions. Katie was removed from her father's abusive household and placed in foster care.

Since then, the girl had thrived. Her bruises, both physical and emotional, finally faded. Claire had counted Katie as one of her triumphs. Why would the girl switch doctors?

She found Katie in X-ray. Through the small viewing window, Claire saw the girl lying on the table, her lower leg positioned beneath the X-ray tube.

'Can I ask what the admitting diagnosis is?' Claire asked the tech.

'They told me cellulitis of the right foot. Her chart's over there, if you want to look at it.'

Claire picked up the medical record and flipped to the admission note. It had been dictated by Adam DelRay at seven A.M. that morning.

Sixteen-year-old white female who stepped on a tack two days ago. This morning she awakened with fever, chills, and swollen foot . . .

Claire skimmed the history and physical, then turned the page and read the therapeutic plan.

Quickly she picked up the phone to page Adam DelRay.

A moment later, he walked into X-ray, looking crisply starched as usual in his long white coat. Though he had always been cordial toward her, he had never displayed any real warmth, and she suspected that under his Yankee reserve burned a masculine sense of competition, perhaps even resentment, that Claire had lured away two of his patients.

Now he had laid claim to one of hers, and she had to suppress her own feelings of competitiveness. Only the well-being of Katie Youmans should concern her now.

'I've been following Katie as an outpatient,' she said. 'I know her pretty well, and –'

'Claire, it's just one of those things.' He lay a reassuring hand on her shoulder. 'I hope you don't take it personally.'

'That's not why I paged you.'

'It was just more convenient for me to admit her. I was in the ER when she came in. And her guardian felt Katie needed an internist.'

'I'm perfectly capable of treating cellulitis, Adam.'

'What if it turns into osteomyelitis? It could get complicated.'

'Are you saying a family physician isn't qualified to take care of this patient?'

'The girl's guardian made the decision. I just happened to be available.'

By now Claire was too angry to respond. Turning, she stared through the window at her patient. At her ex-patient. Suddenly she focused on the girl's IV, and she noticed the handwritten label affixed to the bag of dextrose and water. 'Is she already getting antibiotics?'

'They just hung it,' said the X-ray tech.

'But she's allergic to penicillin! That's why I paged you, Adam!'

'The girl never said anything about allergies.'

Claire ran into the next room, snagged the IV line, and closed off the infusion. Glancing down at Katie, she was alarmed to see the girl's face was flushed. 'I need epinephrine!' Claire called out to the X-ray tech. 'And IV Benadryl!'

Katie was moving restlessly on the table. 'I feel funny, Dr Elliot,' she murmured. 'I'm so hot.' Wheals had swollen on her neck in bright blotches of red.

The tech took one look at the girl, muttered 'Oh, shit,' and yanked open the drawer for the anaphylaxis kit.

'She didn't tell me she was allergic,' said DelRay, defensively.

'Here's the epi,' said the tech, handing Claire the syringe.

'I can't breathe!'

'It's okay, Katie,' soothed Claire, uncapping the needle. 'You'll feel better in just a few seconds . . .' She pierced the girl's skin and injected a tenth of a cc of epinephrine.

'I – can't – *breathe*!'

'Benadryl, twenty-five milligrams IV!' Claire snapped. 'Adam, give her the Benadryl!'

DelRay stared down with stunned eyes at the syringe the X-ray tech had just slapped in his hand. In a daze, he injected the drug into the line.

Claire whipped out her stethoscope. Listening to the girl's lungs, she heard tight wheezes on both sides. 'What's the blood pressure?' she asked the tech.

'I'm getting eighty over fifty. Pulse one-forty.'

'Let's move her to ER, STAT.'

Three pairs of hands reached out to slide the girl onto the gurney.

'Can't breathe – can't breathe –'

'Jesus, she's really swelling up!'

'Just keep moving!' said Claire.

Together they propelled the gurney out of X-ray and ran it down the hallway. They careened around the corner and banged through double doors into the ER. Dr McNally and two nurses looked up, startled, as Claire announced:

'She's going into anaphylactic shock!'

The response was immediate. The ER staff swung

the gurney into a treatment room. An oxygen mask was pressed to the girl's face and EKG leads clapped to her chest. Within minutes a hefty dose of cortisone was dripping into her IV.

Her own heart was still pounding when Claire finally left the room to let McNally and his staff take over. She saw Adam DelRay standing at the nurses' desk, furiously scribbling in Katie's hospital record. As she approached, he quickly shut the chart.

'She never told me she was allergic,' he said.

'The girl is borderline retarded.'

'Then she should be wearing a MedAlert bracelet. Why isn't she?'

'She refuses to.'

'Well, I can't guess these things!'

'Adam, all you had to do was call me when she came in. You knew she was my patient, and that I'm familiar with her history. All you had to do was ask.'

'The guardian should have told me. I can't believe it never even occurred to that woman to –'

He was interrupted by the loud squeal of the ER radio. They both looked up as the transmission came crackling through.

'Knox Hospital, this is unit seventeen, unit seventeen. We have gunshot victim en route, ETA five minutes. Do you copy?'

One of the nurses darted out of the treatment room and snatched up the microphone. 'This is Knox ER. What's that about a gunshot wound?'

'Multiple victims en route. This one's critical – more on the way.'

'How many? Repeat, *how many?*'

'Uncertain. At least three –'

Another voice cut into the frequency. 'Knox Hospital, this is unit nine. En route with gunshot wound to the shoulder. Do you copy?'

In panic, the nurse grabbed the telephone and hit O. 'Disaster code! Call a disaster code! This is not a drill!'

Five doctors. That was all they could round up in the building during the frantic moments before the first ambulance arrived: Claire, DelRay, McNally from the ER, a general surgeon, and one terrified pediatrician. No one knew any details yet, not the location of the shooting, nor the number of victims. All they knew was that something terrible had happened, and that this tiny rural hospital was not prepared to deal with the aftermath. The ER turned into a maelstrom of noise and activity as personnel scrambled to prepare for the injured. Katie, now stabilized, was whisked out and shoved into the hallway to free up the treatment room. Cabinets clanged open, bright lights flared on. Claire pitched in to hang IV bags, lay out instrument trays, and rip open packets of gauze and sutures.

The approaching wail of the first ambulance brought a split second's hush to the ER. Then everyone surged out the double doors to meet the first victim. Standing among that crowd of personnel, Claire heard no one speak; they were all focused on the swelling scream of the siren as it drew near.

Abruptly the siren was cut off and the flashing red light swerved into view.

Claire pushed forward as the ambulance backed up to the entrance. The vehicle's rear door swung open, and the stretcher rolled out with the first victim. It was a woman, already intubated. The surgical tape used to secure the ET tube obscured the lower half of her face. The bandage on her abdomen was soaked with blood.

They rolled her straight into the trauma room and slid her onto the table. A confusing chorus of voices was shouting simultaneously as the woman's clothes were cut away, the EKG leads and oxygen lines connected, a BP cuff wrapped around one arm. A rapid sinus rhythm raced across the cardiac monitor.

'Systolic's seventy!' a nurse called out.

'Drawing the type and cross!' said Claire. She grabbed a sixteen-gauge IV catheter off the tray and snapped a tourniquet around the patient's arm. The vein barely plumped up; the patient was in shock. She stabbed the vein with the IV needle and slid the plastic catheter into place. With a syringe, she withdrew several tubes of blood, then attached the IV tubing to the catheter. 'Another lactated Ringer's going in, wide open!' she called out.

'Systolic's sixty, barely palpable!'

The surgeon said, 'Belly's distended. I think it's full of blood. Open that surgical tray, and get suction ready!' He looked at McNally. 'You're first assist.'

'But she needs to be in the OR –'

'No time. We have to find out where the blood's coming from.'

'I've lost her BP!' a nurse yelled.

The first incision was swift and brutal, one long slash down the center of the abdomen, parting the skin. With a deeper incision, the surgeon cut through the yellow layer of subcutaneous fat, and slit into the peritoneum.

Blood spilled out, streaming onto the floor.

'I can't see where it's coming from!'

The suction wasn't clearing the blood fast enough. In desperation, McNally stuffed two sterile towels into the abdomen and pulled them out again, soaking red and dripping.

'Okay, I think I see it. Bullet nicked the aorta –'

'Jesus, it's gushing!'

A ward clerk yelled through the doorway, 'Two more have arrived! They're wheeling them in now!'

McNally glanced across the table at Claire, and she saw panic in his eyes. 'You're *it*,' he snapped. 'Go, Claire.'

With her heart in her throat, she pushed out of the trauma room and saw the first stretcher being wheeled into one of the treatment rooms.

The patient was a sobbing red-haired boy, shirt cut away, blood soaking through the bandage on his shoulder. Now a second stretcher whisked in the door – a blond teenage girl, half her face covered with blood.

Children, she thought. *These are only children. My god, what has happened?*

She went first to the girl, who was crying but able to move all her extremities. At that first glimpse of blood on the girl's face, Claire nearly panicked, thinking: gunshot wound to the head. She forced herself to pause and take the girl's hand, to calmly ask her name, even while her own heart was thundering. It took only a few questions to confirm that Amelia Reid was fully oriented, and her mental status was clear. The wound was just a superficial graze of the temple, which Claire quickly cleaned and dressed.

Turning her attention to the red-haired boy, she saw that he was already being attended to by the pediatrician.

'Are there any others on the way?' she asked the ward clerk.

'None en route. There may be more at the scene . . .'

A second surgeon arrived, trotting in through the ER doors and announcing: 'I'm here! Who needs me?'

'Trauma room!' said Claire. 'Dr McNally needs to be relieved.'

He was just about to push through the door

when a nurse popped out, almost slamming into him.

'Do we have that O-neg blood for Horatio yet?' she yelled to the ward clerk.

Horatio? Claire hadn't recognized the patient under all that surgical tape, but she knew the name, Dorothy Horatio.

My son's biology teacher. She looked at the clock and saw it was eleven-thirty. Period three. Noah would be in biology – in Mrs Horatio's class.

Another doctor arrived, another pair of hands - the obstetrician from Two Hills. She took one last glance around the room, and saw that the situation was under control.

She made the only decision a panicked mother could make.

She ran outside to her car.

The twenty-mile drive passed in a blur of autumn fields, the mist rising in wisps, stands of pine trees. Here and there farmhouses with tumbling porches. She had driven this country road every day for eight months, but never at this speed, never with her hands shaking and her heart sick with fear. She took the last rise with the accelerator floored and her Subaru leaped past the familiar sign:

You Are Now Leaving Two Hills. Come Back Soon!

And then, a hundred yards beyond that, a second sign, smaller, paint chipping.

She swerved onto School Road and saw the flashing lights of half a dozen emergency vehicles. Police cruisers were parked in a jumble near the high school's red brick front entrance, along with two fire trucks – a full-scale disaster response.

Claire abandoned her car and ran toward the school's front lawn, where dozens of stunned-looking students and teachers had gathered behind a tangle of police tape. Scanning the faces, she didn't see Noah.

A Two Hills policeman stopped her at the front door. 'No one's allowed inside.'

'But I have to go in!'

'Only emergency personnel.'

She took a quick breath. 'I'm Dr Elliot,' she said, her voice steadier. 'I'm a physician from Tranquility.'

He let her pass.

She pushed through the front door into the high school. The building was nearly a century old, and inside hung the musty odors of teenage sweat and dust stirred up by thousands of feet trudging up and down the staircase. She ran up the steps to the second floor.

The doorway to the biology classroom was criss-crossed by strands of police tape. Beyond the tape were overturned chairs, broken glass, and scattered papers. Frogs hopped through the debris.

84

There was blood – pools of it congealing in gelatinous lakes on the floor.

'Mom?'

Her heart leaped at the voice. She whirled to see her son standing at the far end of the hall. In the dim light of that long corridor, he seemed frighteningly small to her, his blood-streaked face pale and thin.

She ran to him and threw her arms around his rigid body, pulling him, forcing him, into an embrace. She felt his shoulders melt first, then his head drooped against her and he was crying. No sound came out; there was just the shuddering of his chest and warm tears sliding onto her neck. At last she felt his arms come around her, circle her waist. His shoulders might be as broad as a man's, but it was a child who clung to her now, a child's grief that spilled out in tears.

'Are you hurt?' she asked. 'Noah, you're bleeding. Are you *hurt*?'

'He's fine, Claire. The blood isn't his. It's the teacher's.'

She looked up and saw Lincoln Kelly standing in the hall, his grim expression reflecting the day's terrible events. 'Noah and I just finished going over what happened. I was about to call you, Claire.'

'I was at the hospital. I heard there was a shooting.'

'Your son grabbed the gun away from the boy,' said Lincoln. 'It was a crazy thing to do. A brave thing to do. He probably saved a few lives.' Lincoln's gaze dropped to Noah, and he added softly: 'You should be proud of him.'

'I wasn't brave,' blurted out Noah. He pulled away from Claire, ashamedly wiping his eyes. 'I was scared. I don't know why I did it. I didn't know what I was doing . . .'

'But you did it, Noah.' Lincoln lay a hand on the boy's shoulder. It was a man's blessing, brusque and matter-of-fact. Noah seemed to draw sustenance from that simple touch. A mother, thought Claire, cannot knight her own son. It must be done by another man.

Slowly Noah straightened, his tears at last under control. 'Is Amelia okay?' he asked her. 'They took her in the ambulance.'

'She's fine. Just a scratch on her face. I think the boy will be fine as well.'

'And . . . Mrs Horatio?'

She shook her head. And said, gently, 'I don't know.'

He took a deep breath and wiped an unsteady hand across his eyes. 'I – I have to go wash my face . . .'

'You do that,' said Lincoln gently. 'Take your time, Noah. Your mom will be waiting for you.'

Claire watched her son walk away down the hall. As he passed the biology classroom he slowed down, his gaze drawn, against his will, to the open doorway. For a few seconds he stood hypnotized by the terrible view beyond that police tape. Then, abruptly, he pushed into the boys' restroom.

'Who was it?' said Claire, turning to Lincoln. 'Who brought the gun to school?'

'It was Taylor Darnell.'

She stared at him. 'Oh god. He's my patient.'

'That's what his father told us. Paul Darnell says the boy can't be held responsible. That he has attention deficit disorder and can't control his impulses. Is that true?'

'ADD doesn't cause violent behavior. And Taylor doesn't have it, anyway. But I can't comment on this case, Lincoln. I'm betraying confidentiality.'

'Well, *something's* wrong with the kid. If you're his doctor, maybe you should take a look at him before he's moved to the Youth Center.'

'Where is he now?'

'We're holding him in the principal's office.' Lincoln paused. 'Just a word of warning, Claire. Don't get too close.'

5

Taylor Darnell sat handcuffed to a chair, swinging his foot, *bam, bam, bam!* against the principal's desk. He didn't look up when Claire and Lincoln walked into the room, didn't even seem to notice they were there. Two Maine state cops were in the room with him. They looked at Lincoln and shook their heads, their thoughts transparent: *This one is totally bonkers.*

'We just got a call from the hospital,' one of the state cops said to Lincoln. 'The teacher's dead.'

No one spoke for a moment; both Claire and Lincoln absorbed the terrible news in silence.

Then Claire asked, softly: 'Where is Taylor's mother?'

'She's still on her way back from Portland. She drove down there on business.'

'And Mr Darnell?'

'I think he's rounding up a lawyer. They're going to need one.'

Taylor was kicking his foot against the desk again in a ceaseless, accelerating beat.

Claire set her medical bag down on a chair and approached the boy. 'You remember me, Taylor, don't you? I'm Dr Elliot.' He didn't answer, just kept up that angry banging. Something was very wrong. This was more than adolescent rage she was looking at. It appeared to be some sort of drug-induced psychosis.

Without warning, Taylor's gaze rose and locked on hers, focusing with predatory intensity. His pupils dilated, irises darkening to ebony pools. His lips curled up, canines gleaming, and from his throat escaped an animal sound, half hiss, half growl.

It happened so fast she had no time to react. He sprang to his feet, dragging the chair up with him, and lunged at her.

The impact of his body slamming into hers sent her toppling backwards to the floor. His teeth sank into her jacket, ripping the fabric, sending goose down and feathers flying in a white cloud. She caught a glimpse of three frantic faces as the cops struggled to separate them. They wrenched Taylor away, dragging him backwards even as he continued to thrash.

Lincoln grasped her arm and lifted her back to her feet. 'Claire – Jesus –'

'I'm okay,' she said, coughing on goose down. 'Really, I'm fine.'

One of the state cops yelped. 'He just bit me! Look, I'm bleeding!'

Even cuffed to the chair, the boy was fighting, bucking against his restraints. 'Let me go!'

he shrieked. 'I'll kill you all if you don't let me *go*!'

'He should be locked up in a freaking kennel!'

'No. No, there's something seriously wrong here,' said Claire. 'It looks like a drug psychosis to me. PCP or amphetamines.' She turned to Lincoln. 'I want this boy moved to the hospital. Now.'

'Too much movement,' said Dr Chapman, the radiologist. 'We're not going to get very clear definition here.'

Claire leaned forward, watching intently as the first cross-section of Taylor Darnell's brain appeared on the computer screen. Each image was a compilation of pixels formed by thousands of tiny X-ray beams. Aimed at different angles along one plane, the beams distinguished between fluid and solid and air, and the various densities were reproduced in the image on the screen.

'See that fuzziness there?' said Chapman, pointing to the movement artifact.

'We can't make him hold still unless we put him under anesthesia.'

'Well, that's an option.'

Claire shook her head. 'His mentation's cloudy enough. I don't want to risk anesthesia right now. I'm just trying to rule out any mass shifts before I do the lumbar puncture.'

'You really think encephalitis could explain these symptoms?' Chapman looked at her, and she saw skepticism in his eyes. In Baltimore, she'd been a respected family practitioner. But here she still had to prove herself. How long would it take before her new colleagues stopped questioning her judgment and learned to trust her?

'At this point, I have no choice,' she said. 'The initial screen for both methamphetamine and PCP came back negative. But Dr Forrest thinks this is clearly an organic psychosis, not psychiatric.'

Chapman was obviously unimpressed by Dr Forrest's clinical skills. 'Psychiatry is hardly an exact science.'

'But I agree with him. The boy's shown alarming personality changes in just the last few days. We have to rule out infection.'

'What's the white cell count?'

'Thirteen thousand.'

'A little high, but not all that impressive. What about the differential?'

'His eosinophil count is high. Way off the scale, in fact, at thirty percent.'

'But he has a history of asthma, right? That could account for it. It's some sort of allergic response.'

Claire had to agree. Eosinophils were a type of white blood cell that proliferated most commonly in response to allergic reactions or asthma. High eosinophil counts could also be caused by a variety of other illnesses such as cancer, parasitic infections, and autoimmune diseases. In some patients, no discernible cause was ever found.

'So what happens now?' asked the Maine state trooper, who'd been watching the procedure with a look of growing impatience. 'Can we move him to the Youth Center or not?'

'We have more tests to run,' said Claire. 'The boy could be seriously ill.'

'Or he could be faking it. That's what it looks like to me.'

'And if he's sick, you could find him dead in his cell. I wouldn't want to make that mistake, would you?'

Without comment, the trooper turned and stared through the CT viewing window at his prisoner.

Taylor was lying on his back, wrists and ankles restrained. His head was hidden inside the CT cradle, but they could see the movement of his feet, twisting against the restraints. *Now comes the hard part*, she thought. *How do we hold him in position long enough for the lumbar puncture?*

'I can't afford to miss a CNS infection,' said Claire. 'With an elevated white blood count and changes in mental status, I have no choice but to do the spinal tap.'

Chapman at last seemed to agree. 'From what I see here on the scan, it looks safe enough to proceed.'

They wheeled Taylor out of X-ray and into a private room. It took two nurses and a male orderly to transfer the struggling boy to the bed.

'Turn him on his side,' said Claire. 'Fetal position.'

'He's not going to lie still for this.'

'Then you'll have to sit on him. We need this spinal tap.'

Together they rolled the boy on his side, his back to Claire. The orderly flexed Taylor's hips, forcibly pushing the knees toward the chest. One nurse pulled the shoulders forward. Taylor snapped at her hand, almost catching her finger in his jaws.

'Watch his teeth!'

'I'm trying to!'

Claire had to work fast; they couldn't keep the boy immobilized much longer. She lifted the hospital gown, exposing his back. With his body curled into a fetal position, the vertebral spines poked out clearly under the skin. In rapid order she identified the space between the fourth and fifth spinous processes in the lower back, and swabbed the skin with Betadine, then alcohol. She snapped on sterile gloves and picked up the syringe with local anesthetic.

'I'm putting in the Xylocaine now. He's not going to like this.'

Claire pricked the skin with the twenty-five-gauge needle and gently injected the local anesthetic. At the first sting of the drug, Taylor shrieked with rage. Claire saw one of the nurses glance up, fear in her eyes. None of them had ever dealt with anything like this, and the violence coursing through this boy's body was frightening them all.

Claire reached for the spinal needle. It was three inches long, twenty-two-gauge gleaming steel, the hub end open to allow cerebrospinal fluid to drip out.

'Steady him. I'm doing the tap now.'

She pierced the skin. The Xylocaine had numbed the area, so he didn't feel any pain – not yet. She kept pushing the needle deeper, aiming the tip between the spinous processes, toward the dura mater of the spinal cord. She felt a slight resistance, then a distinct pop as the needle penetrated the protective dura.

Taylor screamed again and began to thrash.

'Hold him! You have to hold him!'

'We're trying! Can you hurry it up?'

'I'm already in. It'll just be another minute now.' She held a test tube under the open hub of the needle and caught the first drop of CSF as it slid out. To her surprise, the fluid was crystal clear with no blood, no telltale cloudiness of infection. This was not an obvious case of meningitis. *So what am I dealing with?* she wondered as she carefully collected CSF in three different test tubes. The fluid would be sent immediately to the lab, where it would be analyzed for cell count and bacteria, glucose and protein. Just by looking at the fluid in the tubes, she knew that the results would be normal.

She withdrew the needle and applied a bandage to the puncture site. Everyone in the room seemed to give a simultaneous sigh of relief; the procedure was over.

But the answer was no closer.

*   *   *

Later that evening, she found Taylor's mother downstairs in the tiny hospital chapel, gazing numbly at the altar. They had spoken earlier, when Claire had requested the mother's consent for the lumbar puncture. At the time, Wanda Darnell had been a bundle of nerves, all jittery hands and trembling lips. She had been on the road all day, first the two-hundred mile drive to Portland to visit her divorce attorney, and then the harrowing drive back, after the police had contacted her with the terrible news.

Now Wanda seemed exhausted, all her adrenaline depleted. She was a small woman, dressed in an ill-fitting skirt suit that made her look like a child playing grown-up in her mother's clothes. She looked up as Claire came into the chapel and barely managed a nod of greeting.

Claire sat down and gently placed her hand on Wanda's. 'The lab results have come back on the spinal tap, and they're completely normal. Taylor doesn't have meningitis.'

Wanda Darnell released a deep sigh, her shoulders slumping forward in the oversize suit jacket. 'That's good, then?'

'Yes. And judging by the CT scan, he has no tumors or signs of hemorrhage in his brain. So that's good, too.'

'Then what's wrong with him? Why did he do it?'

'I don't know, Wanda. Do you?'

She sat very still, as though struggling to come

up with an answer. 'He hasn't been . . . right. For almost a week.'

'What do you mean?'

'He's been out of control, angry at everyone. Cursing and slamming doors. I thought it was because of the divorce. He's had such a hard time of it . . .'

Claire was reluctant to bring up the next subject, but it had to be addressed. 'What about drugs, Wanda? That could change a child's personality. Do you think he's been experimenting with anything?'

Wanda hesitated. 'No.'

'You don't sound sure.'

'It's just that . . .' She swallowed, tears flashing in her eyes. 'I feel like I hardly know him anymore. He's my son, and I don't even recognize him.'

'Have you seen any warning signs?'

'He's always been a little difficult. That's why Dr Pomeroy thought he might have attention deficit disorder. Lately, it seems he's gotten worse. Especially since he started hanging out with those awful boys.'

'Which boys?'

'They live up the road from us. J.D. and Eddie Reid. And then there's that Scotty Braxton. All four of them got into trouble with the police back in March. Last week, I told Taylor he had to stay away from the Reid brothers. That's when we got into our first really big fight. That's when he slapped me.'

'*Taylor* did?'

Wanda's head drooped, the victim ashamed she'd been abused. 'We've hardly spoken to each other since then. And when we do talk, it's so obvious that . . .' Her voice slid to a whisper. 'That we hate each other.'

Gently Claire touched Wanda's arm. 'Believe it or not, disliking your own teenager isn't all that abnormal.'

'But I'm also afraid of him! That's what makes it even worse. I dislike him *and* I'm scared of him. When he hit me, it was like having his father back in the house.' She touched her fingers to her mouth, as though remembering some long-faded bruise. 'Paul and I are still in a custody fight. Two of us battling over a boy who doesn't like either of us.'

Claire's beeper went off. She glanced at the digital readout and saw the lab was paging her. 'Excuse me,' she said, and left the chapel to make the call from the hospital lobby.

Anthony, the lab supervisor, answered the phone. 'The Bangor lab just called with more of Taylor's results, Dr Elliot.'

'Did anything turn up positive on the specific screens?'

'I'm afraid not. There's no alcohol, cannabis, opioids, or amphetamines in his blood. That's a negative for every drug you wanted screened.'

'I was so sure,' she said in bewilderment. 'I don't know what else could cause this behavior.

There must be some drug I've forgotten to test for.'

'There *may* be something. I ran his blood through our hospital gas chromatography machine, and an abnormal peak showed up at one minute, ten seconds' retention time.'

'What does that mean?'

'It doesn't pinpoint any particular drug. But there is a peak, which indicates something out of the ordinary is circulating in his blood. It could be completely innocuous – an herbal supplement, for instance.'

'How do we find out what it is?'

'We'd need more extensive analysis. The Bangor lab isn't equipped to do that. We have to draw more blood and send it to our reference lab in Boston. They can simultaneously screen for hundreds of different drugs.'

'Then let's do it.'

'Well, here's the problem. It's the other reason I paged you. I just got an order to cancel any and all remaining drug tests. It's signed by Dr DelRay.'

'What?' She shook her head in disbelief. '*I'm* Taylor's doctor.'

'But DelRay's writing orders, and his are contradictory to yours. So I'm not sure what to do.'

'Look, let me talk to the mother and I'll clear this up right now.' She hung up and returned to the chapel.

Even before she opened the door, she could hear a man's voice, raised in anger.

'. . . never exerted any control! Completely useless, that's what you are. No wonder he's so screwed up!'

Claire pushed into the chapel. 'Is there a problem here, Wanda?'

The man turned to her. 'I'm Taylor's father.'

Personal crises bring out the worst in people, but Paul Darnell was probably not likable even at his best. A partner in the largest accounting firm in Two Hills, he was far more stylishly garbed than his wife, who seemed to shrink to inconsequential size in her ill-fitting suit. The brief interaction Claire had witnessed between these two ex-spouses told her what this marriage must have been like: Paul the aggressor, full of demands and complaints. Wanda always appeasing, retreating.

'What is this about my son taking illegal drugs?' he asked.

'I'm trying to find a reason for what happened today, Mr Darnell. I was just asking your wife –'

'Taylor hasn't been taking any drugs. Not since you stopped the Ritalin.' He paused. 'And he was fine on the Ritalin. I never understood why you took him off it.'

'It's been two months since I discontinued it. This personality change is more recent.'

'Two months ago, he was fine.'

'No he wasn't. He was tired and listless. And that diagnosis of ADD was never really established. It's

99

not the same as diagnosing hypertension, where there are definite parameters to go by.'

'Dr Pomeroy was certain of the diagnosis.'

'ADD has turned into a catchall for all childhood misbehavior. When a student's failing in class, or he gets into mischief, parents want to find a reason. I didn't agree with Pomeroy's diagnosis. When in doubt, I prefer not to push pills on children.'

'And look what's happened. He's out of control. He's been out of control for weeks.'

'How would you know, Paul?' said Wanda. 'How long has it been since you actually spent time with your own son?'

Paul turned to his ex-wife with such a look of hatred, Wanda shrank back. 'You're the one who's supposed to be in charge,' he said. 'I knew you couldn't handle him. You screwed it up as usual, and now our son's going to end up in jail!'

'At least I didn't provide him with the gun,' she said softly.

'What?'

'It was your gun he brought to school. Did you ever notice it was missing?'

He stared at her. 'The little *shit*! How did he get –'

'This isn't helping!' Claire cut in. 'We need to focus on Taylor. On how to explain his behavior.'

Paul turned to his wife. 'I've asked Adam DelRay to take over. He's upstairs looking at Taylor now.'

Paul's blunt announcement left Claire speechless. So this was why DelRay had written orders;

he was the new attending. She'd just been fired from the case.

'But Dr Elliot's his doctor!' Wanda protested.

'I know Adam, and I trust his judgment.'

Meaning he doesn't trust mine?

'I don't even like Adam DelRay,' said Wanda. 'He's your friend, not mine.'

'You don't have to like him.'

'If he's taking care of my son, I do.'

Paul's laughter was grating. 'Is that how you choose a doctor, Wanda? Pick whoever gives you the most warm fuzzies?'

'I'm doing what's best for Taylor!'

'And that's exactly why he ended up *here*.'

Claire's temper at last burst through. 'Mr Darnell,' she said, 'this is *not* the time to be attacking your wife!'

He turned to Claire, and his contempt was clearly meant for her as well. '*Ex*-wife,' he corrected. And he turned and walked out of the chapel.

She found Adam DelRay sitting at the nurses' station, writing in Taylor's chart. Although it was late in the evening, his white coat was starched and fresh, and Claire felt rumpled by comparison. Whatever embarrassment he'd suffered earlier that day during the crisis with Katie Youmans had been conveniently forgotten, and he regarded Claire with his usual irritating self-confidence.

'I was about to page you,' he said. 'Paul Darnell just decided –'

'I've already spoken to him.'

'Oh. So you know.' He gave an apologetic shrug. 'I hope you don't take it personally.'

'It's the parents' decision. They have a right to make it,' she acknowledged grudgingly. 'But since you're taking over, I thought you should know the boy has an abnormal peak on gas chromatography. I suggest you order a comprehensive drug screen.'

'I don't think that's necessary.' He set the chart down and stood up. 'The most likely drugs have been ruled out.'

'That peak needs to be identified.'

'Paul doesn't want any more drug tests.'

She shook her head, puzzled. 'I don't understand his objections.'

'I believe he reached that decision after speaking with his attorney.'

She waited for him to walk away before picking up the chart. She flipped to the progress notes and with growing dismay read DelRay's entry.

History and physical dictated.
Assessment:
1. Acute psychosis secondary to abrupt Ritalin withdrawal.
2. Attention Deficit Disorder.

Claire dropped into the nearest chair, her legs suddenly unsteady, her stomach queasy. So this was their criminal defense strategy. That the boy was not responsible for his actions. That Claire should be blamed, because she took him off the Ritalin, triggering a psychotic break. That she was the one who should be blamed. *I'm going to end up in court.*

This was why Paul didn't want to find any drug in the boy's bloodstream. It would shift the blame away from Claire.

Agitated, she flipped to the front of the chart and read DelRay's orders.

Cancel comprehensive drug/tox screen.
Refer all future questions and lab reports to me.
Dr Elliot is no longer the attending physician.

She slapped the chart shut and felt her nausea intensify. Now it was no longer just Taylor's life on the line; it was her practice, and her reputation as well.

She thought of the first rule of defensive medicine: cover your ass. You can't get sued if you can prove you didn't make a mistake. If you can back up your diagnosis with lab tests.

She had to get a sample of Taylor's blood. This was her last chance to draw the specimen; by tomorrow, any drug would be cleared from his system, and there'd be nothing left to detect.

She crossed the nurses' station to the supply room, pulled open a drawer, and collected a Vacutainer syringe, alcohol swabs, and three red-top blood tubes. Her heart was racing as she walked up the hall to Taylor's room. The boy was no longer her patient, and she had no right to be doing this, but she needed to know what drug, if any, was circulating in his bloodstream.

The state trooper gave her a nod of greeting as she approached.

'I need to draw blood,' she said. 'Would you mind holding down his arm for me?'

He didn't look happy about it, but he followed her into the room.

Draw it quick and get out of here. With shaking hands she snapped on the tourniquet and twisted off the needle cap. *Get out of here before someone finds out what you're doing.* She swabbed Taylor's arm with alcohol and he gave a shout of rage, twisting against the trooper's restraining grip. Claire's pulse accelerated as she pierced the skin and felt that subtle and satisfying pop as the needle penetrated the vein. *Hurry. Hurry.* She filled one tube, slipped it into her lab coat pocket, then squeezed another into the Vacutainer. Dark blood streamed out.

'I can't hold him still,' said the trooper, wrestling for control as the boy bucked and cursed.

'I'm almost done.'

'He's trying to bite me!'

'Just keep him still!' she snapped, her ears ringing with the boy's shrieks. She slipped the third tube into place and watched as a fresh stream of blood shot out. *Just one more. Come on, come on.*

'What the hell is going on in here?'

Claire looked up, so startled she let the needle

slip out of the vein. Blood dribbled from the puncture wound and dripped onto the sheets. Quickly she snapped off the tourniquet and applied gauze to the boy's arm. Cheeks burning with shame, she turned to face Paul Darnell and Adam DelRay, who were staring at her incredulously from the doorway. Two nurses peered over their shoulders.

The trooper said, 'She was just drawing some blood. The boy got a little noisy.'

'Dr Elliot isn't supposed to be in here,' said Paul. 'Didn't you hear about the new orders?'

'What orders?'

'I'm the boy's physician now,' snapped DelRay. 'Dr Elliot has no authority. She shouldn't even be in here.'

The trooper stared at Claire, and his anger was unmistakable. *You used me.*

Paul thrust out his hand. 'Give me the blood tubes, Dr Elliot.'

She shook her head. 'I'm following up an abnormal test. It could affect your son's treatment.'

'You're no longer his doctor! Give me the tubes.'

She swallowed hard. 'I'm sorry, Mr Darnell. But I can't.'

'This is assault!' Paul turned to the others in the room, and his face was florid with outrage. 'That's what this is, you know! She assaulted my son with that needle, and she knows she has no authority!' He looked at Claire. 'You'll be hearing from my attorney.'

'Paul,' interjected DelRay, playing the role of

diplomat to the hilt. 'I'm sure Dr Elliot doesn't want this kind of complication in her life.' He turned to her and spoke with the smug voice of reason. 'Come on, Claire. This is turning into a circus. Just give me the tubes.'

She looked down at the two tubes she was holding, weighing their value against a charge of assault. Against the probable loss of her hospital privileges. She felt the gaze of everyone in the room watching, even enjoying, her humiliation.

In silence she handed over the blood tubes.

DelRay took them with a look of triumph. Then he turned to the Maine state trooper. 'The boy is my patient. Is that clear?'

'Perfectly clear, Dr DelRay.'

No one said a word to Claire as she walked out of the ward, but she knew they were staring at her. She kept her gaze focused straight ahead as she turned the corner and punched the down button. Only when she'd stepped into the elevator and the door slid shut did she finally allow her hand to slip into her coat pocket.

The third blood tube was still there.

She rode the elevator to the basement lab and found Anthony sitting at his lab bench, surrounded by racks of test tubes.

'I've got a sample of the boy's blood,' she told him.

'For the drug screen?'

'Yes. I'll fill out the requisition myself.'

'The forms are on that shelf over there.'

She took one off the stack and frowned at the letterhead, Anson Biologicals. 'Are we using a new reference lab? I've never seen one of these forms before.'

He glanced up from a whirring centrifuge. 'We just switched over to Anson a few weeks ago. The hospital signed a new contract with them for our complex chem and radioimmunoassay work.'

'Why?'

'I think it was a cost issue.'

She scanned the form, then checked off the box for *gas chromatography/mass spectrometry; comprehensive drug and tox screen*. In the space for comments at the bottom of the page, she wrote: 'Fourteen-year-old boy with apparent drug-induced psychosis and aggression. This lab test is for my personal research only. Report results directly to me.' And she signed her name.

Noah answered the knock on his front door and found Amelia standing outside in the dark. She was wearing a bandage, a bright slash of white across her temple, and he could tell it hurt her to smile. In her discomfort, the best she could muster was a crooked lifting of one side of her mouth.

He was so surprised by her unexpected visit, he couldn't think of a single intelligent thing to say, so he just gaped at her, as dazzled as a peasant who suddenly finds himself in the presence of royalty.

'This is for you,' she said, and she held out a

small brown package. 'I'm sorry I couldn't find anything nice to wrap it in.'

He took the package, but his gaze remained on her face. 'Are you all right?'

'I'm okay. I guess you heard that Mrs Horatio . . .' She paused, swallowing back tears.

He nodded. 'My mom told me.'

Amelia touched the bandage on her face. Again he saw a flash of tears in her eyes. 'I met your mom. In the emergency room. She was really nice to me . . .' She turned and glanced over her shoulder at the darkness, as though expecting to see someone watching her. 'I've got to go now –'

'Did someone drive you here?'

'I walked.'

'You walked? In the dark?'

'It's not so far. I live just the other side of the lake, right past the boat ramp.' She backed away from the door, blond hair swaying. 'I'll see you in school.'

'Wait. Amelia!' He held up the gift. 'What's this for?'

'To thank you. For what you did today.' She took another retreating step, and was almost swallowed up in darkness.

'Amelia!'

'Yes?'

Noah paused, not knowing what to say. The silence was broken only by the rustle of dead leaves scattering across the lawn. Amelia stood on the farthest edge of the light spilling from the open doorway, her face a pale oval eclipsing into night.

'You want to come inside?' he asked.

To his surprise she seemed to consider the invitation. For a moment she lingered between darkness and light, advance and retreat. She looked over her shoulder again, as though seeking permission. Then she nodded.

Noah found himself panicking over the disorder in the front parlor. His mom had been home for only a few hours that afternoon, to comfort him and cook dinner. Then she'd driven back to the hospital to see Taylor. No one had tidied up the parlor, and everything was still lying where Noah had dropped it that afternoon – backpack on the couch, sweatshirt on the coffee table, dirty tennis shoes in front of the fireplace. He decided to bypass the parlor and led Amelia into the kitchen instead.

They sat down, not looking at each other, two foreign species struggling to find a common language.

She glanced up as the phone rang. 'Aren't you going to answer that?'

'Naw. It's another one of those reporters. They've been calling all afternoon, ever since I got home.'

The answering machine picked up, and as he'd predicted, a woman's voice came on: 'This is Damaris Horne of the *Weekly Informer*. I'd really, really like to talk to Noah Elliot, if I could, about that amazing act of heroism today in the classroom.

The whole country wants to hear about it, Noah. I'll be staying at the Lakeside B and B, and I could offer some financial compensation for your time, if that would make it more worth your while . . .'

'She's offering to pay you just to talk?' asked Amelia.

'Crazy, isn't it? My mom says it's a sure sign I *shouldn't* talk to that lady.'

'But people do want to hear about it. About what you did.'

What I did.

He gave a shrug, feeling unworthy of all the praise, of Amelia's praise, most of all. He sat listening as the call ended. The silence returned, interrupted only by the soft beep of the message reminder.

'You can open it now. If you want,' said Amelia.

He looked down at the gift. Though the wrapping was plain brown paper, he took great effort not to tear it, because it seemed uncouth to go ripping it open in front of her. Gingerly he peeled off the tape and folded back the wrapping.

The pocket knife was neither large nor impressive. He saw scratches on the handle, and realized it was not even new. She'd given him a used knife.

'Wow,' he managed to say with some measure of enthusiasm. 'This is a nice one.'

'It belonged to my dad.' She added, quietly: 'My real dad.'

He looked up as the implication of those words sank in.

'Jack is my stepfather.' She uttered that last word as though it were an object of disgust.

'Then J.D. and Eddie . . .'

'They're not my real brothers. They're Jack's boys.'

'I guess I wondered about it. They don't look like you.'

'Thank god.'

Noah laughed. 'Yeah, that's not a family resemblance I'd want to have, either.'

'I'm not even allowed to talk about my real dad, because it makes Jack mad. He hates to be reminded there was someone else before him. But I want people to know. I want them to know Jack has nothing to do with who I am.'

Gently he placed the knife back in her hand. 'I can't take this, Amelia.'

'I want you to.'

'But it's got to mean a lot to you, if it belonged to him.'

'That's why I want you to have it.' She touched the bandage on her temple, as though pointing to the evidence of her debt to him. 'You were the only one who did anything. The only one who didn't run.'

He didn't confess the humiliating truth: *I wanted to run, but I was so terrified I couldn't move my legs.*

She looked up at the kitchen clock. With a start of panic, she abruptly stood up. 'I didn't know it was so late.'

He followed her to the front door. Amelia had

111

just stepped out when headlights suddenly cut through the trees. She spun around to face them, and then seemed to freeze as the pickup truck roared up the driveway.

The door swung open and Jack Reid stepped out, whippet thin and scowling. 'Get in the truck, Amelia,' he said.

'Jack, how did you –'

'Eddie told me you'd be here.'

'I was just about to walk home.'

'Get in the truck *now*.'

Instantly she clammed up and obediently slid into the passenger seat.

Her stepfather was about to climb back behind the wheel when he met Noah's gaze.

'She doesn't hang out with boys,' he said. 'I want you to know that.'

'She only came by to say hello,' said Noah angrily. 'What's the big deal?'

'The deal, boy, is that my daughter's off limits.' He climbed in and slammed the door.

'She's not even your daughter!' Noah yelled, but he knew the man couldn't hear him over the revving engine.

As the truck swung around in the driveway, Noah caught one last glimpse of Amelia's profile, framed by the passenger window, her terrified gaze focused straight ahead.

6

The first snowflakes spiraled down through the bare branches and gently dusted the excavation site. Lucy Overlock glanced up at the sky and said, 'This snow's going to stop, isn't it? It has to stop, or it'll obscure everything.'

'It's already melting,' said Lincoln. He sniffed the air and knew, by some instinct developed during a lifetime in these woods, that the snow would not last long. These flakes were merely a whispered warning, deceptively gentle, of the wintry months to come. He did not mind the snow, did not even resent all the inconveniences that came with it, the shoveling, the plowing out, the nights without power when the lines went down from the weight of it. It was the darkness he disliked. Darkness fell so early these days. Already daylight was fading, and the trees were featureless black slashes against the sky.

'Well, we might as well pack it up for the day,' said Lucy. 'And hope it's not buried under a foot of snow by tomorrow.'

Now that the bones were no longer of interest to the police, Lucy and her grad students had assumed the responsibility of protecting the dig. The two students pulled a tarp over the excavation site and staked it in place. It was a futile precaution; a marauding raccoon could rip it away with one slash of its claws.

'When will you finish here?' asked Lincoln.

'I'd like to take several weeks,' said Lucy. 'But with the weather turning bad, we'll have to rush. One hard freeze, and that's it for the season.'

Headlights flickered through the trees. Lincoln saw that another vehicle had pulled into Rachel Sorkin's driveway.

He tramped back through the woods, toward the house. In the last few days, the front yard had become a parking lot. Next to Lincoln's vehicle was Lucy Overlock's Jeep and a beat-up Honda, which he assumed belonged to her grad student.

At the far end of the driveway, parked under the trees, was yet another vehicle – a dark blue Volvo. He recognized it, and he crossed the yard to the driver's side.

The window hummed open an inch. 'Lincoln,' the woman said.

'Evening, Judge Keating.'

'You have time to talk?' He heard the locks click open.

Lincoln circled to the passenger side and slid in, shutting the door. They sat for a moment, cocooned in silence.

'Have they found anything else?' she asked. She didn't look at him but gazed straight ahead, her eyes focused somewhere among the trees. In the car's gloom, she seemed younger than her sixty-six years, the lines in her face fading to uniform smoothness. Younger and not so formidable.

'There were only the two skeletons,' said Lincoln.

'Both were children?'

'Yes. Dr Overlock estimates their ages at around nine or ten years old.'

'Not a natural death?'

'No. Both deaths were violent.'

There was a long pause. 'And when did this happen?'

'That's not so easy to determine. All they have to go on are some artifacts found with the remains. They've dug up some buttons, a coffin handle. Dr Overlock thinks it's probably part of a family cemetery.'

She took her time absorbing this information. Her next question came out softly tentative: 'So the remains are quite old?'

'A hundred years, more or less.'

She released a deep breath. Was it Lincoln's imagination or did the tension suddenly melt from her silhouette? She seemed to fall almost limp with relief, her head tilting back against the neck rest. 'A hundred years,' she said. 'Then it's nothing to worry about. It's not from –'

'No. It's unrelated.'

She gazed ahead, at the congealing darkness.

'Still, it's such a strange coincidence, isn't it? That very same part of the lake . . .' She paused. 'I wonder if it happened in the fall.'

'People die every day, Judge Keating. A century's worth of skeletons – they all have to be buried somewhere.'

'I heard there was a hatchet mark on one of the thigh bones.'

'That's true.'

'It will have people wondering. Remembering.'

Lincoln heard the woman's fear, and he wanted to reassure her, but could not bring himself to make physical contact. Iris Keating was not a touchable woman. Her emotional barrier was so thick, it would not have surprised him to reach out and feel a shell.

He said, 'It was a long time ago. No one remembers.'

'This town remembers.'

'Only a few. The older ones. And they don't want to talk about it any more than you do.'

'Still, it's a matter of public record. And now all those reporters are in town. They'll be asking questions.'

'What happened half a century ago isn't relevant.'

'Isn't it?' She looked at him. 'This is how it began last time. The killings. It started in the fall.'

'You can't interpret every violent act as history repeating itself.'

'But history *is* violence.' Once again, she faced

116

forward, her gaze directed toward the lake. Night had fallen and through the bare trees, the water was only a faint glimmer. 'Don't you feel it, Lincoln?' she asked softly. 'There's something wrong about this place. I don't know what it is, but I've felt it since I was small. I didn't like living here, even then. And now . . .' She reached for the ignition and started the engine.

Lincoln stepped out of the car. 'It's a slippery road tonight. Drive carefully.'

'I will. Oh, and Lincoln?'

'Yes?'

'I'm told there's a new opening in that alcohol rehab program in Augusta. It might be the place for Doreen. If you can talk her into it.'

'I'll try. I just keep hoping that one of these days it'll take.'

He thought he saw pity in her eyes. 'I wish you luck. You deserve a lot better, Lincoln.'

'I'm managing all right.'

'Of course you are.' He realized, then, that it wasn't pity, but admiration he heard in her voice. 'You're one of the few men in this world who would.'

A photo of Mrs Horatio was propped up on the coffin, a picture of her as a young woman of eighteen, smiling, almost pretty. Noah had never thought of his biology teacher as pretty, nor had he imagined her as ever having been young. In his mind, Dorothy Horatio had sprung up on this earth already middle-aged, and now, in death, she would remain eternally so.

Moving with the long line of students, he shuffled dutifully toward the coffin, past the photo of Mrs Horatio in her past incarnation as an actual human female. It was a shock to confront that eerily familiar image of Mrs Horatio before the extra pounds and wrinkles and gray hair. To realize that the photo had been taken when she was not much older than Noah. What happens when we get old? he wondered. Where does the kid part of us go?

He stopped before the coffin. It was closed, which was a mercy; he didn't think he could handle seeing his dead teacher's face. It was terrible enough just to imagine how she must look, hidden beneath that mahogany lid. He had not particularly liked Dorothy Horatio. Not at all, in fact. But today he had met her husband and adult daughter, had seen them both sobbing, their arms flung around each other, and had come to realize a startling truth: that even the Mrs Horatios of this world have people who love them.

In the coffin's polished surface, he could see his own face, bland and composed. Emotions hidden beneath an expressionless mask.

He had not been so composed at the last funeral he'd attended.

Two years ago, he and his mother had stood holding hands as they gazed at his father's coffin. The lid had been left open, so people could gaze down at his gaunt face as they said their good-byes. When the time had come to leave, Noah had refused to go. His mother had tried to lead him away, but he had sobbed: *You can't leave Daddy in there! Go back, go back!*

He blinked and touched his hand to Mrs Horatio's coffin. It was smooth and glossy. Like fine furniture.

Where does the kid part of us go?

He realized that the line ahead of him had vanished, that people behind him were waiting for him to move forward. He continued past the coffin, walked up the aisle, and fled out the mortuary doors.

Outside it was lightly snowing, the cold kiss of flakes soothing to his face. He was relieved none of the reporters had followed him out. All afternoon, they'd chased him around with their tape recorders, wanting just a sentence from the boy who'd courageously wrestled the gun away from the killer. The hero of Knox High School.

What a joke.

He stood across the street from the mortuary, shivering in the gloom as he watched people walk out of the building. They each performed the identical into-the-cold ritual: the appraising glance at the sky, the shudder, the hugging close of one's coat. Just about everyone in town had come to pay their last respects, but he scarcely recognized some of them, so transformed were they by their suits and ties and mourning dresses. No one wearing the usual flannels and jeans. Even Chief Kelly was wearing a suit and tie.

Noah watched as Amelia Reid stepped out the mortuary doors. She was breathing quickly, deeply, and she sagged against the building as though she'd been pursued and was desperately trying to catch her breath.

A car drove by, its tires crunching across the crystalline snow as it passed between them.

Noah called out to her: 'Amelia?'

She looked up, startled, and saw him. She hesitated, glancing up and down the street, as though to assure herself it was safe to proceed. He felt his heart beat faster as she crossed the street to join him.

'Pretty grim in there,' he said.

She nodded. 'I couldn't listen to it anymore. I didn't want to start crying in front of everyone.'

Neither did I, he thought, but would never admit it.

They stood together in the gloom, not looking at each other, both of them moving their feet to stay warm. Both of them searching for some thread of conversation. He took a deep breath and said, suddenly, 'I hate funerals. They remind me of . . .' He stopped.

'They remind me of my dad's funeral, too,' she said softly. And she looked up as snowflakes spiraled down from the darkening sky.

*   *   *

Warren Emerson walked on the side of the road, his boots crunching the frost-stiffened grass. He wore a blaze-orange vest and an orange cap, yet he couldn't help flinching every time another gun went off in the woods. Bullets, after all, were colorblind. It was cold this morning, far colder than yesterday, and his fingers ached in their thin woolen gloves. He shoved his hands into his pockets and kept trudging, not worried about the cold, knowing that in another mile he would cease to notice it.

He had walked this road over a thousand times, in every season of the year, and could trace his progress by the landmarks he passed. The toppled stone wall was four hundred paces from his front yard. The Murrays' tumbledown barn was nine hundred fifty paces. At two thousand paces, the turnoff to Toddy Point Road, he reached the halfway mark. The landmarks became more frequent as he approached the outskirts of town. So did the traffic, every so often a car or truck rattling by, tires spitting up dirt.

Local drivers seldom stopped to offer Warren a ride into town. In the summertime he caught plenty of rides, from tourists who considered Warren Emerson, shuffling along in his boots and baggy trousers, an example of living, breathing local color. They'd pull over and invite him to climb in for a lift. During the drive they'd ply him with an endless stream of questions, always the same ones: 'What do you folks do in the winter?' 'You lived here all your life?' 'You ever met Stephen

King?' Warren's answers never went beyond a simple yes or no, an economy of words which the tourists invariably found amusing. They'd pull into town, let him off at the general store, and wave so sincerely you'd think they were saying good-bye to their best friend. Wicked friendly people, those tourists; every autumn, he was sorry to see them go, because it meant another nine months of walking down this road, with not a single driver who'd stop for him.

The townspeople were all afraid.

Were he licensed to drive, he often thought, he would not be so unsympathetic to an old man. But Warren could not drive. He had a perfectly fine old Ford gathering dust in the barn – his father's car, a 1945, scarcely driven – yet Warren could not use it. A danger to himself and to others. That's what the doctors had said about his driving.

So the Ford stayed in the barn, over fifty years now, and it was as shiny as the day his father had parked it there. Time was kinder to chrome than it was to a man's face. To a man's heart. *I am a danger to myself and to others.*

His hands at last were starting to feel warm.

He pulled them from his pockets and swung his arms as he walked, heart pumping faster, sweat gathering under his cap. Even on the most frigid of days, if he walked fast enough, far enough, the cold would cease to matter.

By the time he reached town, he'd unbuttoned his coat and removed the cap. When he walked into Cobb and Morong's General Store, he found it almost unbearably hot inside.

As soon as the door swung shut behind him, the store seemed to fall silent. The clerk looked up, then looked away. Two women standing by the vegetable bin ceased their chatter. Though no one was staring, he could feel their attention focused on him as he picked up a shopping basket and walked up the aisle, toward the canned goods. He filled his basket with the same items he bought every week. Cat food. Chili with beef. Tuna. Corn. He went down the next row for the dried beans and oatmeal, then to the vegetable bin for a sack of onions.

He carried the basket, now heavy, to the checkout counter.

The cashier avoided looking at him as she tallied up the items. He stood before the register, his blaze orange vest screaming out to the world, *Look at me, look at me*. Yet no one did. No one met his gaze.

In silence he paid the cashier, picked up the plastic grocery sacks, and turned to leave, steeling himself for the long walk home. At the door, he stopped.

On the newsstand was this week's issue of the *Tranquility Gazette*. There was one copy left. He stared at the headline and suddenly the grocery sacks slipped out of his grasp and thudded to the floor. With shaking hands he reached for the newspaper.

HIGH SCHOOL SHOOTING LEAVES TEACHER DEAD, TWO

STUDENTS WOUNDED: 14-YEAR-OLD BOY ARRESTED.

'Hey! You gonna pay for that paper?' the clerk called out.

Warren didn't answer. He just stood by the door, his eyes fixed in horror on a second headline, almost lost in the bottom right corner: YOUTH BEATS PUPPY TO DEATH: CITED FOR CRUELTY.

And he thought: *It's happening again.*

Damaris Horne was stuck in purgatory, and all she could think about was how to get back to Boston. So this is how my editor punishes me, she thought. We get into a tiff, and he assigns me to the story no one else wants. Welcome to Hicksville-by-the-Lake, otherwise known as Tranquility, Maine. Good name. The place was so tranquil, they should issue it a death certificate. She drove up Main Street, thinking that this was the perfect model for how a town would look after a neutron bomb hit it: no people, no signs of life, just standing buildings and deserted sidewalks. Nine hundred ten residents supposedly lived in this town, so where were they all? In the woods, gnawing lichen off the trees?

She drove past Monaghan's Diner, and through the front window she caught a glimpse of a plaid shirt. Yes! A sighting of the local natives in their ceremonial dress. (What was the mystical significance of plaid, anyway?) Further up the street, she had another sighting: a shabbily dressed old geezer came out of Cobb and Morong's, clutching his grocery sacks. She stopped to let him cross the street, and he shuffled past, head bent in a look of permanent weariness. She watched him walk along the lakeshore, a slow-moving silhouette laboring across a bleak backdrop of bare trees and gray water.

She drove on, to the Lakeside Bed and Breakfast, her home for the indefinite future. It was the only local inn still open this late in the year, and although she sneeringly referred to it as the Bates Motel, she knew she was lucky to have found any room at all, what with the other regional reporters arriving in town.

She walked into the dining room and saw that most of her competition were still stuffing themselves at the breakfast buffet. Damaris always skipped breakfast, which put her ahead of the game this morning. It was eight A.M., and she'd already been up for two and a half hours. At six, she'd been at the hospital to observe the boy being transferred out to his new home, the Maine Youth Center. At seven-fifteen, she'd driven over to the high school. There she'd sat in her parked car and watched the kids in their baggy clothes gather in front of the building, waiting for first bell, looking like teenagers everywhere.

Damaris crossed to the coffee pot and poured herself a cup. Sipping it black, she glanced around the room at the other reporters until her gaze settled on the freelancer, Mitchell Groome. Though he couldn't be much older than forty-five, Groome's face was all sad droops, like a hound in mourning. Still, he seemed fit enough – perhaps even athletic. Best of all, he had noticed her gaze, and was looking back at her, albeit with puzzlement.

She set down her empty cup and strolled out of the dining room, knowing, without even a backward glance, that Groome was watching her.

Hicksville had just gotten a little more interesting.

Up in her room, she took a few minutes to review her notes from the interviews she'd conducted over the last few days. Now came the hard part – putting it all together in an article that would make her editor happy and catch the eyes of bored New England housewives cruising past the tabloid stands.

She sat at her desk and stared out the window, wondering how to turn this tragic but nonetheless commonplace tale into something a little more titillating. What made this case special? What new angle would entice a reader to reach for a copy of the *Weekly Informer*?

She suddenly realized she was staring straight at it.

Across the street was a rundown old building, the windows boarded up. The faded sign said Kimball's Furniture.

The address was 666.

The sign of the Beast.

As her laptop computer powered up, she quickly shuffled through her notes, searching for the quote she remembered from yesterday. Something a woman had said in the local grocery store.

She found it. 'I know the explanation for what happened at the school,' the woman had said. 'Everyone knows it, but no one wants to admit it. They don't want to sound superstitious or uneducated. But I'll tell you what it is: it's this new Godlessness. People have pushed the Lord out of their lives. They've replaced Him with something else. Something no one dares speak of.'

Yes! thought Damaris, and she was grinning as she began to type.

'Last week, Satan arrived in the bucolic town of Tranquility, Maine . . .'

Sitting in her wheelchair before the living room window, Faye Braxton watched her thirteen-year-old son step off the school bus and begin to hike up the long dirt driveway to the house. It was a daily event she usually looked forward to, seeing Scotty's slight figure at last emerge through the bus doors, his shoulders weighed down by the heavy backpack, his head craned forward with the effort to lug his burden of books up the weedy and sloping front yard.

He was still so small. It pained her to see how little he had grown in the last year. While many of his classmates had shot past him in both height and bulk, there was her Scotty, left behind in pale adolescence, and so anxious to grow up he had nicked his chin last week while trying to shave his nonexistent beard. He was her firstborn, her best friend. She wouldn't have minded at all if time suddenly stood still, and she could keep him as he'd always been, a sweet and loving child. But she knew the child would soon be gone.

The transformation had already begun.

She'd seen the first hint of it a few days ago, when he had stepped off the bus as usual. She'd been at the window, watching him walk toward the house, when she saw something happen that was both inexplicable and frightening. In the front yard, he had suddenly halted and gazed up at a tree in which three gray squirrels perched. She'd thought he was merely curious. That like his younger sister Kitty, he would try to coax them down to be petted. So she was startled when he bent down, picked up a rock, and flung it at the tree.

The squirrels scampered to higher branches.

As she'd watched in dismay, Scotty had hurled another rock, and another, his thin body winding up like a tautly coiled spring of fury, the stones flying into the branches. When at last he stopped, he was breathing hard and exhausted. Then he'd turned to the house.

The look on his face had made her jerk back from the window. For one horrifying moment she'd thought: *That is not my son.*

Now, as she watched him approach the house, she wondered which boy would step through the door. Her son, her *real* son, sweet and smiling, or the ugly stranger who looked like Scotty? In the past, she would have dealt firmly with him for throwing rocks at animals.

In the past, she was never afraid of her own child.

Faye heard Scotty's footsteps on the porch. Heart pounding, she swiveled her wheelchair around to face him as he came in the door.

7

Anyone could see that fourteen-year-old Barry Knowlton was his mother's child. The resemblance was startling enough to take in with a single glance. Barry and Louise were like a pair of cheerful dumplings, both of them red-haired and apple-cheeked, both with pliant pink mouths. Their smiles of greeting promised to dispel even Claire's gloom.

Since the classroom shooting nearly a week ago, Claire had awakened each morning to the awful realization that her move to Tranquility had been a mistake. Only eight months ago, she had arrived here full of confidence, had used most of her savings to buy a medical practice she was certain would succeed. And why wouldn't it? She'd had a thriving practice in Baltimore. But one very public lawsuit would destroy everything.

Every day at work, when she saw the mailman stride up the front walk, she braced herself for the delivery of a letter she dreaded receiving.

Paul Darnell had said she'd be hearing from his attorney, and she had no doubt he'd follow up on his threat.

Is it too late to leave? That was the question she asked herself every day now. *Is it too late to move back to Baltimore?*

She forced herself to smile as she stepped into the exam room to see Barry and his mother. Here, at least, was a bright spot in her day.

They both looked genuinely pleased to see her. Barry had already pulled off his boots and was standing on the scale, watching expectantly as the counterweight arm bobbed up and down.

'Hey, I think I lost another pound!' he announced.

Claire checked the chart, then glanced at the reading. 'Down to two hundred forty-seven pounds. That's two pounds you've lost. Good for you!'

Barry stepped off the scale, which sent the counterweight tilting up with a loud clap. 'I think my belt feels looser already!'

'Let me listen to your heart,' said Claire.

Barry waddled over to the exam table, carefully climbed up onto the footstool, and plopped onto the table. He peeled off his shirt, baring folds of pale and sagging flesh. As Claire listened to his heart and lungs and took his blood pressure, she felt his gaze, curious and engaged, following her every move. The first time they'd met, Barry had told her he wanted to be a doctor, and he seemed to relish these bimonthly visits as field trips into his future profession. The occasional blood test, an ordeal for most patients, was a fascinating procedure for Barry, an opportunity to ask in sometimes endless detail about needle gauges and syringe volumes and the purpose of each different colored blood tube.

If only Barry would pay as much attention to what he put in his mouth.

She finished her exam, then stood back and regarded him for a moment. 'You're doing a good job, Barry. How is the diet coming?'

He gave a shrug. 'Okay, I guess. I'm trying real hard.'

'Oh, he loves to eat! That's the problem,' said Louise. 'I try my best cooking low-fat meals. But then his daddy comes home with a box of dough-nuts and, well . . . it's so hard to resist. It just about breaks my heart to see the way Barry looks at us, with those big hungry eyes of his.'

'Could you discourage your husband from bringing home doughnuts?'

'Oh, no. Mel, he's got this . . .' She leaned forward and said, confidentially: 'Overeating prob-lem.'

'Is that so?'

'I gave up on Mel long ago. But Barry, he's still so young. It's not good for a boy his age to carry around all that weight. And the other kids, they can be so mean about it.'

Claire looked sympathetically at Barry. 'You're having problems at school?'

A light seemed to dim in the boy's eyes. He

looked down, all cheerfulness gone. 'I don't much like school anymore.'

'The other kids tease you?'

'They don't ever *stop* with the fat boy jokes.'

Claire glanced at Louise, who shook her head sadly. 'He has an IQ of a hundred thirty-five, and he doesn't want to go to school. I don't know what to do about it.'

'I'll tell you what, Barry,' said Claire. 'We're going to show everyone how determined you are. You're too intelligent to let those other kids defeat you.'

'Well, they aren't all that bright,' he agreed hopefully.

'You have to outsmart your own body as well. That's the part that takes effort. And Mom and Dad have to work with you, not against you.' She looked at Louise. 'Mrs Knowlton, you have a smart and wonderful boy here, but he can't do this alone. This takes the whole family.'

Louise sighed, already preparing for the daunting task ahead. 'I know,' she said. 'I'll talk to Mel. No more doughnuts.'

After the Knowltons left, Claire walked into Vera's office. 'Don't we have a patient at three o'clock?'

'We did,' said Vera, looking puzzled as she hung up the phone. 'That was Mrs Monaghan. It's the second cancellation we've had today.'

Claire glimpsed movement in the waiting room. Through the sliding business window, she saw a man sitting on the couch. Large, homely, his sad-clown face emphasized by an unflattering crewcut, he looked as if he'd rather be anywhere else than in a doctor's office. 'Well, who's that?'

'Oh, he's just some magazine reporter who wants to talk to you. His name's Mitchell Groome.'

'I hope you told him I'm not available.'

'I gave him your standard "no comment" line. But this guy insists on waiting around for you.'

'Well, he can wait all he wants. I'm not talking to any more reporters. Is there anyone left on the schedule?'

'Elwyn Clyde. Wound check on his foot.'

Elwyn. Claire pressed her hand to her head, already anticipating a headache. 'Do we have air freshener on hand?'

Vera laughed and clapped a can of Glade on the desk. 'We're all ready for Elwyn. After him, you're free for the day. Which works out well, because you have a meeting with Dr Sarnicki this afternoon. He just called a little while ago.'

Dr Sarnicki was chief of staff at the hospital. This was the first Claire had heard about any meeting.

'Did he say what it's about?'

'Something about a letter he just received. He said it was urgent.' Vera's gaze suddenly shot to the front window and she jumped to her feet. 'Damn it, there they are again!' she said, and dashed out the side door.

Claire looked out the window to see Vera, all flashing bangles and earrings, shaking her fist at

134

two boys with skateboards. One of the boys was yelling back at her now, his voice cracking in adolescent outrage.

'We didn't do anything to your stupid car!'

'Then who left that giant scratch on the door, huh? Who?' demanded Vera.

'Why're you always blaming us? Like kids are always the ones who get dumped on!'

'I see you here again, I'm calling the police!'

'This is a public sidewalk! We gotta right to skate here!'

A tapping on glass drew Claire's attention. Mitchell Groome's hang-dog face was gazing at her through the receptionist's window.

She slid the window open. 'Mr Groome, I'm not talking to any reporters.'

'I just wanted to tell you something.'

'If it's about Taylor Darnell, you can talk to Dr Adam DelRay. He's the boy's physician now.'

'No, it's about your receptionist's car. The one that got scratched. Those boys out there didn't do it.'

'How do you know?'

'I saw it happen yesterday. Some old woman scraped past it with her car. I assumed she was going to leave a note on the windshield. Obviously she didn't, and I think your receptionist has already reached her own conclusions.' He glanced out the window, at the argument raging outside, and he shook his head. 'Why do we always treat kids like the enemy?'

'Because they so often behave like an alien species?'

He gave her a sympathetic smile. 'Spoken like someone who has an alien living in the house.'

'Fourteen years old. You can probably tell by all the gray hairs on my head.' They regarded each other for a moment through the window.

'Are you sure you won't talk to me?' he asked. 'It would just be for a few minutes.'

'I can't discuss my patients. It's a confidentiality issue.'

'No, I'm not going to ask about Taylor Darnell specifically. I'm after more general information, about the other kids in town. You're the only doctor in Tranquility, and I assume you have a good idea of what's going on around here.'

'I've only been in town eight months.'

'But you'd be aware of drug abuse among the local kids, wouldn't you? It could explain the boy's behavior.'

'I hardly think one incident, tragic as it was, means that this town has a drug problem.' Her gaze suddenly focused on the view through the front window. The boys with the skateboards were gone. The mail carrier had arrived, and was chatting with Vera on the sidewalk. He handed Vera an armful of mail. Was there a letter from Paul Darnell's attorney in that stack?

Groome said something, and she realized he had moved closer, and was practically leaning through the open business window.

'Let me tell you a story, Dr Elliot. It's about a perfect little town called Flanders, Iowa. Population four thousand. A clean, decent place where everyone knows everyone else. The sort of people who go to church and join the PTA. Four murders later – all of them committed by teenagers – the shell-shocked residents of Flanders finally got around to facing up to reality.'

'Which was?'

'Methamphetamine. An epidemic of abuse in the local schools. It turned that town into the dark side of America.'

'But what does that have to do with Tranquility?'

'Haven't you been reading your own newspaper? Look around at what's happening to your neighbors. First, there was that street brawl on Halloween night. Then a boy beats his dog to death, and fistfights are breaking out in the school. Finally, there's the shooting.'

She was focused on the front sidewalk again, where the mailman was still shooting the breeze with Vera. *For heaven's sakes, bring in the mail!*

'I followed the Flanders story for months,' said Groome. 'I watched that town implode on itself. Parents blaming the schools. Kids turning on their teachers, on their own families. When I heard about the problems in your town, methamphetamine was the first thing I thought of. I know you must have run a drug screen on that Darnell boy. Could you just tell me one thing: Did methamphetamine turn up in his system?'

Still distracted, she answered: 'No, it didn't.'

'Did anything else?'

She didn't answer. In truth, she didn't know, because she hadn't heard back from the lab in Boston.

'Then there *was* something,' he said, picking up on her silence.

'I'm not the boy's physician. You have to ask Dr DelRay.'

Groome gave a dismissive snort. 'DelRay says it's Ritalin withdrawal psychosis. Something so rare, there's only a few anecdotal reports that it even exists.'

'You don't accept his diagnosis?'

He looked her straight in the eye. 'Don't tell me you do?'

She was beginning to like Mitchell Groome.

The front door opened and Vera stomped in, carrying the mail. Unceremoniously she dumped the whole pile on her desk. Claire eyed the stack of business-size envelopes, and her throat went dry.

'Excuse me,' she said to Groome. 'I have work to do.'

'Flanders, Iowa. Just keep it in mind,' he said, and with a wave, walked out of the building.

Claire picked up the mail, headed straight to her office, and shut the door.

Sitting at her desk, she swiftly shuffled through the envelopes, then sank back with a sigh of relief. Another day's reprieve; no attorney's name was on any of the return addresses. Maybe Paul Darnell

had been bluffing; maybe there would be no repercussions after all.

For a moment she sat with her head tilted back,
her tension melting. Then she reached for the first
envelope and tore it open. Seconds later she was
sitting up, rigid, in her chair.

Inside was a short note from Rachel Sorkin, the
woman who'd reported Elwyn Clyde's gunshot
wound.

Dr Elliot,
    This letter came in my mail today. I thought
you should know about it.

Rachel.
    P.S. I don't believe a word of it.

Attached to it was a typewritten letter:

To whom it may concern,
    I am writing to inform you of a disturbing
incident. On November third, Dr Claire Elliot
assaulted a hospital patient. Although there
were a number of witnesses, this event has
not been made public. If Dr Elliot is your
physician, you may wish to reconsider your
options. Patients have a right to know.
            A concerned health care professional

There were three men waiting for her in the
medical staff office. She knew Dr Sarnicki only

slightly, but her impressions of him had been favorable. A comfortably rumpled man with a gentle voice, he was known to be a caring physician as well as a skillful diplomat who had helped ease tensions during the hospital's recent contract negotiations with the nurses. The second man was Roger Hayes, the hospital administrator, whom she scarcely knew at all except as a bland and smiling man.

The third man she knew only too well. It was Adam DelRay.

They greeted her with polite nods as she sat down at the conference table. She was already strung so tight she felt close to snapping in two. On the table in front of Sarnicki was a copy of the same anonymous letter that Rachel had forwarded to her.

'You've seen this already?' he said.

She gave a grim nod. 'One of my patients sent me a copy. I've called around, and so far I've confirmed that at least six others have received it.'

'Mine arrived in the departmental mail this morning.'

'This has been blown completely out of proportion,' said Claire. 'I certainly did not assault the patient. The letter's designed to do only one thing, and that's to damage my reputation.' She looked directly at Adam DelRay. He returned her gaze without flinching, without even a flicker of guilt in his eyes.

'What exactly happened on November third?' asked Hayes.

She answered evenly: 'I drew blood from Taylor Darnell, to send off for a comprehensive drug and tox screen. I've already told Dr Sarnicki who else was in the room. Who witnessed it. I didn't abuse the patient. It was just a blood draw.'

'Tell them the rest,' said DelRay. 'Or are you going to leave out the most important detail? Which is, you had no authority to draw his blood.'

'So why did you?' asked Hayes.

'The boy had a drug-induced psychosis. I wanted that drug identified.'

'There is no drug,' said DelRay.

'You don't know that,' she said. 'You never ran the test.'

'There is no drug.' He slapped a sheet of paper on the table. She stared in dismay at the letterhead: Anson Biologicals.

'I have the results right here. Apparently, Dr Elliot managed to get a blood tube out to the reference lab without the father's knowledge. Or permission. Anson faxed the report to the hospital this morning.' He added, with a note of smugness, 'It's negative. No drugs, no toxins.'

Why had the lab disregarded her instructions? Why had they sent the report to the hospital?

She said, 'Our own lab found an unidentified peak on gas chromatography. There *was* something in his blood.'

DelRay laughed. 'Have you seen our lab's gas

chromatography machine? It's an antique. A hand-me-down from Eastern Maine Medical Center. You can't trust our results.'

'But it did need a followup test.' She looked at Sarnicki. 'That's why I drew the blood. Because Adam refused to.'

'She made an unauthorized blood draw,' said DelRay.

Hayes sighed. 'It's a mountain out of a molehill, Adam. The boy wasn't harmed, and he's doing fine at the Youth Center.'

'She ignored the father's wishes.'

'But one blood draw does not make a lawsuit.'

Claire's chin snapped up in alarm. 'Is Paul Darnell talking about legal action?'

'No, not at all,' said Hayes. 'I spoke to him this morning, and he reassured me he wasn't suing anyone.'

'I'll tell you why he's not suing,' said DelRay. 'It's because that ex-wife of his threatened to sabotage any lawsuit. It's an automatic reflex for bitter ex-wives. Whatever the husband wants, the wife blindly opposes.'

Thank you, Wanda, thought Claire.

'Then this whole incident is now a nonissue,' said Sarnicki, looking relieved. 'As far as I can see, no action is necessary.'

'What about the letter?' said Claire. 'Someone is trying to ruin my practice.'

'I'm not sure what we can do about an anonymous letter.'

'It's signed "A health care professional."' She looked pointedly at DelRay.

'Now wait a *minute*,' he snapped. 'I had nothing to do with it.'

'Paul Darnell, then,' she said.

'There were a couple of nurses who were there too, remember? In fact, this sort of sneaky letter is more a woman's style.'

'What the hell does that mean?' she shot back in outrage. '"A woman's style?"'

'I'm just calling it as I see it. Men are upfront about these things.'

Sarnicki warned, 'Adam, this isn't helping.'

'I think it is helping,' said Claire. 'It shows us exactly what he thinks about women. Are you implying, Adam, that we're all liars?'

'Now this really isn't helping,' said Sarnicki.

'She's putting words in my mouth! I didn't send those letters, and neither did Paul! Why should we? Everyone in town's already heard the gossip!'

'I'm cutting off this meeting *now*,' said Sarnicki, banging on the table for silence.

That's when they all heard the announcement over the hospital address system. It was barely audible through the closed doors of the meeting room.

'Code blue, ICU. Code blue, ICU.'

Instantly Claire shot to her feet. She had a stroke patient in the ICU.

She bolted out of the meeting room and ran for

the stairwell. Two flights up, she stepped into the intensive care unit and was relieved to see that her patient was not the one being coded. The crisis was in cubicle six, where a crowd of personnel had massed around the doorway.

They parted to let Claire enter.

The first thing she noticed was the smell. It was the odor of smoke and singed hair, and it came from the massive, soot-streaked man lying in the bed. McNally from the ER was crouched behind the patient's head, trying without success to insert an endotracheal tube. Claire looked up at the heart monitor.

The rhythm was sinus bradycardia. The patient's heart was beating, but slowly.

'Does he have a blood pressure?' she asked.

'I think I'm getting a systolic of ninety,' said a nurse. 'He's so big, I'm having trouble hearing it.'

'I can't get him intubated!' said McNally. 'Go ahead, bag him again.'

The respiratory tech clapped an oxygen mask on the patient's face and squeezed the reservoir bag, forcing oxygen into the lungs.

'His neck's so short and fat I can't even see the vocal cords,' said McNally.

'Anesthesia's coming in from home,' a nurse said. 'Should I also call a surgeon?'

'Yeah, call him. This one's gonna need an emergency tracheotomy.' He looked at Claire. 'Unless you think you can intubate him.'

She doubted she could, but she was willing to try.

Heart pounding, she circled around to the patient's head and was about to insert the laryngoscope into his mouth when she noticed the man's eyelids were flickering.

She straightened in surprise. 'He's conscious.'

'What?'

'I think he's awake!'

'Then why isn't he breathing?'

'Bag him again!' said Claire, stepping aside to let the respiratory tech back in. As the mask was replaced, as more oxygen was forced into the man's lungs, Claire swiftly reviewed the situation. The man's eyelids were indeed twitching, as though he was struggling to open them. Yet he was not breathing, and his limbs remained flaccid.

'What's the history?' she asked.

'Came in through the ER this afternoon,' said McNally. 'He's a volunteer fireman who collapsed at the scene. We don't know if it was smoke inhalation or a cardiac event – they had to drag him out of the building. We admitted him for superficial burns and a possible MI.'

'He's been doing fine up here,' an ICU nurse said. 'In fact, he was talking to me just a little while ago. I gave him his dose of gentamicin and he suddenly went bradycardic. That's when I realized he'd stopped breathing.'

'Why's he getting gentamicin?' asked Claire.

'The burns. One of the wounds got pretty contaminated.'

'Look, we can't keep bagging him all night,' said McNally. 'Did you call the surgeon?'

'Done,' a nurse answered.

'Then let's get him prepped for the tracheotomy.'

Claire said, 'He may not need one, Gordon.'

McNally looked skeptical. 'I couldn't get that ET tube in. Can you?'

'Let's try something else first.' Claire turned to the nurse. 'Give him an amp of calcium chloride, IV.'

The nurse glanced questioningly at McNally, who shook his head in puzzlement.

'Why on earth are you giving calcium?' he asked.

'Just before he stopped breathing,' said Claire, 'he got the antibiotic, right?'

'Yeah, for the open burn wound.'

'Then he had the respiratory arrest. But he *hasn't lost consciousness*. I think he's still awake. What does that mean?'

Suddenly McNally understood. 'Neuromuscular paralysis. From the gentamicin?'

She nodded. 'I've never seen it happen, but it's been reported. And it's reversed by calcium.'

'I'm giving the calcium chloride now,' said the nurse.

Everyone watched. The prolonged silence was broken only by the intermittent whoosh of oxygen being bagged through the mask. The patient's eyelids responded first. Slowly they fluttered open, and he looked up, struggling to focus on Claire's face.

'He's moving air!' said the respiratory tech.

Seconds later, the patient coughed, took a noisy breath, and coughed again. He reached up and tried to push away the mask.

'I think he wants to talk,' said Claire. 'Let him speak.'

The patient responded with a look of profound relief as the mask was removed from his face.

'Sir, did you want to say something?' Claire asked.

The man nodded. Everyone leaned forward, eager to hear his first words.

'Please,' he whispered.

'Yes?' prompted Claire.

'Let's not . . . do that . . . again.'

As laughter broke out all around her, Claire patted the man on the shoulder. Then she looked at the nurses. 'I think we can cancel the tracheotomy.'

'I'm glad someone around here still has a sense of humor,' McNally said as he and Claire walked out of the cubicle a few minutes later. 'It's been pretty grim recently.' He paused in the nurses' station and looked at the bank of monitors. 'I don't know where we're going to put anyone else.'

Claire was startled to see eight cardiac rhythms tracing across the screens. She swung around, her gaze sweeping the ICU in disbelief.

Every bed was filled.

'What on earth has been going on?' said Claire. 'When I made rounds this morning, there was only my one patient in here.'

'It started on my shift. First a little girl with a skull fracture. Then a wreck up on Barnstown Road. Then some nutty kid sets his house on fire.' McNally shook his head. 'It's been going nonstop in the ER all day, and the patients still keep coming in.'

Over the hospital address system, they heard the page: 'Dr McNally to the ER. Dr McNally to the ER.'

He sighed and turned to leave. 'It must be the full moon.'

Noah shed his jacket and lay it across the boulder. The granite felt warm, a day's worth of sunshine radiating back from the stone. Turning, he squinted across the lake. The afternoon was windless, the water a glassy, brilliant mirror reflecting sky and leafless trees.

'I wish it was summer again,' said Amelia.

He looked up at her. She was perched on the highest rock, chin resting on her blue-jeaned knees. Her blond hair was tucked behind one ear, revealing the streak of healing flesh on her temple. He wondered if she'd have a scar, and almost wished there would be one – just a small scar, so she would never forget him. Every morning, looking in her mirror, she'd see that faint trace of the bullet and would remember Noah Elliot.

Amelia tilted her face toward the sun. 'I wish we could skip winter. Just one winter.'

He clambered up onto her rock and sat down beside her. Not too close, not too far. Almost, but not quite, touching. 'I don't know, I'm kind of looking forward to it.'

'You haven't seen what it's like here.'

'So what is it like?'

She stared across the lake with what was almost an expression of dread. 'In a few weeks, it'll start to freeze over. First there'll be patches of ice along the shore. By December, it'll be frozen all the way across, thick enough to walk on. That's when it starts to make these sounds at night.'

'What sounds?'

'Like someone moaning. Like someone in pain.'

He started to laugh, but then she looked at him, and he fell silent.

'You don't believe me, do you?' she said. 'Sometimes I wake up at night and I think I'm having a nightmare. But it's just the lake. Making those horrible sounds.'

'How can it?'

'Mrs Horatio says . . .' She stopped, remembering that Mrs Horatio was dead. She looked back at the water. 'It's because of the ice. The water freezes and expands. It's always pushing, pushing against the banks, trying to escape, but it can't because it's trapped. That's when you hear the moaning. It's the pressure building up, building until it can't take any more. Until it finally crushes itself.' She murmured: 'No wonder it makes such terrible sounds.'

He tried to imagine what the lake would look like in January. The snow drifting against the banks, the water turned to a glaring sheet of ice. But today the sun was bright in his eyes, and with the warmth radiating off the stone, the only images that came to mind were of summer.

'Where do the frogs go?' he asked.

She turned to him. 'What?'

'The frogs. And the fish and things. I mean, the ducks all migrate, they get away from here. But what do the frogs do? Do you think they just freeze up like green Popsicles?'

He'd meant to make her laugh, and he was glad to see a smile appear on her face. 'No, they don't become Popsicles, silly. They bury themselves in the mud, way at the bottom.' She picked up a pebble and tossed it into the water. 'We used to have lots and lots of frogs around here. I remember catching bucketfuls of them when I was little.'

'Used to?'

'There aren't so many now. Mrs Horatio says . . .' Again, that pause of remembered loss. Again, that sad sigh before she continued. 'She said that it could be acid rain.'

'But I heard plenty of frogs this summer. I used to sit here and listen to them.'

'I wish I'd known about you then,' she said wistfully.

'I knew about you.'

She looked at him in puzzlement. Reddening, he averted his gaze. 'I used to watch you in school,' he said. 'Every lunchtime in the cafeteria, I'd be looking at you. I guess you didn't notice.'

He felt his face flush hotter, and he stood up, his gaze on the water, avoiding hers. 'You ever go swimming? I used to come here every day.'

'This is where all the kids hang out.'

'So where were you last summer?'

She gave a shrug. 'Ear infection. The doctor wouldn't let me swim.'

'Bummer.'

There was a silence. 'Noah?' she said.

'Yeah?'

'Do you ever feel like . . . not going home?'

'You mean like running away?'

'No, it's more like *staying* away.'

'Staying away from what?'

She didn't answer his question. When he turned to look at her, she had already risen to her feet and was hugging her arms to her chest. 'It's getting cold.'

Suddenly he too noticed the chill. Only the rock retained any warmth, and he could feel it quickly dissipating as the sun dropped behind the trees.

The surface of the water rippled, then flattened to black glass. The lake seemed alive at that moment, a single fluid organism. He wondered if everything she'd said about the lake was true, if it really did moan on winter nights. He supposed it could happen. Water expands as it freezes – a scientific fact. The ice would solidify at the surface first, a fine crust that slowly thickens through the dark months of winter, layer building upon layer. And far below, deep in the bottom mud, the frogs would burrow with nowhere else to go. They would be trapped beneath the ice. Entombed.

Sweat filmed Claire's face as she strained at the oars. She felt them drag evenly through the water, felt the satisfying lurch of the rowboat as it cut across the surface of the lake. Over the months her rowing had grown smoothly efficient. Back in May, when she'd first dipped oars into water, it had been a humbling experience. One or both oars would whip wildly across the water, throwing up spray, or she'd favor one oar over the other and would end up rowing in circles. Control was the key. Power, perfectly balanced. Fluid movements, gliding, not splashing.

She had it down, now.

She rowed to the center of the lake. There she raised the oars, lay them in the boat, and sat back to drift. The sun had just dropped behind the trees, and she knew the sweat would soon feel like rime against her skin, but for these few moments, while she was still flushed from exertion, she enjoyed dusk without noticing its chill. The water rippled, black as oil. On the opposite shore, she saw the lights of houses where suppers were being prepared, where families came together in warm and complete universes. *The way we three used to be when you were alive, Peter. Not shattered, but whole.*

She stared across at the glow of those houses, her longing for Peter suddenly so overwhelming it hurt her to breathe. On summer days, when they had gone rowing in their neighborhood pond, Peter had always been the one to wield the oars. Claire would perch in the bow and admire his graceful rhythm, the way his muscles stood out and his smiling face glowed with perspiration. She'd been the pampered passenger, magically ferried across the water by her lover.

She listened to the ripples slap the hull, and could almost imagine Peter was sitting across from her now, his gaze focused sadly on hers. *You have to learn to row alone, Claire. You must be the one to guide the boat.*

How can I, Peter? I'm already foundering. Someone's trying to drive me from this place. And Noah, our darling Noah, has grown so distant.

She felt tears chilling on her face. Felt his presence so clearly, she thought if she could just reach out, he'd be there. Warm and alive, flesh and blood.

But he wasn't there, and she was alone in the boat.

She continued to drift, nudged toward land by the wind. Overhead the stars grew brilliant. Now the boat slowly rotated and she saw, in the distance, the northern shoreline, where seasonal cottages stood dark and boarded up for the winter.

A sudden splash made her sit up in surprise. Turning, she stared at the nearby shore, and made out a man's silhouette. He was standing on the bank, his thin frame slightly bent, as though peering down at the water. He jerked and lunged sideways. There was another loud splash, and his silhouette dropped from sight. It could be only one person.

Quickly Claire wiped the tears from her face and called out: 'Dr Tutwiler? Are you all right?'

The man's head popped back up into view. 'Who's there?'

'Claire Elliot. I thought you'd fallen in the water.'

He finally seemed to locate her in the gloom and he gave a wave. She had met the wetlands biologist only a few weeks before, soon after he'd moved into the Alford cottage, which he was renting for the month. They'd both been rowing on the lake that morning, and as their boats drifted past each other through the mist, they had waved in greeting. Ever since, whenever she rowed past his cottage, they would say hello. Sometimes he'd bring out jars with the latest addition to his amphibian collection. *The frog dweeb*, Noah called him.

Her boat drifted closer to shore, and she saw Max's glass jars lined up on the bank. 'How is your frog collection coming?' she asked.

'It's getting too cold now. They're all heading for deep water.'

'Have you found any more six-legged specimens?'

'One this week. It really makes me worry about this lake.'

Now her rowboat had reached the shore and bumped up against the mud. Max stood above her, a spindly silhouette, moonlight reflecting off his glasses.

'It's happening in all these northern lakes,' he said. 'Amphibian deformities. A massive die-off.'

'How did the lake samples turn out? The ones you collected last week?'

'I'm still waiting for the results. It can take months.' He paused, glancing around at the sudden sound of chirping. 'What's that?'

Claire sighed. 'My beeper.' She'd almost forgotten it was still clipped to her belt. She saw a local exchange on the luminous readout.

'It's a long row back to your house,' he said. 'Why don't you use my telephone?'

She made the call from his kitchen, the whole time staring at the glass jars sitting on his countertop. These were not cucumbers floating in brine. She picked up a jar and saw an eye staring back at her. The frog was strangely pale, the color of human flesh, mottled with purplish blotches. Both hind legs branched into two, forming four separate flippers. She looked at the label: 'Locust Lake. November 10.' Shuddering, she put down the jar.

On the phone, a woman answered, her voice slurred, obviously drunk. 'Hello? Who's this calling?'

'This is Dr Elliot. Did you page me?' Claire winced as the receiver was slammed down. She heard footsteps, then recognized Lincoln Kelly's voice, speaking to the woman.

'Doreen, can I have my phone?'

'Who are all these women calling you?'

'Give me the phone.'

'You're not sick. Why's the doctor calling?'

'Is that Claire Elliot?'

'Oh, it's *Claire* now. First names!'

'Doreen, I'm going to drive you home in a minute. Now let me speak to her.'

At last he came on the line, sounding embarrassed. 'Claire, are you still there?'

'I'm here.'

'Look, I'm sorry about what just happened.'

'Don't worry about it,' she said, and thought: *You have enough things in your life to worry about.*

'Lucy Overlock suggested I give you a call. She's finished the dig.'

'Any interesting conclusions?'

'I think you've already heard most of it. The burial's at least a hundred years old. The remains were of two children. Both of them had obvious signs of trauma.'

'So it was an old homicide.'

'Apparently. She's presenting the details tomorrow, to her undergraduate class. It may be more than you care to hear, but she thought I should invite you. Since you're the one who found the first bone.'

'Where's the class held?'

'In the museum lab, at Orono. I'm driving there, if you'd care to ride with me. I'll leave around noon.'

In the background, Doreen whined, 'But tomorrow's Saturday! Since when do you work on Saturday?'

'Doreen, let me finish this call.'

'That's how it always is! You're always too busy. Never here for me –'

'Put on your coat, and get in the car. I'll take you home.'

'Hell, I can drive myself.' A door slammed shut.

'Doreen!' said Lincoln. 'Give me back those car keys! Doreen!' His voice came back on the line, hurried. Frantic. 'I have to go. Will I see you tomorrow?'

'Noon. I'll be waiting.'

8

'Doreen tries,' said Lincoln, his gaze fixed on the road. 'She really does. But it's not easy for her.'

'Or for you either, I imagine,' said Claire.

'No, it's been hard all around. It has been for years.'

It had been raining when they left Tranquility. Now the rain was thickening to sleet, and they heard it tick-ticking against the windshield. The road had turned treacherous as the temperature dropped to that dangerous transition between freeze and thaw, the blacktop collecting a frosting of watery ice. She was glad Lincoln was behind the wheel, not her. A man who has lived forty-five winters in this climate knows enough to respect its perils.

He reached down to turn up the defroster and streaks of condensation began to clear from the glass.

'We've been separated two years,' he said. 'The

problem is, she just can't let go. And I don't have the heart to force it.'

They both tensed as the car ahead suddenly braked and began to fishtail, sliding from one side of the road to the other. It barely pulled out of its skid in time to avoid an oncoming truck.

Claire sat back, her heart pounding. 'Jesus.'

'Everyone's driving too damn fast.'

'Do you think we should turn around and go home?'

'We're more than halfway there. Might as well keep going. Or do you want to call it off?'

She swallowed. 'I'm okay with this if you are.'

'We'll just take our time. It means we'll probably be home late.' He glanced at her. 'What about Noah?'

'He's pretty self-sufficient these days. I'm sure he'll be fine.'

Lincoln nodded. 'He seems like a great kid.'

'Yes he is,' she said. And amended her answer with a rueful smile. 'Most of the time.'

'Guess it's not as easy as it looks,' said Lincoln. 'I hear that all the time from parents. That raising a kid is the hardest job in the world.'

'And it's a hundred times harder when you're doing it alone.'

'So where's Noah's dad?'

Claire paused. The answer to that question almost had to be forced out. 'He died. Two years ago.' She barely registered his murmured response of, 'I'm sorry.' For a moment, the only sound was the windshield wiper scraping sleet from the glass. Two years, and she still had trouble talking about it. She still couldn't bring herself to use the word *widow*. Women should not be made widows at the age of thirty-eight.

And laughing, loving, thirty-nine-year-old men should not die of lymphoma.

Through the freezing mist, she saw emergency lights flashing ahead. An accident. Yet she felt strangely safe riding in this man's car. Protected and insulated from harm. They inched past a string of emergency vehicles: two police cruisers, a tow truck, and an ambulance. A Ford Bronco had slid off the road and now lay on its side, glistening with rime. They drove past it in silence, both of them sobered by that stark reminder of how quickly life can be altered. Ended. It was one more gloomy note to an already depressing day.

Lucy Overlock arrived late to her own class. Fifteen minutes after her two graduate and ten undergraduate students stood assembled in the university museum's basement lab, Lucy herself strode in, her slicker dripping. 'With this weather, I probably should have canceled,' she said. 'I'm glad you all made it anyway.' She hung up her rain gear, under which she wore her usual jeans and flannel shirt, practical attire considering their surroundings. The museum basement was both dank and dusty, a cluttered cavern that smelled like the artifacts it contained. Along both walls were shelves lined with hundreds of wooden boxes, contents labeled in faded type-script: 'Stonington #11: shell implements, arrow-heads, miscellaneous.' 'Pittsfield #32: partial skel-etal remains, adult male.'

At the center of the room, on a broad work table draped with a plastic tarpaulin, lay the new additions to this neatly catalogued charnel house.

Lucy flicked on a wall switch. Fluorescent lamps hummed on, their unnatural glare illuminating the table. Claire and Lincoln joined the circle of students. The lights were unforgiving, casting the faces around the table in harsh relief.

Lucy removed the tarp.

The skeletal remains of the two children had been laid out side by side, the bones placed in their approximate anatomical positions. One skeleton was missing its rib cage, one lower leg, and the right upper extremity. The other skeleton appeared to be largely intact except for the missing small bones of the hands.

Lucy took her position at the head of the table, near the skulls. 'What we have here is a sampled assemblage of human remains from dig number seventy-two at the southern end of Locust Lake. The dig was completed yesterday. For reference purposes, I've tacked the site map over there, on the wall. As you can see, the site is located right on the edge of the Meegawki Stream. That area had heavy rains and flooding this past spring, which is probably the reason this gravesite became exposed.' She looked down at the table. 'So, let's begin. First, I want all of you to examine the remains. Feel free to pick them up, look them over carefully. Ask any questions you have about the site. Then let's hear your conclusions as to age, race, and length of burial. Those of you who took part in the dig – please hold your tongues. Let's see what the others can deduce on their own.'

One of the students reached for a skull.

Lucy stepped back and quietly circled the table, sometimes glancing over her students' shoulders to watch them work. This assembly made Claire think of some grotesque dining ritual: the remains laid out like a feast on the table, all those eager hands reaching for the bones, turning them under the light, passing them to other hands. At first there was no conversation, the silence broken only by the occasional whisk of a tape measure being extended, retracted.

One of the skulls, missing its mandible, was handed to Claire.

The last time she'd held a human skull was in medical school. She rotated it beneath the light. Once she could name every foramen, every protuberance, but like so many other facts crammed into her memory during four years of training, those anatomical names had been forgotten, displaced by more practical data like billing codes and hospital phone numbers. She turned the skull upside down and saw that the upper teeth were still in place. The third molars had not yet erupted. *A child's mouth.*

Gently she set down the skull, shaken by the reality of what she'd just cradled in her hands. She thought of Noah at age nine, his hair a whorl of dark curls, his face silky smooth against hers, and she stared at that skull of a child whose flesh had long since rotted away.

She was suddenly aware of Lincoln's hand, resting on her shoulder. 'You all right?' he asked, and she nodded. His gaze was sad, almost mournful under the harsh lights. Are we the only ones haunted by this child's life? she wondered. The only ones who see more than an empty shell of calcium and phosphate?

One of the female students, a younger, slimmer version of Lucy, asked the first question. 'Was this a coffin burial? And was the terrain field or woods?'

'The terrain was moderately wooded, all new growth,' answered Lucy. 'We did find iron nails and fragments of the coffin, but the wood was mostly rotted away.'

'And the soil?' a male student asked.

'Clay, moderately saturated. Why do you ask?'

'A high clay content helps preserve remains.'

'Correct. What other factors affect the preservation of remains?' Lucy glanced around the table. Her students responded with an eagerness that struck Claire as almost unseemly. They were so focused on mineralized remains, they had forgotten

163

what these bones represented. Living, laughing children.

'Soil compaction – moisture –'

'Ambient temperature.'

'Carnivores.'

'Depth of burial. Whether it's exposed to sunlight.'

'The age at time of death.'

Lucy's gaze shot to the student who'd spoken. It was the young Lucy clone, also dressed in jeans and a plaid shirt. 'How does the deceased's age affect the bony remains?'

'The skulls of young adults remain intact longer than skulls of elderly people, perhaps because of heavier mineralization.'

'That doesn't tell me how long these particular skeletons have been lying in the ground. When did these individuals die?'

There was silence.

Lucy did not seem disappointed by their lack of response. 'The correct answer,' she said, 'is: We can't tell. After a hundred years, some skeletons may crumble to dust, while others will show almost no weathering. But we can still draw a number of conclusions.' She reached across the table and picked up a tibia. 'Note the flaking and peeling in some of the long bones, where circumferential lamellar bone has natural cleavage lines. What does this indicate to you?'

'Changing wet and dry periods,' said the Lucy clone.

'Right. These remains were temporarily protected by the coffin. But then the coffin rotted, and the bones were exposed to water, especially near that streambed.' She glanced at a young man Claire recognized as one of the grad students who'd helped excavate the site. With his long blond hair tied back in a ponytail, and three gold earrings in one ear, he could easily have passed for a rogue sailor in an earlier century. The one incongruous note to his appearance was his scholarly wire-rim spectacles. 'Vince,' said Lucy, 'tell us about the flood data for that area.'

'I've searched back as far as the records go, to the 1920s,' said Vince. 'There were two episodes of catastrophic flooding: in the spring of 1946, and then again, this past spring, when the Locust River overflowed its banks. I assume that's how this burial site became exposed. Erosion of the Meegawki streambed due to heavy rain.'

'So we have two recorded periods of site saturation, followed by drier years, which have caused this flaking and peeling of cortical bone.' Lucy set down the tibia and picked up the femur. 'And now for the most interesting finding of all. I'm referring to this gash here, on the back of the femoral shaft. It looks like a cut mark, but the bone is so badly weathered, the gash has lost its definition. So we can't tell if there's been a green bone response.' She noticed Lincoln's questioning look. 'A green bone response is what happens when living bone bends or twists while being stabbed. It tells you whether the bone was cut postmortem or antemortem.'

'And you can't tell from this bone?'

'No. It's been exposed too long to the elements.'

'So how can you determine if this was a homicide?'

'We have to turn our attention to the other bones. And here we'll find your answer.' She reached for a small paper bag. Tipping it sideways, she emptied the contents on the table.

Small bones clattered out like gray dice.

'The carpals,' she said. 'These are from the right hand. Carpals are quite dense – they don't disintegrate as quickly as other bones. These were found buried deep and packed in a dense clump of clay, which further preserved them.' She began to shuffle through the carpals like a seamstress searching for just the right button. 'Here,' she said, choosing one pebble and holding it up to the light.

The gash was immediately apparent, and so deep it had nearly cleaved the bone in two.

'This is a defense injury,' said Lucy. 'This child – let's call her a girl – raised her arms to defend herself against her attacker. The blade stabbed her in the hand – deeply enough to almost split the carpal bone. The girl is only eight or nine and rather small in stature, so she can hardly fight back. And whoever plunged that knife in is quite strong – strong enough to stab right through her hand.

'The girl turns. Maybe the blade is still lodged in her flesh, or maybe the attacker has pulled it out and is preparing to stab again. The girl would try to run away, but she is pursued. Then she stumbles, or he brings her down, and she falls to the ground, prone. I assume it's prone, because there are cut marks on the thoracic vertebrae, a broad blade, possibly a hatchet, sinking in from behind. There is also the cut mark in the femur – a blow to the back of the thigh, which means she's lying on the ground now. None of these injuries are necessarily fatal. If she is still alive, she's bleeding heavily. What happens next, we don't know, because the bones don't tell us. What we do know is that she is lying face down on the ground and she can't run, she can't defend herself. And someone has just sunk a hatchet or an ax into her thigh.' Gently she placed the carpal bone on the table. It was only the size of a pebble, the broken remnant of a terrible death. 'That's what these bones tell me.'

For a moment no one spoke. Then Claire said, softly: 'What happened to the other child?'

Lucy seemed to rouse herself from a trance, and she looked at the second skull. 'This was a child of similar age. Many of its bones are missing, and those we do have are severely weathered, but I can tell you this much: he – or she – suffered a crushing and probably fatal blow to the skull. These two children were buried together, in the same coffin. I suspect they died during the same attack.'

'There must be records of it,' said Lincoln. 'Some old news account of who these children were.'

'As a matter of fact, we do know their names.' It was Vince talking, the ponytailed grad student. 'Because of the date on a coin found in the same soil stratum, we knew their deaths occurred sometime after 1885. I searched the county deed records and learned that a family by the name of Gow owned that entire tract of land extending along the southern curve of Locust Lake. These bones are the mortal remains of Joseph and Jennie Gow, siblings, ages eight and ten.' Vince gave a sheepish grin. 'It seems that what we've dug up here, folks, is the Gow family cemetery.'

This revelation did not strike Claire as a particularly humorous revelation, and she was disturbed by the fact several of the students laughed.

'Because it was a coffin burial,' explained Lucy, 'we suspected this might be a family cemetery. I'm afraid we've disturbed their final resting place.'

'Then you know how these children died?' asked Claire.

'News accounts are hard to come by, because that particular area was sparsely populated at the time,' said Vince. 'What we do have available are the county death records. The Gow children's deaths were both recorded on the same day: November fifteenth, 1887. Along with the deaths of three other members of their family.'

There was a moment of horrified silence.

'Are you saying all five people died on the *same* day?' asked Claire.

Vince nodded. 'It appears this family was massacred.'

9

Carrot sticks and boiled potatoes and a microscopic sliver of chicken breast.

Louise Knowlton gazed down at the barren plate she'd just set before her son and she ached with maternal guilt. She was starving her own child. She saw it in his face, in those hungry eyes, the weak slump of his shoulders. Sixteen hundred calories a day! How could anyone survive on that! Barry had indeed lost weight, but at what price? He was but a shadow of his formerly robust 265-pound self, and even though she knew he needed to lose weight, it was clear to her, the one person in the world who knew him best, that her darling child was suffering.

She sat down at her own plate, on which she'd piled fried chicken and buttered biscuits. A solid, healthy meal for a cold night. Looking across the table, she met her husband's gaze. Mel was silently shaking his head. He couldn't stand it either, watching their son go hungry.

'Barry, sweetie, why don't you have just one biscuit?' offered Louise.

'No, Mom.'

'It's not so many calories. You can scrape off the gravy.'

'I don't want any.'

'Look how flaky they are! It's that recipe from Barbara Perry's mom. It's the bacon fat that makes them so good. One little bite, Barry. Just try one bite!' She held out a steaming biscuit to his lips. She could not stop herself, could not suppress the impulse, reinforced by fourteen years of motherhood, to feed that pink and needy mouth. This was more than food; this was love, in the shape of a crusty biscuit dripping butter onto her fingers. She waited for him to accept the offering.

'I told you, I don't want any!' he yelled.

It was as shocking as a slap in the face. Louise sat back, stunned. The biscuit tumbled from her fingers and plopped into the lake of gravy glistening on her plate.

'Barry,' said his father.

'She's always shoving food at me! No wonder I look like this! Look at both of you!'

'Your mother loves you. Look how you've hurt her feelings.'

Louise sat with trembling lips, trying not to cry. She gazed down at the bountiful dinner she had set on the table. It represented two hours of work in the kitchen, a labor of love, and oh how she loved her son! Now she saw the meal for what it

171

was: the wasted efforts of a fat and stupid mother. She began to cry, her tears dribbling into the cream cheese mashed potatoes.

'Mom.' Barry groaned. 'Ah geez. I'm sorry.'

'Never mind.' She held up a hand to ward off his pity. 'I understand, Barry. I understand, and I won't do it again. I swear I won't.' She blotted away the tears with the napkin and for a few seconds managed to regain her dignity. 'But I try so hard and – and—' She buried her face in the napkin, her whole body quaking with the effort not to cry. It took a moment for her to realize Barry was talking to her.

'Mom. Mom?'

She gulped in a breath and forced herself to look at him.

'Can I have a biscuit?'

Wordlessly she held out the platter. She watched him take a biscuit, split it open, and slather it with butter. She held her breath as he took the first bite, as the look of bliss rippled across his face. He had craved it all along, but had denied himself the pleasure. Now he gave himself up to it, eating a second. And a third. She watched him take every bite, and she felt a mother's satisfaction, deep and primal.

Noah leaned against the side of the school building, smoking a cigarette. It had been months since he'd last lit up, and it made him cough, his lungs rebelling against the smoke. He imagined all those poisons swirling into his chest, the ones his mom was always lecturing him about, but in the general scheme of his life in this dreary town, he figured a little poison was hardly worth worrying about. He took another drag and coughed some more, not really enjoying the experience. But there wasn't much else to do between classes, not since the skateboards were banned. At least out here, standing alone by the Dumpster, no one would hassle him.

He heard the soft growl of an engine, and he glanced toward the street. A dark green car was creeping by, so slowly it barely seemed to move. The windows were too darkly tinted to see through, and Noah couldn't tell if it was a man or woman behind the wheel.

The car stopped right across the street. Somehow Noah knew the driver was staring at him, just as surely as Noah was staring back.

He dropped the cigarette and quickly crushed it under his shoe. No sense getting caught; the last thing he needed was another detention. The evidence now obliterated, he turned and brazenly faced the unseen driver. He felt a sense of victory when the car drove away.

Noah looked down at the crushed cigarette, only half smoked. What a waste. He was weighing the chances of salvaging what remained when he heard the school bell ring, signaling the end of break.

Then he heard the shouting. It came from the front of the school.

He rounded the corner of the building and saw a crowd of kids milling on the lawn, chanting: 'Cat fight! Cat fight!'

This should be something to see.

He pushed forward, trying to get a peek at the action before the teachers broke it up, and the two battling girls practically flew right into him. Noah stumbled backwards to a safer distance, shocked by the viciousness of the fight. This was worse than any brawl between two boys; this really *was* a cat fight, the girls clawing at each other's faces, yanking at hair. The shouts of the crowd rang in his ears. He looked around at the circle of spectators, and saw their frenzied faces, smelled the blood lust, strong as musk.

A strange excitement coiled inside him. He felt his hand close into a fist, felt heat rush to his face. Both the girls were bloodied now, and the sight of it enthralled him. Provoked him. He pushed forward, jostling with the crowd for a better view, and was angry when he could not get closer.

'Cat fight! Cat fight!'

He began to chant too, his excitement building with every glimpse of a bloodied face.

Then his gaze froze on Amelia, standing at the far edge of the lawn, and instantly he fell silent. She was staring at the crowd in disbelief and horror.

Shamefaced, he turned before she could see him, and he fled into the building.

In the boys' restroom, he stared at himself in

the mirror. *What happened to everyone out there?* he thought. *What happened to me?*

He splashed icy water on his face, and scarcely felt its sting.

'They were fighting over a boy,' said Fern. 'At least, that's the story I got. It started off with a few insults, and the next thing you know, they were clawing each other's faces.' She shook her head. 'After Mrs Horatio's funeral, I was hoping the kids would support each other. Stand by each other. But this is the fourth fight we've had in two days, Lincoln. I can't control them. I need a policeman to stand watch in this school.'

'Well, it seems like overkill,' he responded doubtfully, 'but I can have Floyd Spear drop in a few times during the school day, if you want.'

'No, you don't understand. We need someone here all day. I don't know what else is going to work.'

Lincoln sighed and ran his hand through his hair. It seemed to Fern that he was getting grayer every day, just as she was. This morning, she had noticed the telltale hairs sprouting among her blond ones, had realized that the face she saw in the mirror was that of a middle-aged woman. Seeing the changes in Lincoln's face, though, was somehow more painful than confronting her own aging image, because she carried such vivid memories of the man he'd been at twenty-five: dark-haired, dark-eyed, already a face of strength and character. The days before Doreen caught his eye. She regarded the deepening lines in his face and thought, as she so often did: *I could have made you so much happier than Doreen has.*

Together they walked to her office. Fourth period classes had started, and their footsteps echoed in the empty hallway. A banner sagged overhead: Harvest Dance November 20! From Mr Rubio's classroom came the sound of bored voices raised in unison: *Me llamo Pablo. Te llamas Pablo. Se llama Pablo . . .*

Her office was her private territory, and it reflected the way she lived her life, everything neat and in its place. Books lined up, spines out, no stray papers on the desk. Controlled. Children thrived on order, and Fern believed that only through absolute order could a school function properly.

'I know it's asking for a manpower commitment,' she said, 'but I want you to consider assigning a full-time officer to this school.'

'It means pulling a man off patrol, Fern, and I'm not convinced it's necessary.'

'And what are you patrolling out there? Empty roads! The trouble in this town is right here, in this building. This is where we need a policeman.'

At last he nodded. 'I'll do what I can,' he said, and stood up. His shoulders seemed to sag with the burdens they carried. All day he wrestles with the problems of this town, she thought guiltily, and he gets no praise, only demands and criticism. Then he has no one to go home to, no one to comfort him. A man who makes the mistake of marrying the wrong woman should not have to suffer for the rest of his life. Not a man as decent as Lincoln.

She walked him to the door. They were close enough to touch each other, and the temptation to reach out, to throw her arms around him, was so overwhelming she had to close her hands into fists to resist it.

'I look at what's happening,' she said, 'and I can't help but wonder what I'm doing wrong.'

'You haven't done anything wrong.'

'Six years as principal, and suddenly I'm fighting to keep order in my school. Fighting to keep my job.'

'Fern, I really think it's just a temporary reaction to the shooting. The kids need time to recover.' He gave her shoulder a reassuring pat and he turned to the door. 'It'll pass.'

Once again Claire was staring into Mairead Temple's mouth. It seemed like familiar territory to her now, the furry tongue, the tonsillar pillars, the uvula hanging down in a quivering flap of pink flesh. And that smell, like an old ashtray, the same smell that permeated Mairead's kitchen, where they were now sitting. It was Tuesday, the day Claire made house calls, and Mairead was the next to last patient on her schedule. When one's medical practice is failing, when patients are switching to other doctors, desperate measures are called for. A home visit to Mairead Temple's smoky kitchen qualified as a desperate measure. Anything to keep a patient happy.

Claire turned off her pen light. 'Your throat looks about the same to me. It's just a little red.'

'Still hurts wicked bad.'

'The culture came back negative.'

'You mean I don't get any more penicillin?'

'I'm sorry, but I can't justify it.'

Mairead clacked her dentures together and glared at Claire with pale eyes. 'What kinda treatment is that?'

'Well, I'll tell you, Mairead, the best treatment is prevention.'

'So?'

'So . . .' Claire eyed the pack of menthol cigarettes lying on the kitchen table. In the advertisements, it was a brand usually associated with slim sophisticates, women in slinky gowns trailing furs and men. 'I think it's time for you to quit smoking.'

'What's wrong with penicillin?'

Claire ignored the question, turning her attention instead to the wood-burning stove in the center of the overheated kitchen. 'That's not good for your throat, either. It dries out the air and fills it with smoke and irritants. You do have an oil furnace, don't you?'

'Wood's cheaper.'

'You'd feel better.'

'I get the wood free, from my nephew.'

'All right,' sighed Claire. 'So how about just quitting the cigarettes?'

'How about the penicillin?'

They looked at each other, budding enemies over a handful of three-buck pills.

In the end, Claire surrendered. She didn't have the stamina for an argument this late in the afternoon, not with someone as mulish as Mairead Temple. *Just this once* was what she told herself as she rummaged for the appropriate antibiotic samples.

Mairead crossed to the woodstove and threw in another log. Smoke puffed out, adding to the general haze hanging over the room.

Even Claire's throat was beginning to feel sore.

Mairead picked up a pair of tongs and poked at the logs on the fire. 'I heard more talk about those bones,' she said.

Claire was still counting out sample tablets. Only when she looked up did she see Mairead was studying her, eyes strangely alert. Feral.

Mairead turned and slapped the stove's cast-iron door shut. 'Old bones, that's what I heard.'

'Yes, they are.'

'How old?' The pale eyes were once again locked on hers.

'A hundred years, maybe more.'

'They sure about that?'

'I believe they're quite sure. Why?'

The unsettling gaze slid away from hers again. 'You never know what goes on around these parts. No big surprise they found the bones on her property. You know what she is, don't you? She's not the only one around here, either. Last Halloween, they lit themselves a big bonfire, over in Warren Emerson's cornfield. That Emerson, he's another one.'

'Another what?'

'What do you call 'em when they're men? A warlock.'

Claire burst out laughing. It was the wrong thing to do.

'You go ask around town,' insisted Mairead, now angry. 'They'll all tell you there was a bonfire up in Emerson's field that night. And right afterwards, those kids caused all that trouble in town.'

'It happens everywhere. Kids always get rowdy on Halloween.'

'It's their holy night. Their black Christmas.'

Looking into the other woman's eyes, Claire realized she didn't like Mairead Temple. 'Everyone is entitled to their beliefs. As long as no one gets hurt.'

'Well, that's the question, isn't it? We just don't know. Look what's happened around here since then.'

Abruptly Claire shut her medical bag and stood up. 'Rachel Sorkin minds her own business, Mairead. I think everyone else in this town should do likewise.'

The bones again, thought Claire as she drove to her last house call of the day. Everyone wants to know about the bones. Whom they belonged to, when they were buried. And today a new question, one that had taken her by surprise: why were they found in Rachel Sorkin's yard.

It's their holy night, their black Christmas.

In Mairead's kitchen, Claire had laughed. Now, driving through the deepening gloom, she found nothing humorous about the conversation. Rachel Sorkin was the outsider, the black-haired woman from away who lived alone by the lake. That's how it had always been through the ages; the young woman alone was an object of suspicion, the subject of gossip. In a small town she is the anomaly that requires explanation. She is the town siren, the irresistible temptation for otherwise virtuous husbands. Or she is the shrew no man wants to marry, or the twisted female with unnatural desires. And if one is also attractive, like Rachel, or exotic, or peculiar of taste and whim, then suspicion is mixed with fascination. Fascination which could turn to obsession for someone like Mairead Temple, who brooded all day in her grim kitchen, smoking cigarettes that promised glamor but delivered bronchitis and yellow teeth. Rachel did not have yellow teeth. Rachel was beautiful and unencumbered and a little eccentric.

Rachel must therefore be a witch.

Since Warren Emerson had lit a bonfire in his cornfield on Halloween night, he must be a witch as well.

Though dusk had not yet fallen, Claire turned on her headlights and drew some measure of reassurance from the glow of her dashboard. This time of year, she thought, brings out irrational fears in all of us. And the season hasn't yet reached its darkest point. As the nights grow longer and the first heavy snows begin to fall, cutting off all access to the outside world, this bleak and lonely landscape becomes our universe. And it's an unforgiving one, where a patch of black ice, and a night's bitter cold, can act as both judge and executioner.

She arrived at a rural mailbox labeled 'Braxton' and turned onto the dirt road. Her patient's house stood surrounded by neglected fields. The clap-boards were stripped bare, the wood weathered to silver. On the front porch, half a cord of firewood was stacked up precariously against the crooked railing. It would all come tumbling down one of these days – the railing, the porch, the house itself. Divorced, forty-one-year-old Faye Braxton, who lived here with her two children, was as structurally unsound as her dwelling. Both her hips had been destroyed by rheumatoid arthritis, and she could not even step out of this dismal home without assistance.

Carrying her medical bag, Claire climbed the steps to the front porch. Only then did she realize something was not right.

It was thirty-five degrees outside, and the front door was open.

She poked her head inside the house and called into the gloom: 'Mrs Braxton?' She heard a shutter banging in the wind. And she heard something else – the faint patter of footsteps, running in an upstairs room. One of the children?

Claire stepped into the house and closed the door against the cold. No lamps were on, and the fading daylight glowed dimly through thin living room curtains. She felt her way down the hall, searching for the light switch. At last she found it and flicked it on.

At her feet, a naked Barbie doll lay on the threadbare runner. Claire reached down for it. 'Mrs Braxton? It's Dr Elliot.'

Her announcement was met with silence.

She looked down at the Barbie doll and saw that half of its blond hair had been cut away. When she had last visited this house, three weeks ago, she had seen Faye Braxton's seven-year-old daughter Kitty clutching a Barbie doll like this one. It had been dressed in a pink prom gown and the long blond hair had been tied back with a scrap of green rickrack.

A chill slithered up her spine.

She heard it again: the rapid *thump-thump-thump* of footsteps moving across the ceiling. She looked up toward the stairs, toward the second floor. Someone was home, yet the heat was off, the house was freezing, and none of the lights were on.

Slowly she backed away, then turned and fled the house.

Sitting in her car, she used her cell phone to call the police.

Officer Mark Dolan answered.

'This is Dr Elliot. I'm at the Braxton residence. Something's wrong here.'

'What do you mean, Dr Elliot?'

'I found the front door open, and there's no heat on, no lights. But I heard someone moving around upstairs.'

'Is the family home? Have you checked?'

'I'd rather not go upstairs.'

'All you'd have to do is take a look. We're already swamped with calls, and I don't know when I can get a man over there.'

'Look, could you just send someone? I'm telling you, it doesn't feel right.'

Officer Dolan gave a loud sigh. She could almost see him at his desk, rolling his eyes in derision. Now that she had actually voiced her fears, they did not seem significant. Perhaps she hadn't heard footsteps at all, but merely that loose shutter swinging in the wind. Perhaps the family was away. The police will arrive and find nothing, she thought, and tomorrow the whole town will be laughing at the cowardly doctor. Her reputation had already suffered enough blows this week.

'Lincoln's somewhere over that way,' Dolan finally said. 'I'll ask him to swing by when he gets the chance.'

She hung up, already regretting the call. Stepping out of the car again, she looked up at the house. Dusk had thickened to night. I'll cancel the

184

dispatch and save myself the embarrassment, she thought. She went back into the house.

Standing at the foot of the stairs, she gazed up toward the second-floor landing, but heard no sound from above. She grasped the banister. It was oak, solid and reassuring. She began to climb, driven upward by pride, by grim determination not to be the butt of the latest town joke.

On the second floor, she turned on the light switch and confronted a narrow hallway, the walls dingy from little hands trailing smudges. She poked her head into the first room on the right.

It was Kitty's bedroom. Ballerinas danced across the curtains. Scattered on the bed were girl things: plastic barrettes, a red sweater embroidered with snowflakes, a child's backpack in pink and purple. On the floor was Kitty's beloved Barbie doll collection. But these were not pampered recipients of a young girl's love. These dolls had been viciously abused, their clothes ripped to shreds, their limbs splayed out as though in horror. A single doll's head, torn from its body, stared up at her with bright blue eyes.

The chill was back in her spine.

She backed into the hall, and her gaze suddenly shifted to another doorway, to the unlit room beyond. Something shimmered in the darkness, a strange luminescence, like the green glow of a watch face. She stepped into the room and turned on the light. The green glow vanished. She was in a boy's room, untidy, with books

185

and dirty socks scattered on the bed and floor. A rubbish can overflowed with crumpled papers and Coke cans. It was the typical disarray left by a thirteen-year-old. She turned off the light.

And saw it again – the green glow. It came from the bed.

She stared down at the pillow, splashed with a bright luminescence, and touched the linen; it was cool, but not damp. Now she noticed the faint streaks of luminescence on the wall as well, just above the bed, and one brilliant emerald splash on the sheet.

Thump, thump, thump. Her gaze shot upward, and she heard a whimper, a child's soft cry.

The attic. The children were in the attic.

She left the boy's room, stumbling over a tennis shoe as she reemerged in the hallway. The attic stairs were steep and narrow; she had to grasp the flimsy handrail as she climbed. When she reached the top, she was standing in impenetrable darkness.

She took a step forward, and brushed past a hanging light chain. One tug, and the bare lightbulb came on, its dim glow illuminating only a small circle of the attic. In the shadowy periphery she could make out a jumble of old furniture and cardboard boxes. A coat rack, its prongs wide as elk's antlers, cast a threatening shadow across the floor.

Next to one of the boxes, something moved.

Quickly she shoved aside the box. Behind it,

curled up on a bundle of old coats, was seven-year-old Kitty. The girl's skin felt icy, but she was still alive, her throat issuing soft little moans with every breath. Claire reached down to pick her up, and realized the girl's clothes were saturated. In horror she lifted her glistening hand to the light.

Blood.

The only warning she had was the creak of the floorboard. *Someone is standing behind me.*

Claire turned just as the shadow exploded toward her. The impact slammed hard against her chest and she flew backwards, pinned under the weight of her attacker. Claws grappled at her throat. She tried to tear them away, frantically thrashing left, then right, a dozen shadowy images swirling before her eyes. The coat rack slammed to the floor. Under the swaying light, she caught sight of her attacker's face.

The boy.

He tightened his grip around her throat, and as her vision began to blacken, she saw his lips curl back, his eyes narrow to angry slits.

She clawed at his eye. Shrieking, the boy released her, stumbling away. She scrambled to her feet just as the boy lunged at her again. She dodged sideways and he flew past her and landed among the cardboard boxes, scattering books and tools across the floor.

They both spotted the screwdriver at the same time.

Simultaneously they sprang toward it, but he

was closer. He snatched it up and brought it high over his head. As it came stabbing down, she raised both hands to catch the boy's wrist. His strength shocked her. She was forced down to her knees. The blade of the screwdriver wavered closer, even as she fought to keep it at bay.

Then, through the roar of her own pulse, she heard a voice calling her name. She screamed out: 'Help me!'

Footsteps thudded up the stairs. Suddenly the weapon was no longer stabbing toward her. The boy pivoted, his weapon redirected as Lincoln flew toward him. She saw the boy fall backwards, sprawling to the floor. Saw the boy and Lincoln rolling over and over in a blur of thrashing limbs, furniture and boxes scattering around them. The screwdriver skittered off into the shadows. Lincoln pinned the boy facedown on the floorboards and Claire heard the metallic click of handcuffs snapping shut. Even then, the boy continued to struggle, kicking out blindly. Lincoln dragged him over to an attic support post and tightly lashed him there with his belt.

When at last he turned to Claire, he was breathing hard, and a bruise was swelling up on one cheek. For the first time he noticed the girl, lying among the boxes.

'She's bleeding!' said Claire. 'Help me get her downstairs, where there's light!'

He scooped the girl into his arms.

By the time he lay her on the kitchen table, she

had stopped breathing. Claire gave her three quick breaths, then felt for a carotid pulse, but could not detect one. 'Get an ambulance here now!' she said to Lincoln. Positioning her hands over the girl's sternum, Claire began chest compressions. The blouse was soaked, and her hands kept slipping as she pumped. Fresh blood seeped through the fabric. *She is only seven years old. How much blood can a child lose? How much longer can I keep her brain cells alive?*

'Ambulance is on the way!' said Lincoln.

'Okay, I need you to cut off her blouse. We have to see where she's bleeding.' Claire paused to give the girl three more breaths. She heard fabric ripping and saw that Lincoln had already bared the girl's chest.

'Jesus,' he murmured.

Blood dribbled from half a dozen stab wounds.

She placed her hands back on the sternum and resumed cardiac compressions, but with every pump, more blood spilled out of the girl's body.

A siren wailed closer, and through the kitchen window they saw strobelike flashes of light as the ambulance pulled into the front yard. Two EMTs swept into the house, took one look at the child on the table, and threw open their emergency kit. Claire continued pumping on the chest as the EMTs intubated, inserted an IV, slapped on EKG leads.

'Have we got a rhythm?' Claire asked, holding compressions.

'Rapid sinus tach.'

'BP?'

She heard the *whiff, whiff* of the blood pressure cuff, then the answer. 'Barely palpable at fifty. Ringer's lacate going wide open in this IV. Having trouble getting this second line started . . .'

Another siren screamed into the yard, and more footsteps banged into the house. Officers Mark Dolan and Pete Sparks crowded into the kitchen. Dolan met Claire's gaze, and he quickly looked away, sensing her reproach. *I told you something was wrong!*

'There's a boy upstairs in the attic,' said Lincoln. 'I've already got him cuffed. Now we have to find the mother.'

'I'll check the barn,' said Dolan.

Claire protested, 'Faye's in a wheelchair! She couldn't get out to the barn. She's got to be somewhere in this house.'

Ignoring her, Dolan turned and headed straight out the door.

She focused her attention back on the girl. Now that they were getting a pulse, she could stop pumping on the chest, and she was acutely aware that her hands were sticky with blood. She heard Lincoln and Pete running from room to room in search of Faye, heard the EMT's radio crackle with questions from the Knox Hospital ER.

'How much blood loss?' It was McNally's voice on the radio.

'Her clothes are saturated,' answered the EMT.

'At least six stab wounds to the chest. We've got sinus tach at one-sixty, BP palpable at fifty. One IV in. We can't get a second line started.'

'Breathing?'

'No. She's tubed and we're bagging her. Dr Elliot's here with us.'

'Gordon,' Claire called out. 'She needs immediate thoracotomy! Get a surgeon there, and let's just *move* her!'

'We'll be waiting for you.'

Though it took only seconds to transfer the girl into the ambulance, Claire felt as if everything were moving in excruciatingly slow motion. She saw it all through a cloud of panic: the heartbreakingly small body being strapped into the stretcher, the tangle of EKG wires and IV line, the tense faces of the EMTs as they ran the girl down the porch steps and slid her into the ambulance.

Claire and one of the EMTs climbed in beside the girl and the door slammed shut. She knelt beside the stretcher, bagging the lungs and fighting to keep her balance as they bumped down the Braxton driveway, then swung onto the main road.

On the cardiac monitor, the girl's heart rhythm stumbled. Two premature ventricular beats. Then three more.

'PVCs,' said the EMT.

'Go ahead with the lidocaine.'

The EMT had just started to inject the drug when the ambulance hit a pothole. He sprawled backwards, his arm snagging the IV line. The catheter slid out of the girl's vein, sending a spray of Ringer's lactate into Claire's face.

'Shit, I've lost the line!' he said.

An alarm beeped on the monitor. Claire glanced up to see a string of PVCs skipping across the screen. At once she began cardiac compressions. 'Hurry with that second line!'

Already he was ripping open a package, pulling out a fresh catheter. He tied a tourniquet on Kitty's arm and slapped the flesh a few times, trying to get a vein to plump up. 'I can't find one! She's lost too much blood.'

The girl was in shock. Her veins had collapsed.

The alarm squealed. Ventricular tachycardia was racing across the screen.

In panic, Claire gave Kitty's chest a sharp thump. Nothing changed.

She heard the whine of the defibrillator. The EMT had already punched the charge button and was slapping contact pads on Kitty's chest. Claire pulled away as he positioned the paddles and discharged the current.

On the monitor, the tracing shot up, then slid back to a rapid sinus tachycardia. Both Claire and the EMT released loud sighs of relief.

'That rhythm's not going to hold,' said Claire. 'We need the IV.'

Fighting to keep his balance in the swaying ambulance, he wound the tourniquet around the opposite arm and again searched for a vein. 'I can't find one.'

'Not even the antecubital?'

'It's already blown. We lost it trying to get the IV started earlier.'

She glanced up at the monitor. PVCs were beginning to march across the screen again. They were still miles away from the ER, and the girl's rhythm was deteriorating. They had to get an IV in her now.

'Take over CPR,' she said. 'I'll start a subclavian line.'

They scrambled to switch positions.

Claire's heart was hammering as she crouched beside Kitty's chest and stared down at the collarbone. It had been years since she'd inserted a child's central venous line. She would have to insert a needle under the clavicle, angling the tip toward the large subclavian vein, while running the danger of puncturing the lung. Her hands were already trembling; in the swaying ambulance, they would be even less steady.

The girl is in shock, and dying. I have no choice.

She opened the central venous line kit, swabbed the skin with Betadine, and snapped on sterile gloves. Then she took a shaky breath. 'Hold compressions,' she said. She placed the tip of the needle beneath the collarbone and pierced the skin. With steady pressure she advanced the needle, the whole time gently applying suction to the attached syringe.

Dark blood suddenly flashed back.

'I'm in the vein.'

The alarm squealed. 'Hurry! She's in V. tach!' said the EMT.

Lord, don't send us over a pothole. Not now.

Holding the needle absolutely still, she removed the syringe and threaded the J wire through the hollow needle, into the subclavian vein. Her guide wire was in position; the most delicate part of the procedure was over. Moving swiftly now, she slid the catheter into place, withdrew the wire, and connected the IV tubing.

'Good show, doc!'

'Lidocaine's going in. Ringer's at wide open.' Claire glanced at the monitor.

Still in V. tach. She reached for the paddles, and was just placing them on Kitty's chest when the EMT said, 'Wait.'

She looked at the monitor. The lidocaine was taking effect; the V. tach had stopped.

The abrupt lurch of the braking ambulance alerted them to their arrival. Claire braced herself as the vehicle swung around and backed up into the ER bay.

The door swung open and suddenly McNally and his staff were there, half a dozen pairs of hands reaching to pull the stretcher out of the vehicle.

They had only a bare-bones surgical team waiting in the trauma room, but it was the best McNally could round up on such short notice: an anesthetist, two obstetrical nurses, and Dr Byrne, a general surgeon.

At once Byrne moved into action. With a scalpel, he slashed the skin above Kitty's rib and with almost savage force shoved in a plastic chest tube. Blood gushed through the tube and poured into the glass reservoir. He took one look at the rapidly accumulating blood and said, 'We have to crack the chest.'

They had no time for the ritual hand scrub. While McNally performed a cutdown on the girl's arm for another IV line, and a unit of O-neg blood pumped in, Claire slipped into a surgical gown, thrust her hands into sterile gloves, and took her place across from Byrne. She could see from his white face that he was scared. He was not a thoracic surgeon, and clearly he knew he was in over his head. But Kitty was dying, and there was no one else to turn to.

'Hail Mary, full of grace,' he muttered, and started up the sternal saw.

Wincing at the whine of the saw, Claire squinted against the spray of bone dust, into the widening gap of Kitty's chest cavity. All she could see was blood, glistening like red satin under the lights. A massive hemothorax. As Byrne positioned the retractors, widening the gap, Claire suctioned, temporarily clearing the cavity.

'Where's it coming from?' muttered Byrne. 'The heart looks undamaged.'

And so small, thought Claire with sudden anguish. *This child is so very small* . . .

'We've got to clear away this blood.'

As Claire suctioned deeper, a tiny spurt suddenly appeared from the lacerated lung, pumping out an arc of blood.

'I see it,' he said, and snapped on a clamp.

Another spurt appeared, fresh blood swirling bright red into the darker pool.

'That's two,' he said with a tense note of triumph, clamping off the second bleeder.

'I'm hearing a BP!' said a nurse. 'Systolic's seventy!'

'Hanging the second unit of O-neg.'

'There,' said Claire, and Byrne clamped off the third telltale spurt.

Claire suctioned again. For a moment they watched the open chest, waiting in dread for the blood to reaccumulate. Everyone in the room fell silent. The seconds ticked by.

Then Byrne glanced across at her. 'You know that Hail Mary I just said?'

'Yes?'

'It seems to be working.'

Pete Sparks was waiting for her when Claire finally emerged from the trauma room. Her clothes were splattered with blood, but he didn't seem to notice it; they had seen so much violence that night, perhaps they could no longer be shocked by the sight of gore.

'How's the girl?' he asked.

'She made it through surgery. As soon as her blood pressure's stabilized, they'll be transferring her to Bangor.' Claire gave him a tired smile. 'I think she'll be fine, Pete.'

'We brought the boy here,' he said.

'Scotty?'

He nodded. 'The nurses put him in that exam room over there. Lincoln thought you'd better take a look at him. There's something wrong.'

With growing apprehension, she crossed the ER and came to an abrupt halt in the exam room doorway. There she stood staring into the room, saying nothing, a chill rising up her spine.

She almost jumped when Pete said, quietly, 'You see what I mean?'

'What about his mother?' she asked. 'Did you find Faye?'

'Yes, we found her.'

'Where?'

'In the cellar. She was still in her wheelchair.' Pete looked into the exam room, and as if repelled by what he saw, he took a fearful step backwards. 'Her neck was broken. He pushed her down the stairs.'

10

From the other side of the X-ray viewing window, Claire and the CT technician watched Scotty Braxton's head disappear into the mouth of the scanner. His limbs and chest were firmly strapped to the table, but his hands continued to twist against the leather restraints and his wrists had already been chafed raw, streaking the leather with blood.

'We're not going to get any decent shots,' said the tech. 'Still too much movement. Maybe you can give him some more Valium?'

'He's already got five milligrams on board. I hate to obscure his neuro status,' said Claire.

'It's either that or no CT.'

She had no choice. She filled the syringe and entered the scan room. Through the window, she saw the state trooper watching her. She approached the table and reached for the IV port. Without warning the boy's hand shot open. She jerked away just as his fingers clamped down like a trap.

The cop stepped into the room. 'Dr Elliot?'

'I'm okay,' she said, heart pounding. 'He just startled me.'

'I'm right here. Go ahead and give him the medicine.'

Quickly she snatched up the IV line, plunged the needle in the rubber dam, and injected the full two milligrams.

The boy's hand finally fell still.

From behind the window, she watched as the scanner began to whir and click, bombarding his head with a shifting sequence of X-ray beams. The first slice, from the top of the cranium, appeared on the computer screen.

'Looks normal so far,' said the tech. 'What are you expecting to see?'

'Any anatomical abnormality that might explain his behavior. A mass, a tumor. There has to be a reason for this. He's the second boy I've seen with uncontrollable aggression.'

They all turned as Lincoln came into the CT room. The tragedy had taken its toll on him; she could see it in his face, in the shadows under his eyes and the sadness of his gaze. For him, the death of Faye Braxton had been only the start of an endless night of press conferences and meetings with state police investigators. He shut the door and seemed to breathe a sigh of relief that he had at last found a quiet, albeit temporary, retreat.

He crossed to the window and gazed at the boy lying on the table. 'What have you found so far?'

'The preliminary drug screens were just called back from Bangor. His blood's negative for amphetamines, phencyclidine, and cocaine. The usual drugs associated with violence. Now we have to rule out other causes for his behavior.' She looked through the glass at her patient. 'It's just like Taylor Darnell. And this boy has never been on Ritalin.'

'Are you sure?'

'I'm their family doctor. I have all Scotty's records from Dr Pomeroy's files.'

They both stood with shoulders propped wearily against the window, conserving energy for the hours that lay ahead. It was the only time they ever seemed to interact, she realized. When they were both tired or scared or distracted by crisis. Neither one of them looking his best. They held no illusions about each other, because they had been through the worst together. *And I've only learned to admire him more*, she thought with surprise.

The tech said, 'Here come the final cuts.'

Both Claire and Lincoln stirred from their exhausted daze and crossed to the computer terminal. She sat down to watch as the cross sections of brain appeared on the screen. Lincoln moved behind her, his hands resting on the back of her chair, his breath warming her hair.

'So what do you see?' asked Lincoln.

'No midline shift,' she said. 'No masses. No bleeding.'

'How can you tell what you're looking at?'

'The whiter it is, the denser it is. Bone is white,

air is black. As you cut lower in the cranium, you'll begin to see parts of the sphenoid bone appearing, at the base of the brain. What I'm looking for is symmetry. Since most pathology affects only one side of the brain, I check for differences between the two sides.'

A new cut appeared. Lincoln said, 'That view doesn't look symmetrical to me.'

'You're right, it isn't. But I don't worry about that particular asymmetry because it doesn't involve the brain. It's in one of the bony sinuses.'

'What are you looking at?' asked the tech.

'The right maxillary sinus. You see? It's not completely lucent. There seems to be something clouding it.'

'A mucoid cyst, I'd guess,' said the tech. 'We see that sometimes in patients with chronic allergies.'

'It certainly wouldn't explain his behavior,' said Claire.

The phone rang. It was Anthony, calling from the lab.

'You might want to come down and look at this, Dr Elliot,' he said. 'It's the gas chromatogram on your patient.'

'Has something shown up in his blood?'

'I'm not sure.'

'Explain this test to me,' said Lincoln. 'What are you measuring here?'

Anthony patted the boxlike gas chromatograph and grinned like a proud father. The tabletop instrument was a recent acquisition, a valuable hand-me-down from Eastern Maine Medical Center in Bangor, and he hovered over it protectively. 'What this piece of equipment does,' he explained, 'is separate mixtures into their individual components. It does this by making use of each molecule's known equilibrium between the liquid phase and the gas phase. You remember high school chemistry?'

'It wasn't my favorite subject,' Lincoln admitted.

'Well, every substance can exist either as a liquid or a gas. For instance, if you heat water, you make steam – which is the gas phase of H-two-oh.'

'Okay, I'm following you.'

'Coiled inside this machine is a capillary column – a very long, very thin tube that, if you laid it out straight, would stretch about half the length of a football field. It's filled with an inert gas that won't react with anything. Now, what I do is inject the sample to be tested into this port here. It gets heated and vaporized to gas, and the different types of molecules travel along that tube at different rates of speed, depending on their mass. That separates them. As they come out the other end of the tube, they pass through a detector and it's recorded on a strip-chart. The time it takes for each substance to emerge is called "retention time." We already know the retention times for hundreds of different drugs and toxins. This test clues us in to the presence of a particular substance in a patient's blood.' He picked up a syringe and screwed it into the port. 'Watch the screen. See what happens when I inject the patient's sample.' Anthony squeezed down on the syringe.

On the computer screen, an uneven line appeared. They watched the tracing for a moment, but it only looked like 'noise' to Claire – minor, nonspecific readings indicating the biochemical soup that makes up human plasma.

'Just be patient,' said Anthony. 'It shows up at about one minute, ten seconds.'

'What does?' asked Claire.

He pointed to the screen. 'That.'

Claire stared as the line suddenly shot up to a peak and promptly dropped back down again to the uneven baseline. 'What *was* that?' she asked.

Anthony went to the printer, where a hard copy was being simultaneously recorded on paper. He tore off the sheet and spread it out on the lab counter for Claire and Lincoln to see.

'That peak,' he said, 'is something I can't identify. The retention time places it in the steroid class, but you can also see a similar peak for certain vitamins and endogenous testosterone. It'd take a more sophisticated lab to identify exactly what this is.'

'You mentioned endogenous testosterones,' said Claire. 'Could this be an anabolic steroid? Something a teenage boy might abuse?' She looked at Lincoln. 'It would explain the symptoms. Body builders sometimes use steroids to bulk up their muscle mass. Unfortunately it has side effects, one of them being uncontrollable aggression. They call it '*roid rage*.'

'It's something to consider,' said Anthony. 'Some sort of anabolic steroid. Now look at this.' He went to his desk and retrieved another sheet of graph paper.

'What is it?'

'It's Taylor Darnell's gas chromatogram, taken the day he was admitted.' He lay the second sheet next to Scotty Braxton's tracing.

The pattern was identical. A single, well-defined peak at one minute, ten seconds.

'Whatever this substance is,' said Anthony, 'it's in the blood of both boys.'

'The comprehensive drug screen on Taylor's blood was reported negative.'

'Yeah, I called the reference lab about that. They questioned *our* results. As if I'm imagining this peak or something. I admit, this is an older machine, but these results are reproducible every time.'

'Who did you talk to?'

'A biochemist at Anson Biologicals.'

Claire looked down at the two graphs, the papers laid out one over the other, the tracings practically superimposed. Two boys with the same bizarre behavior. The same unidentifiable substance in their bloodstreams. 'Send them Scotty Braxton's blood,' she said. 'I want to know what this peak is.'

Anthony nodded. 'I've got the requisition right here for you to sign.'

By two A.M., Claire had reviewed every X-ray, every blood test, and was no closer to an answer. In exhaustion she lingered beside the boy's bed, silently studying her patient. She tried to think of what she might have missed. The lumbar puncture was normal, as were the blood chemistries and EEG. The CT scan had shown only the mucoid cyst in the right maxillary sinus – probably a result of chronic allergies. Allergies would also explain the one abnormality in his white blood cell count: a high percentage of eosinophils. *Like Taylor Darnell*, she suddenly recalled.

Scotty stirred from his Valium-induced sleep and opened his eyes. A few blinks, and his gaze fixed on Claire.

She turned off the light to leave. Even in the darkness, she could see the gleam of his eyes focused on her.

Then she realized it was not his eyes she saw glowing.

Slowly she crossed back to the bed. She could make out the white linen beneath his head, the darker shape of his head against the pillow. On his upper lip shimmered a brilliant patch of phos-phorescent green.

'Sit down, Noah,' said Fern Cornwallis. 'There's something we need to discuss.'

Noah hesitated in the doorway, reluctant to step into the principal's office. Enemy territory. He didn't know why he'd been pulled out of class to see her, but judging by the expression on Miss C.'s face, he suspected it couldn't be anything good.

The other kids had eyed him with speculative looks when the message had crackled over the intercom in band class: *Noah Elliot, Miss Cornwallis wants to see you in her office. Now.* Acutely aware of everyone's gaze, he had set down his saxophone and made his way through the maze of chairs and music stands to the door. He knew his classmates were wondering what he'd done wrong.

He had no idea.

'Noah?' said Miss C., pointing to the chair.

He sat down. He didn't look at her, but at her desk, which was neat beyond belief. No human had a desk like that.

'I received something in the mail today,' she said. 'I need to ask you about it. I don't know who sent it. But I'm glad they did, because I need to know when one of my students requires extra guidance.'

'I don't know what you're talking about, Miss C.'

In answer, she slid a photocopied news clipping across the desk. He took one glance and felt his face blanch. It was from *The Baltimore Sun*:

ONE YOUTH IN CRITICAL CONDITION
AFTER CRASH OF STOLEN CAR: FOUR
YOUTHS IN CUSTODY.

Who knew about it? he thought. And, more important: *Why are they doing this to me?*

Miss Cornwallis said, 'You moved here from Baltimore. Didn't you?'

Noah swallowed. 'Yes, ma'am,' he whispered.

'There are no names mentioned in this article. But there was a note attached, suggesting I talk to you about this.' She looked straight at him. 'This is about you, isn't it?'

'Who sent it?'

'That's not important right now.'

'It's one of those reporters.' His chin suddenly jutted up in anger. 'They've been following me around, asking questions. Now they're trying to get back at me!'

'For what?'

'For not talking to them.'

She sighed. 'Noah, three teachers had their cars broken into yesterday. Do you know anything about it?'

'You're looking for someone to blame. Aren't you?'

'I'm just asking if you know anything about the cars.'

He stared her straight in the eye. 'No,' he said, and stood up. 'Now can I go?'

She didn't believe him; he could see it in her face. But there was nothing more she could say.

She nodded. 'Go back to class.'

He walked out of her office, past the snoopy

school secretary, and stormed into the hallway. Instead of returning to band class, he fled outside and sat down, shaking, on the front steps. He wasn't wearing a jacket, but he scarcely noticed the cold; he was fighting too hard not to cry.

I can't live here any more, either, he thought. *I can't live anywhere. No matter where I go, someone will find out about me. About what I did.* He hugged his knees and rocked back and forth, wanting desperately to go home, now, but it was too far to walk, and his mom couldn't come and get him.

He heard the gym door slam shut, and he turned to see a woman with wild blond hair walk out of the building. He recognized her; it was that reporter, Damaris Horne. She crossed the street and climbed into a car. A dark green car.

She's the one.

He ran across the street. 'Hey!' he yelled, and slapped her door in fury. 'You stay the hell away from me!'

She rolled down her window and looked at him with almost predatory interest. 'Hello, Noah. You want to talk about something?'

'I just want you to stop trying to ruin my life!'

'How am I ruining your life?'

'Following me around! Telling people about Baltimore!'

'What does Baltimore have to do with anything?'

He stared at her, suddenly realizing she had no

idea what he was talking about. He backed away. 'Forget about it.'

'Noah, I haven't been following you around.'

'Yes you have. I've seen your car. You drove past my house yesterday. And the day before.'

'No, I didn't.'

'You were tailing my mom and me in town!'

'Okay, that time I just happened to be behind you. So what? Do you know how many reporters are in town right now? How many green cars are cruising around?'

He backed away some more. 'Just stay away from me.'

'Why don't we talk? You can tell me what's really going on in the school. What all the fights are about. Noah? Noah!'

He turned and fled into the building.

Two pit bulls growled and barked at Claire's car, their claws scraping at her door. She stayed safely shut inside and stared across the front yard, at the ramshackle farmhouse. In the front yard, years of junk had accumulated. She saw a trailer propped up on bricks and three broken-down cars, in various states of being cannibalized. A cat peered fearfully through the open door of a rusting clothes dryer. In the land of Yankee thrift, it was not unusual to find front yards like this. Families who have known poverty hoard their junk like treasure.

She honked, then rolled down her window a

few inches and called out through the crack: 'Hello? Is anyone home?'

A tattered curtain flicked aside in the window, and a moment later, the door opened and a blond man of about forty stepped out. He crossed the yard and regarded her with unsmiling eyes as the dogs barked and jumped at his feet. Everything about him seemed thin – his face, his receding hair, his pencil-sketch mustache. Thin and resentful.

'I'm Dr Elliot,' she said. 'Are you Mr Reid?'

'Yeah.'

'I'd like to talk to your sons, if I may. It's about Scotty Braxton.'

'What about him?'

'He's in the hospital. I'm hoping your sons can tell me what's wrong with him.'

'You're the doctor. Don't you know?'

'I believe it's a drug psychosis, Mr Reid. I think he and Taylor Darnell both took the same drug. Mrs Darnell said Scotty and Taylor spent a lot of time with your sons. If I can talk to them –'

'They can't help you,' said Jack Reid, and he stepped away from her car.

'They may all have been experimenting with the same drug.'

'My boys know better than that.' He turned back to the house, his contempt for her apparent in the angry set of his shoulders.

'I don't want to get your sons in trouble, Mr Reid!' she called·out. 'I'm just trying to get information!'

210

A woman stepped out onto the porch. She cast a worried look at Claire, then said something to Reid. In reply, he shoved her back into the house. The dogs trotted away from Claire now, and were watching the porch, attracted by the promise of new conflict.

Claire rolled down her window and stuck her head out. 'If I can't talk to your sons, I'll call the police to do it for me. Would you prefer to speak to Chief Kelly?'

He turned to look at her, his face tight with anger. Now the woman cautiously poked her head out and stared at Claire as well.

'This will be strictly confidential,' said Claire. 'Let me talk to them, and I'll keep the police out of it.'

The woman said something to Reid – a plea, by the look of her body language. He gave a snort of disgust and stomped into the house.

The woman crossed to Claire's car. Like Reid she was blond, her face washed-out and colorless, but there was no hostility in her eyes. Rather, there was a disturbing lack of any emotion, as though she had long ago buried her feelings in some deep, safe place.

'The boys just got home from school,' the woman said.

'Are you Mrs Reid?'

'Yes, ma'am. I'm Grace.' She looked at the house. 'Those boys've been in enough trouble. Chief Kelly said if it happened again . . .'

'He doesn't have to know about this. I'm here only because of my patient, Scotty. I need to know what drug he's taken, and I think your boys can tell me.'

'They're Jack's boys, not mine.' She turned to face Claire, as though it was very important that this fact be understood. 'I can't force them to talk to you. But you can come inside. First let me tie up these dogs.'

She grabbed both pit bulls by their collars and pulled them over to the maple tree, where she restrained them. They shot to the ends of their chains, barking wildly as Claire stepped out of the car and followed the woman up to the porch.

Stepping into the house was like entering a warren of caves, low-ceilinged and cluttered.

'I'll get them,' said Grace, and she disappeared up a narrow stairway, leaving Claire alone in the living room. The TV was on, tuned to the shopper's channel. On the coffee table, someone had written on a notepad: 'Chanel #5, 4 oz., $14.99.' She breathed in the air of that house, with its odors of mildew and cigarettes, and wondered if perfume alone could mask this smell of poverty.

Heavy footsteps thudded on the stairs, and two teenage boys slouched into the room. Matching buzz cuts made their blond heads seem unnaturally small. They said nothing, but stood looking at her with incurious blue eyes. The blandness of teenagers.

'This is Eddie and J.D.,' said Grace.

'I'm Dr Elliot,' said Claire. She looked at Grace, who understood the meaning of that glance, and quietly left the room.

The boys plopped down on the couch, their gazes automatically shifting to the TV. Even when Claire reached for the remote and turned it off, their gazes remained fixed on the blank screen, as though by habit.

'Your friend Scotty Braxton's in the hospital,' she said. 'Did you know that?'

There was a long silence. Then Eddie, the younger boy, perhaps fourteen, said: 'We heard he went crazy last night.'

'That's right. I'm his doctor, Eddie, and I'm trying to find out why. Whatever you tell me, it's just between us. I need to know what drug he's taken.'

The boys exchanged a look that Claire didn't understand.

'I know he took something,' she said. 'So did Taylor Darnell. It showed up in both their blood tests.'

'So why're you asking us?' It was J.D. talking now, his voice deeper than Eddie's, and vibrating with contempt. 'Sounds like you already know.'

'I don't know what the drug is.'

'Is it a pill?' asked Eddie.

'Not necessarily. I believe it's some kind of hormone. It could be a pill, a shot, or even a plant of some kind. Hormones are chemicals made by living things. Plants and animals, insects.

They affect our bodies in a lot of different ways. This particular hormone makes people violent. It makes them kill. Do you know how he got it?'

Eddie's gaze dropped, as though he was suddenly afraid to look at her.

In frustration she said, 'I just saw Scotty this morning, at the hospital, and he's tied down like an animal. Oh, it's bad for him now, but it's going to be a lot worse when the drug wears off. When he wakes up and remembers what he did to his mother. To his sister.' She paused, hoping her words were penetrating their thick skulls. 'His mother is dead. His sister is still recovering from her wounds. For the rest of her life, Kitty will remember her brother as the boy who tried to kill her. This drug has ruined Scotty's life. And Taylor's. You have to tell me where they got it.'

Both boys stared down at the coffee table, and she saw only the bristly tops of their heads. In boredom, J.D. picked up the remote and turned on the TV. The shopping channel blared out a sales pitch for a genuine man-made emerald pendant on a fourteen-carat gold chain. High-fashion elegance for only seventy-nine ninety-nine.

Claire snatched the remote from J.D.'s hand and angrily shut off the TV. 'Since you two don't have anything to say to me, I guess you'll have to talk to Chief Kelly.'

Eddie started to speak, then glanced at his older

214

brother and clammed up again. Only then did Claire notice the essential difference between the two. Eddie was afraid of J.D.

She set her business card down on the coffee table. 'If you change your minds, that's where you can reach me,' she said, her gaze directed at Eddie. Then she walked out of the house.

As she stepped off the porch, the two pit bulls came charging at her, only to be yanked to a stop by their chains. Jack Reid was chopping kindling in the front yard, his ax ringing out against a tree stump. He made no effort to quiet his animals; maybe he enjoyed the spectacle of watching them terrify this unwanted visitor. Claire continued across the yard, past the rusting clothes dryer and a car gutted of engine parts. As she walked past Reid, he stopped swinging his ax and looked at her. Sweat beaded his brow and dampened the pale mustache. He leaned against the ax handle, the blade at rest on the stump, and there was mean satisfaction in his eyes.

'Had nothing to say to you, did they?'

'I think they have plenty to say. It will all come out eventually.'

The dogs were barking with renewed agitation, their chains scraping against the maple tree. She cast a glance their way, then looked back at Reid, whose hands had tightened around the ax handle.

'If you're hunting for trouble,' he said, 'best check under your own roof.'

'What?'

He gave her an ugly smile, then raised his ax and brought it down, hard, on a log of firewood.

Claire was in her office later that afternoon when the call came. She heard the phone ringing in the outer office, and then Vera appeared in the doorway.

'She wants to talk to you. She says you were over at her house today.'

'Who's calling?'

'Amelia Reid.'

At once Claire picked up her extension. 'This is Dr Elliot.'

Amelia's voice was muffled. 'My brother Eddie – he asked me to call you. He's afraid to do it himself.'

'And what does Eddie want to tell me?'

'He wants you to know—' There was a pause, as though the girl had stopped to listen. Then her voice came back on, so soft it was almost inaudible. 'He said to tell you about the mushrooms.'

'What mushrooms?'

'They were all eating them. Taylor and Scotty and my brothers. The little blue mushrooms, in the woods.'

Lincoln Kelly stepped out of his truck and his boot landed on a twig, the snap of dead wood echoing like gunshot across the still lake. It was

216

late afternoon, the sky leaden with rain clouds, the water flat as black glass. 'A little late in the year to go hunting for mushrooms, Claire,' he said dryly.

'But a-hunting we will go.' She reached into the back of her pickup and grabbed two leaf rakes, one of which she handed to Lincoln. He took it with obvious reluctance. 'They're supposed to be a hundred yards upstream from the Boulders,' she said. 'They're growing under some oak trees. Little blue mushrooms with narrow stalks.'

She turned to face the woods. They were not at all inviting, the trees bare and absolutely still, the gloom thickening beneath them. She had not wanted to come out here this late in the day, but a storm was predicted. Already a half inch of rain had fallen, and with the temperature expected to plummet tonight, by tomorrow everything would be covered with snow. This was their last chance to comb bare ground.

'This could be the common factor, Lincoln. A natural toxin from plants growing right in these woods.'

'And the kids were eating these mushrooms?'

'They made it some sort of ritual. Eat a mushroom, prove you're a man.'

They walked along the riverbed, hiking through ankle-deep leaves and thickets of wild raspberry canes. Twigs littered the forest floor, and every step made a sharp explosion of sound. A walk in the woods in late fall is not a silent experience.

The forest opened to a small clearing, where the oak trees had grown to towering heights.

'I think this is the place,' she said.

They began to rake aside the leaves. They worked with quiet urgency as sleet fell, stinging pellets of it mixed with rain, coating everything with a glaze of ice. They uncovered toadstools and white fairy rings and brilliant orange fungi.

It was Lincoln who found the blue one. He spotted the tiny nubbin poking up from a crevice formed by two tree roots. He brushed away the oak leaves and uncovered the cap. Darkness was already falling, and the mushroom's color was apparent only under the direct beam of his flashlight. They crouched side by side, battered by rain and sleet, both of them too chilled and miserable to feel much sense of triumph as Claire slipped the specimen into a Ziploc bag.

'There's a wetlands biologist up the road,' she said. 'Maybe he'll know what it is.'

In silence they sloshed back through the mud and emerged from the woods. On the bank of Locust Lake, they both halted in surprise. Half the shoreline was almost completely dark. Where the lights of houses should have glowed, there was only the occasional glimmer of candlelight through a window.

'It's a bad night to lose power,' said Lincoln. 'Temperature's going to drop into the twenties.'

'Looks like my end of the lake still has electricity,' she noted with relief.

'Well, keep the firewood handy. There's probably ice building up on the lines. You could lose yours next.'

She threw the rakes in the back of her truck, and was circling around to the door when something in the lake caught her eye. It was only a faint glimmer, and she might have missed it had it not been for the contrasting blackness of the Boulders jutting into the water.

'Lincoln,' she said. *'Lincoln!'*

He turned from his cruiser. 'What?'

'Look at the lake.' Slowly she walked toward the small tongue of water lapping at the mud.

He followed her.

At first he couldn't seem to comprehend what he was seeing. It was only a vague shimmer, like moonlight dancing on the surface. But there was no moon out tonight, and the streak of light wavering on the water was a phosphorescent green. They climbed onto one of the rocks and looked across the water. In wonder, they watched the streak undulate like a snake on the surface, its coils a swirl of bright emerald. Not a purposeful movement, but a lazy drifting, its form contracting, then expanding.

Suddenly the clatter of sleet intensified, and needles of ice stippled the lake.

The phosphorescent coils shattered into a thousand bright fragments and disintegrated.

For a long time, neither Claire nor Lincoln spoke. Then he whispered, 'What the hell was that?'

'You've never seen it before?'

'I've lived here all my life, Claire. I've never seen anything like it.'

The water was dark, now. Invisible. 'I have,' she said.

11

'I'm not an expert on mushrooms,' said Max Tutwiler. 'But I might recognize a toxic variety if I saw one.'

Claire took the mushroom out of the Ziploc bag and handed it to him. 'Can you tell us what this is?'

He slipped on his spectacles, and by the light of a kerosene lamp, studied the specimen. He turned it over, examining every detail of the delicate stalk, the blue-green cap.

Sleet *tick-ticked* against the cottage windows and wind moaned in the chimney. The power had gone out an hour before, and Max's cottage was getting colder by the minute. The rising storm seemed to make Lincoln restless. Claire could hear him moving around the room, fussing with the cold woodstove, tightening the window latches. The ingrained habits of a man who has known hard winters. He lit newspapers and kindling in the stove and threw in a log, but the wood was green, and produced more smoke than heat.

Max did not look well. He sat clutching a blanket, a box of Kleenex by his chair. A shivering testament to the miseries of a winter flu and a cottage without heat.

At last he looked up with rheumy eyes. 'Where did you find this mushroom?'

'Upstream from the Boulders.'

'Which boulders?'

'That's the name for the place – the Boulders. It's a hangout for the local kids. They found dozens of those mushrooms this summer. It's the first year they've noticed them. But then, it's been a strange year.'

'How so?' asked Max.

'We had all those floods last spring. And then the hottest summer on record.'

Max nodded soberly. 'Global warming. The signs are everywhere.'

Lincoln glanced at the window, where needles of sleet tapped at the glass, and laughed. 'Not tonight.'

'You have to look at the big picture,' said Max. 'Weather patterns changing all over the world. Catastrophic droughts in Africa. Floods in the Midwest. Unusual growing conditions lead to unusual things growing.'

'Like blue mushrooms,' said Claire.

'Or eight-legged amphibians.' He pointed to the bookshelf, where his specimen jars were displayed. There were eight jars now, each containing a freak of nature.

Lincoln picked up one of the jars and stared at a two-headed salamander. 'Jesus. You found this in our lake?'

'In one of the vernal ponds.'

'And you think this is because of global warming?'

'I don't know what's causing it. Or which species will be affected next.' Max refocused his bleary eyes on the mushroom. 'It's not surprising that plant life would be affected.' He turned the mushroom over and gave it a sniff. 'This damn cold has blocked up my nose. But I think I can smell it.'

'What?'

'The scent of anise.' He held it out to her.

'I smell it too. What does it mean?'

He rose and pulled down *An Illustrated Textbook of Mycology* from the bookshelf. 'This species grows in both hardwood and coniferous forests, from midsummer through fall.' He opened the book to a color plate. '*Clitocybe odora*. The anise funnel cap. It contains a small amount of muscarine, that's all.'

'Is that our toxin, then?' asked Lincoln.

Claire sank back in her chair and gave a sigh of disappointment. 'No, it's not. Muscarine causes mostly gastrointestinal or cardiac symptoms. Not violent behavior.'

Max returned the mushroom to the Ziploc bag. 'Sometimes,' he said, 'there is no explanation for violence. And that's the frightening thing about it. How unexpected it can be. How often it happens without rhyme or reason.'

Wind rattled the door. Outside, the sleet had turned to snow, and it tumbled past the window in a thick whirl of white. The wood stove gave off only the barest suggestion of heat. Lincoln crouched down to check the fire.

It had gone out.

'Lincoln and I saw something tonight. On the lake,' said Claire. 'It was almost like an hallucination.'

She and Max sat facing the hearth in Claire's parlor, their backs turned against the shadows. She had coaxed him out of his unheated cottage, had offered him a bed in her guest room, and now that dinner was over, they sat before the fire and took turns pouring from a bottle of brandy. Flames hissed brightly around a log, but for all that light, all that combustion, precious little heat seemed to penetrate the room's chill. Outside, snowflakes skittered against the window and stray branches of forsythia, bone bare, clawed at the glass.

'What did you see in the lake?' he asked.

'It was floating on the surface of the water, near the Boulders. This swirl of green light, just drifting by. Not solid, but liquid. Changing shape, like a slick of oil.' She took a sip of brandy and stared at the fire. 'Then the sleet began to fall, churning the water. And the green light, it just disintegrated.' She looked at him. 'It sounds crazy, doesn't it?'

'It could be a chemical spill. Fluorescent paint in the lake, for instance. Or it could be a biological phenomenon.'

'Biological?'

He pressed his hand to his forehead, as though to ease a headache beginning to build there. 'There are bioluminescent strains of algae. And certain bacteria glow in the dark. There's one species that forms a symbiotic relationship with luminescent squid. The squid attracts mates by flashing a light organ powered by glowing bacteria.'

Bacteria, she thought. A floating mass of them.

'Scotty Braxton's pillow was stained with a luminescent substance,' she said. 'At first I thought he'd been using some sort of hobby paint. Now I wonder if it was bacterial.'

'Have you cultured it?'

'I cultured his nasal discharge. I asked the lab to identify every organism that grows out, so it will take time to get the results. What have you found in the lake water?'

'None of the cultures are back yet, but maybe I should take a few more samples before I pack up and leave.'

'When are you leaving?'

'I rented the cottage through the end of this month. But with the weather turning so cold, I might as well cut it short and go back to Boston. To central heating. I have enough data already. Samples from a dozen different Maine lakes.' He looked at the window, at the snow falling outside, thick as a curtain. 'I leave this place to hardier souls like you.'

The flames were dying. She stood up, took a

birch log from the pile, and threw it onto the fire. The papery bark caught instantly, snapping and sparkling. She watched it for a moment, savoring the heat, feeling it flush her cheeks. 'I'm not such a hardy soul,' she said softly. 'I'm not sure I belong here, either.'

He poured more brandy into his glass. 'There's a lot about this place that takes getting used to. The isolation. The people. They're not easy to get to know. In the month I've been here, you're the only one who's invited me to dinner.'

She sat down and regarded him with a new measure of sympathy. She recalled her own introduction to Tranquility. After eight months, how many people here did she really know? She'd been warned it would be this way, that the locals were wary of outsiders. People from away drift to Maine like loose bits of fluff, linger for a season or two, and then scatter to the four winds. They have no roots here, no memories. No permanence. Mainers know this, and they greet each new resident with suspicion. They wonder what has driven this stranger into their midst, what secrets lie hidden in some past life. They wonder if the stranger has somehow carried with him the very contagion he is trying to escape. Lives that fall apart in one city often fall apart yet again in another.

Mainers can see the progression. First the new house, enthusiastically purchased, the garden with freshly tamped-down daffodil beds, the snow boots and L.L. Bean jackets. A winter or two goes by.

The daffodils bloom, fade, bloom untended. The heating bill astounds. The storm windows linger months past thaw. The stranger begins to shuffle pale-faced around town, to talk longingly of Florida, to recall beaches he has lolled upon, and to dream of towns that have neither mud season nor snowplows. And the house, so lovingly restored, soon collects one more decoration: a For Sale sign.

People from away have no permanence. Even she was not sure she would stay here.

'Why did you want to move here, then?' he asked.

She settled back in her chair and watched the flames engulf the birch log. 'I didn't move here because of me. It was because of Noah.' She looked up toward the second floor, toward her son's bedroom. It was silent upstairs, just as Noah had been silent all evening. At dinner he had scarcely said a word to their guest. And afterwards, he had gone straight to his room and shut the door.

'He's a handsome boy,' said Max.

'His father was very good-looking.'

'And his mother isn't?' Max's glass of brandy was almost empty, and he seemed flushed in the firelight. 'Because you are.'

She smiled. 'I think you're drunk.'

'No, what I'm feeling right now is . . . comfortable.' He set his glass on the table. 'It was Noah who wanted to move?'

'Oh, no. He had to be dragged, kicking and

screaming. He didn't want to leave his old school or his friends. But that's exactly why we *had* to leave.'

'The wrong crowd?'

She nodded. 'He got into trouble. The whole group of them did. I was taken completely by surprise when it happened. I couldn't control him, couldn't discipline him. Sometimes . . .' She sighed. 'Sometimes I think I've lost him entirely.'

The birch log slid, sizzling into the embers. Sparks leaped up and drifted gently down into the ashes.

'I had to take some sort of drastic action,' she said. 'It was my last chance to exert control. In another year or two, he would have been too old. Too strong.'

'Did it work?'

'You mean, did all our troubles go away? Of course not. Instead, I've taken on a whole new slew of troubles. This creaky old house. A medical practice that I seem to be slowly killing.'

'Don't they need a doctor here?'

'They had a town doctor. Old Dr Pomeroy, who died last winter. They can't seem to accept me as even a pale substitute.'

'It takes time, Claire.'

'It's been eight months, and I can't even turn a profit. Someone with a grudge has been sending anonymous letters to my patients. Warning them off.' She looked at the bottle of brandy, thought: *What the hell*, and poured herself another glass. 'Out of the frying pan, into the fire.'

'Then why do you stay?'

'Because I keep hoping it'll get better. That winter will pass, it'll be summer again, and we'll both be happy. That's the dream, anyway. It's the dreams that keep us going.' She sipped her brandy, noticing that the flames were now pleasantly out of focus.

'And what is your dream?'

'That my son will love me the way he used to.'

'You sound as if you have doubts.'

She sighed, and raised the glass to her lips. 'Parenthood,' she said, 'is nothing but doubts.'

Lying in bed, Amelia could hear the sound of slapping in her mother's room, could hear the stifled sobs and whimpers and the angry grunts that punctuated each blow.

Dumb bitch. Don't you ever go against me. You hear? You hear?

Amelia thought of all the things she could do about it – all the things she'd already done in the past. None of them had worked. Twice she'd called the police; twice they'd taken Jack away to jail, but within days he'd returned, welcomed back by her mother. It was no use. Grace was weak. Grace was afraid of being alone.

I will never, ever, let a man hurt me and get away with it.

She covered her ears and buried her head under the sheets.

*   *   *

J.D. listened to the sound of blows and could feel himself getting excited. Yeah, that's the way to treat 'em, Dad. It's what you always told me. A firm hand keeps 'em in line. He rolled up close to the wall, placing his ear against the plaster. His dad's bed was right on the other side. As he had on so many other nights, J.D. would press up close, listening to the rhythmic squeak of his father's bed, knowing exactly what was going on in the next room. His dad was something else, a man like no other, and although J.D. was a little afraid of him, he also admired him. He admired the way ol' Jack took control of his household and never let the females get high and mighty. It's the way the Good Book meant it to be, Jack always said, the man as master and protector of his house. It made sense. The man was larger, stronger, of course he was meant to be in charge.

The slapping had stopped, and now it was just the bed squeaking up and down. That's how it always ended. A little discipline and then some good old-fashioned making up. J.D. was getting more and more excited, and the ache down there got to be unbearable.

He got up and felt his way past Eddie's bed, toward the door. Eddie was sound asleep, the dumb cluck. It was embarrassing to have such a weak wuss for a brother. He went into the hall and headed toward the bathroom.

Halfway there, he paused outside his stepsister's closed door. He pressed his ear to it, wondering if Amelia was awake, if she too was listening to the squeaking of their parents' bed. Juicy little Amelia, the untouchable. Right under the same roof. So close he could almost hear the sound of her breathing, could smell her girl-scent wafting out from under the door. He tried the knob and found it was locked. She always kept it locked, ever since that night he'd sneaked into her room to watch her sleep, and she'd awakened to find him unbuttoning her pajama top. The little tease had screamed, and his dad had come tearing into the room with a loaded shotgun, eager to blow away some intruder.

When all the female caterwauling had died down, and J.D. had slunk back to his own room, he'd heard his dad say, 'The boy's always been a sleepwalker. Didn't know what he was doing.' J.D. had thought he was off the hook. Then his dad had come into J.D.'s room and whacked him so hard across the face, he'd seen exploding lights.

Amelia got a lock put in her door the next day.

J.D. closed his eyes and felt sweat dampen his upper lip as he pictured his luscious stepsister lying in her bed, slender arms flung out. He thought of her legs as he'd seen them this summer, long and tan in her white shorts, just the softest hint of golden down on her thighs. Sweat was breaking out on his forehead now, and on his palms. He felt his heart beat hard. His senses had sharpened to such acuteness, he could hear the night humming around him, fields of energy looping and swirling in electric flashes.

He had never felt so powerful.

Again he gripped the doorknob, and its resistance suddenly enraged him. *She* enraged him, with her superior ways and her disapproval. He reached down and touched himself, but really, he was touching *her*, taking command of *her*. Making her do what he wanted. And even though sex was what his body craved, when he finally released himself, the image that came unbidden into his mind was of his own fingers, like thick ropes, wrapped around Amelia's slender neck.

12

Noah shoved two slices of bread in the toaster and jammed down the lever. 'He stayed all night, didn't he?'

'It was too cold for him to sleep in the cottage. He'll be going back today.'

'So are we taking in every strange guy who doesn't know how to keep his woodstove lit?'

'Please keep your voice down. He's still sleeping.'

'It's my home too! Why should I have to whisper?'

Claire sat at the breakfast table, staring at her son's back. Noah refused to look at her and stood hulking by the kitchen counter, as though the toaster required all his concentration.

'You're mad because I had a houseguest? Is that it?'

'You don't even know him, and you invite some strange guy to spend the night.'

'He's not a strange guy, Noah. He's a scientist.'

'Like scientists aren't strange?'

'Your father was a scientist.'

'Is that supposed to make me like this guy?'

The toast popped up. Noah threw the slices onto a plate and sat down at the table. She watched in puzzlement as he picked up a knife and began to slash the toast into smaller and smaller squares. It was bizarre, and she'd never seen him do this before. He's transferring his rage, she thought. Taking it out on the bread.

'I guess my mother isn't so perfect after all,' he said, and she flushed, stung by the cruel comment. 'You're always telling me to keep *my* nose clean. I'm not the one having sleepovers.'

'He's just a friend, Noah. I have a right to have friends, don't I?' She added, recklessly, 'I even have a right to boyfriends.'

'Go ahead!'

'In four years, you'll be in college. You'll have your own life. Why can't I have mine?'

Noah crossed back to the sink. 'You think I have a life?' He laughed. 'I'm on permanent probation. Being watched all the time. By *everyone*.'

'What do you mean?'

'My teachers all look at me like I'm some kind of criminal. Like it's just a matter of time before I screw up.'

'Did you do something to draw their attention?'

In fury he whirled around to face her. 'Yeah, it's my fault! It's always my fault!'

'Noah, is there something you aren't telling me?'

With an angry sweep of his hand, he knocked two coffee cups off the counter and into the dish-water. 'You already think I'm a screw-up! You're never happy with me. No matter how perfect I try to be.'

'Don't whine to me about having to be perfect. I'm not allowed to screw up either. Not as a mother, not as a doctor, and I'm getting pretty sick of it. Especially when no matter how hard I try, you always blame me for *something*.'

'What I blame you for,' he shot back, 'is dragging me to this dump of a town.' He stalked out of the house, and the slam of the front door seemed to echo forever.

She reached for her coffee, which by now was lukewarm, and sipped it fiercely, hands shaking around the cup. What had just happened? Where did all that rage come from? They'd argued in the past, but never had he tried so hard to hurt her. Never had he cut so close to the bone.

She heard the rumble of the school bus as it drove away.

She looked down at his plate, at the uneaten toast. It had been slashed to crumbs.

'This isn't the right place for him, Dr Elliot,' said the nursing supervisor. Eileen Culkin was short but powerfully built for a woman, and with her boom-ing voice and background as an army nurse, she commanded instant respect. When Eileen spoke, the doctors listened.

Though Claire was in the middle of reviewing Scotty Braxton's chart, she set it aside and turned to face Eileen. 'I haven't seen Scotty yet this morning,' she said. 'Have there been more problems?'

'Even after you ordered that extra sedation at midnight, he didn't sleep. He's quiet now, but last night, he was awake the entire shift, screaming at the guard to unlock his handcuffs. Disturbing all the other patients. Dr Elliot, that boy needs to be in juvenile lockup, or a psychiatric unit. Not a medical ward.'

'I haven't finished the evaluation. There are labs still pending.'

'If he's stable, couldn't you move him? The nurses are afraid to go in the room. They can't even change his sheets without three people restraining him. We'd like him moved, the sooner the better.'

Time to make a decision, thought Claire as she walked down the hall to Scotty's room. Unless she could diagnose a life-threatening illness, she couldn't keep him in the hospital any longer.

The state trooper stationed outside Scotty Braxton's hospital room gave Claire a nod of greeting. 'Morning, doc.'

'Good morning. I understand he's been quite a handful.'

'He's been better the last hour. Not a peep out of him.'

'I need to examine him again. Could you stand by, just in case?'

'Sure thing.' He pushed open the door and managed to take one step into the room before he froze. '*Jesus Christ.*'

At first all Claire registered was the horror in his voice. Then she pushed past him, into the room. She felt the rush of cold air coming through the open window, and saw the blood. It was spattered across the empty bed, a shocking spray of it staining the pillow and the sheets, thickly smearing the empty handcuff dangling from the side rail. On the floor just below the handcuff, a pool of red had gathered. The human tissue lying at the edge of that pool would have been unrecognizable, save for the fingernail and the white nubbin of bone protruding from one end of the torn flesh. It was the boy's thumb; he had chewed it off.

Groaning, the trooper sank to the floor and dropped his head into his lap. 'Jesus,' he kept murmuring. 'Jesus . . .'

Claire saw the prints of bare feet tracking across the room. She ran to the open window and stared down at the ground one story below.

There was blood mixed with the churned-up snow. Footprints, and more blood, trailed away from the building, toward the forested perimeter of the hospital grounds.

'He's gone into the woods!' she said, and ran out of the room to the stairwell.

She dashed down to the first floor, and pushed out through the fire exit, sinking at once into ankle-deep wet snow. By the time she'd circled around the building to Scotty's window, icy water had seeped into her shoes. She picked up the trail of Scotty's blood and followed it across the wide expanse of snow.

At the edge of the woods she halted, trying to see what lay in the shadow of the evergreens. She could make out the boy's footprints, trailing into the underbrush, and here and there a bright splash of blood.

Heart thudding, she eased into the woods. The most dangerous animal is the one in pain.

Her ungloved hands were numb from cold, from fear, as she moved aside a branch and peered deeper into the woods. Behind her, a twig snapped sharply. She spun around and almost cried out with relief when she saw it was the trooper, who'd followed her out of the building.

'Did you see him?' he asked.

'No. His footprints lead into the woods.'

He waded toward her through the snow. 'Security's on the way. So's the emergency room staff.'

She turned to face the trees. 'Do you hear that?'

'What?'

'Water. I hear water.' She began to run, ducking under low branches, stumbling through underbrush. The boy's footprints were weaving back and forth now, as though he had been staggering. Here was churned-up snow, where he'd fallen. Too much blood loss, she thought. He's stumbling and on the verge of collapse.

The sound of rushing water grew louder.

She broke through a tangle of evergreens and emerged on the bank of a creek. Rain and melting snow had swollen it to a torrent. Frantically she scanned the snow for the boy's prints and spotted them moving parallel to the creek for several yards.

Then, at the water's edge, the footprints abruptly vanished.

'You see him?' the guard yelled.

'He's gone into the water!' She splashed knee-deep into the creek. Reaching underwater, she blindly grabbed whatever her hands encountered. She came up with branches, beer bottles. An old boot. She waded in deeper, up to her thighs, but the water was moving too fast and she felt the torrent pulling her downstream.

Stubbornly she braced her foot against a rock. Once again, she plunged her arms deep into the icy water.

And found an arm.

At her scream, the trooper came splashing to her side. The boy's hospital gown had snagged on a branch; they had to rip the fabric free. Together they lifted him from the creek and dragged him up the bank, onto the snow. His face was blue. He was not breathing, nor did he have a pulse.

She began CPR. Three breaths, filling his lungs, then cardiac compressions. One-one-thousand, two-one-thousand, the sequence automatic and well rehearsed. As she pumped on his chest, blood gushed from his nostril and spilled to the snow. Reestablish circulation, and blood flows to the brain, to the vital organs, but it also means the body bleeds again. She saw a fresh stream of dark red trickle from his torn hand.

Voices drew near, and then footsteps were running toward them. Claire stepped back, wet and shivering, as the ER personnel lifted Scotty onto a stretcher.

She followed them back to the building, and into a trauma room exploding with noise and chaos. On the monitor, the cardiac tracing showed a pattern of ventricular fibrillation.

A nurse hit the defibrillator charge button and slapped paddles on the boy's chest. Scotty jerked as the electrical current shot through his body.

'Still in V. fib,' said Dr McNally. 'Resume compressions. Did you get the bretylium in?'

'Going in now,' a nurse said.

'Everyone back!' Another shock to the heart.

'Still in V. fib,' said McNally. He glanced at Claire. 'How long was he underwater?'

'I don't know. Possibly up to an hour. But he's young, and that water's close to freezing.' Even an apparently dead child could sometimes be revived after cold-water immersion. They couldn't give up yet.

'Core body temp's up to thirty-two degrees centigrade,' a nurse said.

'Maintain CPR and get him warmed up. We might have a chance.'

'What's all this blood from the nose?' a nurse asked. 'Did he hit his head?'

A trickle of bright red slid down the boy's cheek and splattered to the floor.

'He was bleeding when we pulled him out,' said Claire. 'He could have fallen on the rocks.'

'There's no scalp or facial trauma.'

McNally reached for the paddles. 'Stand back. Let's shock him again.'

Lincoln found her in the doctors' lounge. She had changed into hospital scrubs, and was huddled on the couch, numbly sipping coffee, when she heard the door swing shut. He moved so quietly she did not realize it was him until he sat down beside her and said, 'You should go home, Claire. There's no reason for you to stay. Please, go home.'

She blinked and dropped her head in her hands, fighting not to cry. To weep in public over a patient's death was to show loss of control. A breach of professional facade. Her body went rigid with the struggle to hold back tears.

'I have to warn you,' he said. 'When you leave the building, you'll find a mob scene downstairs. The TV crews have parked their vans right outside the exit. You can't walk to the parking lot without running their gauntlet.'

'I have nothing to say to them.'

'Then don't say anything. I'll help you get through it, if you want me to.' She felt Lincoln's hand settle on her arm. A gentle reminder that it was time to leave.

'I called Scotty's next of kin,' she said, wiping a

hand across her eyes. 'There's only his mother's cousin. She just came up from Florida, to be with Kitty while she recovers. I told her Scotty was dead, and you know what she said? She said, "It's a blessing."' She looked at Lincoln and saw disbelief in his eyes. 'That's what she called it, *a blessing*. Divine punishment.'

He slipped his arm around her, and she pressed her face to his shoulder. He was silently granting her permission to cry, but she didn't allow herself that luxury. There was still that gauntlet of reporters to confront, and she would not show them a face swollen with tears.

He was right beside her as they walked out of the hospital. As soon as the cold air hit them, so did the barrage of questions.

'Dr Elliot! Is it true Scotty Braxton was abusing drugs?'

'—rumors of a teenage murder ring?'

'Did he really chew off his own thumb?'

Dazed by the assault of shouts, Claire waded blindly into the gathering, not seeing any of the faces as she pushed through. A cassette recorder was thrust into her face, and she found herself staring at a woman with a lion's mane of blond hair.

'Isn't it true this town has a history of murder going back hundreds of years?'

'What?'

'Those old bones they found by the lake. It was a mass murder. And a century before that –'

Swiftly Lincoln stepped between them. 'Get out of here, Damaris.'

The woman gave a sheepish laugh. 'Hey, I'm just doing my job, Chief.'

'Then go write about alien babies! Leave her alone.'

A new voice called out: 'Dr Elliot?'

Claire turned to focus on the man's face, and she recognized Mitchell Groome. The reporter stepped toward her, his gaze searching hers. 'Flanders, Iowa,' he said quietly. 'Is it happening here?'

She shook her head. And said, softly: 'I don't know.'

13

Warren Emerson's lungs hurt from the cold. His outdoor thermometer had registered nine degrees this morning, so he had dressed warmly. He was wearing two shirts and a sweater under his jacket, had pulled on a hat and mittens and wound a scarf around and around his neck, but you could not protect against the cold air you breathed in. It seared his throat and made his chest ache, his lungs spasm. He sounded like a locomotive chugging down the road. *Wheeze-cough, wheeze-cough.* Not even winter yet, he thought, and already the world has turned to ice. The bare trees were encased in it, their branches glittering and crystalline. He had to walk with care on the slick road, deliberately planting each footstep on the speckled ice, where the county trucks had left their spray of sand. It took twice the effort just to stay on his feet, and by the time he reached the edge of town, the muscles in his legs were trembling.

The check-out lady at Cobb and Morong's General Store raised her head as Warren walked into the store. He smiled at her, as he did each week, always in hope that she would return the greeting. He saw her lips start to tilt up in an automatic welcome, then her eyes focused on Warren's face and her smile froze, not quite formed. She looked away.

In silent defeat, Warren turned and reached for a shopping cart.

He followed the same tired routine he always did, his boots shuffling across the creaky floorboards. He stopped in the aisle of canned vegetables and stared at the array of creamed corn and green beans and beets, at the labels with their bright illustrations of summer succulence. Labels lie, he thought. There is no comparison between that can of orange cubes and a carrot pulled fresh and sweet from warm soil. He stood there without reaching for a single item, his thoughts drifting instead to the summer vegetables he had grown and now missed so much. He counted the months until spring, added on the months needed for a new crop to mature. His whole life, it seemed, was spent waiting for winter to pass, or preparing for winter to come. He thought: *Enough is enough. I've lived too many winters already. I cannot bear to live through another one.*

He left his cart where it was standing, and he walked past the eternally unsmiling cashier and out the door.

He stood on the sidewalk outside Cobb and Morong's and gazed across the road, at the newly frozen lake. Its surface was as bright as a polished mirror, flawlessly silvered, unmarred by even a wisp of snow. Skating ice, he thought, remembering the winters of his childhood, his feet gliding, the delicious scrape, scrape of his blades. Soon there would be children skating out there with their hockey sticks and their bright winter jackets, like confetti blowing across the ice.

But I have had enough of winter. I want no more of it.

He breathed in and felt, deep in his lungs, the sting of cold air. Sharp. Punishing.

The cat was back in the window of the five-and-dime on Elm Street. He was cleaning himself, his fur glossy and raven-black in the sunshine. As Claire walked past, he paused from his self-administered bath and stared at her in disdain.

She glanced up at the sky. It was a hard blue, the kind of sky that precedes a wretchedly cold night. Since Scotty Braxton's death four days ago, winter had asserted itself with cruel finality. A dull sheen of ice now covered the entire lake, and in the newspaper obituaries this morning, the announcements of funeral arrangements had all concluded with the same phrase: 'Burial will be in the spring.' When the ground has thawed. When the earth reawakens.

Will I still be here in the spring?

She turned into Tannery Alley. Over a doorway hung a sign, swaying like a tavern placard in the wind:

Police, Town of Tranquility

She walked straight into Lincoln's office, and placed the latest issue of the *Weekly Informer* on his desk.

He looked over his glasses at her. 'Problem, Claire?'

'I just came from Monaghan's Diner, where everyone was talking about *that*. Damaris Horne's latest piece of trash.'

He glanced down at the headline: SMALL TOWN GRIPPED BY EVIL. 'It's just a Boston tabloid,' he said. 'No one takes that stuff seriously.'

'Have you read it?'

'No.'

'Everyone at Monaghan's has. And they're so scared, they're talking about keeping loaded guns handy, just in case some devil-possessed teenager tries to steal their precious truck or something.'

Lincoln groaned and pulled off his glasses. 'Oh, hell. This is the last thing I need.'

'I sewed up three patients with lacerations yesterday. One of them was a *nine*-year-old who punched his fist through a window. We're having enough trouble with the kids in this town. Now the adults have gone crazy, too.' She planted both hands on his desk. 'Lincoln, you can't wait until the town meeting to talk to these people. You have to head off the hysteria now. Those Dinosaurs have declared open season on children.'

'Even imbeciles have a right to free speech.'

'Then at least gag your own men! Who's this cop Damaris quotes from your department?' She pointed to the tabloid. 'Read it.'

He looked down at the section she'd indicated.

What is behind this small town's epidemic of violence?

Many here think they know the reason for it, but their explanations are so disturbing to local authorities that few will speak on the record. One local policeman (who wishes to remain unidentified) privately confirmed the harrowing claims made by local citizens: that Satanists have taken hold of Tranquility.

'We're well aware there are witches living here,' he said. 'Sure, they call themselves "wiccans" and claim they're innocently worshiping earth spirits or some such. But witchcraft has been linked to devil worship through the ages, and you can't help but wonder what these so-called earth worshipers are really doing out there in the woods at night.' When asked to elaborate, he said, 'We've had a number of complaints from citizens who've heard drumming in the woods. Some people have seen lights flickering up on Beech Hill, which is uninhabited forest.'

Late-night drumming and weird lights in the woods aren't the only alarming signs that something is amiss in this isolated village. Rumors of Satanic rituals have long been part of local lore. One woman recalls hearing whispered stories from her childhood of secret ceremonies and infants vanishing soon after birth. Others in town recount horrifying childhood tales of ceremonies in which small animals or even children have been offered up in the name of Satan . . .

'Which one of your officers is talking to this reporter?' Claire demanded.

His face suddenly dark with anger, Lincoln shot to his feet and stalked to the doorway. 'Floyd! Floyd! Who the hell talked to that Damaris Horne woman?'

Floyd's response was slightly tremulous. 'Uh . . . you did, Lincoln. Last week.'

'Someone else in this department has too. Who was it?'

'It wasn't me.' Floyd paused, and added confidentially, 'She kinda scares me, that Damaris lady. Gives you the impression she'd like to eat y'up alive.'

Lincoln returned to his desk and sat down, his anger still evident. 'We've got six men in this department,' he said to Claire. 'I'll do my best to track it down. But anonymous leaks are next to impossible to trace.'

'Could she have made up the quotes?'

'She might. Knowing Damaris.'

'How well *do* you know her?'

'Better than I care to.'

'What does that mean?'

'Well, we're not running off to Rio together,' he snapped back. 'She's a goddamn persistent woman, and she seems to get whatever she goes after.'

'Including the local police.'

She saw fresh anger flare up in his eyes. Their gazes held for a moment, and she felt an unexpected spark of attraction. It surprised her, coming as it did at that instant. This morning he was not looking his best. His hair was ruffled, as though he'd been running his hands through it in frustration, and he was more rumpled than usual, his shirt wrinkled, his eyes bleary from lack of sleep. All the stress of his job, of his personal life, was written right there on his face.

In the next room, the phone rang. Floyd reappeared in Lincoln's doorway. 'The cashier from Cobb and Morong's just called. Dr Elliot, you might want to head over there.'

'Why?' asked Claire. 'What happened?'

'Oh, it's that old Warren Emerson again. He's having another seizure.'

A crowd of bystanders had gathered on the sidewalk. At their center lay an old man dressed in frayed clothes, his limbs jerking in a grand mal seizure. A scalp wound was oozing blood, and in the bitter wind, an alarming splash of red had flash-frozen on the sidewalk. None of the bystanders had attempted to help the man; instead they were all standing back, as though afraid to touch him, afraid even to approach him.

Claire knelt down, and her first concern was to prevent him from injuring himself or aspirating secretions into his lungs. She rolled the man onto his side, loosened his scarf, and wedged it under his cheek to protect it from the icy sidewalk. His skin was florid from the cold, not cyanotic; his pulse was rapid but strong.

'How long has he been seizing?' she called out.

Her question was met with silence. She glanced up at the bystanders and saw that they had backed away even farther, that their gazes were focused not on her, but on the man. The only sound was the wind, blowing in from the lake, whipping at coats and scarves.

'How long?' she repeated, her voice now sharp with impatience.

'Five, maybe ten minutes,' someone finally answered.

'Has an ambulance been called?'

There was a shaking of heads, a collective shrug of shoulders.

'It's just old Warren,' said a woman whom Claire recognized as the cashier from the general store. 'He never needed an ambulance before.'

'Well, he needs one now!' snapped Claire. 'Call one!'

'Seizures are slowing down,' said the cashier. 'It'll be over in a minute.'

The man's limbs were jerking only intermittently now, his brain firing off the final bursts of its electrical storm. At last he lay flaccid. Claire again checked his pulse and found it still strong, still steady.

'See, he's okay,' said the cashier. 'Always comes out of it fine.'

'He needs stitches. And he needs neurological evaluation,' said Claire. 'Who's his doctor?'

'It used to be Pomeroy.'

'Well, someone must be prescribing seizure meds for him now. What's his medical history? Does anyone know?'

'Why don't you ask Warren? He's waking up.'

She looked down and saw Warren Emerson's eyes slowly open. Though he was surrounded by people, he gazed straight up at the sky, as though seeing it for the first time.

'Mr Emerson,' she said. 'Can you look at me?'

For a moment he didn't respond; he seemed lost in wonder, his eyes following the slow drift of a cloud overhead.

'Warren?'

At last he focused on her, his brow wrinkling as though he was struggling to understand why this strange woman was talking to him.

'I had another one,' he murmured. 'Didn't I?'

'I'm Dr Elliot. The ambulance is on its way, and we'll be taking you to the hospital.'

'I want to go home . . .'

'You've split open your scalp and you need stitches.'

'But my cat – my cat's at home.'

'Your cat will be fine. Who's your doctor, Warren?'

He seemed to be struggling to remember. 'Dr Pomeroy.'

'Dr Pomeroy has passed away. Who is your doctor now?'

He shook his head and closed his eyes. 'Doesn't matter. It doesn't matter anymore.'

Claire heard the wail of the approaching ambulance. It pulled to a stop at the curb and two EMTs stepped out.

'Oh, it's just Warren Emerson,' one of them said, as though he ran into the same patient every day. 'He have another seizure?'

'And a pretty deep scalp wound.'

'Okay, Warren, ol' buddy,' said the EMT. 'Looks like you're going for a ride.'

By the time the ambulance drove away, Claire's fury was boiling over. She looked down at the blood, solidified on the ice. 'I can't believe you people,' she said. 'Did anyone try to help him? Does anyone give a damn?'

'They're just scared,' said the cashier.

Claire turned to look at the woman. 'At the very least you could have protected his head. A seizure's nothing to be afraid of.'

'We're not afraid of that. It's *him*.'

She shook her head in disbelief. 'You're afraid of an old man? What possible threat could he be?'

Her question was met with silence. Claire looked around at the other faces, but no one returned her gaze.

No one said a thing.

By the time Claire arrived at the hospital, the ER physician had already sutured Warren Emerson's lacerated scalp and was scribbling notes on a clipboard. 'Needed eight stitches,' said McNally. 'Plus he had some minor frostbite of the nose and ears. Must've been lying in the cold for a while.'

'At least twenty minutes,' said Claire. 'You think he needs admission?'

'Well, the seizures are a chronic problem, and he seems to be neurologically intact. But he did hit his head. I can't tell if the loss of consciousness was due to the seizure or the head bonk.'

'Does he have a primary care physician?'

'Not currently. According to our records, his last hospitalization was back in '89, when Dr Pomeroy admitted him.' McNally signed off on the ER sheet and looked at Claire. 'You want to take him?'

'I was about to suggest it,' she said.

McNally handed her Emerson's old hospital chart. 'Happy reading.'

The file contained the record for Emerson's 1989 hospitalization as well as the summaries from numerous ER visits over the years. She turned first to the 1989 admission history and physical and recognized Dr Pomeroy's spidery handwriting. It was a skimpy entry, recording only the essential facts:

History: 57-year-old white male, accidentally struck left foot with ax while chopping kindling five days ago. Wound has turned swollen and painful and patient now unable to bear weight.

Physical: Temperature 99 degrees. Left foot has two-inch laceration, skin edges closed. Surrounding skin is warm, red, tender. Enlarged groin nodes on left.

Diagnosis: Cellulitis.

Rx: Intravenous antibiotics.

There was no past medical history, no social history, nothing to indicate that a living, breathing human was attached to that infected foot.

She flipped to the ER records. There were twenty-five sheets for twenty-five visits going back thirty years, all the visits for the same reasons: *'Chronic epileptic with seizure . . .' 'Seizure, scalp wound . . .' 'Seizure, lacerated cheek . . .'* Seizure, seizure, seizure. In every case, Dr Pomeroy had simply released him without further investigation. Nowhere did she find a record of any diagnostic workup.

Pomeroy may have been beloved by his patients, but in this case, he had clearly been negligent.

She stepped into the exam room.

Warren Emerson was lying on his back on the

treatment table. Surrounded by all that gleaming equipment, his clothes seemed even more frayed, more shabby. A large patch of his hair had been shaved, and the newly sutured scalp laceration was now dressed with gauze. He heard Claire enter the room and slowly turned to look at her. He seemed to recognize her; a faint smile formed on his lips.

'Mr Emerson,' she said. 'I'm Dr Elliot.'

'You were there.'

'Yes, when you had the seizure.'

'I wanted to thank you.'

'For what?'

'I don't like waking up alone. I don't like it when . . .' He fell silent and stared at the ceiling. 'Can I go home now?'

'That's what we have to talk about. Since Dr Pomeroy died, no one's been following you. Would you like me to be your doctor?'

'Don't much need a doctor anymore. Nothing anyone can do for me.'

Smiling, she squeezed his shoulder. He seemed buried, mummified beneath all those musty layers of clothes. 'I think I can help you. The first thing we have to do is get your seizures controlled. How often do you have them?'

'I don't know. Sometimes I wake up on the floor, and I figure that's what happened.'

'There's no one else at home? You live alone?'

'Yes, ma'am.' He gave her a sad wisp of a smile. 'I mean, except for my cat, Mona.'

'How often do you *think* you've had seizures?'

He hesitated. 'A few times a month.'

'And what medicines do you take?'

'I gave them up years ago. Weren't doing me any good, all those pills.'

She gave an exasperated sigh. 'Mr Emerson, you can't just stop taking medications.'

'But I don't need them anymore. I'm ready to die now.' He said it quietly, without fear, without the faintest note of self-pity. It was merely a statement of fact. *I am going to die soon, and there's nothing to be done about it.*

She had heard other patients make such predictions. They would enter the hospital in far-from-terminal condition, yet they'd say to Claire, with quiet conviction, 'I am not going home this time.' She would try to reassure them, but would already be feeling that premonitory chill of death. Patients always seem to know. When they say they are going to die, they do.

Looking into Warren Emerson's calm eyes, she felt that chill. She shook it off, and proceeded to do the physical exam.

'I have to look in your eyes,' she said, reaching for the ophthalmoscope.

He sighed in resignation and allowed her to examine his retinas.

'Have you ever seen a neurologist about your seizures? A brain specialist?'

'I saw one way back. When I was seventeen.'

She straightened in surprise and flipped off the

ophthalmoscope light. 'That's almost fifty years ago.'

'He said I had epilepsy. That I'd have it for the rest of my life.'

'Have you seen a neurologist since then?'

'No, ma'am. Dr Pomeroy, he took care of me after I moved back to Tranquility.'

She continued her exam, finding no neurologic abnormalities. His heart and lungs were normal, his abdomen without masses.

'Did Dr Pomeroy ever do a brain scan on you?'

'He did an X-ray, few years ago, after I fell down and hit my head. He thought maybe I'd cracked my skull, but I didn't. Got too hard a head, I guess.'

'Have you been to any other hospital?'

'No, Ma'am. Been in Tranquility most all my life. Never had call to go anywhere else.' He sounded regretful. 'Now it's too late.'

'Too late for what, Mr Emerson?'

'God doesn't give us a second chance.'

She had found nothing abnormal. Still, she felt uneasy about letting him go home to an empty house.

Also, what he'd said still bothered her: *I'm ready to die now.*

'Mr Emerson,' she said, 'I want to keep you in the hospital overnight and run a few tests. Just to make sure there's nothing new causing these seizures.'

'I been having them most of my life.'

'But you haven't been checked out in years. I want to start you on medication again, and get some pictures of your brain. If everything looks fine, I'll let you go home tomorrow.'

'Mona doesn't like to go hungry.'

'Your cat will be fine. Right now you have to think about yourself. Your own health.'

'Haven't fed her since last night. She'll be yowling –'

'I'll make sure your cat's fed, if that'll keep you here. How about it?'

He studied her for a moment, trying to decide whether he could entrust the welfare of his best, perhaps only, friend to a woman he scarcely knew.

'The tuna,' he said finally. 'Today, she'll expect the tuna.'

Claire nodded. 'The tuna it is.'

Back in the nurses' station, the first call she made was to the X-ray department. 'I'm admitting a patient named Warren Emerson, and I want to order a CT scan of his head.'

'Diagnosis?'

'Seizures. Rule out brain tumor.'

She was writing Warren's history and physical when Adam DelRay strolled into the ER, shaking his head. 'I just saw them wheel Warren Emerson out of the elevator,' he said to one of the nurses. 'Who on earth admitted him?'

Claire looked up, her feelings of dislike for him

stronger than ever. 'I did,' she said coolly. 'He had a seizure today.'

He snorted. 'Emerson's had seizures for years. He's a lifelong epileptic.'

'One can always grow a new brain tumor.'

'Hey, if you want to take him on, you get the halo. Pomeroy complained about him for years.'

'Why?'

'Never took his meds. That's why he keeps seizing. Plus he's on Medicaid, so good luck getting paid. But I guess there are worse ways to spend our tax dollars than serving old Emerson breakfast in bed.' He laughed and walked away.

She signed her name so hard the tip of her pen almost sliced through the paper. All these tests she'd ordered, plus a night's stay in the hospital, added up to an expensive hunch on her part. Perhaps Emerson's memory was faulty; perhaps Dr Pomeroy had performed a recent diagnostic workup, though she doubted it. From what she'd seen of his charts, Pomeroy had been a lackadaisical clinician, more likely to write a prescription for some new pill than to painstakingly investigate the reasons for a patient's symptoms.

She left the hospital and drove back to Tranquility. By the time she reached her office, she was focused on only one thing: reviewing Emerson's outpatient chart and proving to herself that her decision to admit him was justified.

Vera was on the telephone when Claire walked

in. Waving the phone, Vera said, 'You've got a call from a Max Tutwiler.'

'I'll take it in my office. Could you get Warren Emerson's file for me?'

'Warren *Emerson*?'

'Yes, I've just admitted him for seizures.'

'Why?'

Claire halted in her office doorway and turned to glare at Vera. 'Why does everyone in this town question my judgment?'

'Well, I was just *wondering*,' said Vera.

Claire shut the door and sank behind her desk. Now she'd have to apologize to Vera. Add it to her ever-growing list of mea culpas. She was in no mood to talk to anyone right now; reluctantly she picked up the telephone.

'Hello, Max?'

'Good time to call?'

'Don't even ask.'

'Oh. I'll keep it short, then. I thought you'd want to know they've confirmed the identity of that blue mushroom. I sent it to a mycologist, and he agreed it's *Clitocybe odora*, the anise funnel cap.'

'How toxic is it?'

'Only mildly so. The small amounts of muscarine wouldn't cause much beyond some mild gastrointestinal upset.'

She sighed. 'So that's a dead end.'

'It would appear so.'

'What about those lake water samples? Are the results back?'

'Yes, I have some of the preliminary findings here. Let me get the printout . . .'

Vera knocked on the door and came in with Warren Emerson's chart. She didn't say a word, just dropped the folder on the desk and walked out again. While waiting for Max to come back on the line, Claire opened the chart and glanced at the first page. It was dated 1932, the year of Emerson's birth. It described the uncomplicated labor and delivery of a healthy boy to a Mrs Agnes Emerson. The doctor's name was Higgins. The next few pages were devoted to well-baby checks and routine childhood visits.

She turned to a new page in the chart and frowned at the date: 1956. There had been a ten-year gap between the previous entry and this one. For the first time, Dr Pomeroy's signature appeared in the chart. She started to read Pomeroy's entry, but was interrupted by Max's voice on the line.

'Bacterial cultures are still pending,' he said. 'So far I see that dioxin, lead, and mercury levels are all within safe limits . . .'

Claire's attention was suddenly riveted on the chart. On what Pomeroy had written in the last paragraph: *'Has committed no other violent acts since his arrest in 1946.'*

'. . . by next week, we should know more,' Max said. 'But so far, the water quality seems pretty good. No evidence of any chemical contamination.'

262

'I've got to go,' she cut in. 'I'll call you later.'

She hung up and reread Pomeroy's entry from beginning to end. It was written in the year Warren Emerson had turned twenty-five years old.

The year he'd been released from the State Mental Hospital in Augusta.

Nineteen forty-six. In which month had Warren Emerson committed violence?

Claire stood in the basement archives room of the *Tranquility Gazette*, staring at a wooden cabinet that took up an entire wall. Each drawer was labeled by year. She opened the drawer for 1946, July to December.

Inside lay six issues of the *Gazette*. In 1946, it had been a monthly newspaper. The pages were brittle and yellow, the ads adorned with wasp-waisted women in bouffant skirts and smart little hats. Gingerly she leafed through the July issue, scanning the headlines: RECORD HEAT MAKES UP FOR RAINY SPRING ... BIGGEST SUMMER VISITOR COUNT EVER ... MOSQUITO ALERT ... BOYS CAUGHT WITH ILLEGAL FIREWORKS ... JULY 4TH PARADE DRAWS RECORD CROWDS. The same headlines that seem to appear every July, she thought. Summer has always been the season for parades and biting bugs, and these headlines brought back memories of her first summer in Maine. The crunch of sweet corn on the cob and snap peas, the tang of citronella on her skin. It had been a good summer, as it had been in 1946.

She turned to the August and September issues, where she read more of the same, news of fish fries and church dances and swim races in the lake. There was unpleasant news as well: a three-car accident had sent two visitors to the hospital and a house had burned down due to a cooking mishap. Shoplifters had taken their toll on area stores. Life was not perfect in Vacationland.

She turned to the October issue and found herself staring at a headline in bold print:

15-YEAR-OLD BOY SLAYS PARENTS, THEN FALLS TO HIS DEATH; YOUNGER SISTER'S ACTIONS 'CLEARLY SELF-DEFENSE.'

The juvenile was not named, but there were photographs of the murdered parents, a handsome, dark-haired couple smiling in their Sunday best. She focused on the caption beneath the photo, identifying the murdered couple: Martha and Frank Keating. Their last name was familiar; she knew of a local judge named Iris Keating. Were they related?

Her gaze dropped to another headline below it:

FISTFIGHT BREAKS OUT IN HIGH SCHOOL CAFETERIA.

Then another: BOSTON VISITOR MISSING; GIRL LAST SEEN WITH AREA YOUTHS.

The basement was unheated, and her hands felt like ice. But the chill came from within.

She reached for the November issue and stared at the front page. At the headline screaming up at her.

14-YEAR-OLD ARRESTED FOR MURDER OF

The chill had spread all the way up her spine. She thought: *It's happening all over again.*

14

'Why didn't you tell me? Why did you keep it a secret?'

Lincoln crossed the room to shut his office door. Then he turned to face Claire. 'It was a long time ago. I didn't see the point of dredging up old history.'

'But it's the history of this town! Considering what's happened in the last month, it strikes me as relevant.'

She placed the photocopied articles from the *Tranquility Gazette* on his desk. 'Look at this. In 1946, seven people were murdered and one girl from Boston was never found. Obviously violence is nothing new to this town.' She tapped the stack of papers. 'Read the articles, Lincoln. Or do you already know the details?'

Slowly he sat down, staring at the pages. 'Yes, I know most of the details,' he said softly. 'I've heard the stories.'

'Who told you?'

'Jeff Willard. He was chief of police when I was first hired twenty-two years ago.'

'You hadn't heard about it before then?'

'No. And I grew up here. I knew nothing about it until Chief Willard told me. People just don't talk about it.'

'They'd rather pretend it never happened.'

'There's also our reputation to consider.' He looked up, at last meeting her gaze. 'This is a resort town, Claire. People come here to escape the big city, escape crime. We're not eager to reveal to the world that we've had our own problems. Our own murder epidemic.'

She sat down, her gaze now level with his. 'Who knows about this?'

'The people who were here then. The older ones, now in their sixties and seventies. But not their children. Not my generation.'

She shook her head in amazement. 'They kept it a secret all these years?'

'You understand why, don't you? It's not just the town they're protecting. It's their families. The kids who committed those crimes were all local. Their families still live here, and maybe they're still ashamed. Still suffering the aftermath.'

'Like Warren Emerson.'

'Exactly. Look at the life he's had. He lives alone, and has no friends. He's never committed another crime, yet he's shunned by everyone. Even by the kids, who have no idea why they're supposed to steer clear of him. They just know from their grandparents that Emerson is a man to be avoided.' He looked down at the photocopied article. 'So that's the background on your patient. Warren Emerson is a murderer. But he wasn't the only one.'

'You must have seen the parallels, Lincoln.'

'Okay, I admit there are some.'

'Too many to list.' She reached for the photocopied articles and flipped to the October issue. 'In 1946, it started off with fights in the schools. Two kids were expelled. Then there were windows smashed in town, homes vandalized – again, adolescents were blamed. Finally, the last week of October, a fifteen-year-old boy hacks his parents to death. His younger sister pushes him out the window in self-defense.' She looked up at him. 'It only gets worse from there. How do you explain it?'

'When violence occurs, Claire, it's only human nature to ask why. But the truth is, we don't always know why people kill each other.'

'Look at the sequence of events. Last time it started off with a quiet town. Then here and there, kids start to misbehave. Hurt each other. In a matter of weeks, they're killing people. The town's in an uproar, everyone demanding that something be done. And suddenly – magically – it all just *stops*. And the town goes back to sleep again.' She fell silent, her gaze dropping to the headline. 'Lincoln, there's something else that's strange about it. In the city, the most dangerous time of year is the summer, when the heat makes everyone's temper flare. Crime always takes a nosedive when it gets cold. But in this town, it's different. The violence starts in October, and peaks in November.' She looked up at him. 'Both times, the killing started in the fall.'

The beeping of her pocket pager startled her. She glanced at the number on the display, and reached for Lincoln's phone.

A CT technician answered her call. 'We just finished the brain scan on your patient, Warren Emerson. Dr Chapman's on his way over to read it now.'

'You see anything?' asked Claire.

'It's definitely abnormal.'

Dr Chapman clipped the CT films to the X-ray viewing box and flipped on the switch. The light flickered on, illuminating the transverse cuts of Warren Emerson's brain. 'This is what I'm talking about,' he said. 'Right here, extending into the left frontal lobe. You see it?'

Claire stepped closer. What he'd pointed out was a small, spherelike density located at the front of the brain, just behind the eyebrow. It appeared to be solid, not cystic. She glanced at the other cuts on view, but saw no other masses. If this was a tumor, then it appeared to be localized. 'What do you think?' she asked. 'A meningioma?'

He nodded. 'Most likely. See how smooth the edges are? Of course you'll need tissue diagnosis to confirm it's benign. It's about two centimeters in diameter, and it seems to be thickly encapsulated. Walled off by fibrous tissue. I suspect it can be removed without any residual tumor left behind.'

'Could this be the cause of his seizures?'

'How long has he had them?'

'Since his late teens. Which would make it close to fifty years.'

Chapman glanced at her in surprise. 'And this mass was never picked up?'

'No. Since he's had the seizures most of his life, I think Pomeroy assumed it wasn't worth pursuing.'

Chapman shook his head. 'That makes me rethink my diagnosis. First of all, you rarely see meningiomas in young adults. Also, a meningioma would continue to grow. So either this isn't the cause of his seizures, or this is not a meningioma.'

'What else could it be?'

'A glioma. A metastasis from some other primary.' He shrugged. 'It could even be an old walled-off cyst.'

'This mass looks solid.'

'If this was from TB, for instance, or a parasite, the body would launch an inflammatory reaction. Surround it or bind it up with scar tissue. Have you checked his TB status?'

'He was PPD-negative ten years ago.'

'Well, in the end, it's still a pathologic diagnosis. This patient needs a craniotomy and excision.'

'I guess this means we have to transfer him to Bangor.'

'We don't do craniotomies in this hospital. Our docs usually refer neurosurgery cases to Clarence Rothstein, out at Eastern Maine Medical Center.'

'You'd recommend him?'

Chapman nodded and flicked off the light box. 'He's got very good hands.'

Steamed broccoli and rice and a pathetic little dab of cod.

Louise Knowlton didn't know if she could bear it any longer, watching her son slowly starve. He had lost two more pounds, and the strain showed in his grim expression, his flashes of irritability. He was no longer her cheerful Barry.

Louise looked across the table at her husband and read the same thought in Mel's eyes: *It's the diet. He's behaving this way because of the diet.*

Louise pointed to the platter of french fries that she and Mel had been sharing. 'Barry, sweetie, you look so hungry! A few of those won't matter.'

Barry ignored her, and kept scraping his plate with the fork, eliciting teeth-shattering squeals against the china.

'Barry, stop that!'

He looked up. Not just a glance, but the coldest, flattest stare she had ever seen.

With trembling hands, Louise extended the platter of french fries. 'Oh please, Barry,' she murmured. 'Eat one. Eat them all. It will make you feel so much better if you just eat something.'

She gave a startled gasp as Barry shoved his chair

back and abruptly stood up. Without a word he walked away and slammed his bedroom door shut. A moment later they heard the incessant gunfire of the video game as their son blasted away hordes of virtual enemies.

'Did something happen in school today?' asked Mel. 'Those kids picking on him again?'

Louise sighed. 'I don't know. I don't know anything anymore.'

They sat listening to the accelerating blast of gunfire. To the cries and moans of virtual victims as they lay dying in some Super Nintendo hell.

Louise looked down at the pile of limp and soggy french fries and she shuddered. For the first time in her life, she pushed her dinner away, unfinished.

Noah's stereo was playing full blast when Claire arrived home. The headache that had been building all afternoon seemed to tighten around her cranium, digging its claws into her forehead. She hung up her coat and stood at the bottom of the steps, listening to the relentless pounding of drums, the chanting of lyrics. She couldn't understand a single word. How am I supposed to monitor my child's music when I don't even know what the songs are saying?

This could not go on. She couldn't deal with the noise, not tonight. She called up the stairs: 'Noah, turn it down!'

The music played on, unabating. Unbearable.

She climbed the steps, her irritation swelling to anger. Reaching his room, she found the door locked. She pounded on it and yelled: 'Noah!'

It took a moment before the door swung open. The music rushed at her, engulfing her in a tidal wave of noise. Noah hulked in the doorway, his shirt and trousers so baggy they hung like tattered ceremonial robes.

'Turn it down!' she yelled.

He flipped the amplifier switch and the music abruptly went dead. Her ears were still ringing in the silence.

'What are you trying to do, make yourself deaf? And drive me totally nuts in the process?'

'You weren't home.'

'I *was* home. I've been yelling, but you couldn't hear me.'

'I'm hearing you now, okay?'

'In ten years you're not going to hear a thing if you keep playing your music that loud. You're not the only one who lives under this roof.'

'How can I forget when you keep reminding me?' He dropped like a stone into a chair and swiveled around to face his desk. Turning his back on her.

She stood watching him. Even though he was flipping the pages of a magazine, she knew by the muscles tensed in his shoulders that he wasn't really reading. He was too aware of *her*, of her anger toward him.

She came into his room and wearily sat down

on the bed. After a moment she said, 'I'm sorry I yelled at you.'

'You do it all the time now.'

'Do I?'

'Yeah.' He flipped a page.

'I don't mean to, Noah. I have so many things going wrong at once, I can't seem to deal with them all.'

'Everything's all screwed up since we moved here, Mom. *Everything*.' He slapped the magazine shut and dropped his head in his hands. His voice was barely a whisper. 'I wish Dad was here.'

For a moment they were both silent. She heard his tears fall on the page of the magazine, heard his sharp intake of breath as he struggled for control.

She stood up and placed her hands on his shoulders. They were tense, all his muscles knotted with the effort not to cry. We are so much alike, she realized, both of us constantly fighting to rein in our emotions, to stay in control. Peter had been the exuberant member of the family, the one who screamed with delight on roller coasters and roared with laughter in movie theaters. The one who sang in the shower and set off smoke alarms with his cooking. The one who had never hesitated to say 'I love you.'

How sad you would be to see us now, Peter. Afraid to reach out to each other. Still mourning, still crippled by your death.

'I miss him too,' she whispered. She let her arms slip around her son and she rested her cheek in his hair, inhaling the boy-smell she loved so much. 'I miss him too.'

Downstairs, the doorbell rang.

Not now. Not now.

She held on, ignoring the sound, shutting out everything but the warmth of her son in her arms.

'Mom,' said Noah, shrugging her off. 'Mom, someone's at the door.'

Reluctantly she released her hold on him and straightened. The moment, the opportunity, had passed, and she was staring once again at his rigid shoulders.

She went downstairs, angry at this new intrusion, at yet another demand tugging her away from her son. She opened the front door to find Lincoln standing in the bitterly cold wind, his gloved hand poised to ring the bell again. He had never stopped in at her house before, and she was both surprised and puzzled by his visit.

'I have to talk to you,' he said. 'Can I come in?'

She had not yet lit a fire in the front parlor, and the room was cold and depressingly dark. Quickly she turned on all the lamps, but light was poor compensation for the chill.

'After you left my office,' he said, 'I got to thinking about what you'd said. That there's a pattern to the violence in this town. That there's some sort of connection between 1946 and this year.' He reached in his jacket and took out the sheaf of photocopied news articles she'd left him. 'Guess what? The answer was staring right at us.'

'What answer?'

'Look at the first page. The October issue, 1946.'

'I've already read that article.'

'No, not the story about the murder. The article at the bottom. You probably didn't notice it.'

She smoothed the page on her lap. The article he'd referred to was partly cut off; only the top half had been included in the photocopy. The headline read: REPAIRS ON LOCUST RIVER BRIDGE COMPLETED.

'I don't know what you're getting at,' she said.

'We had to repair that same bridge this year. Remember?'

'Yes.'

'So *why* did we have to repair it?'

'Because it was broken?'

He ran his hand through his hair in frustration. 'Geez, Claire. Think about it! Why'd the bridge need repairs? Because it got washed away. We had record rainfall this past spring, and it flooded the Locust River, washed out two homes, tore out a whole series of footbridges. I called the U.S. Geological Survey to confirm it. This year was the heaviest rainfall we've had *in fifty-two years*.'

She looked up, suddenly registering what he was trying to tell her. 'Then the last time the rainfall was this heavy . . .'

'Was the spring of 1946.'

She sat back, stunned by the coincidence. 'Rainfall,' she murmured. 'Moist soil. Bacteria. Fungi . . .'

'Mushrooms are fungi. What about those blue ones?'

She shook her head. 'Max had their identity confirmed. They're not very toxic. But heavy rains would encourage the growth of other fungi. In fact, it's a fungus that caused mass occurrences of St Vitus' dance.'

'Is that a seizure?'

'The medical term for St Vitus' dance is *chorea*. It's a writhing, dancelike movement of the limbs. Occasionally, there'll be reports of mass occurrences. It may even have inspired the witchcraft accusations in Salem.'

'A medical condition?'

'Yes. After a cold, wet spring, rye crops can be infected by this fungus. People eat the rye, and they develop chorea.'

'Could we be dealing with a form of St Vitus' dance?'

'No, I'm just saying there are examples throughout history of human diseases linked to climate. Everything in nature is intimately bound together. We may *think* we control our environment, but we're affected by so many organisms we can't see.' She paused, thinking about Scotty Braxton's negative cultures. So far nothing had grown out from either his blood or spinal fluid. Could there be a locus of infection she had missed? An organism so unusual, so unexpected, the lab would have discounted it as error?

'There must be a common factor among these children,' she said. 'Exposure to the same contaminated food, for instance. All we have is this apparent association between rainfall and violence. It could be just coincidence.'

He sat in silence for a moment. She had often studied his face, admiring the strength she saw there, the calm self-confidence. Today she saw the intelligence in his eyes. He had taken two completely disparate bits of information and had recognized a pattern that she had not even noticed.

'Then what we need to find,' he said, 'is the common factor.'

She nodded. 'Could you get me into the Maine Youth Center? So I can talk to Taylor?'

'That could be a problem. You know Paul Darnell still blames you.'

'But Taylor's not the only child affected. Paul can't blame me for everything else that's gone wrong in this town.'

'Not now, he can't.' Lincoln rose to his feet. 'We need answers before the town meeting. I'll get you in to see the boy, Claire. One way or another.'

Standing at the parlor window, she watched him walk down the icy driveway to his truck. He moved with the balanced stride of a man who'd grown up in this unforgiving climate, each step planted squarely, the boot sole stamped down to catch the ice. He reached the truck, opened the door, and for some reason glanced back at her house.

Just for an instant, their gazes met.

And she thought, with a strange sense of wonder, *How long have I been attracted to him? When did it start? I can't remember.* Now it was one more complication in her life.

As he drove away, she remained at the window, staring at a landscape bled of all color. Snow and ice and bare trees, all of it fading to black.

Upstairs, Noah's music had started again.

She turned from the window and flicked off the parlor lamp. That's when she suddenly remembered the promise she'd made to Warren Emerson, and she groaned.

The cat.

Night had fallen by the time she drove up the lower slope of Beech Hill and pulled into Emerson's front yard. She parked next to the woodpile, a perfectly circular tower of stacked logs. She thought of the many hours it must have taken him to arrange his wood with such precision, each log placed with the same care one usually gave to constructing a stone wall. And then to pull it down again, bit by bit, as winter consumed his annual work of art.

She turned off her engine and looked up at the old farmhouse. No lights were on inside. She used a flashlight to guide herself up the icy front steps to the porch. Everything seemed to sag and she had the strange illusion that she was tilting sideways, sliding toward the edge, toward oblivion. Warren had told her the door would be unlocked, and it was. She stepped inside and turned on the lights.

The kitchen sprang into view with its worn linoleum and chipped appliances. A small gray cat stared up at her from the floor. They had startled each other, she and the cat, and for a few seconds they both froze.

Then the cat shot out of the room and vanished somewhere into the house.

'Here, kitty, kitty! You want your dinner, don't you? Mona?'

She had planned to take Mona to a kennel for boarding. Warren Emerson had already been transferred to Eastern Maine Medical Center for his craniotomy, and would remain hospitalized for at least a week. Claire didn't relish the thought of driving here every day just to feed a cat. But it appeared the cat had different ideas.

Her frustration mounted as she went from room to room in search of the uncooperative Mona, turning on lights as she went. Like so many other farmhouses of its era, this one had been built to house a large family, and it consisted of many small rooms, made even more claustrophobic by the clutter. She saw piles of old newspapers and magazines, bundled grocery sacks, crates filled with empty bottles. In the hallway she had to turn sideways to navigate a narrow tunnel between stacked books. Such hoarding was usually a sign of mental illness, but Warren had organized his clutter in a logical fashion, the books segregated from the magazines, the brown paper bags all folded and bound together with twine. Perhaps this was merely Yankee frugality carried to an extreme.

It provided plenty of cover for a fugitive cat.

She'd made a complete circuit of the downstairs without spotting Mona. The cat must be hiding in one of the upstairs rooms.

She started up the steps, then halted, her hands suddenly sweating. *Deja vu*, she thought. I have lived this before. A strange house, a strange staircase. Something terrible waiting for me in the attic . . .

But this was not Scotty Braxton's house, and the only thing lurking upstairs was a frightened animal.

She forced herself to continue climbing as she called out, 'Here, kitty!' if only to prop up her faltering courage. There were four doors on the second floor, but only one was open. If the cat had fled upstairs, she had to be in that room.

Claire stepped through the doorway and turned on the light.

Her gaze was drawn at once to the black and white photographs – dozens of them hanging on the wall or propped up on the dresser and nightstand. A gallery of Warren Emerson's memories. She crossed the room and stared at three faces smiling back at her from one of the photos, a middle-aged couple with a young boy. The woman was round-faced and plain, her hat tilted at a comically drunken pitch. The man beside her seemed to be sharing in the joke; his eyes were bright with laughter. They each rested one hand on the shoulders of the boy standing between them, physically claiming him as their own, their shared possession.

And the boy with the cowlick and the missing front teeth – this must be young Warren, basking in the glow of his parents' attention.

Her gaze moved to the other photographs and she saw the same faces again and again, different seasons, different places. Here a shot of the mother proudly holding up a pie. There a shot of father and son on a riverbank with their fishing poles. Finally, a school photo of a young girl, apparently Warren's sweetheart, for at the bottom someone had drawn in a heart containing the words *Warren and Iris forever*. Through tears, Claire stared at the nightstand, at a glass of water resting there, half full. At the bed, where gray hairs had been shed on the pillow. Warren's bed.

Every morning he would wake up alone in this room, to the sight of his parents' photos. And every night, the last image he'd register was of their faces, smiling at him.

She was crying now, for the child he once was. A lonely little boy trapped in an old man's body.

She went back downstairs to the kitchen.

There was no sense chasing after a cat that didn't want to be captured. She would simply

282

leave food in the dish, and come back another time. Opening the pantry door, she found herself staring at dozens of cans of cat food stacked on the shelves. There was scarcely anything in the kitchen for a man to eat, but pampered Mona was certainly well-supplied.

Today she'll he expecting tuna.

Tuna it would be. She emptied the can into the cat dish and placed it on the floor next to the bowl of water. She filled another bowl with dried cat food, enough to last several days. She cleaned out the litterbox. Then she turned off the lights and walked out.

Sitting in her car, she glanced one last time at the house. For most of his life, Warren Emerson had lived within those walls, without human companionship, without love. He would probably die in that house alone, with only a cat to witness his exit.

She wiped the tears from her eyes. Then she turned the car around and drove down the dark road for home.

That night Lincoln called her.

'I spoke to Wanda Darnell,' he said. 'I told her there may be a biological reason for her son's actions. That other children in town have been affected, and we're trying to track down the cause.'

'How did she react?'

'I think she's relieved. It means there's something external to blame. Not the family. Not her.'

'I understand that perfectly.'

'She's given permission for you to interview her son.'

'When?'

'Tomorrow. At the Maine Youth Center.'

A long row of beds lined the wall of the silent dormitory room. The morning sun shone in through windows above, one bright square of light spilling down on the boy's thin shoulders. He sat on the bed with his legs tucked up against his chest. His head was bowed. This was not the same boy she had seen four weeks ago, cursing and thrashing. This was a child who'd been beaten down, hopes and dreams trampled, only his physical shell remaining.

He did not look up as Claire approached, her footsteps echoing on the worn planks. She stopped beside his bed. 'Hello, Taylor. Do you feel like talking to me?'

The boy lifted one shoulder, barely a shrug, but at least it was the semblance of an invitation.

She reached for a chair, her gaze falling briefly on the small pine desk next to his bed. It was a badly abused piece of furniture, its surface gouged with four-letter words and the initials of countless young residents. She wondered if Taylor had already carved his mark into this permanent record of despair.

She slid the chair to his bed and sat down. 'Whatever we talk about today, Taylor, is just between us, okay?' He gave a shrug, as if it hardly mattered. 'Tell me about what happened, that day in school. Why did you do it?'

He turned his cheek against his knees, as though suddenly too exhausted to hold up his head. 'I don't know why.'

'Do you remember that day?'

'Uh-huh.'

'Everything?'

He swallowed hard, but didn't say anything. His face suddenly rippled with anguish and he closed his eyes, squeezing them so tight his whole face seemed to collapse on itself. He took a deep breath and what should have been a howl of pain came out only as a high, thin keening.

'I don't know. I don't know why I did it.'

'You brought a gun to school that day.'

'To prove I had one. They didn't believe me. They said I was making it up.'

'Who didn't believe you?'

'J.D. and Eddie. They're always bragging that their dad lets them shoot his guns.'

Jack Reid's sons again. Wanda Darnell had said they were a bad influence, and she'd been right.

'So you brought the gun to school,' said Claire. 'Did you plan to use it?'

He shook his head. 'I just had it in my backpack. But then I got a D on my test. And Mrs Horatio – she started yelling at me about that stupid frog.' He began to rock, hugging his knees, every breath catching in a sob. 'I wanted to kill them all. It was like I couldn't stop myself. I wanted to make them all pay.' He stopped rocking and went very still, his eyes unfocused, gazing at nothing. 'I'm not mad at them anymore. But now it's too late.'

'It may not be your fault, Taylor.'

'Everyone knows I did it.'

'But you just told me you weren't in control.'

'It's still my fault . . .'

'Taylor, look at me. I don't know if anyone's told you about your friend, Scotty Braxton.'

Slowly the boy's gaze lifted to hers.

'The same thing happened to him. And now his mother is dead.'

She saw, by his look of shock, that he had not been told the news.

'No one can explain why he snapped. Why he attacked her. You're not the only one it's happened to.'

'My dad says it's because you took away my medicine.'

'Scotty wasn't taking any medicine.' She paused, searching his eyes. 'Or was he?'

'No.'

'This is very important. You have to tell me the truth, Taylor. Did either of you boys take any drugs?'

'I *am* telling the truth.'

He looked at her, his gaze unflinching. And she believed him.

'What about Scotty?' he asked. 'Is Scotty coming here?'

Tears suddenly stung her eyes. She said, softly: 'I'm sorry, Taylor. I know you two were good friends . . .'

'The best. We're best friends.'

'He was in the hospital. And something happened. We tried to help him, but there was – there was nothing –'

'He's dead. Isn't he?'

His direct question was a plea for an honest answer. She admitted, quietly: 'Yes. I'm afraid so.'

He dropped his face against his knees, and the words spilled out between sobs. 'Scotty never did anything wrong! He was such a wuss. That's what J.D. always called him, the dumb wuss. I never stood up for him. I should've said something, but I never did . . .'

'Taylor. Taylor, I need to ask you another question.'

'. . . I was afraid to.'

'You and Scotty were together a lot. Where did you two spend your time?'

He didn't answer; he just kept rocking on the bed.

'I really need to know this, Taylor. Where did you two hang out?'

He took in a shaky breath. 'With – with the other kids.'

'Where?'

'I don't know! All over.'

'In the woods? At someone's house?'

He stopped rocking, and for a moment she thought he hadn't heard the last question. Then he raised his head and looked at her. 'The lake.'

Locust Lake. It was the center of all activity in Tranquility, the place for picnics and swim races, for boaters and fishermen. Without it, there would be no summer visitors, no flow of money. The town itself would not exist.

It all has something to do with the lake, she thought suddenly. Water and rainfall. Floods and bacteria.

The night the water glowed.

'Taylor,' she said, 'did you and Scotty both swim in the lake?'

He nodded. 'Every day.'

15

The town meeting was scheduled for seven-thirty, and by seven-fifteen, every seat in the high school cafeteria was filled. People were crowding into the aisles, lining up along the walls, and spilling out the rear doors into the cold wind. From where Claire was standing, off to the side, she had a good view of the speakers' table at the front. There Lincoln, Fern Cornwallis, and the chairman of the Town Board of Selectmen, Glen Ryder, were seated. The five members of the board were clustered in the front row.

Claire recognized many of the faces in the audience. Most of them were other parents, whom she'd met at high school functions. She also saw a number of her colleagues from Knox Hospital. The dozen teenagers in attendance had chosen to stand at the rear of the cafeteria, and were tightly clustered together as though to ward off attack by their elders.

Glen Ryder banged his gavel, but the crowd was

too large, too agitated, to hear him. The frustrated Ryder had to climb onto a chair and yell: 'This meeting will come to order *now*!'

The cafeteria at last fell silent, and Ryder continued. 'I know there aren't enough seats for everyone in here. I know there are people outside who are upset about having to stand in eight-degree weather. But the fire chief says we've already exceeded this room's occupancy limit. We just can't allow anyone else to enter, unless someone else exits first.'

'Seems to me some of those kids in the back could leave and make room for adults,' a man grumbled.

One of the teenagers retorted: 'We've got a right to be here too!'

'You kids're the reason we're here in the first place!'

'If you're going to talk about us, then we want to hear what you're saying!'

Half a dozen people started to speak at once.

'No one's being kicked out of here!' yelled Ryder. 'It's a public meeting, Ben, and we can't exclude people. Now let's get on with it.' Ryder looked at Lincoln. 'Chief Kelly, why don't you bring us up to date with the problems in town.'

Lincoln rose to his feet. The last few days had drained him, both physically and emotionally, and it showed in the drooping slope of his shoulders. 'It hasn't been a good month,' he said. A typical Lincoln Kelly understatement. 'What everyone seems to focus on are the murders. The shooting at the high school on November second, and then the Braxtons on November fifteenth. That's two murders in two weeks. What scares me even more is, I don't think we've seen the worst of it yet. Last night, my officers responded to eight different calls involving juveniles assaulting others. I've never seen this before. I've been a cop in this town for twenty-two years. I've seen minor crime waves come and go. But what I'm seeing now – kids trying to hurt each other, *kill* each other – trying to kill the people they love . . .' He shook his head and sat down without another word.

'Miss Cornwallis?' said Ryder.

The high school principal rose to her feet. Fern Cornwallis was a handsome woman, and she had taken pains to look her best tonight. Her blond hair was swept into a gleaming French twist, and she was one of the few women in the room who'd bothered to apply makeup. But that touch of bright lipstick only emphasized the anxious pallor of her face.

'I want to echo everything Chief Kelly just said. What's happening in this town – the anger, the violence – I've never seen it before, either. And it's not just a problem in the school. It's also a problem in your homes. I know these children! I've watched them grow up. I've seen them around town, in the school hallways. Or in my office, as the occasion warranted. And the ones who are getting into fights now, none of them are kids I would have labeled troublemakers. None of them gave any hint, in past years, of being violent. But suddenly I find I don't know these children anymore. I don't recognize them.' She paused and swallowed hard. 'I'm afraid of them,' she said quietly.

'So whose fault is it?' yelled Ben Doucette.

'We're not saying it's anyone's fault,' Fern said. 'We're just trying to understand why this is happening. Between our school and the middle school, we've brought in five new guidance counselors on an emergency basis. The high school has a district psychologist, Dr Lieberman, working intensively with our staff. Trying to come up with a plan of action.'

Ben stood up. A sour-faced bachelor in his fifties, he had lost an arm in Vietnam, and he was always clutching the stump with his good hand, as though to emphasize his sacrifice. 'I can tell you what the problem is,' he said. 'It's the same problem we've got all over this country. No goddamn discipline. When I was thirteen, you think I'd have dared to pick up a knife, threaten my mother? My old man woulda whapped me up the side of the head.'

'What are you suggesting, Mr Doucette?' said Fern. 'That we spank fourteen-year-olds?'

'Why not?'

'Try it!' yelled one of the teenage boys, and he was joined by the other kids in a chorus of jeers: *'Try it, try it, try it!'*

The meeting was out of control. Lincoln stood

up, raising his hand in a plea for order. It was a measure of the respect the town held for him that the crowd finally quieted down to hear him speak.

'It's time to talk about realistic solutions,' he said.

Jack Reid stood up. 'Can't talk about solutions till we talk about why it's happening in the first place. I hear from my boys that it's the new kids in school, the ones who moved here from other cities, who're causing most of the problems. Starting up gangs, maybe bringing in drugs.'

Lincoln's response was lost in a sudden crescendo of voices. Claire could see the frustration in his face, the deepening flush of anger.

'This is not a problem from away,' said Lincoln. 'This crisis is local. It's *our* problem, and *our* kids getting into trouble.'

'But who got them started?' said Reid. 'Who got 'em going? Some folks just don't belong here!'

Glen Ryder's gavel banged again and again, to no avail. Jack Reid had pushed a hot button with this crowd, and now everyone was yelling at once.

A woman's voice cut through the bedlam. 'What about the rumors of a centuries-old Satanic cult?' said Damaris Horne, rising to her feet. It was hard to miss that wild mane of blond hair. Also hard to miss were the interested glances men cast her way. 'We've all heard about those old bones they dug up by the lake. I understand it was a mass murder. Maybe even a ritual slaying.'

'That was over a hundred years ago,' said Lincoln. 'It's completely unrelated.'

'Maybe not. New England has a long history of Satanic cults.'

Lincoln was fast losing control of his temper. 'The only cult around here,' he shot back, 'is the one you made up for your trashy tabloid!'

'Then perhaps you'll explain all the disturbing rumors I've been hearing,' said Damaris, keeping her cool. 'For instance, the number *six-six-six* painted on the side of the high school.'

Lincoln aimed a startled glance at Fern. Claire realized at once what that look meant. Clearly they were both surprised by the reporter's knowledge of a real event.

'There was a barn found splashed with blood last month,' said Damaris. 'What about that?'

'That was a can of red paint. Not blood.'

'And those lights flickering at night up on Beech Hill. Which, I've been told, is nothing but forest reserve.'

'Now wait a minute,' interjected Lois Cuthbert, one of the town selectmen. 'That I can explain. It's that biologist fella, Dr Tutwiler, collecting salamanders at night. I almost ran over him in the dark a few weeks ago, when he came hiking back down.'

'All right,' conceded Damaris. 'Forget the lights up on Beech Hill. But I still say there's a lot of strange and unexplained things happening in this town. If anyone here wants to talk to me about it later, I'm ready to listen.' Damaris sat down again.

'I agree with her,' said a tremulous voice. The woman stood at the back of the room, a small, white-faced figure clutching at her coat. 'There's something wrong in this town. I've felt it for a long time. You can deny it all you want, Chief Kelly, but what we have here is *evil*. I'm not saying it's Satan. I don't know what it is. But I know I can't live here anymore. I've put my house up for sale, and I'm leaving next week. Before something happens to *my* family.' She turned and walked out of the hushed room.

The high-pitched beeping of Claire's pocket pager cut through the silence. She glanced down and saw it was the hospital trying to reach her. She pushed her way through the crowd and stepped outside to make the call on her cell phone.

After the overheated cafeteria, the wind felt piercingly cold, and she huddled, shivering, against the building, waiting for an answer.

'Laboratory, Clive speaking.'

'This is Dr Elliot. You paged me.'

'I wasn't sure if you still wanted us to call you on these results, since this patient's deceased. But I've got some reports back on Scotty Braxton.'

'Yes, I want to hear all the results.'

'First, I have a final report here from Anson Biologicals on the boy's comprehensive drug and tox screen. None were detected.'

'There's nothing about the peak on his chroma-togram?'

'Not on this report.'

'This has to be a mistake. There must be something in his drug screen.'

'That's all it says here: "None detected." We've also got the final culture result on the boy's nasal discharge. It's a pretty long list of organisms, since you wanted everything identified. Mostly the usual colonizers. *Staph epidermidis*, alpha *strep*. Bugs we don't normally bother to report.'

'Is there anything unusual growing out?'

'Yes. *Vibrio fischeri.*'

She scribbled the name down on a scrap of paper. 'I've never heard of that organism.'

'Neither had we. It's never turned up in a culture here. It has to be a contaminant.'

'But I collected the specimen straight from the patient's nasal mucosa.'

'Well, I doubt this contamination came from our lab. This bacteria isn't something you'd find floating around in a hospital.'

'What is *Vibrio fischeri*? Where does it normally grow?'

'I checked with the microbiologist in Bangor, where they did the cultures. She says this species is usually a colonizer of invertebrates like squid or marine worms. It forms a symbiotic relationship. The host invertebrate provides a safe environment.'

'And what does the *Vibrio* do in exchange?'

'It provides the power for the host's light organ.'

It took a few seconds for the significance of that fact to sink in. She asked, sharply: 'Are you saying this bacteria is bioluminescent?'

'Yeah. The squid collects it in a translucent sac. It

uses the bacteria's glow to attract other squid. Sort of like a neon sign for sex.'

'I've got to go,' she cut in. 'I'll talk to you later.' She disconnected and hurried back into the school cafeteria.

Glen Ryder was trying to quiet down the audience again, his gavel thumping ineffectually against a chorus of competing voices. He looked startled as Claire pushed her way to the speakers' table.

'I have to make an announcement,' she said. 'I have a health alert for the town.'

'It's not exactly relevant to this meeting, Dr Elliot.'

'I believe it is relevant. Please let me speak.'

He nodded and resumed banging the gavel with new urgency. 'Dr Elliot has an announcement!'

Claire moved front and center, acutely aware that everyone's gaze was on her. She took a deep breath and began. 'These attacks are scaring us all, causing us to point fingers at our neighbors, at the school. At people from away. But I believe there's a medical explanation. I've just spoken to the hospital lab, and I have a clue to what's going on.' She held up the scrap of paper with the organism's name. 'It's a bacteria called *Vibrio fischeri*. It was growing in Scotty Braxton's nasal mucus. What we're seeing now – this aggressive behavior in our children – may be a symptom of infection. *Vibrio fischeri* could cause a case of meningitis we can't detect with our usual tests. It could also cause what doctors call a "neighborhood reaction" – an infection of the sinuses, extending into the brain –'

'Wait a minute,' said Adam DelRay, rising to his feet. 'I've been practicing medicine here for ten years. I've never come across an infection of this – what is it?'

'*Vibrio fischeri*. It's not normally seen in humans. But the lab's identified it as an organism infecting my patient.'

'And where did your patient pick up this bug?'

'I believe it was the lake. Scotty Braxton and Taylor Darnell both swam in that lake almost every day last summer. So did a lot of other kids in this town. If that lake has a high bacterial count of *Vibrio*, that could explain how they're getting infected.'

'I went swimming last summer,' said a woman. 'A lot of adults did. Why would only the kids get infected?'

'It may have to do with what part of the lake you swim in. I also know there's a similar infectious pattern for amoebic meningitis. That's a brain infection caused by amoebas growing in fresh water. Children and teenagers are most often infected. When they swim in contaminated water, the amoeba enters their nasal mucosa. From there it reaches the brain by passing through a porous barrier called the cribriform plate. Adults don't get infected, because their cribriform plates are sealed over, protecting their brains. Children don't have that protection.'

'So how do you treat this? With antibiotics or something?'

'That would be my guess.'

Adam DelRay let out an incredulous laugh. 'Are you suggesting we dispense antibiotics to every irritable kid in town? You have no proof anyone's infected!'

'I do have a positive culture.'

'*One* positive culture. And it's not from the spinal fluid, so how can you call this meningitis?' He looked at the audience. 'I can assure this town there is no epidemic. Last month, the Two Hills Pediatric Group got a lab grant to survey blood counts and hormone levels in kids. They've been drawing blood on all their teenage patients in the area. Any infection would have shown up in their blood counts.'

'What grant are you talking about?' asked Claire.

'From Anson Biologicals. To confirm baseline normals. They haven't reported anything unusual.' He shook his head. 'This infection theory of yours is the most crackpot thing I've heard yet, and it comes without a shred of evidence. You don't even know if *Vibrio* is growing in the lake.'

'I know it is,' said Claire. 'I've seen it.'

'You *saw* a bacteria? What, do you have microscopic vision?'

'*Vibrio fischeri* is bioluminescent. It glows. I've seen bioluminescence in Locust Lake.'

'Where are the cultures to back it up? Have you collected water samples?'

'I saw it just before the lake froze over. It's probably too cold now to grow out viable cultures. Which means we won't have confirmation until we do water sampling in the spring. These cultures take time to grow. It could be weeks or months after that before we get an answer.' She paused, reluctant to make her next suggestion. 'Until we rule out the lake as the source of this bacteria,' she said, 'I recommend we keep our children from swimming in it.'

The uproar was expected and immediate.

'Are you crazy? We can't let an announcement like that get out!'

'What about the tourists? You'll scare off the tourists!'

'How the hell are we s'posed to make a living?'

Glen Ryder was on his feet, banging at the table. 'Order! I will have *order*!' His face florid, he turned to confront Claire. 'Dr Elliot, this isn't the time or place to suggest such drastic action. It needs to be discussed by the Board of Selectmen.'

'This is a public health issue,' said Claire. 'It's a decision for the health department. Not politicians.'

'There's no need to involve the state!'

'It's irresponsible not to.'

Lois Cuthbert shot to her feet. 'I'll tell you what's irresponsible! It's getting up there, without any evidence, with all these reporters in the room, and claiming there's some deadly bacteria in our lake. You're going to destroy this town.'

'If there's a health risk, we have no other choice.'

Lois turned to Adam DelRay. 'What's your opinion, Dr DelRay? Is there a health risk?'

DelRay gave a derisive laugh. 'The only risk that I can see is that we'll be made laughingstocks if we take this seriously. Bacteria that glow in the dark? Do they sing and dance too?'

Claire flushed as laughter burst out all around her. 'I know what I saw,' she insisted.

'Right, Dr Elliot! Psychedelic bacteria.'

Lincoln's voice suddenly rang through the laughter. 'I saw it too.'

Everyone fell silent as he rose to his feet. Startled, Claire turned to look at him and he gave her a wry nod, a gesture that said: We might as well hang together.

'I was there that night, with Dr Elliot,' he said. 'We both saw the glow on the lake. I can't tell you what it was. It only lasted for a few minutes, and then it vanished. But there *was* a glow.'

'I've lived on that lake all my life,' said Lois Cuthbert. 'I've never seen any glow.'

'Me neither!'

'—or me!'

'Hey, Chief, you and the doc sniffing the same thing?'

New laughter erupted, and this time it was directed at both of them. The outrage had turned to ridicule, but Lincoln didn't back down; he bore the insults with calm equanimity.

'It may be an episodic occurrence,' said Claire.

301

'Something that doesn't happen every year. It could be related to weather conditions. Spring flooding or a particularly hot summer – we had both this year. The very same conditions that occurred fifty-two years ago.' She paused, and her challenging gaze swept the audience. 'I know there are people in this room who remember what happened fifty-two years ago.'

The crowd went silent.

The reporter from the *Portland Press Herald* asked, loudly: 'What happened fifty-two years ago?'

Abruptly Glen Ryder shot to his feet. 'The board will take it under advisement. Thank you, Dr Elliot.'

'This should be addressed now,' said Claire. 'The health department should be called in to test the water –'

'We will discuss it at our next board meeting,' Ryder repeated firmly. 'That's *all*, Dr Elliot.'

Cheeks burning, she walked away from the speakers' table.

The meeting continued, loud and rancorous, as suggestions were tossed out. There was no further mention of her theory; they had unanimously dismissed it as not worth further discussion. Someone suggested a nine P.M. curfew – all kids off the streets. The teens protested, 'Civil rights!' 'What about our civil rights?'

'You kids have no civil rights!' shot back Lois. 'Not until you learn responsibility!'

It went downhill from there.

At ten P.M., with everyone hoarse from shouting, Glen Ryder finally adjourned the meeting.

Claire remained standing at the side of the room, watching as the crowd exited. No one looked at her as they filed past. I've ceased to exist in this town, she thought wretchedly, except as an object of scorn. She wanted to thank Lincoln for supporting her, but she saw that he was under siege, surrounded by the Board of Selectmen, who were plying him with questions and complaints.

'Dr Elliot!' called out Damaris Horne. 'What happened fifty-two years ago?'

Claire fled toward the exit, Damaris and the other reporters trailing after her as she kept repeating, 'No comment. No comment.' She was relieved when no one pursued her out the door.

Outside, the chill wind seemed to slice right through her coat. Her car was parked some distance from the school. Thrusting her hands in her pockets, she began to walk as quickly as she dared along the icy road, squinting against the intermittent glare of headlights as other cars pulled away. By the time she reached her vehicle, she already had the keys out, and was about to unlock the door when she realized something was not right.

She took a step back and stared in shock at the pools of flaccid rubber that had been her tires. All four of them had been slashed. In fury, in frustration, she slammed her hand down on the car. Once, twice.

Across the road, a man walking back to his own car turned and looked at her in surprise. It was Mitchell Groome.

'Something wrong, Dr Elliot?' he called out.

'Look at my tires!'

He paused to let a car drive past, then crossed the road to join her. 'Jesus,' he murmured. 'Someone doesn't like you.'

'They slashed *all* of them!'

'I'd help you change them. But I don't suppose you'd have four spare tires in the trunk.'

She did not appreciate his weak attempt at humor. She turned her back on him and stared down at the ruined tires. Her exposed face stung from the wind, and the chill of the frozen ground seemed to seep through the soles of her boots. It was too late to call Joe Bartlett's garage; he wouldn't be able to get four new tires till morning, anyway. She was stranded, furious, and growing colder by the minute.

She turned to Groome. 'Could you give me a ride home?'

It was a deal with the devil, and she knew it. A journalist must ask questions, and barely ten seconds into the drive, he asked the one she'd expected:

'So what did happen in this town fifty-two years ago?'

She averted her eyes. 'I'm really not in the mood for this.'

'I'm sure you're not, but it's going to come out eventually. Damaris Horne will track it down, one way or the other.'

'That woman has no sense of ethics.'

'But she does have an inside source.'

Claire looked at him. 'Are you talking about the police department?'

'You already know about it?'

'Not the name of the officer. Which one is it?'

'Tell me what happened in 1946.'

She faced forward again. 'It's in the local newspaper archives. You can look it up for yourself.'

He drove for a moment in silence. 'It's happened to this town before, hasn't it?' he said. 'The killings.'

'Yes.'

'And you believe there's a biological reason for it?'

'It has something to do with that lake. It's some sort of natural phenomenon. A bacteria, or an algae.'

'What about my theory? That this is another Flanders, Iowa?'

'It's not drug abuse, Mitchell. I thought we'd turned up something in both boys' blood – an anabolic steroid of some kind. But the final tox screens on both of them came back negative. And Taylor denies any drug abuse.'

'Kids do lie.'

'Blood tests don't.'

They pulled into her driveway, and he turned to look at her. 'You've picked an uphill fight, Dr Elliot. Maybe you didn't sense the depth of anger in that room, but I certainly did.'

'Not only did I sense it, I have four slashed tires to prove it.' She stepped out. 'Thank you for the ride. Now you owe *me* something.'

'Do I?'

'The name of the cop who's been talking to Damaris Horne.'

He gave an apologetic shrug. 'I don't know his name. All I can tell you is that I've seen them together in, shall we say, close contact. Dark hair, medium build. Works the night shift.'

She nodded grimly. 'I'll figure it out.'

Lincoln climbed the stairs to the handsome Victorian, each step bringing him closer to exhaustion. It was well past midnight. He had spent the last few hours at an emergency meeting of the Board of Selectmen, held at Glen Ryder's house, where Lincoln had been told in no uncertain terms that his job was in jeopardy. The board had hired him, and they could fire him. He was an employee of the Town of Tranquility, and therefore a guardian of its welfare. How could he support Dr Elliot's suggestion to close down the lake?

I was just stating my honest opinion, he'd told them.

But in this case, honesty was clearly not the best policy.

What had followed was a mind-numbing litany of financial statistics, provided by the town treasurer. How much money came in every summer from tourists. How many jobs were created as a result. How many local businesses existed only to service the visitor trade.

Where Lincoln's salary came from.

The town lived and died by Locust Lake, and there would be no calls to close it, no health alerts, not even a whisper of public debate.

He'd left the meeting uncertain whether he still had a job, uncertain whether he even wanted the job. He'd climbed into his cruiser, had been halfway home, when he'd received the message from Dispatch that someone else wanted to speak to him tonight.

He rang the bell. As he waited for the door to open, he glanced up the street and saw that every house was dark, all the curtains drawn against this black and frigid night.

The door swung open, and Judge Iris Keating said: 'Thank you for coming, Lincoln.'

He stepped into the house. It felt airless, suffocating. 'You said it was urgent.'

'You've already met with the board?'

'A little while ago.'

'And they won't consider closing the lake. Will they?'

He gave her a resigned smile. 'Was there any doubt?'

'I know this town too well. I know how people

think, and what they're afraid of. How far they'll go to protect their own.'

'Then you know what I'm dealing with.'

She gestured toward the library. 'Let's sit down, Lincoln. I have something to tell you.'

A fire was dying behind the grate, only a few listless flames puffing up from the mound of cinders. Still, the room felt overwarm, and as Lincoln sank deeply into an overstuffed chair, he wondered if he could summon the energy to stay awake. To rise to his feet again and walk back out into the cold. Iris sat across from him, her face illuminated only by the fire's glow. The dim light was kind to her features, deepening her eyes, smoothing the wrinkles of sixty-six years into velvety shadow. Only her hands, thin and gnarled by arthritis, betrayed her age.

'I should have said something at the meeting tonight, but I didn't have the courage,' she confessed.

'Courage to say what?'

'When Claire Elliot spoke about the lake – about the night she saw the water glow – I should have added my voice to hers.'

Lincoln sat forward, the meaning of her words at last piercing his fatigue. 'You've seen it too.'

'Yes.'

'When?'

She looked down at her hands, grasping the armrests. 'It was in late summer. I was fourteen years old, and we had a house by the Boulders.

It's gone, now. Torn down years ago.' Her gaze shifted to the fire and remained there, focused on the sputtering flames. She leaned back, her hair like a halo of silver against the dark fabric of the chair. 'I remember that night, it was raining hard. I woke up, and I heard thunder. I went to the window, and there was something in the water. A light. A glow. It was there for only a few minutes, and then . . .' She paused. 'By the time I woke my parents, it was gone, and the water was dark again.' She shook her head. 'Of course they didn't believe me.'

'Did you ever see the glow again?'

'Once. A few weeks later, also during a rainstorm. Just the briefest shimmer, and then nothing.'

'The night Claire and I saw it, it was raining hard, too.'

Her gaze lifted to Lincoln's. 'All these years, I thought it was lightning. Or a trick of the eyes. But then tonight, for the first time, I learned I'm not the only one who's seen it.'

'Why didn't you say something? The town would have listened to *you*.'

'And people would ask all sorts of questions. When I saw it, which year it was.'

'Which year was it, Judge Keating?'

She looked away, but he saw the flash of tears in her eyes. 'Nineteen forty-six,' she whispered. 'It was the summer of '46.'

The year Iris Keating's parents had died at the hands of her fifteen-year-old brother. The year Iris, too, had killed, but in self-defense. She had pushed her own brother through the turret window, had watched him fall to his death.

'You understand now why I didn't speak,' she said.

'You could have made a difference.'

'No one wants to hear about it. I don't want to talk about it.'

'It was so long ago. Fifty-two years –'

'Fifty-two years is *nothing*! Look at how they still treat Warren Emerson. I'm just as guilty of it. When we were children, he and I were so close. I used to think that someday, we would . . .' She suddenly stopped. Her gaze settled on the fire, by now little more than glowing ashes. 'All these years, I've avoided him. Pretended he didn't exist. And now I hear it may not have been his fault at all, but merely a sickness. An infection of the brain. And it's too late to make it up to him.'

'It's not too late. Warren had surgery last week, and he's fine now. You could visit him.'

'I don't know what I'd say after all these years. I don't know that he'd want to see me.'

'Let Warren make that decision.'

She thought it over, her eyes glistening in the dying light of the embers. Then she rose stiffly from the chair. 'I believe the fire's gone out,' she said. And she turned and left the room.

There was a car parked in Lincoln's driveway.

He pulled up behind it and groaned. Though he

had not been home all day, the lights were on in his living room, and he knew what awaited him inside the house. Not again, he thought. Not tonight.

He trudged up the steps to his porch and found the front door was unlocked. When had Dorcen stolen his new key?

He found her asleep on the couch. The sour stench of liquor permeated the room. If he woke her now, there would be another drunken scene, crying and shouting, neighbors awakened. Better to let her sleep it off, and deal with it in the morning when she was sober and he wasn't reeling from exhaustion. He stood looking down at her, regarding, with a sense of sad bewilderment, the woman he'd married. Her red hair was matted, shot through with gray. Her mouth hung open. Her sleep was a noisy rhythm of whistles and grunts. And yet he did not feel disgust when he looked at her. Rather he felt pity, and disbelief that he had ever been in love with her.

And a sense of stifling and never-ending responsibility for her welfare.

She would need a blanket. He turned toward the hall closet and heard the telephone ring. Quickly he answered it, afraid that it would wake Doreen and ignite the scene he dreaded.

It was Pete Sparks on the line. 'I'm sorry to call you so late,' he said, 'but Dr Elliot insisted. She was going to call you herself if I didn't.'

'Is this about the slashed tires? Mark already called me about it.'

'No, it's something else.'

'What happened?'

'I'm at her medical building. Someone's smashed all the windows.'

16

Glass was everywhere, bright shards littering the carpet, the magazine table, the waiting room couch. Through the broken windows, now open to the night air, wisps of snow slithered in and settled like fine lace on the furniture.

Stunned and silent, Claire moved through the waiting room to the business office. The window above Vera's desk had been smashed as well, and slivers of glass and broken icicles sparkled on the computer keyboard. Wind had blown loose papers and snow into drifts throughout the room, a blizzard of white that would soon melt to soggy heaps on the carpet.

She heard Lincoln's boots crunch across the glass. 'Plywood's on the way, Claire. There's more snow predicted, so they'll get those windows boarded up tonight.'

She just kept staring down at the snow on her carpet. 'It's because of what I said at the meeting tonight. Isn't it?'

'This isn't the only building that's been vandalized. There've been several this week.'

'But this is the second time for me in one night. First my tires. Now this. Don't you dare tell me this is a coincidence.'

Officer Pete Sparks came into the room. 'Not having much luck with the neighbors, Lincoln. They called in when they heard the breaking glass, but they didn't see who did it. It's like that incident down at Bartlett's garage last week. Smash and run.'

'But Joe Bartlett had only one broken window,' she said. 'They've smashed all of mine. This is going to shut me down for weeks.'

Sparks tried to be reassuring. 'It should only take a few days to get those windows replaced.'

'What about my computer? The ruined carpet? The snow's gotten into everything. The data will have to be replaced, and all my billing records reconstructed. I don't know if it's worth it. I don't know if I even *want* to start over again.'

She turned and walked out of the building.

She was huddled in her truck when Lincoln and Sparks emerged a short time later. They exchanged a few words, then Lincoln crossed the street to her pickup truck and slid into the seat beside her.

For a moment neither of them spoke. She kept her gaze focused straight ahead, and her vision blurred, the twirling lights of Sparks's cruiser softening to a pulsating haze. Quickly, angrily, she wiped her hand across her eyes. 'I'd say the message came through loud and clear. This town doesn't want me here.'

'Not the whole town, Claire. One vandal. One person –'

'Who probably speaks for a lot of other people. I might as well pack up and leave tonight. Before they decide to burn down my house.'

He said nothing.

'That's what you're thinking, isn't it?' she said, and she finally looked at him. 'That I've lost any chance of making it here.'

'You made it hard on yourself tonight. When you talk about shutting down the lake, it threatens a lot of people.'

'I shouldn't have said anything.'

'No, you had to say it, Claire. You did the right thing, and I'm not the only one who thinks so.'

'No one's come up to shake my hand.'

'Take my word for it. There are others who have concerns about the lake.'

'But they're not going to close it down, are they? They can't afford to. So they shut me up instead, by doing this. By trying to drive me out of town.' She looked at her building. 'It's going to work, too.'

'You've been here less than a year. It takes time –'

'How long does it take to be accepted in this town? Five years, ten? A lifetime?' Reaching down, she turned on the ignition, and felt the initial blast of cold air from the heater.

'Your office can be repaired.'

'Yes, buildings are easy to fix.'

'It can all be replaced. The windows, the computer.'

'And what about my patients? I don't think I have any left after tonight.'

'You don't know that. You haven't given Tranquility a chance.'

'Haven't I?' She straightened and looked at him in fury. 'I've given it nine months of my life! Every minute, I worry about my practice, about why my appointment book is still half empty. Why someone hates me enough to send anonymous letters to my patients. There are people here who want me to fail, and they're doing their best to drive me out of town. It's taken me this long to realize it's never going to get better. Tranquility doesn't want me, Lincoln. They want another Dr Pomeroy, or maybe Marcus Welby. But not me.'

'It takes time, Claire. You're from away, and people need to get used to you, to feel confident you're not going to abandon them. That's where Adam DelRay has the advantage. He's a local boy, and everyone assumes he'll stay. The last doctor who came here from another state left after eighteen months. Couldn't take the winters. The doctor before him stayed less than a year. The town doesn't think you'll last, either. They're holding back, waiting to see if you make it through the winter. Or if you'll give up and leave town like the other two did.'

'It's not winter that's driving me away. I can take

the darkness and the cold. What I can't take is the feeling I don't belong. That I'll never belong.' She released a deep breath, and her anger suddenly dissolved, leaving only a feeling of weariness. 'I don't know why I thought this would work. Noah didn't want to move here, but I forced him. And now I see what a stupid thing it was to do . . .'

'Why *did* you come, Claire?' He'd asked the question so softly it was almost lost in the whisper of air from the heater.

It was a question he had never asked her, an elementary piece of information about herself she had never shared. *Why I came to Tranquility*. Now as he waited for her answer, the silence stretched between them, magnifying her reluctance to confide in him.

He sensed her discomfort and shifted his gaze to the street, granting her some measure of privacy. When he spoke again, it was almost as if the words weren't directed at her, that he was merely sharing his thoughts with no one in particular.

'The people who move here, from other places,' he said, 'most times it seems to me they're running away from something. A job they hate, an ex-husband. An ex-wife. Some tragedy that's shaken their lives.'

She sagged sideways and felt the icy window against her cheek. How does he know? she wondered. How much has he guessed?

'They come here, these people from away, and they think they've found paradise. Maybe they're on summer vacation. Maybe they're just driving through, and the name of the town catches their fancy. Tranquility. It sounds safe, a place to run to, a place to hide. They stop at the local realty office and look at the photos on the wall. All the farmhouses for sale, the cottages on the lake.'

It was a picture of a white farmhouse with daffodils nodding in the front yard and a maple tree just beginning to show its spring blush. I'd never had a house with a maple tree. I'd never lived in a town where I could look up at the sky at night and see stars, instead of the glare of city lights.

'They wonder what it'd be like, to live in a small town,' said Lincoln. 'A place where no one locks their doors, and neighbors welcome you with casseroles. A place that's more fantasy than reality, because the small town they imagine doesn't exist. And the problems they're trying to leave behind just follow them to their next home. And the next.'

Noah told me he didn't want to come. He told me he'd hate me if I forced him to leave Baltimore, to leave behind all his friends. But you can't let a fourteen-year-old boy run your life. I'm the parent. I'm in charge. I knew what was good for him, good for both of us.

I thought I did.

'For a while, maybe, it seems to work out,' he said. 'A new house, a new town – it keeps your mind off the things you were running away from. Everyone hopes for a new beginning, a chance to make things right. And they think, what better time and place to start a new life than a summer by the lake?'

'He stole a car,' she said.

He didn't respond. She wondered what she'd see in his eyes if she were to turn and look at him now. Surely not surprise; somehow he had already known or guessed that her coming to Tranquility had been an act of desperation.

'It wasn't the only crime he committed, of course. After he was arrested, I learned about all the other things he'd done. The shoplifting. The graffiti. The break-ins at the neighborhood grocery store. They did it together, Noah and his friends. Three boys who just got bored and decided to add a little excitement to their lives. To their parents' lives.' She leaned back, her gaze focused on the empty street. Snow was beginning to fall, and as the flakes slithered onto the windshield they melted and slid down like tears on the glass. 'The worst part about it was I didn't know. That's how little he told me, how completely out of touch I was with my own son.

'When the police called me that night, and told me there'd been an accident – that Noah had been in a stolen car – I told them it was a mistake. My son wouldn't do something like that. My son was spending the night at a friend's house. But he wasn't. He was sitting in the emergency room with a scalp laceration. And his friend – one of the boys – was in a coma. I guess I should be grateful for the fact that my son never forgets to buckle his seat belt. Even in the act of stealing a car.' She shook her head and gave an ironic sigh. 'The other parents were as stunned as I was. They couldn't believe their boys would do such a thing. They thought Noah talked them into it. Noah was the bad influence. What could you expect from a boy who has no father?

'It made no difference to them that my son was the youngest of the three. They blamed it on his lack of a father. And the fact I was too busy working as a doctor, taking care of other peoples' families, to pay attention to my own.'

Outside the snow was falling more thickly now, blanketing the windshield, cutting off her view of the street.

'The worst part about it was, I agreed with them. I had to be doing something wrong, failing him in some way. And all I could think of was, how could I set things right again?'

'Packing up and leaving home is a pretty drastic measure.'

'I was looking for a miracle. A magic solution. We'd gotten to the point where we hated each other. I couldn't control where he went or what he did. Worst of all, I couldn't choose his friends. I could see where it was leading. Another stolen car, another arrest. Another round of useless family counseling . . .' She took a deep breath. The windshield was covered by snow now, and she felt buried away, entombed with this man beside her.

'And then,' she said, 'we visited Tranquility.'

'When?'

'It was a weekend in fall. A little over a year ago. Most of the tourists were gone, and the weather was still nice. Indian summer. Noah and I rented a cottage on the lake. Every morning, when I woke up, I'd hear the loons. And nothing else. Just the loons, and silence. That's what I loved most about that weekend, the feeling of complete peace. For once we didn't argue. We actually enjoyed being together. That's when I knew I wanted to leave Baltimore . . .' She shook her head. 'I guess you had me pegged right, Lincoln. I'm like every other outsider who moves to this town, who's running away from another life, another set of problems. I wasn't sure where I was going. I only knew I couldn't stay where I was.'

'And now?'

'I can't stay here either,' she said brokenly.

'It's too soon to make that decision, Claire. You haven't been here long enough to build up the practice.'

'I've had nine months. All summer and fall, I sat in that office waiting for the flood of patients. Almost all I got were tourists. Summer people coming in for a sprained ankle or an upset stomach. When summer was over, they all went home. And I suddenly realized how few of my patients actually lived in this town. I thought I could hang on, that people would learn to trust me. It might've happened in another year or two. But after tonight, there's no chance of it. I said what I had to say at

321

that meeting and the town didn't like it. Now my best option is to pack up and leave. And hope it's not too late to go back to Baltimore.'

'You're giving up so easily?'

It was a statement designed to provoke. Angry, she turned to look at him. 'So easily? And when does it get hard?'

'It's not the whole town attacking you. It's a few disturbed individuals. You have more support than you realize.'

'Where is it? Why didn't anyone else stand up for me at the meeting? You were the only one.'

'Some of them are confused. Or they're afraid to speak up.'

'No wonder. They could get their tires slashed as well,' she said sarcastically.

'It's a very small town, Claire. People here think they know each other, but when you get right down to it, we really don't. We keep our secrets to ourselves. We stake out our private territory and we don't let others cross the line. Speaking up at a town meeting is opening ourselves to the public. Most choose to say nothing at all, even though they may agree with you.'

'All that silent support won't help me earn a living.'

'No, it won't.'

'There's no guarantee any patients will walk into my office now.'

'It'd be a gamble, yes.'

'So why should I? Give me one reason why I should stay in this town?'

'Because I don't want you to leave.'

This was not the answer she had expected. She stared at him, straining to read his expression in the gloom.

'This town needs someone like you,' he said. 'Someone who comes in and stirs things up a little. Who makes us ask ourselves questions we've never had the nerve to ask. It would be a loss if you left us, Claire. It would be a loss to us all.'

'So you're speaking on behalf of the town?'

'Yes.' He paused. And added softly, 'And for myself as well.'

'I'm not sure what that means.'

'I'm not sure what it means, either. I don't even know why I'm saying it. It doesn't do either of us any good.' Abruptly he grasped the door handle and was about to open it when she reached out and touched his arm. At once he fell still, his hand clutching the door, his body poised to step into the cold.

'I used to think you didn't like me,' she said.

He looked at her in surprise. 'I gave you that impression?'

'It wasn't anything you said.'

'What was it, then?'

'You never talked about anything personal. As if you didn't want me to know things about you. It didn't bother me. I realized that's just how it is up here. People keep to themselves, the way you did. But after a while, after we'd known each other, and that invisible wall still seemed to stand between us, I thought: Maybe it's not just the fact I'm an outsider. Maybe it's me. Something he doesn't like about *me*.'

'It is because of you, Claire.'

She paused. 'I see.'

'I knew what would happen if I didn't keep that wall up between us.' His shoulders sagged, as though under the weight of his unhappiness. 'A person gets used to anything, even misery, if it goes on long enough. I've been married to Doreen so long, I guess I accepted it as the way things are supposed to be. I made a bad choice, I took on a responsibility, and I've done the best I could.'

'One mistake shouldn't ruin your life.'

'When there's someone else who'll be hurt, it's not easy to be selfish, to think only of yourself. It's almost easier to do nothing and just let things slide. Add on another layer of numbness.'

A gust swept the windshield, leaving streaks of melting snow on the glass. Fresh snow swirled down, whitening over that fleeting glimpse of the night.

'If it seems I didn't warm up to you, Claire,' he said, 'it's only because I was trying so hard not to.'

He reached, once again, to open the door.

Once again, she stopped him with a touch, her hand lingering on his arm.

He turned to face her. This time their gazes held, neither one flinching away, neither one retreating.

He cupped her face in his hand and kissed her. Before he could pull away, before he had time to regret the impulse, she leaned toward him, welcoming his kiss with one of her own.

His lips, the taste of his mouth, were new and unfamiliar to her. The kiss of a stranger. A man whose longing for her, so long concealed, now burned like a fever. She too had caught the sickness, felt the same heat flush her face, her whole body, as he pulled her against him. He said her name once, twice, a murmur of wonder that she was the one in his arms.

The glare of headlights suddenly penetrated the snow-covered windshield. They pulled apart and sat in guilty silence, listening to the sound of footsteps approaching the truck. Someone rapped on the passenger side. Snowflakes slithered in as Lincoln rolled down the window.

Officer Mark Dolan stared into the truck. His gaze took in both Lincoln and Claire, and all he said was, 'Oh.' One syllable, an ocean's worth of meaning.

'I, uh, I saw the doc's engine running and wondered if everything was okay,' Dolan explained. 'You know, carbon monoxide poisoning and all . . .'

'Everything's fine,' said Lincoln.

'Yeah. All right.' Dolan backed away from the window. ''Night, Lincoln.'

'Good night.'

After Dolan had walked away, Claire and Lincoln sat without speaking for a moment. Then Lincoln said, 'It'll be all over town tomorrow.'

'I'm sure it will be. I'm sorry.'

'I'm not.' As he stepped out of her truck, he gave a reckless laugh. 'Truth is, Claire, I don't give a damn. Everything that's gone wrong in my life has been public knowledge in this town. Now, for once, something's gone right for me, and it might as well be public knowledge as well.'

She turned on the windshield wipers. Through the clearing glass she watched him wave good-night, then walk away to his car. Officer Dolan was still parked nearby, and Lincoln stopped to speak to him.

As she drove away, she suddenly remembered what Mitchell Groome had told her earlier that evening about Damaris Horne's inside source.

Dark-haired, medium build. Works the night shift.

Mark Dolan, she thought.

The next morning Lincoln drove south, to Orono. He had not slept well, had lain awake for hours mulling over the night's events. The town meeting. His conversation with Iris Keating. The damage to Claire's office. And Claire herself.

Most of all, he'd thought about Claire.

At seven he'd awakened unrefreshed, and gone downstairs. It was a cold slap of reality to find Doreen still asleep on his living room couch. She lay with one arm dangling off the side, her red hair

326

dull and greasy, her mouth half open. He stood for a moment, looking down at her, pondering how to convince her to leave with a minimum of yelling and crying on her part, but he was too weary to deal with the problem at that moment. Worrying about Doreen had already drained so much energy from his life. Just the sight of her seemed to drag down on his limbs, making them hang heavy, as though Doreen and the force of gravity were intimately connected.

'I'm sorry, Honey,' he said softly. 'But I'm going on with my life.'

He made one phone call, then he left Doreen sleeping on the couch and walked out of the house. As he drove away, he felt the first layers of depression peel away like a worn outer skin. The roads were plowed, the pavement sanded; he pressed the accelerator, and as he picked up speed he felt he was shedding more and more layers, that if he just drove far enough, fast enough, the real Lincoln, the man he used to be, would finally emerge, scrubbed and clean and reborn. He sped past fields where the snow, so freshly fallen, puffed up in clouds of white powder with the slightest gust of wind. *Keep driving, don't stop, don't look back.* He had a destination in mind, and a purpose to this journey, but for now, what he experienced was the joyful rush of escape.

When he reached the University of Maine campus an hour later, he felt renewed and refreshed, as though he had enjoyed a long night's sleep in a comfortable bed. He parked his car and walked onto the campus, and the cold air, the crystalline morning, invigorated him.

Lucy Overlock was in her office in the physical anthropology department. With her six-foot frame clad in her usual attire of blue jeans and flannel shirt, she looked more like a lumberjack than a college professor.

She greeted him with a calloused hand and a no-nonsense nod and sat down behind her desk. Even seated, she was an imposing woman of Amazonian proportions. 'You said on the phone you had questions about the Locust Lake remains.'

'I want to know about the Gow family. How they died. Who killed them.'

She raised an eyebrow. 'It's about a hundred years too late to arrest anyone for that crime.'

'I'm bothered by the circumstances of their deaths. Did you ever locate any news articles about the murders?'

'Vince did – my grad student. He's using the Gow case for his doctoral thesis. A reconstruction of an old murder, based on the remains. It took him weeks to track down an account. Not every old newspaper, you see, has been archived. Your particular area was so sparsely populated at that time, there wasn't much news coverage.'

'So how did the Gow family die?'

She shook her head. 'I'm afraid it's the same old story. Unfortunately, family violence is not a modern phenomenon.'

'The father did it?'

'No. It was their seventeen-year-old son. His body was found weeks later, hanging from a tree. Apparently a suicide.'

'What about motive? Was the boy disturbed?'

Lucy leaned back, her tanned face catching the light from the window. Years of work in the outdoors had taken their toll on her complexion, and the wintry light illuminated every freckle, every deepening crease. 'We don't know. The family apparently lived in relative isolation. According to the deed maps for that period, the Gows' property encompassed the whole south shore of the lake. There may not have been any neighbors around who'd know the boy very well.'

'Then the family was wealthy?'

'I wouldn't say wealthy, but they'd be considered land rich. Vince said the property came into the Gow family in the late 1700s, and stayed with them until this . . . event. It was later sold off piece by piece. Developed.'

'Is Vince that scruffy kid with the ponytail?'

She laughed. 'All my students are scruffy. It's almost a prerequisite for graduation.'

'And where can I find Vince right now?'

'At nine o'clock, he should be in his office. The museum basement. I'll call and let him know you're coming.'

Lincoln had been here before. The broad wooden table was covered with pottery shards this time, not human remains, and the basement windows were blotted over by drifted snow. The lack of natural light, and the damp stone steps, made Lincoln feel he had descended into some vast underground cavern. He walked into the maze of storage shelves, past towering stacks of artifact boxes, their labels feathered by mold. 'Human mandible (male)' was all he could make out on one label. A wooden box, he thought, is a sadly anonymous resting place for what had once been a man's jaw. He moved deeper into the maze, his throat already scratchy from the dust and mildew and a faintly smoky odor that grew stronger as he progressed through the shadows, toward the far end of the basement. Marijuana.

'Mr Brentano?' he called out.

'I'm back here, Chief Kelly,' a voice answered. 'Take a left at the stuffed owl.'

Lincoln walked a few more paces and came to a great horned owl mounted in a glass case. He turned left.

Vince Brentano's 'office' was little more than a desk and a filing cabinet crammed in between artifact shelves. Though there was no ashtray in sight, the aroma of pot hung heavy in the air, and the young man, clearly uneasy in the presence of a cop, had assumed a defensive posture, barricaded behind his desk, arms braced in front of him. Looking the boy straight in the eye, Lincoln held out his hand in greeting.

After a hesitation, Vince shook it. They both

understood the meaning of that gesture: a treaty between them was now in force.

'Sit down,' offered Vince. 'You can set that box on the floor, but watch the chair – it wobbles a little. Everything in here wobbles. As you can see, I got the deluxe office.'

Lincoln removed the box from the chair and set it down. The contents gave an ominous clatter.

'Bones,' said Vince.

'Human?'

'Lowland gorilla. I use them for comparison teaching. I hand them to the undergrads and ask them for a diagnosis, but I don't tell them the bones aren't human. You should hear some of the crazy answers I get. Everything from acromegaly to syphilis.'

'That's a trick question.'

'Hey, all of life is a trick question.' Vince sat back, thoughtfully regarding Lincoln. 'I take it this visit is a trick question, too. The police don't usually waste their time on century-old murders.'

'The Gow family interests me for other reasons.'

'Which are?'

'I believe their deaths may be related to our current problems in Tranquility.'

Vince looked puzzled. 'Are you referring to the recent murders?'

'They were committed by otherwise normal kids. Teenagers who lost control and killed. We've got child psychologists psychoanalyzing every kid in town, but they can't explain it. So I got to thinking about what happened to the Gows. The parallels.'

'You mean the part about teenage killers?' Vince shrugged. 'The underdog will only take so much abuse. When authority clamps down too hard, young people rebel. It's happened again and again.'

'This isn't rebellion. It's kids going berserk, killing friends and family.' He paused. 'The same thing happened fifty-two years ago.'

'What did?'

'Nineteen forty-six, in Tranquility. Seven murders committed during the month of November.'

'*Seven?*' Vince's eyes widened behind the wire-rim glasses. 'In a town of how many people?'

'In 1946, there were seven hundred living in Tranquility. Now we're facing the same crisis, all over again.'

Vince gave a startled laugh. 'Man, you've obviously got some major sociological issues in your town, Chief. But don't blame it on the kids. Look to the adults. When children grow up with violence, they learn that violence is how they solve problems. Dad worships the almighty gun, goes out and blasts a deer to smithereens for sport. Junior gets the message: Killing is fun.'

'That's too pat an explanation.'

'Our society glorifies violence! And then we put guns in the hands of children. Ask any sociologist.'

'I don't think the sociologists can explain this.'

'Okay. What's your explanation, Chief Kelly?'

'Rainfall.'

There was a long silence. 'Excuse me?'

'In 1946, and again this year, we've had identical weather patterns. It started off in April, with heavy rains. The local bridge was washed out, livestock were drowned –'

Vince rolled his eyes heavenward. 'A flood of *Biblical* proportions?'

'Look, I'm not a religious man –'

'I'm not a believer, either, Chief Kelly. I'm a scientist.'

'Then you're always looking for patterns in nature, right? Correlations. Well, here's the pattern I'm seeing, both this year and in 1946. In April and May, our town has record rainfall. The Locust River floods, and there's major damage to homes along the riverbank. Then the rains stop, and in July and August, there's no rain at all. In fact, it's unusually hot, with temperatures high enough to make it into the record books, both those years.' He took a breath, slowly released it. 'Finally, in November,' he said, 'it starts to happen.'

'What does?'

'The killing.'

Vince said nothing, his expression shuttered.

'I know it sounds crazy,' said Lincoln.

'You have no idea how crazy it sounds.'

'But the correlation's there. Dr Elliot thinks it could be a natural phenomenon. A new bacteria or algae in the lake, causing personality changes. I read about a similar thing happening, in rivers down south. A microorganism's killing fish by the millions. It makes a toxin that affects humans as well. It damages their concentration, sometimes causes rage attacks.'

'You must mean the dinoflagellate, *Pfiesteria*.'

'Yes. It could parallel what's happening here. That's why I want to know about the Gows. Specifically, whether there were heavy rains the year they died. Government flood data doesn't go back that far. I need historical news accounts.'

Vince finally understood. 'You want to see my newspaper clippings.'

'It might have the information I'm looking for.'

'A flood.' Vince sat back, frowning, as though a memory had just floated to the surface. 'This is weird. I do seem to recall something about a flood . . .' He swiveled around to the filing cabinet, yanked open the drawer, and shuffled through folders. 'Where did I see that? Where, where . . .' He pulled out a file labeled: 'November, 1887, *Two Hills Herald*.' It contained a stack of photocopied news articles.

'The rain would have happened in the springtime,' said Lincoln. 'You wouldn't see it in the November clippings –'

'No, this had something to do with the Gow case. I remember jotting it down.' He flipped through the photocopies, then paused, staring at a wrinkled page. 'Okay, here's the article, dated November twenty-third. Headline: SEVENTEEN-YEAR-OLD SLAUGHTERS OWN FAMILY. FIVE DEAD. Goes on to mention the victims, Mr and Mrs Theodore Gow, their children, Jennie and Joseph, and Mrs Gow's mother, Althea Frick.' He set the page aside. 'I remember now. It was in the obituaries.'

'What was?'

Vince flipped to another photocopied page. 'The one for Mrs Gow's mother. "Althea Frick, age sixty-two, slain early last week, was buried November thirtieth at a combined graveside service for the Theodore Gow family. Born in Two Hills, she was a daughter of Petras and Maria Gosse, and was a devoted wife and mother of two. She was married for forty-one years to Donat Frick, who drowned this past spring . . ."' Vince's voice suddenly faded, and he looked up with startled eyes at Lincoln. '". . . in the Locust River flood."'

They stared at each other, both of them stunned by this confirmation. At Vince's feet, a space heater hummed on, its element glowing bright orange. But nothing could penetrate the chill Lincoln felt at that moment. He wondered if he would ever feel warm again.

'A few weeks ago,' said Lincoln, 'you mentioned the Penobscot Indians. You said they refused to settle anywhere near Locust Lake.'

'Yes. It was taboo, as was the lower half of Beech Hill, where the Meegawki Stream runs. They considered it an unhealthy place.'

'Do you know why it was considered unhealthy?'

'No.'

Lincoln thought it over for a moment. 'The

name *Meegawki* – I assume that's from a Penobscot word?'

'Yes. It's a bastardization of *Sankade'lak Migah'ke*, their name for the area. *Sankade'lak*, loosely translated, is their word for stream.'

'And what does the other word mean?'

'Let me look it up again.' Vince swiveled around and took down from the shelf a battered copy of *The Penobscot Language*. Quickly he flipped to the appropriate page. 'Okay. I'm right about *Sankade'lak*. It's the Penobscot word for "river" or "stream."'

'And the other?'

'*Migah'ke* means "to fight" or . . .' Vince paused. He looked up at Lincoln. '"To slaughter."'

They stared at each other.

'That would explain the taboo,' said Lincoln softly.

Vince swallowed. 'Yes. It's the Stream of Slaughter.'

17

'Fat ass,' whispered J.D. Reid from the trombone section. 'Barry's got a fat ass!'

Noah glanced up from his music and sneaked a peek at his stand partner, Barry Knowlton. The poor shlump was tightly gripping his saxophone, trying hard to concentrate on staying with the beat, but his face had turned red, and he was sweating again, which was what Barry did whenever he got stressed. Barry Knowlton sweated in gym. He sweated while conjugating verbs in French class. He sweated whenever a girl just *spoke* to him. First he'd blush, then little droplets would bead up on his forehead and temples, and before you knew it, Barry would be dripping like an ice cream cone in a heat wave.

'Man, that ass is so fat, you could launch it into space and we'd have ourselves another *moon*.'

A drop of sweat slid down Barry's face and plopped onto his sax. He was gripping the instrument so hard his fingers looked like bare bone.

Noah turned and said, 'Lay off him, J.D.'

'Ooh. Now skinny ass is jealous of all the attention. I got some view back here. Fat ass and skinny ass, side by side.'

'I said, lay off!'

The rest of the band had suddenly stopped playing, and Noah's *lay off* seemed to shout out across the abrupt silence.

'Noah, what is going on back there?'

Noah turned to see Mr Sanborn frowning at him. Mr Sanborn was a cool guy, one of Noah's favorite teachers, in fact, but the man was blind when it came to seeing what was happening in his own classroom.

'Noah's trying to pick a fight, sir,' said J.D.

'*What?* He's the one trying to pick a fight!' protested Noah.

'I don't *think* so,' jeered J.D.

'He won't let up! He keeps making stupid comments!'

Wearily Mr Sanborn crossed his arms. 'What comments, if I may ask?'

'He said – he said—' Noah stopped and looked at Barry, who was tensed up like a bomb about to explode. 'Insults.'

To everyone's shock, Barry suddenly kicked the stand over and it clanged to the floor, scattering sheets of music everywhere. 'He called me a fat ass! That's what he called me!'

'Hey, it's not an insult if it's true, is it?' said J.D.

Laughter erupted in the band room.

'Stop it!' yelled Barry. 'Stop laughing at me!'

'Barry, please settle down.'

Barry turned on Mr Sanborn. 'You never do anything! No one does! You let him screw around with my head, and no one gives a shit!'

'Barry, you have to calm down. Please go into the hall and cool off.'

Barry slammed his saxophone down on the chair. 'Thanks for *nothing*, Mr Sanborn,' he said, and walked out of the room.

'Ooh. Full moon receding,' whispered J.D.

Noah finally snapped. 'Shut up!' he yelled. 'You just shut up!'

'Noah!' said Mr Sanborn, whacking his baton against the stand.

'It's his fault, not Barry's! J.D. never lets up! None of the kids do!' He looked around at his classmates. 'All of you, you're always screwing around with Barry's head!'

Mr Sanborn's baton was now whipping the stand furiously.

'You're all jerks!'

J.D. laughed. 'Look who's talkin'.'

Noah shot to his feet, every muscle tensed to lunge at J.D. *I'm gonna kill him!*

A hand grabbed Noah by the shoulder. 'That's enough!' shouted Mr Sanborn, hauling Noah backwards. 'Noah, I'll deal with J.D.! You go cool off in the hallway.'

Noah shook him away. The rage that had peaked

so dangerously was still pumping through his body, but he managed to wrestle it under control. He shot a last look at J.D., a look that said: *Cross me again and you're toast*, and he walked out.

He found Barry standing by the lockers, sweating and sniffling as he struggled with his combination. In frustration, Barry punched the locker, then turned and sagged back against it, his weight threatening to buckle the metal. 'I'm going to kill him,' he said.

'You and me both,' said Noah.

'I mean it.' Barry looked at him, and Noah suddenly realized, *he does mean it*.

The bell rang, signaling the end of the period. A flood of kids spilled out of the classrooms, eddying into the halls. Noah just stood there, staring as Barry walked away, a sweating blimp swallowed up in the crowd. He didn't notice Amelia until she was standing right beside him. Touching his arm.

He gave a startled jerk and looked at her.

'I heard about you and J.D.,' she said.

'Then I guess you heard I'm the one who got kicked out of class.'

'J.D.'s a jerk. No one's ever stood up to him before.'

'Yeah, well I'm sorry I did.' He spun his combination and opened the locker. The door swung open with a bang. 'Not worth opening my big mouth.'

'It is worth it. I wish everyone was brave enough.'

Her head drooped, the golden hair sliding across her cheek. She turned away.

'Amelia?'

She looked at him. So many times before, he had sneaked furtive glances at her, just for the pleasure of looking at her face. So many times, he had fantasized about what it would be like to touch that face, that hair. To kiss her. He'd had opportunities, but had never mustered the courage to actually *do* it. Now she was gazing at him with such quiet intensity, he could not stop himself. His locker door hung open, concealing them from the hallway. He reached out, took her hand, and gently tugged her toward him.

She came willingly, her eyes wide, her cheeks flushing as she leaned close. Their lips brushed so softly, it was almost as if it didn't happen. They looked at each other, a wordless confirmation that it had not been long enough. That they were both willing to try again.

They came together in another kiss. Firmer, deeper, drawing courage from each other's lips. He put his arm around her, and she was as soft as he'd imagined, like sweet-smelling, lustrous silk. Now she had her arm around him as well, her hand clinging to the back of his neck, claiming him.

The locker door slammed wide open, and suddenly there was someone else standing there.

'What a *touching* scene,' sneered J.D.

Amelia jumped back, staring at her stepbrother.

341

'You cheap little tease,' said J.D., and he gave her a shove.

Amelia shoved right back. 'Don't you touch me!'

'Oh. You'd rather have Noah Elliot feel you up?'

'That's it!' said Noah. He advanced on J.D., his hand already closed in a fist. Then he froze. Mr Sanborn had just walked out of the band room and was standing in the hall, eyeing them both.

'Outside,' said J.D. softly, eyes glittering. 'The parking lot. *Now.*'

Fern Cornwallis dashed out of the building and ran through ankle-deep snow toward the faculty parking lot. By the time she reached the brawling boys, her brand new leather pumps were soaked through and her toes were numb. She was in no mood to be reasonable. She shoved her way into the circle of spectators and grabbed one of the boys by his jacket. *It's Noah Elliot again*, she thought furiously as she hauled him away from J.D. Reid. J.D. snorted like a mad bull and rammed his shoulder into Noah's chest, sending both Noah and Fern sprawling.

Fern landed flat on her back on the pavement, grinding sand and dirt into her wool suit. She scrambled to her feet, snagging her nylons in the process. Uncontrollable rage pulsing through her, she charged right back into the fight, this time grabbing hold of J.D.'s collar. She yanked him back so hard his face turned purple and he made choking sounds, but he continued to flail his arms, fists waving in Noah's general direction.

Two teachers dashed to Fern's aid, each one grabbing an arm, and they dragged J.D. backwards across the pavement.

'You stay away from my sister, Elliot!'

'I never touched your sister!' Noah yelled back.

'That's not what I saw!'

'Then you're blind *and* stupid!'

'I see you two together again, I kick both your asses!'

'Stop it! Both of you!' screamed Amelia, pushing forward and planting herself between the two boys. 'You're such a loser, J.D.!'

'Better a loser than the school slut.'

Amelia's face flushed bright red. 'Shut up.'

'Slut,' J.D. spat out. 'Slut, *slut*.'

Noah broke free and rammed his fist into J.D.'s mouth. The loud *thunk* of bone on flesh was as startling as gunshot in the crisp air.

Blood splattered on the snow.

'Some sort of action has to be taken,' said Mrs Lubec, the sophomore history teacher. 'We can't keep putting out small fires, Fern, while the whole forest burns down around us.'

Fern huddled in a borrowed sweatsuit and gulped her cup of tea. She knew everyone sitting around the conference table was watching her and waiting for some sort of decision, but they could damn well wait a little longer. She had to get warm first, had to get the feeling back in her frostbitten bare feet, which were now swaddled in a towel under the table. The sweatsuit smelled like perspiration and stale perfume. It smelled like its owner, chubby Miss Boodles, the gym teacher, and it was stretched and saggy around the hips. Fern suppressed a shudder and focused on the five people sitting around the conference table. In two hours, she was scheduled to meet with the district superintendent of schools, and she had to present him with a new plan of action. For that, she needed guidance from her staff.

In the room with her now was the vice principal, two teachers, the school guidance counselor, and the district psychologist, Dr Lieberman. Lieberman was the only man in the room, and he'd assumed that superior attitude that men often adopt when they're the lone rooster among hens.

The freshmen English teacher said, 'I think it's time to clamp down harder. Be draconian. If it takes armed guards in the hallways and permanent expulsion of troublemakers, then that's what we do.'

'That's not the approach I would take,' said Dr Lieberman, adding with a noted lack of humility, 'in my humble opinion.'

'We've tried intensive counseling,' said Fern. 'We've tried conflict resolution classes. We've tried suspension, detention, and pleading. We've even taken desserts off the menu to cut down on their sugar. These kids are out of control, and I don't know whose fault it is. I do know that my staff is wrung out, and I'm ready to call in the cavalry.' She glanced at the vice principal. 'Where's Chief Kelly? Isn't he joining us?'

'I left a message with the dispatcher. Chief Kelly's been delayed this morning.'

'Must be those late-night vehicle inspections,' Mrs Lubec wisecracked.

Fern looked at her. 'What?'

'I heard it over at Monaghan's. The Dinosaurs were all talking about it.'

'What did they say?' Fern's question came out more sharply than she'd intended. She fought to regain her composure, to keep the flush from rising to her cheeks.

'Oh, Chief Kelly and that Dr Elliot were really steaming up the car windows last night. I mean, it's not like the poor man doesn't deserve a break, after all these years . . .' Mrs Lubec's voice trailed off as she saw Fern's thunderstruck face.

'Look, can we get back to the problem at hand?' cut in Lieberman.

'Yes. By all means,' whispered Fern. *It's only gossip. Lincoln defends the woman in public, and the next thing you know, the town thinks they're sleeping together.* Just a few months ago, Fern herself had been the rumored woman in his life. More false gossip, based on the long hours they'd worked together on the student DARE project. She forced the subject of Claire Elliot out of her mind, and focused her irritation on Lieberman, who was trying to wrest control of her meeting.

'Brute authority doesn't work well with this age group,' he was saying. 'We're talking about a stage of development where authority is precisely what they rebel against. Clamping down on these kids – asserting your power – doesn't give them the right message.'

'I'm beyond caring what message I give these kids,' said Fern. 'My responsibility is to keep them from killing each other.'

'Then threaten them with the loss of something that matters to them. Sports, class trips. What about that dance you had on the schedule? That's a pretty major social event for them, isn't it?'

'We've canceled the harvest dance twice already,' said Fern. 'The first time because of Mrs Horatio, the second time because of all these fights.'

'But don't you see, it's something positive you can hold out to them. A carrot for good behavior. I wouldn't cancel it. What other incentives do they have?'

'How about the threat of death?' muttered the English teacher.

'Positive reinforcement,' said Lieberman. 'That's the mantra we have to keep in mind. Positive. Positive.'

'The dance could be a disaster,' said Fern. 'Two hundred kids in a crowded gym. All it takes is one fistfight, and we'd end up with a scream-ing mob.'

'Then you weed out the troublemakers ahead of time. That's what I mean by positive reinforcement. Any kid steps one inch out of line, they don't get to go.' He paused. 'Those two boys today – the ones who got in the fight.'

'Noah Elliot and J.D. Reid.'

'Start off by making examples of them.'

'I've suspended them for the rest of the week,' said Fern. 'Their parents are coming to pick them up now.'

'If I were you, I'd make it clear to the whole school that those boys won't be allowed into the dance, and neither will any other troublemakers. Turn them into poster boys for what *not* to do.'

In the prolonged silence, everyone looked to Fern for a decision. She was tired of being the one in charge, the one who got blamed when things went wrong. Now here was this Ph.D. Lieberman, telling her exactly what to do, and she almost welcomed the chance to defer to his judgment. To pass the responsibility to someone else.

'All right. The dance is back on the schedule,' she said.

There was a knock on the door. Fern's pulse quickened as Lincoln Kelly stepped into the room. He was out of uniform today, dressed in jeans and his old hunting jacket, and he brought with him the scent of winter, the sparkle of snowflakes on his hair. He looked tired, but fatigue only emphasized his appeal. It made her think, as she had so many times before: *You need a good woman to take care of you.*

'Sorry I'm late,' he said. 'I got back into town a few minutes ago.'

'We're just finishing up the meeting,' said Fern. 'But you and I need to talk, if you have the time right now.' She stood up, and instantly felt embarrassed when she saw him glance in surprise at her shabby attire. 'I had to break up another fight, and ended up getting shoved to the ground,' she explained. She tugged on the sweatshirt. 'Emergency change of clothes. Not exactly my most flattering color.'

'You weren't hurt, were you?'

'No. Although it is painful to ruin a good pair of Italian shoes.'

He smiled, an affirmation that despite her bedraggled appearance, she could still project both charm and wit, and that this man appreciated it.

'I'll wait for you in the other office,' he said, and stepped out again.

She could not just walk out of the room and join him. First she had to make the necessary graceful exit. By the time she'd successfully disengaged herself, it was five minutes later, and Lincoln was no longer alone in the outer office.

Claire Elliot was with him.

The two of them didn't seem to notice Fern as she came out of the conference room; their attention was focused so completely on each other.

They didn't touch, but Fern saw, in Lincoln's face, a vibrant intensity she'd never seen before. It was as if he'd suddenly awakened after a long hibernation to rejoin the living.

The pain she felt at that instant was almost physical. She took a step toward them, but found she had nothing to say. *What is it he sees in you that he never saw in me*? she wondered, looking at Claire. All these years she had watched Lincoln's marriage deteriorate, had thought that in the end, time would be her ally. Doreen would fade from the picture and Fern would step into the void. Instead here was this outsider, such an ordinary-looking woman in her snow boots and brown turtleneck, moving straight to the head of the line. *You don't fit in here*, thought Fern spitefully as Claire turned to face her. *You've never fit in*.

'Mary Delahanty called me,' said Claire. 'I understand Noah was in another fight.'

'Your son's been suspended,' said Fern, pulling no punches. If anything, she felt the urge to inflict damage on this woman, and she was glad to see Claire flinch.

'What happened?'

'He got into a fight over a girl. Apparently Noah's been playing fast and easy with his hands, and the girl's brother stepped in to protect his sister.'

'I have trouble believing this. My son's never mentioned any girl –'

'It's not easy for kids to communicate these days, when parents are so busy with their jobs.' Fern had wanted to hurt Claire Elliot, and it was obvious she had, because a guilty flush appeared on Claire's cheeks. Fern had known exactly what target to aim for, a parent's sorest point, where self-blame and overwhelming responsibility have already left them vulnerable.

'Fern,' said Lincoln. She heard reproval in his voice. Turning to look at him, she felt suddenly, deeply, ashamed. She'd lost control, had unleashed her anger, showing off her worst side, while Claire played the role of the innocent party.

In a subdued voice, she said, 'Your son's waiting in the detention room. You can take him home now.'

'When can he return to school?'

'I haven't decided. I'll meet with his teachers and consider their recommendations. The punishment has to be severe enough to make him think twice before he causes trouble again.' She gave Claire a knowing look. 'He's been in trouble before, hasn't he?'

'There was just that skateboarding incident –'

'No, I mean before. In Baltimore.'

Claire stared at her in shock. So it was true, thought Fern with satisfaction. The boy has always been a problem.

'My son,' said Claire with quiet defiance, 'is not a troublemaker.'

'Yet he does have a juvenile record.'

'How do you know that?'

'I received some newspaper clippings, taken from a Baltimore paper.'

'Who sent them?'

'I don't know. That's not relevant.'

'It's very relevant! Someone's trying to ruin my reputation, drive me out of town. Now they're going after my *son*.'

'But the clippings are true, aren't they? He did steal a car.'

'It happened right after his father died. Do you have any idea what it's like for a twelve-year-old boy to watch his father waste away? How completely it can break a child's heart? Noah has never recovered. Yes, he's still angry. He's still grieving. But I know him, and I'm telling you, *my son is not bad*.'

Fern held back a retort. There was no point arguing with an enraged mother. It was obvious to her that Dr Elliot was blind, unable to see beyond her love.

Lincoln asked, 'Who was the other boy?'

'Does that matter?' said Fern. 'Noah has to face the consequences of his own behavior.'

'You implied the other boy started the fight.'

'Yes, to protect his sister.'

'Have you spoken with the girl? Confirmed that she needed defending?'

'I don't need to confirm anything. I saw two boys fighting. I ran out to stop it, and I was shoved to the ground. What happened out there was ugly.

Brutal. I can't believe you're sympathizing with a boy who attacked me –'

'Attacked?'

'There was physical contact. I fell.'

'Do you wish to press charges?'

She opened her mouth to say yes, then stopped herself at the last instant. Pressing charges meant testifying in court. And what would she say under oath? She'd seen the rage in Noah's face, knew that he'd wanted to strike her. The fact he hadn't actually raised a hand against her was only a technicality; what mattered was his intent, the violence in his eyes. But had anyone else seen it?

'No, I don't wish to press charges,' she said. And added, magnanimously, 'I'll give him another chance.'

'I'm sure Noah will thank you for it, Fern,' he said.

And she thought miserably: *It's not the boy's approval I want. It's yours.*

'Do you want to talk about it?' Claire asked.

Noah's response was to draw away like an amoeba, shrinking to his side of the car.

'We have to talk about it sometime, Hon.'

'What's the point?'

'The point is, you've been suspended. We don't know when, or even if, you can go back to school.'

'So I don't go back, so what? I wasn't learning

anything anyway.' He turned and stared out the window, shutting her off.

She drove a mile without speaking, her gaze fixed on the road, but not really seeing it. She saw, instead, a vision of her son as a five-year-old child curled up, mute, on the couch, too upset to tell her about the teasing he'd endured in school that day. He has never been a communicator, she thought. He has always wrapped himself in silence, and now the silence has grown deeper, more impenetrable.

She said, 'I've been thinking about what we should do, Noah. I need you to tell me what you want: Whether you think I'm doing the right thing. You know my practice isn't going well. And now, with those broken windows, and the damage to the carpets, it'll be weeks before I can see patients again. If they even want to see me . . .' She sighed. 'All I was trying to do was find a place where you'd fit in, where we'd both fit in. And now it seems like I've made a mess of things.' She pulled into their driveway and turned off the engine. They sat without speaking for a moment. She turned to look at him. 'You don't have to tell me right away. But we need to talk about it soon. We need to decide.'

'Decide what?'

'Whether we should move back to Baltimore.'

'What?' His chin snapped up, his gaze focused at last on hers. 'You mean, *leave?*'

'It's what you've been saying for months, that

you want to go back to the city. I called Grandma Elliot this morning. She said you could move back early and stay with her. I'd join you after I get our things packed, and put the house up for sale.'

'You're doing the same thing again. Making decisions about *my* life.'

'No, I'm asking you to help me choose.'

'You're not asking. You've already decided.'

'That's not true. I've made that mistake once already, and I'm not going to repeat it.'

'You want to leave, don't you? All these months, I've wanted to go back to Baltimore, and you didn't listen to me. Now *you* decide it's time, and suddenly you ask, *What do you want, Noah?*'

'I'm asking because it does matter to me! What you want has always mattered.'

'What if I said I want to stay? What if I told you I've got a friend I really care about, and she's *here*?'

'All you've talked about for the past nine months is how much you hate this place.'

'And you didn't care then.'

'What do you want? What can I do to make you happy? Is there anything that'll make you happy?'

'You're yelling at me.'

'I try so hard, and nothing ever satisfies you!'

'Stop yelling at me!'

'You think I like being your mother these days? You think you'd be happier with a different mother?'

He slammed his fist on the dashboard, punching it again and again as he roared: '*Stop – yelling – at – me!*'

She stared, shocked by the violence of his rage. And by the bright drop of blood that suddenly trickled from his nostril. It fell, spattering the front of his jacket.

'You're bleeding –'

Automatically he touched his upper lip and gazed down at the blood on his fingers. Another drop slid from his nostril and landed on his jacket in a bright splash of red.

He shoved open the door and ran into the house.

She followed him inside, and found he'd locked himself in the bathroom. 'Noah, let me in.'

'Leave me alone.'

'I want to stop the bleeding.'

'It's already stopped.'

'Can I take a look? Are you all right?'

'Jesus Christ,' he yelled, and she heard something crash to the floor and shatter. 'Can't you just *go away*?'

She stared at the closed door, silently demanding it swing open, knowing that it wouldn't. There were already too many closed doors between them, and this was just another one she couldn't hope to break through.

The telephone rang. As she hurried to the kitchen to answer it, she thought wearily: *In how many directions can I be pulled at once?*

Over the phone, a familiar voice blurted out in panic: 'Doc, you gotta come out here! She needs to be looked at!'

'Elwyn?' said Claire. 'Is this Elwyn Clyde?'

'Yes, ma'am. I'm over at Rachel's. She don't wanna go to the hospital, so's I thought I better call you.'

'What happened?'

'I don't know, exactly. But you better come here quick, 'cause she's bleeding all over the kitchen.'

18

Dusk had fallen when Claire arrived at Rachel Sorkin's house. She found Elwyn Clyde standing outside on the porch, watching his dogs run around in the front yard. 'Bad business,' he muttered darkly as Claire came up the steps.

'How is she?'

'Oh, she's wicked ornery. Gone and ordered me outside when all's I'm trying to do is help, y'know. Just wanta help, but she says, "You go outside Elwyn, you're smelling up my kitchen."' He looked down, his homely face drooping. 'She was good to me, what with my foot and all. I was just looking to return the favor.'

'You already have,' said Claire, and patted his shoulder. It felt like a bundle of twigs through the ratty coat. 'I'll go in and have a look at her.'

Claire stepped into the kitchen. At once her gaze shot to the far wall. *Blood* was her automatic reaction upon seeing the bright splashes. Then she saw the words, spray-painted in red across the cabinet doors:

SATAN'S WHORE

'I knew it was coming,' said Rachel softly. She was sitting at the kitchen table, clutching a plastic bag of ice to her head. Blood had dried on her cheek and matted the strands of her black hair. Broken glass littered the floor around her feet. 'It was just a matter of time.'

Claire pulled up a chair next to Rachel. 'Let me see your head.'

'People are so unbelievably ignorant. All it takes is one idiot to get them started, and it turns into a . . .' She gave a choked laugh. 'Witch hunt.'

Gently Claire lifted the ice pack from Rachel's scalp. Though the laceration wasn't deep, it had bled profusely and would require at least half a dozen stitches. 'Is this from the flying glass?'

Rachel nodded, then winced as though that simple motion had set off new stabs of pain. 'I didn't see the rock coming. I was so angry about the paint, about the mess they'd left in here. I didn't realize they were right outside, watching me walk into the house. I was standing there, looking at the cabinets, when the rock came through.' She gestured toward the broken window, now boarded over. 'Elwyn put up the boards.'

'How did he happen to come by?'

'Oh, that crazy Elwyn's always tramping through my yard with those dogs of his. He saw the broken window and came in to see if I was all right.'

'That was good of him. You could have a worse neighbor.'

Rachel answered with a grudging, 'I suppose. His heart's in the right place.'

Claire opened her medical bag and took out the suture set. She began dabbing Betadine on Rachel's wound. 'Did you lose consciousness?'

'I don't remember.'

'You're not sure?'

'I guess I was a little stunned. I found myself sitting on the floor, but I don't recall how I got there.'

'You should be under observation tonight. If there's any bleeding inside your skull –'

'I can't go to the hospital. I don't have insurance.'

'You can't be home alone. I can arrange a direct admission.'

'But I don't have the money, Dr Elliot. I can't pay for the hospital.'

Claire regarded her patient for a moment, wondering how hard she should push the issue. 'All right. But if you stay home, someone will have to be with you tonight.'

'There's no one.'

'A friend? A neighbor?'

'I can't think of anyone.'

They heard a loud knock. 'Hey!' yelled Elwyn through the closed door. 'Can I come in and use the bathroom?'

'Are you absolutely sure about that?' Claire

asked with a meaningful glance in Elwyn's direction.

Rachel closed her eyes and sighed.

A police car had just pulled up in the darkness when Claire came back out onto Rachel's porch. She and Elwyn watched as the officer stepped out of the cruiser and crossed the front yard toward them. He came into the light, and she recognized Mark Dolan. She was surprised to see him, because he normally worked the late night shift. She had never liked Dolan, and she wasn't kindly disposed to him today, either, when she remembered what Mitchell Groome had told her.

'Had some trouble here?' he asked.

'Called ya over an hour ago,' Elwyn said crossly.

'Yeah, well, we're up to our eyeballs in calls. Vandalism takes a lower priority. So what happened? Someone went and broke a window?'

'This is more than just vandalism,' said Claire. 'This is a hate crime. They threw a rock in the window, and Rachel Sorkin was hit in the head. She could have been seriously hurt.'

'How is that a hate crime?'

'They attacked her for her religious beliefs.'

'What religion?'

Elwyn blurted out, 'She's a witch, you goddamn imbecile! Everyone knows that!'

Dolan's smile was condescending. 'Elwyn, that's not very nice of you to call her that.'

'Nothing wrong with calling her a witch, if that's

what she is! If it's okay with her, hell, it's okay with me. I figure, better a witch than a vegetarian. I don't hold that against her, neither.'

'I wouldn't exactly call her beliefs a religion.'

'Don't matter what you call it. Just 'cause a woman wantsta believe some airy-fairy stuff don't mean people can throw rocks at her!'

'This *is* a hate crime,' insisted Claire. 'Don't pass it off as simple vandalism.'

Dolan's smile had thinned to a sneer. 'This will get the attention it deserves,' he said. And he walked up the porch steps and into the house.

Claire and Elwyn stood together for a moment in silence.

'She deserves better,' he said. 'She's a good woman, and she deserves better 'n this town has dealt her.'

Claire looked at him. 'And you're a good man, Elwyn. Thank you for staying with her tonight.'

'Yeah, well, it's turned into somethin' of a major operation now, hasn't it?' he muttered as he headed down the steps. 'I'll just take these dogs on home first, seein' as how they make her all tetchy like. Might as well get that other fool business over with, too. Since I did promise her.'

'What business?'

'Bath,' he grunted, and tramped off into the woods, the dogs trotting at his heels.

It was late at night, and Noah was asleep, when Lincoln finally called her.

'I've picked up the phone a dozen times to talk to you,' he said, 'but something always came up. We're pulling double shifts here, just to keep up with the calls.'

'Did you hear about the attack on Rachel Sorkin?'

'Mark mentioned it in passing.'

'Did he also mention he was a total jerk?'

'What did he do?'

'It's what he didn't do. He didn't take the attack seriously. He passed it off as simple vandalism.'

'He told me it was just a broken window.'

'The vandals spray-painted a message in her kitchen. It said, "Satan's Whore."'

There was a silence. When he spoke again, she heard barely controlled anger in his voice. 'These devil rumors have gone too goddamn far. I'm going to have it out with that Damaris Horne, before she starts writing about Penobscot Indian curses.'

'You haven't told her about your conversation with Vince, have you?'

'Hell, no. I've been trying to avoid her.'

'If you do talk to her, you might ask her about her good buddy, Officer Dolan.'

'Does that mean what I think it means?'

'I heard it from one of the reporters, Mitchell Groome. He saw them together.'

'I've already asked Mark whether he's been talking to her. He absolutely denies it. I can't take action against him without proof.'

'Do you trust his word?'

A pause. 'I honestly don't know, Claire,' he

sighed. 'Lately I've been learning things about my neighbors, about my friends, I never knew before. Things I didn't want to know.' The anger faded from his voice. 'I'm not calling to talk about Mark Dolan.'

'Why are you calling?'

'To talk about what happened last night. Between you and me.'

She closed her eyes, bracing herself to hear words of regret. Part of her wanted to be cut off, cut free. It meant she could leave this town without looking back, without struggling for the right decision.

But another part of her, the largest part, wanted *him*.

'Have you thought about what I said?' he asked. 'About whether you'll stay?'

'Are you still asking me to?'

'Yes.'

He said it without hesitation. He was not cutting her free, and she felt both joy and apprehension.

'I don't know, Lincoln. I keep thinking of all the reasons I should leave this town.'

'What about all the reasons you should stay?'

'Besides you, what other reasons are there?'

'We can talk about it. I can come over now.'

She wanted him to come, but was afraid of what would happen if he did. Afraid that she'd make a premature decision, that just his presence alone would prove to be the most convincing argument of all for her to stay in Tranquility. So many things were driving her away. Just to look out her window, to see the impenetrable darkness of a November night and to know that that night is cold enough to kill . . .

'I can be there in ten minutes.'

She swallowed. Nodded to the empty room. 'All right.'

The instant she hung up, a sense of panic seized her. Was she presentable? Was her hair combed, was the house tidy? She recognized these scattering thoughts for what they were, the feminine longing to impress one's lover, and she was startled to be experiencing it at this late stage of her life. Middle age, she thought with a rueful smile, does not automatically confer dignity.

She deliberately avoided even a glance at her mirror, and went downstairs to the front parlor, where she forced herself to occupy the next moments building a fire in the hearth. If Lincoln insisted on paying a visit at this late hour, he'd have to be satisfied with what he found. A woman with soot on her hands and the smell of wood smoke in her hair. The real Claire Elliot, beleaguered and unglamorous. Let him see me this way, she thought rebelliously, and let's see if he still wants me.

She lay down wood and kindling, then struck a match and touched the flame to the crumpled newspapers. The fire was well set and would burn without further attention, but she remained by the hearth, watching with primitive satisfaction as the kindling caught, and then the logs. The wood was fully seasoned and would burn hot and swift. She was like this wood, left dry and untouched for too long. She scarcely remembered what it was like to burn at all.

She heard him ring the doorbell. Instantly she was a bundle of nerves. She clapped her sooty hands, then rubbed them against her hips and succeeded only in transferring the soot to her slacks.

Let him see the real Claire. Let him decide if this is what he wants.

She went to the front hall, paused to regain her composure, and opened the door. 'Come in,' she said.

'Hello, Claire,' he answered, equally at a loss for words. They just looked at each other for a second, then broke eye contact, gazes drifting off to safer territory. He stepped inside, and she saw that his jacket was dusted with fine snow, that the darkness outside swirled with a powdery whiteness, like mist.

She closed the door. 'I've got a fire going in the other room. Can I hang up your jacket?'

He took it off and as she slipped it onto a hanger, she felt the heat of his body in the lining. So many times before, they had met, had spoken, yet this was the first time her awareness of him extended to all her senses, to the warmth of his body lingering in the jacket, to his scent of wood smoke and melting snow. To the certainty of knowing, even with her back turned, that at that moment, his gaze was on her.

She led the way into the parlor.

By now the fire was fully ablaze, throwing its bright circle of light against the gloom. Claire took a seat on the couch and turned off the lamp burning beside her. The fire gave off light enough; it was in shadow she sought refuge. Lincoln sat down beside her, a comfortable space apart, a statement of neutrality that did not distinguish between friend, lover, or mere acquaintance.

'How is Noah doing?' he finally asked, neutrality maintained even in conversation.

'He went to bed angry. In some ways, he wants to be a victim, he wants to feel like the world's against him. There's nothing I can do to change his mind.' She sighed and dropped her head against her hand. 'For nine months he's made me the villain for forcing him to move here. This afternoon, when I told him I was thinking of moving back to Baltimore, he blew up. Said I wasn't thinking of his needs, what he wanted. No matter what I do, I can't win. I can't please him.'

'Then all you can do is please yourself.'

'It feels selfish.'

'Does it?'

'It feels as if I'm not being the best mother I could be.'

'I see you trying so hard, Claire. As hard as any parent could.' He paused, and sighed as well. 'And now I suppose I'm throwing another complication into your life, at a time when you least need it. But Claire, there is no other time for me. I had to say it before you made a decision. Before you left Tranquility.' He added softly: 'Before it's too late for me to say anything at all.'

At last she looked at him. He was sitting with his gaze downcast, his head tilted wearily against his hand.

'Not that I blame you for wanting to leave,' he said. 'This town is slow to warm up to strangers, slow to trust them. There are a few who are just plain mean. But for the most part, they're like people everywhere else. Some of them are unbelievably generous. The best folks you could ever hope to find . . .' His voice faded to silence, as though he'd run out of things to say.

A moment passed between them.

'Are you speaking on behalf of the whole town again, Lincoln? Or yourself?'

He shook his head. 'It's not coming out right. I came to say something, and here I am, beating around the bush. I think about you a lot, Claire. The fact is, I think about you all the time. I'm not sure what to make of this, because it's a new experience for me. Walking around with my head in the clouds.'

She smiled. For so long she had thought of him as the stoic Yankee, plain-spoken and practical. A man whose boots were planted too firmly on earth to ever lose his head to the clouds.

He rose to his feet and stood, unsure of himself,

by the fire. 'That's all I came to tell you. I know there are complications. Doreen, mainly. And I know I don't have any experience being a father. But I have all the patience in the world when it comes to things I really care about.' He cleared his throat. 'I'll let myself out.'

He had already gone to the closet door and was reaching for his jacket when she caught up to him in the front hall. She put her hand on his shoulder, and he turned to look at her. His jacket slipped from the hanger and fell, unnoticed, to the floor.

'Come back and sit with me.' That whispered request, the smile on her lips, was all the invitation he needed. He touched her face, caressed her cheek. She had forgotten what it felt like, the touch of a man's hand against her flesh. It awakened a longing that was deep and unexpected and so powerful that she gave a sigh and closed her eyes. Gave another sigh as he kissed her, as their bodies folded into each other.

They kissed all the way to the front parlor and were still kissing as they sank onto the couch. In the hearth a log tipped over, and a shower of sparks and flames leapt up with startling brilliance. *Seasoned wood makes the hottest fire.* The heat of their own fire was consuming her now, reducing to ashes any resistance. They lay on the couch, bodies pressed together, hands exploring, discovering. She pulled his shirt loose and slid her hand across the breadth of his back. His skin there felt startlingly cool, as if all the heat he possessed was radiating toward her, in the kisses he pressed to her face, her throat. She unbuttoned his shirt, inhaling his scent. Those all-too-brief whiffs she'd had of him over the weeks had somehow been branded into her memory, and now the smell of him was both familiar and intoxicating.

'If we're going to stop,' he murmured, 'we'd better stop now.'

'I don't want to stop.'

'I'm not ready – I mean, I didn't come prepared –'

'It's all right. It's all right,' she heard herself saying, without knowing or caring if it *was* all right, so hungry was she for the touch of him.

'Noah,' he said. 'What if Noah wakes up . . .'

At that she opened her eyes and found herself looking directly into his. It was a view of him she'd never seen before, his face lit by the fire's glow, his gaze stark with need.

'Upstairs,' she said. 'My bedroom.'

Slowly he smiled. 'Is there a lock on the door?'

They made love three times that night. The first was a mindless collision of bodies, limbs tangled together, then the shuddering explosion deep within. The second time was the slower coupling of lovers, gazes locked, the touch and scent of each other now familiar.

The third time they made love, it was to say good-bye.

They'd awakened in the hours before dawn, and knowingly reached for each other in the darkness.

They spoke no words, their bodies joining of their own accord, two halves gliding together into one whole. When, in silence, he emptied himself into her, it was as though he was spilling tears of both joy and sorrow. The joy of having found her. The sorrow of what they would now have to face. Doreen's wrath. Noah's resistance. A town that might never accept her.

He did not want Noah to find them in bed together when morning came; neither he nor Claire was ready to deal with the repercussions. It was still dark when Lincoln got dressed and left the house.

From her bedroom window she watched his truck drive away. She heard the loud crackle of ice under his wheels and knew that the night had turned even colder, that this morning, to merely draw in a breath would be painful. For a long time, even after the taillights had vanished, she remained at the window, staring out through moonlit-silvered icicles. Already she felt his absence. And she felt something else, both unexpected and troubling: a mother's guilt that she was selfishly pursuing her own needs, her own passions.

She walked down the hall to Noah's door. There was silence within; knowing how deeply he slept, she felt certain he'd heard nothing of what had gone on in her bedroom last night. She stepped inside and crossed the darkness to kneel beside his bed.

When he was still a child, Claire had often lingered over her sleeping son, stroking his hair, inhaling the scent of warm linen and soap. He allowed so little contact between them now; she had almost forgotten what it was like to touch him and not have him automatically pull away. *If only I could have you back again.* She leaned over and kissed him on the eyebrow. He gave a moan and rolled over, turning his back to her. Even in his sleep, she thought, he pulls away from me.

She was about to rise to her feet when she suddenly froze, her gaze fixed on his pillow. On the streak of phosphorescent green where Noah's face had rested against the linen.

In disbelief she touched the streak and felt moistness there, like the warm leavings of tears. She stared at the tips of her fingers.

They glimmered with spectral light in the darkness.

19

'I need to know what's growing in that lake, Max. And I need to know *today*.'

Max gestured her into his cottage and shut the door against the bitter wind. 'How is Noah this morning?'

'I examined him from head to toe, and he seems perfectly healthy except for a stuffed-up nose. I left him in bed with juice and decongestants.'

'And the phosphorescence? Did you culture it?'

'Yes. I sent the swab off right away.' She took off her coat. Max had finally been able to get a fire going in the woodstove, and the cottage felt stiflingly hot. She almost preferred the bone-chilling wind outside. In here, surrounded by Max's clutter, the air hazy with smoke, she thought she might suffocate.

'I've just made coffee,' he said. 'Have a seat – if you can find an empty chair.'

She took one glance around the claustrophobic room and followed him, instead, into the kitchen.

'So tell me about those water culture results. The ones you took before the lake froze.'

'The report came back this morning.'

'Why didn't you call me right away?'

'Because there was nothing much to report.' He shuffled through a stack of papers on the kitchen counter, and handed her a computer printout. 'There. The final ID from the lab.'

She glanced down the long list of microorganisms. 'I don't recognize most of these,' she said.

'That's because they're not pathogens – they don't cause disease in humans. What's on that list are just the typical bacteria and algae you'd find in any northern freshwater pond. The coliform count is borderline high, which may indicate that someone's septic system is leaking from the shoreline, or into one of the feeder streams. But overall, it's an unremarkable bacterial spectrum.'

'No phosphorescent *Vibrio?*'

'No. If *Vibrio* was ever in that lake, then it didn't survive very long, which makes it an unlikely source of disease. Most likely the *Vibrio* isn't a pathogen, but an incidental bacteria. Harmless, like all the other bacteria we carry around in our bodies.'

She sighed. 'That's what the state health department told me.'

'You called them?'

'First thing this morning. I was in such a panic about Noah.'

He handed her a cup of coffee. She took one

sip, then set it down, wondering if Max had used bottled water to brew it, or if he had unthinkingly drawn the water from the tap.

From the lake.

Her gaze drifted out the window, to the unbroken expanse of white that was Locust Lake. In so many ways, that wide body of water defined the everyday course of their lives. In summer they swam and bathed in its water, pulled struggling fish from its depths. In winter they glided over its surface on skates, insulated their homes against the merciless winds that howled across its ice. Without the lake, the Town of Tranquility would not exist, and this would be only another valley in a dark expanse of forest.

Her beeper went off. On the digital readout was a number she didn't recognize, with a Bangor exchange.

She made the call from Max's phone, and a nurse from Eastern Maine Medical Center answered.

'Dr Rothstein asked us to call you, Dr Elliot. It's about that craniotomy patient you referred here last week, Mr Emerson.'

'How's Warren been doing since his surgery?'

'Well, the psychiatrist and the social worker have seen him several times, but nothing seems to be helping. That's why we're calling you. We thought, since he's your patient, you might know how to handle this situation.'

'What situation?'

'Mr Emerson refuses all his medications. Even

worse, he's stopped eating. All he'll take now is water.'

'Does he give a reason?'

'Yes. He says it's his time to die.'

Warren Emerson seemed to have shrunken since the last time she'd seen him, as though life itself was slowly leaking from him like air from a balloon. He sat in a chair by the window, his gaze focused on the parking lot below, where snow-covered cars were lined up like soft bread loaves. He did not turn to look at her when she walked into the room, but just kept staring out the window, a tired man bathed in the light of a gray day. She wondered if he realized she was there.

Then he said, 'It doesn't do any good, you know. So you might as well leave me alone. When your time comes, it comes.'

'But it isn't your time yet, Mr Emerson,' said Claire.

At last he turned, and if he was surprised to see her, he didn't show it. She had the feeling he was beyond surprise. Beyond pleasure or pain. He watched with bland indifference as she crossed toward him.

'Your operation was a success,' she said. 'They took out the brain mass, and the chances are, it's benign. You have every hope of a complete recovery. A normal life.'

Her words seemed to have no effect on him. He

simply turned back to the window. 'A man like me can't have a normal life.'

'But we can control the seizures. We might even be able to stop them from ever –'

'They're all afraid of me.'

That statement, spoken with such resignation, explained everything. This was the malady for which there was no cure, from which he could never recover. She could offer no surgery that would resect the fear and revulsion his neighbors felt toward him.

'I see it in their eyes,' he said. 'I see it whenever I pass them on the street, or brush against them in the grocery store. It's like they've been burned by acid. No one will touch me. No one has touched me in thirty years. Only doctors and nurses. People who have no choice. I'm poison, you see. I'm dangerous. They all stay away, because they know I'm the town monster.'

'No, Mr Emerson. You're not a monster. You blame yourself for what happened all those years ago, but I don't believe it was your fault. It was a sickness. You had no control over your actions.'

He didn't look at her, and she wondered if he had even heard her.

'Mr Emerson?'

He was still gazing out the window. 'It's kind of you to visit,' he murmured. 'But there's no need to lie to me, Dr Elliot. I know what I did.' He drew in a deep breath and slowly released it, and with that sigh he seemed to shrink even smaller.

'I'm so tired. Every night I go to sleep expecting not to wake up again. Hoping not to. And every morning, when I open my eyes, I'm disappointed. People think it's such a struggle to stay alive. But you know, that's the easy part. The hard part is the dying.'

There was nothing she could say. She looked down at the untouched meal tray by the window. A chicken breast in congealed gravy, a mound of rice, kernels glistening like tiny pearls. And bread, the staff of life. A life Warren Emerson no longer wished to experience or to suffer. I cannot make you want to go on living, she thought. I can force feed liquid nourishment, inject it into a tube that threads up your nostril and into your stomach, but I cannot breathe joy into your lungs.

'Dr Elliot?'

Turning, Claire saw a nurse standing in the doorway.

'Dr Clevenger from Pathology is on the phone, trying to reach you. He's on line three.'

Claire left Warren Emerson's room and picked up the extension in the nurses' station. 'This is Claire Elliot.'

'I'm glad I caught you,' said Clevenger. 'Dr Rothstein told me you'd be driving over this afternoon, and I thought you might want to come down to Pathology and take a look at these slides. Rothstein's on his way down now.'

'Which slides?'

'From your craniotomy patient's brain mass. It

took a week to fully fix the tissue. I just got the slides back today.'

'Is it a meningioma?'

'Not even close.'

'Then what is it?'

She heard the undertone of excitement in his voice. 'This you've got to see to believe.'

Fern Cornwallis looked up at the banner hanging from the gym rafters and she sighed.

KNOX HIGH SCHOOL – YOUR THE BEST!!!

How ironic that the students had gone to such effort to prepare the banner, had crawled up dizzyingly tall ladders to hang it on those rafters, but had neglected to double-check the grammar. It reflected badly on the school, on the teachers, and on Fern herself, but it was too much trouble to pull it down now and correct it. No one would notice it once the lights were turned down, the music was thudding, and the air turned to a steamy vapor of teen hormones.

'There's snow predicted tonight,' Lincoln said. 'Are you sure you don't want to cancel this event?'

Speaking of hormones. Fern turned and her stomach fluttered as it always did when she looked at him. It was a wonder he couldn't see the longing in her eyes. Men are so blind.

'We've postponed this dance twice already,' she

said. 'The kids need some sort of reward, just for getting through this awful month.'

'They're saying four to six inches, the worst of it coming around midnight.'

'The dance will be over by then. They'll all be home.'

Lincoln nodded, but he was obviously uneasy as he looked around at the gym, decorated with blue and white crepe streamers and silver balloons. The chilly colors of winter. A half dozen girls – why was it always the girls who did the work? – were setting up the refreshment table, lugging out the punch bowl, the trays of cookies, the paper plates and napkins. In the far corner, a shaggy student was adjusting the sound equipment, setting off ear-splitting squeals from the amplifier.

'Please keep it down!' yelled Fern, pressing her hand to her head. 'These kids are going to make me deaf.'

'It may be a blessing, considering the music they play.'

'Yeah, urban rap in the woods. Maybe they can mosh into a pile of leaves.'

'Do you know how many will show up tonight?'

'The first dance of the year? I expect a full house. Four grades, minus the thirty-eight troublemakers who've been suspended.'

'It's that many already?'

'I'm taking a proactive stance here, Lincoln. One false move and they're out of here for a week. Not even allowed on the school grounds.'

'That will make my job easier. I'm bringing in both Dolan and Pete Sparks for patrol shift tonight, so you'll have at least two of us here to keep an eye on things.'

The loud crash of a tray made them both turn, and they saw broken cookies scatter across the floor. A blond girl stared down in disbelief at the mess. She spun around and focused on a black-haired girl standing nearby. 'You tripped me.'

'No, I didn't.'

'You've been bumping into me all afternoon!'

'Look, Donna, don't blame me if you can't walk without falling over your own feet!'

'That's it!' said Fern. 'Clean up that mess or you're both suspended!'

Two angry faces stared at her. Almost simultaneously, they said, 'But Miss Cornwallis, she —'

'You heard me.'

The girls exchanged poisonous glances, and Donna stormed out of the gym.

'This is what it's come to,' Fern sighed. 'This is what I'm dealing with.' She looked up, at the high gym windows. At the fading daylight.

The first flakes of snow had begun to fall.

Nightfall was the time of day she dreaded most, for it was with the coming of darkness that all Doreen Kelly's fears seemed to rush forth like demons from their tightly lidded prisons. In the light of day, she could still feel flutterings of hope, and though it was thin as gossamer, she could plot out fantasy scenarios in which she was young again, charming again, and so irresistible she would surely lure Lincoln back home to her, as she had a dozen times before. Staying sober was the key. Oh, she had tried to hold the course! Again and again, she'd managed to convince Lincoln that this time she was dry for good. But then she'd get that familiar thirst, like an itch in her throat that needed scratching, and finally there'd be one little slip of the old willpower, the sweet taste of coffee brandy on the tongue, and she'd be spiraling downward, helpless to pull out of the descent. In the end, what hurt most wasn't the sense of failure or the loss of dignity. It was seeing the look of resignation in Lincoln's eyes.

Come back to me. I'm still your wife and you promised to love and cherish me. Come back just one more time.

Outside, the gray light of afternoon faded, and with it faded the hopes she'd nursed all day. The hopes that, in her more lucid moments, she knew were false. With nightfall came lucidity.

And despair.

She sat down at her kitchen table and poured the first drink. As soon as the coffee brandy hit her stomach, she could feel its heat racing through her veins, bringing with it the welcome flood of numbness. She poured another, felt the numbness spread to her lips, her face. Her fears.

By the fourth drink, she was no longer in pain, no longer in despair. Rather, she was feeling more sure of herself with every sip. Liquid confidence.

She'd made him fall in love with her once before; she could do it again. She still had her figure – a good one. He was a man, wasn't he? He could be coaxed. All it took was to catch him at a moment of weakness.

She stumbled to her feet and pulled on her coat.

Outside, it was starting to snow, soft and lacy flakes drifting down from a black sky. Snow was her friend; what better decoration for her hair than a few glittery snowflakes? She would step into his house with her hair long and loose, her cheeks prettily flushed from the cold. He would invite her in – he'd have to invite her in – and perhaps a spark of lust would leap between them. Yes, yes, that's how she saw it happening, with snowflakes in her hair.

But his house was too far to walk to. It was time to pick up a car.

She headed up the street to Cobb and Morong's. It was an hour before closing, and the evening rush was on to pick up that extra carton of milk, that emergency bag of sugar, on the way home. As Doreen had expected, there were several cars parked along the sidewalk in front of the general store, some of them with their engines running, the heaters blowing. There is nothing so disheartening on a cold night than to walk out and climb into your car, only to find your engine doesn't start.

Doreen walked along the street, eyeing the cars,

deciding which one to choose. Not the pickup –
it wasn't a lady's vehicle, nor the VW, because
she had more important things on her mind than
wrestling with a stick shift.

The green sedan. That was just the car for her.

She glanced at the general store, saw that no
one was coming out the door, and quickly slid
into the sedan. The seat was nice and warm, the
heater's breath toasty against her knees. She put it
in gear, hit the gas, and jolted up and off the curb.
Something in the trunk gave a loud thump.

She drove off just as a voice on the street yelled:
'Hey! Hey, come back with my car!'

It took her a few blocks of weaving back and
forth to figure out how to turn on the headlights,
another block to get the windshield wipers going.
At last her view cleared, and she could actually
see the road ahead. She accelerated, the sedan
fishtailing on the newly fallen snow. She could
hear things rolling around in the trunk, the sound
of glass clinking together as she swerved around
corners. She drove to Lincoln's house and skidded
to a stop in his driveway.

The house was dark.

She climbed out of the car, stumbled onto the
porch, and banged on the front door. 'Lincoln!
Lincoln, I gotta talk to you! You're still my husband!' She banged again and again, but no lights
came on, and the door was locked. He'd taken
away her key, the bastard, and she couldn't
get in.

She went back to the car and sat there for a long time with the engine running, the heater blowing. Snow continued to fall, just a dusting of it, fluttering soundlessly on the windshield. Saturday night was not Lincoln's usual shift, so where was he? She thought of all the places he might be spending the evening, and the possibilities gnawed at her with cruel teeth. She wasn't stupid; she knew that Fern Cornwallis had always had her predatory eye on Lincoln. There must be other women as well, dozens of women who'd find a cop in uniform irresistible. Agitation mounting, Doreen began to rock back and forth, moaning, in her seat. *Come home, come home. Come back to me.*

Even the heater wasn't enough to ward off the chill seeping into her bones, into her soul. She longed for the warmth of brandy, for the welcome flush of alcohol in her veins. Then she remembered the clink of glass in the trunk. Please let it be something worth drinking. Something stronger than soda pop.

She staggered out of the car, went around to the rear, and opened the trunk. It took her a moment to focus her eyes, and even when she did, she wondered if she was hallucinating. *So beautiful, so green. Like jars of emeralds glowing in the darkness.* She started to reach down for one, then turned at the sound of a car engine.

Approaching headlights blinded her. Dazed, she put up her hand to shield her eyes.

A silhouette stepped out of the car.

*　　*　　*

Dr Francis Clevenger was a man in miniature, small-boned, sparrow-faced, his lab coat drooping like a parent's oversize raincoat on his frail shoulders. That, and his absolutely beardless face, made him seem far younger than he was. He looked more like a pale adolescent than a board-certified pathologist. With quick grace he rose from his chair to greet Claire and Warren Emerson's neurosurgeon, Dr Rothstein.

'These slides are *so* cool,' Clevenger said. 'It was the last thing I expected to see. Go on, take a look!' He pointed to the dual-headed teaching microscope.

Claire and Rothstein sat on opposite sides of the scope and leaned into the eyepieces.

'So what do you see?' asked Clevenger, practically dancing beside them in anticipation.

'A mixture of cells,' said Rothstein. 'Astrocytes, I'd guess. Plus what looks to me like an interweaving of scar tissue.'

'That's a start. Dr Elliot, you see anything worth noting?'

Claire focused her eyepiece and gazed at the field of tissue. She was able to identify most of the cells, based on what she remembered from medical school histology classes years before. She recognized starshaped astrocytes, and the presence of macrophages – the cleanup crew, whose function is to tidy up after infection. She also saw what Rothstein had noticed: there were swirls of granulation tissue or scarring, possibly the aftermath of acute inflammation.

Reaching for the slide position knob, she shifted the field, scanning new cells. An unfamiliar pattern appeared under her gaze, a swirl of fibrous matter several cells thick, forming a microscopic rind of tissue. 'I see encapsulation here,' she said. 'A layer of scar tissue. Is this a cyst, maybe? Some sort of infectious process that his immune system managed to wall off and encase?'

'You're getting warm. Remember the CT scan?'

'Yes. It looked like he had a discrete brain mass, with calcifications.'

'An MRI was done here after transfer,' said Rothstein. 'It showed essentially the same thing. A discrete lesion, encapsulated, with calcifications.'

'Right,' said Clevenger. 'And what Dr Elliot has just identified is the cyst wall. Scar tissue formed by the body's immune system, surrounding and closing off the infection.'

'Infection by what organism?' asked Rothstein, raising his head to look at Clevenger.

'Well, that's the mystery here, isn't it?'

Slowly Claire moved the slide, shifting the field again. What appeared through her eyepiece was so startling her gaze froze in amazement. 'What on earth is *this*?' she said.

Clevenger made a sound of almost childish delight. 'You found it!'

'Yes, but I don't know what it is.'

Rothstein pressed his face back to the eyepiece. 'My god. I don't know what it is, either.'

'Describe it for us, Dr Elliot,' said Clevenger.

Claire was silent for a moment as she shifted the position knob and slowly scanned the field. What she saw was a strangely twisted architecture, partially calcified. 'It's some sort of degraded tissue. I don't know if this is all artifact or what – it's as if some organism collapsed into an accordion shape, and then became petrified.'

'Good. Good!' said Clevenger. 'I like that description – petrified. Like a fossil.'

'Yes, but of what?'

'Back off, look at the larger picture.'

She reduced magnification, trying to get an over-all view. The shape took more complete form, became a spiral that had folded upon itself. The realization of what she was looking at made her straighten in shock and stare at Clevenger. 'It's some sort of parasite,' she said.

'Yeah! And isn't it cool?'

'What on earth was a parasite doing in my patient's brain?' said Rothstein.

'It's probably been there for years. Invaded the gray matter, caused a temporary encephalitis. The immune system launched an inflammatory response. You get an influx of white blood cells, eosinophils, everything the host can muster to fight back. Eventually the host wins, and his body walls off the critter, encases it in granulation tissue, forming a sort of cyst. The parasite dies. Parts of it become calcified – petrified, if you will. Years later, that's what you have left.' He nodded at the microscope. 'A dead parasite, trapped in an envelope of scar tissue. It's probably the reason behind his seizures. The mass effect of that little pocket of dead worm and scar.'

'What parasite are we talking about?' asked Claire. 'The only one I can think of that invades the brain is cysticercus.'

'Exactly. I can't conclusively identify this species – it's too far degraded. But this is almost certainly the disease cysticercosis, caused by the larva of *Taenia solium*. The pork tapeworm.'

Rothstein looked disbelieving. 'I thought *Taenia solium* was only found in underdeveloped countries.'

'For the most part it is. You'll find it in Mexico, South America, sometimes in Africa and Asia. That's why I was so excited when I saw that slide. To find a case of cysticercosis here, in northern Maine, is unbelievable. It's definitely worth an article in *The New England Journal of Medicine*. What we need to figure out is when and where he got exposed to pork tapeworm eggs.'

'There's nothing in his history about foreign travel,' said Claire. 'He told me he's lived all his life in this state.'

'Which would make it a truly unusual case. I'll run antibody tests to confirm this is the right diagnosis. If it is *Taenia solium*, he'll have a positive ELISA test on his serum and CSF. Is there any history of an initial inflammatory response? Symptoms that might tell us when he was first infected?'

'What symptoms, specifically?' asked Rothstein.

'It could be a clinical picture as dramatic as full-blown meningitis or encephalitis. Or new onset epilepsy.'

'His first seizures occurred sometime before age eighteen.'

'That's one clue.'

'What other symptoms might show up?'

'Subtler signs, possibly. It can mimic brain tumors, cause a variety of psychiatric disorders.'

The back of Claire's neck was suddenly tingling. 'Violent behavior?' she asked.

'Possibly,' said Clevenger. 'I didn't see that specifically mentioned in my references. But it could be a sign of acute illness.'

'When Warren Emerson was fourteen years old,' said Claire, 'he murdered both his parents.'

The men stared at her. 'I didn't know that,' said Rothstein. 'You never mentioned it.'

'It wasn't relevant to his medical condition. At least, I didn't think so.' She looked down at the microscope, the image of the parasite still vivid in her mind. *An initial infection of parasitic eggs, followed by symptoms of encephalitis. Irritability. Even violence.*

'It's been a long time since medical school,' she said. 'I don't remember much about *Taenia solium*. What's the life cycle of this organism?'

'*Taenia solium* is a cestode,' said Clevenger. 'A tapeworm that usually lives in the intestinal tract of its host. People get it by eating undercooked pork that's been infected with the larvae. The larva has sucking caps that hook on to the wall of the human small intestine, which is where it sets up housekeeping, absorbing food. The worms can live there for decades without causing symptoms, and grow as long as three meters – over nine feet long! Sometimes the worms will be passed or expelled. You can imagine what it'd be like to wake up one morning and find one of those critters lying in the sheets with you.'

Rothstein and Claire exchanged slightly nauseated glances. 'Sweet dreams,' muttered Rothstein.

'So how does the larva reach the brain?' asked Claire.

'It happens during a different part of the worm's life cycle. After the worm matures to adulthood in the human intestine, it begins to produce eggs. When those eggs are passed, they contaminate soil and food sources. People ingest them, the eggs hatch and penetrate the intestinal wall, and are then carried through the bloodstream to any number of organs, including the brain. There, after a few months, they develop into larvae. But it's a dead end, because they can't grow in that confined space, without nutrients. So they just sit there until they die, forming little cystlike pockets in the brain. The cause of this patient's seizures.'

'You said these eggs contaminate the soil,' said Claire. 'How long can the eggs stay alive outside of a host?'

'A number of weeks.'

'What about in water? Could they stay alive in a lake, for instance?'

'It's not mentioned in any of my reference books, but I suppose it's possible.'

'Would the *Taenia solium* ELISA test be a screen for infection? Because we should order it on another patient. A boy at the Maine Youth Center.'

'You think there's *another* case in this state?'

'Maybe a number of other cases in Tranquility. It would explain why so many of our children are suddenly showing violent behavior.'

'An epidemic of cysticercosis in Maine?' Rothstein looked skeptical.

Claire's excitement was rising. 'Both the boys I admitted had the same abnormality in their white blood cell count: a high percentage of eosinophils. At the time, I thought it was because of asthma or allergies. Now I realize it was caused by something else.'

'A parasitic infection,' said Rothstein. 'That raises the eosinophil count.'

'Exactly. And Warren Emerson could be the source of the infection. If he's been harboring a nine-foot tapeworm in his intestines, then he's been shedding parasitic eggs for years. A leak in his septic tank would contaminate the soil and groundwater. The eggs would find their way into the lake, exposing anyone who swims there. Anyone who accidentally takes in a gulp of water.'

'That's a lot of *ifs*,' said Clevenger. 'It's a house of cards you're building.'

'Even the time frame makes sense! The kids would have been infected during the summer, when they swam in the lake. You said the eggs take several months to develop into larvae. Now it's fall, and the symptoms are just starting to show up. A November syndrome.' She paused, suddenly frowning. 'The only thing I can't explain is their negative CT scans.'

'Maybe it was too early in the infection,' said Clevenger. 'During the acute symptoms, the larvae may still be too small to detect. And there wouldn't be any cyst formation yet.'

'Well, there's a simple screen for the parasite,' added Rothstein. 'The ELISA test.'

Claire nodded. 'If anyone shows antibodies to *Taenia solium*, then this theory is more than just a house of cards.'

'We can start by testing Warren Emerson,' said Rothstein. 'And that boy at the Youth Center. If they both come back negative, that kills your theory right there. But if they're positive . . .'

Clevenger, ever the scientist, eagerly rubbed his hands at the possibility. 'Then we'll get out the needles and tourniquets, folks,' he said. 'Because there are a whole lot of arms we have to poke.'

20

J.D. was jeering at her through her bedroom door, calling her a slut, a cheap lay, a whore. Amelia sat on the bed with her hands clapped over her ears, trying to shut out her stepbrother's voice, knowing that if she yelled back at him, it would only make things worse. J.D. was mad at everyone these days, looking to pick a fight with whoever was in reach.

Yesterday, the day he'd been sent home from school, she'd made the mistake of calling him a bastard. He'd slapped her so hard her ears had rung for hours. She'd run sobbing to her mother, but of course there'd been no support from Grace. 'You know how he is,' Grace had said in her I've-got-troubles-of-my-own voice. 'Just stay away from him.'

All day, Amelia had kept her distance by locking herself in her room and trying to concentrate on her homework, but now it was impossible to think. Earlier that day she'd heard J.D. raise hell downstairs, shoving Eddie around, yelling at Mom, even yelling at Jack. Maybe one of these days Jack and J.D. would kill each other. Like father, like son. She wouldn't mourn either one of them.

But now J.D. stood out in the hall, insulting her through the door. 'You like tiny weenies? That why you doing it with that loser, Noah Elliot? I'll show you a big dick! I'll show you how it's done! Or do you want Noah's little weenie?' He laughed, and began chanting, 'Little weenie! Little weenie!' until even Jack had had enough and he yelled up the stairs, 'Shut up, J.D.! I'm trying to watch TV!'

At which point J.D. went tearing downstairs to pick a fight with Jack. Amelia could hear them in the living room, their voices crescendoing to shouts. One big happy family. Now things were being knocked onto the floor. She heard furniture thudding, glass breaking. Jesus, how much worse could it get? Her mother was part of the chaos now, sobbing about her precious broken lamp. Amelia looked down at the school books spread open on her bed, at the list of assignments she'd hoped to complete by Monday, and knew she couldn't possibly finish them. I should have gone to the dance instead, she thought. If I can't do my homework, I might as well have some fun tonight.

Except the dance wouldn't be any fun either, since Noah Elliot wasn't there.

She heard another lamp smash to the floor, then her mother wailing: 'Why don't you do something,

Jack? Why don't you ever do anything?' There was a loud slap, and then Grace was sobbing.

In disgust, Amelia stuffed her books in her backpack, grabbed her jacket, and stalked out of her room. They didn't even hear her come down the stairs. She caught a glimpse of the living room, the floor littered with broken glass, J.D. red-faced and huffing like an angry bull as he faced his father and stepmother.

Amelia slipped out the front door and into a snowy night.

She began to walk down Toddy Point Road, not caring at first where she was going, just wanting to get away from *them*. By the time she'd passed the boat ramp, the cold was starting to penetrate her clothes, and melting snow dripped down her face. She had to go *somewhere*; walking aimlessly on a night like this was stupid and dangerous. But there was only one place she really wanted to go, one home where she knew she'd be welcomed.

Just the thought made her heart lift. She walked faster.

Since when did schoolgirls go out in public wearing fancy underwear? wondered Lincoln as he watched the students gather on the dance floor. He remembered the school dances of his own youth, the girls in their shiny hair and pastel dresses and satin miniskirts. Tonight the girls looked like a gathering of tarted-up vampires in their black lace and spaghetti straps. A few of them had painted their lips black too, and with their white winter faces, they reminded Lincoln of corpses wandering around the murky gym. As for the boys, well, they were just as likely to be wearing earrings as the girls were.

Pete Sparks, standing beside him, said, 'You'd think they'd catch pneumonia in those getups. Can't believe their mothers let 'em out looking like that.'

'I bet their mothers have no idea,' said Lincoln. He had seen many of the girls arrive modestly dressed, only to duck into the bathroom and emerge stripped down to the skimpiest of outfits.

Loud music suddenly blasted from the speakers in a driving beat. After only a few minutes of that racket, Lincoln was desperate to escape.

He stepped through the double doors of the gym, into the relative peace of a cold night.

The snowfall was gentle, just a fluttering of silver past the street-lamp. Standing beneath the building's overhang, he turned up his jacket collar and gratefully inhaled air that was sharp and clean.

Behind him, the door opened and shut, and he heard Fern say, 'Too much for you too?'

'I had to take a breather.'

She came to stand beside him. She was wearing her coat, which meant she'd come out with the intention of staying for a while.

'Does it ever feel like it's all just too much responsibility, Lincoln? Like you're ready to call it quits and just walk away?'

He gave a rueful laugh. 'At least twice a day.'

'Yet you're still here.'

He looked at her. 'So are you.'

'Not because I want to be. It's because I don't see any alternatives.' She looked up at the falling snow, and said softly, 'Doreen doesn't deserve you. She never did.'

'It's not a matter of people deserving good luck or bad, Fern.'

'Still, you should've had better. All these years, I've watched how miserable she's made you, and I kept thinking how unfair it was. How selfish she was. Life doesn't have to be unfair. We can choose happiness.' She paused, marshaling the nerve for what she had to say. He knew what it was; he'd always known, and had always avoided hearing the words spoken aloud, because he knew the aftermath would be humiliating for her, and painful for him. 'It's not too late for us,' she said.

He released a regretful sigh. 'Fern –'

'We could pick up where we left off. Before Doreen.'

He shook his head. 'We can't.'

'Why not?'

He heard the neediness in her voice, the desperation, and he had to force himself to meet her gaze. 'There's someone else I care about.'

She took a step back, retreating into the shadows, but not before he'd seen the tears in her eyes. 'I suppose I already knew that.'

'I'm sorry.'

'No. No, there's no reason to be sorry.' She shook her head and laughed. 'It's just the story of my life.'

He watched her turn back to the building. She paused to square her shoulders, regain her pride. *Why couldn't Fern have been the one*? he thought. Had he fallen in love with her, had they married, it might have been a reasonably happy union. She was attractive enough, intelligent enough. Yet something between them had always been missing. The magic.

In sorrow he watched her cross to the gym door and pull it open. At that instant, the sounds of shouting and running feet suddenly spilled out the open doorway.

'What's going on now?' said Fern, and she ran into the building with Lincoln right behind her.

Inside, they found mass confusion. The punch bowl had tipped over, and a pool of strawberry-colored liquid was spreading across the gym floor. The music was still pounding away, but half the students had retreated against one wall, where they milled together in alarm. Others were clustered in a circle near the sound system. Lincoln couldn't see what was happening at their center, but he heard a loudspeaker thud to the floor, and heard Pete Sparks and the chaperones all shouting: 'Break it up! Back off, back off!'

As Lincoln pushed into the circle, another amplifier tipped over and splashed into the river of punch. There was a deafening squeal and the crowd clapped their hands to their ears, backing away as electrical sparks shot up.

In the next instant, the music died. So did the gym lights.

The darkness lasted only a few seconds, but in that brief pause before the emergency lamp came on, panic seized the crowd. Lincoln felt screaming kids slam into him in their rush to reach the exits. He couldn't see who was coming at him, could only hear the sound of stampeding. He felt someone go down near his feet, and he blindly reached down and hauled a girl back up by her dress.

The emergency lamp at last flared on, one inadequate spotlight in the far corner of the gym. It was just enough light to see the shadowy chaos of running figures, kids stumbling back to their feet.

Then Lincoln focused on a scene that chilled him to the marrow. Pete Sparks had fallen to his knees and seemed too dazed to notice the overweight boy standing beside him. The boy reached down and removed the weapon from Pete's holster.

Lincoln was too far away to disarm the boy with a tackle. He managed to take only two steps forward, then froze as the boy turned to face him, rage glowing in his eyes. Lincoln recognized him. It was Barry Knowlton.

'Put it down, son,' said Lincoln quietly. 'Just put the gun down on the floor.'

'No. No, I'm tired of being kicked around!'

'We can talk about it. But first you have to put it down.'

'Like anyone ever bothers to talk to me!' Barry turned, his gaze circling wildly around the gym. 'You girls, you never bother. You just laugh at me! All the time, that's all I hear, the laughing.' His focus shot to another part of the room. 'Or you, stud! What'd you call me? Fat ass? Say it now! Go ahead, say it now!'

'Put the gun down,' Lincoln repeated, slowly reaching for his own weapon. It was the last resort; he didn't want to shoot the boy. He had to talk him down. Negotiate. Anything to keep the bullets from flying. Footsteps scurried in the shadows and he caught a glimpse of Fern's blond hair as she rushed a group of students out the door. But there were still dozens of people trapped against the far wall, unable to flee.

He took another step forward. Instantly the boy turned to face him.

'You've made your point, Barry,' said Lincoln. 'Let's go in the other room and talk, okay?'

'He called me fat ass.' Anguish had crept into the boy's voice. The desolation of the outsider.

'We'll talk, just the two of us,' said Lincoln.

'No.' The boy turned toward the trapped students, cowering against the wall. 'It's my turn to call the shots.'

Claire drove with her radio turned off, the silence interrupted only by the sweep of her windshield wipers as they cleared away the dusting of snow. She had spent the hour's drive from Bangor deep in thought, and by the time she reached the Tranquility town line, she had pieced it all together. Her theory centered on Warren Emerson.

Emerson's farmhouse was located on the lower slopes of Beech Hill, only a mile upstream from the lake. It was remote enough that it required its own septic system, which drained into a leach field. If a parasite had matured in his intestines, he would have been a continuing source of parasitic eggs. All it took was a leak in his aging septic tank, a year of heavy flooding, and those eggs could have been washed into the nearby Meegawki Stream.

Into the lake.

An elegantly logical explanation, she thought. It's not an epidemic of madness. Nor is it a centuries-old curse on this town. It's a microorganism, a parasitic larva lodging itself in the human brain, wreaking havoc as it grows. All they needed to confirm the diagnosis was a positive ELISA blood test. One more day, and they'd be certain.

A siren alerted her to an approaching police car. She looked up at the lights flashing in her rearview mirror, and saw a cruiser from Two Hills. It barreled past her and raced toward Tranquility. A moment later, a second cruiser screamed by, going in the same direction, followed by an ambulance.

Up ahead, she saw that the flashing lights had turned onto the road toward the high school.

She followed them.

It was a replay of the frightening scene from a month before, emergency vehicles parked at crazy angles outside the gym, clusters of teenagers standing in the road, crying and hugging each other. But this time snow was fluttering from the night sky, and the vehicles' flashing lights were muted, as though seen through white gauze.

Claire grabbed her medical bag and hurried toward the building. She was stopped half a block from the gym by Officer Mark Dolan, decked out in body armor. The look he gave her confirmed what she'd long suspected: their dislike for each other was mutual.

'Everyone has to stay back,' he said. 'We've got a hostage situation.'

'Has anyone been hurt?'

'Not yet, and we want to keep it that way.'

'Where's Lincoln?'

'He's trying to talk the kid down. Now you have to move back, Dr Elliot. Away from the building.'

Claire retreated to where the crowd had gathered. She watched Dolan turn and confer with the police chief from Two Hills. The men in uniform were in charge here, and she was merely another annoying civilian.

'Lincoln's all alone,' said Fern. 'And these goddamn heroes aren't doing anything to help him.'

Claire turned and saw that Fern's blond hair was in disarray, the loose strands crusted with snow. 'I left him in there,' said Fern softly. 'I didn't have a choice. I had to get the kids out . . .'

'Who else is inside?'

'At least a few dozen other kids.' She stared at

the building, melting snow dripping down her cheeks. 'Lincoln has a gun. Why doesn't he just use it?'

Claire looked back at the gym, the situation inside that building now vividly clear to her. An unstable boy. A room with dozens of hostages. Lincoln would not act rashly, nor would he shoot a boy in cold blood, if he could avoid it. The fact that there had been no gunfire yet meant there was still hope of avoiding bloodshed.

She glanced at the policemen gathered behind their parked cruisers, and she saw their agitation, heard the excitement in their voices. These were small-town cops, facing a big-city crisis, and they were champing at the bit to take action, any action.

Mark Dolan signaled to two officers, who were already in position on either side of the gym doors. With his chief trapped inside, Dolan had assumed authority, and he was letting his testosterone take command.

Claire ran through the snow to the cruisers. Dolan and the Two Hills police chief stared at her in surprise as she dropped to a crouch beside them.

'You're supposed to stay back!' said Dolan.

'Don't tell me you're going to send armed men in there!'

'The boy has a gun.'

'You're going to get people killed, Dolan!'

'They'll get killed if we *don't* do something,' said the Two Hills chief. He signaled to three cops crouched behind the next car.

Claire watched in alarm as the officers scrambled toward the building and took position by the doors.

'Don't do this,' she said to Dolan. 'You don't know the situation in there –'

'And you do?'

'There's been no gunfire. Give Lincoln a chance to negotiate.'

'Lincoln's not in charge, Dr Elliot. Now get out of my face or I'll have you arrested!'

She stared straight ahead at the gym doors. The snow was falling faster now, obscuring her view of the building, and through that gauzy curtain of white, the cops looked like ghostly figures floating toward the entrance.

One of them reached for the door.

Lincoln and the boy were at a stalemate. They faced each other across the shadowy gym, the distant beam from the emergency lamp slashing the darkness between them. The boy was still holding the gun, but so far all he'd done was wave it around in the air, eliciting terrified shrieks from the students huddled near the wall. He had not yet aimed at anyone, not even at Lincoln, who had his hand on his weapon, and was prepared to draw it. Two girls were standing just behind the boy, making any shot risky. Lincoln was relying on his instincts now, and they told him this boy could still be talked down, that even as the boy raged on, there was some part of him struggling for control, needing only a calm voice to guide him.

Slowly, Lincoln lowered his hand from his holster. He was facing the boy with his arms at his sides now, a position of neutrality. Trust. 'I don't want to hurt you, son. And I don't think you want to hurt anyone. You're above that. You're better than that.'

The boy wavered. He started to kneel, to place the gun on the floor, then he changed his mind and straightened again. He turned to look at the classmates who cowered in the shadows. 'I'm not like you. I'm not like *any* of you.'

'Then prove it, son,' said Lincoln. 'Put the weapon down.'

The boy turned to look at him. At that moment, the flames of his anger seemed to flicker, grow dim. He was drifting between rage and reason, and in Lincoln's gaze he desperately sought anchor.

Lincoln moved toward him and held out his hand. 'I'll take it now,' he said quietly.

The boy nodded. Gazing steadily into Lincoln's eyes, he reached out to surrender the weapon.

The door crashed open, followed by the rapid-fire staccato of running footsteps. Lincoln saw a confusing blur of movement as men burst into the room from every direction. Shrieking students ran for cover. And caught in the knifelike beam of the emergency lamp stood a dazed Barry Knowlton, his arm still extended, the weapon gripped in his hand. In that split-second, Lincoln saw with sickening clarity what was about to happen. He saw the boy, still clutching the gun, as he turned toward the cops. He saw the men, pumped on adrenaline, weapons raised.

Lincoln screamed, '*Hold your fire!*'

His voice was lost in the deafening blast.

The thunder of gunfire momentarily paralyzed the crowd in the street. Then everyone reacted at once, the bystanders hysterical and screaming, the cops rushing toward the building.

A teacher ran out of the gym and shouted: 'We need an ambulance!'

Claire had to fight a stream of terrified kids pushing out the door as she struggled into the building. At first all she saw was a confusing jumble of silhouettes, men padded with body armor, paper streamers drifting, ghostlike, in the shadows above. The darkness smelled of sweat and fear.

And blood. She almost stepped in a pool of it as she forced her way into the gathering of cops. At their center was Lincoln, crouched on the floor, cradling a limp boy in his arms.

'Who gave the order?' he demanded, his voice hoarse with fury.

'Officer Dolan thought –'

'Mark?' Lincoln looked at Dolan.

'It was a joint decision,' said Dolan. 'Chief Orbison and I – we knew the boy was armed –'

'He was about to surrender!'

'We didn't know!'

'Get out of here,' said Lincoln. 'Go on, get *out* of here!'

Dolan turned and shoved Claire aside as he walked out the door.

She knelt down beside Lincoln. 'The ambulance is right outside.'

'It's too late,' he said.

'Let me see if I can help him!'

'There's nothing you can do.' He looked at her, his eyes glistening with tears.

She reached down for the boy's wrist and felt no pulse. Then Lincoln opened his arms and she saw the boy's head. What was left of it.

21

That night he needed her. After Barry Knowlton's body had been removed, after the ordeal of meeting the shattered parents, Lincoln had found himself trapped in the bright glare of reporters' flashbulbs. Twice he'd broken down and cried in front of the TV cameras. He was not ashamed of his tears, nor was he stinting in his angry condemnation of how the crisis had been resolved. He knew he was laying the groundwork for a wrongful death suit against his own employer, the Town of Tranquility. He didn't care. All he knew was that a boy had been shot down like a deer in November, and someone should have to pay.

Driving through a galaxy of falling snow, he realized he could not bear the thought of going home, of spending this night, like so many other nights, alone.

He drove instead to Claire's house.

Stumbling from his car through the calf-deep snow, he felt like some wretched pilgrim struggling toward sanctuary. He climbed to her porch and knocked again and again on the door, and when there was no response, he was suddenly gripped by despair at the thought she was not home, that this house was empty. That he faced the rest of the night without her.

Then above, a light came on, its warm halo filtering down through the falling snow. A moment later the door opened and she stood before him.

He stepped inside. Neither one of them said a word. She simply opened her arms to him, accepted him. He was dusted with snow, and it melted against her heat, trickling in cold rivulets to soak the flannel of her gown. She just kept holding him, even as melted snow puddled on the floor around her bare feet.

'I waited for you,' she said.

'I couldn't stand the thought of going home.'

'Then stay here. Stay with me.'

Upstairs they shed their clothes and slid between sheets still warm from her sleeping body. He had not come to make love, had come seeking only comfort. She gave him both, granting him the welcome exhaustion that eased him into sleep.

He awakened to a view through the window of a sky so sharply blue it hurt his eyes. Claire lay curled up asleep beside him, her hair an unruly tangle of curls on the pillow. He could see strands of gray mingled among the brown, and that first silvering of age in her hair was so unexpectedly touching that he found himself blinking back tears.

Half a lifetime of not knowing you, he thought. Half a lifetime wasted, until now.

He kissed her softly on the head, but she didn't awaken.

He got dressed while gazing out the window, at a world transformed by the night's storm. A fluffy mantle of snow had buried his car, turning it into an indistinct mound of white. The snow-covered branches of trees drooped under their heavy cloaks, and where once there'd been the front lawn, now there seemed to be a bright field of diamonds, glittering in the sunlight.

A pickup truck came up the road and turned onto Claire's property. It had a winter plow mounted in front, and Lincoln assumed at first that this was someone Claire had hired to clear her driveway. Then the driver stepped out, and Lincoln saw the Tranquility police department uniform. It was Floyd Spear.

Floyd waded over to the mound that was Lincoln's vehicle and brushed away the snow from the license plate. Then he looked up, questioningly, at the house. *Now the whole town will know where I spent the night.*

Lincoln went downstairs and opened the front door just as Floyd raised his gloved hand to knock. 'Morning,' said Lincoln.

'Uh . . . morning.'

'You looking for me?'

'Yeah, I – I drove over to your house, but you weren't home.'

410

'My pager's been on.'

'I know. But I – well, I didn't want to break the news over the phone.'

'What news?'

Floyd looked down at his own boots, crusted with snow. 'It's bad news, Lincoln. I'm real sorry. It's about Doreen.'

Lincoln said nothing. And strangely enough, he felt nothing, as if the cold air he was breathing in had somehow numbed his heart, and his brain as well. Floyd's voice seemed to be speaking to him from across a great distance, the words fading in and out of hearing.

'. . . found her body over on Slocum Road. Don't know how she got all the way out there. We think it must've happened early last night, 'round the same time as that trouble over at the school. But it's up to the ME to determine.'

Lincoln could barely force words from his throat. 'How . . . how did it happen?'

Floyd hesitated, his gaze rising, then dropping again to his boots. 'It looks like a hit-and-run to me. The state police are heading out to the scene.'

By Floyd's prolonged silence, Lincoln understood there was still more that hadn't been said. When Floyd looked up at last, his next words came out with painful reluctance. 'Last night, around nine, the dispatcher got a call about a drunken driver, weaving all over Slocum Road. Same vicinity where we found Doreen. That call came in

411

while we were all over at the high school, so no one managed to follow up on it –'

'Did the witness get a license number?'

Floyd nodded. And added miserably: 'The vehicle was registered to Dr Elliot.'

Lincoln felt the blood drain from his face. *Claire's car?*

'According to the registration, it's a brown Chevy pickup.'

'But she wasn't driving the pickup! I saw her last night at the school. She was driving that old Subaru sedan.'

'All I'm saying, Lincoln, is that the witness gave Dr Elliot's license number. So maybe – maybe I should take a look at the pickup?'

Lincoln stepped outside in his shirtsleeves, but scarcely felt the cold as he waded across to the barn. He reached elbow deep into the snow, found the handle, and raised the door.

Inside, both of Claire's vehicles were parked side by side, the pickup on the right. The first thing Lincoln noticed was the snowmelt puddled beneath both vehicles. Both of them had been driven sometime in the last day or two, recently enough so that the puddles had not yet evaporated.

His numbness was quickly giving way to a nauseating sense of dread. He circled around to the front of the pickup truck. At his first glimpse of the blood smeared across the fender, the world seemed to drop away from under his feet, to collapse beneath him.

Without a word, he turned and walked out of the barn.

Halting in calf-deep snow, he looked up at the house where Claire and her son now slept. He could think of no way to avoid the ordeal to come, no way to spare her from the pain he himself would now have to inflict. He had no choice in the matter. Surely she would understand. Perhaps some day she would even forgive him.

But today – today she would hate him.

'You know you're gonna have to step away from this,' said Floyd, softly. 'Hell, you're gonna have to stay *miles* away. Doreen was your wife. And you just spent the night with . . .' His voice faded. 'It's a state police case, Lincoln. They'll be wanting to talk to you. To both of you.'

Lincoln took a deep breath and welcomed the punishing sharpness of cold air in his lungs. Welcomed the physical pain. 'Then you get them on the radio,' he said. And he started, reluctantly, toward the house. 'I have to talk to Noah.'

She didn't understand how this could have happened. She had awakened to a parallel universe where people she knew, people she loved, were behaving in ways she did not recognize. There was Noah slouched in the kitchen chair, his whole body so electric with rage the air around him seemed to hum. There was Lincoln, grim and distant as he asked another question, and another. Neither one of them looked at her; clearly they both preferred she be out of the room, but they hadn't asked her to leave. She would not leave in any event; she saw the direction Lincoln's questions were taking, and she understood the dangerous nature of this drama now being played out in her kitchen.

'I need you to be honest with me, son,' said Lincoln. 'I'm not trying to play tricks on you. I'm not trying to trap you. I just have to know where you drove the truck last night, and what happened.'

'Who says I drove it anywhere?'

'The pickup has obviously been out of the barn. There's snowmelt under it.'

'My mom –'

'Your mom was driving the Subaru last night, Noah. She confirms it.'

Noah's gaze shot to Claire, and she saw the accusation in his eyes. *You're on his side.*

'Who gives a shit if I did take it out for a drive?' said Noah. 'I brought it back in one piece, didn't I?'

'Yes, you did.'

'So I drove without a license. Send me to the electric chair.'

'Where did you drive the truck, Noah?'

'Around.'

'Where?'

'Just around, okay?'

'Why are you asking him these questions?' said Claire. 'What are you trying to get him to say?'

Lincoln didn't answer; his attention remained

414

fixed on her son. That's how far he's pulled away from me, she thought. That's how little I know this man. Welcome to the morning after, the hard light of regret.

'This isn't about a simple joyride, is it?' said Claire.

At last Lincoln looked at her. 'There was a hit-and-run accident last night. Your pickup truck may have been involved.'

'How do you know that?'

'A witness saw your truck driving erratically and called it in. It was on the same road where the body was found.'

She sat back in her chair, as though someone had shoved her. *A body. Someone has been killed.*

'Where did you take the pickup last night, Noah?' Lincoln asked.

Suddenly Noah looked terrified. 'The lake,' he said, almost too softly to be heard.

'Where else?'

'Just the lake. Toddy Point Road. I parked for a while, on the boat ramp. Then it started to snow too hard, and we didn't want to get stuck there, so I – I drove home. I was already here when mom got back.'

'We? You said *we* didn't want to get stuck.'

Noah looked confused. 'I meant *me*.'

'Who was in the truck with you?'

'Nobody.'

'The truth, Noah. Who was with you when you hit Doreen?'

415

'Who?'

'Doreen Kelly.'

Lincoln's wife? Claire stood up so abruptly her chair toppled backwards. 'Stop it. Stop the questions!'

'They found her body this morning, Noah,' Lincoln continued, as though Claire hadn't spoken at all, and his quiet monotone barely disguised his pain. 'She was lying at the side of Slocum Road. Not far from where the witness saw you driving last night. You could have stopped to help her. You could have called someone, anyone. She didn't deserve to die that way, Noah. Not all alone, in the cold.' Claire heard more than pain in his voice; she heard guilt. His marriage may have been over, but Lincoln had never lost his sense of responsibility toward Doreen. With her death, he had taken on the new burden of self-blame.

'Noah wouldn't leave her there,' said Claire. 'I know he wouldn't.'

'You may think you know him.'

'Lincoln, I understand you're hurting. I understand you're in shock. But now you're lashing out, trying to assign blame to the nearest target.'

Lincoln looked at Noah. 'You've been in trouble before, haven't you? You've stolen cars.'

Noah's hands clenched into fists. 'You know?'

'Yes, I do. Officer Spear called your juvenile intake officer down in Baltimore.'

'So why are you bothering with the questions? You've already decided I'm guilty!'

'I want to hear your side.'

'I told you my side!'

'You say you drove around the lake. You also drove out to Slocum Road, didn't you? Did you realize you'd hit her? Did you ever think to get out and just take a goddamn *look*?'

'Stop it,' said Claire.

'I have to know!'

'I won't have a cop interrogating my son without legal counsel!'

'I'm not asking this as a cop.'

'You *are* a cop! And there'll be no more questions!' She stood behind her son, her hands on Noah's shoulders as she gazed straight at Lincoln. 'He has nothing more to say to you.'

'He'll have to come up with answers eventually, Claire. The state police will be asking him all these questions and more.'

'Noah won't be talking to them either. Not without an attorney.'

'Claire,' he said, anguish spilling into his voice. 'She was my wife. I need to know.'

'Are you placing my son under arrest?'

'It's not my decision –'

Claire's hands tightened on Noah's shoulders. 'If you're not arresting him, and you have no search warrant, then I want you to leave my house. I want you and Officer Spear off my property.'

'There's physical evidence. If Noah would just come clean with me and admit –'

'What physical evidence?'

'Blood. On your pickup truck.'

She stared at him, the shock like a vise crushing her chest.

'Your truck was driven recently. The blood on the front fender –'

'You had no right,' she said. 'You had no search warrant.'

'I didn't need one.'

The meaning of his words was instantly clear to her. *He was my guest last night. I gave him implied permission to be here. To search my property. I allowed him in my house as a lover, and he's turned against me.*

She said, 'I want you to leave.'

'Claire, please –'

'Get out of my house!'

Slowly Lincoln rose to his feet. There was no anger in his expression, just profound sadness. 'They'll be coming to talk to him,' he said. 'I suggest you call an attorney soon. I don't know how likely it is you'll find one on a Sunday morning . . .' He looked down at the table, then back up at her. 'I'm sorry. If there was any way I could change things – any way I could make this turn out right . . .'

'I have my son to think of,' she said. 'Right now he has to be my only concern.'

Lincoln turned to Noah. 'If you did anything wrong, it will come out. And you'll be punished. I won't have any sympathy for you, not one bit. I'm just sorry it's going to break your mother's heart.'

*　　*　　*

The men were not leaving. Claire stood in the front parlor, gazing out the window at Lincoln and Floyd, who lingered at the end of her driveway. They are not going to leave us unguarded, she thought. They're afraid Noah will slip away.

Lincoln turned to look at the house, and Claire stepped back from the window, not wanting him to see her, not allowing even the briefest eye contact. There could be nothing between them now. Doreen's death had changed everything.

She went back into the kitchen where Noah sat, and sank into the chair across from him. 'Tell me what happened, Noah. Tell me everything.'

'I did tell you.'

'You took the pickup out last night. Why?'

He shrugged.

'Have you done this before?'

'No.'

'The truth, Noah.'

His gaze shot up, dark with anger. 'You're calling me a liar. Just like he did.'

'I'm trying to get a straight answer out of you.'

'I gave you a straight answer, and you don't believe me! Okay, fine, believe what you want. I take the truck out every night for a joyride. Rack up thousands of miles – haven't you noticed? But why would you? You're never home for me anyway!'

Claire was stunned by the rage in his voice. Is that really how he sees me? she wondered. The mother who's never here, never home for her only child? She swallowed the hurt, forcing herself to focus on the events of last night.

'All right, I'll accept your word that it was the only time you took out the truck. You still haven't told me why you did.'

Noah's gaze dropped to the table, a clear indication he was being evasive. 'I felt like it.'

'You drove to the boat ramp and just parked there?'

'Yeah.'

'Did you see Doreen Kelly?'

'I don't even know what she looks like!'

'Did you see anyone?'

A pause. 'I didn't see any lady named Doreen. Stupid name.'

'She was not just a name. She was a person, and she's dead. If you know anything at all –'

'I don't.'

'Lincoln seems to think you do.'

Again that angry gaze slanted up at her. 'And you believe *him*, don't you?' He shoved the chair back and stood up.

'Sit down.'

'You don't want me around. You want Mr Cop instead.' She saw the flash of tears in his eyes as he turned for the kitchen door.

'Where are you going?'

'What difference does it make?' He walked out, slamming the door behind him.

She stepped outside and saw that he was already stumbling away into the woods. He had no jacket, only those tattered jeans and a long-sleeved cotton shirt, but he didn't seem to care about the cold. His anger and hurt were driving him recklessly forward through the snow.

'Noah!' she yelled.

Now he had reached the lake's edge and he veered left, following its curve, crossing into the woods of the neighboring property.

'Noah!' She plunged into the snow after him. He was already far ahead and with each angry stride he increased the distance between them. *He's not coming back.* She began to run, shouting his name.

Now two figures, off to her left, caught her eye. Lincoln and Floyd had heard her voice and were in pursuit as well. They had nearly caught up when Noah glanced back and saw them.

He began to run, toward the lake.

Claire cried out: 'Don't hurt him!'

Floyd grabbed him just as they both reached the edge of the ice and he hauled him backwards. They both tumbled into deep snow. Noah scrambled back to his feet first and he flew at Floyd, fists swinging, his rage out of control. He thrashed, howling, as Lincoln grabbed him from behind and wrestled him to the ground.

Floyd scrambled back to his feet and drew his weapon.

'No!' screamed Claire, and terror sent her churning through the snow. She reached her son just as Lincoln cuffed the boy's hands behind his back.

'Don't fight them, Noah!' she pleaded. 'Stop fighting!'

Noah twisted around to look at her, his face so contorted by fury she didn't recognize him. *Who is this boy?* she thought in horror. *I don't know him.*

'*Let – me – go!*' he shrieked. A bright drop of blood slid from his nostril and splattered onto the snow.

She stared down in shock at the splash of red, then looked at her son, heaving like an exhausted beast, his breath steaming the air. A fine line of blood glistened on his upper lip.

New voices called out to them from a distance. Claire turned, and saw men crossing toward them. As they came closer, she recognized the uniforms.

State police.

22

The noise was driving her crazy. Amelia Reid leaned on her desk and clutched her head, wishing she could block out all the sounds assaulting her from different parts of the house. From the room next door came the thump of J.D.'s god-awful music, pounding like a demon's heartbeat against her wall. And from the living room downstairs came the shout of the TV, its volume turned up to the max. She could deal with the music, because it was just noise, an irritant that chewed away at the farthest margins of her concentration. The TV, though, insinuated itself right into her mind because it was the voices of people talking, their words distracting her from the book she was trying to read.

In frustration, she slammed it shut and went downstairs. She found Jack in his usual position for the evening, slumped in the plaid BarcaLounger, a beer in his hand. His Royal Highness, farting in his throne. What awful desperation had driven her mother to marry him? Amelia could not imagine ever choosing such an option, could not even bear to contemplate a future with such a man under her roof, belching at her table, discarding his filthy socks like droppings on the living room floor.

And at night, to lie in bed with him, to feel his hands on her flesh . . .

An involuntary sound of disgust escaped her throat, drawing Jack's attention from the evening news. He looked at her, and his blank expression changed to one of interest, maybe even speculation. She knew the reason for it, and almost felt the need to cross her arms over her chest.

'Can you turn it down?' she said. 'I can't study.'

'So shut your door.'

'I did shut my door. The TV's too loud.'

'It's my house, y'know. You're lucky I let you live here. I work hard all day. I deserve to relax in my own home.'

'I can't concentrate. I can't do my homework.'

Jack let out a half-belch, half-laugh. 'A girl like you doesn't need to blow a circuit in her brain. You don't even need a brain.'

'What's that supposed to mean?'

'Find a rich man, toss that pretty hair of yours, you got a meal ticket for the rest of your life.'

She bit back an angry retort. Jack was baiting her. She could see that smirk on his lips, the thin mustache tilting up at one corner. He liked to get her angry, enjoyed seeing her upset. He couldn't get her attention any other way, and

Amelia knew he was titillated by any flash of emotion she displayed, even if it was rage.

With a shrug, she focused instead on the TV. Icy withdrawal was the way to deal with Jack. Show no anger, no feelings at all, and it drove him crazy. It showed him exactly what he was: irrelevant. Inconsequential. Staring at the screen, she felt herself regain a measure of control over him. To hell with him. He couldn't get to her, or at her, because she wouldn't let him.

It took a few seconds for her brain to register the images on the screen. She saw a brown pickup being towed by a police truck, saw the blurred figure of a boy, face covered, as he was escorted into the Tranquility police station. When she finally understood what she was looking at, she forgot about Jack entirely.

'. . . the fourteen-year-old boy is currently being held for questioning. The body of forty-three-year-old Doreen Kelly was found this morning on a remote stretch of Slocum Road, east of Tranquility. According to an anonymous eyewitness report, the suspect's truck was seen weaving erratically on that same stretch of road around nine P.M. last night, and unspecified physical evidence has led police to take the youth into custody. The victim, wife of Tranquility Police Chief Lincoln Kelly, had a long and troubling history of alcoholism, according to several town residents . . .'

A new face appeared onscreen, a woman Amelia recognized as a cashier from Cobb and Morong's.

'Doreen was sort of the local tragic figure around here. She'd never, ever harm a soul, and I just can't believe someone would do this. Only a monster would leave her out there to die.'

Now the TV showed a stretcher bearing a shrouded body being loaded into an ambulance.

'In a community already rocked by the tragedy of last night's high school violence, this latest death is just one more blow to a town ironically named Tranquility . . .'

Amelia said, 'What are they talking about? What happened?'

Jack's colorless eyes showed an ugly flicker of amusement. 'Heard about it in town today,' he said. 'That doctor's kid is dead meat.'

Noah? Surely he's not talking about Noah.

'Ran over the police chief's wife last night, over on Slocum Road. That's what some witness says.'

'Who's saying that?'

Jack's expression of amusement had spread to the rest of his face, tugging his lips into an ugly smile. 'Well, that's the question, isn't it? Just who did see it?' He raised his eyebrows in mock surprise. 'Oh! I almost forgot. That's the boy you're all sweet on, isn't it? The one you think is something special. Well, I guess you're right.' He looked back at the TV and laughed. 'He's gonna be *real* special in prison.'

'Fuck you,' said Amelia, and she ran out of the room and up the stairs.

'Hey! Hey, you come back here and apologize!'

yelled Jack. 'You show me a little goddamn *respect*!'

Ignoring the demands he was hurling after her, she headed straight into her mother's bedroom and shut the door. *If he'll just leave me alone for five minutes. If he'll let me make this one call . . .*

She picked up the telephone and called Noah Elliot's house.

To her dismay, it rang four times and then an answering machine picked up with a recording of his mother's voice.

'This is Dr Elliot. I'm unable to answer the phone, so please leave a message. If this is an emergency, you can page me through the Knox Hospital operator, and I'll return your call as soon as I can.'

At the beep, Amelia blurted out: 'Dr Elliot, this is Amelia Reid. Noah didn't run over that woman! He couldn't have, because he was with –'

The bedroom door flew open. 'What the hell are you doing in my room, you little bitch?' Jack roared.

Amelia slammed the phone down and turned to face him.

'You apologize,' said Jack.

'For what?'

'For cussing at me, goddamn it.'

'You mean for saying *fuck you*?'

His slap made her head whip sideways. She raised a hand to her stinging cheek, then she focused her gaze back on his. She stared at him for a moment, and something deep inside her, some

427

core of molten steel, at last seemed to solidify. When he reached up to slap her again, she didn't even flinch. She just looked at him, her eyes telling him that one more blow on his part would make him very, very sorry.

Slowly he lowered his hand, the blow never struck. He didn't try to stop her as she walked out and went to her own room. He was still standing there, motionless, as she swung the door shut behind her.

Claire and Max Tutwiler stood in front of Lincoln's desk, refusing to leave. They had walked into the police station together, and now Max had his briefcase open, and as Lincoln watched in bewilderment, Max unrolled a topographical map and spread it across the desk.

'What's this supposed to show me?' Lincoln asked.

'It's the explanation for my son's illness. For what's happening in this town,' said Claire urgently. 'Noah needs to be hospitalized. You *have* to release him.'

Reluctantly Lincoln looked up at her. Only twelve hours ago, they had been lovers. Now it was apparent he could barely bring himself to meet her gaze.

'He didn't look ill to me, Claire. In fact, he almost outran us this morning.'

'The sickness is in his brain. It's a parasite called *Taenia solium*, and during the initial infection, it can cause personality changes. If Noah's infected, he needs to be treated. *Taenia solium* cysts cause brain swelling and symptoms of meningitis. That's what I've been seeing in him these past few days. The irritability, the rage. If I don't get him to a hospital, if he's developed a cyst and it ruptures . . .' She stopped, struggling to hold back tears. 'Please,' she whispered. 'I don't want to lose my son.'

'What it means,' said Max, 'is that he's not responsible for his actions. Neither are the other children.'

'But how did the kids get this parasite?' asked Lincoln.

'From Warren Emerson,' said Claire. 'A pathologist at Eastern Maine Medical Center is almost certain his brain lesion was caused by *Taenia solium*, the pork tapeworm. Emerson's probably been infected for years. Which means he's also been a carrier of the disease.'

'And this is how the kids got it from Emerson,' said Max. He smoothed out the topographical map, which he'd spread across Lincoln's desk. 'Claire came up with this theory. This shows the lower Meegawki Stream. The elevations, the flood pattern, even the subterranean sections of its flow.'

'What is this supposed to tell me?'

'Look here.' Max placed his finger on the map. 'It's the approximate location of Warren Emerson's farm, about a mile upstream from the lake. Elevation two hundred feet. The Meegawki Stream runs right past his property, close to the leach field for his septic system. It's probably a very old septic system.' Max looked up at Lincoln. 'Do you understand the significance of his farm's location?'

'Contamination of the stream?'

'Exactly. This past spring, you had record rainfall, and the stream would have flooded right up to Emerson's leach field. It could have washed parasitic eggs into the stream and carried it away. To the lake.'

'How would these eggs get into the leach field?'

'From Warren Emerson himself,' said Claire. 'He was probably infected years ago, when he ate undercooked pork containing the tapeworm larvae. The larvae grow and live in human intestines, sometimes for decades. They produce eggs.'

'If Emerson's harbored a tapeworm in his digestive tract,' said Max, 'then he's been passing parasitic eggs into his septic system. A leak in the tank, a heavy flood, could wash them into the feeder stream. And eventually, into the lake. They'd be at their highest concentration right here, where the Meegawki Stream empties in.' Max pointed to the Boulders. 'Precisely the spot where your local teenagers like to swim. Am I right?'

Lincoln suddenly looked up, his attention drawn to a commotion elsewhere in the building. They all turned as the door flew open and a panicked-looking Floyd Spear stuck his head in.

'The boy's having seizures! We're calling the ambulance now.'

Claire shot one terrified glance at Lincoln and ran out of the office. One of the state policemen tried to stop her, but Lincoln snapped, 'She's a doctor! Let her through!' Claire pushed into the hallway leading to the three-cell jail.

The door to the first cell was open. Inside, two policemen were crouched down. All she could see of her son was his legs, jerking in electric spasms. Then she noticed the blood on the floor, near his head, and saw that half his face was smeared with it.

'What did you do to him?' she cried.

'Nothing! We found him like this. He must've hit his head on the floor –'

'Get back. Get out of my way!'

The cops moved aside and Claire dropped to her knees beside Noah. The panic almost paralyzed her. She had to force herself to think, to shove aside the terrifying fact that this was her son, her only child, and that he might be dying before her eyes. *A grand mal seizure. Breathing's erratic.* She heard the gurgle of fluid in his throat, and his chest was seized by violent spasms as he struggled to suck air into his starved lungs.

Get him off his back. Don't let him aspirate!

She grabbed his shoulder. Another pair of hands came to her aid. Glancing sideways, she saw Lincoln kneeling beside her. Together they log-rolled Noah onto his side. He was still convulsing, still battering his head against the floor.

'I need padding to protect his head!' she yelled.

Max, who'd also pushed into the cell, yanked a blanket from the cot and tossed it to her. Gently she raised Noah's head and slid the blanket underneath. Many times before, when he was a child, she would find him asleep on the couch and would slide a pillow under his hair. This was not the head of a sleeping boy; with each new spasm, his neck turned rigid, the muscles taut and corded. And the blood – where was the blood coming from?

Again, she heard the gurgle and saw his chest heave as a fresh stream of red trickled out his nostril. So he hadn't cut himself; it was the nosebleed again. Was it blood she heard gurgling in his throat? She turned his face downward, hoping to clear any blood from his mouth, but only a trickle spilled out, mixed with saliva. The seizures were fading now, his limbs no longer jerking with such violence, but the sound of choking intensified.

Heimlich maneuver. Before he suffocates.

She left him lying on his side, placed one hand on his upper abdomen, and braced her other hand against his back. She gave a forceful thrust against his belly, aiming it toward the rib cage.

Air wheezed out of his throat. It wasn't a complete obstruction, she thought with relief. His lungs were still getting air.

She repeated the maneuver. Again, she positioned the heel of her hand against his belly and gave a firm thrust. She heard air rush out of his lungs, heard the wheeze clear as the reason for the obstruction was suddenly expelled from his throat and spilled partway out one nostril. When she saw what it was, she jerked back with a gasp of horror.

'Jesus Christ!' yelled the state cop. 'What the fuck is *that*?'

The worm was moving, lashing back and forth in a pink froth of blood and mucus. Now more of it slithered out, twisting into glistening loops as it frantically worked itself free. Claire was so shocked she could only stare as it wriggled out of her son's nose and slid to the floor. There it coiled up on itself, one end rising like a cobra as though to test the air.

In the next instant it whipped away and vanished under the nearby cot.

'Where is it? Get it!' yelled Claire.

Max was already scrambling on hands and knees, trying to peer under the cot. 'I don't see it –'

'We need it identified!'

'There, I see it,' said Lincoln, who'd dropped to his knees beside Max. 'It's still moving –'

The cut-off wail of an ambulance drew Claire's attention. She glanced toward the sound of approaching voices and the metallic rattle of a rolling stretcher. Noah was breathing easier now, his chest rising and falling without spasms, his pulse rapid but steady.

The EMTs pushed into the cell. Claire moved aside as they went to work, establishing an intravenous line, administering oxygen.

'Claire,' said Lincoln. 'You'd better take a look at this.'

She moved to his side and knelt down, peering into the narrow space beneath the cot. The cell was poorly lit, and it was hard to see much detail in the shadow of that sagging mattress. Where the light just slanted under the edge, she made out a few dust balls and a crumpled tissue. Beyond that, in the farthest recess, a bright green line was moving, forming hallucinogenic curlicues in the darkness.

'It's glowing, Claire,' said Lincoln. 'That's what we saw. That night, on the lake.'

'Bioluminescence,' said Max. 'Some worms have the capability.'

Claire heard a restraint buckle snap into place. Turning, she saw that the EMTs had already strapped Noah on the stretcher and were man-euvering him through the cell door.

'He seems stable,' said the EMT. 'We're taking him to Knox ER.'

'I'll be driving right behind you,' she said, then glanced at Max. 'I need that specimen.'

'You go on ahead with Noah,' said Max. 'I'll bring the worm to the pathology department.'

She nodded, and followed her son out of the building.

Claire stood in the X-ray department, frowning at the films clipped to the viewing box. 'What do you think?' she said.

'This CT scan looks normal,' said Dr Chapman, the radiologist. 'All the cuts appear symmetrical. I see no masses, no cysts. No evidence of bleeding into the brain.' He glanced up as Dr Thayer, the neurologist whom Claire had asked to be Noah's physician, walked into the room. 'We're just looking at the CT scan now. No abnormalities that I can see.'

Thayer slipped on his glasses and surveyed the films. 'I agree,' he said. 'What about you, Claire?'

Claire trusted both these men, but this was her son they were discussing, and she could not completely relinquish control. They understood this, and were careful to share with her the results of every blood test and X-ray. They were now sharing their bewilderment as well. She could see it in Chapman's face as he focused once again on the films. The light box cast back twin reflections of the X-rays on his glasses, obscuring his eyes, but his frown told her he did not have an answer.

'I see nothing here to explain the seizures,' he said.

'And nothing to contraindicate a spinal tap,' said Thayer. 'Given the clinical picture, I'd say a tap is definitely called for.'

'I don't understand. I was almost certain of the diagnosis,' said Claire. 'You don't see any indication of cysticercosis?'

'No,' said Chapman. 'No larval cysts. As I said, the brain looks normal.'

'So are the blood tests,' said Thayer. 'All except a slightly elevated white count, and that could be due to stress.'

'His differential wasn't normal,' Claire pointed

out. 'He has a high eosinophil count, which would go along with a parasitic infection. The other boys had high eosinophil counts as well. At the time I didn't pay attention to it. Now I think I missed the vital clue.' She looked at the CT scan. 'I *saw* that parasite with my own eyes. I saw it come out of my son's nostril. All we need is species identification.'

'It may have nothing to do with his seizures, Claire. That parasite could be an unrelated illness. Most likely it's just a common *Ascaris* infection. Those can turn up anywhere in the world. I saw a kid in Mexico cough up one of those worms and expel it from his nostril. *Ascaris* wouldn't cause neurologic symptoms.'

'But *Taenia solium* would.'

'Have they identified Warren Emerson's parasite?' asked Chapman. 'Is it *Taenia solium*?'

'His ELISA test should be done by tomorrow. If he has antibodies to *Taenia*, we'll know that's the parasite we're dealing with.'

Thayer, still looking at the X-ray, shook his head. 'This CT scan shows no evidence of larval cysts. True, it may be too early a stage to visualize yet. But in the meantime, we have to rule out other possibilities. Encephalitis. Meningitis.' He reached up and flicked off the light box. 'It's time to do a spinal tap.'

An X-ray clerk stuck her head in the room. 'Dr Thayer, Pathology's on the line for you.'

Thayer picked up the wall phone. A moment

later he hung up, and turned to Claire. 'Well, we have an answer on that worm. The one that your son expelled.'

'They've identified it?'

'They transmitted photos and microscopic sections online to Bangor. A parasitologist at Eastern Maine Medical Center just confirmed the ID. It's not *Taenia*.'

'Is it *Ascaris*, then?'

'No, it's from the Annelida phylum.' He shook his head in bewilderment. 'This has to be a mistake. Obviously they've misidentified it.'

Claire frowned in puzzlement. 'I'm not familiar with Annelida. What is it?'

'It's just a common earthworm.'

23

Claire sat in the darkness of Noah's hospital room, listening to her son rock side to side on the bed. Since the spinal tap earlier that evening, he had continued to fight against his restraints, and had dislodged two IVs. Thayer had finally relented to the nurses' requests and allowed them to administer a sedative. Even with sedation, even with the lights turned off, he didn't sleep, but continued rocking back and forth, uttering curses. It exhausted her just to hear his ceaseless struggle.

A little after midnight, Lincoln came into the room. She saw the door swing open, the light spill in from the hall, and recognized his silhouette as he hesitated in the doorway. He came in and sat down in the chair across from her.

'I spoke to the nurse,' he said. 'She says everything is stable.'

Stable. Claire shook her head at the word. *Unchanging* was all it meant, a state of constancy, good or bad. *Despair* could be thought of as a stable condition.

'He seems quieter,' said Lincoln.

'They've pumped him full of sedatives. They had to, after the spinal tap.'

'Have the results come back?'

'No meningitis. No encephalitis. Nothing in the CSF to explain what's happened to him. And now the parasite theory is dead as well.' She leaned back, her body heavy with fatigue, and gave a bewildered laugh. 'No one can explain it to me. How he managed to inhale an earthworm. It doesn't make sense, Lincoln. Earthworms don't glow. They don't use humans as hosts. There has to be some kind of mistake . . .'

'You need to go home and sleep,' he said.

'No, I need answers. I need my son. I need him back the way he was before his father died, before all this trouble, when he still loved me.'

'He does love you, Claire.'

'I don't know that anymore. I haven't felt it in so long. Not since we moved to this place.' She kept staring at Noah, remembering all the times in his childhood when she had watched him sleep. When her love for him had felt almost like obsession. Even desperation. 'You don't know what he was like, before,' she said. 'You've only seen him at his worst. His ugliest. A suspect in a crime. You can't imagine how warm and loving he was as a small child. He was my very best friend . . .' She brought her hand up and wiped her eyes, grateful for the darkness. 'I'm just waiting for that boy to come back to me.'

Lincoln rose and went to her. 'I know you think of him as your best friend, Claire,' he said. 'But he's not your only friend.'

She allowed him to put his arms around her, to kiss her on the forehead, but even as he did she thought: *I can no longer trust you or depend on you.*

I have no one now, but myself. And my son.

He seemed to sense the barrier she had erected against him and slowly he released her. In silence he left the room.

She stayed all night at Noah's bedside, dozing in the chair, waking up every so often when a nurse came in to check his vital signs.

When she opened her eyes to a startlingly bright dawn, she found her thoughts had somehow crystallized. Noah was at last sleeping quietly. Though she too had managed to sleep, her brain had not shut down. It had, in fact, been working all night, trying to explain the puzzle of the earthworm, and how it could have found its way into her son's body. Now, as she stood at the window and gazed at the snow, she wondered how she'd missed an answer so obvious.

From the nurses' station, she called EMMC and asked to speak to Dr Clevenger in Pathology.

'I tried calling you last night,' he said. 'Left a message on your home phone.'

'Was it about Warren Emerson's ELISA test? Because that's why I'm calling you.'

'Yes, we got the results. I hate to disappoint you, but it's negative for *Taenia solium*.'

She paused. 'I see.'

'You don't sound too surprised. I am.'

'Could the test be wrong?'

'That's possible, but it's unlikely. Just to be certain, we also ran an ELISA test for that boy, Taylor Darnell.'

'And it was negative, too.'

'Oh, so you already knew that.'

'No, I didn't. It was a guess.'

'Well, that house of cards we were talking about the other day, it just collapsed. Neither patient has antibodies to the pork tapeworm. I can't explain why those kids are going berserk. I know it's not from cysticercosis. I can't explain how Mr Emerson got that cyst in his brain, either.'

'But you do think it was a larva of some kind?'

'Either that or a hell of a weird artifact from staining.'

'Could it be a different parasite – not *Taenia*?'

'What kind of parasite?'

'One that invades its host via the nasal passages. It could coil up inside one of the sinuses and hide there indefinitely. Until it's expelled or it dies. Any biological toxins it released would be absorbed right through the sinus membranes, into the host's bloodstream.'

'Wouldn't you see it on CT scan?'

'No. You'd miss it on CT, because it would look completely innocuous. Like nothing more than a mucoid cyst.' Like Scotty Braxton's CT scan.

'If it was coiled up in a sinus, how would it get into Warren Emerson's brain?'

'Think about the anatomy. There's only a thin layer of bone separating the brain from the frontal sinus. The parasite could have eroded through.'

'You know, it's a marvelous theory. But there's no parasite that fits that clinical picture. Nothing I can find in the textbooks.'

'What about something that's not in the textbooks?'

'You mean an entirely new parasite?' Clevenger laughed. 'I wish! It'd be like hitting the scientific jackpot. I'd get my name immortalized for discovering it. *Taenia clevengeria*. It's got a nice ring, doesn't it? But all I've got is a degraded and unidentifiable larva on microscopic. And no living specimen for show and tell.'

Just an earthworm.

On the drive back to Tranquility, she realized she was still missing a number of pieces to the puzzle. Max Tutwiler would have to supply them. She would give him the opportunity to explain in private; he had been her friend, and she owed him the benefit of the doubt. She'd been married to a scientist, and she knew the fever that sometimes consumes them, that intense rush of excitement when they scent the first whiff of a discovery. Yes, she understood *why* Max might hoard the

442

specimen, might keep it a secret until he could confirm it was a new species. What she could not understand, and could never forgive, was the fact he had concealed information from her, and from Noah's physicians. Information that might have been vital to her son's health.

She was growing angrier by the mile.

Talk to him first, she reminded herself. *You could be wrong. This could have nothing to do with Max.*

By the time she reached the Tranquility town line, she was too agitated to put off the meeting any longer. She wanted to have it out with him now.

She drove directly to Max's cottage.

His car wasn't there. She parked in his driveway and was crossing to the porch when she noticed, off to her right, footprints tracking away from the building. She followed them a short distance into the woods, where they halted at a churned up section of snow mixed with dirt. She squatted down, and with her gloved hand dug into the disturbed snow. About six inches deep, she reached a layer of loose soil and dead leaves. She picked up a handful of dirt and saw something glistening, moving in her palm. An earthworm. She buried it and retraced her steps out of the woods.

On the porch, she glanced around for a shovel, knowing one had to be there. She spotted it, along with a pickaxe, leaning against the woodpile, frozen soil still caked to the blade.

The door was unlocked; she stepped into the cottage and saw at once why Max hadn't bothered

443

to secure the place. It had been cleaned out of almost all his belongings. What remained – the furniture, the cookware – had probably come with the rental. She walked through the bedrooms, the kitchen, and found only a few of his things left: a box of books, a basket of dirty clothes, and some food in the refrigerator. And tacked to the wall, his topographical map of the Meegawki Stream. He'll be coming back for these things, she thought. And I'll be waiting for him.

Her gaze fell to the box of books. To the corporate mailing label still affixed to the cardboard flap: ANSON BIOLOGICALS.

It was the name of the reference lab that had analyzed Scotty's and Taylor's blood, and had returned negative reports on both their drug screens. False negatives? she wondered, and if so, what were they trying to hide? It was the same lab that had recently paid a grant to the Two Hills Pediatric Group, to collect blood samples from the area's teenagers. What was Anson's interest in the children of Tranquility?

She took out her cell phone and called Anthony at the Knox Hospital lab. 'What do you know about Anson Biologicals?' she asked him. 'How did it end up with the contract for our hospital?'

'Well, it was a funny thing. We used to send all our GC-MS and radioimmunoassay tests to BloodTek, in Portland. Then about two months ago, we suddenly switched to Anson.'

'Who made the decision?'

'Our chief of pathology. The change made sense,

since Anson's charges are discounted. The hospital couldn't resist. We're probably saving tens of thousands of bucks.'

'Could you find out more about them? I need to know as soon as possible. You can reach me on beeper.'

'What do you want to know, exactly?'

'Everything. Whether they're more than just a diagnostic lab. And what other ties they have to Tranquility.'

'I'll see what I can find out.'

She hung up. Even with the electric heat turned on, the room felt cold. She built a fire in the woodstove and made breakfast out of Max's meager food supplies. Coffee and buttered toast and a slightly shriveled apple. By the time she'd finished eating, so much warmth was radiating from the woodstove, she was starting to feel drowsy from the heat. She called the hospital again to check on Noah's condition, then she sat down by the window to wait.

He couldn't avoid her forever.

It seemed like only moments later when she startled awake in the chair, her neck hurting from uncomfortable slumber. It was three o'clock, and the morning sunlight had shifted to the slanting rays of afternoon.

She rose and massaged her neck as she wandered restlessly around the cottage. Into the bedroom, back to the kitchen. Where was he? Surely he'd come back for his dirty laundry.

She stopped in the living room and her gaze rose to the topographical map, tacked on the wall. She moved closer to it, suddenly focusing on Beech Hill, elevation 980 feet. What was it Lois Cuthbert had said at the town meeting? It had to do with the lights people had seen flickering up on the hill, and the rumors that satanic cults were gathering in the woods at night.

Lois had explained the lights. *It's just that biologist fella, Dr Tutwiler, collecting salamanders at night. I almost ran over him in the dark a few weeks ago, when he came hiking back down.*

Claire had only an hour of daylight left; she would need it to find what she was looking for. She already knew where to start.

She left the cottage and got back in her car.

The snow would make her search easy. She turned onto the road leading up Beech Hill. As she neared Emerson's property, she slowed down and observed that the driveway to his house was unplowed. It had snowed since her last visit to feed the cat, and there were no new tire tracks. She drove on, past his property. There were no other homes beyond his on the hill, and the road became a dirt track. Decades before, this had been a logging road; it was now used only by hunters or hikers on their way to the panoramic lookout at the top. The town plows had not cleared the recent snowfall, and the road was barely navigable in her Subaru. Another vehicle had been up this road before her; she saw the tire tracks.

A few hundred yards past the Emerson property, the tracks veered off the road and ended abruptly at a stand of pine trees. There was no vehicle parked there now; whoever had been here had since departed. But he had left behind ankle-deep footprints in the snow.

She climbed out of her car to study the prints. They'd been made by large boots – a man's size. They led into the woods and back out again in several round trips.

She'd often heard that snow on the ground is a hunter's best friend. She was a hunter now, following a clear trail of broken snow through the forest. She wasn't afraid of getting lost. She had a penlight in case darkness fell, her cell phone was in her pocket, and she had the footprints to lead her back to the car. Off to the right, she heard water, and realized the streambed was nearby. The footprints ran parallel to the stream, climbing slightly toward a massive tumble of boulders.

She halted and looked up in wonder. Melting snow had dripped down and flash-frozen again into a rippling blue sculpture of waterfalls. Standing at the base of that ancient landslide, she puzzled over the abrupt disappearance of the footprints. Had Max scaled those boulders? Wind had polished the ice to a hard glaze. It would be a treacherously difficult climb.

The sound of the stream again drew her attention. She looked down, where the running water had dissolved the snow, and saw the faint mark of a heel in the mud. If he had waded into the stream, why did his footprints not reappear on the opposite bank?

She took a step into the stream and felt icy water seep through the lacing holes into her boots. She took another step, and the water was at her boot tops and already soaking into her trouser cuffs. Only then did she see the opening in the rocks.

The cleft was partly shielded by a bush that would be lush with foliage in summer. To reach the opening, she had to wade calf-deep into the stream. She pulled herself up onto a lip of rock, then squeezed under the low entrance into the wider chamber beyond.

It was just large enough for her to raise her head. Though scarcely any light shone through the small opening behind her, she found she could make out vague details of her surroundings. She heard the steady drip of moisture and saw trickles of water glistening on the walls. Sunlight must be filtering in some other way. Was there another opening up ahead? Beyond the shadowy outline of an archway, faint light seemed to glimmer. Another chamber.

She squeezed under the arch, and almost immediately tumbled off the ledge and began to roll, down and down, until she landed hard on wet stone. Pain rang like a bell in her skull. She lay stunned for a moment, waiting for her head to clear, for the lights to stop flashing in her eyes. Something fluttered overhead and whooshed away with a beat of frantic wings. *Bats*.

Slowly the throbbing in her head faded to a dull ache, but the lights were still flashing in streaks of psychedelic green. Symptoms of a retinal detachment, she thought in alarm. Impending blindness.

Slowly she rose to her feet, reaching out to the cave wall to steady herself. Instead of touching stone, her hand met something slimy and yielding. She screamed and jerked away, and more beating wings fluttered out of the cave.

It moved. The wall moved.

What she'd felt on the wall was cold, not the fur of a wriggling bat. She could still feel the wetness on her fingers. Shuddering, she started to wipe her hand on her trousers when she noticed the glow. It clung to her skin, outlining the shape of her hand in the darkness. In amazement, she looked up at the cave ceiling, and she saw a multitude of lights, like soft green stars in the night sky. Except these stars moved, swaying back and forth in gentle waves.

She stepped forward, splashing through puddles, to stand in the center of the chamber, and had to close her eyes for a moment; the swaying of those stars above her head made the ground seem to rock beneath her feet.

The source, she thought in wonderment. Max has found the source of the parasite, the cave that has probably harbored this species for millennia. Heat generated by organic decay, by the warm-blooded bodies of hundreds of bats, would keep this world constant, even as the seasons cycled on the surface above.

She took out her penlight and aimed the beam at a cluster of green stars on the wall. In that circle of light, the stars were extinguished, and what she saw in their place was a clump of worms, like a many-tentacled medusa, waving gently from the dripping stone. She turned off the light. In the restored blackness, the stars reappeared, rejoining that vast galaxy of green.

Bioluminescence. The worms used *Vibrio fischeri* bacteria as their source of light. Whenever this cave flooded, worm larvae and *Vibrio* together would be washed into the stream. Into Locust Lake. *We are just the accidental hosts*, she thought. A summer's swim, an unlucky inhalation of water, and a larva would find its way through the nasal passages into a human host. There, lodged in one of the sinuses, the larva would grow, releasing a hormone as it matured and died. That would account for the chromatographic peak in Taylor Darnell's and Scotty Braxton's blood: a hormone secreted by this parasite.

Tutwiler, and perhaps Anson, knew about that hormone, and about these worms, yet they didn't tell her. They had put her and her son through hell.

In fury, she reached down, grasped a rock, and hurled it at the green stars. It bounced off the cave ceiling, clattered across the ground, and landed with a strangely metallic clang. A fresh flurry of bats whooshed out of the chamber.

She stood immobilized for a moment, trying to process what she'd just heard. Moving cautiously through the gloom, she stepped toward the far end of the chamber, where she'd heard the rock clang. There were not as many worms here, and in the absence of their glow, the darkness seemed to thicken and almost solidify as she progressed.

Once again she turned on her penlight and shone it at the ground. Something reflected back at her. She bent down for a closer look and saw it was a camp stove coffee cup.

Next to it was the toe of a man's boot.

She jerked back, gasping. The beam of light zigzagged wildly as she brought it up in panic to shine on Max Tutwiler's sightless eyes. He'd slumped to the ground with his back propped up against the cave wall. His legs were sprawled out in front of him. Froth had spilled from his mouth and dribbled onto the front of his jacket. There it joined the blacker stain of blood, which had poured from the bullet wound torn into his throat.

She stumbled backwards, turned, and splashed to her knees in the puddled water.

Run. Run.

In an instant she was back on her feet and scrambling in panic up the sloping passage to the next chamber. Bats flapped past her head. She wriggled under the archway and rolled into the entrance chamber. The sound of her own gasping echoed back at her from the walls. On hands and knees, she scuttled like a frantic insect toward the opening.

The cleft grew brighter, closer.

Then her head emerged into daylight. She took in a desperate breath of air, and looked up, just as the blow came crashing down on her skull.

24

'We haven't seen Dr Elliot all day, Chief Kelly,' said the nurse. 'And frankly, we're starting to get a little concerned.'

'When did you last speak to her?'

'According to the day shift, she called around noon or so to check on Noah's condition. But there's been no word from her since, and we've been paging her for hours. We called her house, but all we get is her answering machine. We really think she should be here. The boy's been asking for her.'

Something was wrong, thought Lincoln as he walked up the hall to Noah's room. Claire would not let so much time pass without a visit, or at least a call, to her son. He'd driven by her house earlier that evening, and her car was not there, so he'd assumed she was at the hospital.

But she had not been here all day.

He nodded to the state cop guarding the door, and walked into Noah's room.

The bedside lamp was on, and caught in its brightness, the boy's face looked pale, exhausted. At the sound of the door closing, he looked up at Lincoln, and disappointment at once clouded his eyes. The rage is gone, thought Lincoln, and the difference was startling. Thirty-six hours ago, Noah had been beyond reason, possessed by such strength and fury it had taken two men to wrestle him to the ground. Now he looked like nothing more than a tired boy. A frightened boy.

His question was barely a whisper. 'Where is my mom?'

'I don't know where she is, son.'

'Call her. Please, can you call her?'

'We're trying to reach her.'

The boy blinked, and looked up at the ceiling. 'I want to tell her I'm sorry. I want to tell her . . .' He blinked again, then turned away, his voice almost muffled against the pillow. 'I want to tell her the truth.'

'About what?'

'About what happened. That night . . .'

Lincoln remained silent. This confession could not be forced; it had to spill out of its own accord.

'I took the truck because I had to drive a friend home. She walked all the way to see me, and we were gonna wait for my mom to drive her back. But then it got late, and Mom didn't get home. And it started to snow really hard . . .'

'So you drove the girl home yourself?'

'It was only two miles. It's not like I haven't driven before.'

'And what happened, Noah? On that drive?'

'Nothing. It was just a quick trip both ways. I swear it.'

'Did you drive to Slocum Road?'

'No, sir. I stayed on Toddy Point Road the whole way. I dropped her off at the end of her driveway, so her dad wouldn't see me. And then I came straight home.'

'What time was this?'

'I don't know. Ten o'clock, I guess.'

An hour after the anonymous witness had seen Claire's pickup weaving on Slocum Road.

'This doesn't fit the facts, son. It doesn't explain the blood on the fender.'

'I don't know how the blood got there.'

'You're not telling the whole truth.'

'I am telling the truth!' The boy turned to him, his frustration building toward rage. But this time his anger was somehow different. This time it was rooted in reason.

'If you are telling the truth,' said Lincoln, 'then the girl will support your story. Who is she?'

Noah averted his gaze and stared once again at the ceiling. 'I can't tell you.'

'Why not?'

'Her father will *kill* her. That's why not.'

'She could clear this up with one statement.'

'She's scared of him. I can't get her in trouble.'

'You're the one who's in trouble, Noah.'

'I have to talk to her first. I have to give her the chance to –'

'To what? Get her story to line up with yours?'

They regarded each other in silence, Lincoln waiting for an answer, the boy refusing to yield the information.

Through the closed door, Lincoln barely heard the page announced over the hospital address system:

'Dr Elliot, extension seven-one-three-three. Dr Elliot . . .'

Lincoln left Noah's room and went to the nurses' station to pick up the phone. He dialed 7133.

It was answered by Anthony, in the laboratory. 'Dr Elliot?'

'This is Chief Kelly. How long have you been paging Dr Elliot?'

'All afternoon. I tried her beeper, but she must have it turned off. No one answers at her house, so I thought I'd try paging her on the overhead. Just in case she's in the building.'

'If she does call you, could you tell her I'm trying to reach her too?'

'Sure thing. I'm kind of surprised she hasn't called me back.'

Lincoln paused. 'What do you mean, called you back? Did you talk to her earlier?'

'Yes, sir. She asked me to track down some information.'

'When was this?'

'She called about noon today. She seemed pretty anxious to get the answer. I thought she'd get back to me by now.'

'What information did she want?'

'About a company called Anson Biologicals.'

'What's that?'

'It turns out it's just the R and D branch of Sloan-Routhier. You know, the big pharmaceutical firm. But I have no idea why she wanted to know about it.'

'Do you know where she was when she called you?'

'Chief Kelly, I haven't got a clue.'

Lincoln hung up. No one had spoken to Claire since noon – nine hours ago.

He walked out to the hospital parking lot. It had been a clear day, with no snowfall, and all the cars were lightly glazed with frost. Driving slowly in his cruiser, he searched the parking lot row by row for Claire's Subaru. Her car was not there.

She left the hospital, then what? Where would she go?

He started back toward Tranquility, his apprehension mounting. Though the road was clear, the pavement free of ice, he took the drive slowly, scanning the snowy shoulders for any sign that a car might have slid off. He stopped at Claire's house only long enough to confirm that she was not there.

By now his apprehension was turning to dread.

From his house, he made another flurry of phone calls, to the hospital, to Max Tutwiler's cottage, to the police dispatcher. Claire was nowhere to be found.

He sat in his living room, staring at the telephone, the sense of dread growing, gnawing at him. To whom would she go? She no longer trusted *him*, and that was what hurt him most of all. He dropped his head in his hands, struggling to make sense of her disappearance.

She'd been distraught about Noah. She would do anything for her son.

Noah. This had something to do with Noah.

He reached for the phone again and called Fern Cornwallis.

She had barely picked up when he asked, 'Who was the girl Noah Elliot was fighting over?'

'Lincoln? What time is it?'

'Just the name, Fern. I need to know the girl's name.'

Fern gave a weary sigh. 'It was Amelia Reid.'

'Is that Jack Reid's girl?'

'Yes. He's her stepfather.'

There was blood on the snow.

As Lincoln turned into the front yard of the Reid farmhouse, the beams of his headlights swept across an ominously dark blot in the otherwise pristine expanse of white. He braked to a stop, his gaze fixed on the stained snow, fear suddenly coiling like a serpent in his stomach. Jack Reid's truck was parked in the driveway, but the house was dark. Was the family asleep?

Slowly he stepped out of the cruiser and aimed the beam of his flashlight at the ground. At first he saw only the one bright splash of red, a bleeding Rorschach butterfly. Then he saw the other splashes, a series of them, leading around the side of the house, accompanied by footprints, both human and canine. He stared at the footprints and suddenly thought: Where were the dogs? Jack Reid owned two of them, a pair of troublesome pit bulls who had the nasty habit of ripping apart any neighborhood cats they came across. Were these bloodstains left by some unfortunate creature who'd wandered into the wrong yard?

He knelt down for a closer look and saw that, mingled with the broken snow, was a clump of dark fur, bloodied flesh still attached. Just a dead animal – a cat, or a raccoon, he thought, his tension easing, but not entirely fading. Those pit bulls could still be loose somewhere in the yard, could even now be watching him.

The sensation of being observed was suddenly so strong he quickly straightened and swung his flashlight in a wide arc, cutting a circle through the darkness. As the beam swept past the trunk of the maple tree, he spotted the second clump of fur, this one larger, the animal recognizable. He moved toward it, and his fear was suddenly back full force, tension screaming along every nerve. The steel collar studs reflected back at him, as did the gleam of white teeth protruding from the open and lifeless jaw. *One of the pit bulls. Half of it, anyway.* It had been wearing a collar which was still fastened to the chain. The animal had been unable to escape, unable to avoid slaughter.

He didn't recall drawing his weapon; he knew only that it was suddenly in his hand, and that the fear was so thick it seemed to coat his throat. He swept the beam of his flashlight in a wider circle around the yard, and found the other half of the dog, and its intestines, lying in a bundle by the porch steps. He crossed to the bloody heap and forced himself to press a bare finger to the offal. The tissue was cold, but not yet frozen. Less than an hour old. Whatever had ripped apart this animal could still be lurking nearby.

The muffled explosion of breaking glass made him wheel around, his heart slamming against his chest. The sound had come from inside the house. He glanced up at the dark windows. There were five people living in there, one of them a fourteen-year-old girl. What had happened to them?

He climbed the porch steps to the front door. It was unlocked – another disturbing detail. He gave the knob a twist and nudged the door open. A quick sweep of his flashlight revealed a threadbare carpet and several pairs of shoes cluttering the front hall. Nothing alarming. He reached up and flicked the light switch. No lights. Had the power been shut off?

For a moment he hesitated near the front door, debating the wisdom of announcing his presence. He knew Jack Reid owned a shotgun, and the man would not hesitate to use it if he thought a prowler was in his house. Lincoln drew a breath, preparing to call out: 'Police!' when his gaze froze on something that instantly killed his voice.

There was a bloody handprint on the wall.

The gun suddenly felt slick in his hand. He moved toward the print. A closer look revealed it was indeed blood, and that there was more of it smeared along the wall, leading toward the kitchen.

Five people live in this house. Where are they?

Stepping into the kitchen, he found the first member of the family. Jack Reid lay sprawled on the floor, his throat cut ear to ear. The arterial spray of his blood had splattered all four walls of the room. He was still clutching his shotgun.

Something clattered, rolled across the floor. At once, Lincoln's weapon was up, his pulse roaring in his ears. The noise had come from below. From the cellar.

His lungs were like bellows, air rushing in and out in quick breaths. He eased toward the cellar door, paused for a one-two-three count, his heart accelerating, his sweating fingers clamped like a vise around his weapon. He took a breath, and with a burst of force, kicked the door.

It flew open, slamming into the opposite wall.

A set of steps dropped away into blackness.

Someone was down there. The darkness seemed charged with an alien energy. He could almost smell the other presence, lurking at the bottom of those stairs. He aimed his flashlight downward, the beam quickly sweeping the cellar. He caught only the flash of movement, a shadow slipping toward cover under the stairs.

'Police!' yelled Lincoln. 'Come out where I can see you!' He kept the beam steady, his weapon aimed at the bottom of the stairs. 'Come on, come on. Do it *now*!'

Slowly the darkness congealed into a solid shape. A single arm, materializing in the beam's circle. Then a face inched into view, peering out with terrified eyes from beneath the stairs. A boy.

'My mom,' whimpered Eddie Reid. 'Please, help me get my mom out of here.'

Now a woman's voice whispered from beneath the stairs. 'Help us. God in heaven, help us!'

Lincoln descended the stairs and shone his light directly at the woman. Grace Reid stared back at him, her face white as a corpse, her expression almost catatonic with terror.

'No light,' she pleaded. 'Turn off the lights or he'll find us!' She backed away. Behind her, the circuit breaker box hung open. She had flipped off the switches, cutting all power to the house.

Eddie tugged his mother toward the stairs. 'Mom, it's okay now. We gotta get out of here. Please, please *move*.'

Grace shook her head in almost violent protest.

'No, he's waiting for us.' She pulled away, refusing to budge. 'J.D.'s up there.'

Again Eddie grabbed his mother's arm and dragged her toward the steps. 'Now, Mom!'

'Wait,' cut in Lincoln. 'What about Amelia? Mrs Reid, where's Amelia?'

Grace looked at him with wide eyes. 'Amelia?' she murmured, as though she'd suddenly remembered her own daughter. 'In her room.'

'Let's get your mom out of the house,' Lincoln said to Eddie. 'My cruiser's parked right outside.'

'But what about –'

'I'll find your sister. First, I'll get you both into the car and I'll radio for help. Now let's go. Stay right behind me.' He turned and started slowly up the stairs. He could hear Grace and Eddie following behind him, Grace's breath coming out in frantic whimpers, Eddie murmuring words of encouragement.

J.D. They were both terrified of J.D.

Lincoln reached the top of the stairs. There was no way around it; he'd have to lead them through the blood-splattered kitchen, right past Jack Reid's body. If Grace was going to collapse in hysterics, it would be here.

Thank god for Eddie. The boy draped his arm around his stepmother, hugging her face against his chest. 'Go, Chief Kelly,' he whispered urgently. 'Please, just get us out of here.'

Lincoln led them through the kitchen, into the hallway. There he halted, every nerve suddenly giving off panic alarms. By the beam of his flashlight, he saw that the front door hung open. *Did I close it when I came in the house?*

He whispered, 'Wait here,' and he inched toward the front door. Glancing outside, he saw moonlit-silvered snow. The cruiser was parked about thirty feet away. Everything lay still, as silent as air trapped in a bell jar.

Something is wrong. We are being watched. We are being stalked.

He turned to Eddie and Grace and whispered: 'Run to the car. *Now!*'

But Grace didn't run. Instead she backed away, and as she stumbled past a moonlit window, Lincoln saw her face was gazing upward. Toward the stairs.

He pivoted, just as the shadow came hurtling down at him. He was slammed backwards so hard the breath whooshed from his lungs. Pain sliced across his cheek. He staggered sideways, just as the knife blade came down again, stabbing deep into the wall near his head. His weapon had fallen, knocked from his grasp by that first tackle. Now he scrabbled frantically on the floor, trying to locate the gun in the dark.

He heard the squeak of the knife being pried free from the wood, and spun around to see the shadow rushing at him. He brought his left arm up just as the knife came stabbing down. The blade struck bone, and he heard his own gasp of pain like a distant, foreign sound.

Somehow he grasped the boy's wrist in his right hand and twisted the knife free. It thudded to the floor. The boy wrenched away, stumbling backwards.

Lincoln dropped down and grabbed the knife. His sense of triumph lasted only for an instant.

The boy had risen to his feet as well, his silhouette framed by the window. He was holding Lincoln's gun. He swung it around, aiming the barrel straight at Lincoln.

The explosion was so loud it shattered the window. Glass blew out in a hail of shards, raining down onto the porch.

No pain. Why was he feeling no pain?

Frozen in bewilderment, Lincoln watched as J.D. Reid, backlit by moonlight through the broken window, slowly crumpled to the floor. A footstep creaked behind him, then he heard Eddie's tremulous voice ask:

'Did I kill him?'

'We need light,' said Lincoln.

He heard Eddie stumble through the darkness into the kitchen and down the cellar steps. Seconds later, he flipped the circuit breakers, and all the lights came on.

One look at the body told Lincoln J.D. was dead.

Eddie came back out of the kitchen, still holding Jack Reid's shotgun. He slowed, halted beside his stepmother. They were both unable to pry their gazes from the dead boy, unable to utter a sound, as the terrible vision of J.D. Reid, collapsed in a pool of blood, burned its way forever into their brains.

'Amelia,' said Lincoln, and he glanced up the stairs, toward the second floor. 'Which bedroom is hers?'

Eddie looked at him with dazed eyes. 'The second one. On the right . . .'

Lincoln ran up the stairs. At his first glimpse of Amelia's bedroom door, he knew the worst had already happened. The door had been hacked open, and splinters of wood littered the hallway. The girl must have tried to lock J.D. out, but a few swings of an ax had shattered the wood. Dreading the scene he knew lay within, he stepped into the girl's room.

He saw the ax, embedded in a chair, almost cleaving it in two. He saw the shattered mirror, the ripped dresses, the closet door hanging askew on a broken hinge. Then he stared at the girl's bed.

It was empty.

Mitchell Groome was behind the wheel of Claire Elliot's Subaru as he drove slowly down Beech Hill. He had waited until midnight, an hour when no witnesses would be awake, but unfortunately the sky was clear, and the light of the full moon reflected with alarming brilliance off the snow. It made him feel exposed and vulnerable. Full moon or not, he had to finish this tonight. Too much had already gone wrong, and he had been forced to take far more drastic measures than he'd planned.

His job had started off as a simple assignment, to keep an eye on Dr Tutwiler's work, and, posing as a journalist asking questions, to quietly and discreetly assess the natural course of parasitic infection in the youth of Tranquility. His job had suddenly become complicated by Claire Elliot, whose suspicions had veered dangerously close to the truth. Then Doreen Kelly had added an even worse complication.

He would definitely have some explaining to do when he returned to Boston.

He felt certain he could come up with a reasonable explanation for Max Tutwiler's disappearance. He could hardly tell his superiors at Anson Biologicals what had actually happened: that Max had wanted to quit after he'd learned how Doreen Kelly really died. *I was hired to find the worms for you, Max had protested. Anson told me this was nothing more than a biological treasure hunt. No one said anything about murder, and for what? To keep this species a corporate secret?*

What Max refused to understand was that the development of a new drug was like prospecting for gold. Secrecy was paramount. You cannot let the competition know you are closing in on a fresh vein of treasure.

The treasure, in this case, was a hormone produced by a unique invertebrate, a hormone whose defining effect was the enhancement of aggression.

A minute dose was all it took to hone the fighting edge of a soldier in battle. It was a killing potion with obvious military applications.

Only two months ago, Anson Biologicals and its parent company, Sloan-Routhier Pharmaceuticals, had learned of the worms' existence when the teenage sons of a Virginia couple were admitted to the psychiatric wing of a military hospital. One of the boys had expelled a worm – a bioluminescent species that none of the military pathologists could identify.

The family had spent the month of July in a lakeside cottage in Maine.

Groome turned onto Toddy Point Road. In the seat beside him, Claire groaned and moved her head. He hoped, for her sake, that she didn't fully regain consciousness, because the end that awaited her was not a merciful one. It was another unpleasant necessity. The death of a woman as pitiful as Doreen Kelly had raised few eyebrows in town. But a local doctor couldn't simply vanish without questions being asked. It was important for the authorities to find her body, and to conclude her death was accidental.

The road was only gentle rises and dips now, a lonely drive at this hour of night. Groome's headlights skimmed across deserted blacktop crusted with ice and road sand, the beams illuminating an arc just wide enough to see the trees pressing in on both sides. A black tunnel, the only opening a swath of stars overhead.

He approached another curve, where the black-top veered sharply left, and braked to a stop at the top of the boat ramp.

Claire groaned again as he dragged her from the passenger seat and positioned her behind the steering wheel. He buckled her seat belt. Then, with the engine still running, he put the car in gear, released the hand brake, and let the door swing shut.

The car began to roll forward, down the gentle grade of the boat ramp.

Groome stood on the roadside, watching as the car reached the lake and continued rolling. There was snow on the ice, and the tires slowly churned through it, the headlights jittery on the barren expanse. Ten yards. Twenty. How far before it reached thin ice? It was only the first week of December; the lake would not yet be frozen thick enough to support the weight of a car.

Thirty yards. That's when Groome heard the *crack*, sharp as gunfire. The front of the car dipped down, its headlights suddenly swallowed up by snow and fracturing ice. Another *crack*, and the car tilted crazily forward, the red glow of its taillights pointing toward the sky. Now the ice beneath the rear wheels snapped, disintegrated, and the car splashed through. The headlights died, the circuits shorted out.

The end was played out in the glow of moon-light, in a landscape silvered by the luminous whiteness of snow, the car bobbing for a moment, engine flooding, the water dragging it down, claiming it as its own. Now the sound of splashing, the liquid turmoil as the car slipped deeper and began to turn over, rotated by the buoyancy of the tires. It sank upside down, its roof settling into the mud, and he imagined the swirl of dark sediment, blacking out the watery moonlight filtering from above.

Tomorrow, thought Groome, someone will spot the break in the ice and will put two and two together. Poor tired Dr Elliot, driving home in the dark, missed the curve in the road and veered onto the boat ramp instead. A tragedy.

He heard the distant wail of a police siren and he turned, his pulse suddenly racing. Only when the siren passed and then faded did he allow himself to breathe easier. The police had been called elsewhere; no one had witnessed his crime.

He turned and began to walk at a brisk pace up the road, toward the blackness of Beech Hill. It was a three-mile hike back to the cave, and he still had work to do.

25

She felt the darkness lurch around her, felt the shocking embrace of icy water as it engulfed her body, and she jolted awake into a reality far more horrifying than any nightmare could be.

She was trapped in blackness, in a coffinlike space, and was so disoriented she had no sense of up or down. All she knew was that water was creeping up around her in a numbing flood, lapping at her waist, now her chest. She flailed out in panic, instinctively craning her neck to keep her head above it, but found her body was strapped in. She tore at the restraints but could not free herself. The water was licking at her neck, now. Her breathing turned to frantic gasps and half-sobs of panic.

Then it all turned upside down.

She had time for one deep breath before she felt herself rolling sideways, before the water rushed over her head, flooding into her nostrils.

The darkness that swallowed her was total, a

world of liquid blackness. She thrashed, trapped head-down underwater. Her lungs ached, straining to hold on to that final breath.

Again she clawed at the strap across her chest, but it would not loosen, would not release her. *Air. I need air!* Her pulse roared in her ears and streaks of light exploded in her brain, the warning flashes of oxygen depletion. Already she was losing strength in her limbs, her efforts reduced to tugging uselessly at the restraint. Through thickening layers of confusion, she realized she was grasping something hard in her hand, something she recognized by its contours. A seat belt buckle. She was in her car. Strapped in her car.

Thousands of times before she had unbuckled that belt and now her fingers automatically found the release button. The strap fell away from her chest.

She kicked, limbs thrashing, battering against the inside of the car. Blinded by water, disoriented in the darkness, she could not even tell which way was up. Her frantically clawing fingers brushed against the steering wheel, the dashboard.

I need AIR!

She felt her lungs rebel and begin to draw in a fatal breath of water when she suddenly twisted around, and her face popped through the surface, into an air pocket. She gasped in a breath, then another, and another. There were only a few inches of air, and even that was rapidly filling with water. A few more gasps, and there would be nothing left to breathe.

With the fresh inrush of oxygen, her brain was functioning again. She forced back the panic, forced herself to think. The car was upside down. She had to find the latch – had to get the door open.

She held her breath and plunged into the water. Quickly she located the door release and gave it a tug. She felt the latch pop free, but the door wouldn't swing open. The roof of the vehicle was sunk too deeply in mud, miring the door shut.

Out of breath!

She surfaced back in the air pocket and found it reduced to a bare six inches. As she gasped in the last of the oxygen, she desperately tried to reorient herself to an upside-down world. *The window. Roll open the window.*

Last breath, last chance.

She sank back underwater, feeling frantically for the window crank. By now her fingers were so deadened from the cold, she could barely feel the handle, even when she finally managed to grasp it. Each revolution seemed to take an eternity, but she could feel the glass slide open, the gap widen. By the time she had cranked it all the way open, her hunger for air was growing desperate. She wriggled her head and shoulders through the opening, and suddenly could go no farther.

Her jacket! It was snagged!

She thrashed, trying to squeeze all the way

through, but her body was trapped, half in, half out of the car. She reached for the zipper, loosened the jacket.

All at once she slithered free, and suddenly she was shooting toward the surface, toward the faint glow of light far above.

She burst through into the air, water splashing like a million diamonds in the moonlight, and grasped the nearest broken edge of ice. There she clung for a moment, shaking and wheezing in the frigid night. Already she'd lost feeling in her legs, and her hands were so numb she could barely grasp the ice.

She tried to pull herself out, managed to lift her shoulders a few inches, but immediately fell back into the water. There was nothing to hold on to, nothing to pull against, only slick ice covered with powdery snow. Scrabbling uselessly at the ice, she found no purchase.

Again she tried to lift herself out; again she slid back with a splash, sinking in over her head. She resurfaced, sputtering, coughing, her legs almost paralyzed.

She couldn't do it. She couldn't pull herself out.

Half a dozen times more she struggled to climb out, but her clothes were soaked, dragging her down, and she was shaking so hard she could not even hold on to the ice. A profound lethargy was taking hold of her limbs, turning them wooden. Dead. She felt herself go under again, the blackness sucking her down, welcoming her into a cold sleep. All her energy was spent. Nothing was left.

She sank, drifting deeper, exhaustion claiming her body. Looking up, she saw with strange detachment the shimmer of moonlight above, and felt the darkness pull her down into its embrace. She no longer felt the cold; she felt only a weary sense of inevitability.

Noah.

In the shimmering circle of light above, she imagined she saw his face, as he was when he was a child. Calling to her, reaching for her with needy arms. The circle of light seemed to fracture into fragments of silver.

Noah. Think of Noah.

Though she had no strength left, she reached up toward that phantom hand. It dissolved like liquid in her grasp. *You are too far away. I can't reach you.*

She felt herself sliding downward again, dragged into the murk. Noah's arms receded, but his voice continued to call to her. She reached up to him again, and saw the circle of light grow brighter, a halo of silver just within reach. If I can touch it, she thought, I will reach heaven. I will reach my baby.

She struggled toward it, limbs thrashing against the pull of darkness, every muscle straining toward the light.

Her arm broke through the surface, shattering

it to ripples, her head bursting through for one gasp of air. She caught a glimpse of the moon, so beautiful and brilliant it hurt her eyes, and she felt herself sink for the last time, her arm still outstretched toward heaven.

A hand grasped hers. A real hand, its grip solid around her wrist. *Noah*, she thought. *I've found my son.*

Now the hand dragged her upward, out of the murk. She stared in wonder as the light blossomed brighter, and then her head surfaced and she saw the face staring down at her. Not Noah's face, but a girl's. A girl with long hair, bright as silver in the moonlight.

Mitchell Groome poured half a can of gasoline over Max Tutwiler's body. Not that destroying the corpse really mattered. This cave had lain untouched all these millennia; Max's remains would not be found anytime soon. Still, as long as he was destroying the worm colony, he might as well dispose of a dead body as well.

Wearing a mask against the fumes and a headlamp to light the dim cave, he took his time emptying the contents of the three gasoline cans. He had no reason to rush; the doctor's submerged vehicle would not be found until daylight, and even if it was found before then, no one would link Groome to her death. If anyone were to draw suspicion, it would be Max, whose sudden disappearance would only solidify those suspicions.

Groome didn't like being forced to improvise; he had not planned this move, had not planned to kill anyone. But then, he hadn't counted on Doreen Kelly stealing his car, either.

One murder sometimes necessitates another.

He finished splashing the walls and tossed the last empty container into the shallow pool of gasoline at the center of the cavern. It was right beneath the thickest colony of worms. Already they seemed to sense impending disaster, for they were wriggling frantically in the rising fumes. The bats had long since fled, abandoning their invertebrate companions to the flames. Groome took one last look around the cavern, assuring himself he'd forgotten no detail. The last box of specimens, as well as Max's scientific log books, were in the trunk of his car, parked at the trailhead. With the strike of a match, everything in this cave would go up in flames.

It would be instant extinction of the species, except for the surviving specimens now being nurtured in the labs at Anson Biologicals. The hormone these worms secreted was worth a fortune in Defense Department contracts, but only if it stayed out of the hands of Anson's competitors.

With the destruction of this cave, only Anson would possess the species. To the rest of the world, the reason for this epidemic of violence, and for all the epidemics that came before it, would remain a mystery.

He crawled up the passageway leading to the

exit, dribbling a fine line of accelerant as he backed toward the opening. Crouching in the entrance chamber, he lit a match and touched the flame to the ground. A line of fire licked all the way down the tunnel, and then there was a *whoosh* as the cavern below exploded in flames. Groome felt the inrush of air as oxygen was sucked in to feed the conflagration. He turned off his headlamp and watched the fire burn for a moment, imagining the worms turning black, their charred carcasses dropping from the ceiling. And he thought of Max's corpse, reduced to unidentifiable bone and ash.

He backed out of the cave, his feet dropping into the icy stream, and pulled the branches over the opening. Beyond these thick woods, the glow of the fire in the cavern would be invisible. He waded to the streambank and stumbled onto land. His eyes were still dazzled by the fire, and he had not yet readjusted to the darkness. He turned on his headlamp, to light his way back to the car.

Only then, as his beam flared on, did he see the policemen standing among the trees, weapons drawn.

Expecting him.

Warren Emerson opened his eyes and thought: At last I have died. But why am I in heaven? It was a discovery that greatly surprised him, because he had always assumed that if there was

478

existence after death, he would find himself in some dark and terrible place. An afterlife that was merely an extension of his despairing existence on earth.

Here there were flowers. Vases and vases of them.

He saw blood-red roses. Orchid blossoms like white butterflies fluttering on stalks across the window. And lilies, their fragrance sweeter than any perfume he had ever inhaled. He stared in wonder, for he had never seen anything so beautiful.

Then he heard a chair creak beside his bed, and he turned to see a woman smiling at him. A woman he had not seen in years.

Her hair was more silver than black, and age had left its deep engraving in the lines on her face. But he saw none of this. Looking into her eyes, what he saw instead was a laughing girl of fourteen. The girl he had always loved.

'Hello, Warren,' whispered Iris Keating. She reached out to take his hand in hers.

'I'm alive,' he said.

She heard the question in his voice, and with a smile she nodded. 'Yes. You most certainly are alive.'

He looked down at her hand, grasping his. Remembered how their fingers once had entwined all those years ago, when they had both been young, and they had sat together by the lake. So many changes in our hands, he thought. Mine are now scarred and leathery; hers are knobby with arthritis. But here we are, holding hands again, and she is still my Iris.

Through his tears, he looked at her. And decided he was not ready to die after all.

Lincoln knew where he would find her, and there she was, sitting in a chair at her son's bedside. Sometime in the night, Claire had climbed out of her own hospital bed, had shuffled down the long hallway in her robe and slippers, and found her way to Noah's room. Now she sat hugging a blanket to her shoulders, looking very tired and pale in the afternoon sunlight. God help the soul who dares to come between a mother bear and her cub, thought Lincoln.

He sat down in the chair across from her, and their gazes met over Noah's sleeping figure. It hurt him to see that she was still wary, still untrusting of him, but he understood the reason for it. Only a day ago, he had threatened to take from her the one thing in the world she loved most. Now she was watching him with an expression that was both fierce and, at the same time, afraid.

'My son didn't do it,' she said. 'He told me, this morning. He swore it to me, and I know he's telling the truth.'

He nodded. 'I spoke to Amelia Reid. They were together that night until after ten. And then he drove her home.'

By which time, Doreen was already dead.

Claire released a breath, tension melting from her body. She sank back in the chair and placed her hand protectively on Noah's head. At the touch of her fingers stroking his hair, his eyes flickered open, and he focused on Claire. Neither mother nor son spoke; their quiet smiles conveyed everything that needed to be said.

I could have spared them both this ordeal, thought Lincoln. If only he had known the truth. If only Noah had come right out and confessed he'd spent the evening with Amelia. But he had been protecting the girl from her stepfather's wrath. Lincoln knew of Jack Reid's temper, and he understood why Amelia would be afraid of him.

Afraid or not, the girl had been ready to share the truth with Claire. Last night, just before J.D.'s rage had exploded in murder, Amelia had slipped out of her house and walked through the clear, cold night, toward Claire's house. Her route had taken her along Toddy Point Road.

Right past the boat ramp.

The girl's fortunate journey had saved Claire's life. And in the process, Amelia had saved her own.

Noah had once again fallen asleep.

Claire looked at Lincoln. 'Is Amelia's word going to be enough? Will anyone believe a fourteen-year-old girl?'

'I believe her.'

'Yesterday you said you had physical evidence. The blood –'

'We also found blood in the trunk of Mitchell Groome's car.'

She paused as the significance of that fact sank in. 'Doreen's?' she said softly.

He nodded. 'I think Groome meant to implicate you, not Noah, when he smeared the blood on your pickup. He didn't know which car you'd been driving that night.'

They were both quiet for a moment, and he wondered if this was how it would end between them, with silence on her part, and longing on his. There was so much he still had to tell her about Mitchell Groome. There'd been the items they'd found in Groome's trunk: the jars of specimens and Max's handwritten log books. Both Anson Biologicals and Sloan-Routhier had denied any connection to the two men, and now Groome, angered by that disavowal, was threatening to drag the pharmaceutical giant down with him. Lincoln had come to tell Claire all this and more, but instead he remained silent, his unhappiness weighing down on him so heavily it seemed a burden just to take a deep breath.

He said, hopefully, 'Claire?'

She raised her eyes to his, and this time she did not look away.

'I can't turn back the clock,' he said. 'I can't erase the hurt I caused you. I can only say that I'm sorry. I wish there was some way we could go back to . . .' He shook his head. 'The way we were.'

'I'm not sure what that means, Lincoln. The way we were.'

He thought about it. 'Well, for one thing,' he said, 'we were friends.'

'Yes, that's true,' she admitted.

'Good friends. Weren't we?'

A faint smile touched her lips. 'Good enough to sleep together, anyway.'

He felt himself flush. 'That's not what I'm talking about! It's not just the sleeping together. It's—' He gazed at her with painful honesty. 'It's knowing there's a *possibility* for us. A possibility that I'll be seeing you every morning when I wake up. I can wait, Claire. I can live with the uncertainty. It's not easy, but I can stand it, as long as there's a chance we'll be together. That's all I'm really asking for.'

Something sparkled in her eyes. Tears of forgiveness? he wondered. She reached out and stroked his face. It was the gentle caress of a lover. Even better than that, it was the touch of a friend.

'Anything's possible, Lincoln,' she said softly. And she smiled.

He was actually whistling when he walked out of the hospital. And why shouldn't he? The sky was blue, the sun was shining, and the ice-encrusted branches of willow trees clacked and glittered like hanging crystals. In two weeks would come the longest night of the year. Then the days would open up again, the earth cycling back toward light and warmth. Toward hope.

Anything's possible.

Lincoln Kelly was a patient man, and he could wait.